ZANE GREY
the Complete and Unabridged Novels

Riders of the Purple Sage

The Trail Driver

Rangers of the Lone Star

PRION

Published in 2009 by Prion
An imprint of the Carlton Publishing Group
20 Mortimer Street
London W1T 3JW

1 3 5 7 9 10 8 6 4 2

A CIP catalogue record for this book is available from the British Library.

ISBN 978-1-85375-746-4

Typeset by Ellipsis, Glasgow

Printed in Thailand

Contents

INTRODUCTION

A qualified dentist, accomplished baseball player and record-breaking sports fisherman might not be the sort of person you would expect to produce the most popular novels of the 'wild west' ever written but, while Zane Grey's prolific writing career ultimately overshadowed all of his other achievements, dentistry, baseball and fishing all played a vital part in the creative process that made him a best-selling author.

Born in Ohio, far from the deserts, mountain ranges and cattle trails of the old west that were to become the landscape of his most famous novels, Zane was a feisty youth and a reluctant student who regularly incurred the wrath of his father. Lewis M Grey was a dentist in Zanesville, Ohio, married to Alice Zane, whose ancestors had given their name to the city in 1797. Zane was actually Grey's middle name, his first name being Pearl, which may go some way to explaining why he is reputed to have become involved in so many fights as a youngster. He was later to drop his first name, although his pride in the name Zane would become apparent in his first two novels *Betty Zane* (1903) and *Spirit of the Border* (1906) which, along with *The Last Trail* (1909), formed his 'Ohio River Trilogy' based on the experiences of his forebears. Betty Zane had been a heroine of the war against the British, saving the besieged Fort Henry in Virginia by making a dash outside the stronghold in the face of the enemy to collect gunpowder and ammunition from a secret store.

Zane's prowess as a baseball player won him a scholarship to the University of Pennsylvania where he followed in his father's footsteps to study dentistry, having already acquired some basic skills when he travelled the countryside performing extractions as an unlicensed teenager, supplementing the family income after his father's investments had resulted in financial ruin in 1889. Although he graduated from university, Zane's dentistry studies had always taken third place to both baseball and his passion for creative writing. As a boy he had devoured adventure novels and, while he did establish a dentistry practice in New York in 1896 as Dr Zane Grey, his free time was spent writing or playing amateur baseball.

Setting up a practice in New York may have brought Zane closer to the publishing houses that did business in the city, but the lure of the great outdoors was always difficult for Zane to resist. He and his brother, Romer (Zane was one of five siblings), took themselves off on regular camping and fishing trips, one such trip resulting in the 28-year-old Zane meeting 17-year-old Dolly Roth, whom he was to marry in 1905. On their honeymoon, Zane visited California for the first time and was overwhelmed by the grandeur of the scenery. He was to follow up this trip with several more during which he went hunting mountain lions, trekking through the wilderness and making detailed notes about the places and the people he came across. The way people talked, the phrases they used and the varied pronunciation that he encountered would, along with the vivid descriptions of the mountains and deserts through which he travelled, add the kind of colour to his novels that drew readers into the stories. The reluctant student was now driven by a passion for his chosen subject.

Before long, Dolly, who had trained as a teacher, had given up her work to raise a family with Zane as well as supporting him in his efforts to become a writer. Abandoning his dentistry practice, they set up home in Lackawaxen, Pennsylvania, using an inheritance that had come to Dolly to maintain them while Zane's literary career began to bear fruit. There was, however, to be no overnight success. Dolly helped Zane to refine his writing style, editing his work when necessary but, after some initial encouragement when Zane had an article about a fishing trip published in a magazine, his debut novel, *Betty Zane,* failed to find a publisher. Eventually, Zane published the book himself, although he could ill afford such expense and had taken the trauma of rejection very badly.

Prone to mood swings that could take him to the depths of depression, Zane's relationship with Dolly had always suffered due to his erratic temperament. She had also always endured his philandering nature. Zane remained in contact with several girlfriends during their courtship and would take a number of mistresses during their marriage.

Zane's career progressed through the writing of magazine articles and stories for younger readers, with Dolly acting as his secretary, editor and business manager, dealing with publishers, negotiating contracts and managing finances, an amalgamation of roles that she would maintain throughout their marriage. Then, in 1910, came the publication of *The Heritage of the Desert*, which became a bestseller, establishing Zane as a major author of popular fiction. Altogether Zane was to write almost 100 books, including books on the outdoors, hunting, fishing, baseball and a handful of children's books.

It is for his tales of the wild west, of course, that he is most famous and these formed the bulk of his work, with more than fifty of his western novels being turned into movies. He even formed his own movie company at one time, having moved to California with Dolly and their three children in 1918 to be near the film studios. The movies, which starred names such as Randolph Scott, Gary Cooper, Shirley Temple and Fay Wray, served to increase the sales of Zane's books and it has been estimated that total sales of his work now exceed 40 million worldwide.

Zane's love of fishing came to dominate his life as he began to spend most of the year away from home, sometimes with his mistresses, but more often travelling the Pacific, visiting Tahiti, Tonga, Australia and New Zealand where he set world records for catching swordfish, marlin and shark. He used the fishing trips as 'down time' between intense periods of writing and kept in regular contact with Dolly by letter. Theirs was a far from conventional relationship, but then Zane was a far from conventional character. The wanderer did, however, finally return home to California, where Zane Grey died at the age of 67 in October 1939.

Rod Green
Series Editor

RIDERS OF THE PURPLE SAGE

CHAPTER ONE

Lassiter

A SHARP clip-clop of iron-shod hoofs deadened and died away, and clouds of yellow dust drifted from under the cottonwoods out over the sage.

Jane Withersteen gazed down the wide purple slope with dreamy and troubled eyes. A rider had just left her and it was his message that held her thoughtful and almost sad, awaiting the churchmen who were coming to resent and attack her right to befriend a Gentile.

She wondered if the unrest and strife that had lately come to the little village of Cottonwoods was to involve her. And then she sighed, remembering that her father had founded this remotest border settlement of southern Utah and that he had left it to her. She owned all the ground and many of the cottages. Withersteen House was hers, and the great ranch, with its thousands of cattle, and the swiftest horses of the sage. To her belonged Amber Spring, the water which gave verdure and beauty to the village and made living possible on that wild purple upland waste. She could not escape being involved by whatever befell Cottonwoods.

That year, 1871, had marked a change which had been gradually coming in the lives of the peace-loving Mormons of the border. Glaze—Stone Bridge—Sterling, villages to the north, had risen against the invasion of Gentile settlers and the forays of rustlers. There had been opposition to the one and fighting with the other. And now Cottonwoods had begun to wake and bestir itself and grown hard.

Jane prayed that the tranquillity and sweetness of her life would not be permanently disrupted. She meant to do so much more for her people than she had done. She wanted the sleepy quiet pastoral days to last always. Trouble between the Mormons and the Gentiles of the community would make her unhappy. She was Mormon-born, and she was a friend to poor and unfortunate Gentiles. She wished only to go on doing good and being happy. And she thought of what that great ranch meant to her. She loved it all—the grove of cottonwoods, the old stone house, the amber-tinted water, and the droves of shaggy, dusty horses and mustangs, the sleek, clean-limbed, blooded racers, and the browsing herds of cattle and the lean, sun-browned riders of the sage.

While she waited there she forgot the prospect of untoward change. The bray of a lazy burro broke the afternoon quiet, and it was comfortingly suggestive of the drowsy farmyard, and the open corrals, and the green alfalfa fields. Her clear sight intensified the purple sage-slope as it rolled before her. Low swells of prairie-like ground sloped up to the west. Dark, lonely cedar-trees, few and far between, stood out strikingly, and at long distances ruins of red rocks. Farther on, up the gradual slope, rose a broken wall, a huge monument, looming dark purple and stretching its solitary, mystic way, a wavering line that faded in the north. Here to the westward was the light and color and beauty. Northward the slope descended to a dim line of cañons from which rose an up-flinging of the earth, not mountainous, but a vast heave of purple uplands, with ribbed and fan-shaped walls, castle-crowned cliffs, and gray escarpments. Over it all crept the lengthening, waning afternoon shadows.

The rapid beat of hoofs recalled Jane Withersteen to the question at hand. A group of riders cantered up the lane, dismounted, and threw their bridles. They were seven in number, and Tull, the leader, a tall, dark man, was an elder of Jane's church.

"Did you get my message?" he asked, curtly.

"Yes," replied Jane.

"I sent word I'd give that rider Venters half an hour to come down to the village. He didn't come."

"He knows nothing of it," said Jane. "I didn't tell him. I've been waiting here for you."

"Where is Venters?"

"I left him in the courtyard."

"Here, Jerry," called Tull, turning to his men, "take the gang and fetch Venters out here if you have to rope him."

The dusty-booted and long-spurred riders clanked noisily into the grove of cottonwoods and disappeared in the shade.

"Elder Tull, what do you mean by this?" demanded Jane. "If you must arrest Venters you might have the courtesy to wait till he leaves my home. And if you do arrest him it will be adding insult to injury. It's absurd to accuse Venters of being mixed up in that shooting fray in the village last night. He was with me at the time. Besides, he let me take charge of his guns. You're only using this as a pretext. What do you mean to do to Venters?"

"I'll tell you presently," replied Tull. "But first tell me why you defend this worthless rider?"

"Worthless!" exclaimed Jane, indignantly. "He's nothing of the kind. He was the best rider I ever had. There's not a reason why I shouldn't champion him and every reason why I should. It's no little shame to me, Elder Tull, that through my friendship he has roused the enmity of my people and become an outcast. Besides, I owe him eternal gratitude for saving the life of little Fay."

"I've heard of your love for Fay Larkin and that you intend to adopt her. But—Jane Withersteen, the child is a Gentile!"

"Yes. But, Elder, I don't love the Mormon children any less because I love a Gentile child. I shall adopt Fay if her mother will give her to me."

"I'm not so much against that. You can give the child Mormon teaching," said Tull. "But I'm sick of seeing this fellow Venters hang around you. I'm going to put a stop to it. You've so much love to throw away on these beggars of Gentiles that I've an idea you might love Venters."

Tull spoke with the arrogance of a Mormon whose power could not be brooked and with the passion of a man in whom jealousy had kindled a consuming fire.

"Maybe I do love him," said Jane. She felt both fear and anger stir her heart. "I'd never thought of that. Poor fellow! he certainly needs some one to love him."

"This'll be a bad day for Venters unless you deny that," returned Tull, grimly.

Tull's men appeared under the cottonwoods and led a young man out into the lane. His ragged clothes were those of an outcast. But he stood tall and straight, his wide shoulders flung back, with the muscles of his bound arms rippling and a blue flame of defiance in the gaze he bent on Tull.

For the first time Jane Withersteen felt Venters's real spirit. She wondered if she would love this splendid youth. Then her emotion cooled to the sobering sense of the issue at stake.

"Venters, will you leave Cottonwoods at once and forever?" asked Tull, tensely.

"Why?" rejoined the rider.

"Because I order it."

Venters laughed in cool disdain.

The red leaped to Tull's dark cheek.

"If you don't go it means your ruin," he said, sharply.

"Ruin!" exclaimed Venters, passionately. "Haven't you already ruined me? What do you call ruin? A year ago I was a rider. I had horses and cattle of my own. I had a good name in Cottonwoods. And now when I come into the village to see this woman you set your men on me. You hound me. You trail me as if I were a rustler. I've no more to lose—except my life."

"Will you leave Utah?"

"Oh! I know," went on Venters, tauntingly, "it galls you, the idea of beautiful Jane Withersteen being friendly to a poor Gentile. You want her all yourself. You're a wiving Mormon. You have use for her—and Withersteen House and Amber Spring and seven thousand head of cattle!"

Tull's hard jaw protruded, and rioting blood corded the veins of his neck.

"Once more. Will you go?"

"*No!*"

"Then I'll have you whipped within an inch of your life," replied Tull, harshly. "I'll turn you out in the sage. And if you ever come back you'll get worse."

Venters's agitated face grew coldly set and the bronze changed to gray.

Jane impulsively stepped forward. "Oh! Elder Tull!" she cried. "You won't do that!"

Tull lifted a shaking finger toward her.

"That'll do from you. Understand, you'll not be allowed to hold this boy to a friendship that's offensive to your Bishop. Jane Withersteen, your father left you wealth and power. It has turned your head. You haven't yet come to see the place of Mormon women. We've reasoned with you, borne with you. We've patiently waited. We've let you have your fling, which is more than I ever saw granted to a Mormon woman. But you haven't come to your senses. Now, once for all, you can't have any further friendship with Venters. He's going to be whipped, and he's got to leave Utah!"

"Oh! Don't whip him! It would be dastardly!" implored Jane with slow certainty of her failing courage.

Tull always blunted her spirit, and she grew conscious that she had feigned a boldness which she did not possess. He loomed up now in different guise, not as a jealous suitor, but embodying the mysterious despotism she had known from childhood—the power of her creed.

"Venters, will you take your whipping here or would you rather go out in the sage?" asked Tull. He smiled a flinty smile that was more than inhuman, yet seemed to give out of its dark aloofness a gleam of righteousness.

"I'll take it here—if I must," said Venters. "But by God!—Tull, you'd better kill me outright. That'll be a dear whipping for you and your praying Mormons. You'll make me another Lassiter!"

The strange glow, the austere light which radiated from Tull's face, might have been a holy joy at the spiritual conception of exalted duty. But there was something more in him, barely hidden, a something personal and sinister, a deep of himself, an engulfing abyss. As his religious mood was fanatical and inexorable, so would his physical hate be merciless.

"Elder, I—I repent my words," Jane faltered. The religion in her, the long habit of obedience, of humility, as well as agony of fear, spoke in her voice. "Spare the boy!" she whispered.

"You can't save him now," replied Tull, stridently.

Her head was bowing to the inevitable. She was grasping the truth, when suddenly there came, in inward constriction, a hardening of gentle forces within her breast. Like a steel bar it was, stiffening all that had been soft and weak in her. She felt a birth in her of something new and unintelligible. Once more her strained gaze sought the sage-slopes. Jane Withersteen loved that wild and purple wilderness. In times of sorrow it had been her strength, in happiness its beauty was her continual delight. In her extremity she found herself murmuring, "Whence cometh my help!" It was a prayer, as if forth from those lonely purple reaches and walls of red and clefts of blue might ride a fearless man, neither creed-bound nor creed-mad, who would hold up a restraining hand in the faces of her ruthless people.

The restless movements of Tull's men suddenly quieted down. Then followed a low whisper, a rustle, a sharp exclamation.

"Look!" said one, pointing to the west.

"A rider!"

Jane Withersteen wheeled and saw a horseman, silhouetted against the western sky, coming riding out of the sage. He had ridden down from the left, in the golden glare of the sun, and had been unobserved till close at hand. An answer to her prayer!

"Do you know him? Does any one know him?" questioned Tull, hurriedly.

His men looked and looked, and one by one shook their heads.

"He's come from far," said one.

"Thet's a fine hoss," said another.

"A strange rider."

"Huh! he wears black leather," added a fourth.

With a wave of his hand, enjoining silence, Tull stepped forward in such a way that he concealed Venters.

The rider reined in his mount, and with a lithe forward-slipping action appeared to reach the ground in one long step. It was a peculiar movement in its quickness and inasmuch that while performing it the rider did not swerve in the slightest from a square front to the group before him.

"Look!" hoarsely whispered one of Tull's companions. "He packs two black-butted guns—low down—they're hard to see—black agin them black chaps."

"A gun-man!" whispered another. "Fellers, careful now about movin' your hands."

The stranger's slow approach might have been a mere leisurely manner of gait or the cramped short steps of a rider unused to walking; yet, as well, it could have been the guarded advance of one who took no chances with men.

"Hello, stranger!" called Tull. No welcome was in this greeting, only a gruff curiosity.

The rider responded with a curt nod. The wide brim of a black sombrero cast a dark shade over his face. For a moment he closely regarded Tull and his comrades, and then, halting in his slow walk, he seemed to relax.

"Evenin', ma'am," he said to Jane, and removed his sombrero with quaint grace.

Jane, greeting him, looked up into a face that she trusted instinctively and which riveted her attention. It had all the characteristics of the range rider's—the leanness, the red burn of the sun, and the set changelessness that came from years of silence and solitude. But it was not these which held her; rather the intensity of his gaze, a strained weariness, a piercing wistfulness of keen, gray sight, as if the man was forever looking for that which he never found. Jane's subtle woman's intuition, even in that brief instant, felt a sadness, a hungering, a secret.

"Jane Withersteen, ma'am?" he inquired.

"Yes," she replied.

"The water here is yours?"

"Yes."

"May I water my horse?"

"Certainly. There's the trough."

"But mebbe if you knew who I was—" He hesitated, with his glance on the listening men. "Mebbe you wouldn't let me water him—though I ain't askin' none for myself."

"Stranger, it doesn't matter who you are. Water your horse. And if you are thirsty and hungry come into my house."

"Thanks, ma'am. I can't accept for myself—but for my tired horse—"

Trampling of hoofs interrupted the rider. More restless movements on the part of Tull's men broke up the little circle, exposing the prisoner Venters.

"Mebbe I've kind of hindered somethin'—for a few moments, perhaps?" inquired the rider.

"Yes," replied Jane Withersteen, with a throb in her voice.

She felt the drawing power of his eyes; and then she saw him look at the bound Venters, and at the men who held him, and their leader.

"In this here country all the rustlers an' thieves an' cut-throats an' gun-throwers an' all-round no-good men jest happen to be Gentiles. Ma'am, which of the no-good class does that young feller belong to?"

"He belongs to none of them. He's an honest boy."

"You *know* that, ma'am?"

"Yes—yes."

"Then what has he done to get tied up that way?"

His clear and distinct question, meant for Tull as well as for Jane Withersteen, stilled the restlessness and brought a momentary silence.

"Ask him," replied Jane, her voice rising high.

The rider stepped away from her, moving out with the same slow, measured stride in which he had approached, and the fact that his action placed her wholly to one side, and him no nearer to Tull and his men, had a penetrating significance.

"Young feller, speak up," he said to Venters.

"Here, stranger, this's none of your mix," began Tull. "Don't try any interference. You've been asked to drink and eat. That's more than you'd have got in any other village of the Utah border. Water your horse and be on your way."

"Easy—easy—I ain't interferin' yet," replied the rider. The tone of his voice had undergone a change. A different man had spoken. Where, in addressing Jane, he had been mild and gentle, now, with his first speech to Tull, he was dry, cool, biting. "I've jest stumbled onto a queer deal. Seven Mormons all packin' guns, an' a Gentile tied with a rope, an' a woman who swears by his honesty! Queer, ain't that?"

"Queer or not, it's none of your business," retorted Tull.

"Where I was raised a woman's word was law. I ain't quite out-growed that yet."

Tull fumed between amaze and anger.

"Meddler, we have a law here something different from woman's whim—Mormon law! . . . Take care you don't transgress it."

"To hell with your Mormon law!"

The deliberate speech marked the rider's further change, this time from kindly

15

interest to an awakening menace. It produced a transformation in Tull and his companions. The leader gasped and staggered backward at a blasphemous affront to an institution he held most sacred. The man Jerry, holding the horses, dropped the bridles and froze in his tracks. Like posts the other men stood, watchful-eyed, arms hanging rigid, all waiting.

"Speak up now, young man. What have you done to be roped that way?"

"It's a damned outrage!" burst out Venters. "I've done no wrong. I've offended this Mormon Elder by being a friend to that woman."

"Ma'am, is it true—what he says?" asked the rider of Jane; but his quiveringly alert eyes never left the little knot of quiet men.

"True? Yes, perfectly true," she answered.

"Well, young man, it seems to me that bein' a friend to such a woman would be what you wouldn't want to help an' couldn't help. . . . What's to be done to you for it?"

"They intend to whip me. You know what that means—in Utah!"

"I reckon," replied the rider, slowly.

With his gray glance cold on the Mormons, with the restive bit-champing of the horses, with Jane failing to repress her mounting agitations, with Venters standing pale and still, the tension of the moment tightened. Tull broke the spell with a laugh, a laugh without mirth, a laugh that was only a sound betraying fear.

"Come on, men!" he called.

Jane Withersteen turned again to the rider.

"Stranger, can you do nothing to save Venters?"

"Ma'am, you ask me to save him—from your own people?"

"Ask you? I beg of you!"

"But you don't dream who you're askin'."

"Oh, sir, I pray you—save him!"

"These are Mormons, an' I . . ."

"At—at any cost—save him. For I—I care for him!"

Tull snarled. "You love-sick fool! Tell your secrets. There'll be a way to teach you what you've never learned. . . . Come men, out of here!"

"Mormon, the young man stays," said the rider.

Like a shot his voice halted Tull.

"What!"

"He stays."

"Who'll keep him? He's my prisoner!" cried Tull, hotly. "Stranger, again I tell you—don't mix here. You've meddled enough. Go your way now or—"

"Listen! . . . He stays."

Absolute certainty, beyond any shadow of doubt, breathed in the rider's low voice.

"Who are you? We are seven here."

The rider dropped his sombrero and made a rapid movement, singular in that it left him somewhat crouched, arms bent and stiff, with the big black gun-sheaths swung round to the fore.

"Lassiter!"

It was Venters's wondering, thrilling cry that bridged the fateful connection between the rider's singular position and the dreaded name.

Tull put out a groping hand. The life of his eyes dulled to the gloom with which men of his fear saw the approach of death. But death, while it hovered over him, did not descend, for the rider waited for the twitching fingers, the downward flash of hand that did not come. Tull, gathering himself together, turned to the horses, attended by his pale comrades.

CHAPTER TWO

Cottonwoods

VENTERS appeared too deeply moved to speak the gratitude his face expressed. And Jane turned upon the rescuer and gripped his hands. Her smiles and tears seemingly dazed him. Presently, as something like calmness returned, she went to Lassiter's weary horse.

"I will water him myself," she said, and she led the horse to a trough under a huge old cottonwood. With nimble fingers she loosened the bridle and removed the bit. The horse snorted and bent his head. The trough was of solid stone, hollowed out, moss-covered and green and wet and cool, and the clear brown water that fed it spouted and splashed from a wooden pipe.

"He has brought you far to-day?"

"Yes, ma'am, a matter of over sixty miles, mebbe seventy."

"A long ride—a ride that—Ah, he is blind!"

"Yes, ma'am," replied Lassiter.

"What blinded him?"

"Some men once roped an' tied him, an' then held white-iron close to his eyes."

"Oh! Men? You mean devils. . . . Were they your enemies—Mormons?"

"Yes, ma'am."

"To take revenge on a horse! Lassiter, the men of my creed are unnaturally cruel. To my everlasting sorrow I confess it. They have been driven, hated, scourged till their hearts have hardened. But we women hope and pray for the time when our men will soften."

"Beggin' your pardon, ma'am—that time will never come."

"Oh, it will! . . . Lassiter, do you think Mormon women wicked? Has your hand been against them, too?"

"No. I believe Mormon women are the best and noblest, the most long-sufferin', and the blindest, unhappiest women on earth."

"Ah!" She gave him a grave, thoughtful look. "Then you will break bread with me?"

Lassiter had no ready response, and he uneasily shifted his weight from one leg to another, and turned his sombrero round and round in his hands. "Ma'am," he began, presently, "I reckon your kindness of heart makes you overlook things. Perhaps I ain't well known hereabouts, but back up North there's Mormons who'd rest oneasy in their graves at the idea of me sittin' to table with you."

"I dare say. But—will you do it, anyway?" she asked.

"Mebbe you have a brother or relative who might drop in an' be offended, an' I wouldn't want to—"

"I've not a relative in Utah that I know of. There's no one with a right to question my actions." She turned smilingly to Venters. "You will come in, Bern, and Lassiter will come in. We'll eat and be merry while we may."

"I'm only wonderin' if Tull an' his men'll raise a storm down in the village," said Lassiter, in his last weakening stand.

"Yes, he'll raise the storm—after he has prayed," replied Jane. "Come."

She led the way, with the bridle of Lassiter's horse over her arm. They entered a grove and walked down a wide path shaded by great low-branching cottonwoods. The last rays of the setting sun sent golden bars through the leaves. The grass was deep and rich; welcome contrast to sage-tired eyes. Twittering quail darted across the path, and from a tree-top somewhere a robin sang its evening song, and on the still air floated the freshness and murmur of flowing water.

The home of Jane Withersteen stood in a circle of cottonwoods, and was a flat, long, red-stone structure with a covered court in the center through which flowed a lively stream of amber-colored water. In the massive blocks of stone and heavy timbers and solid doors and shutters showed the hand of a man who had builded against pillage and time; and in the flowers and mosses lining the stone-bedded stream, in the bright colors of rugs and blankets on the court floor, and the cozy corner with hammock and books, and the clean-linened table, showed the grace of a daughter who lived for happiness and the day at hand.

Jane turned Lassiter's horse loose in the thick grass. "You will want him to be near you," she said, "or I'd have him taken to the alfalfa fields." At her call appeared women who began at once to bustle about, hurrying to and fro, setting the table. Then Jane, excusing herself, went within.

She passed through a huge low-ceiled chamber, like the inside of a fort, and into a smaller one where a bright wood-fire blazed in an old open fireplace, and from this into her own room. It had the same comfort as was manifested in the home-like outer court; moreover, it was warm and rich in soft hues.

Seldom did Jane Withersteen enter her room without looking into her mirror.

She knew she loved the reflection of that beauty which since early childhood she had never been allowed to forget. Her relatives and friends, and later a horde of Mormon and Gentile suitors, had fanned the flame of natural vanity in her. So that at twenty-eight she scarcely thought at all of her wonderful influence for good in the little community where her father had left her practically its beneficent landlord; but cared most for the dream and the assurance and the allurement of her beauty. This time, however, she gazed into her glass with more than the usual happy motive, without the usual slight conscious smile. For she was thinking of more than the desire to be fair in her own eyes, in those of her friend; she wondered if she were to seem fair in the eyes of this Lassiter, this man whose name had crossed the long, wild brakes of stone and plains of sage, this gentle-voiced, sad-faced man who was a hater and a killer of Mormons. It was not now her usual half-conscious vain obsession that actuated her as she hurriedly changed her riding-dress to one of white, and then looked long at the stately form with its gracious contours, at the fair face with its strong chin and full firm lips, at the dark-blue, proud, and passionate eyes.

"If by some means I can keep him here a few days, a week—he will never kill another Mormon," she mused. "Lassiter! . . . I shudder when I think of that name, of him. But when I look at the man I forget who he is—I almost like him. I remember only that he saved Bern. He has suffered. I wonder what it was—did he love a Mormon woman once? How splendidly he championed us poor misunderstood souls! Somehow he knows—much."

Jane Withersteen joined her guests and bade them to her board. Dismissing her woman, she waited upon them with her own hands. It was a bountiful supper and a strange company. On her right sat the ragged and half-starved Venters; and though blind eyes could have seen what he counted for in the sum of her happiness, yet he looked the gloomy outcast his allegiance had made him, and about him there was the shadow of the ruin presaged by Tull. On her left sat black-leather-garbed Lassiter looking like a man in a dream. Hunger was not with him, nor composure, nor speech, and when he twisted in frequent unquiet movements the heavy guns that he had not removed knocked against the table-legs. If it had been otherwise possible to forget the presence of Lassiter those telling little jars would have rendered it unlikely. And Jane Withersteen talked and smiled and laughed with all the dazzling play of lips and eyes that a beautiful, daring woman could summon to her purpose.

When the meal ended, and the men pushed back their chairs, she leaned closer to Lassiter and looked square into his eyes.

"Why did you come to Cottonwoods?"

Her question seemed to break a spell. The rider arose as if he had just remembered himself and had tarried longer than his wont.

"Ma'am, I have hunted all over the southern Utah and Nevada for—somethin'. An' through your name I learned where to find it—here in Cottonwoods."

"My name! Oh, I remember. You did know my name when you spoke first. Well, tell me where you heard it and from whom?"

"At the little village—Glaze, I think it's called—some fifty miles or more west of here. An' I heard it from a Gentile, a rider who said you'd know where to tell me to find—"

"What?" she demanded, imperiously, as Lassiter broke off.

"Milly Erne's grave," he answered low, and the words came with a wrench.

Venters wheeled in his chair to regard Lassiter in amazement, and Jane slowly raised herself in white, still wonder.

"Milly Erne's grave?" she echoed, in a whisper. "What do you know of Milly Erne, my best-beloved friend—who died in my arms? What were you to her?"

"Did I claim to be anythin'?" he inquired. "I know people—relatives—who have long wanted to know where she's buried. That's all."

"Relatives? She never spoke of relatives, except a brother who was shot in Texas. Lassiter, Milly Erne's grave is in a secret burying-ground on my property."

"Will you take me there? . . . You'll be offendin' Mormons worse than by breakin' bread with me."

"Indeed yes, but I'll do it. Only we must go unseen. To-morrow, perhaps."

"Thank you, Jane Withersteen," replied the rider, and he bowed to her and stepped backward out of the court.

"Will you not stay—sleep under my roof?" she asked.

"No, ma'am, an' thanks again. I never sleep indoors. An' even if I did there's that gatherin' storm in the village below. No, no. I'll go to the sage. I hope you won't suffer none for your kindness to me."

"Lassiter," said Venters, with a half-bitter laugh, "my bed, too, is the sage. Perhaps we may meet out there."

"Mebbe so. But the sage is wide an' I won't be near. Good night."

At Lassiter's low whistle the black horse whinnied, and carefully picked his blind way out of the grove. The rider did not bridle him, but walked beside him, leading him by touch of hand, and together they passed slowly into the shade of the cottonwoods.

"Jane, I must be off soon," said Venters. "Give me my guns. If I'd had my guns—"

"Either my friend or the Elder of my church would be lying dead," she interposed.

"Tull would be—surely."

"Oh, you fierce-blooded, savage youth! Can't I teach you forbearance, mercy? Bern, it's divine to forgive your enemies. 'Let not the sun go down upon thy wrath.'"

"Hush! Talk to me no more of mercy or religion—after to-day. To-day this strange coming of Lassiter left me still a man, and now I'll die a man! . . . Give me my guns."

Silently she went into the house, to return with a heavy cartridge-belt and gun-filled sheath and a long rifle; these she handed to him, and as he buckled on the belt she stood before him in silent eloquence.

"Jane," he said, in gentler voice, "don't look so. I'm not going out to murder your churchman. I'll try to avoid him and all his men. But can't you see I've reached the end of my rope? Jane, you're a wonderful woman. Never was there a woman so unselfish and good. Only you're blind in one way. . . . Listen!"

From behind the grove came the clicking sound of horses in a rapid trot.

"Some of your riders," he continued. "It's getting time for the night shift. Let us go out to the bench in the grove and talk there."

It was still daylight in the open, but under the spreading cottonwoods shadows were obscuring the lanes. Venters drew Jane off from one of these into a shrub-lined trail, just wide enough for the two to walk abreast, and in a roundabout way led her far from the house to a knoll on the edge of the grove. Here in a secluded nook was a bench from which, through an opening in the tree-tops, could be seen the sage-slope and the wall of rock and the dim lines of cañons. Jane had not spoken since Venters had shocked her with his first harsh speech; but all the way she had clung to his arm, and now, as he stopped and laid his rifle against the bench, she still clung to him.

"Jane, I'm afraid I must leave you."

"Bern!" she cried.

"Yes, it looks that way. My position is not a happy one—I can't feel right— I've lost all—"

"I'll give you anything you—"

"Listen, please. When I say loss I don't mean what you think. I mean loss of good-will, good name—that which would have enabled me to stand up in this village without bitterness. Well, it's too late. . . . Now, as to the future, I think you'd do best to give me up. Tull is implacable. You ought to see from his intention to-day that—But you can't see. Your blindness—your damned religion! . . . Jane, forgive me—I'm sore within and something rankles. Well, I fear that invisible hand will turn its hidden work to your ruin."

"Invisible hand? Bern!"

"I mean your Bishop." Venters said it deliberately and would not release her as she started back. "He's the law. The edict went forth to ruin me. Well, look at me! It'll now go forth to compel you to the will of the Church."

"You wrong Bishop Dyer. Tull is hard, I know. But then he has been in love with me for years."

"Oh, your faith and your excuses! You can't see what I know—and if you did see it you'd not admit it to save your life. That's the Mormon of you. These elders and bishops will do absolutely any deed to go on building up the power and wealth of their church, their empire. Think of what they've done to the Gentiles here, to me—think of Milly Erne's fate!"

"What do you know of her story?"

"I know enough—all, perhaps, except the name of the Mormon who brought her here. But I must stop this kind of talk."

She pressed his hand in response. He helped her to a seat beside him on the bench. And he respected a silence that he divined was full of woman's deep emotion, beyond his understanding.

It was the moment when the last ruddy rays of the sunset brightened momentarily before yielding to twilight. And for Venters the outlook before him was in some sense similar to a feeling of his future, and with searching eyes he studied the beautiful purple, barren waste of sage. Here was the unknown and the perilous. The whole scene impressed Venters as a wild, austere, and mighty manifestation of nature. And as it somehow reminded him of his prospect in life, so it suddenly resembled the woman near him, only in her there were greater beauty and peril, a mystery more unsolvable, and something nameless that numbed his heart and dimmed his eye.

"Look! A rider!" exclaimed Jane, breaking the silence. "Can that be Lassiter?"

Venters moved his glance once more to the west. A horseman showed dark on the sky-line, then merged into the color of the sage.

"It might be. But I think not—that fellow was coming in. One of your riders, more likely. Yes, I see him clearly now. And there's another."

"I see them, too."

"Jane, your riders seem as many as the bunches of sage. I ran into five yesterday 'way down near the trail to Deception Pass. They were with the white herd."

"You still go to that cañon? Bern, I wish you wouldn't. Oldring and his rustlers live somewhere down there."

"Well, what of that?"

"Tull has already hinted to your frequent trips into Deception Pass."

"I know." Venters uttered a short laugh. "He'll make a rustler of me next. But, Jane, there's no water for fifty miles after I leave here, and the nearest is in the cañon. I must drink and water my horse. There! I see more riders. They are going out."

"The red herd is on the slope, toward the Pass."

Twilight was fast falling. A group of horsemen crossed the dark line of low ground to become more distinct as they climbed the slope. The silence broke to a clear call from an incoming rider, and, almost like the peal of a hunting-horn, floated back the answer. The outgoing riders moved swiftly, came sharply into sight as they topped a ridge to show wild and black above the horizon, and then passed down, dimming into the purple of the sage.

"I hope they don't meet Lassiter," said Jane.

"So do I," replied Venters. "By this time the riders of the night shift know what happened to-day. But Lassiter will likely keep out of their way."

"Bern, who is Lassiter? He's only a name to me—a terrible name."

"Who is he? I don't know, Jane. Nobody I ever met knows him. He talks a little like a Texan, like Milly Erne. Did you note that?"

"Yes. How strange of him to know of her! And she lived here ten years and has been dead two. Bern, what do you know of Lassiter? Tell me what he has done—why you spoke of him to Tull—threatening to become another Lassiter yourself?"

"Jane, I only heard things, rumors, stories, most of which I disbelieved. At Glaze his name was known, but none of the riders or ranchers I knew there ever met him. At Stone Bridge I never heard him mentioned. But at Sterling and villages north of there he was spoken of often. I've never been in a village which he had been known to visit. There were many conflicting stories about him and his doings. Some said he had shot up this and that Mormon village, and others denied it. I'm inclined to believe he has, and you know how Mormons hide the truth. But there was one feature about Lassiter upon which all agree—that he was what riders in this country call a gun-man. He's a man with a marvelous quickness and

24

accuracy in the use of a Colt. And now that I've seen him I know more. Lassiter was born without fear. I watched him with eyes which saw him my friend. I'll never forget the moment I recognized him from what had been told me of his crouch before the draw. It was then I yelled his name. I believe that yell saved Tull's life. At any rate, I know this, between Tull and death then there was not the breadth of the littlest hair. If he or any of his men had moved a finger downward . . ."

Venters left his meaning unspoken, but at the suggestion Jane shuddered.

The pale afterglow in the west darkened with the merging of twilight into night. The sage now spread out black and gloomy. One dim star glimmered in the southwest sky. The sound of trotting horses had ceased, and there was silence broken only by a faint, dry pattering of cottonwood leaves in the soft night wind.

Into this peace and calm suddenly broke the high-keyed yelp of a coyote, and from far off in the darkness came the faint answering note of a trailing mate.

"Hello! the sage-dogs are barking," said Venters.

"I don't like to hear them," replied Jane. "At night, sometimes, when I lie awake, listening to the long mourn or breaking bark or wild howl, I think of you asleep somewhere in the sage, and my heart aches."

"Jane, you couldn't listen to sweeter music, nor could I have a better bed."

"Just think! Men like Lassiter and you have no home, no comfort, no rest, no place to lay your weary heads. Well! . . . Let us be patient. Tull's anger may cool, and time may help us. You might do some service to the village—who can tell? Suppose you discovered the long-unknown hiding-place of Oldring and his band, and told it to my riders? That would disarm Tull's ugly hints and put you in favor. For years my riders have trailed the tracks of stolen cattle. You know as well as I how dearly we've paid for our ranges in this wild country. Oldring drives our cattle down into the network of deceiving cañons, and somewhere far to the north or east he drives them up and out to Utah markets. If you will spend time in Deception Pass try to find the trails."

"Jane, I've thought of that. I'll try."

"I must go now. And it hurts, for now I'll never be sure of seeing you again. But to-morrow, Bern?"

"To-morrow surely. I'll watch for Lassiter and ride in with him."

"Good night."

Then she left him and moved away, a white, gliding shape that soon vanished in the shadows.

Venters waited until the faint slam of a door assured him she had reached the house; and then, taking up his rifle, he noiselessly slipped through the bushes, down the knoll, and on under the dark trees to the edge of the grove. The sky was now turning from gray to blue; stars had begun to lighten the earlier blackness; and from the wide flat sweep before him blew a cool wind, fragrant with the breath of sage. Keeping close to the edge of the cottonwoods, he went swiftly and silently westward. The grove was long, and he had not reached the end when he heard something that brought him to a halt. Low padded thuds told him horses were coming this way. He sank down in the gloom, waiting, listening. Much before he had expected, judging from sound, to his amazement he descried horsemen near at hand. They were riding along the border of the sage, and instantly he knew the hoofs of the horses were muffled. Then the pale starlight afforded him indistinct sight of the riders. But his eyes were keen and used to the dark, and by peering closely he recognized the huge bulk and black-bearded visage of Oldring and the lithe, supple form of the rustler's lieutenant, a masked rider. They passed on; the darkness swallowed them. Then, farther out on the sage, a dark, compact body of horsemen went by, almost without sound, almost like specters, and they, too, melted into the night.

CHAPTER THREE

Amber Spring

No unusual circumstances was it for Oldring and some of his men to visit Cottonwoods in the broad light of day, but for him to prowl about in the dark with the hoofs of his horses muffled meant that mischief was brewing. Moreover, to Venters the presence of the masked rider with Oldring seemed especially ominous. For about this man there was mystery; he seldom rode through the village, and when he did ride through it was swiftly; riders seldom met by day on the sage; but wherever he rode there always followed deeds as dark and mysterious as the mask he wore. Oldring's band did not confine themselves to the rustling of cattle.

Venters lay low in the shade of the cottonwoods, pondering this chance meeting, and not for many moments did he consider it safe to move on. Then, with sudden impulse, he turned the other way and went back along the grove. When he reached the path leading to Jane's home he decided to go down to the village. So he hurried onward, with quick soft steps. Once beyond the grove he entered the one and only street. It was wide, lined with tall poplars, and under each row of trees, inside the foot-path, were ditches where ran the water from Jane Withersteen's spring.

Between the trees twinkled lights of cottage candles, and far down flared bright windows of the village stores. When Venters got closer to these he saw knots of men standing together in earnest conversation. The usual lounging on the corners and benches and steps was not in evidence. Keeping in the shadow, Venters went closer and closer until he could hear voices. But he could not distinguish what was said. He recognized many Mormons, and looked hard for Tull and his men, but looked in vain. Venters concluded that the rustlers had not passed along the village street. No doubt these earnest men were discussing Lassiter's coming. But Venters felt positive that Tull's intention toward himself that day had not been and would not be revealed.

So Venters, seeing there was little for him to learn, began retracing his steps. The church was dark, Bishop Dyer's home next to it was also dark, and likewise

Tull's cottage. Upon almost any night at this hour there would be lights here, and Venters marked the unusual omission.

As he was about to pass out of the street to skirt the grove, he once more slunk down at the sound of trotting horses. Presently he descried two mounted men riding toward him. He hugged the shadow of a tree. Again the starlight, brighter now, aided him, and he made out Tull's stalwart figure, and beside him the short, froglike shape of the rider Jerry. They were silent, and they rode on to disappear.

Venters went his way with busy, gloomy mind, revolving events of the day, trying to reckon those brooding in the night. His thoughts overwhelmed him. Up in that dark grove dwelt a woman who had been his friend. And he skulked about her home, gripping a gun stealthily as an Indian, a man without place or people or purpose. Above her hovered the shadow of grim, hidden, secret power. No queen could have given more royally out of a bounteous store than Jane Withersteen gave her people, and likewise to those unfortunates whom her people hated. She asked only the divine right of all women—freedom; to love and to live as her heart willed. And yet prayer and her hope were vain.

"For years I've seen a storm clouding over her and the village of Cottonwoods," muttered Venters, as he strode on. "Soon it'll burst. I don't like the prospects." That night the villagers whispered in the street—and night-riding rustlers muffled horses—and Tull was at work in secret—and out there in the sage hid a man who meant something terrible—Lassiter!

Venters passed the black cottonwoods, and, entering the sage, climbed the gradual slope. He kept his direction in line with a western star. From time to time he stopped to listen and heard only the usual familiar bark of coyote and sweep of wind and rustle of sage. Presently a low jumble of rocks loomed up darkly somewhat to his right, and, turning that way, he whistled softly. Out of the rocks glided a dog that leaped and whined about him. He climbed over rough, broken rock, picking his way carefully, and then went down. Here it was darker, and sheltered from the wind. A white object guided him. It was another dog, and this one was asleep, curled up between a saddle and a pack. The animal awoke and thumped his tail in greeting. Venters placed the saddle for a pillow, rolled in his blankets, with his face upward to the stars. The white dog snuggled close to him. The other whined and pattered a few yards to the rise of ground and there crouched on guard. And in that wild covert Venters shut his eyes under the great white stars and intense vaulted blue, bitterly comparing their loneliness to his own, and fell asleep.

When he awoke, day had dawned and all about him was bright steel-gray. The air had a cold tang. Arising, he greeted the fawning dogs and stretched his cramped body, and then, gathering together bunches of dead sage sticks, he lighted a fire. Strips of dried beef held to the blaze for a moment served him and the dogs. He drank from a canteen. There was nothing else in his outfit; he had grown used to a scant fire. Then he sat over the fire, palms outspread, and waited. Waiting had been his chief occupation for months, and he scarcely knew what he waited for, unless it was the passing of the hours. But now he sensed action in the immediate present; the day promised another meeting with Lassiter and Jane, perhaps news of the rustlers; on the morrow he meant to take the trail to Deception Pass.

And while he waited he talked to his dogs. He called them Ring and Whitie; they were sheep-dogs, half collie, half deer-hound, superb in build, perfectly trained. It seemed that in his fallen fortunes these dogs understood the nature of their value to him, and governed their affection and faithfulness accordingly. Whitie watched him with somber eyes of love, and Ring, crouched on the little rise of ground above, kept tireless guard. When the sun rose, the white dog took the place of the other, and Ring went to sleep at his master's feet.

By and by Venters rolled up his blankets and tied them and his meager pack together, then climbed out to look for his horse. He saw him, presently, a little way off in the sage, and went to fetch him. In that country, where every rider boasted of a fine mount and was eager for a race, where thoroughbreds dotted the wonderful grazing ranges, Venters rode a horse that was sad proof of his misfortunes.

Then, with his back against a stone, Venters faced the east, and, stick in hand and idle blade, he waited. The glorious sunlight filled the valley with purple fire. Before him, to left, to right, waving, rolling, sinking, rising, like low swells of a purple sea, stretched the sage. Out of the grove of cottonwoods, a green patch on the purple, gleamed the dull red of Jane Withersteen's old stone house. And from there extended the wide green of the village gardens and orchards marked by the graceful poplars; and farther down shone the deep, dark richness of the alfalfa fields. Numberless red and black and white dots speckled the sage, and these were cattle and horses.

So, watching and waiting, Venters let the time wear away. At length he saw a horse rise above a ridge, and he knew it to be Lassiter's black. Climbing to the highest rock, so that he would show against the sky-line, he stood and waved his hat. The almost instant turning of Lassiter's horse attested to the quickness of that rider's eye. Then Venters climbed down, saddled his horse, tied on his pack, and, with a word to his dogs, was about to ride out to meet Lassiter, when he concluded to wait for him there, on higher ground, where the outlook was commanding.

It had been long since Venters had experienced friendly greeting from a man. Lassiter's warmed in him something that had grown cold from neglect. And when he had returned it, with a strong grip of the iron hand that held his, and met the gray eyes, he knew that Lassiter and he were to be friends.

"Venters, let's talk awhile before we go down there," said Lassiter, slipping his bridle. "I ain't in no hurry. Them's sure fine dogs you've got." With a rider's eye he took in the points of Venter's horse, but did not speak his thought. "Well, did anythin' come off after I left you last night?"

Venters told him about the rustlers.

"I was snug hid in the sage," replied Lassiter, "an' didn't see or hear no one. Oldrin's got a high hand here, I reckon. It's no news up in Utah how he holes in cañons an' leaves no track." Lassiter was silent a moment. "Me an' Oldrin' wasn't exactly strangers some years back when he drove cattle into Bostil's Ford, at the head of the Rio Virgin. But he got harassed there an' now he drives some place else."

"Lassiter, you knew him? Tell me, is he Mormon or Gentile?"

"I can't say. I've knowed Mormons who pretended to be Gentiles."

"No Mormon ever pretended that unless he was a rustler," declared Venters.

"Mebbe so."

"It's a hard country for any one, but hardest for Gentiles. Did you ever know or hear of a Gentile prospering in a Mormon community?"

"I never did."

"Well, I want to get out of Utah. I've a mother living in Illinois. I want to go home. It's eight years now."

The older man's sympathy moved Venters to tell his story. He had left Quincy, run off to seek his fortune in the gold fields, had never gotten any farther than Salt Lake City, wandered here and there as helper, teamster, shepherd, and drifted southward over the divide and across the barrens and up the rugged plateau through the passes to the last border settlements. Here he became a rider of the sage, had stock of his own, and for a time prospered, until chance threw him in the employ of Jane Withersteen.

"Lassiter, I needn't tell you the rest."

"Well, it'd be no news to me. I know Mormons. I've seen their women's strange love an' patience an' sacrifice an' silence an' what I call madness for their idea of God. An' over against that I've seen the tricks of men. They work hand in hand, all together, an' in the dark. No man can hold out against them, unless he takes to packin' guns. For Mormons are slow to kill. That's the only good I ever seen in their religion. Venters, take this from me, these Mormons ain't just right in their minds. Else could a Mormon marry one woman when he already has a wife, an' call it duty?"

"Lassiter, you think as I think," returned Venters.

"How'd it come then that you never throwed a gun on Tull or some of them?" inquired the rider, curiously.

"Jane pleaded with me, begged me to be patient, to overlook. She even took my guns from me. I lost all before I knew it," replied Venters, with the red color in his face. "But, Lassiter, listen.

"Out of the wreck I saved a Winchester, two Colts, and plenty of shells. I packed these down into Deception Pass. There, almost every day for six months, I have practised with my rifle till the barrel burnt my hands. Practised the draw— the firing of a Colt, hour after hour!"

"Now that's interestin' to me," said Lassiter, with a quick uplift of his head and a concentration of his gray gaze on Venters. "Could you throw a gun before you began that practisin'?"

"Yes. And now . . ." Venters made a lightning-swift movement.

Lassiter smiled, and then his bronzed eyelids narrowed till his, eyes seemed mere gray slits. "You'll kill Tull!" He did not question; he affirmed.

"I promised Jane Withersteen I'd try to avoid Tull. I'll keep my word. But sooner or later Tull and I will meet. As I feel now, if he even looks at me I'll draw!"

"I reckon so. There'll be hell down there, presently." He paused a moment and flicked a sage-brush with his quirt. "Venters, seein' as you're considerable worked up, tell me Milly Erne's story."

Venters's agitation stilled to the trace of suppressed eagerness in Lassiter's query.

"Milly Erne's story? Well, Lassiter, I'll tell you what I know. Milly Erne had been in Cottonwoods years when I first arrived there, and most of what I tell you happened before my arrival. I got to know her pretty well. She was a slip of a woman, and crazy on religion. I conceived an idea that I never mentioned—I thought she was at heart more Gentile than Mormon. But she passed as a Mormon, and certainly she had the Mormon woman's locked lips. You know, in every Mormon village there are women who seem mysterious to us, but about Milly there was more than the ordinary mystery. When she came to Cottonwoods she had a beautiful little girl whom she loved passionately. Milly was not known openly in Cottonwoods as a Mormon wife. That she really was a Mormon wife I have no doubt. Perhaps the Mormon's other wife or wives would not acknowledge Milly. Such things happen in these villages. Mormon wives wear yokes, but they get jealous. Well, whatever had brought Milly to this country—love or madness of religion—she repented of it. She gave up teaching the village school. She quit the church. And she began to fight Mormon upbringing for her baby girl. Then the Mormons put on the screws—slowly, as is their way. At last the child disappeared. Lost, was the report. The child was stolen, I know that. So do you. That wrecked Milly Erne. But she lived on in hope. She became a slave. She worked her heart and soul and life out to get back her child. She never heard of it again. Then she sank. . . . I can see her now, a frail thing, so transparent you could almost look through her—white like ashes—and her eyes! . . . Her eyes have always haunted me. She had one real friend—Jane Withersteen. But Jane couldn't mend a broken heart, and Milly died."

For moments Lassiter did not speak, or turn his head.

"The man!" he exclaimed, presently, in husky accents.

"I haven't the slightest idea who the Mormon was," replied Venters; "nor has any Gentile in Cottonwoods."

"Does Jane Withersteen know?"

"Yes. But a red-hot running-iron couldn't burn that name out of her!"

Without further speech Lassiter started off, walking his horse, and Venters followed with his dogs. Half a mile down the slope they entered a luxuriant growth of willows, and soon came into an open space carpeted with grass like deep green velvet. The rushing of water and singing of birds filled their ears. Venters led his comrade to a shady bower and showed him Amber Spring. It was a magnificent outburst of clear, amber water pouring from a dark, stone-lined hole. Lassiter knelt and drank, lingered there to drink again. He made no comment, but Venters did not need words. Next to his horse a rider of the sage loved a spring. And this spring was the most beautiful and remarkable known to the upland riders of southern Utah. It was the spring that made old Withersteen a feudal lord and now enabled his daughter to return the toll which her father had exacted from the toilers of the sage.

The spring gushed forth in a swirling torrent, and leaped down joyously to make its swift way along a willow-skirted channel. Moss and ferns and lilies overhung its green banks. Except for the rough-hewn stones that held and directed the water, this willow thicket and glade had been left as nature had made it.

Below were artificial lakes, three in number, one above the other in banks of raised earth; and round about them rose the lofty green-foliaged shafts of poplar trees. Ducks dotted the glassy surface of the lakes; a blue heron stood motionless on a water-gate; kingfishers darted with shrieking flight along the shady banks; a white hawk sailed above; and from the trees and shrubs came the song of robins and cat-birds. It was all in strange contrast to the endless slopes of lonely sage and the wild rock environs beyond. Venters thought of the woman who loved the birds and the green of the leaves and the murmur of the water.

Next on the slope, just below the third and largest lake, were corrals and a wide stone barn and open sheds and coops and pens. Here were clouds of dust, and cracking sounds of hoofs, and romping colts and heehawing burros. Neighing horses trampled to the corral fences. And from the little windows of the barn projected bobbing heads of bays and blacks and sorrels. When the two men entered the immense barnyard, from all around the din increased. This welcome, however, was not seconded by the several men and boys who vanished on sight.

Venters and Lassiter were turning toward the house when Jane appeared in the lane leading a horse. In riding-skirt and blouse she seemed to have lost some of her statuesque proportions, and looked more like a girl rider than the mistress of Withersteen. She was brightly smiling, and her greeting was warmly cordial.

"Good news," she announced. "I've been to the village. All is quiet. I expected—I don't know what. But there's no excitement. And Tull has ridden out on his way to Glaze."

"Tull gone?" inquired Venters, with surprise. He was wondering what could have taken Tull away. Was it to avoid another meeting with Lassiter that he went? Could it have any connection with the probable nearness of Oldring and his gang?

"Gone, yes, thank goodness," replied Jane. "Now I'll have peace for a while. Lassiter, I want you to see my horses. You are a rider, and you must be a judge of horseflesh. Some of mine have Arabian blood. My father got his best strain in Nevada from Indians who claimed their horses were bred down from the original stock left by the Spaniards."

"Well, ma'am, the one you've been ridin' takes my eye," said Lassiter, as he walked round the racy, clean-limbed, and fine-pointed roan.

"Where are the boys?" she asked, looking about. "Jerd, Paul, where are you? Here, bring out the horses."

The sound of dropping bars inside the barn was the signal for the horses to jerk their heads in the windows, to snort and stamp. Then they came pounding out of the door, a file of thoroughbreds, to plunge about the barnyard, heads and tails up, manes flying. They halted afar off, squared away to look, came slowly forward with whinnies for their mistress, and doubtful snorts for the strangers and their horses.

"Come—come—come," called Jane, holding out her hands. "Why Bells— Wrangle, where are your manners? Come, Black Star—come, Night. Ah, you beauties! My racers of the sage!"

Only two came up to her; those she called Night and Black Star. Venters never looked at them without delight. The first was soft dead black, the other glittering black, and they were perfectly matched in size, both being high and long-bodied, wide through the shoulders, with lithe, powerful legs. That they were a woman's pets showed in the gloss of skin, the fineness of mane. It showed, too, in the light of big eyes and the gentle reach of eagerness.

"I never seen their like," was Lassiter's encomium, "an' in my day I've seen a sight of horses. Now, ma'am, if you was wantin' to make a long an' fast ride across the sage—say to elope—"

Lassiter ended there with dry humor, yet behind that was meaning. Jane blushed and made arch eyes at him.

"Take care, Lassiter, I might think that a proposal," she replied, gaily. "It's dangerous to propose elopement to a Mormon woman. Well, I was expecting you. Now will be a good hour to show you Milly Erne's grave. The day-riders have gone, and the night-riders haven't come in. Bern, what do you make of that? Need I worry? You know I have to be made worry."

"Well, it's not usual for the night shift to ride in so late," replied Venters, slowly, and his glance sought Lassiter's. "Cattle are usually quiet after dark. Still, I've known even a coyote to stampede your white herd."

"I refuse to borrow trouble. Come," said Jane.

They mounted, and, with Jane in the lead, rode down the lane, and, turning off into a cattle trail, proceeded westward. Venters's dogs trotted behind them. On this side of the ranch the outlook was different from that on the other; the immediate foreground was rough and the sage more rugged and less colorful;

there were no dark-blue lines of cañons to hold the eye, nor any uprearing rock walls. It was a long roll and slope into gray obscurity. Soon Jane left the trail and rode into the sage, and presently she dismounted and threw her bridle. The men did likewise. Then, on foot, they followed her, coming out at length on the rim of a low escarpment. She passed by several little ridges of earth to halt before a faintly defined mound. It lay in the shade of a sweeping sage-brush close to the edge of the promontory; and a rider could have jumped his horse over it without recognizing a grave.

"Here!"

She looked sad as she spoke, but she offered no explanation for the neglect of an unmarked, uncared-for grave. There was a little bunch of pale, sweet lavender daisies, doubtless planted there by Jane.

"I only come here to remember and to pray," she said. "But I leave no trail!"

A grave in the sage! How lonely this resting-place of Milly Erne! The cotton-woods or the alfalfa fields were not in sight, nor was there any rock or ridge or cedar to lend contrast to the monotony. Gray slopes, tinging the purple, barren and wild, with the wind waving the sage, swept away to the dim horizon.

Lassiter looked at the grave and then out into space. At that moment he seemed a figure of bronze.

Jane touched Venters's arm and led him back to the horses.

"Bern!" cried Jane, when they were out of hearing. "Suppose Lassiter were Milly's husband—the father of that little girl lost so long ago!"

"It might be, Jane. Let us ride on. If he wants to see us again he'll come."

So they mounted and rode out to the cattle trail and began to climb. From the height of the ridge, where they had started down, Venters looked back. He did not see Lassiter, but his glance, drawn irresistibly farther out on the gradual slope, caught sight of a moving cloud of dust.

"Hello, a rider!"

"Yes, I see," said Jane.

"That fellow's riding hard. Jane, there's something wrong."

"Oh yes, there must be. . . . How he rides!"

The horse disappeared in the sage, and then puffs of dust marked his course.

"He's short-cut on us—he's making straight for the corrals."

Venters and Jane galloped their steeds and reined in at the turning of the lane. This lane led down to the right of the grove. Suddenly into its lower entrance flashed a bay horse. Then Venters caught the fast rhythmic beat of pounding hoofs. Soon his keen eye recognized the swing of the rider in his saddle.

"It's Judkins, your Gentile rider!" he cried. "Jane, when Judkins rides like that it means hell!"

CHAPTER FOUR

Deception Pass

THE rider thundered up and almost threw his foam-flecked horse in the sudden stop. He was a giant form, and with fearless eyes.

"Judkins, you're all bloody!" cried Jane, in affright. "Oh, you've been shot!"

"Nothin' much, Miss Withersteen. I got a nick in the shoulder. I'm some wet an' the hoss's been throwin' lather, so all this ain't blood."

"What's up?" queried Venters, sharply.

"Rustlers sloped off with the red herd."

"Where are my riders?" demanded Jane.

"Miss Withersteen, I was alone all night with the herd. At daylight this mornin' the rustlers rode down. They began to shoot at me on sight. They chased me hard an' far, burnin' powder all the time, but I got away."

"Jud, they meant to kill you," declared Venters.

"Now I wonder," returned Judkins. "They wanted me bad. An' it ain't regular for rustlers to waste time chasin' one rider."

"Thank heaven you got away," said Jane. "But my riders—where are they?"

"I don't know. The night-riders weren't there last night when I rode down, an' this mornin' I met no day-riders."

"Judkins! Bern they've been set upon—killed by Oldring's men!"

"I don't think so," replied Venters, decidedly. "Jane, your riders haven't gone out in the sage."

"Bern, what do you mean?" Jane Withersteen turned deathly pale.

"You remember what I said about the unseen hand?"

"Oh! . . . Impossible!"

"I hope so. But I fear—" Venters finished, with a shake of his head.

"Bern, you're bitter; but that's only natural. We'll wait to see what's happened to my riders. Judkins, come to the house with me. Your wound must be attended to."

"Jane, I'll find out where Oldring drives the herd," vowed Venters.

"No, no! Bern, don't risk it now—when the rustlers are in such shooting mood."

"I'm going. Jud, how many cattle in that red herd?"

"Twenty-five hundred head."

"Whew! What on earth can Oldring do with so many cattle? Why, a hundred head is a big steal. I've got to find out."

"Don't go," implored Jane.

"Bern, you want a hoss thet can run. Miss Withersteen, if it's not too bold of me to advise, make him take a fast hoss or don't let him go."

"Yes, yes, Judkins. He must ride a horse that can't be caught. Which one—Black Star—Night?"

"Jane, I won't take either," said Venters, emphatically. "I wouldn't risk losing one of your favorites."

"Wrangle, then?"

"Thet's the hoss," replied Judkins. "Wrangle can outrun Black Star an' Night. You'd never believe it, Miss Withersteen, but I know. Wrangle's the biggest an' fastest hoss on the sage."

"Oh no, Wrangle can't beat Black Star. But, Bern, take Wrangle, if you will go. Ask Jerd for anything you need. Oh, be watchful, careful. . . . God speed you!"

She clasped his hand, turned quickly away, and went down the lane with the rider.

Venters rode to the barn, and, leaping off, shouted for Jerd. The boy came running. Venters sent him for meat, bread, and dried fruits, to be packed in saddlebags. His own horse he turned loose into the nearest corral. Then he went for Wrangle. The giant sorrel had earned his name for a trait the opposite of amiability. He came readily out of the barn, but once in the yard he broke from Venters, and plunged about with ears laid back. Venters had to rope him, and then he kicked down a section of fence, stood on his hind legs, crashed down and fought the rope. Jerd returned to lend a hand.

"Wrangle don't git enough work," said Jerd, as the big saddle went on. "He's unruly when he's corralled, an' wants to run. Wait till he smells the sage!"

"Jerd, this horse is an iron-jawed devil. I never straddled him but once. Run? Say, he's swift as wind!"

When Venters's boot touched the stirrup the sorrel bolted, giving him the rider's flying mount. The swing of this fiery horse recalled to Venters days that were not really long past, when he rode into the sage as the leader of Jane

Withersteen's riders. Wrangle pulled hard on a tight rein. He galloped out of the lane, down the shady border of the grove, and hauled up at the watering-trough, where he pranced and champed his bit. Venters got off and filled his canteen while the horse drank. The dogs, Ring and Whitie, came trotting up for their drink. Then Venters remounted and turned Wrangle toward the sage.

A wide, white trail wound away down the slope. One keen, sweeping glance told Venters that there was neither man nor horse nor steer within the limit of his vision, unless they were lying down in the sage. Ring loped in the lead and Whitie loped in the rear. Wrangle settled gradually into an easy swinging canter, and Venters's thoughts, now that the rush and flurry of the start were past, and the long miles stretched before him, reverted to a calm reckoning of late singular coincidences.

There was the night ride of Tull's, which, viewed in the light of subsequent events, had a look of his covert machinations; Oldring and his Masked Rider and his rustlers riding muffled horses; the report that Tull had ridden out that morning with his man Jerry on the trail to Glaze, the strange disappearance of Jane Withersteen's riders, the unusually determined attempt to kill the one Gentile still in her employ, an intention frustrated, no doubt, only by Judkin's magnificent riding of her racer, and lastly the driving of the red herd. These events, to Venters's color of mind, had a dark relationship. Remembering Jane's accusation of bitterness, he tried hard to put aside his rancor in judging Tull. But it was bitter knowledge that made him see the truth. He had felt the shadow of an unseen hand; he had watched till he saw its dim outline, and then he had traced it to a man's hate, to the rivalry of a Mormon Elder, to the power of a Bishop, to the long, far-reaching arm of a terrible creed. That unseen hand had made its first move against Jane Withersteen. Her riders had been called in, leaving her without help to drive seven thousand head of cattle. But to Venters it seemed extraordinary that the power which had called in these riders had left so many cattle to be driven by rustlers and harried by wolves. For hand in glove with that power was an insatiate greed; they were one and the same.

"What can Oldring do with twenty-five hundred head of cattle?" muttered Venters. "Is he a Mormon? Did he meet Tull last night? It looks like a black plot to me. But Tull and his churchmen wouldn't ruin Jane Withersteen unless the Church was to profit by that ruin. Where does Oldring come in? I'm going to find out about these things."

Wrangle did the twenty-five miles in three hours and walked little of the way. When he had gotten warmed up he had been allowed to choose his own gait.

The afternoon had well advanced when Venters struck the trail of the red herd and found where it had grazed the night before. Then Venters rested the horse and used his eyes. Near at hand were a cow and a calf and several yearlings, and farther out in the sage some straggling steers. He caught a glimpse of coyotes skulking near the cattle. The slow, sweeping gaze of the rider failed to find other living things within the field of sight. The sage about him was breast-high to his horse, oversweet with its warm, fragrant breath, gray where it waved to the light, darker where the wind left it still, and beyond the wonderful haze-purple lent by distance. Far across that wide waste began the slow lift of uplands through which Deception Pass cut its tortuous many-cañoned way.

Venters raised the bridle of his horse and followed the broad cattle trail. The crushed sage resembled the path of a monster snake. In a few miles of travel he passed several cows and calves that had escaped the drive. Then he stood on the last high bench of the slope with the floor of the valley beneath. The opening of the cañon showed in a break of the sage, and the cattle trail paralleled it as far as he could see. That trail led to an undiscovered point where Oldring drove cattle into the pass, and many a rider who had followed it had never returned. Venters satisfied himself that the rustlers had not deviated from their usual course, and then he turned at right angles off the cattle trail and made for the head of the pass.

The sun lost its heat and wore down to the western horizon, where it changed from white to gold and rested like a huge ball about to roll on its golden shadows down the slope. Venters watched the lengthening of the rays and bars, and marveled at his own league-long shadow. The sun sank. There was instant shading of brightness about him, and he saw a kind of cold purple bloom creep ahead of him to cross the cañon, to mount the opposite slope and chase and darken and bury the last golden flare of sunlight.

Venters rode into a trail that he always took to get down into the cañon. He dismounted and found no tracks but his own made days previous. Nevertheless he sent the dog Ring ahead and waited. In a little while Ring returned. Whereupon Venters led his horse on to the break in the ground.

The opening into Deception Pass was one of the remarkable natural phenomena in a country remarkable for vast slopes of sage, uplands insulated by gigantic red walls, and deep cañons of mysterious source and outlet. Here the valley floor was level, and here opened a narrow chasm, a ragged vent in yellow walls of stone. The trail down the five hundred feet of sheer depth always tested Venters's nerve. It was bad going for even a burro. But Wrangle, as Venters led him, snorted defiance or disgust rather than fear, and, like a hobbled horse on the jump, lifted his ponderous iron-shod fore hoofs and crashed down over the first rough step. Venters warmed to greater admiration of the sorrel; and, giving him a loose bridle, he stepped down foot by foot. Oftentimes the stones and shale started by Wrangle buried Venters to his knees; again he was hard put to it to dodge a rolling boulder; there were times when he could not see Wrangle for dust, and once he and the horse rode a sliding shelf of yellow, weathered cliff. It was a trail on which there could be no stops, and, therefore, if perilous, it was at least one that did not take long in the descent.

Venters breathed lighter when that was over, and felt a sudden assurance in the success of his enterprise. For at first it had been a reckless determination to achieve something at any cost, and now it resolved itself into an adventure worthy of all his reason and cunning, and keenness of eye and ear.

Piñon pines clustered in little clumps along the level floor of the pass. Twilight had gathered under the walls. Venters rode into the trail and up the cañon. Gradually the trees and caves and objects low down turned black, and this blackness moved up the walls till night enfolded the pass, while day still lingered above. The sky darkened; and stars began to show, at first pale and then bright. Sharp notches of the rim-wall, biting like teeth into the blue, were landmarks by which Venters knew where his camping site lay. He had to feel his way through a thicket of slender oaks to a spring where he watered Wrangle and drank himself. Here he unsaddled and turned Wrangle loose, having no fear that the horse would leave the thick, cool grass adjacent to the spring. Next he satisfied his own hunger, fed Ring and Whitie, and, with them curled beside him, composed himself to await sleep.

There had been a time when night in the high altitude of these Utah uplands had been satisfying to Venters. But that was before the oppression of enemies had made the change in his mind. As a rider guarding the herd he had never thought of the night's wildness and loneliness; as an outcast, now when the full silence set in, and the deep darkness, and trains of radiant stars shone cold and calm, he lay with an ache in his heart. For a year he had lived as a black fox, driven from his kind. He longed for the sound of a voice, the touch of a hand. In the daytime there was riding from place to place, and the gun practice to which something drove him, and other tasks that at least necessitated action; at night, before he won sleep, there was strife in his soul. He yearned to leave the endless sage slopes, the wilderness of cañons; and it was in the lonely night that this yearning grew unbearable. It was then that he reached forth to feel

Ring or Whitie, immeasurably grateful for the love and companionship of two dogs.

On this night the same old loneliness beset Venters, the old habit of sad thought and burning unquiet had its way. But from it evolved a conviction that his useless life had undergone a subtle change. He had sensed it first when Wrangle swung him up to the high saddle, he knew it now when he lay in the gateway of Deception Pass. He had no thrill of adventure, rather a gloomy perception of great hazard, perhaps death. He meant to find Oldring's retreat. The rustlers had fast horses, but none that could catch Wrangle. Venters knew no rustler could creep upon him at night when Ring and Whitie guarded his hiding-place. For the rest, he had eyes and ears, and a long rifle and an unerring aim, which he meant to use. Strangely his foreshadowing of change did not hold a thought of the killing of Tull. It related only to what was to happen to him in Deception Pass; and he could no more lift the veil of that mystery than tell where the trails led to in that unexplored cañon. Moreover, he did not care. And at length, tired out by stress of thought, he fell asleep.

When his eyes unclosed, day had come again, and he saw the rim of the opposite wall tipped with the gold of sunrise. A few moments sufficed for the morning's simple camp duties. Near at hand he found Wrangle, and to his surprise the horse came to him. Wrangle was one of the horses that left his viciousness in the home corral. What he wanted was to be free of mules and burros and steers, to roll in dust-patches, and then to run down the wide, open, windy sage-plains, and at night browse and sleep in the cool wet grass of a springhole. Jerd knew the sorrel when he said of him, "Wait till he smells the sage!"

Venters saddled and led him out of the oak thicket, and, leaping astride, rode up the cañon, with Ring and Whitie trotting behind. An old grass-grown trail followed the course of a shallow wash where flowed a thin stream of water. The cañon was a hundred rods wide; its yellow walls were perpendicular; it had abundant sage and a scant growth of oak and piñon. For five miles it held to a comparatively straight bearing, and then began a heightening of rugged walls and a deepening of the floor. Beyond this point of sudden change in the character of the cañon Venters had never explored, and here was the real door to the intricacies of Deception Pass.

He reined Wrangle to a walk, halted now and then to listen, and then proceeded cautiously with shifting and alert gaze. The cañon assumed proportions that dwarfed those of its first ten miles. Venters rode on and on, not losing in the interest of his wide surroundings any of his caution or keen search for tracks or sight of living thing. If there ever had been a trail here, he could not find it. He rode through sage and clumps of piñon trees and grassy plots where long-petaled purple lilies bloomed. He rode through a dark constriction of the pass no wider than the lane in the grove at Cottonwoods. And he came out into a great amphitheater into which jutted huge towering corners of a confluence of intersecting cañons.

Venters sat his horse, and, with a rider's eye, studied this wild cross-cut of huge stone gullies. Then he went on, guided by the course of running water. If it had not been for the main stream of water flowing north he would never have been able to tell which of those many openings was a continuation of the pass. In crossing this amphitheater he went by the mouths of five cañons, fording little streams that flowed into the larger one. Gaining the outlet which he took to be the pass, he rode on again under overhanging walls. One side was dark in shade, the other light in sun. This narrow passageway turned and twisted and opened into a valley that amazed Venters.

Here again was a sweep of purple sage, richer than upon the higher levels. The valley was miles long, several wide, and in-closed by unscalable walls. But it was the background of this valley that so forcibly struck him. Across the sage-flat rose a strange up-flinging of yellow rocks. He could not tell which were close and which were distant. Scrawled mounds of stone, like mountain waves, seemed to roll up to steep bare slopes and towers.

In this plain of sage Venters flushed birds and rabbits, and when he had proceeded about a mile he caught sight of the bobbing white tails of a herd of running antelope. He rode along the edge of the stream which wound toward the western end of the slowly looming mounds of stone. The high slope retreated out of sight behind the nearer projection. To Venters the valley appeared to have been filled in by a mountain of melted stone that had hardened in strange shapes of rounded outline. He followed the stream till he lost it in a deep cut. Therefore Venters quit the dark slit which baffled further search in that direction, and rode out along the curved edge of stone where it met the sage. It was not long before he came to a low place, and here Wrangle readily climbed up.

All about him was ridgy roll of wind-smoothed, rain-washed rock. Not a tuft of grass or a bunch of sage colored the dull rust-yellow. He saw where, to the right, this uneven flow of stone ended in a blunt wall. Leftward, from the hollow that lay at his feet, mounted a gradual slow-swelling slope to a great height topped by leaning, cracked, and ruined crags. Not for some time did he grasp the wonder of that acclivity. It was no less than a mountain-side, glistening in the sun like polished granite, with cedar-trees springing as if by magic out of the denuded surface. Winds had swept it clear of weathered shale, and rains had washed it free of dust. Far up the curved slope its beautiful lines broke to meet the vertical rim-wall, to lose its grace in a different order and color of rock, a stained yellow cliff of cracks and caves and seamed crags. And straight before Venters was a scene less striking but more significant to his keen survey. For beyond a mile of the bare, hummocky rock began the valley of sage, and the mouths of cañons, one of which surely was another gateway into the pass.

He got off his horse, and, giving the bridle to Ring to hold, he commenced a search for the cleft where the stream ran. He was not successful and concluded the water dropped into an underground passage. Then he returned to where he had left Wrangle, and led him down off the stone to the sage. It was a short ride to the opening cañons.

There was no reason for a choice of which one to enter. The one he rode into was a clear, sharp shaft in yellow stone a thousand feet deep, with wonderful wind-worn caves low down and high above buttressed and turreted ramparts. Farther on Venters came into a region where deep indentations marked the line of cañon walls. These were huge, cove-like blind pockets extending back to a sharp corner with a dense growth of underbrush and trees.

Venters penetrated into one of these offshoots, and, as he had hoped, he found abundant grass. He had to bend the oak saplings to get his horse through. Deciding to make this a hiding-place if he could find water, he worked back to the limit of the shelving walls. In a little cluster of silver spruces he found a spring. This inclosed nook seemed an ideal place to leave his horse and to camp at night, and from which to make stealthy trips on foot. The thick grass hid his trail; the dense growth of oaks in the opening would serve as a barrier to keep Wrangle in, if, indeed, the luxuriant browse would not suffice for that.

So Venters, leaving Whitie with the horse, called Ring to his side, and, rifle in hand, worked his way out to the open. A careful photographing in mind of the formation of the bold outlines of rimrock assured him he would be able to return to his retreat even in the dark.

Bunches of scattered sage covered the center of the cañon, and among these Venters threaded his way with the step of an Indian. At intervals he put his hand on the dog and stopped to listen.

There was a drowsy hum of insects, but no other sound disturbed the warm midday stillness. Venters saw ahead a turn, more abrupt than any yet. Warily he rounded this corner, once again to halt bewildered.

The cañon opened fan-shaped into a great oval of green and gray growths. It was the hub of an oblong wheel, and from it, at regular distances, like spokes, ran the outgoing cañons. Here a dull red color predominated over the fading yellow. The corners of wall bluntly rose, scarred and scrawled, to taper into towers and serrated peaks and pinnacled domes.

Venters pushed on more heedfully than ever. Toward the center of this circle the sage-brush grew smaller and farther apart. He was about to sheer off to the right, where thickets and jumbles of fallen rock would afford him cover, when he ran right upon a broad cattle trail. Like a road it was, more than a trail; and the cattle tracks were fresh. What surprised him more, they were wet! He pondered over this feature. It had not rained. The only solution to this puzzle was that the cattle had been driven through water, and water deep enough to wet their legs.

Suddenly Ring growled low. Venters rose cautiously and looked over the sage. A band of straggling horsemen were riding across the oval. He sank down, startled and trembling. "Rustlers!" he muttered. Hurriedly he glanced about for a place to hide. Near at hand there was nothing but sage-brush. He dared not risk crossing the open patches to reach the rocks. Again he peeped over the sage. The rustlers—four—five—seven—eight in all, were approaching, but not directly in line with him. That was relief for a cold deadness which seemed to be creeping inward along his veins. He crouched down with bated breath and held the bristling dog.

He heard the click of iron-shod hoofs on stone, the coarse laughter of men, and then voices gradually dying away. Long moments passed. Then he rose. The rustlers were riding into a cañon. Their horses were tired, and they had several pack animals; evidently they had traveled far. Venters doubted that they were the rustlers who had driven the red herd. Olding's band had split. Venters watched these horsemen disappear under a bold cañon wall.

The rustlers had come from the northwest side of the oval. Venters kept a steady gaze in that direction, hoping, if there were more, to see from what cañon they rode. A quarter of an hour went by. Reward for his vigilance came when he descried three more mounted men, far over to the north. But out of what cañon they had ridden it was too late to tell. He watched the three ride across the oval and round the jutting red corner where the others had gone.

"Up that cañon!" exclaimed Venters. "Oldring's den! I've found it!"

A knotty point for Venters was the fact that the cattle tracks all pointed west. The broad trail came from the direction of the cañon into which the rustlers had ridden, and undoubtedly the cattle had been driven out of it across the oval.

There were no tracks pointing the other way. It had been in his mind that Oldring had driven the red herd toward the rendezvous, and not from it. Where did that broad trail come down into the pass, and where did it lead? Venters knew he wasted time in pondering the question, but it held a fascination not easily dispelled. For many years Oldring's mysterious entrance and exit to Deception Pass had been all-absorbing topics to sage-riders.

All at once the dog put an end to Venters's pondering. Ring sniffed the air, turned slowly in his tracks with a whine, and then growled. Venters wheeled. Two horsemen were within a hundred yards, coming straight at him. One, lagging behind the other, was Oldring's Masked Rider.

Venters cunningly sank, slowly trying to merge into sage-brush. But, guarded as his action was, the first horse detected it. He stopped short, snorted, and shot up his ears. The rustler bent forward, as if keenly peering ahead. Then, with a swift sweep, he jerked a gun from its sheath and fired.

The bullet zipped through the sage-brush. Flying bits of wood struck Venters, and the hot, stinging pain seemed to lift him in one leap. Like a flash the blue barrel of his rifle gleamed level and he shot once—twice.

The foremost rustler dropped his weapon and toppled from his saddle, to fall with his foot catching in a stirrup. The horse snorted wildly and plunged away, dragging the rustler through the sage.

The Masked Rider huddled over his pommel, slowly swaying to one side, and then, with a faint, strange cry, slipped out of the saddle.

CHAPTER FIVE

The Masked Rider

Venters looked quickly from the fallen rustlers to the cañon where the others had disappeared. He calculated on the time needed for running horses to return to the open, if their riders heard shots. He waited breathlessly. But the estimated time dragged by and no riders appeared. Venters began presently to believe that the rifle reports had not penetrated into the recesses of the cañon, and felt safe for the immediate present.

He hurried to the spot where the first rustler had been dragged by his horse. The man lay in deep grass, dead, jaw fallen, eyes protruding—a sight that sickened Venters. The first man at whom he had ever aimed a weapon he had shot through the heart. With the clammy sweat oozing from every pore Venters dragged the rustler in among some boulders and covered him with slabs of rock. Then he smoothed out the crushed trail in grass and sage. The rustler's horse had stopped a quarter of a mile off and was grazing.

When Venters rapidly strode toward the Masked Rider not even the cold nausea that gripped him could wholly banish curiosity. For he had shot Oldring's infamous lieutenant, whose face had never been seen. Venters experienced a grim pride in the feat. What would Tull say to this achievement of the outcast who rode too often to Deception Pass?

Venters's curious eagerness and expectation had not prepared him for the shock he received when he stood over a slight, dark figure. The rustler wore the black mask that had given him his name, but he had no weapons. Venters glanced at the drooping horse; there were no gun-sheaths on the saddle.

"A rustler who didn't pack guns!" muttered Venters. "He wears no belt. He couldn't pack guns in that rig . . . Strange!"

A low, gasping intake of breath and a sudden twitching of body told Venters the rider still lived.

"He's alive! . . . I've got to stand here and watch him die. And I shot an unarmed man."

Shrinkingly Venters removed the rider's wide sombrero and the black cloth mask. This action disclosed bright chestnut hair, inclined to curl, and a white, youthful face. Along the lower line of cheek and jaw was a clear demarcation, where the brown of tanned skin met the white that had been hidden from the sun.

"Oh, he's only a boy! . . . What! Can he be Oldring's Masked Rider?"

The boy showed signs of returning consciousness. He stirred; his lips moved; a small brown hand clenched in his blouse.

Venters knelt with a gathering horror of his deed. His bullet had entered the rider's right breast, high up to the shoulder. With hands that shook, Venters untied a black scarf and ripped open the blood-wet blouse.

First he saw a gaping hole, dark red against a whiteness of skin, from which welled a slender red stream. Then the graceful, beautiful swell of a woman's breast!

"A woman!" he cried. "A girl! . . . I've killed a girl!"

She suddenly opened eyes that transfixed Venters. They were fathomless blue. Consciousness of death was there, a blended terror and pain, but no consciousness of sight. She did not see Venters. She stared into the unknown.

Then came a spasm of vitality. She writhed in a torture of reviving strength, and in her convulsions she almost tore from Venters's grasp. Slowly she relaxed and sank partly back. The ungloved hand sought the wound, and pressed so hard that her wrist half buried itself in her bosom. Blood trickled between her spread fingers. And she looked at Venters with eyes that saw him.

He cursed himself and the unerring aim of which he had been so proud. He had seen that look in the eyes of a crippled antelope which he was about to finish with his knife. But in her it had infinitely more—a revelation of mortal spirit. The instinctive clinging to life was there, and the divining helplessness and the terrible accusation of the stricken.

"Forgive me! I didn't know!" burst out Venters.

"You shot me—you've killed me!" she whispered, in panting gasps. Upon her lips appeared a fluttering, bloody froth. By that Venters knew the air in her lungs was mixing with blood. "Oh, I knew—it would—come—some day! . . . Oh, the burn! . . . Hold me—I'm sinking—it's all dark . . . Ah, God! . . . Mercy—"

Her rigidity loosened in one long quiver and she lay back limp, still, white as snow, with closed eyes.

Venters thought then that she died. But the faint pulsation of her breast assured him that life yet lingered. Death seemed only a matter of moments, for the bullet had gone clear through her. Nevertheless, he tore sageleaves from a bush, and, pressing them tightly over her wounds, he bound the black scarf round her shoulder, tying it securely under her arm. Then he closed the blouse, hiding from his sight that blood-stained, accusing breast.

"What—now?" he questioned, with flying mind. "I must get out of here. She's dying—but I can't leave her."

He rapidly surveyed the sage to the north and made out no animate object. Then he picked up the girl's sombrero and the mask. This time the mask gave him as great a shock as when he first removed it from her face. For in the woman he had forgotten the rustler, and this black strip of felt-cloth established the identity of Oldring's Masked Rider. Venters had solved the mystery. He slipped his rifle under her, and, lifting her carefully upon it, he began to retrace his steps. The dog trailed in his shadow. And the horse, that had stood drooping by, followed without a call. Venters chose the deepest tufts of grass and clumps of sage on his return. From time to time he glanced over his shoulder. He did not rest. His concern was to avoid jarring the girl and to hide his trail. Gaining the narrow cañon, he turned and held close to the wall till he reached his hiding-place. When he entered the dense thicket of oaks he was hard put to it to force a way through. But he held his burden almost upright, and by slipping sidewise and bending the saplings he got in. Through sage and grass he hurried to the grove of silver spruces.

He laid the girl down, almost fearing to look at her. Though marble pale and cold, she was living. Venters then appreciated the tax that long carry had been to his strength. He sat down to rest. Whitie sniffed at the pale girl and whined and crept to Venters's feet. Ring lapped the water in the runway of the spring.

Presently Venters went out to the opening, caught the horse, and, leading him through the thicket, unsaddled him and tied him with a long halter. Wrangle left his browsing long enough to whinny and toss his head. Venters felt that he could not rest easily till he had secured the other rustler's horse; so, taking his rifle and calling for Ring, he set out. Swiftly yet watchfully he made his way through the cañon to the oval and out to the cattle trail. What few tracks might have betrayed him he obliterated, so only an expert tracker could have trailed him. Then, with many a wary backward glance across the sage, he started to round up the rustler's horse. This was unexpectedly easy. He led the horse to lower ground, out of sight from the opposite side of the oval, along the shadowy western wall, and so on into his cañon and secluded camp.

The girl's eyes were open; a feverish spot burned in her cheeks; she moaned something unintelligible to Venters, but he took the movement of her lips to mean that she wanted water. Lifting her head, he tipped the canteen to her lips. After that she again lapsed into unconsciousness or a weakness which was its counterpart. Venters noted, however, that the burning flush had faded into the former pallor.

The sun set behind the high cañon rim, and a cool shade darkened the walls. Venters fed the dogs and put a halter on the dead rustler's horse. He allowed Wrangle to browse free. This done, he cut spruce boughs and made a lean-to for the girl. Then, gently lifting her upon a blanket, he folded the sides over her. The other blanket he wrapped about his shoulders and found a comfortable seat against a spruce-tree that upheld the little shack. Ring and Whitie lay near at hand, one asleep, the other watchful.

Venters dreaded the night's vigil. At night his mind was active, and this time he had to watch and think and feel beside a dying girl whom he had all but murdered. A thousand excuses he invented for himself, yet not one made any difference in his act or his self-reproach.

It seemed to him that when night fell black he could see her white face so much more plainly.

"She'll go, presently," he said, "and be out of agony—thank God!"

Every little while certainty of her death came to him with a shock; and then he would bend over and lay his ear on her breast. Her heart still beat.

The early night blackness cleared to the cold starlight. The horses were not moving, and no sound disturbed the deathly silence of the cañon.

"I'll bury her here," thought Venters, "and let her grave be as much a mystery as her life was."

For the girl's few words, the look of her eyes, the prayer, had strangely touched Venters.

"She was only a girl," he soliloquized. "What was she to Oldring? Rustlers don't have wives nor sisters nor daughters. She was bad—that's all. But somehow . . . well, she may not have willingly become the companion of rustlers. That prayer of hers to God for mercy! . . . Life is strange and cruel. I wonder if other members of Oldring's gang are women? Likely enough. But what was his game? Oldring's Masked Rider! A name to make villagers hide and lock their doors. A name credited with a dozen murders, a hundred forays, and a thousand stealings of cattle. What part did the girl have in this? It may have served Oldring to create mystery."

Hours passed. The white stars moved across the narrow strip of dark-blue sky above. The silence awoke to the low hum of insects. Venters watched the immovable white face, and as he watched, hour by hour waiting for death, the infamy of her passed from his mind. He thought only of the sadness, the truth of the moment. Whoever she was—whatever she had done—she was young and she was dying.

The after-part of the night wore on interminably. The starlight failed and the gloom blackened to the darkest hour. "She'll die at the gray of dawn," muttered Venters, remembering some old woman's fancy. The blackness paled to gray, and the gray lightened and day peeped over the eastern rim. Venters listened at the breast of the girl. She still lived. Did he only imagine that her heart beat stronger, ever so slightly, but stronger? He pressed his ear closer to her breast. And he rose with his own pulse quickening.

"If she doesn't die soon—she's got a chance—the barest chance—to live," he said.

He wondered if the internal bleeding had ceased. There was no more film of blood upon her lips. But no corpse could have been whiter. Opening her blouse, he untied the scarf, and carefully picked away the sageleaves from the wound in her shoulder. It had closed. Lifting her lightly, he ascertained that the same was true of the hole where the bullet had come out. He reflected on the fact that clean wounds closed quickly in the healing upland air. He recalled instances of riders who had been cut and shot, apparently to fatal issues; yet the blood had clotted, the wounds closed, and they had recovered. He had no way to tell if internal hemorrhage still went on, but he believed that it had stopped. Otherwise she would surely not have lived so long. He marked the entrance of the bullet, and concluded that it had just touched the upper lobe of her lung. Perhaps the wound in the lung had also closed. As he began to wash the blood stains from her breast and carefully rebandage the wound, he was vaguely conscious of a strange, grave happiness in the thought that she might live.

Broad daylight and a hint of sunshine high on the cliff-rim to the west brought him to consideration of what he had better do. And while busy with his few camp tasks he revolved the thing in his mind. It would not be wise for him to remain long in his present hiding-place. And if he intended to follow the cattle trail and try to find the rustlers he had better make a move at once. For he knew that rustlers, being riders, would not make much of a day's or night's absence from camp for one or two of their number; but when the missing ones failed to show up in reasonable time there would be a search. And Venters was afraid of that.

"A good tracker could trail me," he muttered. "And I'd be cornered here. Let's see. Rustlers are a lazy set when they're not on the ride. I'll risk it. Then I'll change my hiding-place."

He carefully cleaned and reloaded his guns. When he rose to go he bent a long glance down upon the unconscious girl. Then, ordering Whitie and Ring to keep guard, he left the camp.

The safest cover lay close under the wall of the cañon, and here through the dense thickets Venters made his slow, listening advance toward the oval. Upon gaining the wide opening he decided to cross it and follow the left wall till he came to the cattle trail. He scanned the oval as keenly as if hunting for antelope. Then, stooping, he stole from one cover to another, taking advantage of rocks and bunches of sage, until he had reached the thickets under the opposite wall. Once there, he exercised extreme caution in his surveys of the ground ahead, but increased his speed when moving. Dodging from bush to bush, he passed the mouths of two cañons, and in the entrance of a third cañon he crossed a wash of swift, clear water, to come abruptly upon the cattle trail.

It followed the low bank of the wash, and, keeping it in sight, Venters hugged the line of sage and thicket. Like the curves of a serpent the cañon wound for a mile or more and then opened into a valley. Patches of red showed clear against the purple of sage, and farther out on the level dotted strings of red led away to the wall of rock.

"Ha, the red herd!" exclaimed Venters.

Then dots of white and black told him there were cattle of other colors in this inclosed valley. Oldring, the rustler, was also a rancher. Venters's calculating eye took count of stock that outnumbered the red herd.

"What a range!" went on Venters. "Water and grass enough for fifty thousand head, and no riders needed!"

After his first burst of surprise and rapid calculation Venters lost no time there, but slunk again into the sage on his back trail. With the discovery of Oldring's hidden cattle-range had come enlightenment on several problems. Here the rustler kept his stock; here was Jane Withersteen's red herd; here were the few cattle that had disappeared from the Cottonwoods slopes during the last two years. Until Oldring had driven the red herd his thefts of cattle for that time had not been more than enough to supply meat for his men. Of late no drives had been reported from Sterling or the villages north. And Venters knew that the riders had wondered at Oldring's inactivity in that particular field. He and his band had been active enough in their visits to Glaze and Cottonwoods; they always had gold; but of late the amount gambled away and drunk and thrown away in the villages had given rise to much conjecture. Oldring's more frequent visits had resulted in new saloons, and where there had formerly been one raid or shooting fray in the little hamlets there were now many. Perhaps Oldring had another range farther on up the pass, and from there drove the cattle to distant Utah towns where he was little known. But Venters came finally to doubt this. And, from what he had learned in the last few days, a belief began to form in Venters's mind that Oldring's intimidations of the villages and the mystery of the Masked Rider, with his alleged evil deeds, and the fierce resistance offered any trailing riders, and the rustling of cattle—these things were only the craft of the rustler-chief to conceal his real life and purpose and work in Deception Pass.

And like a scouting Indian Venters crawled through the sage of the oval valley, crossed trail after trail on the north side, and at last entered the cañon out of which headed the cattle trail, and into which he had watched the rustlers disappear.

If he had used caution before, now he strained every nerve to force himself to creeping stealth and to sensitiveness of ear. He crawled along so hidden that he could not use his eyes except to aid himself in the toilsome progress through the brakes and ruins of cliff-wall. Yet from time to time, as he rested, he saw the massive red walls growing higher and wilder, more looming and broken. He made note of the fact that he was turning and climbing. The sage and thickets of oak and brakes of alder gave place to piñon pine growing out of rocky soil. Suddenly a low, dull murmur assailed his ears. At first he thought it was thunder, then the slipping of a weathered slope of rock. But it was incessant, and as he progressed it filled out deeper and from a murmur changed into a soft roar.

"Falling water," he said. "There's volume to that. I wonder if it's the stream I lost."

The roar bothered him, for he could hear nothing else. Likewise, however, no rustlers could hear him. Emboldened by this, and sure that nothing but a bird could see him, he arose from his hands and knees to hurry on. An opening in the piñons warned him that he was nearing the height of slope.

He gained it, and dropped low with a burst of astonishment. Before him stretched a short cañon with rounded stone floor bare of grass or sage or tree, and with curved, shelving walls. A broad rippling stream flowed toward him, and at the back of the cañon a waterfall burst from a wide rent in the cliff, and, bounding down in two green steps, spread into a long white sheet.

If Venters had not been indubitably certain that he had entered the right cañon his astonishment would not have been so great. There had been no breaks in the walls, no side cañons entering this one where the rustlers' tracks and the cattle trail had guided him, and, therefore, he could not be wrong. But here the cañon ended, and presumably the trails also.

"That cattle trail headed out of here," Venters kept saying to himself. "It headed out. Now what I want to know is how on earth did cattle ever get in here?"

If he could be sure of anything it was of the careful scrutiny he had given that cattle track, every hoofmark of which headed straight west. He was now looking east at an immense round boxed corner of cañon down which tumbled a thin, white veil of water, scarcely twenty yards wide. Somehow, somewhere, his calculations had gone wrong. For the first time in years he found himself doubting his rider's skill in finding tracks, and his memory of what he had actually seen. In his anxiety to keep under cover he must have lost himself in this offshoot of Deception Pass, and thereby, in some unaccountable manner, missed the cañon with the trails. There was nothing else for him to think. Rustlers could not fly, nor cattle jump down thousand-foot precipices. He was only proving what the sage-riders had long said of this labyrinthine system of deceitful cañons and valleys—trails led down into Deception Pass, but no rider had ever followed them.

On a sudden he heard above the soft roar of the waterfall an unusual sound that he could not define. He dropped flat behind a stone and listened. From the direction he had come swelled something that resembled a strange muffled pounding and splashing and ringing. Despite his nerve the chill sweat began to dampen his forehead. What might not be possible in this stonewalled maze of mystery? The unnatural sound passed beyond him as he lay gripping his rifle and fighting for coolness. Then from the open came the sound, now distinct and different. Venters recognized a hobblebell of a horse, and the cracking of iron on submerged stones, and the hollow splash of hoofs in water.

Relief surged over him. His mind caught again at realities, and curiosity prompted him to peep from behind the rock.

In the middle of the stream waded a long string of packed burros driven by three superbly mounted men. Had Venters met these dark-clothed, dark-visaged, heavily armed men anywhere in Utah, let alone in this robbers' retreat, he would have recognized them as rustlers. The discerning eye of a rider saw the signs of a long, arduous trip. These men were packing in supplies from one of the northern villages. They were tired, and their horses were almost played out, and the burros plodded on, after the manner of their kind when exhausted, faithful and patient, but as if every weary, splashing, slipping step would be their last.

All this Venters noted in one glance. After that he watched with a thrilling eagerness. Straight at the waterfall the rustlers drove the burros, and straight through the middle, where the water spread into a fleecy, thin film like dissolving smoke. Following closely, the rustlers rode into this white mist, showing in bold black relief for an instant, and then they vanished.

Venters drew a full breath that rushed out in brief and sudden utterance.

"Good Heaven! Of all the holes for a rustler! . . . There's a cavern under that waterfall, and a passageway leading out to a cañon beyond. Oldring hides in there. He needs only to guard a trail leading down from the sage-flat above. Little danger of this outlet to the pass being discovered. I stumbled on it by luck, after I had given up. And now I know the truth of what puzzled me most—why that cattle trail was wet!"

He wheeled and ran down the slope, and out to the level of the sage-brush. Returning, he had no time to spare, only now and then, between dashes, a moment when he stopped to cast sharp eyes ahead. The abundant grass left no trace of his trail. Short work he made of the distance to the circle of cañons. He doubted that he would ever see it again; he knew he never wanted to; yet he looked at the red corners and towers with the eyes of a rider picturing landmarks never to be forgotten.

Here he spent a panting moment in a slow-circling gaze of the sage-oval and the gaps between the bluffs. Nothing stirred except the gentle wave of the tips of the brush. Then he pressed on past the mouths of several cañons and over ground new to him, now close under the eastern wall. This latter part proved to be easy traveling, well screened from possible observation from the north and west, and he soon covered it and felt safer in the deepening shade of his own cañon. Then the huge, notched bulge of red rim loomed over him, a mark by which he knew again the deep cove where his camp lay hidden. As he penetrated the thicket, safe again for the present, his thoughts reverted to the girl he had left there. The afternoon had far advanced. How would he find her? He ran into camp, frightening the dogs.

The girl lay with wide-open, dark eyes, and they dilated when he knelt beside her. The flush of fever shone in her cheeks. He lifted her and held water to her dry lips, and felt an inexplicable sense of lightness as he saw her swallow in a slow, choking gulp. Gently he laid her back.

"Who—are—you?" she whispered, haltingly.

"I'm the man who shot you," he replied.

"You'll—not—kill me—now?"

"No, no."

"What—will—you—do—with me?"

"When you get better—strong enough—I'll take you back to the cañon where the rustlers ride through the waterfall."

As with a faint shadow from a flitting wing overhead, the marble whiteness of her face seemed to change.

"Don't—take—me—back—there!"

CHAPTER SIX

The Mill-Wheel of Steers

MEANTIME, at the ranch, when Judkins's news had sent Venters on the trail of the rustlers, Jane Withersteen led the injured man to her house and with skilled fingers dressed the gunshot wound in his arm.

"Judkins, what do you think happened to my riders?"

"I—I'd rather not say," he replied.

"Tell me. Whatever you'll tell me I'll keep to myself. I'm beginning to worry about more than the loss of a herd of cattle. Venters hinted of—but tell me, Judkins."

"Well, Miss Withersteen, I think as Venters thinks—your riders have been called in."

"Judkins! . . . By whom?"

"You know who handles the reins of your Mormon riders."

"Do you dare insinute that my churchmen have ordered in my riders?"

"I ain't insinuatin' nothin', Miss Withersteen," answered Judkins, with spirit. "I know what I'm talking about. I didn't want to tell you."

"Oh, I can't believe that! I'll not believe it! Would Tull leave my herds at the mercy of rustlers and wolves just because—because—? No, no! It's unbelievable."

"Yes, thet particular thing's onheard of around Cottonwoods. But, beggin' pardon, Miss Withersteen, there never was any other rich Mormon woman here on the border, let alone one thet's taken the bit between her teeth."

That was a bold thing for the reserved Judkins to say, but it did not anger her. This rider's crude hint of her spirit gave her a glimpse of what others might think. Humility and obedience had been hers always. But had she taken the bit between her teeth? Still she wavered. And then, with a quick spurt of warm blood along her veins, she thought of Black Star when he got the bit fast between his iron jaws and ran wild in the sage. If she ever started to run! Jane smothered the glow and burn within her, ashamed of a passion for freedom that opposed her duty.

"Judkins, go to the village," she said, "and when you have learned anything definite about my riders please come to me at once."

When he had gone Jane resolutely applied her mind to a number of tasks that of late had been neglected. Her father had trained her in the management of a hundred employees and the working of gardens and fields; and to keep record of the movements of cattle and riders. And beside the many duties she had added to this work was one of extreme delicacy, such as required all her tact and ingenuity. It was an unobtrusive, almost secret aid which she rendered to the Gentile families of the village. Though Jane Withersteen never admitted so to herself, it amounted to no less than a system of charity. But for her invention of numberless kinds of employment, for which there was no actual need, these families of Gentiles, who had failed in a Mormon community, would have starved.

In aiding these poor people Jane thought she deceived her keen churchmen, but it was a kind of deceit for which she did not pray to be forgiven. Equally as difficult was the task of deceiving the Gentiles, for they were as proud as they were poor. It had been a great grief to her to discover how these people hated her people; and it had been a source of great joy that through her they had come to soften in hatred. At any time this work called for a clearness of mind that precluded anxiety and worry; but under the present circumstances it required all her vigor and obstinate tenacity to pin her attention upon her task.

Sunset came, bringing with the end of her labor a patient calmness and power to wait that had not been hers earlier in the day. She expected Judkins, but he did not appear. Her house was always quiet; to-night, however, it seemed unusually so. At supper her women served her with a silent assiduity; it spoke what their sealed lips could not utter—the sympathy of Mormon women. Jerd came to her with the key of the great door of the stone stable, and to make his daily report about the horses. One of his daily duties was to give Black Star and Night and the other racers a ten-mile run. This day it had been omitted, and the boy grew confused in explanations that she had not asked for. She did inquire if he would return on the morrow, and Jerd, in mingled surprise and relief, assured her he would always work for her. Jane missed the rattle and trot, canter and gallop of the incoming riders on the hard trails. Dusk shaded the grove where she walked; the birds ceased singing; the wind sighed through the leaves of the cottonwoods, and the running water murmured down its stone-bedded channel. The glimmering of the first star was like the peace and beauty of the night. Her faith welled up in her heart and said that all would soon be right in her little world. She pictured Venters about his lonely camp-fire sitting between his faithful dogs. She prayed for his safety, for the success of his under-taking.

Early the next morning one of Jane's women brought in word that Judkins wished to speak to her. She hurried out, and in her surprise to see him armed with rifle and revolver, she forgot her intention to inquire about his wound.

"Judkins! Those guns? You never carried guns."

"It's high time, Miss Withersteen," he replied. "Will you come into the grove? It ain't jest exactly safe for me to be seen here."

She walked with him into the shade of the cottonwoods.

"What do you mean?"

"Miss Withersteen, I went to my mother's house last night. While there, some one knocked, an' a man asked for me. I went to the door. He wore a mask. He said I'd better not ride any more for Jane Withersteen. His voice was hoarse an' strange, disguised, I reckon, like his face. He said no more, an' ran off in the dark."

"Did you know who he was?" asked Jane, in a low voice.

"Yes."

Jane did not ask to know; she did not want to know; she feared to know. All her calmness fled at a single thought.

"Thet's why I'm packin' guns," went on Judkins. "For I'll never quit ridin' for you, Miss Withersteen, till you let me go."

"Judkins, do you want to leave me?"

"Do I look thet way? Give me a hoss—a fast hoss, an' send me out on the sage."

"Oh, thank you, Judkins! You're more faithful than my own people. I ought not accept your loyalty—you might suffer more through it. But what in the world can I do? My head whirls. The wrong to Venters—the stolen herd—these masks, threats, this coil in the dark! I can't understand! But I feel something dark and terrible closing in around me."

"Miss Withersteen, it's all simple enough," said Judkins, earnestly. "Now please listen—an' beggin' your pardon—jest turn thet deaf Mormon ear aside, an' let me talk clear an' plain in the other. I went around to the saloons an' the stores an' the loafin' places yesterday. All your riders are in. There's talk of a vigilance band organized to hunt down rustlers. They call themselves 'The Riders.' Thet's the report—thet's the reason given for your riders leavin' you. Strange thet only a few riders of other ranchers joined the band! An' Tull's man, Jerry Card—he's the leader. I seen him an' his hoss. He 'ain't been to Glaze. I'm not easy to fool on the looks of a hoss thet's traveled the sage. Tull an' Jerry didn't ride to Glaze! . . . Well, I met Blake an' Dorn, both good friends of mine, usually, as far as their Mormon lights will let 'em go. But these fellers couldn't fool me, an' they didn't try very hard. I asked them, straight out like a man, why they left you like thet. I didn't forget to mention how you nursed Blake's poor old mother when she was sick, an' how good you was to Dorn's kids. They looked ashamed, Miss Withersteen. An' they jest froze up—thet dark set look thet makes them strange an' different to me. But I could tell the difference between thet first natural twinge of conscience an' the later look of some secret thing. An' the difference I caught was thet they couldn't help themselves. They hadn't no say in the matter. They looked as if their bein' unfaithful to you was bein' faithful to a higher duty. An' there's the secret. Why, it's as plain as—as sight of my gun here."

"Plain! . . . My herds to wander in the sage—to be stolen! Jane Withersteen a poor woman! Her head to be brought low and her spirit broken! . . . Why, Judkins, it's plain enough."

"Miss Withersteen, let me get what boys I can gather, an' hold the white herd. It's on the slope now, not ten miles out—three thousand head, an' all steers. They're wild, an' likely to stampede at the pop of a jack-rabbit's ears. We'll camp right with them, an' try to hold them."

"Judkins, I'll reward you some day for your service, unless all is taken from me. Get the boys and tell Jerd to give you pick of my horses, except Black Star and Night. But—do not shed blood for my cattle nor heedlessly risk your lives."

Jane Withersteen rushed to the silence and seclusion of her room, and there could not longer hold back the bursting of her wrath. She went stone-blind in the fury of a passion that had never before showed its power. Lying upon her bed, sightless, voiceless, she was a writhing, living flame. And she tossed there while her fury burned and burned, and finally burned itself out.

Then, weak and spent, she lay thinking, not of the oppression that would break her, but of this new revelation of self. Until the last few days there had been little in her life to rouse passions. Her forefathers had been Vikings, savage chieftains who bore no cross and brooked no hindrance to their will. Her father had inherited that temper; and at times, like antelope fleeing before fire on the slope, his people fled from his red rages. Jane Withersteen realized that the spirit of wrath and war had lain dormant in her. She shrank from black depths hitherto unsuspected. The one thing in man or woman that she scorned above all scorn, and which she could not forgive, was hate. Hate headed a flaming pathway straight to hell. All in a flash, beyond her control there had been in her a birth of fiery hate. And the man who had dragged her peaceful and loving spirit to this degradation was a minister of God's word, an Elder of her church, the counselor of her beloved Bishop.

The loss of herds and ranges, even of Amber Spring and the Old Stone House, no longer concerned Jane Withersteen; she faced the foremost thought of her life, what she now considered the mightiest problem—the salvation of her soul.

She knelt by her bedside and prayed; she prayed as she had never prayed in all her life—prayed to be forgiven for her sin; to be immune from that dark, hot hate; to love Tull as her minister, though she could not love him as a man; to do her duty by her church and people and those dependent upon her bounty; to hold reverence of God and womanhood inviolate.

When Jane Withersteen rose from that storm of wrath and prayer for help she was serene, calm, sure—a changed woman. She would do her duty as she saw it, live her life as her own truth guided her. She might never be able to marry a man of her choice, but she certainly never would become the wife of Tull. Her churchmen might take her cattle and horses, ranges and fields, her corrals and stables, the house of Witherseen and the water that nourished the village of Cottonwoods; but they could not force her to marry Tull, they could not change her decision or break her spirit. Once resigned to further loss, and sure of herself, Jane Withersteen attained a peace of mind that had not been hers for a year. She forgave Tull, and felt a melancholy regret over what she knew he considered duty, irrespective of his personal feeling for her. First of all, Tull, as he was a man, wanted her for himself; and secondly, he hoped to save her and her riches for his church. She did not believe that Tull had been actuated solely by his minister's zeal to save her soul. She doubted her interpretation of one of his dark sayings— that if she were lost to him she might as well be lost to heaven. Jane Withersteen's common sense took arms against the binding limits of her religion; and she doubted that her Bishop, whom she had been taught had direct communication with God—would damn her soul for refusing to marry a Mormon. As for Tull and his churchmen, when they had harassed her, perhaps made her poor, they would find her unchangeable, and then she would get back most of what she had lost. So she reasoned, true at last to her faith in all men, and in their ultimate goodness.

The clank of iron hoofs upon the stone courtyard drew her hurriedly from her retirement. There, beside his horse, stood Lassiter, his dark apparel and the great black gun-sheaths contrasting singularly with his gentle smile. Jane's active mind took up her interest in him and her half-determined desire to use what charm she had to foil his evident design in visiting Cottonwoods. If she could mitigate his hatred of Mormons, or at least keep him from killing more of them, not only would she be saving her people, but also be leading back this bloodspiller to some semblance of the human.

"Mornin', ma'am," he said, black sombrero in hand.

"Lassiter, I'm not an old woman, or even a madam," she replied, with her bright smile. "If you can't say Miss Withersteen—call me Jane."

"I reckon Jane would be easier. First names are always handy for me."

"Well, use mine, then. Lassiter, I'm glad to see you. I'm in trouble."

Then she told him of Judkins's return, of the driving of the red herd, of Venters's departure on Wrangle, and the calling-in of her riders.

"'Pears to me you're some smilin' an' pretty for a woman with so much trouble," he remarked.

"Lassiter! Are you paying me compliments? But, seriously, I've made up my mind not to be miserable. I've lost much, and I'll lose more. Nevertheless, I won't be sour, and I hope I'll never be unhappy—again."

Lassiter twisted his hat round and round, as was his way, and took his time in replying.

"Women are strange to me. I got to back-trailin' myself from them long ago. But I'd like a game woman. Might I ask, seein' as how you take this trouble, if you're goin' to fight?"

"Fight! How? Even if I would, I haven't a friend except that boy who doesn't dare stay in the village."

"I make bold to say, ma'am—Jane—that there's another, if you want him."

"Lassiter! . . . Thank you. But how can I accept you as a friend? Think! Why, you'd ride down into the village with those terrible guns and kill my enemies—who are also my churchmen."

"I reckon I might be riled up to jest about that," he replied, dryly.

She held out both hands to him.

"Lassiter! I'll accept your friendship—be proud of it—return it—if I may keep you from killing another Mormon."

"I'll tell you one thing," he said, bluntly, as the gray lightning formed in his eyes. "You're too good a woman to be sacrificed as you're goin' to be. . . . No, I reckon you an' me can't be friends on such terms."

In her earnestness she stepped closer to him, repelled yet fascinated by the sudden transition of his moods. That he would fight for her was at once horrible and wonderful.

"You came here to kill a man—the man whom Milly Erne—"

"The man who dragged Milly Erne to hell—put it that way! . . . Jane Witifersteen, yes, that's why I came here. I'd tell so much to no other livin' soul. . . . There're things such a woman as you'd never dream of—so don't mention her again. Not till you tell me the name of the man!"

"Tell you! I? Never!"

"I reckon you will. An' I'll never ask you. I'm a man of strange beliefs an' ways of thinkin', an' I seem to see into the future an' feel things hard to explain. The trail I've been followin' for so many years was twisted an' tangled, but it's straightenin' out now. An', Jane Witifersteen, you crossed it long ago to ease poor Milly's agony. That, whether you want or not, makes Lassiter your friend. But you cross it now strangely to mean somethin' to me—God knows what!—unless by your noble blindness to incite me to greater hatred of Mormon men."

Jane felt swayed by a strength that far exceeded her own. In a clash of wills with this man she would go to the wall. If she were to influence him it must be wholly through womanly allurement. There was that about Lassiter which commanded her respect; she had abhorred his name; face to face with him, she found she feared only his deeds. His mystic suggestion, his foreshadowing of something that she was to mean to him, pierced deep into her mind. She believed fate had thrown in her way the lover or husband of Milly Erne. She believed that through her an evil man might be reclaimed. His allusion to what he called her blindness terrified her. Such a mistaken idea of his might unleash the bitter, fatal mood she sensed in him. At any cost she must placate this man; she knew the die was cast, and that if Lassiter did not soften to a woman's grace and beauty and wiles, then it would be because she could not make him.

"I reckon you'll hear no more such talk from me," Lassiter went on, presently. "Now, Miss Jane, I rode in to tell you that your herd of white steers is down on the slope behind them big ridges. An' I seen somethin' goin' on that'd be mighty interestin' to you, if you could see it. Have you a field-glass?"

"Yes, I have two glasses. I'll get them and ride out with you. Wait, Lassiter, please," she said, and hurried within. Sending word to Jerd to saddle Black Star and fetch him to the court, she then went to her room and changed to the riding-clothes she always donned when going into the sage. In this male attire her mirror showed her a jaunty, handsome rider. If she expected some little need of admiration from Lassiter, she had no cause for disappointment. The gentle smile that she liked, which made of him another person, slowly overspread his face.

"If I didn't take you for a boy!" he exclaimed. "It's powerful queer what difference clothes make. Now I've been some scared of your dignity, like when the other night you was all in white, but in this rig—"

Black Star came pounding into the court, dragging Jerd half off his feet, and he whistled at Lassiter's black. But at sight of Jane all his defiant lines seemed to soften, and with tosses of his beautiful head he whipped his bridle.

"Down, Black Star, down," said Jane.

He dropped his head, and, slowly lengthening, he bent one foreleg, then the other, and sank to his knees. Jane slipped her left foot in the stirrup, swung lightly into the saddle, and Black Star rose with a ringing stamp. It was not easy for Jane to hold him to a canter through the grove, and like the wind he broke when he saw the sage. Jane let him have a couple of miles of free running on the open trail, and then she coaxed him in and waited for her companion. Lassiter was not long in catching up, and presently they were riding side by side. It reminded her how she used to ride with Venters. Where was he now? She gazed far down the slope to the curved purple lines of Deception Pass, and involuntarily shut her eyes with a trembling stir of nameless fear.

"We'll turn off here," Lassiter said, "an' take to the sage a mile or so. The white herd is behind them big ridges."

"What are you going to show me?" asked Jane. "I'm prepared—don't be afraid."

He smiled as if he meant that bad news came swiftly enough without being presaged by speech.

When they reached the lee of a rolling ridge Lassiter dismounted, motioning to her to do likewise. They left the horses standing, bridles down. Then Lassiter, carrying the field-glasses, began to lead the way up the slow rise of ground. Upon nearing the summit he halted her with a gesture.

"I reckon we'd see more if we didn't show ourselves against the sky," he said. "I was here less than an hour ago. Then the herd was seven or eight miles south, an' if they 'ain't bolted yet—"

"Lassiter! . . . Bolted?"

"That's what I said. Now let's see."

Jane climbed a few more paces behind him and then peeped over the ridge. Just beyond began a shallow swale that deepened and widened into a valley and then swung to the left. Following the undulating sweep of sage, Jane saw the straggling lines and then the great body of the white herd. She knew enough about steers, even at a distance of four or five miles, to realize that something was in the wind. Bringing her field-glass into use, she moved it slowly from left to right, which action swept the whole herd into range. The stragglers were restless; the more compactly massed steers were browsing. Jane brought the glass back to the big sentinels of the herd, and she saw them trot with quick steps, stop short and toss wide horns, look everywhere, and then trot in another direction.

"Judkins hasn't been able to get his boys together yet," said Jane. "But he'll be there soon. I hope not too late. Lassiter, what's frightening those big leaders?"

"Nothin' jest on the minute," replied Lassiter. "Them steers are quietin' down. They've been scared, but not bad yet. I reckon the whole herd has moved a few miles this way since I was here."

"They didn't browse that distance—not in less than an hour. Cattle aren't sheep."

"No, they jest run it, an' that looks bad."

"Lassiter, what frightened them?" repeated Jane, impatiently.

"Put down your glass. You'll see at first better with a naked eye. Now look along them ridges on the other side of the herd, the ridges where the sun shines bright on the sage. . . . That's right. Now look an' look hard an' wait."

Long-drawn moments of straining sight rewarded Jane with nothing save the low, purple rim of ridge and the shimmering sage.

"It's begun again!" whispered Lassiter, and he gripped her arm. "Watch. . . . There, did you see that?"

"No, no. Tell me what to look for?"

"A white flash—a kind of pin-point of quick light—a gleam as from sun shinin' on somethin' white."

Suddenly Jane's concentrated gaze caught a fleeting glint. Quickly she brought her glass to bear on the spot. Again the purple sage, magnified in color and size and wave, for long moments irritated her with its monotony. Then from out of the sage on the ridge flew up a broad, white object, flashed in the sunlight, and vanished. Like magic it was, and bewildered Jane.

"What on earth is that?"

"I reckon there's some one behind that ridge throwin' up a sheet or a white blanket to reflect the sunshine."

"Why?" queried Jane, more bewildered than ever.

"To stampede the herd," replied Lassiter, and his teeth clicked.

"Ah!" She made a fierce, passionate movement, clutched the glass tightly, shook as with the passing of a spasm, and then dropped her head. Presently she raised it to greet Lassiter with something like a smile. "My righteous brethren are at work again," she said, in scorn. She had stifled the leap of her wrath, but for perhaps the first time in her life a bitter derision curled her lips. Lassiter's cool gray eyes seemed to pierce her. "I said I was prepared for anything; but that was hardly true. But why would they—anybody stampede my cattle?"

"That's a Mormon's godly way of bringin' a woman to her knees."

"Lassiter, I'll die before I ever bend my knees. I might be led; I won't be driven. Do you expect the herd to bolt?"

"I don't like the looks of them big steers. But you can never tell. Cattle sometimes stampede as easily as buffalo. Any little flash or move will start them. A rider gettin' down an' walkin' toward them sometimes will make them jump an' fly. Then again nothin' seems to scare them. But I reckon that white flare will do the biz. It's a new one on me, an' I've seen some ridin' an' rustlin'. It jest takes one of them God-fearin' Mormons to think of devilish tricks."

"Lassiter, might not this trick be done by Oldring's men?" asked Jane, ever grasping at straws.

"It might be, but it ain't," replied Lassiter. "Oldring's an honest thief. He don't skulk behind ridges to scatter your cattle to the four winds. He rides down on you, an' if you don't like it you can throw a gun."

Jane bit her tongue to refrain from championing men who at the very moment were proving to her that they were little and mean compared even with rustlers.

"Look! . . . Jane, them leadin' steers have bolted. They're drawin' the stragglers, an' that'll pull the whole herd."

Jane was not quick enough to catch the details called out by Lassiter, but she saw the line of cattle lengthening. Then, like a stream of white bees pouring from a huge swarm, the steers stretched out from the main body. In a few moments, with astonishing rapidity, the whole herd got into motion. A faint roar of trampling hoofs came to Jane's ears, and gradually swelled; low, rolling clouds of dust began to rise above the sage.

"It's a stampede, an' a hummer," said Lassiter.

"Oh, Lassiter! The herd's running with the valley! It leads into the cañon! There's a straight jump-off!"

"I reckon they'll run into it, too. But that's a good many miles yet. An' Jane, this valley swings round almost north before it goes east. That stampede will pass within a mile of us."

The long, white, bobbing line of steers streaked swiftly through the sage, and a funnel-shaped dust-cloud arose at a low angle. A dull rumbling filled Jane's ears.

"I'm thinkin' of millin' that herd," said Lassiter. His gray glance swept up the slope to the west. "There's some specks an' dust way off toward the village. Mebbe that's Judkins an' his boys. It ain't likely he'll get here in time to help. You'd better hold Black Star here on this high ridge."

He ran to his horse and, throwing off saddle-bags and tightening the cinches, he leaped astride and galloped straight down across the valley.

Jane went for Black Star and, leading him to the summit of the ridge, she mounted and faced the valley with excitement and expectancy. She had heard of milling stampeded cattle, and knew it was a feat accomplished by only the most daring riders.

The white herd was now strung out in a line two miles long. The dull rumble of thousands of hoofs deepened into continuous low thunder, and as the steers swept swiftly closer the thunder became a heavy roll. Lassiter crossed in a few moments the level of the valley to the eastern rise of ground and there waited the coming of the herd. Presently, as the head of the white line reached a point opposite to where Jane stood, Lassiter spurred his black into a run.

Jane saw him take a position on the off side of the leaders of the stampede, and there he rode. It was like a race. They swept on down the valley, and when the end of the white line neared Lassiter's first stand the head had begun to swing round to the west. It swung slowly and stubbornly, yet surely, and gradually assumed a long, beautiful curve of moving white. To Jane's amaze she saw the leaders swinging, turning till they headed back toward her and up the valley. Out to the right of these wild, plunging steers ran Lassiter's black, and Jane's keen eye appreciated the fleet stride and sure-footedness of the blind horse. Then it seemed that the herd moved in a great curve, a huge half-moon, with the points of head and tail almost opposite, and a mile apart. But Lassiter relentlessly crowded the leaders, sheering them to the left, turning them little by little. And the dust-blinded wild followers plunged on madly in the tracks of their leaders. This ever-moving, ever-changing curve of steers rolled toward Jane, and when below her, scarce half a mile, it began to narrow and close into a circle. Lassiter had ridden parallel with her position, turned toward her, then aside, and now he was riding directly away from her, all the time pushing the head of that bobbing line inward.

It was then that Jane, suddenly understanding Lassiter's feat, stared and gasped at the riding of this intrepid man. His horse was fleet and tireless, but blind. He had pushed the leaders around and around till they were about to turn in on the inner side of the end of that line of steers. The leaders were already running in a circle; the end of the herd was still running almost straight. But soon they would be wheeling. Then, when Lassiter had the circle formed, how would he escape? With Jane Withersteen prayer was as ready as praise; and she prayed for this man's safety. A circle of dust began to collect. Dimly, as through a yellow veil, Jane saw Lassiter press the leaders inward to close the gap in the sage. She lost sight of him in the dust; again she thought she saw the black, riderless now, rear and drag himself and fall. Lassiter had been thrown—lost! Then he reappeared running out of the dust into the sage. He had escaped, and she breathed again.

Spellbound, Jane Withersteen watched this stupendous millwheel of steers. Here was the milling of the herd. The white running circle closed in upon the open space of sage. And the dust circles closed above into a pall. The ground quaked and the incessant thunder of pounding hoofs rolled on. Jane felt deafened, yet she thrilled to a new sound. As the circle of sage lessened the steers began to bawl, and when it closed entirely there came a great upheaval in the center, and a terrible thumping of heads and clicking of horns. Bawling, climbing, goring, the great mass of steers on the inside wrestled in a crashing din, heaved and groaned under the pressure. Then came a deadlock. The inner strife, ceased, and the hideous roar and crash. Movement went on in the outer circle, and that, too, gradually stilled. The white herd had come to a stop, and the pall of yellow dust began to drift away on the wind.

Jane Withersteen waited on the ridge with full and grateful heart. Lassiter appeared, making his weary way toward her through the sage. And up on the slope Judkins rode into sight with his troop of boys. For the present, at least, the white herd would be looked after.

When Lassiter reached her and laid his hand on Black Star's mane, Jane could not find speech.

"Killed—my—hoss," he panted.

"Oh! I'm sorry," cried Jane. "Lassiter! I know you can't replace him, but I'll give you any one of my racers—Bells, or Night, even Black Star."

"I'll take a fast hoss, Jane, but not one of your favorites," he replied. "Only— will you let me have Black Star now an' ride him over there an' head off them fellers who stampeded the herd?"

He pointed to several moving specks of black and puffs of dust in the purple sage.

"I can head them off with this hoss, an' then—"

"Then, Lassiter?"

"They'll never stampede no more cattle."

"Oh! No! No! . . . Lassiter, I won't let you go!"

But a flush of fire flamed in her cheeks, and her trembling hands shook Black Star's bridle, and her eyes fell before Lassiter's.

CHAPTER SEVEN

The Daughter of Withersteen

"LASSITER, will you be my rider?" Jane had asked him.

"I reckon so," he had replied.

Few as the words were, Jane knew how infinitely much they implied. She wanted him to take charge of her cattle and horses and ranges, and save them if that were possible. Yet, though she could not have spoken aloud all she meant, she was perfectly honest with herself. Whatever the price to be paid, she must keep Lassiter close to her; she must shield from him the man who had lured Milly Erne to Cottonwoods. In her fear she so controlled her mind that she did not whisper this Mormon's name to her own soul, she did not even think it. Besides, beyond this thing she regarded as a sacred obligation thrust upon her, was the need of a helper, of a friend, of a champion in this critical time. If she could rule this gun-man, as Venters had called him, if she could even keep him from shedding blood, what strategy to play his name and his presence against the game of oppression her churchmen were waging against her? Never would she forget the effect upon Tull and his men when Venters shouted Lassiter's name. If she could not wholly control Lassiter, then what she could do might put off the fatal day.

One of her safe racers was a dark bay, and she called him Bells because of the way he struck his iron shoes on the stones. When Jerd led out this slender, beautifully built horse Lassiter suddenly became all eyes. A rider's love of a thoroughbred shone in them. Round and round Bells he walked, plainly weakening all the time in his determination not to take one of Jane's favorite racers.

"Lassiter, you're half horse, and Bells sees it already," said Jane, laughing. "Look at his eyes. He likes you. He'll love you, too. How can you resist him? Oh, Lassiter, but Bells can run! It's nip and tuck between him and Wrangle, and only Black Star can beat him. He's too spirited a horse for a woman. Take him. He's yours."

"I jest am weak where a hoss's concerned," said Lassiter. "I'll take him, an' I'll take your orders, ma'am."

"Well, I'm glad, but never mind the ma'am. Let it still be Jane."

From that hour, it seemed, Lassiter was always in the saddle, riding early and late; and coincident with his part in Jane's affairs the days assumed their old tranquillity. Her intelligence told her this was only the lull before the storm, but her faith would not have it so.

She resumed her visits to the village, and upon one of these she encountered Tull. He greeted her as he had before any trouble came between them, and she, responsive to peace if not quick to forget, met him halfway with manner almost cheerful. He regretted the loss of her cattle; he assured her that the vigilantes which had been organized would soon rout the rustlers; when that had been accomplished her riders would likely return to her.

"You've done a headstrong thing to hire this man Lassiter," Tull went on, severely. "He came to Cottonwoods with evil intent."

"I had to have somebody. And perhaps making him my rider may turn out best in the end for the Mormons of Cottonwoods."

"You mean to stay his hand?"

"I do—if I can."

"A woman like you can do anything with a man. That would be well, and would atone in some measure for the errors you have made."

He bowed and passed on. Jane resumed her walk with conflicting thoughts. She resented Elder Tull's cold, impassive manner that looked down upon her as one who had incurred his just displeasure. Otherwise he would have been the same calm, dark-browed, impenetrable man she had known for ten years. In fact, except when he had revealed his passion in the matter of the seizing of Venters, she had never dreamed he could be other than the grave, reproving preacher. He stood out now a strange, secretive man. She would have thought better of him if he had picked up the threads of their quarrel where they had parted. Was Tull what he appeared to be? The question flung itself involuntarily over Jane Withersteen's inhibitive habit of faith without question. And she refused to answer it. Tull could not fight in the open. Venters had said, Lassiter had said, that her Elder shirked fight and worked in the dark. Just now in this meeting Tull ignored the fact that he had sued, exhorted, demanded that she marry him. He made no mention of Venters. His manner was that of the minister who had been outraged, but who overlooked the frailties of a woman. Beyond question he seemed unutterably aloof from all knowledge of pressure being brought to bear upon her, absolutely guiltless of any connection with secret power over riders, with night journeys, with rustlers and stampedes of cattle. And that convinced her again of unjust suspicions. But it was convincement through an obstinate faith. She shuddered as she accepted it, and that shudder was the nucleus of a terrible revolt.

Jane turned into one of the wide lanes leading from the main street and entered a huge, shady yard. Here were sweet-smelling clover, alfalfa, flowers, and vegetables, all growing in happy confusion. And like these fresh green things were the dozens of babies, tots, toddlers, noisy urchins, laughing girls, a whole multitude of children of one family. For Collier Brandt, the father of all this numerous progeny, was a Mormon with four wives.

The big house where they lived was old, solid, picturesque, the lower part built of logs, the upper of rough clapboards, with vines growing up the outside stone chimneys. There were many wooden-shuttered windows, and one pretentious window of glass, proudly curtained in white. As this house had four mistresses, it likewise had four separate sections, not one of which communicated with another, and all had to be entered from the outside.

In the shade of a wide, low, vine-roofed porch Jane found Brandt's wives entertaining Bishop Dyer. They were motherly women, of comparatively similar ages, and plain-featured, and just at this moment anything but grave. The Bishop was rather tall, of stout build, with iron-gray hair and beard, and eyes of light blue. They were merry now; but Jane had seen them when they were not, and then she feared him as she had feared her father.

The woman flocked around her in welcome.

"Daughter of Withersteen," said the Bishop, gaily, as he took her hand, "you have not been prodigal of your gracious self of late. A Sabbath without you at service! I shall reprove Elder Tull."

"Bishop, the guilt is mine. I'll come to you and confess," Jane replied, lightly; but she felt the undercurrent of her words.

"Mormon love-making!" exclaimed the Bishop, rubbing his hands. "Tull keeps you all to himself."

"No. He is not courting me."

"What? The laggard! If he does not make haste I'll go a-courting myself up to Withersteen House."

There was laughter and further bantering by the Bishop, and then mild talk of village affairs, after which he took his leave, and Jane was left with her friend, Mary Brandt.

"Jane, you're not yourself. Are you sad about the rustling of the cattle? But you have so many, you are so rich."

Then Jane confided in her, telling much, yet holding back her doubts of fear.

"Oh, why don't you marry Tull and be one of us?"

"But, Mary, I don't love Tull," said Jane, stubbornly.

"I don't blame you for that. But, Jane Withersteen, you've got to choose between the love of man and love of God. Often we Mormon women have to do that. It's not easy. The kind of happiness you want I wanted once. I never got it, nor will you, unless you throw away your soul. We've all watched your affair with Venters in fear and trembling. Some dreadful thing will come of it. You don't want him hanged or shot—or treated worse, as that Gentile boy was treated in Glaze for fooling round a Mormon woman. Marry Tull. It's your duty as a Mormon. You'll feel no rapture as his wife—but think of Heaven! Mormon women don't marry for what they expect on earth. Take up the cross, Jane. Remember your father found Amber Spring, built these old houses, brought Mormons here, and fathered them. You are the daughter of Withersteen!"

Jane left Mary Brandt and went to call upon other friends. They received her with the same glad welcome as had Mary, lavished upon her the pent-up affection of Mormon women, and let her go with her ears ringing of Tull, Venters, Lassiter, of duty to God and glory in Heaven.

"Verily," murmured Jane, "I don't know myself when, through all this, I remain unchanged—nay, more fixed of purpose."

She returned to the main street and bent her thoughtful steps toward the center of the village. A string of wagons drawn by oxen was lumbering along. These "sage-freighters," as they were called, hauled grain and flour and merchandise from Sterling; and Jane laughed suddenly in the midst of her humility at the thought that they were her property, as was one of the three stores for which they freighted goods. The water that flowed along the path at her feet, and turned into each cottage-yard to nourish garden and orchard, also was hers, no less her private property because she chose to give it free. Yet in this village of Cottonwoods, which her father had founded and which she maintained, she was not her own mistress; she was not able to abide by her own choice of a husband. She was the daughter of Withersteen. Suppose she proved it, imperiously! But she quelled that proud temptation at its birth.

Nothing could have replaced the affection which the village people had for her; no power could have made her happy as the pleasure her presence gave. As she went on down the street, past the stores with their rude platform entrances, and the saloons, where tired horses stood with bridles dragging, she was again assured of what was the bread and wine of life to her—that she was loved. Dirty boys playing in the ditch, clerks, teamsters, riders, loungers on the corners, ranchers on dusty horses, little girls running errands, and women hurrying to the stores all looked up at her coming with glad eyes.

Jane's various calls and wandering steps at length led her to the Gentile quarter of the village. This was at the extreme southern end, and here some thirty Gentile families lived in huts and shacks and log-cabins and several dilapidated cottages. The fortunes of these inhabitants of Cottonwoods could be read in their abodes. Water they had in abundance, and therefore grass and fruit-trees and patches of alfalfa and vegetable gardens. Some of the men and boys had a few stray cattle, others obtained such intermittent employment as the Mormons reluctantly tendered them. But none of the families was prosperous, many were very poor, and some lived only by Jane Withersteen's beneficence.

As it made Jane happy to go among her own people, so it saddened her to come in contact with these Gentiles. Yet that was not because she was unwelcome; here she was gratefully received by the women, passionately by the children. But poverty and idleness, with their attendant wretchedness and sorrow, always hurt her. That she could alleviate this distress more now than ever before proved the adage that it was an ill wind that blew nobody good. While her Mormon riders were in her employ she had found few Gentiles who would stay with her, and now she was able to find employment for all the men and boys. No little shock was it to have man after man tell her that he dare not accept her kind offer.

"It won't do," said one Carson, an intelligent man who had seen better days. "We've had our warning. Plain and to the point! Now there's Judkins, he packs guns, and he can use them, and so can the daredevil boys he's hired. But they've little responsibility. Can we risk having our homes burned in our absence?"

Jane felt the stretching and chilling of the skin of her face as the blood left it.

"Carson, you and the others rent these houses?" she asked.

"You ought to know, Miss Withersteen. Some of them are yours."

"I know? . . . Carson, I never in my life took a day's labor for rent or a yearling calf or a bunch of grass, let alone gold."

"Bivens, your store-keeper, sees to that."

"Look here, Carson," went on Jane, hurriedly, and now her cheeks were burning. "You and Black and Willet pack your goods and move your families up to my cabins in the grove. They're far more comfortable than these. Then go to work for me. And if aught happens to you there I'll give you money—gold enough to leave Utah!"

The man choked and stammered, and then, as tears welled into his eyes, he found the use of his tongue and cursed. No gentle speech could ever have equaled that curse in eloquent expression of what he felt for Jane Withersteen. How strangely his look and tone reminded her of Lassiter!

"No, it won't do," he said, when he had somewhat recovered himself. "Miss Withersteen, there are things that you don't know, and there's not a soul among us who can tell you."

"I seem to be learning many things, Carson. Well, then, will you let me aid you—say till better times?"

"Yes, I will," he replied, with his face lighting up. "I see what it means to you, and you know what it means to me. Thank you! And if better times ever came I'll be only too happy to work for you."

"Better times will come. I trust God and have faith in man. Good day, Carson."

The lane opened out upon the sage-inclosed alfalfa fields, and the last habitation, at the end of that lane of hovels, was the meanest. Formerly it had been a shed; now it was a home. The broad leaves of a wide-spreading cottonwood sheltered the sunken roof of weathered boards. Like an Indian hut, it had one floor. Round about it were a few scanty rows of vegetables, such as the hand of a weak woman had time and strength to cultivate. This little dwelling-place was just outside the village limits, and the widow who lived there had to carry her water from the nearest irrigation ditch. As Jane Withersteen entered the unfenced yard a child saw her, shrieked with joy, and came tearing toward her with curls flying. This child was a little girl of four called Fay. Her name suited her, for she was an elf, a sprite, a creature so fairy-like and beautiful that she seemed unearthly.

"Muvver sended for oo," cried Fay, as Jane kissed her, "an' oo never tome."

"I didn't know, Fay; but I've come now."

Fay was a child of outdoors, of the garden and ditch and field, and she was dirty and ragged. But rags and dirt did not hide her beauty. The one thin little bedraggled garment she wore half covered her fine, slim body. Red as cherries were her cheeks and lips; her eyes were violet blue, and the crown of her childish loveliness was the curling golden hair. All the children of Cottonwoods were Jane Withersteen's friends; she loved them all. But Fay was dearest to her. Fay had few playmates, for among the Gentile children there were none near her age, and the Mormon children were forbidden to play with her. So she was a shy, wild, lonely child.

"Muvver's sick," said Fay, leading Jane toward the door of the hut.

Jane went in. There was only one room, rather dark and bare, but it was clean and neat. A woman lay upon a bed.

"Mrs. Larkin, how are you?" asked Jane, anxiously.

"I've been pretty bad for a week, but I'm better now."

"You haven't been here all alone—with no one to wait on you?"

"Oh no! My women neighbors are kind. They take turns coming in."

"Did you send for me?"

"Yes, several times."

"But I had no word—no messages ever got to me."

"I sent the boys, and they left word with your women that I was ill and would you please come."

A sudden deadly sickness seized Jane. She fought the weakness, as she fought to be above suspicious thoughts, and it passed, leaving her conscious of her utter impotence. That, too, passed as her spirit rebounded. But she had again caught a glimpse of dark underhand domination, running its secret lines this time into her own household. Like a spider in the blackness of night an unseen hand had begun to run these dark lines, to turn and twist them about her life, to plait and weave a web. Jane Withersteen knew it now, and in the realization further coolness and sureness came to her, and the fighting courage of her ancestors.

"Mrs. Larkin, you're better, and I'm so glad," said Jane. "But may I not do something for you—a turn at nursing, or send you things, or take care of Fay?"

"You're so good. Since my husband's been gone what would have become of Fay and me but for you? It was about Fay that I wanted to speak to you. This time I thought surely I'd die, and I was worried about Fay. Well, I'll be around all right shortly, but my strength's gone and I won't live long. So I may as well speak now. You remember you've been asking me to let you take Fay and bring her up as your daughter?"

"Indeed yes, I remember. I'll be happy to have her. But I hope the day—"

"Never mind that. The day'll come—sooner or later. I refused your offer, and now I'll tell you why."

"I know why," interposed Jane. "It's because you don't want her brought up as a Mormon."

"No, it wasn't altogether that." Mrs. Larkin raised her thin hand and laid it appealingly on Jane's. "I don't like to tell you. But—it's this: I told all my friends what you wanted. They know you, care for you, and they said for me to trust

Fay to you. Women will talk, you know. It got to the ears of Mormons—gossip of your love for Fay and your wanting her. And it came straight back to me, in jealousy, perhaps, that you wouldn't take Fay as much for love of her as because of your religious duty to bring up another girl for some Mormon to marry."

"That's a damnable lie!" cried Jane Withersteen.

"It was what made me hesitate," went on Mrs. Larkin, "but I never believed it at heart. And now I guess I'll let you—"

"Wait! Mrs. Larkin, I may have told little white lies in my life, but never a lie that mattered, that hurt any one. Now believe me. I love little Fay. If I had her near me I'd grow to worship her. When I asked for her I thought only of that love. . . . Let me prove this. You and Fay come to live with me. I've such a big house, and I'm so lonely. I'll help nurse you, take care of you. When you're better you can work for me. I'll keep little Fay and bring her up—without Mormon teaching. When she's grown, if she should want to leave me, I'll send her, and not empty-handed, back to Illinois where you came from. I promise you."

"I knew it was a lie," replied the mother, and she sank back upon her pillow with something of peace in her white, worn face. "Jane Withersteen, may Heaven bless you! I've been deeply grateful to you. But because you're a Mormon I never felt close to you till now. I don't know much about religion as religion, but your God and my God are the same."

CHAPTER EIGHT

Surprise Valley

Back in that strange cañon, which Venters had found indeed a valley of surprises, the wounded girl's whispered appeal, almost a prayer, not to take her back to the rustlers crowned the events of the last few days with a confounding climax. That she should not want to return to them staggered Venters. Presently, as logical thought returned, her appeal confirmed his first impression—that she was more unfortunate than bad—and he experienced a sensation of gladness. If he had known before that Oldring's Masked Rider was a woman his opinion would have been formed and he would have considered her abandoned. But his first knowledge had come when he lifted a white face quivering in a convulsion of agony; he had heard God's name whispered by blood-stained lips; through her solemn and awful eyes he had caught a glimpse of her soul. And just now had come the entreaty to him, "Don't—take—me—back—there!"

Once for all Venters's quick mind formed a permanent conception of this poor girl. He based it, not upon what the chances of life had made her, but upon the revelation of dark eyes that pierced the infinite, upon a few pitiful, halting words that betrayed failure and wrong and misery, yet breathed the truth of a tragic fate rather than a natural leaning to evil.

"What's your name?" he inquired.

"Bess," she answered.

"Bess what?"

"That's enough—just Bess."

The red that deepened in her cheeks was not all the flush of fever. Venters marveled anew, and this time at the tint of shame in her face, at the momentary drooping of long lashes. She might be a rustler's girl, but she was still capable of shame; she might be dying, but she still clung to some little remnant of honor.

"Very well, Bess. It doesn't matter," he said. "But this matters—what shall I do with you?"

"Are—you—a rider?" she whispered.

"Not now. I was once. I drove the Withersteen herds. But I lost my place—lost all I owned—and now I'm—I'm a sort of outcast. My name's Bern Venters."

"You won't—take me—to Cottonwoods—or Glaze? I'd be—hanged."

"No, indeed. But I must do something with you. For it's not safe for me here. I shot that rustler who was with you. Sooner or later he'll be found, and then my tracks. I must find a safer hiding-place where I can't be trailed."

"Leave me—here."

"Alone—to die!"

"Yes."

"I will not." Venters spoke shortly with a kind of ring in his voice.

"What—do you want—to do—with me?" Her whispering grew difficult, so low and faint that Venters had to stoop to hear her.

"Why, let's see," he replied, slowly. "I'd like to take you some place where I could watch by you, nurse you, till you're all right again."

"And—then?"

"Well, it'll be time to think of that when you're cured of your wound. It's a bad one. And—Bess, if you don't want to live—if you don't fight for life—you'll never—"

"Oh! I want—to live! I'm afraid—to die. But I'd rather—die—than go back—to—to—"

"To Oldring?" asked Venters, interrupting her in turn.

Her lips moved in an affirmative.

"I promise not to take you back to him or to Cottonwoods or to Glaze."

The mournful earnestness of her gaze suddenly shone with unutterable gratitude and wonder. And as suddenly Venters found her eyes beautiful as he had never seen or felt beauty. They were as dark blue as the sky at night. Then the flashing changed to a long, thoughtful look, in which there was a wistful, unconscious searching of his face, a look that trembled on the verge of hope and trust.

"I'll try—to live," she said. The broken whisper just reached his ears. "Do what—you want—with me."

"Rest then—don't worry—sleep," he replied.

Abruptly he arose, as if words had been decision for him, and with a sharp command to the dogs he strode from the camp. Venters was conscious of an indefinite conflict of change within him. It seemed to be a vague passing of old moods, a dim coalescing of new forces, a moment of inexplicable transition. He was both cast down and uplifted. He wanted to think and think of the meaning, but he resolutely dispelled emotion. His imperative need at present was to find a safe retreat, and this called for action.

So he set out. It still wanted several hours before dark. This trip he turned to the left and wended his skulking way southward a mile or more to the opening of the valley, where lay the strange scrawled rocks. He did not, however, venture boldly out into the open sage, but clung to the right-hand wall and went along that till its perpendicular line broke into the long incline of bare stone.

Before proceeding farther he halted, studying the strange character of this slope and realizing that a moving black object could be seen far against such background. Before him ascended a gradual swell of smooth stone. It was hard, polished, and full of pockets worn by centuries of eddying rain-water. A hundred yards up began a line of grotesque cedar-trees, and they extended along the slope clear to its most southerly end. Beyond that end Venters wanted to get, and he concluded the cedars, few as they were, would afford some cover.

Therefore he climbed swiftly. The trees were farther up than he had estimated, though he had from long habit made allowance for the deceiving nature of distances in that country. When he gained the cover of cedars he paused to rest and look, and it was then he saw how the trees sprang from holes in the bare rock. Ages of rain had run down the slope, circling, eddying in depressions, wearing deep round holes. There had been dry seasons, accumulations of dust, wind-blown seeds, and cedars rose wonderfully out of solid rock. But these were not beautiful cedars. They were gnarled, twisted into weird contortions, as if growth were torture, dead at the tops, shrunken, gray, and old. Theirs had been a bitter fight, and Venters felt a strange sympathy for them. This country was hard on trees—and men.

He slipped from cedar to cedar, keeping them between him and the open valley. As he progressed, the belt of trees widened, and he kept to its upper margin. He passed shady pockets half full of water, and, as he marked the location for possible future need, he reflected that there had been no rain since the winter snows. From one of these shady holes a rabbit hopped out and squatted down, laying its ears flat.

Venters wanted fresh meat now more than when he had only himself to think of. But it would not do to fire his rifle there. So he broke off a cedar branch and threw it. He crippled the rabbit, which started to flounder up the slope. Venters did not wish to lose the meat, and he never allowed crippled game to escape, to die lingeringly in some covert. So after a careful glance below, and back toward the cañon, he began to chase the rabbit.

The fact that rabbits generally ran uphill was not new to him. But it presently seemed singular why this rabbit, that might have escaped downward, chose to ascend the slope. Venters knew then that it had a burrow higher up. More than once he jerked over to seize it, only in vain, for the rabbit by renewed effort eluded his grasp. Thus the chase continued on up the bare slope. The farther Venters climbed the more determined he grew to catch his quarry. At last, panting and sweating, he captured the rabbit at the foot of a steeper grade. Laying his rifle on the bulge of rising stone, he killed the animal and slung it from his belt.

Before starting down he waited to catch his breath. He had climbed far up that wonderful smooth slope, and had almost reached the base of yellow cliff that rose skyward, a huge scarred and cracked bulk. It frowned down upon him as if to forbid furthur ascent. Venters bent over for his rifle, and, as he picked it up from where it leaned against the steeper grade, he saw several little nicks cut in the solid stone.

They were only a few inches deep and about a foot apart. Venters began to count them—one—two—three—four—on up to sixteen. That number carried his glance to the top of his first bulging bench of cliff-base. Above, after a more level offset, was still steeper slope, and the line of nicks kept on, to wind round a projecting corner of wall.

A casual glance would have passed by these little dents; if Venters had not known what they signified he would never have bestowed upon them the second glance. But he knew they had been cut there by hand, and, though age-worn, he recognized them as steps cut in the rock by the cliff-dwellers. With a pulse beginning to beat and hammer away his calmness, he eyed that indistinct line of steps, up to where the buttress of wall hid further sight of them. He knew that behind the corner of stone would be a cave or a crack which could never be suspected from below. Chance, that had sported with him of late, now directed him to a probable hiding-place. Again he laid aside his rifle, and, removing boots and belt, he began to walk up the steps. Like a mountain goat, he was agile, sure-footed, and he mounted the first bench without bending to use his hands. The next ascent took grip of fingers as well as toes, but he climbed steadily, swiftly, to reach the projecting corner, and slipped around it. Here he faced a notch in the cliff. At the apex he turned abruptly into a ragged vent that split the ponderous wall clear to the top, showing a narrow streak of blue sky.

At the base this vent was dark, cool, and smelled of dry, musty dust. It zigzagged so that he could not see ahead more than a few yards at a time. He noticed tracks of wildcats and rabbits in the dusty floor. At every turn he expected to come upon a huge cavern full of little square stone houses, each with a small aperture like a staring dark eye. The passage lightened and widened, and opened at the foot of a narrow, steep, ascending chute.

Venters had a moment's notice of the rock, which was of the same smoothness and hardness as the slope below, before his gaze went irresistibly upward to the precipitous walls of this wide ladder of granite. These were ruined walls of yellow sandstone, and so split and splintered, so overhanging with great sections of balancing rim, so impending with tremendous crumbling crags, that Venters caught his breath sharply, and, appalled, he instinctively recoiled as if a step upward might jar the ponderous cliffs from their foundation. Indeed, it seemed that these ruined cliffs were but awaiting a breath of wind to collapse and come tumbling down. Venters hesitated. It would be a foolhardy man who risked his life under the leaning, waiting avalanches of rock in that gigantic split. Yet how many years had they leaned there without falling! At the bottom of the incline was an immense heap of weathered sandstone all crumbling to dust, but there were no huge rocks as large as houses, such as rested so lightly and frightfully above, waiting patiently and inevitably to crash down. Slowly split from the parent rock by the weathering process, and carved and sculptured by ages of wind and rain, they waited their moment. Venters felt how foolish it was for him to fear these broken walls; to fear that, after they had endured for thousands of years, the moment of his passing should be the one for them to slip. Yet he feared it.

"What a place to hide!" muttered Venters. "I'll climb—I'll see where this thing goes. If only I can find water!"

With teeth tight shut he essayed the incline. And as he climbed he bent his eyes downward. This, however, after a little grew impossible; he had to look to obey his eager, curious mind. He raised his glance and saw light between row on row of shafts and pinnacles and crags that stood out from the main wall. Some leaned against the cliff, others against each other; many stood sheer and alone; all were crumbling, cracked, rotten. It was a place of yellow, ragged ruin. The passage narrowed as he went up; it became a slant, hard for him to stick on; it was smooth as marble. Finally he surmounted it, surprised to find the walls still several hundred feet high, and a narrow gorge leading down on the other side. This was a divide between two inclines, about twenty yards wide. At one side stood an enormous rock. Venters gave it a second glance, because it rested on a pedestal. It attracted closer attention. It was like a colossal pear of stone standing on its stem. Around the bottom were thousands of little nicks just distinguishable to the eye. They were marks of stone hatchets. The cliff-dwellers had chipped and chipped away at this boulder till it rested its tremendous bulk upon a mere pin-point of its surface. Venters pondered. Why had the little stone-men hacked away at that big boulder? It bore no semblance to a statue or an idol or a godhead or a sphinx. Instinctively he put his hands on it and pushed; then his shoulder and heaved. The stone seemed to groan, to stir, to grate, and then to move. It tipped a little downward and hung balancing for a long instant, slowly returned, rocked slightly, groaned, and settled back to its former position.

Venters divined its significance. It had been meant for defense. The cliff-dwellers, driven by dreaded enemies to this last stand, had cunningly cut the rock until it balanced perfectly, ready to be dislodged by strong hands. Just below it leaned a tottering crag that would have toppled, starting an avalanche on an acclivity where no sliding mass could stop. Crags and pinnacles, splintered cliffs, and leaning shafts and monuments, would have thundered down to block forever the outlet to Deception Pass.

"That was a narrow shave for me," said Venters, soberly. "A balancing rock! The cliff-dwellers never had to roll it. They died, vanished, and here the rock stands, probably little changed. . . . But it might serve another lonely dweller of the cliffs. I'll hide up here somewhere, if I can only find water."

He descended the gorge on the other side. The slope was gradual, the space narrow, the course straight for many rods. A gloom hung between the up-sweeping walls. In a turn the passage narrowed to scarce a dozen feet, and here was darkness of night. But light shone ahead; another abrupt turn brought day again, and then wide open space.

Above Venters loomed a wonderful arch of stone bridging the cañon rims, and through the enormous round portal gleamed and glistened a beautiful valley shining under sunset gold reflected by surrounding cliffs. He gave a start of surprise. The valley was a cove a mile long, half that wide, and its enclosing walls were smooth and stained, and curved inward, forming great caves. He decided that its floor was far higher than the level of Deception Pass and the intersecting cañons. No purple sage colored this valley floor. Instead there were the white of aspens, streaks of branch and slender trunk glistening from the green of leaves, and the darker green of oaks, and through the middle of this forest, from wall to wall, ran a winding line of brilliant green which marked the course of cotton-woods and willows.

"There's water here—and this is the place for me," said Venters. "Only birds can peep over those walls. I've gone Oldring one better."

Venters waited no longer, and turned swiftly to retrace his steps. He named the cañon Surprise Valley and the huge boulder that guarded the outlet Balancing

Rock. Going down he did not find himself attended by such fears as had beset him in the climb; still, he was not easy in mind and could not occupy himself with plans of moving the girl and his outfit until he had descended to the notch. There he rested a moment and looked about him. The pass was darkening with the approach of night. At the corner of the wall, where the stone steps turned, he saw a spur of rock that would serve to hold the noose of a lasso. He needed no more aid to scale that place. As he intended to make the move under cover of darkness, he wanted most to be able to tell where to climb up. So, taking several small stones with him, he stepped and slid down to the edge of the slope where he had left his rifle and boots. He placed the stones some yards apart. He left the rabbit lying upon the bench where the steps began. Then he addressed a keen-sighted, remembering gaze to the rim-wall above. It was serrated, and between two spears of rock, directly in line with his position, showed a zigzag crack that at night would let through the gleam of sky. This settled, he put on his belt and boots and prepared to descend. Some consideration was necessary to decide whether or not to leave his rifle there. On the return, carrying the girl and a pack, it would be added encumbrance; and after debating the matter he left the rifle leaning against the bench. As he went straight down the slope he halted every few rods to look up at his mark on the rim. It changed, but he fixed each change in his memory. When he reached the first cedar-tree, he tied his scarf upon a dead branch, and then hurried toward camp, having no more concern about finding his trail upon the return trip.

Darkness soon emboldened and lent him greater speed. It occurred to him, as he glided into the grassy glade near camp and heard the whinny of a horse, that he had forgotten Wrangle. The big sorrel could not be gotten into Surprise Valley. He would have to be left here.

Venters determined at once to lead the other horses out through the thicket and turn them loose. The farther they wandered from this cañon the better it would suit him. He easily descried Wrangle through the gloom, but the others were not in sight. Venters whistled low for the dogs, and when they came trotting to him he sent them out to search for the horses, and followed. It soon developed that they were not in the glade nor the thicket. Venters grew cold and rigid at the thought of rustlers having entered his retreat. But the thought passed, for the demeanor of Ring and Whitie reassured him. The horses had wandered away.

Under the clump of silver spruces a denser mantle of darkness, yet not so thick that Venters' night-practiced eyes could not catch the white oval of a still face. He bent over it with a slight suspension of breath that was both caution lest he frighten her and chill uncertainty of feeling lest he find her dead. But she slept, and he arose to renewed activity.

He packed his saddle-bags. The dogs were hungry, they whined about him and nosed his busy hands; but he took no time to feed them nor to satisfy his own hunger. He slung the saddle-bags over his shoulders and made them secure with his lasso. Then he wrapped the blankets closer about the girl and lifted her in his arms. Wrangle whinnied and thumped the ground as Venters passed him with the dogs. The sorrel knew he was being left behind, and was not sure whether he liked it or not. Venters went on and entered the thicket. Here he had to feel his way in pitch blackness and to wedge his progress between the close saplings. Time meant little to him now that he had started, and he edged along with slow side movement till he got clear of the thicket. Ring and Whitie stood waiting for him. Taking to the open aisles and patches of the sage, he walked guardedly, careful not to stumble or step in dust or strike against spreading sage-branches.

If he were burdened he did not feel it. From time to time, when he passed out of the black lines of shade into the wan starlight, he glanced at the white face of the girl lying in his arms. She had not awakened from her sleep or stupor. He did not rest until he cleared the black gate of the cañon. Then he leaned against a stone breast-high to him and gently released the girl from his hold. His brow and hair and the palms of his hands were wet, and there was a kind of nervous contraction of his muscles. They seemed to ripple and string tense. He had a desire to hurry and no sense of fatigue. A wind blew the scent of sage in his face. The first early blackness of night passed with the brightening of the stars. Somewhere back on his trail a coyote yelped, splitting the dead silence. Venters's faculties seemed singularly acute.

He lifted the girl again and pressed on. The valley afforded better traveling than the cañon. It was lighter, freer of sage, and there were no rocks. Soon, out of the pale gloom shone a still paler thing, and that was the low swell of slope. Venters mounted it, and his dogs walked beside him. Once upon the stone he slowed to snail pace, straining his sight to avoid the pockets and holes. Foot by foot he went up. The weird cedars, like great demons and witches chained to the rock and writhing in silent anguish, loomed up with wide and twisting naked arms. Venters crossed this belt of cedars, skirted the upper border, and recognized the tree he had marked, even before he saw his waving scarf.

Here he knelt and deposited the girl gently, feet first, and slowly laid her out full length. What he feared was to reopen one of her wounds. If he gave her a violent jar, or slipped and fell! But the supreme confidence so strangely felt that night admitted no such blunders.

The slope before him seemed to swell into obscurity, to lose its definite outline in a misty, opaque cloud that shaded into the over-shadowing wall. He scanned the rim where the serrated points speared the sky, and he found the zigzag crack. It was dim, only a shade lighter than the dark ramparts; but he distinguished it, and that served.

Lifting the girl, he stepped upward, closely attending to the nature of the path under his feet. After a few steps he stopped to mark his line with the crack in the rim. The dogs clung closer to him. While chasing the rabbit this slope had appeared interminable to him; now, burdened as he was, he did not think of length or height or toil. He remembered only to avoid a misstep and to keep his direction. He climbed on, with frequent stops to watch the rim, and before he dreamed of gaining the bench he bumped his knees into it, and saw, in the dim gray light, his rifle and the rabbit. He had come straight up without mishap or swerving off his course, and his shut teeth unlocked.

As he laid the girl down in the shallow hollow of the little ridge, with her white face upturned, she opened her eyes. Wide, staring, black, at once like both the night and the stars, they made her face seem still whiter.

"Is—it—you?" she asked, faintly.

"Yes," replied Venters.

"Oh! Where—are we?"

"I'm taking you to a safe place where no one will ever find you. I must climb a little here and call the dogs. Don't be afraid. I'll soon come for you."

She said no more. Her eyes watched him steadily for a moment and then closed. Venters pulled off his boots and then felt for the little steps in the rock. The shade of the cliff above obscured the point he wanted to gain, but he could see dimly a few feet before him. What he had attempted with care he now went at with surpassing lightness. Buoyant, rapid, sure, he attained the corner of wall and slipped around it. Here he could not see a hand before his face, so he groped along, found a little flat space, and there removed the saddle-bags. The lasso he took back with him to the corner and looped the noose over the spur of rock.

"Ring—Whitie—come," he called, softly.

Low whines came up from below.

"Here! Come, Whitie—Ring," he repeated, this time sharply.

Then followed scraping of claws and pattering of feet; and out of the gray gloom below him swiftly climbed the dogs to reach his side and pass beyond.

Venters descended, holding to the lasso. He tested its strength by throwing all his weight upon it. Then he gathered the girl up, and, holding her securely in his left arm, he began to climb, at every few steps jerking his right hand upward along the lasso. It sagged at each forward movement he made, but he balanced himself lightly during the interval when he lacked the support of a taut rope. He climbed as if he had wings, the strength of a giant, and knew not the sense of fear. The sharp corner of cliff seemed to cut out of the darkness. He reached it and the protruding shelf, and then, entering the black shade of the notch, he moved blindly but surely to the place where he had left the saddle-bags. He heard the dogs, though he could not see them. Once more he carefully placed the girl at his feet. Then, on hands and knees, he went over the little flat space, feeling for stones. He removed a number, and, scraping the deep dust into a heap, he unfolded the outer blanket from around the girl and laid her upon this bed. Then he went down the slope again for his boots, rifle, and the rabbit, and, bringing also his lasso with him, he made short work of that trip.

"Are—you—there?" The girl's voice came low from the blackness.

"Yes," he replied, and was conscious that his laboring breast made speech difficult.

"Are we—in a cave?"

"Yes."

"Oh, listen! . . . The waterfall! . . . I hear it! You've brought me back!"

Venters heard a murmuring moan that one moment swelled to a pitch almost softly shrill and the next lulled to a low, almost inaudible sigh.

"That's—wind blowing—in the—cliffs," he panted. "You're far—from Oldring's—cañon."

The effort it cost him to speak made him conscious of extreme lassitude following upon great exertion. It seemed that when he lay down and drew his blanket over him the action was the last before utter prostration. He stretched inert, wet, hot, his body one great strife of throbbing, stinging nerves and bursting veins. And there he lay for a long while before he felt that he had begun to rest.

Rest came to him that night, but no sleep. Sleep he did not want. The hours of strained effort were now as if they had never been, and he wanted to think. Earlier in the day he had dismissed an inexplicable feeling of change; but now, when there was no longer demand on his cunning and strength and he had time to think, he could not catch the illusive thing that had sadly perplexed as well as elevated his spirit.

Above him, through a V-shaped cleft in the dark rim of the cliff, shone the lustrous stars that had been his lonely accusers for a long, long year. To-night they were different. He studied them. Larger, whiter, more radiant they seemed; but that was not the difference he meant. Gradually it came to him that the distinction was not one he saw, but one he felt. In this he divined as much of the baffling change as he thought would be revealed to him then. And as he lay there, with the singing of the cliff-winds in his ears, the white stars above the dark, bold vent, the difference which he felt was that he was no longer alone.

CHAPTER NINE

Silver Spruce and Aspens

THE rest of that night seemed to Venters only a few moments of starlight, a dark overcasting of sky, an hour or so of gray gloom, and then the lighting of dawn.

When he had bestirred himself, feeding the hungry dogs and breaking his long fast, and had repacked his saddle-bags, it was clear daylight, though the sun had not tipped the yellow wall in the east. He concluded to make the climb and descent into Surprise Valley in one trip. To that end he tied his blanket upon Ring and gave Whitie the extra lasso and the rabbit to carry. Then, with the rifle and saddle-bags slung upon his back, he took up the girl. She did not awaken from heavy slumber.

That climb up under the rugged, menacing brows of the broken cliffs, in the face of a grim, leaning boulder that seemed to be weary of its age-long wavering, was a tax on strength and nerve that Venters felt equally with something sweet and strangely exulting in its accomplishment. He did not pause until he gained the narrow divide and there he rested. Balancing Rock loomed huge, cold in the gray light of dawn, a thing without life, yet it spoke silently to Venters: "I am waiting to plunge down, to shatter and crash, roar and boom, to bury your trail, and close forever the outlet to Deception Pass!"

On the descent of the other side Venters had easy going, but was somewhat concerned because Whitie appeared to have succumbed to temptation, and while carrying the rabbit was also chewing on it. And Ring evidently regarded this as an injury to himself, especially as he had carried the heavier load. Presently he snapped at one end of the rabbit and refused to let go. But his action prevented Whitie from further misdoing, and then the two dogs pattered down, carrying the rabbit between them.

Venters turned out of the gorge, and suddenly paused stock-still, astounded at the scene before him. The curve of the great stone bridge had caught the sunrise, and through the magnificent arch burst a glorious stream of gold that shone with a long slant down into the center of Surprise Valley. Only through the arch did any sunlight pass, so that all the rest of the valley lay still asleep, dark green, mysterious, shadowy, merging its level into walls as misty and soft as morning clouds.

Venters then descended, passing through the arch, looking up at its tremendous height and sweep. It spanned the opening to Surprise Valley, stretching in almost perfect curve from rim to rim. Even in his hurry and concern Venters could not but feel its majesty, and the thought came to him that the cliff-dwellers must have regarded it as an object of worship.

Down, down, down Venters strode, more and more feeling the weight of his burden as he descended, and still the valley lay below him. As all other cañons and coves and valleys had deceived him, so had this deep, nestling oval. At length he passed beyond the slope of weathered stone that spread fan-shape from the arch, and encountered a grassy terrace running to the right and about on a level with the tips of the oaks and cottonwoods below. Scattered here and there upon this shelf were clumps of aspens, and he walked through them into a glade that surpassed, in beauty and adaptability for a wild home, any place he had ever seen. Silver spruces bordered the base of a precipitous wall that rose loftily. Caves indented its surface, and there were no detached ledges or weathered sections that might dislodge a stone. The level ground, beyond the spruces, dropped down into a little ravine. This was one dense line of slender aspens from which came the low splashing of water. And the terrace, lying open to the west, afforded unobstructed view of the valley of green tree-tops.

For his camp Venters chose a shady, grassy plot between the silver spruces and the cliff. Here, in the stone wall, had been wonderfully carved by wind or washed by water several deep caves above the level of the terrace. They were clean, dry, roomy. He cut spruce boughs and made a bed in the largest cave and laid the girl there. The first intimation that he had of her being aroused from sleep or lethargy was a low call for water.

He hurried down into the ravine with his canteen. It was a shallow, grass-green place with aspens growing up everywhere. To his delight he found a tiny brook of swift-running water: Its faint tinge of amber reminded him of the spring at Cottonwoods, and the thought gave him a little shock. The water was so cold it made his fingers tingle as he dipped the canteen. Having returned to the cave, he was glad to see the girl drink thirstily. This time he noted that she could raise her head slightly without his help.

"You were thirsty," he said. "It's good water. I've found a fine place. Tell me—how do you feel?"

"There's pain—here," she replied, and moved her hand to her left side.

"Why, that's strange! Your wounds are on your right side. I believe you're hungry. Is the pain a kind of dull ache—a gnawing?"

"It's like—that."

"Then it's hunger." Venters laughed, and suddenly caught himself with a quick breath and felt again the little shock. When had he laughed? "It's hunger," he went on. "I've had that gnaw many a time. I've got it now. But you mustn't eat. You can have all the water you want, but no food just yet."

"Won't I—starve?"

"No, people don't starve easily. I've discovered that. You must lie perfectly still and rest and sleep—for days."

"My hands—are dirty; my face feels—so hot and sticky; my boots hurt." It was her longest speech as yet, and it trailed off in a whisper.

"Well, I'm a fine nurse!"

It annoyed him that he had never thought of these things. But then, awaiting her death and thinking of her comfort were vastly different matters. He unwrapped the blanket which covered her. What a slender girl she was! No wonder he had been able to carry her miles and pack her up that slippery ladder of stone. Her boots were of soft, fine leather, reaching clear to her knees. He recognized the make as one of a bootmaker in Sterling. Her spurs, that he had stupidly neglected to remove, consisted of silver frames and gold chains, and the rowels, large as silver dollars, were fancifully engraved. The boots slipped off rather hard. She wore heavy woollen rider's stockings, half length, and these were pulled up over the ends of her short trousers. Venters took off the stockings to note her little feet were red and swollen. He bathed them. Then he removed his scarf and bathed her face and hands.

"I must see your wounds now," he said, gently.

She made no reply, but watched him steadily as he opened her blouse and untied the bandage. His strong fingers trembled a little as he removed it. If the wounds had reopened! A chill struck him as he saw the angry red bullet-mark, and a tiny stream of blood winding from it down her white breast. Very carefully he lifted her to see that the wound in her back had closed perfectly. Then he washed the blood from her breast, bathed the wound, and left it unbandaged, open to the air.

Her eyes thanked him.

"Listen," he said, earnestly. "I've had some wounds, and I've seen many. I know a little about them. The hole in your back has closed. If you lie still three days the one in your breast will close and you'll be safe. The danger from hemorrhage will be over."

He had spoken with earnest sincerity, almost eagerness.

"Why—do you—want me—to get well?" she asked, wonderingly.

The simple question seemed unanswerable except on grounds of humanity. But the circumstances under which he had shot this strange girl, the shock and realization, the waiting for death, the hope, had resulted in a condition of mind wherein Venters wanted her to live more than he had ever wanted anything. Yet he could not tell why. He believed the killing of the rustler and the subsequent excitement had disturbed him. For how else could he explain the throbbing of his brain, the heat of his blood, the undefined sense of full hours, charged, vibrant with pulsating mystery where once they had dragged in loneliness?

"I shot you," he said, slowly, "and I want you to get well so I shall not have killed a woman. But—for your own sake, too—"

A terrible bitterness darkened her eyes, and her lips quivered.

"Hush," said Venters. "You've talked too much already."

In her unutterable bitterness he saw a darkness of mood that could not have been caused by her present weak and feverish state. She hated the life she had led, that she probably had been compelled to lead. She had suffered some unforgivable wrong at the hands of Oldring. With that conviction Venters felt a flame throughout his body, and it marked the rekindling of fierce anger and ruthlessness. In the past long year he had nursed resentment. He had hated the wilderness—the loneliness of the uplands. He had waited for something to come to pass. It had come. Like an Indian stealing horses he had skulked into the recesses of the cañons. He had found Oldring's retreat; he had killed a rustler; he had shot an unfortunate girl, then had saved her from this unwitting act, and he meant to save her from the consequent wasting of blood, from fever and weakness. Starvation he had to fight for her and for himself. Where he had been sick at the letting of blood, now he remembered it in grim, cold calm. And as he lost that softness of nature, so he lost his fear of men. He would watch for Oldring, biding his time, and he would kill this great black-bearded rustler who had held a girl in bondage, who had used her to his infamous ends.

Venters surmised this much of the change in him—idleness had passed; keen, fierce vigor flooded his mind and body; all that had happened to him at Cottonwoods seemed remote and hard to recall; the difficulties and perils of the present absorbed him, held him in a kind of spell.

First, then, he fitted up the little cave adjoining the girl's room for his own comfort and use. His next work was to build a fireplace of stones and to gather a store of wood. That done, he spilled the contents of his saddle-bags upon the grass and took stock. His outfit consisted of a small-handled axe, a hunting-knife, a large number of cartridges for rifle or revolver, a tin plate, a cup, and a fork and spoon, a quantity of dried beef and dried fruits, and small canvas bags containing tea, sugar, salt, and pepper. For him alone this supply would have been bountiful to begin a sojourn in the wilderness, but he was no longer alone. Starvation in the uplands was not an unheard-of thing; he did not, however, worry at all on that score, and feared only his possible inability to supply the needs of a woman in a weakened and extremely delicate condition.

If there was no game in the valley—a contingency he doubted—it would not be a great task for him to go by night to Oldring's herd and pack out a calf. The exigency of the moment was to ascertain if there were game in Surprise Valley. Whitie still guarded the dilapidated rabbit, and Ring slept near by under a spruce. Venters called Ring and went to the edge of the terrace, and there halted to survey the valley.

He was prepared to find it larger than his unstudied glances had made it appear; for more than a casual idea of dimensions and a hasty conception of oval shape and singular beauty he had not had time. Again the felicity of the name he had given the valley struck him forcibly. Around the red perpendicular walls, except under the great arc of stone, ran a terrace fringed at the cliff-base by silver spruces; below that first terrace sloped another wider one densely overgrown with aspens, and the center of the valley was a level circle of oaks and alders, with the glittering green line of willows and cottonwood dividing it in half. Venters saw a number and variety of birds flitting among the trees. To his left, facing the stone bridge, an enormous cavern opened in the wall; and low down, just above the tree-tops, he made out a long shelf of cliff-dwellings, with little black, staring windows or doors. Like eyes they were, and seemed to watch him. The few cliff-dwellings he had seen—all ruins—had left him with haunting memory of age and solitude and of something past. He had come, in a way, to be a cliff-dweller himself, and those silent eyes would look down upon him, as if in surprise that after thousands of years a man had invaded the valley. Venters felt sure that he was the only white man who had ever walked under the shadow of the wonderful stone bridge, down into that wonderful valley with its circle of caves and its terraced rings of silver spruce and aspens.

The dog growled below and rushed into the forest. Venters ran down the declivity to enter a zone of light shade streaked with sunshine. The oak-trees were slender, none more than half a foot thick, and they grew close together, intermingling their branches. Ring came running back with a rabbit in his mouth. Venters took the rabbit and, holding the dog near him, stole softly on. There were fluttering of wings among the branches and quick bird-notes, and rustling of dead leaves and rapid patterings. Venters crossed well-worn trails marked with fresh tracks; and when he had stolen on a little farther he saw many birds and running quail, and more rabbits than he could count. He had not penetrated the forest of oaks for a hundred yards, had not approached anywhere near the line of willows and cottonwoods which he knew grew along a stream. But he had seen enough to know that Surprise Valley was the home of many wild creatures.

Venters returned to camp. He skinned the rabbits, and gave the dogs the one they had quarreled over, and the skin of this he dressed and hung up to dry, feeling that he would like to keep it. It was a particularly rich, furry pelt with a beautiful white tail. Venters remembered that but for the bobbing of that white tail catching his eye he would not have espied the rabbit, and he would never have discovered Surprise Valley. Little incidents of chance like this had turned him here and there in Deception Pass; and now they had assumed to him the significance and direction of destiny.

His good fortune in the matter of game at hand brought to his mind the necessity of keeping it in the valley. Therefore he took the axe and cut bundles of aspens and willows, and packed them up under the bridge to the narrow outlet of the gorge. Here he began fashioning a fence, by driving aspens into the ground and lacing them fast with willows. Trip after trip he made down for more building material, and the afternoon had passed when he finished the work to his satisfaction. Wildcats might scale the fence, but no coyote could come in to search for prey, and no rabbits or other small game could escape from the valley.

Upon returning to camp he set about getting his supper at ease, around a fine fire, without hurry or fear of discovery. After hard work that had definite purpose, this freedom and comfort gave him peculiar satisfaction. He caught himself often, as he kept busy round the camp-fire, stopping to glance at the quiet form in the cave, and at the dogs stretched cozily near him, and then out across the beautiful valley. The present was not yet real to him.

While he ate, the sun set beyond a dip in the rim of the curved wall. As the morning sun burst wondrously through a grand arch into this valley, in a golden, slanting shaft, so the evening sun, at the moment of setting, shone through a gap of cliffs, sending down a broad red burst to brighten the oval with a blaze of fire. To Venters both sunrise and sunset were unreal.

A cool wind blew across the oval, waving the tips of oaks, and, while the light lasted, fluttering the aspen leaves into millions of facets of red, and sweeping the graceful spruces. Then with the wind soon came a shade and a darkening, and suddenly the valley was gray. Night came there quickly after the sinking of the sun. Venters went softly to look at the girl. She slept, and her breathing was quiet and slow. He lifted Ring into the cave, with stern whisper for him to stay there on guard. Then he drew the blanket carefully over her and returned to the camp-fire.

Though exceedingly tired, he was yet loath to yield to lassitude, but this night it was not from listening, watchful vigilance; it was from a desire to realize his position. The details of his wild environment seemed the only substance of a strange dream. He saw the darkening rims, the gray oval turning black, the undulating surface of forest, like a rippling lake, and the spear-pointed spruces. He heard the flutter of aspen leaves and the soft, continuous splash of falling water. The melancholy note of a cañon bird broke clear and lonely from the high cliffs. Venters had no name for this night singer, and he had never seen one; but the few notes, always pealing out just at darkness, were as familiar to him as the cañon silence. Then they ceased, and the rustle of leaves and the murmur of water hushed in a growing sound that Venters fancied was not of earth. Neither had he a name for this, only it was inexpressibly wild and sweet. The thought came that it might be a moan of the girl in her last outcry of life, and he felt a tremor shake him. But no! This sound was not human, though it was like despair. He began to doubt his sensitive perceptions, to believe that he half-dreamed what he thought he heard. Then the sound swelled with the strengthening of the breeze, and he realized it was the singing of the wind in the cliffs.

By and by a drowsiness overcame him, and Venters began to nod, half asleep, with his back against a spruce. Rousing himself and calling Whitie, he went to the cave. The girl lay barely visible in the dimness. Ring crouched beside her, and the patting of his tail on the stone assured Venters that the dog was awake and faithful to his duty. Venters sought his own bed of fragrant boughs; and as he lay back, somehow grateful for the comfort and safety, the night seemed to steal away from him and he sank softly into intangible space and rest and slumber.

Venters awakened to the sound of melody that he imagined was only the haunting echo of dream music. He opened his eyes to another surprise of this valley of beautiful surprises. Out of his cave he saw the exquisitely fine foliage of the silver spruces crossing a round space of blue morning sky; and in this lacy leafage fluttered a number of gray birds with black and white stripes and long tails. They were mocking-birds, and they were singing as if they wanted to burst their throats. Venters listened. One long, silver-tipped branch dropped almost to his cave, and upon it, within a few yards of him, sat one of the graceful birds. Venters saw the swelling and quivering of its throat in song. He arose, and when he slid down out of his cave the birds fluttered and flew farther away.

Venters stepped before the opening of the other cave and looked in. The girl was awake, with wide eyes and listening look, and she had a hand on Ring's neck.

"Mocking-birds!" she said.

"Yes," replied Venters, "and I believe they like our company."

"Where are we?"

"Never mind now. After a little I'll tell you."

"The birds woke me. When I heard them—and saw the shiny trees—and the blue sky—and then a blaze of gold dropping down—I wondered—"

She did not complete her fancy, but Venters imagined he understood her meaning. She appeared to be wandering in mind. Venters felt her face and hands and found them burning with fever. He went for water, and was glad to find it almost as cold as if flowing from ice. That water was the only medicine he had, and he put faith in it. She did not want to drink, but he made her swallow, and then he bathed her face and head and cooled her wrists.

The day began with the heightening of the fever. Venters spent the time reducing her temperature, cooling her hot cheeks and temples. He kept close watch over her, and at the least indication of restlessness, that he knew led to tossing and rolling of the body, he held her tightly, so no violent move could reopen her wounds. Hour after hour she babbled and laughed and cried and moaned in delirium; but whatever her secret was she did not reveal it. Attended by something somber for Venters, the day passed. At night in the cool winds the fever abated and she slept.

The second day was a repetition of the first. On the third he seemed to see her wither and waste away before his eyes. That day he scarcely went from her side for a moment, except to run for fresh, cool water; and he did not eat. The fever broke on the fourth day and left her spent and shrunken, a slip of a girl with life only in her eyes. They hung upon Venters with a mute observance, and he found hope in that.

To rekindle the spark that had nearly flickered out, to nourish the little life and vitality that remained in her, was Venters's problem. But he had little resource other than the meat of the rabbits and quail; and from these he made broths and soups as best he could, and fed her with a spoon. It came to him that the human body, like the human soul, was a strange thing and capable of recovering from terrible shocks. For almost immediately she showed faint signs of gathering strength. There was one more waiting day, in which he doubted, and spent long hours by her side as she slept, and watched the gentle swell of her breast rise and fall in breathing, and the wind stir the tangled chestnut curls. On the next day he knew that she would live.

Upon realizing it he abruptly left the cave and sought his accustomed seat against the trunk of a big spruce, where once more he let his glance stray along the sloping terraces. She would live, and the somber gloom lifted out of the valley, and he felt relief that was pain. Then he roused to the call of action, to the many things he needed to do in the way of making camp fixtures and utensils, to the necessity of hunting food, and the desire to explore the valley.

But he decided to wait a few more days before going far from camp, because he fancied that the girl rested easier when she could see him near at hand. And on the first day her languor appeared to leave her in a renewed grip of life. She awoke stronger from each short slumber; she ate greedily, and she moved about in her bed of boughs; and always, it seemed to Venters, her eyes followed him. He knew now that her recovery would be rapid. She talked about the dogs, about the caves, the valley, about how hungry she was, till Venters silenced her, asking her to put off further talk till another time. She obeyed, but she sat up in her bed, and her eyes roved to and fro, and always back to him.

Upon the second morning she sat up when he awakened her, and would not permit him to bathe her face and feed her, which actions she performed for herself. She spoke little, however, and Venters was quick to catch in her the first intimations of thoughtfulness and curiosity and appreciation of her situation. He left camp and took Whitie out to hunt for rabbits. Upon his return he was amazed and somewhat anxiously concerned to see his invalid sitting with her back to a corner of the cave and her bare feet swinging out. Hurriedly he approached, intending to advise her to lie down again, to tell her that perhaps she might overtax her strength. The sun shone upon her, glinting on the little head with its tangle of bright hair and the small, oval face with its pallor, and dark-blue eyes underlined by dark-blue circles. She looked at him and he looked at her. In that exchange of glances he imagined each saw the other in some different guise. It seemed impossible to Venters that this frail girl could be Oldring's Masked Rider. It flashed over him that he had made a mistake which presently she would explain.

"Help me down," she said.

"But—are you well enough?" he protested. "Wait—a little longer."

"I'm weak—dizzy. But I want to get down."

He lifted her—what a light burden now!—and stood her upright beside him, and supported her as she essayed to walk with halting steps. She was like a stripling of a boy; the bright, small head scarcely reached his shoulder. But now, as she clung to his arm, the rider's costume she wore did not contradict, as it had done at first, his feeling of her femininity. She might be the famous Masked Rider of the uplands, she might resemble a boy; but her outline, her little hands and feet, her hair, her big eyes and tremulous lips, and especially a something that Venters felt as a subtle essence rather than what he saw, proclaimed her sex.

She soon tired. He arranged a comfortable seat for her under the spruce that overspread the camp-fire.

"Now tell me—everything," she said.

He recounted all that had happened from the time of his discovery of the rustlers in the cañon up to the present moment.

"You shot me—and now you've saved my life?"

"Yes. After almost killing you I've pulled you through."

"Are you glad?"

"I should say so!"

Her eyes were unusually expressive, and they regarded him steadily; she was unconscious of that mirroring of her emotions, and they shone with gratefulness and interest and wonder and sadness.

"Tell me—about yourself?" she asked.

He made this a briefer story, telling of his coming to Utah, his various occupations till he became a rider, and then how the Mormons had practically driven him out of Cottonwoods, an outcast.

Then, no longer able to withstand his own burning curiosity, he questioned her in turn.

"Are you Oldring's Masked Rider?"

"Yes," she replied, and dropped her eyes.

"I knew it—I recognized your figure—and mask, for I saw you once. Yet I can't believe it! . . . But you never *were* really that rustler, as we riders knew him? A thief—a marauder—a kidnapper of women—a murderer of sleeping riders!"

"No! I never stole—or harmed any one—in all my life. I only rode and rode—"

"But why—why?" he burst out. "Why the name? I understand Oldring made you ride. But the black mask—the mystery—the things laid to your hands—the threats in your infamous name—the night-riding credited to you—the evil deeds deliberately blamed on you and acknowledged by rustlers—even Oldring himself! Why? Tell me why?"

"I never knew that," she answered low. Her drooping head straightened, and the large eyes, larger now and darker, met Venters's with a clear, steadfast gaze in which he read truth. It verified his own conviction.

"Never knew? That's strange! Are you a Mormon?"

"No."

"Is Oldring a Mormon?"

"No."

"Do you—care for him?"

"Yes. I hate his men—his life—sometimes I almost hate him!"

Venters paused in his rapid-fire questioning, as if to brace himself to ask for a truth that would be abhorrent for him to confirm, but which he seemed driven to hear.

"What are—what _were_ you to Oldring?"

Like some delicate thing suddenly exposed to blasting heat, the girl wilted; her head dropped, and into her white, wasted cheeks crept the red of shame.

Venters would have given anything to recall that question. It seemed so different—his thought when spoken. Yet her shame established in his mind something akin to the respect he had strangely been hungering to feel for her.

"D—n that question!—forget it!" he cried, in a passion of pain for her and anger at himself. "But once and for all—tell me—I know it, yet I want to hear you say so—you couldn't help yourself?"

"Oh no."

"Well, that makes it all right with me," he went on, honestly. "I—I want you to feel that . . . you see—we've been thrown together—and—and I want to help you—not hurt you. I thought life had been cruel to me, but when I think of yours I feel mean and little for my complaining. Anyway, I was a lonely outcast. And now! . . . I don't see very clearly what it all means. Only we are here—together. We've got to stay here, for long, surely till you are well. But you'll never go back to Oldring. And I'm sure helping you will help me, for I was sick in mind. There's something now for me to do. And if I can win back your strength—then get you away, out of this wild country—help you somehow to a happier life—just think how good that'll be for me!"

CHAPTER TEN

Love

DURING all these waiting days Venters, with the exception of the afternoon when he had built the gate in the gorge, had scarcely gone out of sight of camp and never out of hearing. His desire to explore Surprise Valley was keen, and on the morning after his long talk with the girl he took his rifle and, calling Ring, made a move to start. The girl lay back in a rude chair of boughs he had put together for her. She had been watching him, and when he picked up the gun and called the dog Venters thought she gave a nervous start.

"I'm only going to look over the valley," he said.

"Will you be gone long?"

"No," he replied, and started off. The incident set him thinking of his former impression that, after her recovery from fever, she did not seem at ease unless he was close at hand. It was fear of being alone, due, he concluded, most likely to her weakened condition. He must not leave her much alone.

As he strode down the sloping terrace, rabbits scampered before him, and the beautiful valley quail, as purple in color as the sage on the uplands, ran fleetly along the ground into the forest. It was pleasant under the trees, in the gold-flecked shade, with the whistle of quail and twittering of birds everywhere. Soon he had passed the limit of his former excursions and entered new territory. Here the woods began to show open glades and brooks running down from the slope, and presently he emerged from shade into the sunshine of a meadow. The shaking of the high grass told him of the running of animals, what species he could not tell, but from Ring's manifest desire to have a chase they were evidently some kind wilder than rabbits. Venters approached the willow and cottonwood belt that he had observed from the height of slope. He penetrated it to find a considerable stream of water and great half-submerged mounds of brush and sticks, and all about him were old and new gnawed circles at the base of the cottonwoods.

"Beaver!" he exclaimed. "By all that's lucky! The meadow's full of beaver! How did they ever get here?"

Beaver had not found a way into the valley by the trail of the cliff-dwellers, of that he was certain; and he began to have more than curiosity as to the outlet or inlet of the stream. When he passed some dead water, which he noted was held by a beaver-dam, there was a current in the stream, and it flowed west. Following its course, he soon entered the oak forest again, and passed through to find himself before massed and jumbled ruins of cliff-wall. There were tangled thickets of wild plum-trees and other thorny growths that made passage extremely laborsome. He found innumerable tracks of wildcats and foxes. Rustlings in the thick undergrowth told him of stealthy movements of these animals. At length his further advance appeared futile, for the reason that the stream disappeared in a split at the base of immense rocks over which he could not climb. To his relief he concluded that though beaver might work their way up the narrow chasm where the water rushed, it would be impossible for men to enter the valley there.

This western curve was the only part of the valley where the walls had been split asunder, and it was a wildly rough and in-accessible corner. Going back a little way, he leaped the stream and headed toward the southern wall. Once out of the oaks he found again the low terrace of aspens, and above that the wide, open terrace fringed by silver spruces. This side of the valley contained the wind or water worn caves. As he pressed on, keeping to the upper terrace, cave after cave opened out of the cliff; now a large one, now a small one. Then yawned, quite suddenly and wonderfully above him, the great cavern of the cliff-dwellers.

It was still a goodly distance, and he tried to imagine, if it appeared so huge from where he stood, what it would be when he got there. He climbed the terrace and then faced a long, gradual ascent of weathered rock and dust, which made climbing too difficult for attention to anything else. At length he entered a zone of shade, and looked up. He stood just within the hollow of a cavern so immense that he had no conception of its real dimensions. The curved roof, stained by ages of leakage, with buff and black and rust-colored streaks, swept up and loomed higher and seemed to soar to the rim of the cliff. Here again was a magnificent arch, such as formed the grand gateway to the valley, only in this instance it formed the dome of a cave instead of the span of a bridge.

Venters passed onward and upward. The stones he dislodged rolled down with strange, hollow crack and roar. He had climbed a hundred rods inward, and yet he had not reached the base of the shelf where the cliff-dwellings rested, a long half-circle of connected stone house, with little dark holes that he had fancied were eyes. At length he gained the base of the shelf, and here found steps cut in the rock. These facilitated climbing, and as he went up he thought how easily this vanished race of men might once have held that stronghold against an army. There was only one possible place to ascend, and this was narrow and steep.

Venters had visited cliff-dwellings before, and they had been in ruins, and of no great character or size but this place was of proportions that stunned him, and it had not been desecrated by the hand of man, nor had it been crumbled by the hand of time. It was a stupendous tomb. It had been a city. It was just as it had been left by its builders. The little houses were there, the smoke-blackened stains of fires, the pieces of pottery scattered about cold hearths, the stone hatchets; and stone pestles and mealing-stones lay beside round holes polished by years of grinding maize—lay there as if they had been carelessly dropped yesterday. But the cliff-dwellers were gone!

Dust! They were dust on the floor or at the foot of the shelf, and their habitations and utensils endured. Venters felt the sublimity of that marvelous vaulted arch, and it seemed to gleam with a glory of something that was gone. How many years had passed since the cliff-dwellers gazed out across the beautiful valley as he was gazing now? How long had it been since women ground grain in those polished holes? What time had rolled by since men of an unknown race lived, loved, fought, and died there? Had an enemy destroyed them? Had disease destroyed them, or only that greatest destroyer—time? Venters saw a long line of blood-red hands painted low down upon the yellow roof of stone. Here was strange portent, if not an answer to his queries. The place oppressed him. It was light, but full of a transparent gloom. It smelled of dust and musty stone, of age and disuse. It was sad. It was solemn. It had the look of a place where silence had become master and was now irrevocable and terrible and could not be broken. Yet, at the moment, from high up in the carved crevices of the arch, floated down the low, strange wail of wind—a knell indeed for all that had gone.

Venters, sighing, gathered up an armful of pottery, such pieces as he thought strong enough and suitable for his own use, and bent his steps toward camp. He mounted the terrace at an opposite point to which he had left. He saw the girl looking in the direction he had gone. His footsteps made no sound in the deep grass, and he approached close without her being aware of his presence. Whitie lay on the ground near where she sat, and he manifested the usual actions of welcome, but the girl did not notice them. She seemed to be oblivious to everything near at hand. She made a pathetic figure drooping there, with her sunny hair contrasting so markedly with her white, wasted cheeks and her hands listlessly clasped and her little bare feet propped in the framework of the rude seat.

Venters could have sworn and laughed in one breath at the idea of the connection between this girl and Oldring's Masked Rider. She was the victim of more than accident of fate—a victim to some deep plot the mystery of which burned him. As he stepped forward with a half-formed thought that she was absorbed in watching for his return, she turned her head and saw him. A swift start, a change rather than rush of blood under her white cheeks, a flashing of big eyes that fixed their glance upon him, transformed her face in that single instant of turning; and he knew she had been watching for him, that his return was the one thing in her mind. She did not smile; she did not flush; she did not look glad. All these would have meant little compared to her indefinite expression. Venters grasped the peculiar, vivid, vital something that leaped from her face. It was as if she had been in a dead, hopeless clamp of inaction and feeling, and had been suddenly shot through and through with quivering animation. Almost it was as if she had returned to life.

And Venters thought with lightning swiftness, "I've saved her—I've unlinked her from that old life—she was watching as if I were all she had left on earth—she belongs to me!" The thought was startlingly new. Like a blow it was in an unprepared moment. The cheery salutation he had ready for her died unborn, and he tumbled the pieces of pottery awkwardly on the grass, while some unfamiliar, deep-seated emotion, mixed with pity and glad assurance of his power to succor her, held him dumb.

"What a load you had!" she said. "Why, they're pots and crocks! Where did you get them?"

Venters laid down his rifle, and, filling one of the pots from his canteen, he placed it on the smoldering campfire.

"Hope it'll hold water," he said, presently. "Why, there's an enormous cliff-dwelling just across here. I got the pottery there. Don't you think we needed something? That tin cup of mine has served to make tea, broth, soup—everything."

"I noticed we hadn't a great deal to cook in."

She laughed. It was the first time. He liked that laugh, and though he was tempted to look at her, he did not want to show his surprise or his pleasure.

"Will you take me over there, and all around in the valley—pretty soon when I'm well?" she added.

"Indeed I shall. It's a wonderful place. Rabbits so thick you can't step without kicking one out. And quail, beaver, foxes, wild-cats. We're in a regular den. But—haven't you ever seen a cliff-dwelling?"

"No. I've heard about them, though. The—the men say the Pass is full of old houses and ruins."

"Why, I should think you'd have run across one in all your riding around," said Venters. He spoke slowly, choosing his words carefully, and he essayed a perfectly casual manner, and pretended to be busy assorting pieces of pottery. She must have no cause again to suffer shame for curiosity of his. Yet never in all his days had he been so eager to hear the details of anyone's life.

"When I rode—I rode like the wind," she replied, "and never had time to stop for anything."

"I remember that day I—I met you in the Pass—how dusty you were, how tired your horse looked. Were you always riding?"

"Oh, no. Sometimes not for months, when I was shut up in the cabin."

Venters tried to subdue a hot tingling.

"You were shut up, then?" he asked, carelessly.

"When Oldring went away on his long trips—he was gone for months sometimes—he shut me up in the cabin."

"What for?"

"Perhaps to keep me from running away. I always threatened that. Mostly, though, because the men got drunk at the villages. But they were always good to me. I wasn't afraid."

"A prisoner! That must have been hard on you?"

"I liked that. As long as I can remember I've been locked up there at times, and those times were the only happy ones I ever had. It's a big cabin, high up on a cliff, and I could look out. Then I had dogs and pets I had tamed, and books. There was a spring inside, and food stored, and the men brought me fresh meat. Once I was there one whole winter."

It now required deliberation on Venters's part to persist in his unconcern and to keep at work. He wanted to look at her, to volley questions at her.

"As long as you can remember—you've lived in Deception Pass?" he went on.

"I've a dim memory of some other place, and women and children; but I can't make anything of it. Sometimes I think till I'm weary."

"Then you can read—you have books?"

"Oh yes, I can read, and write, too, pretty well. Oldring is educated. He taught me, and years ago an old rustler lived with us, and he had been something different once. He was always teaching me."

"So Oldring takes long trips," mused Venters. "Do you know where he goes?"

"No. Every year he drives cattle north of Sterling—then does not return for months. I heard him accused once of living two lives—and he killed the man. That was at Stone Bridge."

Venters dropped his apparent task and looked up with an eagerness he no longer strove to hide.

"Bess," he said, using her name for the first time, "I suspected Oldring was something besides a rustler. Tell me, what's his purpose here in the Pass? I believe much that he has done was to hide his real work here."

"You're right. He's more than a rustler. In fact, as the men say, his rustling cattle is now only a bluff. There's gold in the cañons!"

"Ah!"

"Yes, there's gold, not in great quantities, but gold enough for him and his men. They wash for gold week in and week out. Then they drive a few cattle and go into the villages to drink and shoot and kill—to bluff the riders."

"Drive a few cattle! But, Bess, the Withersteen herd, the red herd—twenty-five hundred head! That's not a few. And I tracked them into a valley near here."

"Oldring never stole the red herd. He made a deal with Mormons. The riders were to be called in, and Oldring was to drive the herd and keep it till a certain time—I won't know when—then drive it back to the range. What his share was I didn't hear."

"Did you hear *why* that deal was made?" queried Venters.

"No. But it was a trick of Mormons. They're full of tricks. I've heard Oldring's men tell about Mormons. Maybe the Withersteen woman wasn't minding her halter! I saw the man who made the deal. He was a little, queer-shaped man, all humped up. He sat his horse well. I heard one of our men say afterward there was no better rider on the sage than this fellow. What was the name? I forget."

"Jerry Card?" suggested Venters.

"That's it. I remember—it's a name easy to remember—and Jerry Card appeared to be on fair terms with Oldring's men."

"I shouldn't wonder," replied Venters, thoughtfully. Verification of his suspicions in regard to Tull's underhand work—for the deal with Oldring made by Jerry Card assuredly had its inception in the Mormon Elder's brain, and had been accomplished through his orders—revived in Venters a memory of hatred that had been smothered by press of other emotions. Only a few days had elapsed since the hour of his encounter with Tull, yet they had been forgotten and now seemed far off, and the interval one that now appeared large and profound with incalculable change in his feelings. Hatred of Tull still existed in his heart; but it had lost its white heat. His affection for Jane Withersteen had not changed in the least; nevertheless, he seemed to view it from another angle and see it as another thing—what, he could not exactly define. The recalling of these two feelings was to Venters like getting glimpses into a self that was gone; and the wonder of them—perhaps the change which was too illusive for him—was the fact that a strange irritation accompanied the memory and a desire to dismiss it from mind. And straightway he did dismiss it, to return to thoughts of his significant present.

"Bess, tell me one more thing," he said. "Haven't you known any women—any young people?"

"Sometimes there were women with the men; but Oldring never let me know them. And all the young people I ever saw in my life was when I rode fast through the villages."

Perhaps that was the most puzzling and thought-provoking thing she had yet said to Venters. He pondered, more curious the more he learned, but he curbed his inquisitive desires, for he saw her shrinking on the verge of that shame, the causing of which had occasioned him such self-reproach. He would ask no more. Still he had to think, and he found it difficult to think clearly. This sad-eyed girl was so utterly different from what it would have been reason to believe such a remarkable life would have made her. On this day he had found her simple and frank, as natural as any girl he had ever known. About her there was something sweet. Her voice was low and well modulated. He could not look into her face, meet her steady, unabashed, yet wistful eyes, and think of her as the woman she had confessed herself. Oldring's Masked Rider sat before him, a girl dressed as a man. She had been made to ride at the head of infamous forays and drives. She had been imprisoned for many months of her life in an obscure cabin. At times the most vicious of men had been her companions; and the vilest of women, if they had not been permitted to approach her, had, at least, cast their shadows over her. But—but in spite of all this—there thundered at Venters some truth that lifted its voice higher than the clamoring facts of dishonor, some truth that was the very life of her beautiful eyes; and it was innocence.

In the days that followed, Venters balanced perpetually in mind this haunting conception of innocence over against the cold and sickening fact of an unintentional yet actual gift. How could it be possible for the two things to be true? He believed the latter to be true, and he would not relinquish his conviction of the former; and these conflicting thoughts augmented the mystery that appeared to be a part of Bess. In those ensuing days, however, it became clear as clearest light

that Bess was rapidly regaining strength; that, unless reminded of her long association with Oldring, she seemed to have forgotten it; that, like an Indian who
lives solely from moment to moment, she was utterly absorbed in the present.

Day by day Venters watched the white of her face slowly change to brown,
and the wasted cheeks fill out by imperceptible degrees. There came a time when
he could just trace the line of demarcation between the part of her face once
hidden by a mask and that left exposed to wind and sun. When that line disappeared in clear bronze tan it was as if she had been washed clean of the stigma
of Oldring's Masked Rider. The suggestion of the mask always made Venters
remember; now that it was gone he seldom thought of her past. Occasionally he
tried to piece together the several stages of strange experience and to make a
whole. He had shot a masked outlaw the very sight of whom had been ill omen
to riders; he had carried off a wounded woman whose bloody lips quivered in
prayer; he had nursed what seemed a frail, shrunken boy; and now he watched
a girl whose face had become strangely sweet, whose dark-blue eyes were ever
upon him without boldness, without shyness, but with a steady, grave, and growing
light. Many times Venters found the clear gaze embarrassing to him, yet, like
wine, it had an exhilarating effect. What did she think when she looked at him
so? Almost he believed she had no thought at all. All about her and the present
there in Surprise Valley, and the dim yet subtly impending future, fascinated
Venters and made him thoughtful as all his lonely vigils in the sage had not.

Chiefly it was the present that he wished to dwell upon; but it was the call
of the future which stirred him to action. No idea had he of what that future
had in store for Bess and him. He began to think of improving Surprise Valley
as a place to live in, for there was no telling how long they would be compelled
to stay there. Venters stubbornly resisted the entering into his mind of an insistent
thought that, clearly realized, might have made it plain to him that he did not
want to leave Surprise Valley at all. But it was imperative that he consider practical matters; and whether or not he was destined to stay long there, he felt the
immediate need of a change of diet. It would be necessary for him to go farther
afield for a variety of meat, and also that he soon visit Cottonwoods for a supply
of food.

It occurred again to Venters that he could go to the cañon where Oldring kept
his cattle, and at little risk he could pack out some beef. He wished to do this,
however, without letting Bess know of it till after he had made the trip. Presently
he hit upon the plan of going while she was asleep.

That very night he stole out of camp, climbed up under the stone bridge, and entered the outlet to the Pass. The gorge was full of luminous gloom. Balancing Rock loomed dark and leaned over the pale descent. Transformed in the shadowy light, it took shape and dimensions of a spectral god waiting—waiting for the moment to hurl himself down upon the tottering walls and close forever the outlet to Deception Pass. At night more than by day Venters felt something fearful and fateful in that rock, and that it had leaned and waited through a thousand years to have somehow to deal with his destiny.

"Old man, if you must roll, wait till I get back to the girl, and then roll!" he said, aloud, as if the stones were indeed a god.

And those spoken words, in their grim note to his ear, as well as contents to his mind, told Venters that he was all but drifting on a current which he had not power nor wish to stem.

Venters exercised his usual care in the matter of hiding tracks from the outlet, yet it took him scarcely an hour to reach Oldring's cattle. Here sight of many calves changed his original intention, and instead of packing out meat he decided to take a calf out alive. He roped one, securely tied its feet, and swung it over his shoulder. Here was an exceedingly heavy burden, but Venters was powerful— he could take up a sack of grain and with ease pitch it over a pack-saddle—and he made long distance without resting. The hardest work came in the climb up to the outlet and on through to the valley. When he had accomplished it, he became fired with another idea that again changed his intention. He would not kill the calf, but keep it alive. He would go back to Oldring's herd and pack out more calves. Thereupon he secured the calf in the best available spot for the moment and turned to make a second trip.

When Venters got back to the valley with another calf, it was close upon daybreak. He crawled into his cave and slept late. Bess had no inkling that he had been absent from camp nearly all night, and only remarked solicitously that he appeared to be more tired than usual, and more in the need of sleep. In the afternoon Venters built a gate across a small ravine near camp, and here corralled the calves; and he succeeded in completing his task without Bess being any the wiser.

That night he made two more trips to Oldring's range, and again on the following night, and yet another on the next. With eight calves in his corral, he concluded that he had enough; but it dawned upon him then that he did not want to kill one. "I've rustled Oldring's cattle," he said, and laughed. He noted then that all the calves were red. "Red!" he exclaimed. "From the red herd. I've stolen Jane Withersteen's cattle! . . . That's about the strangest thing yet."

One more trip he undertook to Oldring's valley, and this time he roped a yearling steer and killed it and cut out a small quarter of beef. The howling of coyotes told him he need have no apprehension that the work of his knife would be discovered. He packed the beef back to camp and hung it upon a spruce-tree. Then he sought his bed.

On the morrow he was up bright and early, glad that he had a surprise for Bess. He could hardly wait for her to come out. Presently she appeared and walked under the spruce. Then she approached the camp-fire. There was a tinge of healthy red in the bronze of her cheeks, and her slender form had begun to round out in graceful lines.

"Bess, didn't you say you were tired of rabbit?" inquired Venters. "And quail and beaver?"

"Indeed I did."

"What would you like?"

"I'm tired of meat, but if we have to live on it I'd like some beef."

"Well, how does that strike you?" Venters pointed to the quarter hanging from the spruce-tree. "We'll have fresh beef for a few days, then we'll cut the rest into strips and dry it."

"Where did you get that?" asked Bess, slowly.

"I stole that from Oldring."

"You went back to the cañon—you risked—" While she hesitated the tinge of bloom faded out of her cheeks.

"It wasn't any risk, but it was hard work."

"I'm sorry I said I was tired of rabbit. Why! How—When did you get that beef?"

"Last night."

"While I was asleep?"

"Yes."

"I woke last night sometime—but I didn't know."

Her eyes were widening, darkening with thought, and whenever they did so the steady, watchful, seeing gaze gave place to the wistful light. In the former she saw as the primitive woman without thought; in the latter she looked inward, and her gaze was the reflection of a troubled mind. For long Venters had not seen that dark change, that deepening of blue, which he thought was beautiful and sad. But now he wanted to make her think.

"I've done more than pack in that beef," he said. "For five nights I've been working while you slept. I've got eight calves corralled near a ravine. Eight calves, all alive and doing fine!"

"You went five nights!"

All that Venters could make of the dilation of her eyes, her slow pallor, and her exclamation, was fear—fear for herself or for him.

"Yes. I didn't tell you, because I knew you were afraid to be left alone."

"Alone?" She echoed his word, but the meaning of it was nothing to her. She had not even thought of being left alone. It was not, then, fear for herself, but for him. This girl, always slow of speech and action, now seemed almost stupid. She put forth a hand that might have indicated the groping of her mind. Suddenly she stepped swiftly to him, with a look and touch that drove from him any doubt of her quick intelligence or feeling.

"Oldring has men watch the herds—they would kill you. You must never go again!"

When she had spoken, the strength and the blaze of her died, and she swayed toward Venters.

"Bess, I'll not go again," he said, catching her.

She leaned against him, and her body was limp and vibrated to a long, wavering tremble. Her face was upturned to his. Woman's face, woman's eyes, woman's lips—all acutely and blindly and sweetly and terribly truthful in their betrayal! But as her fear was instinctive, so was her clinging to this one and only friend.

Venters gently put her from him and steadied her upon her feet; and all the while his blood raced wild, and a thrilling tingle unsteadied his nerve, and something—that he had seen and felt in her—that he could not understand—seemed very close to him, warm and rich as a fragrant breath, sweet as nothing had ever before been sweet to him.

With all his will Venters strove for calmness and thought and judgment unbiased by pity, and reality unswayed by sentiment. Bess's eyes were still fixed upon him with all her soul bright in that wistful light. Swiftly, resolutely he put out of mind all of her life except what had been spent with him. He scorned himself for the intelligence that made him still doubt. He meant to judge her as she had judged him. He was face to face with the inevitableness of life itself. He saw destiny in the dark, straight path of her wonderful eyes. Here was the simplicity, the sweetness of a girl contending with new and strange and enthralling emotions; here the living truth of innocence; here the blind terror of a woman confronted with the thought of death to her savior and protector. All this Venters saw, but, besides, there was in Bess's eyes a slow-dawning consciousness that seemed about to break out in glorious radiance.

"Bess, are you thinking?" he asked.

"Yes—oh yes!"

"Do you realize we are here alone—man and woman?"

"Yes."

"Have you thought that we may make our way out to civilization, or we may have to stay here—alone—hidden from the world all our lives?"

"I never thought—till now."

"Well, what's your choice—to go—or to stay here—alone with me?"

"Stay!" New-born thought of self, ringing vibrantly in her voice, gave her answer singular power.

Venters trembled, and then swiftly turned his gaze from her face—from her eyes. He knew what she had only half divined—that she loved him.

CHAPTER ELEVEN

Faith and Unfaith

A T Jane Withersteen's home the promise made to Mrs. Larkin to care for little
Fay had begun to be fulfilled. Like a gleam of sunlight through the cottonwoods was the coming of the child to the gloomy house of Withersteen. The big,
silent halls echoed with childish laughter. In the shady court, where Jane spent
many of the hot July days, Fay's tiny feet pattered over the stone flags and splashed
in the amber stream. She prattled incessantly. What difference, Jane thought, a
child made in her home! It had never been a real home, she discovered. Even the
tidiness and neatness she had so observed, and upon which she had insisted to
her women, became, in the light of Fay's smile, habits that now lost their importance. Fay littered the court with Jane's books and papers, and other toys her
fancy improvised, and many a strange craft went floating down the little brook.

And it was owing to Fay's presence that Jane Withersteen came to see more
of Lassiter. The rider had for the most part kept to the sage. He rode for her, but
he did not seek her except on business; and Jane had to acknowledge in pique
that her overtures had been made in vain. Fay, however, captured Lassiter the
moment he first laid eyes on her.

Jane was present at the meeting, and there was something about it which
dimmed her sight and softened her toward this foe of her people. The rider had
clanked into the court, a tired yet wary man, always looking for the attack upon
him that was inevitable and might come from any quarter; and he had walked
right upon little Fay. The child had been beautiful even in her rags and amid the
surroundings of the hovel in the sage, but now, in a pretty white dress, with her
shining curls brushed and her face clean and rosy, she was lovely. She left her
play and looked up at Lassiter.

If there was not an instinct for all three of them in that meeting, an unrea-
soning tendency toward a closer intimacy, then Jane Withersteen believed she had
been subject to a queer fancy. She imagined any child would have feared Lassiter.
And Fay Larkin had been a lonely, a solitary elf of the sage, not at all an ordinary
child, and exquisitely shy with strangers. She watched Lassiter with great, round,

grave eyes, but showed no fear. The rider gave Jane a favorable report of cattle and horses; and as he took the seat to which she invited him, little Fay edged as much as half an inch nearer. Jane replied to his look of inquiry and told Fay's story. The rider's gray, earnest gaze troubled her. Then he turned to Fay and smiled in a way that made Jane doubt her sense of the true relation of things. How could Lassiter smile so at a child when he had made so many children fatherless? But he did smile, and to the gentleness she had seen a few times he added something that was infinitely sad and sweet. Jane's intuition told her that Lassiter had never been a father; but if life ever so blessed him he would be a good one. Fay, also, must have found that smile singularly winning. For she edged closer and closer, and then, by way of feminine capitulation, went to Jane, from whose side she bent a beautiful glance upon the rider.

Lassiter only smiled at her.

Jane watched them, and realized that now was the moment she should seize, if she was ever to win this man from his hatred. But the step was not easy to take. The more she saw of Lassiter the more she respected him, and the greater her respect the harder it became to lend herself to mere coquetry. Yet as she thought of her great motive, of Tull, and of that other whose name she had schooled herself never to think of in connection with Milly Erne's avenger, she suddenly found she had no choice. And her creed gave her boldness far beyond the limit to which vanity would have led her.

"Lassiter, I see so little of you now," she said, and was conscious of heat in her cheeks.

"I've been ridin' hard," he replied.

"But you can't live in the saddle. You come in sometimes. Won't you come here to see me—oftener?"

"Is that an order?"

"Nonsense! I simply ask you to come to see me when you find time."

"Why?"

The query once heard was not so embarrassing to Jane as she might have imagined. Moreover, it established in her mind a fact that there existed actually other than selfish reasons for her wanting to see him. And as she had been bold, so she determined to be both honest and brave.

"I've reasons—only one of which I need mention," she answered. "If it's possible I want to change you toward my people. And on the moment I can conceive of little I wouldn't do to gain that end."

How much better and freer Jane felt after that confession! She meant to show him that there was one Mormon who could play a game or wage a fight in the open.

"I reckon," said Lassiter, and he laughed.

It was the best in her, if the most irritating, that Lassiter always aroused.

"Will you come?" She looked into his eyes, and for the life of her could not quite subdue an imperiousness that rose with her spirit. "I never asked so much of any man—except Bern Venters."

"'Pears to me that you'd run no risk, or Venters, either. But mebbe that doesn't hold good for me."

"You mean it wouldn't be safe for you to be often here? You look for ambush in the cottonwoods?"

"Not that so much."

At this juncture little Fay sidled over to Lassiter.

"Has oo a little dirl?" she inquired.

"No, lassie," replied the rider.

Whatever Fay seemed to be searching for in Lassiter's sun-reddened face and quiet eyes she evidently found. "Oo tan turn to see me," she added, and with that, shyness gave place to friendly curiosity. First his sombrero with its leather band and silver ornaments commanded her attention; next his quirt, and then the clinking, silver spurs. These held her for some time, but presently, true to childish fickleness, she left off playing with them to look for something else. She laughed in glee as she ran her little hands down the slippery, shiny surface of Lassiter's leather chaps. Soon she discovered one of the hanging gun-sheaths, and she dragged it up and began tugging at the huge black handle of the gun. Jane Withersteen repressed an exclamation. What significance there was to her in the little girl's efforts to dislodge that heavy weapon! Jane Withersteen saw Fay's play and her beauty and her love as most powerful allies to her own woman's part in a game that suddenly had acquired a strange zest and a hint of danger. And as for the rider, he appeared to have forgotten Jane in the wonder of this lovely child playing about him. At first he was much the shyer of the two. Gradually her confidence overcame his backwardness, and he had the temerity to stroke her golden curls with a great hand. Fay rewarded his boldness with a smile, and when he had gone to the extreme of closing that great hand over her little brown one, she said, simply, "I like oo!"

Sight of his face then made Jane oblivious for the time to his character as a hater of Mormons. Out of the mother longing that swelled her breast she divined the child hunger in Lassiter.

He returned the next day, and the next; and upon the following he came both at morning and at night. Upon the evening of this fourth day Jane seemed to feel the breaking of a brooding struggle in Lassiter. During all these visits he had scarcely a word to say, though he watched her and played absent-mindedly with Fay. Jane had contented herself with silence. Soon little Fay substituted for the expression of regard, "I like oo," a warmer and more generous one, "I love oo."

Thereafter Lassiter came oftener to see Jane and her little protégée. Daily he grew more gentle and kind, and gradually developed a quaintly merry mood. In the morning he lifted Fay upon his horse and let her ride as he walked beside her to the edge of the sage. In the evening he played with the child at an infinite variety of games she invented, and then, oftener than not, he accepted Jane's invitation to supper. No other visitor came to Withersteen House during those days. So that in spite of watchfulness he never forgot, Lassiter began to show he felt at home there. After the meal they walked into the grove of cottonwoods or up by the lakes, and little Fay held Lassiter's hand as much as she held Jane's. Thus a strange relationship was established, and Jane liked it. At twilight they always returned to the house, where Fay kissed them and went in to her mother. Lassiter and Jane were left alone.

Then, if there were anything that a good woman could do to win a man and still preserve her self-respect, it was something which escaped the natural subtlety of a woman determined to allure. Jane's vanity, that after all was not great, was soon satisfied with Lassiter's silent admiration. And her honest desire to lead him from his dark, blood-stained path would never have blinded her to what she owed herself. But the driving passion of her religion, and its call to save Mormons' lives, one life in particular, bore Jane Withersteen close to an infringement of her womanhood. In the beginning she had reasoned that her appeal to Lassiter must be through the senses. With whatever means she possessed in the way of adornment she enhanced her beauty. And she stooped to artifices that she knew were unworthy of her, but which she deliberately chose to employ. She made of herself a girl in every variable mood wherein a girl might be desirable. In those moods she was not above the methods of an inexperienced though natural flirt. She kept close to him whenever opportunity afforded; and she was forever playfully, yet passionately underneath the surface, fighting him for possession of the great black guns. These he would never yield to her. And so in that manner their hands were often and long in contact. The more of simplicity that she sensed in him the greater the advantage she took.

She had a trick of changing—and it was not altogether voluntary—from this gay, thoughtless, girlish coquettishness to the silence and the brooding, burning mystery of a woman's mood. The strength and passion and fire of her were in her eyes, and she so used them that Lassiter had to see this depth in her, this haunting promise more fitted to her years than to the flaunting guise of a wilful girl.

The July days flew by. Jane reasoned that if it were possible for her to be happy during such a time, then she was happy. Little Fay completely filled a long aching void in her heart. In fettering the hands of this Lassiter she was accomplishing the greatest good of her life, and to do good even in a small way rendered happiness to Jane Withersteen. She had attended the regular Sunday services of her church; otherwise she had not gone to the village for weeks. It was unusual that none of her churchmen or friends had called upon her of late; but it was neglect for which she was glad. Judkins and his boy riders had experienced no difficulty in driving the white herd. So these warm July days were free of worry, and soon Jane hoped she had passed the crisis; and for her to hope was presently to trust, and then to believe. She thought often of Venters, but in a dreamy, abstract way. She spent hours teaching and playing with little Fay. And the activity of her mind centered around Lassiter. The direction she had given her will seemed to blunt any branching off of thought from that straight line. The mood came to obsess her.

In the end, when her awakening came, she learned that she had builded better than she knew. Lassiter, though kinder and gentler than ever, had parted with his quaint humor and his coldness and his tranquillity to become a restless and unhappy man. Whatever the power of his deadly intent toward Mormons, that passion now had a rival, the one equally burning and consuming. Jane Withersteen had one moment of exultation before the dawn of a strange uneasiness. What if she had made of herself a lure, at tremendous cost to him and to her, and all in vain!

That night in the moonlit grove she summoned all her courage and, turning suddenly in the path, she faced Lassiter and leaned close to him, so that she touched him and her eyes looked up to his.

"Lassiter! . . . Will you do anything for me?"

In the moonlight she saw his dark, worn face change, and by that change she seemed to feel him immovable as a wall of stone.

Jane slipped her hands down to the swinging gunsheaths, and when she had locked her fingers around the huge, cold handles of the guns, she trembled as with a chilling ripple over all her body.

"May I take your guns?"

"Why?" he asked, and for the first time to her his voice carried a harsh note. Jane felt his hard, strong hands close round her wrists. It was not wholly with intent that she leaned toward him, for the look of his eyes and the feel of his hands made her weak.

"It's no trifle—no woman's whim—it's deep—as my heart. Let me take them?"

"Why?"

"I want to keep you from killing more men—Mormons. You must let me save you from more wickedness—more wanton bloodshed—" Then the truth forced itself falteringly from her lips. "You must—let—me—help me to keep my vow to Milly Erne. I swore to her—as she lay dying—that if ever any one came here to avenge her—I swore I would stay his hand. Perhaps I—I alone can save the—the man who—who—Oh, Lassiter! . . . I feel that I can't change you—then soon you'll be out to kill—and you'll kill by instinct—and among the Mormons you kill will be the one—who . . . Lassiter, if you care a little for me—let me—for my sake—let me take your guns!"

As if her hands had been those of a child, he unclasped their clinging grip from the handles of his guns, and, pushing her away, he turned his gray face to her in one look of terrible realization and then strode off into the shadows of the cottonwoods.

When the first shock of her futile appeal to Lassiter had passed, Jane took his cold, silent condemnation and abrupt departure not so much as a refusal to her entreaty as a hurt and stunned bitterness for her attempt at his betrayal. Upon further thought and slow consideration of Lassiter's past actions, she believed he would return and forgive her. The man could not be hard to a woman, and she doubted that he could stay away from her. But at the point where she had hoped to find him vulnerable she now began to fear he was proof against all persuasion. The iron and stone quality that she had early suspected in him had actually cropped out as an impregnable barrier. Nevertheless, if Lassiter remained in Cottonwoods she would never give up her hope and desire to change him. She would change him if she had to sacrifice everything dear to her except hope of heaven. Passionately devoted as she was to her religion, she had yet refused to marry a Mormon. But a situation had developed wherein self paled in the great white light of religious duty of the highest order. That was the leading motive, the divinely spiritual one; but there were other motives, which, like tentacles, aided in drawing her will to the acceptance of a possible abnegation. And through the watches of that sleepless night Jane Withersteen, in fear and sorrow and doubt, came finally to believe that if she must throw herself into Lassiter's arms to make him abide by "Thou shalt not kill!" she would yet do well.

In the morning she expected Lassiter at the usual hour, but she was not able to go at once to the court, so she sent little Fay. Mrs. Larkin was ill and required attention. It appeared that the mother, from the time of her arrival at Withersteen House, had relaxed and was slowly losing her hold on life. Jane had believed that absence of worry and responsibility coupled with good nursing and comfort would mend Mrs. Larkin's broken health. Such, however, was not the case.

When Jane did get out to the court, Fay was there alone, and at the moment embarking on a dubious voyage down the stone-lined amber stream upon a craft of two brooms and a pillow. Fay was as delightfully wet as she could possibly wish to get.

Clatter of hoofs distracted Fay and interrupted the scolding she was gleefully receiving from Jane. The sound was not the light-spirited trot that Bells made when Lassiter rode him into the outer court. This was slower and heavier, and Jane did not recognize in it any of her other horses. The appearance of Bishop Dyer startled Jane. He dismounted with his rapid, jerky motion, flung the bridle, and, as he turned toward the inner court and stalked up on the stone flags, his boots rang. In his authoritative front, and in the red anger unmistakably flaming in his face, he reminded Jane of her father.

"Is that the Larkin pauper?" he asked, bruskly, without any greeting to Jane.

"It's Mrs. Larkin's little girl," replied Jane, slowly.

"I hear you intend to raise the child?"

"Yes."

"Of course you mean to give her Mormon bringing-up?"

"No!"

His questions had been swift. She was amazed at a feeling that some one else was replying for her.

"I've come to say a few things to you." He stopped to measure her with stern, speculative eye.

Jane Withersteen loved this man. From earliest childhood she had been taught to revere and love bishops of her church. And for ten years Bishop Dyer had been the closest friend and counselor of her father, and for the greater part of that period her own friend and Scriptural teacher. Her interpretation of her creed and her religious activity in fidelity to it, her acceptance of mysterious and holy

Mormon truths, were all invested in this Bishop. Bishop Dyer as an entity was next to God. He was God's mouthpiece to the little Mormon community at Cottonwoods. God revealed himself in secret to this mortal.

And Jane Withersteen suddenly suffered a paralyzing affront to her consciousness of reverence by some strange, irresistible twist of thought wherein she saw this Bishop as a man. And the train of thought hurdled the rising, crying protests of that other self whose poise she had lost. It was not her Bishop who eyed her in curious measurement. It was a man who tramped into her presence without removing his hat, who had no greeting for her, who had no semblance of courtesy. In looks, as in action, he made her think of a bull stamping cross-grained into a corral. She had heard of Bishop Dyer forgetting the minister in the fury of a common man, and now she was to feel it. The glance by which she measured him in turn momentarily veiled the divine in the ordinary. He looked a rancher; he was booted, spurred, and covered with dust; he carried a gun at his hip, and she remembered that he had been known to use it. But during the long moment while he watched her there was nothing commonplace in the slow-gathering might of his wrath.

"Brother Tull has talked to me," he began. "It was your father's wish that you marry Tull, and my order. You refused him?"

"Yes."

"You would not give up your friendship with that tramp Venters?"

"No."

"But you'll do as *I* order!" he thundered. "Why, Jane Withersteen, you are in danger of becoming a heretic! You can thank your Gentile friends for that. You face the damning of your soul to perdition."

In the flux and reflux of the whirling torture of Jane's mind, that new, daring spirit of hers vanished in the old habitual order of her life. She was a Mormon, and the Bishop regained ascendance.

"It's well I got you in time, Jane Withersteen. What would your father have said to these goings-on of yours? He would have put you in a stone cage on bread and water. He would have taught you something about Mormonism. Remember, you're a *born* Mormon. There have been Mormons who turned heretic—damn their souls!—but no born Mormon ever left us yet. Ah, I see your shame. Your faith is not shaken. You are only a wild girl." The Bishop's tone softened. "Well, it's enough that I got to you in time. . . . Now tell me about this Lassiter. I hear strange things."

"What do you wish to know?" queried Jane.

"About this man. You hired him?"

"Yes, he's riding for me. When my riders left me I had to have any one I could get."

"Is it true what I hear—that he's a gun-man, a Mormon-hater, steeped in blood?"

"True—terribly true, I fear."

"But what's he doing here in Cottonwoods? This place isn't notorious enough for such a man. Sterling and the villages north, where there's universal gun-packing and fights every day—where there are more men like him, it seems to me they would attract him most. We're only a wild, lonely border settlement. It's only recently that the rustlers have made killings here. Nor have there been saloons till lately, nor the drifting in of outcasts. Has not this gun-man some special mission here?"

Jane maintained silence.

"Tell me," ordered Bishop Dyer, sharply.

"Yes," she replied.

"Do you know what it is?"

"Yes."

"Tell me that."

"Bishop Dyer, I don't want to tell."

He waved his hand in an imperative gesture of command. The red once more leaped to his face, and in his steel-blue eyes glinted a pin-point of curiosity.

"That first day," whispered Jane, "Lassiter said he came here to find—Milly Erne's grave!"

With downcast eyes Jane watched the swift flow of the amber water. She saw it and tried to think of it, of the stones, of the ferns; but, like her body, her mind was in a leaden vise. Only the Bishop's voice could release her. Seemingly there was silence of longer duration than all her former life.

"For what—else?" When Bishop Dyer's voice did cleave the silence it was high, curiously shrill, and on the point of breaking. It released Jane's tongue, but she could not lift her eyes.

"To kill the man who persuaded Milly Erne to abandon her home and her husband—and her God!"

With wonderful distinctness Jane Withersteen heard her own clear voice. She heard the water murmur at her feet and flow on to the sea; she heard the rushing of all the waters in the world. They filled her ears with low, unreal murmurings— these sounds that deadened her brain and yet could not break the long and terrible silence. Then, from somewhere—from an immeasurable distance—came a slow, guarded, clinking, clanking step. Into her it shot electrifying life. It released the weight upon her numbed eyelids. Lifting her eyes she saw—ashen, shaken, stricken—not the Bishop but the man! And beyond him, from round the corner came that soft, silvery step. A long black boot with a gleaming spur swept into sight—and then Lassiter! Bishop Dyer did not see, did not hear: he stared at Jane in the throes of sudden revelation.

"Ah, I understand!" he cried, in hoarse accents. "That's why you made love to this Lassiter—to bind his hands!"

It was Jane's gaze riveted upon the rider that made Bishop Dyer turn. Then clear sight failed her. Dizzily, in a blur, she saw the Bishop's hand jerk to his hip. She saw gleam of blue and spout of red. In her ears burst a thundering report. The court floated in darkening circles around her, and she fell into utter blackness.

The darkness lightened, turned to slow-drifting haze, and lifted. Through a thin film of blue smoke she saw the rough-hewn timbers of the court roof. A cool, damp touch moved across her brow. She smelled powder, and it was that which galvanized her suspended thought. She moved, to see that she lay prone upon the stone flags with her head on Lassiter's knee, and he was bathing her brow with water from the stream. The same swift glance, shifting low, brought into range of her sight a smoking gun and splashes of blood.

"Ah-h!" she moaned, and was drifting, sinking again into darkness, when Lassiter's voice arrested her.

"It's all right, Jane. It's all right."

"Did—you—kill—him?" she whispered.

"Who? That fat party who was here? No. I didn't kill him."

"Oh! . . . Lassiter!"

"Say! It was queer for you to faint. I thought you were such a strong woman, not faintish like that. You're all right now—only some pale. I thought you'd never come to. But I'm awkward round women folks. I couldn't think of anythin'."

"Lassiter! . . . the gun there! . . . the blood!"

"So that's troublin' you. I reckon it needn't. You see it was this way. I come round the house an' seen that fat party an' heard him talkin' loud. Then he seen me, an' very impolite goes straight for his gun. He oughtn't have tried to throw a gun on me—whatever his reason was. For that's meetin' me on my own grounds. I've seen runnin' molasses that was quicker 'n him. Now I didn't know who he was, visitor or friend or relation of yours, though I seen he was a Mormon all over, an' I couldn't get serious about shootin'. So I winged him—put a bullet through his arm as he was pullin' at his gun. An' he dropped the gun there, an' a little blood. I told him he'd introduced himself sufficient, an' to please move out of my vicinity. An' he went."

Lassiter spoke with slow, cool, soothing voice, in which there was a hint of levity, and his touch, as he continued to bathe her brow, was gentle and steady. His impassive face, and the kind, gray eyes, further stilled her agitation.

"He drew on you first, and you deliberately shot to cripple him—you wouldn't kill him—you—*Lassiter*?"

"That's about the size of it."

Jane kissed his hand.

All that was calm and cool about Lassiter instantly vanished.

"Don't do that! I won't stand it! An' I don't care a damn who that fat party was."

He helped Jane to her feet and to a chair. Then with the wet scarf he had used to bathe her face he wiped the blood from the stone flags and, picking up the gun, he threw it upon a couch. With that he began to pace the court, and his silver spurs jangled musically, and the great gun-sheaths softly brushed against his leather chaps.

"So—it's true—what I heard him say?" Lassiter asked, presently halting before her. "You made love to me—to bind my hands?"

"Yes," confessed Jane. It took all her woman's courage to meet the gray storm of his glance.

"All these days that you've been so friendly an' like a pardner—all these evenin's that have been so bewilderin' to me—your beauty—an'—an' the way you looked an' came close to me—they were woman's tricks to bind my hands?"

"Yes."

"An' your sweetness that seemed so natural, an' your throwin' little Fay an' me so much together—to make me love the child—all that was for the same reason?"

"Yes."

Lassiter flung his arms—a strange gesture for him.

"Mebbe it wasn't much in your Mormon thinkin', for you to play that game. But to bring the child in—that was hellish!"

Jane's passionate, unheeding zeal began to loom darkly.

"Lassiter, whatever my intention in the beginning, Fay loves you dearly—and I—I've grown to—to like you."

"That's powerful kind of you, now," he said. Sarcasm and scorn made his voice that of a stranger. "An' you sit there an' look me straight in the eyes! You're a wonderful strange woman, Jane Withersteen."

"I'm not ashamed, Lassiter. I told you I'd try to change you."

"Would you mind tellin' me just what you tried?"

"I tried to make you see beauty in me and be softened by it. I wanted you to care for me so that I could influence you. It wasn't easy. At first you were stone-blind. Then I hoped you'd love little Fay, and through that come to feel the horror of making children fatherless."

"Jane Withersteen, either you're a fool or noble beyond my understandin'. Mebbe you're both. I know you're blind. What you meant is one thing—what you *did* was to make me love you."

"Lassiter!"

"I reckon I'm a human bein', though I never loved any one but my sister, Milly Erne. That was long—"

"Oh, are you Milly's brother?"

"Yes, I was, an' I loved her. There never was any one but her in my life till now. Didn't I tell you that long ago I back-trailed myself from women? I was a Texas ranger till—till Milly left home, an' then I became somethin' else—Lassiter! For years I've been a lonely man set on one thing. I came here an' met you. An' now I'm not the man I was. The change was gradual, an' I took no notice of it. I understand now that never-satisfied longin' to see you, listen to you, watch you, feel you near me. It's plain now why you were never out of my thoughts. I've had no thoughts but of you. I've lived an' breathed for you. An' now when I know what it means—what you've done—I'm burnin' up with hell's fire!"

"Oh, Lassiter—no—no—you don't love me that way!" Jane cried.

"If that's what love is, then I do."

"Forgive me! I didn't mean to make you love me like that. Oh, what a tangle of our lives! You—Milly Erne's brother! And I—heedless, mad to melt your heart toward Mormons. Lassiter, I may be wicked but not wicked enough to hate. If I couldn't hate Tull, could I hate you?"

"After all, Jane, mebbe you're only blind—Mormon blind. That only can explain what's close to selfishness—"

"I'm not selfish. I despise the very word. If I were free—"

"But you're not free. Not free of Mormonism. An' in playin' this game with me you've been unfaithful."

"Un-faithful!" faltered Jane.

"Yes, I said unfaithful. You're faithful to your Bishop an' unfaithful to yourself. You're false to your womanhood an' true to your religion. But for a savin' innocence you'd have made yourself low an' vile—betrayin' yourself, betrayin' me—all to bind my hands an' keep me from snuffin' out Mormon life. It's your damned Mormon blindness."

"Is it vile—is it blind—is it only Mormonism to save human life? No, Lassiter, that's God's law, divine, universal for all Christians."

"The blindness I mean is blindness that keeps you from seein' the truth. I've known many good Mormons. But some are blacker than hell. You won't see that even when you know it. Else, why all this blind passion to save the life of that— that. . . ."

Jane shut out the light, and the hands she held over her eyes trembled and quivered against her face.

"Blind—yes, an' let me make it clear an' simple to you," Lassiter went on, his voice losing its tone of anger. "Take, for instance, that idea of yours last night when you wanted my guns. It was good an' beautiful, an' showed your heart— but—why, Jane, it was crazy. Mind I'm assumin' that life to me is as sweet as to any other man. An' to preserve that life is each man's first an' closest thought. Where would any man be on this border without guns? Where, especially, would Lassiter be? Well, I'd be under the sage with thousands of other men now livin' an' sure better men than me. Gun-packin' in the West since the Civil War has growed into a kind of moral law. An' out here on this border it's the difference between a man an' somethin' not a man. Look what your takin' Venters's guns from him all but made him! Why, your churchmen carry guns. Tull has killed a man an' drawed on others. Your Bishop has shot a half dozen men, an' it wasn't through prayers of his that they recovered. An' to-day he'd have shot me if he'd been quick enough on the draw. Could I walk or ride down into Cottonwoods without my guns? This is a wild time, Jane Withersteen, this year of our Lord eighteen seventy-one."

"No time—for a woman!" exclaimed Jane, brokenly. "Oh, Lassiter, I feel helpless—lost—and don't know where to turn. If I *am* blind—then—I need some one—a friend—you, Lassiter—more than ever!"

"Well, I didn't say nothin' about goin' back on you, did I?"

CHAPTER TWELVE

The Invisible Hand

JANE received a letter from Bishop Dyer, not in his own handwriting, which stated that the abrupt termination of their interview had left him in some doubt as to her future conduct. A slight injury had incapacitated him from seeking another meeting at present, the letter went on to say, and ended with a request which was virtually a command, that she call upon him at once.

The reading of the letter acquainted Jane Withersteen with the fact that something within her had all but changed. She sent no reply to Bishop Dyer nor did she go to see him. On Sunday she remained absent from the service—for the second time in years—and though she did not actually suffer there was a dead-lock of feelings deep within her, and the waiting for a balance to fall on either side was almost as bad as suffering. She had a gloomy expectancy of untoward circumstances, and with it a keen-edged curiosity to watch developments. She had a half-formed conviction that her future conduct—as related to her churchmen—was beyond her control and would be governed by their attitude toward her. Something was changing in her, forming, waiting for decision to make it a real and fixed thing. She had told Lassiter that she felt helpless and lost in the fateful tangle of their lives; and now she feared that she was approaching the same chaotic condition of mind in regard to her religion. It appalled her to find that she questioned phases of that religion. Absolute faith had been her serenity. Though leaving her faith unshaken, her serenity had been disturbed, and now it was broken by open war between her and her ministers. That something within her—a whisper—which she had tried in vain to hush had become a ringing voice, and it called to her to wait. She had transgressed no laws of God. Her churchmen, however invested with the power and the glory of a wonderful creed, however they sat in inexorable judgment of her, must now practice toward her the simple, common, Christian virtue they professed to preach, "Do unto others as you would have others do unto you!"

Jane Withersteen, waiting in darkness of mind, remained faithful still. But it was darkness that must soon be pierced by light. If her faith were justified, if her churchmen were trying only to intimidate her, the fact would soon be manifest, as would their failure, and then she would redouble her zeal toward them and toward what had been the best work of her life—work for the welfare and happiness of those among whom she lived, Mormon and Gentile alike. If that secret, intangible power closed its toils round her again, if that great invisible hand moved here and there and everywhere, slowly paralyzing her with its mystery and its inconceivable sway over her affairs, then she would know beyond doubt that it was not chance, nor jealousy, nor intimidation, nor ministerial wrath at her revolt, but a cold and calculating policy thought out long before she was born, a dark, immutable will of whose empire she and all that was hers was but an atom.

Then might come her ruin. Then might come her fall into black storm. Yet she would rise again, and to the light. God would be merciful to a driven woman who had lost her way.

A week passed. Little Fay played and prattled and pulled at Lassiter's big black guns. The rider came to Withersteen House oftener than ever. Jane saw a change in him, though it did not relate to his kindness and gentleness. He was quieter and more thoughtful. While playing with Fay or conversing with Jane he seemed to be possessed of another self that watched with cool, roving eyes, that listened, listened always as if the murmuring amber stream brought messages, and the moving leaves whispered something. Lassiter never rode Bells into the court any more, nor did he come by the lane or the paths. When he appeared it was suddenly and noiselessly out of the dark shadow of the grove.

"I left Bells out in the sage," he said, one day at the end of that week. "I must carry water to him."

"Why not let him drink at the trough or here?" asked Jane, quickly.

"I reckon it'll be safer for me to slip through the grove. I've been watched when I rode in from the sage."

"Watched? By whom?"

"By a man who thought he was well hid. But my eyes are pretty sharp. An', Jane," he went on, almost in a whisper, "I reckon it'd be a good idea for us to talk low. You're spied on here by your women."

"Lassiter!" she whispered in turn. "That's hard to believe. My women love me."

"What of that?" he asked. "Of course they love you. But they're Mormon women."

Jane's old, rebellious loyalty clashed with her doubt.

"I won't believe it," she replied, stubbornly.

"Well then, just act natural an' talk natural, an' pretty soon—give them time to hear us—pretend to go over there to the table, an' then quick-like make a move for the door an' open it."

"I will," said Jane, with heightened color. Lassiter was right; he never made mistakes; he would not have told her unless he positively knew. Yet Jane was so tenacious of faith that she had to see with her own eyes, and so constituted that to employ even such small deceit toward her women made her ashamed, and angry for her shame as well as theirs. Then a singular thought confronted her that made her hold up this simple ruse—which hurt her, though it was well justified—against the deceit she had wittingly and eagerly used toward Lassiter. The difference was staggering in its suggestion of that blindness of which he had accused her. Fairness and justice and mercy, that she had imagined were anchor-cables to hold fast her soul to righteousness, had not been hers in the strange, biased duty that had so exalted and confounded her.

Presently Jane began to act her little part, to laugh and play with Fay, to talk of horses and cattle to Lassiter. Then she made deliberate mention of a book in which she kept records of all pertaining to her stock, and she walked slowly toward the table, and when near the door she suddenly whirled and thrust it open. Her sharp action nearly knocked down a woman who had undoubtedly been listening.

"Hester," said Jane, sternly, "you may go home, and you need not come back."

Jane shut the door and returned to Lassiter. Standing unsteadily, she put her hand on his arm. She let him see that doubt had gone, and how this stab of disloyalty pained her.

"Spies! My own women! . . . Oh, miserable!" she cried, with flashing, tearful eyes.

"I hate to tell you," he replied. By that she knew he had long spared her. "It's begun again—that work in the dark."

"Nay, Lassiter—it never stopped!"

So bitter certainty claimed her at last, and trust fled Withersteen House and fled forever. The women who owed much to Jane Withersteen changed not in love for her, nor in devotion to their household work, but they poisoned both by a thousand acts of stealth and cunning and duplicity. Jane broke out once and caught them in strange, stone-faced, unhesitating falsehood. Thereafter she broke out no more. She forgave them because they were driven. Poor, fettered, and sealed Hagars, how she pitied them! What terrible thing bound them and locked their lips, when they showed neither consciousness of guilt toward their benefactress nor distress at the slow wearing apart of long-established and dear ties?

"The blindness again!" cried Jane Withersteen. "In my sisters as in me! . . . O God!"

There came a time when no words passed between Jane and her women. Silently they went about their household duties, and secretly they went about the underhand work to which they had been bidden. The gloom of the house and the gloom of its mistress, which darkened even the bright spirit of little Fay, did not pervade these women. Happiness was not among them, but they were aloof from gloom. They spied and listened; they received and sent secret messengers; and they stole Jane's books and records, and finally the papers that were deeds of her possessions. Through it all they were silent, rapt in a kind of trance. Then one by one, without leave or explanation or farewell, they left Withersteen House, and never returned.

Coincident with this disappearance Jane's gardeners and workers in the alfalfa fields and stable men quit her, not even asking for their wages. Of all her Mormon employees about the great ranch only Jerd remained. He went on with his duty, but talked no more of the change than if it had never occurred.

"Jerd," said Jane, "what stock you can't take care of turn out in the sage. Let your first thought be for Black Star and Night. Keep them in perfect condition. Run them every day and watch them always."

Though Jane Withersteen gave them such liberality, she loved her possessions. She loved the rich, green stretches of alfalfa, and the farms, and the grove, and the old stone house, and the beautiful, ever-faithful amber spring, and every one of a myriad of horses and colts and burros and fowls down to the smallest rabbit that nipped her vegetables; but she loved best her noble Arabian steeds. In common with all riders of the upland sage Jane cherished two material things—the cold, sweet, brown water that made life possible in the wilderness and the horses which were a part of that life. When Lassiter asked her what Lassiter would be without his guns he was assuming that his horse was part of himself. So Jane loved Black Star and Night because it was her nature to love all beautiful creatures—perhaps all living things; and then she loved them because she herself was of the sage and in her had been born and bred the rider's instinct to rely on his four-footed brother. And when Jane gave Jerd the order to keep her favorites trained down to the day it was a half-conscious admission that presaged a time when she would need her fleet horses.

Jane had now, however, no leisure to brood over the coils that were closing round her. Mrs. Larkin grew weaker as the August days began; she required constant care; there was little Fay to look after; and such household work as was imperative. Lassiter put Bells in the stable with the other racers, and directed his efforts to a closer attendance upon Jane. She welcomed the change. He was always at hand to help, and it was her fortune to learn that his boast of being awkward around women had its root in humility and was not true.

His great, brown hands were skilled in a multiplicity of ways which a woman might have envied. He shared Jane's work, and was of especial help to her in nursing Mrs. Larkin. The woman suffered most at night, and this often broke Jane's rest. So it came about that Lassiter would stay by Mrs. Larkin during the day, when she needed care, and Jane would make up the sleep she lost in night-watches. Mrs. Larkin at once took kindly to the gentle Lassiter, and, without ever asking who or what he was, praised him to Jane. "He's a good man and loves children," she said. How sad to hear this truth spoken of a man whom Jane thought lost beyond all redemption! Yet ever and ever Lassiter towered above her, and behind or through his black, sinister figure shone something luminous that strangely affected Jane. Good and evil began to seem incomprehensibly blended in her judgment. It was her belief that evil could not come forth from good; yet here was a murderer who dwarfed in gentleness, patience, and love any man she had ever known.

She had almost lost track of her more outside concerns when early one morning Judkins presented himself before her in the courtyard.

Thin, hard, burnt, bearded, with the dust and sage thick on him, with his leather wrist-bands shining from use, and his boots worn through on the stirrup side, he looked the rider of riders. He wore two guns and carried a Winchester.

Jane greeted him with surprise and warmth, set meat and bread and drink before him; and called Lassiter out to see him. The men exchanged glances, and the meaning of Lassiter's keen inquiry and Judkins's bold reply, both unspoken, was not lost upon Jane.

"Where's your hoss?" asked Lassiter, aloud.

"Left him down the slope," answered Judkins. "I footed it in a ways, an' slept last night in the sage. I went to the place you told me you 'most always slept, but didn't strike you."

"I moved up some, near the spring, an' now I go there nights."

"Judkins—the white herd?" queried Jane, hurriedly.

"Miss Withersteen, I make proud to say I've not lost a steer. Fer a good while after thet stampede Lassiter milled we hed no trouble. Why, even the sage dogs left us. But it's begun agin—thet flashin' of lights over ridge tips, an' queer puffin' of smoke, an' then at night strange whistles an' noises. But the herd's acted magnificent. An' my boys, say, Miss Withersteen, they're only kids, but I ask no better riders. I got the laugh in the village fer takin' them out. They're a wild lot, an' you know boys hev more nerve than grown men, because they don't know what danger is. I'm not denyin' there's danger. But they glory in it, an' mebbe I like it myself—anyway, we'll stick. We're goin' to drive the herd on the far side of the first break of Deception Pass. There's a great round valley over there, an' no ridges or piles of rocks to aid these stampeders. The rains are due. We'll hev plenty of water fer a while. An' we can hold thet herd from anybody except Oldrin'. I come in fer supplies. I'll pack a couple of burros an' drive out after dark to-night."

"Judkins, take what you want from the store-room. Lassiter will help you. I—I can't thank you enough . . . but—wait."

Jane went to the room that had once been her father's, and from a secret chamber in the thick stone wall she took a bag of gold, and, carrying it back to the court, she gave it to the rider.

"There, Judkins, and understand that I regard it as little for your loyalty. Give what is fair to your boys, and keep the rest. Hide it. Perhaps that would be wisest."

"Oh . . . Miss Withersteen!" ejaculated the rider. "I couldn't earn so much in—in ten years. It's not right—I oughtn't take it."

"Judkins, you know I'm a rich woman. I tell you I've few faithful friends. I've fallen upon evil days. God only knows what will become of me and mine! So take the gold."

She smiled in understanding of his speechless gratitude, and left him with Lassiter. Presently she heard him speaking low at first, then in louder accents emphasized by the thumping of his rifle on the stones. "As infernal a job as even you, Lassiter, ever heerd of."

"Why, son," was Lassiter's reply, "this breakin' of Miss Withersteen may seem bad to you, but it ain't bad—yet. Some of these wall-eyed fellers who look jest as if they was walkin' in the shadow of Christ himself, right down the sunny road, now they can think of things an' do things that are really hell-bent."

Jane covered her ears and ran to her own room, and there like a caged lioness she paced to and fro till the coming of little Fay reversed her dark thoughts.

The following day, a warm and muggy one threatening rain, while Jane was resting in the court, a horseman clattered through the grove and up to the hitching-rack. He leaped off and approached Jane with the manner of a man determined to execute a difficult mission, yet fearful of its reception. In the gaunt, wiry figure and the lean, brown face Jane recognized one of her Mormon riders, Blake. It was he of whom Judkins had long since spoken. Of all the riders ever in her employ Blake owed her the most, and as he stepped before her, removing his hat and making manly efforts to subdue his emotion, he showed that he remembered.

"Miss Withersteen, mother's dead," he said.

"Oh—Blake!" exclaimed Jane, and she could say no more.

"She died free from pain in the end, and she's buried—resting at last, thank God! . . . I've come to ride for you again, if you'll have me. Don't think I mentioned mother to get your sympathy. When she was living and your riders quit, I had to also. I was afraid of what might be done—said to her. . . . Miss Withersteen, we can't talk of—of what's going on now—"

"Blake, do you know?"

"I know a great deal. You understand, my lips are shut. But without explanation or excuse I offer my services. I'm a Mormon—I hope a good one. But—there are some things! . . . It's no use, Miss Withersteen, I can't say any more—what I'd like to. But will you take me back?"

"Blake! . . . You know what it means?"

"I don't care. I'm sick of—of—I'll show you a Mormon who'll be true to you!"

"But, Blake—how terribly you might suffer for that!"

"Maybe. Aren't you suffering now?"

"God knows indeed I am!"

"Miss Withersteen, it's a liberty on my part to speak so, but I know you pretty well—know you'll never give in. I wouldn't if I were you. And I—I must—Something makes me tell you the worst is yet to come. That's all. I absolutely can't say more. Will you take me back—let me ride for you—show everybody what I mean?"

"Blake, it makes me happy to hear you. How my riders hurt me when they quit!" Jane felt the hot tears well to her eyes and splash down upon her hands. "I thought so much of them—tried so hard to be good to them. And not one was true. You've made it easy to forgive. Perhaps many of them really feel as you do, but dare not return to me. Still, Blake, I hesitate to take you back. Yet I want you so much."

"Do it, then. If you're going to make your life a lesson to Mormon women, let me make mine a lesson to the men. Right is right. I believe in you, and here's my life to prove it."

"You hint it may mean your life!" said Jane, breathless and low.

"We won't speak of that. I want to come back. I want to do what every rider aches in his secret heart to do for you. . . . Miss Withersteen, I hoped it'd not be necessary to tell you that my mother on her deathbed told me to have courage. She knew how the thing galled me—she told me to come back. . . . Will you take me?"

"God bless you, Blake! Yes, I'll take you back. And will you—will you accept gold from me?"

"Miss Withersteen!"

"I just gave Judkins a bag of gold. I'll give you one. If you will not take it you must not come back. You might ride for me a few months—weeks—days till the storm breaks. Then you'd have nothing, and be in disgrace with your people. We'll forearm you against poverty, and me against endless regret. I'll give you gold which you can hide—till some future time."

"Well, if it pleases you," replied Blake. "But you know I never thought of pay. Now, Miss Withersteen, one thing more. I want to see this man Lassiter. Is he here?"

"Yes, but, Blake—what—Need you see him? Why?" asked Jane, instantly worried. "I can speak to him—tell him about you."

"That won't do. I want to—I've got to tell him myself. Where is he?"

"Lassiter is with Mrs. Larkin. She is ill. I'll call him," answered Jane, and going to the door she softly called for the rider. A faint, musical jingle preceded his step—then his tall form crossed the threshold.

"Lassiter, here's Blake, an old rider of mine. He has come back to me and he wishes to speak to you."

Blake's brown face turned exceedingly pale.

"Yes, I had to speak to you," he said, swiftly. "My name's Blake. I'm a Mormon and a rider. Lately I quit Miss Withersteen. I've come to beg her to take me back. Now I don't know you, but I know—what you are. So I've this to say to your face. It would never occur to this woman to imagine—let alone suspect me to be a spy. She couldn't think it might just be a low plot to come here and shoot you in the back. Jane Withersteen hasn't that kind of a mind. . . . Well, I've not come for that. I want to help her—to pull a bridle along with Judkins and—and you. The thing is—do you believe me?"

"I reckon I do," replied Lassiter. How this slow, cool speech contrasted with Blake's hot, impulsive words! "You might have saved some of your breath. See here, Blake, cinch this in your mind. Lassiter has met some square Mormons! An' mebbe—"

"Blake," interrupted Jane, nervously anxious to terminate a colloquy that she perceived was an ordeal for him. "Go at once and fetch me a report of my horses."

"Miss Withersteen! . . . You mean the big drove—down in the sage-cleared fields?"

"Of course," replied Jane. "My horses are all there, except the blooded stock I keep here."

"Haven't you heard—then?"

"Heard? No! What's happened to them?"

"They're gone, Miss Withersteen, gone these ten days past. Dorn told me, and I rode down to see for myself."

"Lassiter—did you know?" asked Jane, whirling to him.

"I reckon so. . . . But what was the use to tell you?"

It was Lassiter turning away his face and Blake studying the stone flags at his feet that brought Jane to the understanding of what she betrayed. She strove desperately, but she could not rise immediately from such a blow.

"My horses! My horses! What's become of them?"

"Dorn said the riders report another drive by Oldring. . . . And I trailed the horses miles down the slope toward Deception Pass."

"My red herd's gone! My horses gone! The white herd will go next. I can stand that. But if I lost Black Star and Night, it would be like parting with my own flesh and blood. Lassiter—Blake—am I in danger of losing my racers?"

"A rustler—or—or anybody stealin' hosses of yours would most of all want the blacks," said Lassiter. His evasive reply was affirmative enough. The other rider nodded gloomy acquiescence.

"Oh! Oh!" Jane Withersteen choked, with violent utterance.

"Let me take charge of the blacks?" asked Blake. "One more rider won't be any great help to Judkins. But I might hold Black Star and Night, if you put such store on their value."

"Value! Blake, I love my racers. Besides, there's another reason why I mustn't lose them. You go to the stables. Go with Jerd every day when he runs the horses, and don't let them out of your sight. If you would please me—win my gratitude, guard my black racers."

When Blake had mounted and ridden out of the court Lassiter regarded Jane with the smile that was becoming rarer as the days sped by.

"'Pears to me, as Blake says, you do put some store on them hosses. Now I ain't gainsayin' that the Arabians are the handsomest hosses I ever seen. But Bells can beat Night, an' run neck an' neck with Black Star."

"Lassiter, don't tease me now. I'm miserable—sick. Bells is fast, but he can't stay with the blacks, and you know it. Only Wrangle can do that."

"I'll bet that big raw-boned brute can more'n show his heels to your black racers. Jane, out there in the sage, on a long chase, Wrangle could kill your favorites.

"No, no," replied Jane, impatiently. "Lassiter, why do you say that so often? I know you've teased me at times, and I believe it's only kindness. You're always trying to keep my mind off worry. But you mean more by this repeated mention of my racers?"

"I reckon so." Lassiter paused, and for the thousandth time in her presence moved his black sombrero round and round, as if counting the silver pieces on the band. "Well, Jane, I've sort of read a little that's passin' in your mind."

"You think I might fly from my home—from Cottonwoods—from the Utah border?"

"I reckon. An' if you ever do an' get away with the blacks I wouldn't like to see Wrangle left here on the sage. Wrangle could catch you. I know Venters had him. But you can never tell. Mebbe he hasn't got him now. . . . Besides—things are happenin', an' somethin' of the same queer nature might have happened to Venters."

"God knows you're right! . . . Poor Bern, how long he's gone! In my trouble I've been forgetting him. But, Lassiter, I've little fear for him. I've heard my riders say he's as keen as a wolf. . . . As to your reading my thoughts—well, your suggestion makes an actual thought of what was only one of my dreams. I believe I dreamed of flying from this wild borderland, Lassiter. I've strange dreams. I'm not always practical and thinking of my many duties, as you said once. For instance—if I dared—if I dared I'd ask you to saddle the blacks and ride away with me—and hide me."

"Jane!"

The rider's sunburnt face turned white. A few times Jane had seen Lassiter's cool calm broken—when he had met little Fay, when he had learned how and why he had come to love both child and mistress, when he had stood beside Milly Erne's grave. But one and all they could not be considered in the light of his present agitation. Not only did Lassiter turn white—not only did he grow tense, not only did he lose his coolness, but also he suddenly, violently, hungrily took her into his arms and crushed her to his breast.

"Lassiter!" cried Jane, trembling. It was an action for which she took sole blame. Instantly, as if dazed, weakened, he released her. "Forgive me!" went on Jane. "I'm always forgetting your—your feelings. I thought of you as my faithful friend. I'm always making you out more than human . . . only, let me say—I meant that—about riding away. I'm wretched, sick of this—this—Oh, something bitter and black grows on my heart!"

"Jane, the hell—of it," he replied, with deep intake of breath, "is you *can't* ride away. Mebbe realizin' it accounts for my grabbin' you—that way, as much as the crazy boy's rapture your words gave me. I don't understand myself. . . . But the hell of this game is—you *can't* ride away."

"Lassiter! . . . What on earth do you mean? I'm an absolutely free woman."

"You ain't absolutely anythin' of the kind. . . . I reckon I've got to tell you!"

"Tell me all. It's uncertainty that makes me a coward. It's faith and hope—blind love, if you will, that makes me miserable. Every day I awake believing—still believing. The day grows, and with it doubts, fears, and that black bat hate that bites hotter and hotter into my heart. Then comes night—I pray—I pray for all, and for myself—I sleep—and I awake free once more, trustful, faithful, to believe—to hope! Then, O my God! I grow and live a thousand years till night again! . . . But if you want to see me a woman, tell me why I can't ride away—tell me what more I'm to lose—tell me the worst."

"Jane, you're watched. There's no single move of yours, except when you're hid in your house, that ain't seen by sharp eyes. The cottonwood grove's full of creepin', crawlin' men. Like Indians in the grass. When you rode, which wasn't often lately, the sage was full of sneakin' men. At night they crawl under your windows, into the court, an' I reckon into the house. Jane Withersteen, you know, never locked a door! This here grove's a hummin' bee-hive of mysterious happenin's. Jane, it ain't so much that these spies keep out of my way as me keepin' out of theirs. They're goin' to try to kill me. That's plain. But mebbe I'm as hard to shoot in the back as in the face. So far I've seen fit to watch only. This all means, Jane, that you're a marked woman. You can't get away—not now. Mebbe later, when you're broken, you might. But that's sure doubtful. Jane, you're to lose the cattle that's left—your home an' ranch—an' Amber Spring. You can't even hide a sack of gold! For it couldn't be slipped out of the house, day or night, an' hid or buried, let alone be rid off with. You may lose all. I'm tellin' you, Jane, hopin' to prepare you, if the worst does come. I told you once before about that strange power I've got to feel things."

"Lassiter, what can I do?"

"Nothin', I reckon, except know what's comin' an' wait an' be game. If you'd let me make a call on Tull, an' a long-deferred call on—"

"Hush! . . . Hush!" she whispered.

"Well, even that wouldn't help you any in the end."

"What does it mean? Oh, what does it mean? I am my father's daughter—a Mormon, yet I can't see! I've not failed in religion—in duty. For years I've given with a free and full heart. When my father died I was rich. If I'm still rich it's because I couldn't find enough ways to become poor. What am I, what are my possessions to set in motion such intensity of secret oppression?"

"Jane, the mind behind it all is an empire builder."

"But, Lassiter, I would give freely—all I own to avert this—this wretched thing. If I gave—that would leave me with faith still. Surely my—my churchmen think of my soul? If I lose my trust in them—"

"Child, be still!" said Lassiter, with a dark dignity that had in it something of pity. "You are a woman, fine an' big an' strong, an' your heart matches your size. But in mind you're a child. I'll say a little more—then I'm done. I'll never mention this again. Among many thousands of women you're one who has bucked against your churchmen. They tried you out, an' failed of persuasion, an' finally of threats. You meet now the cold steel of a will as far from Christlike as the universe is wide. You're to be broken. Your body's to be held, given to some man, made, if possible, to bring children into the world. But your soul? . . . What do they care for your soul?"

CHAPTER THIRTEEN

Solitude and Storm

IN his hidden valley Venters awakened from sleep, and his ears rang with innumerable melodies from full-throated mocking-birds, and his eyes opened wide upon the glorious golden shaft of sunlight shining through the great stone bridge. The circle of cliffs surrounding Surprise Valley lay shrouded in morning mist, a dim blue low down along the terraces, a creamy, moving cloud along the ramparts. The oak forest in the center was a plumed and tufted oval of gold.

He saw Bess under the spruces. Upon her complete recovery of strength she always rose with the dawn. At the moment she was feeding the quail she had tamed. And she had begun to tame the mocking-birds. They fluttered among the branches overhead, and some left off their songs to flit down and shyly hop near the twittering quail. Little gray and white rabbits crouched in the grass, now nibbling, now laying long ears flat and watching the dogs.

Venters's swift glance took in the brightening valley, and Bess and her pets, and Ring and Whitie. It swept over all to return again and rest upon the girl. She had changed. To the dark trousers and blouse she had added moccasins of her own make, but she no longer resembled a boy. No eye could have failed to mark the rounded contours of a woman. The change had been to grace and beauty. A glint of warm gold gleamed from her hair, and a tint of red shone in the clear dark brown of cheeks. The haunting sweetness of her lips and eyes, that earlier had been illusive, a promise, had become a living fact. She fitted harmoniously into that wonderful setting; she was like Surprise Valley—wild and beautiful.

Venters leaped out of his cave to begin the day.

He had postponed his journey to Cottonwoods until after the passing of the summer rains. The rains were due soon. But until their arrival and the necessity for his trip to the village he sequestered in a far corner of mind all thought of peril, of his past life, and almost that of the present. It was enough to live. He did not want to know what lay hidden in the dim and distant future. Surprise Valley had enchanted him. In this home of the cliff-dwellers there were peace and quiet and solitude, and another thing, wondrous as the golden morning shaft of sunlight, that he dared not ponder over long enough to understand.

The solitude he had hated when alone he had now come to love. He was assimilating something from this valley of gleams and shadows. From this strange girl he was assimilating more.

The day at hand resembled many days gone before. As Venters had no tools with which to build, or to till the terraces, he remained idle. Beyond the cooking of the simple fare there were no tasks. And as there were no tasks, there was no system. He and Bess began one thing, to leave it; to begin another, to leave that; and then do nothing but lie under the spruces and watch the great cloud-sails majestically move along the ramparts, and dream and dream. The valley was a golden, sunlit world. It was silent. The sighing wind and the twittering quail and the singing birds, even the rare and seldom-occurring hollow crack of a sliding weathered stone, only thickened and deepened that insulated silence.

Venters and Bess had vagrant minds.

"Bess, did I tell you about my horse Wrangle?" inquired Venters.

"A hundred times," she replied.

"Oh, have I? I'd forgotten. I want you to see him. He'll carry us both."

"I'd like to ride him. Can he run?"

"Run? He's a demon. Swiftest horse on the sage! I hope he'll stay in that cañon."

"He'll stay."

They left camp to wander along the terraces, into the aspen ravines, under the gleaming walls. Ring and Whitie wandered in the fore, often turning, often trotting back, open-mouthed and solemn-eyed and happy. Venters lifted his gaze to the grand archway over the entrance to the valley, and Bess lifted hers to follow his, and both were silent. Sometimes the bridge held their attention for a long time. To-day a soaring eagle attracted them.

"How he sails!" exclaimed Bess. "I wonder where his mate is?"

"She's at the nest. It's on the bridge in a crack near the top. I see her often. She's almost white."

They wandered on down the terrace, into the shady, sun-flecked forest. A brown bird fluttered crying from a bush. Bess peeped into the leaves.

"Look! A nest and four little birds. They're not afraid of us. See how they open their mouths. They're hungry."

Rabbits rustled the dead brush and pattered away. The forest was full of a drowsy hum of insects. Little darts of purple, that were running quail, crossed the glades. And a plaintive, sweet peeping came from the coverts. Bess's soft step disturbed a sleeping lizard that scampered away over the leaves. She gave chase and caught it, a slim creature of nameless color but of exquisite beauty.

"Jewel eyes," she said. "It's like a rabbit—afraid. We won't eat you. There—go."

Murmuring water drew their steps down into a shallow shaded ravine where a brown brook brawled softly over mossy stones. Multitudes of strange, gray frogs with white spots and black eyes lined the rocky bank and leaped only at close approach. Then Venters's eye descried a very thin, very long green snake coiled round a sapling. They drew closer and closer till they could have touched it. The snake had no fear and watched them with scintillating eyes.

"It's pretty," said Bess. "How tame! I thought snakes always ran."

"No. Even the rabbits didn't run here till the dogs chased them."

On and on they wandered to the wild jumble of massed and broken fragments of cliff at the west end of the valley. The roar of the disappearing stream dinned in their ears. Into this maze of rocks they threaded a tortuous way, climbing, descending, halting to gather wild plums and great lavender lilies, and going on at the will of fancy. Idle and keen perceptions guided them equally.

"Oh, let us climb there!" cried Bess, pointing upward to a small space of terrace left green and shady between huge abutments of broken cliff. And they climbed to the nook and rested and looked out across the valley to the curling column of blue smoke from their campfire. But the cool shade and the rich grass and the fine view were not what they had climbed for. They could not have told, although whatever had drawn them was well-satisfying. Light, sure-footed as a mountain goat, Bess pattered down at Venters's heels; and they went on, calling the dogs, eyes dreamy and wide, listening to the wind and the bees and the crickets and the birds.

Part of the time Ring and Whitie led the way, then Venters, then Bess; and the direction was not an object. They left the sun-streaked shade of the oaks, brushed the long grass of the meadows, entered the green and fragrant swaying willows, to stop, at length, under the huge old cottonwoods where the beavers were busy.

Here they rested and watched. A dam of brush and logs and mud and stones backed the stream into a little lake. The round, rough beaver houses projected from the water. Like the rabbits, the beavers had become shy. Gradually, however, as Venters and Bess knelt low, holding the dogs, the beavers emerged to swim with logs and gnaw at cottonwoods and pat mud walls with their paddle-like tails, and, glossy and shiny in the sun, to go on with their strange, persistent industry. They were the builders. The lake was a mud-hole, and the immediate environment a scarred and dead region, but it was a wonderful home of wonderful animals.

"Look at that one—he puddles in the mud," said Bess. "And there! See him dive! Hear them gnawing! I'd think they'd break their teeth. How's it they can stay out of the water and under the water?"

And she laughed.

Then Venters and Bess wandered farther, and, perhaps not all unconsciously this time, wended their slow steps to the cave of the cliff-dwellers, where she liked best to go.

The tangled thicket and the long slant of dust and little chips of weathered rock and the steep bench of stone and the worn steps all were arduous work for Bess in the climbing. But she gained the shelf, gasping, hot of cheek, glad of eye, with her hand in Venters's. Here they rested. The beautiful valley glittered below with its millions of wind-turned leaves bright-faced in the sun, and the mighty bridge towered heavenward, crowned with blue sky. Bess, however, never rested for long. Soon she was exploring, and Venters followed; she dragged forth from corners and shelves a multitude of crudely fashioned and painted pieces of pottery, and he carried them. They peeped down into the dark holes of the kivas, and Bess gleefully dropped a stone and waited for the long-coming hollow sound to rise. They peeped into the little globular houses, like mud-wasp nests, and wondered if these had been store-places for grain, or baby cribs, or what; and they crawled into the larger houses and laughed when they bumped their heads on the low roofs, and they dug in the dust of the floors. And they brought from dust and darkness armloads of treasure which they carried to the light. Flints and stones and strange curved sticks and pottery they found; and twisted grass rope that crumbled in their hands, and bits of whitish stone which crushed to powder at a touch and seemed to vanish in the air.

"That white stuff was bone," said Venters, slowly. "Bones of a cliff-dweller."

"No!" exclaimed Bess.

"Here's another piece. Look! . . . Whew! dry, powdery smoke! That's bone."

Then it was that Venters's primitive, childlike mood, like a savage's, seeing, yet unthinking, gave way to the encroachment of civilized thought. The world had not been made for a single day's play or fancy or idle watching. The world was old. Nowhere could be gotten a better idea of its age than in this gigantic silent tomb. The gray ashes in Venters's hand had once been bone of a human being like himself. The pale gloom of the cave had shadowed people long ago. He saw that Bess had received the same shock—could not in moments such as this escape her feeling, living, thinking destiny.

"Bern, people have *lived* here," she said, with wide, thoughtful eyes.

"Yes," he replied.

"How long ago?"

"A thousand years and more."

"What were they?"

"Cliff-dwellers. Men who had enemies and made their homes high out of reach."

"They had to fight?"

"Yes."

"They fought for—what?"

"For life. For their homes, food, children, parents—for their women!"

"Has the world changed any in a thousand years?"

"I don't know—perhaps a little."

"Have men?"

"I hope so—I think so."

"Things crowd into my mind," she went on, and the wistful light in her eyes told Venters the truth of her thoughts. "I've ridden the border of Utah. I've seen people—know how they live—but they must be few of all who are living. I had my books and I studied them. But all that doesn't help me any more. I want to go out into the big world and see it. Yet I want to stay here more. What's to become of us? Are we cliff-dwellers? We're alone here. I'm happy when I don't think. These—these bones that fly into dust—they make me sick and a little afraid. Did the people who lived here once have the same feelings as we have? What was the good of their living at all? They're gone! What's the meaning of it all—of us?"

"Bess, you ask more than I can tell. It's beyond me. Only there was laughter here once—and now there's silence. There was life—and now there's death. Men cut these little steps, made these arrow-heads and mealing-stones, plaited the ropes we found, and left their bones to crumble in our fingers. As far as time is concerned it might all have been yesterday. We're here to-day. Maybe we're higher in the scale of human beings—in intelligence. But who knows? We can't be any higher in the things for which life is lived at all."

"What are they?"

"Why—I suppose relationship, friendship—love."

"Love!"

"Yes. Love of man for woman—love of woman for man. That's the nature, the meaning, the best of life itself."

She said no more. Wistfulness of glance deepened into sadness.

"Come, let us go," said Venters.

Action brightened her. Beside him, holding his hand, she slipped down the shelf, ran down the long, steep slant of sliding stones, out of the cloud of dust, and likewise out of the pale gloom.

"We beat the slide," she cried.

The miniature avalanche cracked and roared, and rattled itself into an inert mass at the base of the incline. Yellow dust like the gloom of the cave, but not so changeless, drifted away on the wind; the roar clapped in echo from the cliff, returned, went back, and came again to die in the hollowness. Down on the sunny terrace there was a different atmosphere. Ring and Whitie leaped around Bess. Once more she was smiling, gay, and thoughtless, with the dream-mood in the shadow of her eyes.

"Bess, I haven't seen that since last summer. Look!" said Venters, pointing to the scalloped edge of rolling purple clouds that peeped over the western wall. "We're in for a storm."

"Oh, I hope not. I'm afraid of storms."

"Are you? Why?"

"Have you ever been down in one of these walled-up pockets in a bad storm?"

"No, now I think of it, I haven't."

"Well, it's terrible. Every summer I get scared to death and hide somewhere in the dark. Storms up on the sage are bad, but nothing to what they are down here in the cañons. And in this little valley—why, echoes can rap back and forth so quick they'll split our ears."

"We're perfectly safe here, Bess."

"I know. But that hasn't anything to do with it. The truth is I'm afraid of lightning and thunder, and thunder-claps hurt my head. If we have a bad storm, will you stay close to me?"

"Yes."

When they got back to camp the afternoon was closing, and it was exceedingly sultry. Not a breath of air stirred the aspen leaves, and when these did not quiver the air was indeed still. The dark-purple clouds moved almost imperceptibly out of the west.

"What have we for supper?" asked Bess.

"Rabbit."

"Bern, can't you think of another new way to cook rabbit?" went on Bess, with earnestness.

"What do you think I am—a magician?" retorted Venters.

"I wouldn't dare tell you. But, Bern, do you want me to turn into a rabbit?"

There was a dark-blue, merry flashing of eyes and a parting of lips; then she laughed. In that moment she was naïve and wholesome.

"Rabbit seems to agree with you," replied Venters. "You are well and strong— and growing very pretty."

Anything in the nature of compliment he had never before said to her, and just now he responded to a sudden curiosity to see its effect. Bess stared as if she had not heard aright, slowly blushed, and completely lost her poise in happy confusion.

"I'd better go right away," he continued, "and fetch supplies from Cottonwoods."

A startlingly swift change in the nature of her agitation made him reproach himself for his abruptness.

"No, no, don't go!" she said. "I didn't mean—that about the rabbit. I—I was only trying to be—funny. Don't leave me all alone!"

"Bess, I must go sometime."

"Wait then. Wait till after the storms."

The purple cloud-bank darkened the lower edge of the setting sun, crept up and up, obscuring its fiery red heart, and finally passed over the last ruddy crescent of its upper rim.

The intense dead silence awakened to a long, low, rumbling roll of thunder.

"Oh!" cried Bess, nervously.

"We've had big black clouds before this without rain," said Venters. "But there's no doubt about that thunder. The storms are coming. I'm glad. Every rider on the sage will hear that thunder with glad ears."

Venters and Bess finished their simple meal and the few tasks around the camp, then faced the open terrace, the valley, and the west, to watch and await the approaching storm.

It required keen vision to see any movement whatever in the purple clouds. By infinitesimal degrees the dark cloud-line merged upward into the golden-red haze of the afterglow of sunset. A shadow lengthened from under the western wall across the valley. As straight and rigid as steel rose the delicate spear-pointed silver spruces; the aspen leaves, by nature pendant and quivering, hung limp and heavy; no slender blade of grass moved. A gentle splashing of water came from the ravine. Then again from out of the west sounded the low, dull, and rumbling roll of thunder.

A wave, a ripple of light, a trembling and turning of the aspen leaves, like the approach of a breeze on the water, crossed the valley from the west; and the lull and the deadly stillness and the sultry air passed away on a cool wind.

The night bird of the cañon, with clear and melancholy notes, announced the twilight. And from all along the cliffs rose the faint murmur and moan and mourn of the wind singing in the caves. The bank of clouds now swept hugely out of the western sky. Its front was purple and black, with gray between, a bulging, mushrooming, vast thing instinct with storm. It had a dark, angry, threatening aspect. As if all the power of the winds were pushing and piling behind, it rolled ponderously across the sky. A red flare burned out instantaneously, flashed from the west to east, and died. Then from the deepest black of the purple cloud burst a boom. It was like the bowling of a huge boulder along the crags and ramparts, and seemed to roll on and fall into the valley to bound and bang and boom from cliff to cliff.

"Oh!" cried Bess, with her hands over her ears. "What did I tell you?"

"Why, Bess, be reasonable!" said Venters.

"I'm a coward."

"Not quite that, I hope. It's strange you're afraid. I love a storm."

"I tell you a storm down in these cañons is an awful thing. I know Oldring hated storms. His men were afraid of them. There was one who went deaf in a bad storm, and never could hear again."

"Maybe I've lots to learn, Bess. I'll lose my guess if this storm isn't bad enough. We're going to have heavy wind first, then lightning and thunder, then the rain. Let's stay out as long as we can."

The tips of the cottonwoods and the oaks waved to the east, and the rings of aspens along the terraces twinkled their myriad of bright faces in fleet and glancing gleam. A low roar rose from the leaves of the forest, and the spruces swished in the rising wind. It came in gusts, with light breezes between. As it increased in strength the lulls shortened in length till there was a strong and steady blow all the time, and violent puffs at intervals, and sudden whirling currents. The clouds spread over the valley, rolling swiftly and low, and twilight faded into a sweeping darkness. Then the singing of the wind in the caves drowned the swift roar of rustling leaves; then the song swelled to a mourning, moaning wail; then with the gathering power of the wind the wail changed to a shriek. Steadily the wind strengthened and constantly the strange sound changed.

The last bit of blue sky yielded to the onsweep of clouds. Like angry surf the pale gleams of gray, amid the purple of that scudding front, swept beyond the eastern rampart of the valley. The purple deepened to black. Broad sheets of lightning flared over the western wall. There were not yet any ropes or zigzag streaks darting down through the gathering darkness. The storm center was still beyond Surprise Valley.

"Listen! . . . Listen!" cried Bess, with her lips close to Venters's ear. "You'll hear Oldring's knell!"

"What's that?"

"Oldring's knell. When the wind blows a gale in the caves it makes what the rustlers call Oldring's knell. They believe it bodes his death. I think he believes so, too. It's not like any sound on earth. . . . It's beginning. Listen!"

The gale swooped down with a hollow unearthly howl. It yelled and pealed and shrilled and shrieked. It was made up of a thousand piercing cries. It was a rising and a moving sound. Beginning at the western break of the valley, it rushed along each gigantic cliff, whistling into the caves and cracks, to mount in power, to bellow a blast through the great stone bridge. Gone, as into an engulfing roar of surging waters, it seemed to shoot back and begin all over again.

It was only wind, thought Venters. Here sped and shrieked the sculptor that carved out the wonderful caves in the cliffs. It was only a gale, but as Venters listened, as his ears became accustomed to the fury and strife, out of it all or through it or above it pealed low and perfectly clear and persistently uniform a strange sound that had no counterpart in all the sounds of the elements. It was not of earth or of life. It was the grief and agony of the gale. A knell of all upon which it blew!

Black night enfolded the valley. Venters could not see his companion, and knew of her presence only through the tightening hold of her hand on his arm. He felt the dogs huddle closer to him. Suddenly the dense, black vault overhead split asunder to a blue-white, dazzling streak of lightning. The whole valley lay vividly clear and luminously bright in his sight. Upreared, vast and magnificent, the stone bridge glimmered like some grand god of storm in the lightning's fire.

Then all flashed black again—blacker than pitch—a thick, impenetrable coal-blackness. And there came a ripping, crashing report. Instantly an echo resounded with clapping crash. The initial report was nothing to the echo. It was a terrible, living, reverberating, detonating crash. The wall threw the sound across, and could have made no greater roar if it had slipped in avalanche. From cliff to cliff the echo went in crashing retort and banged in lessening power, and boomed in thinner volume, and clapped weaker and weaker till a final clap could not reach across the waiting cliff.

In the pitchy darkness Venters led Bess, and, groping his way, by feel of hand found the entrance to her cave and lifted her up. On the instant a blinding flash of lightning illumined the cave and all about him. He saw Bess's face white now, with dark, frightened eyes. He saw the dogs leap up, and he followed suit. The golden glare vanished; all was black; then came the splitting crack and the infernal din of echoes.

Bess shrank closer to him and closer, found his hands, and pressed them tightly over her ears, and dropped her face upon his shoulder, and hid her eyes.

Then the storm burst with a succession of ropes and streaks and shafts of lightning, playing continuously, filling the valley with a broken radiance; and the cracking shots followed each other swiftly till the echoes blended in one fearful, deafening crash.

Venters looked out upon the beautiful valley—beautiful now as never before—mystic in its transparent, luminous gloom, weird in the quivering, golden haze of lightning. The dark spruces were tipped with glimmering lights; the aspens bent low in the winds, as waves in a tempest at sea; the forest of oaks tossed wildly and shone with gleams of fire. Across the valley the huge cavern of the cliff-dwellers yawned in the glare, every little black window as clear as at noonday; but the night and the storm added to their tragedy. Flung arching to the black clouds, the great stone bridge seemed to bear the brunt of the storm. It caught the full fury of the rushing wind. It lifted its noble crown to meet the lightnings. Venters thought of the eagles and their lofty nest in a niche under the arch. A driving pall of rain, black as the clouds, came sweeping on to obscure the bridge and the gleaming walls and the shining valley. The lightning played incessantly, streaking down through opaque darkness of rain. The roar of the wind, with its strange knell and the recrashing echoes, mingled with the roar of the flooding rain, and all seemingly were deadened and drowned in a world of sound.

In the dimming pale light Venters looked down upon the girl. She had sunk into his arms, upon his breast, burying her face. She clung to him. He felt the softness of her, and the warmth, and the quick heave of her breast. He saw the dark, slender, graceful outline of her form. A woman lay in his arms! And he held her closer. He who had been alone in the sad, silent watches of the night was not now and never must be again alone. He who had yearned for the touch of a hand felt the long tremble and the heart-beat of a woman. By what strange chance had she come to love him! By what change—by what marvel had she grown into a treasure!

No more did he listen to the rush and roar of the thunder-storm. For with the touch of clinging hands and the throbbing bosom he grew conscious of an inward storm—the tingling of new chords of thought, strange music of unheard, joyous bells, sad dreams dawning to wakeful delight, dissolving doubt, resurging hope, force, fire, and freedom, unutterable sweetness of desire. A storm in his breast—a storm of real love.

CHAPTER FOURTEEN

West Wind

WHEN the storm abated Venters sought his own cave, and late in the night, as his blood cooled and the stir and throb and thrill subsided, he fell asleep.

With the breaking of dawn his eyes unclosed. The valley lay drenched and bathed, a burnished oval of glittering green. The rain-washed walls glistened in the morning light. Waterfalls of many forms poured over the rims. One, a broad, lacy sheet, thin as smoke, slid over the western notch and struck a ledge in its downward fall, to bound into broader leap, to burst far below into white and gold and rosy mist.

Venters prepared for the day, knowing himself a different man.

"It's a glorious morning," said Bess, in greeting.

"Yes. After the storm the west wind," he replied.

"Last night was I—very much of a baby?" she asked, watching him.

"Pretty much."

"Oh, I couldn't help it!"

"I'm glad you were afraid."

"Why?" she asked, in slow surprise.

"I'll tell you some day," he answered, soberly. Then around the camp-fire and through the morning meal he was silent; afterward he strolled thoughtfully off alone along the terrace. He climbed a great yellow rock raising its crest among the spruces, and there he sat down to face the valley and the west.

"I love her!"

Aloud he spoke—unburdened his heart—confessed his secret. For an instant the golden valley swam before his eyes, and the walls waved, and all about him whirled with tumult within.

"I love her! . . . I understand now."

Reviving memory of Jane Withersteen and thought of the complications of the present amazed him with proof of how far he had drifted from his old life. He discovered that he hated to take up the broken threads, to delve into dark problems and difficulties. In this beautiful valley he had been living a beautiful dream. Tranquillity had come to him, and the joy of solitude, and interest in all the wild creatures and crannies of this incomparable valley—and love. Under the shadow of the great stone bridge God had revealed Himself to Venters.

"The world seems very far away," he muttered, "but it's there—and I'm not yet done with it. Perhaps I never shall be. . . . Only—how glorious it would be to live here always and never think again!"

Whereupon the resurging reality of the present, as if in irony of his wish, steeped him instantly in contending thought. Out of it all he presently evolved these things: he must go to Cottonwoods; he must bring supplies back to Surprise Valley; he must cultivate the soil and raise corn and stock, and, most imperative of all, he must decide the future of the girl who loved him and whom he loved. The first of these things required tremendous effort, the last one, concerning Bess, seemed simply and naturally easy of accomplishment. He would marry her. Suddenly, as from roots of poisonous fire, flamed up the forgotten truth concerning her. It seemed to wither and shrivel up all his joy on its hot, tearing way to his heart. She had been Oldring's Masked Rider. To Venters's question, "What were you to Oldring?" she had answered with scarlet shame and drooping head.

"What do I care who she is or what she was!" he cried, passionately. And he knew it was not his old self speaking. It was this softer, gentler man who had awakened to new thoughts in the quiet valley. Tenderness, masterful in him now, matched the absence of joy and blunted the knife-edge of entering jealousy. Strong and passionate effort of will, surprising to him, held back the poison from piercing his soul.

"Wait! . . . Wait!" he cried, as if calling. His hand pressed his breast, and he might have called to the pang there. "Wait! It's all so strange—so wonderful. Anything can happen. Who am I to judge her? I'll glory in my love for her. But I can't tell it—can't give up to it."

Certainly he could not then decide her future. Marrying her was impossible in Surprise Valley and in any village south of Sterling. Even without the mask she had once worn she would easily have been recognized as Oldring's Rider. No man who had ever seen her would forget her, regardless of his ignorance as to her sex. Then more poignant than all other argument was the fact that he did not want to take her away from Surprise Valley. He resisted all thought of that. He had brought her to the most beautiful and wildest place of the uplands; he had saved her, nursed her back to strength, watched her bloom as one of the valley lilies; he knew her life there to be pure and sweet—she belonged to him, and he loved her. Still these were not all the reasons why he did not want to take her away. Where could they go? He feared the rustlers—he feared the riders—he feared the Mormons. And if he should ever succeed in getting Bess safely away from these immediate perils, he feared the sharp eyes of women and their tongues, the big outside world with its problems of existence. He must wait to decide her future, which, after all, was deciding his own. But between her future and his something hung impending. Like Balancing Rock, which waited darkly over the steep gorge, ready to close forever the outlet to Deception Pass, that nameless thing, as certain yet intangible as fate, must fall and close forever all doubts and fears of the future.

"I've dreamed," muttered Venters, as he rose. "Well, why not? . . . To dream is happiness! But let me just once see this clearly, wholly; then I can go on dreaming till the thing falls. I've got to tell Jane Withersteen. I've dangerous trips to take. I've work here to make comfort for this girl. She's mine. I'll fight to keep her safe from that old life. I've already seen her forget it. I love her. And if a beast ever rises in me I'll burn my hand off before I lay it on her with shameful intent. And, by God! sooner or later I'll kill the man who hid her and kept her in Deception Pass!"

As he spoke the west wind softly blew in his face. It seemed to soothe his passion. That west wind was fresh, cool, fragrant, and it carried a sweet, strange burden of far-off things—tidings of life in other climes, of sunshine asleep on other walls—of other places where reigned peace. It carried, too, sad truth of human hearts and mystery—of promise and hope unquenchable. Surprise Valley was only a little niche in the wide world whence blew that burdened wind. Bess was only one of millions at the mercy of unknown motive in nature and life. Content had come to Venters in the valley; happiness had breathed in the slow, warm air; love as bright as light had hovered over the walls and descended to him; and now on the west wind came a whisper of the eternal triumph of faith over doubt.

"How much better I am for what has come to me!" he exclaimed. "I'll let the future take care of itself. Whatever falls, I'll be ready."

Venters retraced his steps along the terrace back to camp, and found Bess in the old familiar seat, waiting and watching for his return.

"I went off by myself to think a little," he explained.

"You never looked that way before. What—what is it? Won't you tell me?"

"Well, Bess, the fact is I've been dreaming a lot. This valley makes a fellow dream. So I forced myself to think. We can't live this way much longer. Soon I'll simply have to go to Cottonwoods. We need a whole pack train of supplies. I can get—"

"Can you go safely?" she interrupted.

"Why, I'm sure of it. I'll ride through the Pass at night. I haven't any fear that Wrangle isn't where I left him. And once on him—Bess, just wait till you see that horse!"

"Oh, I want to see him—to ride him. But—but, Bern, this is what troubles me," she said. "Will—will you come back?"

"Give me four days. If I'm not back in four days you'll know I'm dead. For that only shall keep me."

"Oh!"

"Bess, I'll come back. There's danger—I wouldn't lie to you—but I can take care of myself."

"Bern, I'm sure—oh, I'm sure of it! All my life I've watched hunted men. I can tell what's in them. And I believe you can ride and shoot and see with any rider of the sage. It's not—not that I—fear."

"Well, what is it, then?"

"Why—why—why should you come back at all?"

"I couldn't leave you here alone."

"You might change your mind when you get to the village—among old friends—"

"I won't change my mind. As for old friends—" He uttered a short, expressive laugh.

"Then—there—there must be a—a woman!" Dark red mantled the clear tan of temple and cheek and neck. Her eyes were eyes of shame, upheld a long moment by intense, straining search for the verification of her fear. Suddenly they drooped, her head fell to her knees, her hands flew to her hot cheeks.

"Bess—look here," said Venters, with a sharpness due to the violence with which he checked his quick, surging emotion.

As if compelled against her will—answering to an irresistible voice—Bess raised her head, looked at him with sad, dark eyes, and tried to whisper with tremulous lips.

"There's no woman," went on Venters, deliberately holding her glance with his. "Nothing on earth, barring the chances of life, can keep me away."

Her face flashed and flushed with the glow of a leaping joy; but like the vanishing of a gleam it disappeared to leave her as he had never beheld her.

"I am nothing—I am lost—I am nameless!"

"Do you *want* me to come back?" he asked, with sudden stern coldness. "Maybe *you* want to go back to Oldring!"

That brought her erect, trembling and ashy pale, with dark, proud eyes and mute lips refuting his insinuation.

"Bess, I beg your pardon. I shouldn't have said that. But you angered me. I intend to work—to make a home for you here—to be a—a brother to you as long as ever you need me. And you must forget what you are—were—I mean, and be happy. When you remember that old life you are bitter, and it hurts me."

"I was happy—I shall be very happy. Oh, you're so good that—that it kills me! If I think, I can't believe it. I grow sick with wondering *why*. I'm only a *let me say it*—only a lost, nameless—girl of the rustlers. *Oldring's Girl*, they called me. That you should save me—be so good and kind—want to make me happy— why, it's beyond belief. No wonder I'm wretched at the thought of your leaving me. But I'll be wretched and bitter no more. I promise you. If only I could repay you even a little—"

"You've repaid me a hundredfold. Will you believe me?"

"Believe you! I couldn't do else."

"Then listen! . . . Saving you, I saved myself. Living here in this valley with you, I've found myself. I've learned to think while I was dreaming. I never troubled myself about God. But God, or some wonderful spirit, has whispered to me here. I absolutely deny the truth of what you say about yourself. I can't explain it. There are things too deep to tell. Whatever the terrible wrongs you've suffered, God holds you blameless. I see that—feel that in you every moment you are near me. I've a mother and a sister 'way back in Illinois. If I could I'd take you to them—to-morrow."

"*If it were true!* Oh, I might—I might lift my head!" she cried.

"Lift it then—you child. For I swear it's true."

She did lift her head with the singular wild grace always a part of her actions, with that old unconscious intimation of innocence which always tortured Venters, but now with something more—a spirit rising from the depths that linked itself to his brave words.

"I've been thinking—too," she cried, with quivering smile and swelling breast. "I've discovered myself—too. I'm young—I'm alive—I'm so full—oh! I'm a woman!"

"Bess, I believe I can claim credit of that last discovery—before you," Venters said, and laughed.

"Oh, there's more—there's something I must tell you."

"Tell it, then."

"When will you go to Cottonwoods?"

"As soon as the storms are past, or the worst of them."

"I'll tell you before you go. I can't now. I don't know how I shall then. But it must be told. I'd never let you leave me without knowing. For in spite of what you say there's a chance you mightn't come back."

Day after day the west wind blew across the valley. Day after day the clouds clustered gray and purple and black. The cliffs sang and the caves rang with Oldring's knell, and the lightning flashed, the thunder rolled, the echoes crashed and crashed, and the rains flooded the valley. Wild flowers sprang up everywhere, swaying with the lengthening grass on the terraces, smiling wanly from shady nooks, peeping wondrously from year-dry crevices of the walls. The valley bloomed into a paradise. Every single moment, from the breaking of the gold bar through the bridge at dawn on to the reddening of rays over the western wall, was one of colorful change. The valley swam in thick, transparent haze, golden at dawn, warm and white at noon, purple in the twilight. At the end of every storm a rainbow curved down into the leaf-bright forest to shine and fade and leave lingeringly some faint essence of its rosy iris in the air.

Venters walked with Bess, once more in a dream, and watched the lights change on the walls, and faced the wind from out of the west.

Always it brought softly to him strange, sweet tidings of far-off things. It blew from a place that was old and whispered of youth. It blew down the grooves of time. It brought a story of the passing hours. It breathed low of fighting men and praying women. It sang clearly the song of love. That ever was the burden of its tidings—youth in the shady woods, waders through the wet meadows, boy and girl at the hedgerow stile, bathers in the booming surf, sweet, idle hours on grassy, windy hills, long strolls down moonlit lanes—everywhere in far-off lands, fingers locked and bursting hearts and longing lips—from all the world tidings of unquenchable love.

Often, in these hours of dreams he watched the girl, and asked himself of what was she dreaming? For the changing light of the valley reflected its gleam and its color and its meaning in the changing light of her eyes. He saw in them infinitely more than he saw in his dreams. He saw thought and soul and nature—strong vision of life. All tidings the west wind blew from distance and age he found deep in those dark-blue depths, and found them mysteries solved. Under their wistful shadow he softened, and in the softening felt himself grow a sadder, a wiser, and a better man.

While the west wind blew its tidings, filling his heart full, teaching him a man's part, the days passed, the purple clouds changed to white, and the storms were over for that summer.

"I must go now," he said.

"When?" she asked.

"At once—to-night."

"I'm glad the time has come. It dragged at me. Go—for you'll come back the sooner."

Late in the afternoon, as the ruddy sun split its last flame in the ragged notch of the western wall, Bess walked with Venters along the eastern terrace, up the long, weathered slope, under the great stone bridge. They entered the narrow gorge to climb around the fence long before built there by Venters. Farther than this she had never been. Twilight had already fallen in the gorge. It brightened to waning shadow in the wider ascent. He showed her Balancing Rock, of which he had often told her, and explained its sinister leaning over the outlet. Shuddering, she looked down the long, pale incline with its closed-in, toppling walls.

"What an awful trail! Did you carry me up here?"

"I did, surely," replied he.

"It frightens me, somehow. Yet I never was afraid of trails. I'd ride anywhere a horse could go, and climb where he couldn't. But there's something fearful here. I feel as—as if the place was watching me."

"Look at this rock. It's balanced here—balanced perfectly. You know I told you the cliff-dwellers cut the rock, and why. But they're gone and the rock waits. Can't you see—feel how it waits here? I moved it once, and I'll never dare again. A strong heave would start it. Then it would fall and bang, and smash that crag, and jar the walls, and close forever the outlet to Deception Pass!"

"Ah! When you come back I'll steal up here and push and push with all my might to roll the rock and close forever the outlet to the Pass!" She said it lightly, but in the undercurrent of her voice was a heavier note, a ring deeper than any ever given mere play of words.

"Bess! . . . You can't dare me! Wait till I come back with supplies—then roll the stone."

"I—was—in—fun." Her voice now throbbed low. "Always you must be free to go when you will. Go now . . . this place presses on me—stifles me."

"I'm going—but you had something to tell me?"

"Yes. . . . Will you—come back?"

"I'll come if I live."

154

"But—but you mightn't come?"

"That's possible, of course. It'll take a good deal to kill me. A man couldn't have a faster horse or keener dog. And, Bess, I've guns, and I'll use them if I'm pushed. But don't worry."

"I've faith in you. I'll not worry until after four days. Only—because you mightn't come—I *must* tell you—"

She lost her voice. Her pale face, her great, glowing, earnest eyes, seemed to stand alone out of the gloom of the gorge. The dog whined, breaking the silence.

"I *must* tell you—because you mightn't come back," she whispered. "You *must* know what—what I think of your goodness—of you. Always I've been tongue-tied. I seemed not to be grateful. It was deep in my heart. Even now—if I were other than I am—I couldn't tell you. But I'm nothing—only a rustler's girl—nameless—infamous. You've saved me—and I'm—I'm yours to do with as you like. . . . With all my heart and soul—I love you!"

CHAPTER FIFTEEN

Shadows on the Sage-Slope

In the cloudy, threatening, waning summer days shadows lengthened down the sage-slope, and Jane Withersteen likened them to the shadows gathering and closing in around her life.

Mrs. Larkin died, and little Fay was left an orphan with no known relative. Jane's love redoubled. It was the saving brightness of a darkening hour. Fay turned now to Jane in childish worship. And Jane at last found full expression for the mother-longing in her heart. Upon Lassiter, too, Mrs. Larkin's death had some subtle reaction. Before, he had often, without explanation, advised Jane to send Fay back to any Gentile family that would take her in. Passionately and reproachfully and wonderingly Jane had refused even to entertain such an idea. And now Lassiter never advised it again, grew sadder and quieter in his contemplation of the child, and infinitely more gentle and loving. Sometimes Jane had a cold, inexplicable sensation of dread when she saw Lassiter watching Fay. What did the rider see in the future? Why did he, day by day, grow more silent, calmer, cooler, yet sadder in prophetic assurance of something to be?

No doubt, Jane thought, the rider, in his almost superhuman power of foresight, saw behind the horizon the dark, lengthening shadows that were soon to crowd and gloom over him and her and little Fay. Jane Withersteen awaited the long-deferred breaking of the storm with a courage and embittered calm that had come to her in her extremity. Hope had not died. Doubt and fear, subservient to her will, no longer gave her sleepless nights and tortured days. Love remained. All that she had loved she now loved the more. She seemed to feel that she was defiantly flinging the wealth of her love in the face of misfortune and of hate. No day passed but she prayed for all—and most fervently for her enemies. It troubled her that she had lost, or had never gained, the whole control of her mind. In some measure reason and wisdom and decision were locked in a chamber of her brain, awaiting a key. Power to think of some things was taken from her. Meanwhile, abiding a day of judgment, she fought ceaselessly to deny the bitter drops in her cup, to tear back the slow, the intangibly slow growth of a hot, corrosive lichen eating into her heart.

On the morning of August 10th, Jane, while waiting in the court for Lassiter, heard a clear, ringing report of a rifle. It came from the grove, somewhere toward the corrals. Jane glanced out in alarm. The day was dull, windless, soundless. The leaves of the cottonwoods drooped, as if they had foretold the doom of Withersteen House and were now ready to die and drop and decay. Never had Jane seen such shade. She pondered on the meaning of the report. Revolver shots had of late cracked from different parts of the grove—spies taking snap-shots at Lassiter from a cowardly distance! But a rifle report meant more. Riders seldom used rifles. Judkins and Venters were the exceptions she called to mind. Had the men who hounded her hidden in her grove, taken to the rifle to rid her of Lassiter, her last friend? It was probable—it was likely. And she did not share his cool assumption that his death would never come at the hands of a Mormon. Long had she expected it. His constancy to her, his singular reluctance to use the fatal skill for which he was famed—both now plain to all Mormons—laid him open to inevitable assassination. Yet what charm against ambush and aim and enemy he seemed to bear about him! No, Jane reflected, it was not charm; only a wonderful training of eye and ear, and sense of impending peril. Nevertheless that could not forever avail against secret attack.

That moment a rustling of leaves attracted her attention; then the familiar clinking accompaniment of a slow, soft, measured step, and Lassiter walked into the court.

"Jane, there's a fellow out there with a long gun," he said, and, removing his sombrero, showed his head bound in a bloody scarf.

"I heard the shot; I knew it was meant for you. Let me see—you can't be badly injured?"

"I reckon not. But mebbe it wasn't a close call! . . . I'll sit here in this corner where nobody can see me from the grove." He untied the scarf and removed it to show a long, bleeding furrow above his left temple.

"It's only a cut," said Jane. "But how it bleeds! Hold your scarf over it just a moment till I come back."

She ran into the house and returned with bandages; and while she bathed and dressed the wound Lassiter talked.

"That fellow had a good chance to get me. But he must have flinched when he pulled the trigger. As I dodged down I saw him run through the trees. He had a rifle. I've been expectin' that kind of gun play. I reckon now I'll have to keep

157

a little closer hid myself. These fellers all seem to get chilly or shaky when they draw a bead on me, but one of them might jest happen to hit me."

"Won't you go away—leave Cottonwoods as I've begged you to—before some one does happen to hit you?" she appealed to him.

"I reckon I'll stay."

"But, oh, Lassiter—your blood will be on my hands!"

"See here, lady, look at your hands now, right now. Aren't they fine, firm, white hands? Aren't they bloody now? Lassiter's blood! That's a queer thing to stain your beautiful hands. But if you could only see deeper you'd find a redder color of blood. Heart color, Jane!"

"Oh! . . . My friend!"

"No, Jane, I'm not one to quit when the game grows hot, no more than you. This game, though, is new to me, an' I don't know the moves yet, else I wouldn't have stepped in front of that bullet."

"Have you no desire to hunt the man who fired at you—to find him—and—and kill him?"

"Well, I reckon I haven't any great hankerin' for that."

"Oh, the wonder of it! . . . I knew—I prayed—I trusted. Lassiter, I almost gave—all myself to soften you to Mormons. Thank God, and thank you, my friend. . . . But, selfish woman that I am, this is no great test. What's the life of one of those sneaking cowards to such a man as you? I think of your great hate toward him who—I think of your life's implacable purpose. Can it be—"

"Wait! . . . Listen!" he whispered. "I hear a hoss."

He rose noiselessly, with his ear to the breeze. Suddenly he pulled his sombrero down over his bandaged head and, swinging his gun-sheaths round in front, he stepped into the alcove.

"It's a hoss—comin' fast," he added.

Jane's listening ear soon caught a faint, rapid, rhythmic beat of hoofs. It came from the sage. It gave her a thrill that she was at a loss to understand. The sound rose stronger, louder. Then came a clear, sharp difference when the horse passed from the sage trail to the hard-packed ground of the grove. It became a ringing run—swift in its bell-like clatterings, yet singular in longer pause than usual between the hoofbeats of a horse.

"It's Wrangle! . . . It's Wrangle!" cried Jane Withersteen. "I'd know him from a million horses!"

Excitement and thrilling expectancy flooded out all Jane Withersteen's calm. A tight band closed round her breast as she saw the giant sorrel flit in reddish-brown flashes across the openings in the green. Then he was pounding down the lane—thundering into the court—crashing his great iron-shod hoofs on the stone flags. Wrangle it was surely, but shaggy and wild-eyed, and sage-streaked, with dust-caked lather staining his flanks. He reared and crashed down and plunged. The rider leaped off, threw the bridle, and held hard on a lasso looped round Wrangle's head and neck. Jane's heart sank as she tried to recognize Venters in the rider. Something familiar struck her in the lofty stature, in the sweep of powerful shoulders. But this bearded, longhaired, unkempt man, who wore ragged clothes patched with pieces of skin, and boots that showed bare legs and feet—this dusty, dark, and wild rider could not possibly be Venters.

"Whoa, Wrangle, old boy! Come down. Easy now. So—so—so. You're home, old boy, and presently you can have a drink of water you'll remember."

In the voice Jane knew the rider to be Venters. He tied Wrangle to the hitching-rack and turned to the court.

"Oh, Bern! . . . You wild man!" she exclaimed.

"Jane—Jane, it's good to see you! Hello, Lassiter! Yes, it's Venters."

Like rough iron his hard hand crushed Jane's. In it she felt the difference she saw in him. Wild, rugged, unshorn—yet how splendid! He had gone away a boy—he had returned a man. He appeared taller, wider of shoulder, deeper-chested, more powerfully built. But was that only her fancy—he had always been a young giant—was the change one of spirit? He might have been absent for years, proven by fire and steel, grown like Lassiter, strong and cool and sure. His eyes—were they keener, more flashing than before?—met hers with clear, frank, warm regard, in which perplexity was not, nor discontent, nor pain.

"Look at me long as you like," he said, with a laugh. "I'm not much to look at. And, Jane, neither you nor Lassiter, can brag. You're paler than I ever saw you. Lassiter, here, he wears a bloody bandage under his hat. That reminds me. Some one took a flying shot at me down in the sage. It made Wrangle run some. . . . Well, perhaps you've more to tell me than I've got to tell you."

Briefly, in few words, Jane outlined the circumstances of her undoing in the weeks of his absence.

Under his beard and bronze she saw his face whiten in terrible wrath.

"Lassiter—what held you back?"

No time in the long period of fiery moments and sudden shocks had Jane Withersteen ever beheld Lassiter as calm and serene and cool as then.

"Jane had gloom enough without my addin' to it by shootin' up the village," he said.

As strange as Lassiter's coolness was Venters's curious, intent scrutiny of them both, and under it Jane felt a flaming tide wave from bosom to temples.

"Well—you're right," he said, with slow pause. "It surprises me a little, that's all."

Jane sensed then a slight alteration in Venters, and what it was, in her own confusion, she could not tell. It had always been her intention to acquaint him with the deceit she had fallen to in her zeal to move Lassiter. She did not mean to spare herself. Yet now, at the moment, before these riders, it was an impossibility to explain.

Venters was speaking somewhat haltingly, without his former frankness. "I found Oldring's hiding-place and your red herd. I learned—I know—I'm sure there was a deal between Tull and Oldring." He paused and shifted his position and his gaze. He looked as if he wanted to say something that he found beyond him. Sorrow and pity and shame seemed to contend for mastery over him. Then he raised himself and spoke with effort. "Jane, I've cost you too much. You've almost ruined yourself for me. It was wrong, for I'm not worth it. I never deserved such friendship. Well, maybe it's not too late. You must give me up. Mind, I haven't changed. I am just the same as ever. I'll see Tull while I'm here, and tell him to his face."

"Bern, it's too late," said Jane.

"I'll *make* him believe!" cried Venters, violently.

"You ask me to break our friendship?"

"Yes. If you don't, I shall."

"Forever?"

"Forever!"

Jane sighed. Another shadow had lengthened down the sage-slope to cast further darkness upon her. A melancholy sweetness pervaded her resignation. The boy who had left her had returned a man, nobler, stronger, one in whom she divined something unbending as steel. There might come a moment later when she would wonder why she had not fought against his will, but just now she yielded to it. She liked him as well—nay, more, she thought, only her emotions were deadened by the long, menacing wait for the bursting storm.

Once before she had held out her hand to him—when she gave it; now she stretched it tremblingly forth in acceptance of the decree circumstance had laid upon them. Venters bowed over it, kissed it, pressed it hard, and half stifled a sound very like a sob. Certain it was that when he raised his head tears glistened in his eyes.

"Some—women—have a hard lot," he said, huskily. Then he shook his powerful form, and his rags lashed about him. "I'll say a few things to Tull—when I meet him."

"Bern—you'll not draw on Tull? Oh, that must not be! Promise me—"

"I promise you this," he interrupted, in stern passion that thrilled while it terrorized her. "If you say one more word for that plotter I'll kill him as I would a mad coyote!"

Jane clasped her hands. Was this fire-eyed man the one whom she had once made as wax to her touch? Had Venters become Lassiter and Lassiter Venters?

"I'll—say no more," she faltered.

"Jane, Lassiter once called you blind," said Venters. "It must be true. But I won't upbraid you. Only don't rouse the devil in me by praying for Tull! I'll try to keep cool when I meet him. That's all. Now there's one more thing I want to ask of you—the last. I've found a valley down in the Pass. It's a wonderful place. I intend to stay there. It's so hidden I believe no one can find it. There's good water, and browse, and game. I want to raise corn and stock. I need to take in supplies. Will you give them to me?"

"Assuredly. The more you take the better you'll please me—and perhaps the less my—my enemies will get."

"Venters, I reckon you'll have trouble packin' anythin' away," put in Lassiter.

"I'll go at night."

"Mebbe that wouldn't be best. You'd sure be stopped. You'd better go early in the mornin'—say, just after dawn. That's the safest time to move round here."

"Lassiter, I'll be hard to stop," returned Venters, darkly.

"I reckon so."

"Bern," said Jane, "go first to the riders' quarters and get yourself a complete outfit. You're a—a sight. Then help yourself to whatever else you need—burros, packs, grain, dried fruits, and meat. You must take coffee and sugar and flour— all kinds of supplies. Don't forget corn and seeds. I remember how you used to starve. Please—please take all you can pack away from here. I'll make a bundle for you, which you mustn't open till you're in your valley. How I'd like to see it! To judge by you and Wrangle, how wild it must be!"

Jane walked down into the outer court and approached the sorrel. Upstarting, he laid back his ears and eyed her.

"Wrangle—dear old Wrangle," she said, and put a caressing hand on his matted mane. "Oh, he's wild, but he knows me! Bern, can he run as fast as ever?"

"Run? Jane, he's done sixty miles since last night at dark, and I could make him kill Black Star right now in a ten-mile race."

"He never could," protested Jane. "He couldn't even if he was fresh."

"I reckon mebbe the best hoss'll prove himself yet," said Lassiter, "an', Jane, if it ever comes to that race I'd like you to be on Wrangle."

"I'd like that, too," rejoined Venters. "But, Jane, maybe Lassiter's hint is extreme. Bad as your prospects are, you'll surely never come to the running point."

"Who knows!" she replied, with mournful smile.

"No, no, Jane, it can't be so bad as all that. Soon as I see Tull there'll be a change in your fortunes. I'll hurry down to the village. . . . Now don't worry."

Jane retired to the seclusion of her room. Lassiter's subtle forecasting of disaster, Venters's forced optimism, neither remained in mind. Material loss weighed nothing in the balance with other losses she was sustaining. She wondered dully at her sitting there, hands folded listlessly, with a kind of numb deadness to the passing of time and the passing of her riches. She thought of Venters's friendship. She had not lost that, but she had lost him. Lassiter's friendship—that was more than love—it would endure, but soon he, too, would be gone. Little Fay slept dreamlessly upon the bed, her golden curls streaming over the pillow. Jane had the child's worship. Would she lose that, too? And if she did, what then would be left? Conscience thundered at her that there was left her religion. Conscience thundered that she should be grateful on her knees for this baptism of fire; that through misfortune, sacrifice, and suffering her soul might be fused pure gold. But the old, spontaneous, rapturous spirit no more exalted her. She wanted to be a woman—not a martyr. Like the saint of old who mortified his flesh, Jane Withersteen had in her the temper for heroic martyrdom, if by sacrificing herself she could save the souls of others. But here the damnable verdict blistered her that the more she sacrificed herself the blacker grew the souls of her churchmen. There was something terribly wrong with her soul, something terribly wrong with her churchmen and her religion. In the whirling gulf of her thought there was yet one shining light to guide her, to sustain her in her hope; and it was that, despite her errors and her frailties and her blindness, she had one absolute and unfaltering hold on ultimate and supreme justice. That was love. "Love your enemies as yourself!" was a divine word, entirely free from any church or creed.

Jane's meditations were disturbed by Lassiter's soft, tinkling step in the court.

Always he wore the clinking spurs. Always he was in readiness to ride. She passed out and called him into the huge, dim hall.

"I think you'll be safer here. The court is too open," she said.

"I reckon," replied Lassiter. "An' it's cooler here. The day's sure muggy. Well, I went down to the village with Venters."

"Already! Where is he?" queried Jane, in quick amaze.

"He's at the corrals. Blake's helpin' him get the burros an' packs ready. That Blake is a good fellow."

"Did—did Bern meet Tull?"

"I guess he did," answered Lassiter, and he laughed dryly.

"Tell me! Oh, you exasperate me! You're so cool, so calm! For Heaven's sake, tell me what happened!"

"First time I've been in the village for weeks," went on Lassiter, mildly. "I reckon there 'ain't been more of a show for a long time. Me an' Venters walkin' down the road! It was funny. I ain't sayin' anybody was particular glad to see us. I'm not much thought of hereabouts, an' Venters he sure looks like what you called him, a wild man. Well, there was some runnin' of folks before we got to the stores. Then everybody vamoosed except some surprised rustlers in front of a saloon. Venters went right in the stores an' saloons, an' of course I went along. I don't know which tickled me the most—the actions of many fellers we met, or Venters's nerve. Jane, I was downright glad to be along. You see *that* sort of thing is my element, an' I've been away from it for a spell. But we didn't find Tull in one of them places. Some Gentile feller at last told Venters he'd find Tull in that long buildin' next to Parsons's store. It's a kind of meetin'-room; and sure enough, when we peeped in, it was half full of men.

"Venters yelled: 'Don't anybody pull guns! We ain't come for that!' Then he tramped in, an' I was some put to keep alongside him. There was a hard, scrapin' sound of feet, a loud cry, an' then some whisperin', an' after that stillness you could cut with a knife. Tull was there, an' that fat party who once tried to throw a gun on me, an' other important-lookin' men, an' that little frog-legged feller who was with Tull the day I rode in here. I wish you could have seen their faces, 'specially Tull's an' the fat party's. But there ain't no use of me tryin' to tell you how they looked.

"Well, Venters an' I stood there in the middle of the room, with that batch of men all in front of us, an' not a blamed one of them winked an eyelash or moved a finger. It was natural, of course, for me to notice many of them packed guns. That's a way of mine, first noticin' them things. Venters spoke up, an' his voice sort of chilled an' cut, an' he told Tull he had a few things to say."

Here Lassiter paused while he turned his sombrero round and round, in his familiar habit, and his eyes had the look of a man seeing over again some thrilling spectacle, and under his red bronze there was strange animation.

"Like a shot, then, Venters told Tull that the friendship between you an' him was all over, an' he was leaving your place. He said you'd both of you broken off in the hope of propitiatin' your people, but you hadn't changed your mind otherwise, an' never would.

"Next he spoke up for you. I ain't goin' to tell you what he said. Only—no other woman who ever lived ever had such tribute! You had a champion, Jane, an' never fear that those thick-skulled men don't know you now. It couldn't be otherwise. He spoke the ringin', lightnin' truth.... Then he accused Tull of the underhand, miserable robbery of a helpless woman. He told Tull where the red herd was, of a deal made with Oldrin', that Jerry Card had made the deal. I thought Tull was goin' to drop, an' that little frog-legged cuss, he looked some limp an' white. But Venters's voice would have kept anybody's legs from bucklin'. I was stiff myself. He went on an' called Tull—called him every bad name ever known to a rider, an' then some. He cursed Tull. I never hear a man get such a cursin'. He laughed in scorn at the idea of Tull bein' a minister. He said Tull an' a few more dogs of hell builded their empire out of the hearts of such innocent an' God-fearin' women as Jane Withersteen. He called Tull a binder of women, a callous beast who hid behind a mock mantle of righteousness—an' the last an' lowest coward on the face of the earth. To prey on weak women through their religion—that was the last unspeakable crime!

"Then he finished, an' by this time he'd almost lost his voice. But his whisper was enough. 'Tull,' he said, '*she* begged me not to draw on you to-day. *She* would pray for you if you burned her at the stake.... But listen! ... I swear if you and I ever come face to face again, I'll kill you!'

"We backed out of the door then, an' up the road. But nobody follered us."

Jane found herself weeping passionately. She had not been conscious of it till Lassiter ended his story, and she experienced exquisite pain and relief in shedding tears. Long had her eyes been dry, her grief deep; long had her emotions been dumb. Lassiter's story put her on the rack; the appalling nature of Venters's act and speech had no parallel as an outrage; it was worse than bloodshed. Men like Tull had been shot, but had one ever been so terribly denounced in public? Overmounting her horror, an uncontrollable, quivering passion shook her very soul. It was sheer human glory in the deed of a fearless man. It was hot, primitive instinct to live—to fight. It was a kind of mad joy in Venters's chivalry. It was close to the wrath that had first shaken her in the beginning of this war waged upon her.

"Well, well, Jane, don't take it that way," said Lassiter, in evident distress. "I had to tell you. There's some things a feller jest can't keep. It's strange you give up on hearin' that, when all this long time you've been the gamest woman I ever seen. But I don't know women. Mebbe there's reason for you to cry. I know this—nothin' ever rang in my soul an' so filled it as what Venters did. I'd like to have done it, but—I'm only good for throwin' a gun, an' it seems you hate that. . . . Well, I'll be goin' now."

"Where?"

"Venters took Wrangle to the stable. The sorrel's shy a shoe, an' I've got to help hold the big devil an' put on another."

"Tell Bern to come for the pack I want to give him—and—and to say good-by," called Jane, as Lassiter went out.

Jane passed the rest of that day in a vain endeavor to decide what and what not to put in the pack for Venters. This task was the last she would ever perform for him, and the gifts were the last she would ever make him. So she picked and chose and rejected, and chose again, and often paused in sad revery, and began again, till at length she filled the pack.

It was about sunset, and she and Fay had finished supper and were sitting in the court, when Venters's quick steps rang on the stones. She scarcely knew him, for he had changed the tattered garments, and she missed the dark beard and long hair. Still he was not the Venters of old. As he came up the steps she felt herself pointing to the pack, and heard herself speaking words that were meaningless to her. He said good-by; he kissed her, released her, and turned away. His tall figure blurred in her sight, grew dim through dark, streaked vision, and then he vanished.

Twilight fell around Withersteen House, and dusk and night. Little Fay slept; but Jane lay with strained, aching eyes. She heard the wind moaning in the cottonwoods and mice squeaking in the walls. The night was interminably long, yet she prayed to hold back the dawn. What would another day bring forth? The blackness of her room seemed blacker for the sad, entering gray of morning light. She heard the chirp of awakening birds, and fancied she caught a faint clatter of hoofs. Then low, dull, distant, throbbed a heavy gunshot. She had expected it, was waiting for it; nevertheless, an electric shock checked her heart, froze the very living fiber of her bones. That vise-like hold on her faculties apparently did not relax for a long time, and it was a voice under her window that released her.

"Jane! . . . Jane!" softly called Lassiter.

She answered somehow.

"It's all right. Venters got away. I thought mebbe you'd heard that shot, an' I was worried some."

"What was it—who fired?"

"Well—some fool feller tried to stop Venters out there in the sage—an' he only stopped lead! . . . I think it'll be all right. I haven't seen or heard of any other fellers round. Venters'll go through safe. An', Jane, I've got Bells saddled, an' I'm going to trail Venters. Mind, I won't show myself unless he falls foul of somebody an' needs me. I want to see if this place where he's goin' is safe for him. He says nobody can track him there. I never seen the place yet I couldn't track a man to. Now, Jane, you stay indoors while I'm gone, an' keep close watch on Fay. Will you?"

"Yes! Oh yes!"

"An' another thing, Jane," he continued, then paused for long—"another thing—if you ain't here when I come back—if you're *gone*—don't fear, I'll trail you—I'll find you."

"My dear Lassiter, where could I be gone—as you put it?" asked Jane, in curious surprise.

"I reckon you might be somewhere. Mebbe tied in an old barn—or corralled in some gulch—or chained in a cave! *Milly Erne was*—till she give in! Mebbe that's news to you. . . . Well, if you're gone I'll hunt for you."

"No, Lassiter," she replied, sadly and low. "If I'm gone just forget the unhappy woman whose blinded selfish deceit you repaid with kindness and love."

She heard a deep, muttering curse, under his breath, and then the silvery tinkling of his spurs as he moved away.

Jane entered upon the duties of that day with a settled, gloomy calm. Disaster hung in the dark clouds, in the shade, in the humid west wind. Blake, when he reported, appeared without his usual cheer; and Jerd wore a harassed look of a worn and worried man. And when Judkins put in appearance, riding a lame horse, and dismounted with the cramp of a rider, his dust-covered figure and his darkly grim, almost dazed expression told Jane of dire calamity. She had no need of words.

"Miss Withersteen, I have to report—loss of the—white herd," said Judkins, hoarsely.

"Come, sit down; you look played out," replied Jane, solicitously. She brought him brandy and food, and while he partook of refreshments, of which he appeared badly in need, she asked no questions.

"No one rider—could hev done more—Miss Withersteen," he went on, presently.

"Judkins, don't be distressed. You've done more than any other rider. I've long expected to lose the white herd. It's no surprise. It's in line with other things that are happening. I'm grateful for your service."

"Miss Withersteen, I knew how you'd take it. But if anythin', that makes it harder to tell. You see, a feller wants to do so much fer you, an' I'd got fond of my job. We hed the herd a ways off to the north of the break in the valley. There was a big level an' pools of water an' tip-top browse. But the cattle was in a high nervous condition. Wild—as wild as antelope! You see, they'd been so scared they never slept. I ain't a-goin' to tell you of the many tricks that were pulled off out there in the sage. But there wasn't a day for weeks thet the herd didn't get started to run. We allus managed to ride 'em close an' drive 'em back an' keep 'em bunched. Honest, Miss Withersteen, them steers was *thin*. They was *thin* when water and grass was everywhere. *Thin* at this season—thet'll tell you how your steers was pestered. Fer instance, one night a strange runnin' streak of fire run right through the herd. That streak was a coyote—*with an oiled an' blazin' tail!* Fer I shot it an' found out. We had hell with the herd that night, an' if the sage an' grass hadn't been wet—we, hosses, steers, an' all would hev burned up. But I said I wasn't goin' to tell you any of the tricks. . . . Strange now, Miss Withersteen, when the stampede did come it was from natural cause—jest a whirlin' devil of dust. You've seen the like often. An' this wasn't no big whirl, fer the dust was mostly settled. It had dried out in a little swale, an' ordinarily no steer would ever hev run fer it. But the herd was nervous an' wild. An' jest as Lassiter said, when that bunch of white steers got to movin' they was as bad as buffalo. I've seen some buffalo stampedes back in Nebraska, an' this bolt of the steers was the same kind.

"I tried to mill the herd jest as Lassiter did. But I wasn't equal to it, Miss Withersteen. I don't believe the rider lives who could hev turned thet herd. We kept along of the herd fer miles, an' more 'n one of my boys tried to get the steers a-millin'. It wasn't no use. We got off level ground, goin' down, an' then the steers ran somethin' fierce. We left the little gullies an' washes level-full of dead steers. Finally I saw the herd was makin' to pass a kind of low pocket between ridges. There was a hog-back—as we used to call 'em—a pile of rocks stickin' up, and I saw the herd was goin' to split round it, or swing out to the left. An' I wanted 'em to go to the right so mebbe we'd be able to drive 'em into the pocket. So, with all my boys except three, I rode hard to turn the herd a little to the right. We couldn't budge 'em. They went on an' split round the rocks, an' the most of 'em was turned sharp to the left by a deep wash we hedn't seen—hed no chance to see.

"The other three boys—Jimmy Vail, Joe Willis, an' thet little Cairns boy—a nervy kid! they, with Cairns leadin', tried to buck thet herd round to the pocket. It was a wild, fool idee. I couldn't do nothin'. The boys got hemmed in between the steers an' the wash—thet they hedn't no chance to see, either. Vail an' Willis was run down right before our eyes. An' Cairns, who rode a fine hoss, he did some ridin' I never seen equaled, an' would hev beat the steers if there'd been any room to run in. I was high up an' could see how the steers kept spillin' by twos an' threes over into the wash. Cairns put his hoss to a place thet was too wide fer any hoss, an' broke his neck an' the hoss's too. We found that out after, an' as fer Vail an' Willis—two thousand steers ran over the poor boys. There wasn't much left to pack home fer buryin'! . . . An', Miss Withersteen, thet all happened yesterday, an' I believe, if the white herd didn't run over the wall of the Pass, it's runnin' yet."

On the morning of the second day after Judkins's recital, during which time Jane remained indoors a prey to regret and sorrow for the boy riders, and a new and now strangely insistent fear for her own person, she again heard what she had missed more than she dared honestly confess—the soft, jingling step of Lassiter. Almost overwhelming relief surged through her, a feeling as akin to joy as any she could have been capable of in those gloomy hours of shadow, and one that suddenly stunned her with the significance of what Lassiter had come to mean to her. She had begged him, for his own sake, to leave Cottonwoods. She might yet beg that, if her weakening courage permitted her to dare absolute loneliness and helplessness, but she realized now that if she were left alone her life would become one long, hideous nightmare.

When his soft steps clinked into the hall, in answer to her greeting, and his tall, black-garbed form filled the door, she felt an inexpressible sense of immediate safety. In his presence she lost her fear of the dim passageways of Witersteen House and of every sound. Always it had been that, when he entered the court or the hall, she had experienced a distinctly sickening but gradually lessening shock at sight of the huge black guns swinging at his sides. This time the sickening shock again visited her, it was, however, because a revealing flash of thought told her that it was not alone Lassiter who was thrillingly welcome, but also his fatal weapons. They meant so much. How she had fallen—how broken and spiritless must she be—to have still the same old horror of Lassiter's guns and his name, yet feel somehow a cold, shrinking protection in their law and might and use.

"Did you trail Venters—find his wonderful valley?" she asked, eagerly.

"Yes, an' I reckon it's sure a wonderful place."

"Is he safe there?"

"That's been botherin' me some. I tracked him an' part of the trail was the hardest I ever tackled. Mebbe there's a rustler or somebody in this country who's as good at trackin' as I am. If that's so Venters ain't safe."

"Well—tell me all about Bern and his valley."

To Jane's surprise Lassiter showed disinclination for further talk about his trip. He appeared to be extremely fatigued. Jane reflected that one hundred and twenty miles, with probably a great deal of climbing on foot, all in three days, was enough to tire any rider. Moreover, it presently developed that Lassiter had returned in a mood of singular sadness and preoccupation. She put it down to a moodiness over the loss of her white herd and the now precarious condition of her fortune.

Several days passed, and as nothing happened, Jane's spirits began to brighten. Once in her musings she thought that this tendency of hers to rebound was as sad as it was futile. Meanwhile, she had resumed her walks through the grove with little Fay.

One morning she went as far as the sage. She had not seen the slope since the beginning of the rains, and now it bloomed a rich deep purple. There was a high wind blowing, and the sage tossed and waved and colored beautifully from light to dark. Clouds scudded across the sky and their shadows sailed darkly down the sunny slope.

Upon her return toward the house she went by the lane to the stables, and she had scarcely entered the great open space with its corrals and sheds when she saw Lassiter hurriedly approaching. Fay broke from her and, running to a corral fence, began to pat and pull the long, hanging ears of a drowsy burro.

One look at Lassiter armed her for a blow.

Without a word he led her across the wide yard to the rise of the ground upon which the stable stood.

"Jane—look!" he said, and pointed to the ground.

Jane glanced down, and again, and upon steadier vision made out splotches of blood on the stones, and broad, smooth marks in the dust, leading out toward the sage.

"What made these?" she asked.

"I reckon somebody has dragged dead or wounded men out to where there was hosses in the sage."

"Dead—or—wounded—men!"

"I reckon—Jane, are you strong? Can you bear up?"

His hands were gently holding hers, and his eyes—suddenly she could no longer look into them. "Strong?" she echoed, trembling. "I—I will be."

Up on the stone-flag drive, nicked with the marks made by the iron-shod hoofs of her racers, Lassiter led her, his grasp ever growing firmer.

"Where's Blake—and—and Jerb?" she asked, haltingly.

"I don't know where Jerb is. Bolted, most likely," replied Lassiter, as he took her through the stone door. "But Blake—poor Blake! He's gone forever! . . . Be prepared, Jane."

With a cold prickling of her skin, with a queer thrumming in her ears, with fixed and staring eyes, Jane saw a gun lying at her feet with chamber swung and empty, and discharged shells scattered near.

Outstretched upon the stable floor lay Blake, ghastly white—dead—one hand clutching a gun and the other twisted in his bloody blouse.

"Whoever the thieves were, whether your people or rustlers—Blake killed some of them!" said Lassiter.

"Thieves?" whispered Jane.

"I reckon. Hoss-thieves! . . . Look!" Lassiter waved his hand toward the stalls.

The first stall—Bells's stall—was empty. All the stalls were empty. No racer whinnied and stamped greeting to her. Night was gone! Black Star was gone!

CHAPTER SIXTEEN

Gold

A s Lassiter had reported to Jane, Venters "went through" safely, and after a toilsome journey reached the peaceful shelter of Surprise Valley. When finally he lay wearily down under the silver spruces, resting from the strain of dragging packs and burros up the slope and through the entrance to Surprise Valley, he had leisure to think, and a great deal of the time went in regretting that he had not been frank with his loyal friend, Jane Withersteen.

But, he kept continually recalling, when he had stood once more face to face with her and had been shocked at the change in her and had heard the details of her adversity, he had not had the heart to tell her of the closer interest which had entered his life. He had not lied; yet he had kept silence.

Bess was in transports over the stores of supplies and the outfit he had packed from Cottonwoods. He had certainly brought a hundred times more than he had gone for; enough, surely, for years, perhaps to make permanent home in the valley. He saw no reason why he need ever leave there again.

After a day of rest he recovered his strength and shared Bess's pleasure in rummaging over the endless packs, and began to plan for the future. And in this planning, his trip to Cottonwoods, with its revived hate of Tull and consequent unleashing of fierce passions, soon faded out of mind. By slower degrees his friendship for Jane Withersteen and his contrition drifted from the active preoccupation of his present thought to a place in memory, with more and more infrequent recalls.

And as far as the state of his mind was concerned, upon the second day after his return, the valley, with its golden hues and purple shades, the speaking west wind and the cool, silent night, and Bess's watching eyes with their wonderful light, so wrought upon Venters that he might never have left them at all.

That very afternoon he set to work. Only one thing hindered him upon beginning, though it in no wise checked his delight, and that in the multiplicity of tasks planned to make a paradise out of the valley he could not choose the one with which to begin. He had to grow into the habit of passing from one dreamy pleasure to another, like a bee going from flower to flower in the valley, and he found this wandering habit likely to extend to his labors. Nevertheless, he made a start.

At the outset he discovered Bess to be both a considerable help in some ways and a very great hindrance in others. Her excitement and joy were spurs, inspirations; but she was utterly impracticable in her ideas, and she flitted from one plan to another with bewildering vacillation. Moreover, he fancied that she grew more eager, youthful, and sweet; and he marked that it was far easier to watch her and listen to her than it was to work. Therefore he gave her tasks that necessitated her going often to the cave where he had stored his packs.

Upon the last of these trips, when he was some distance down the terrace and out of sight of camp, he heard a scream, and then the sharp barking of the dogs.

For an instant he straightened up, amazed. Danger for her had been absolutely out of his mind. She had seen a rattlesnake—or a wildcat. Still she would not have been likely to scream at sight of either; and the barking of the dogs was ominous. Dropping his work, he dashed back along the terrace. Upon breaking through a clump of aspens he saw the dark form of a man in the camp. Cold, then hot, Venters burst into frenzied speed to reach his guns. He was cursing himself for a thoughtless fool when the man's tall form became familiar and he recognized Lassiter. Then the reversal of emotions changed his run to a walk; he tried to call out, but his voice refused to carry; when he reached camp there was Lassiter staring at the white-faced girl. By that time Ring and Whitie had recognized him.

"Hello, Venters! I'm makin' you a visit," said Lassiter, slowly. "An' I'm some surprised to see you've a—a young feller for company."

One glance had sufficed for the keen rider to read Bess's real sex, and for once his cool calm had deserted him. He stared till the white of Bess's cheeks flared into crimson. That, if it were needed, was the concluding evidence of her femininity; for it went fittingly with her sun-tinted hair and darkened, dilated eyes, the sweetness of her mouth, and the striking symmetry of her slender shape.

"Heavens! Lassiter!" panted Venters, when he caught his breath. "What relief—it's only you! How—in the name of all—that's wonderful—did you ever get here?"

"I trailed you. We—I wanted to know where you was, if you had a safe place. So I trailed you."

"Trailed me," cried Venters, bluntly.

"I reckon. It was some of a job after I got to them smooth rocks. I was all day trackin' you up to them little cut steps in the rock. The rest was easy."

"Where's your hoss? I hope you hid him."

"I tied him in them queer cedars down on the slope. He can't be seen from the valley."

"That's good. Well, well! I'm completely dumfounded. It was my idea that no man could track me in here."

"I reckon. But if there's a tracker in these uplands as good as me he can find you."

"That's bad. That'll worry me. But, Lassiter, now you're here I'm glad to see you. And—and my companion here is not a young fellow! . . . Bess, this is a friend of mine. He saved my life once."

The embarrassment of the moment did not extend to Lassiter. Almost at once his manner, as he shook hands with Bess, relieved Venters and put the girl at ease. After Venters's words and one quick look at Lassiter, her agitation stilled, and, though she was shy, if she were conscious of anything out of the ordinary in the situation, certainly she did not show it.

"I reckon I'll only stay a little while," Lassiter was saying. "An' if you don't mind troublin', I'm hungry. I fetched some biscuits along, but they're gone. Venters, this place is sure the wonderfullest ever seen. Them cut steps on the slope! That outlet into the gorge! An' it's like climbin' up through hell into heaven to climb through that gorge into this valley! There's a queer-lookin' rock at the top of the passage. I didn't have time to stop. I'm wonderin' how you ever found this place. It's sure interestin'."

During the preparation and eating of dinner Lassiter listened mostly, as was his wont, and occasionally he spoke in his quaint and dry way. Venters noted, however, that the rider showed an increasing interest in Bess. He asked her no questions, and only directed his attention to her while she was occupied and had no opportunity to observe his scrutiny. It seemed to Venters that Lassiter grew more and more absorbed in his study of Bess, and that he lost his coolness in some strange, softening sympathy. Then, quite abruptly, he arose and announced the necessity for his early departure. He said good-by to Bess in a voice gentle and somewhat broken, and turned hurriedly away. Venters accompanied him, and they had traversed the terrace, climbed the weathered slope, and passed under the stone bridge before either spoke again.

Then Lassiter put a great hand on Venters's shoulder and wheeled him to meet a smoldering fire of gray eyes.

"Lassiter, I couldn't tell Jane! I couldn't," burst out Venters, reading his friend's mind. "I tried. But I couldn't. She wouldn't understand, and she has troubles enough. And I love the girl!"

"Venters, I reckon this beats me. I've seen some queer things in my time, too. This girl—who is she?"

"I don't know."

"Don't know! What is she, then?"

"I don't know that, either. Oh, it's the strangest story you ever heard. I must tell you. But you'll never believe."

"Venters, women were always puzzles to me. But for all that, if this girl ain't a child, an' as innocent, I'm no fit person to think of virtue an' goodness in anybody. Are you goin' to be square with her?"

"I am—so help me God!"

"I reckoned so. Mebbe my temper oughtn't led me to make sure. But, man, she's a woman in all but years. She's sweeter 'n the sage."

"Lassiter, I know, I know. And the *hell* of it is that in spite of her innocence and charm she's—she's not what she seems!"

"I wouldn't want to—of course, I couldn't call you a liar, Venters," said the older man.

"What's more, she was Oldring's Masked Rider!"

Venters expected to floor his friend with that statement, but he was not in any way prepared for the shock his words gave. For an instant he was astounded to see Lassiter stunned; then his own passionate eagerness to unbosom himself, to tell the wonderful story, precluded any other thought.

"Son, tell me all about this," presently said Lassiter as he seated himself on a stone and wiped his moist brow.

Thereupon Venters began his narrative at the point where he had shot the rustler and Oldring's Masked Rider, and he rushed through it, telling all, not holding back even Bess's unreserved avowal of her love or his deepest emotions.

"That's the story," he said, concluding. "I love her, though I've never told her. If I did tell her I'd be ready to marry her, and that seems impossible in this country. I'd be afraid to risk taking her anywhere. So I intend to do the best I can for her here."

"The longer I live the stranger life is," mused Lassiter, with downcast eyes. "I'm reminded of somethin' you once said to Jane about hands in her game of life. There's that unseen hand of power, an' Tull's black hand, an' my red one, an' your indifferent one, an' the girl's little brown, helpless one. An', Venters, there's another one that's all-wise an' all-wonderful. *That's* the hand guidin' Jane Withersteen's game of life! . . . Your story's one to daze a far clearer head than mine. I can't offer no advice, even if you asked for it. Mebbe I can help you. Anyway, I'll hold Oldrin' up when he comes to the village, an' find out about this girl. I knew the rustler years ago. He'll remember me."

"Lassiter, if I ever meet Oldring I'll kill him!" cried Venters, with sudden intensity.

"I reckon that'd be perfectly natural," replied the rider.

"Make him think Bess is dead—as she is to him and that old life."

"Sure, sure, son. Cool down now. If you're goin' to begin pullin' guns on Tull an' Oldin' you want to be cool. I reckon, though, you'd better keep hid here. Well, I must be leavin'.'"

"One thing, Lassiter. You'll not tell Jane about Bess? Please don't!"

"I reckon not. But I wouldn't be afraid to bet that after she'd got over anger at your secrecy—Venters, she'd be furious once in her life!—she'd think more of you. I don't mind sayin' for myself that I think you're a good deal of a man."

In the further ascent Venters halted several times with the intention of saying good-by, yet he changed his mind and kept on climbing till they reached Balancing Rock. Lassiter examined the huge rock, listened to Venters's idea of its position and suggestion, and curiously placed a strong hand upon it.

"Hold on!" cried Venters. "I heaved at it once and have never gotten over my scare."

"Well, you do seem uncommon nervous," replied Lassiter, much amused. "Now, as for me, why I always had the funniest notion to roll stones! When I was a kid I did it, an' the bigger I got the bigger stones I'd roll. Ain't that funny? Honest—even now I often get off my hoss just to tumble a big stone over a precipice, an' watch it drop, an' listen to it bang an' boom. I've started some slides in my time, an' don't you forget it. I never seen a rock I wanted to roll as bad as this one! Wouldn't there jest be roarin', crashin' hell down that trail?"

"You'd close the outlet forever!" exclaimed Venters. "Well, good-by, Lassiter. Keep my secret and don't forget me. And be mighty careful how you get out of the valley below. The rustlers' cañon isn't more than three miles up the Pass. Now you've tracked me here, I'll never feel safe again."

In his descent to the valley, Venters's emotion, roused to stirring pitch by the recital of his love story, quieted gradually, and in its place came a sober, thoughtful mood. All at once he saw that he was serious, because he would never more regain his sense of security while in the valley. What Lassiter could do another skilful tracker might duplicate. Among the many riders with whom Venters had ridden he recalled no one who could have taken his trail at Cottonwoods and have followed it to the edge of the bare slope in the pass, let alone up that glistening smooth stone. Lassiter, however, was not an ordinary rider. Instead of hunting cattle tracks he had likely spent a goodly portion of his life tracking men. It was not improbable that among Oldring's rustlers there was one who shared Lassiter's gift for trailing. And the more Venters dwelt on this possibility the more perturbed he grew.

Lassiter's visit, moreover, had a disquieting effect upon Bess, and Venters fancied that she entertained the same thought as to future seclusion. The breaking of their solitude, though by a well-meaning friend, had not only dispelled all its dream and much of its charm, but had instilled a canker of fear. Both had seen the footprint in the sand.

Venters did no more work that day. Sunset and twilight gave way to night, and the cañon bird whistled its melancholy notes, and the wind sang softly in the cliffs, and the camp-fire blazed and burned down to red embers. To Venters a subtle difference was apparent in all of these, or else the shadowy change had been in him. He hoped that on the morrow this slight depression would have passed away.

In that measure, however, he was doomed to disappointment. Furthermore, Bess reverted to a wistful sadness that he had not observed in her since her recovery. His attempt to cheer her out of it resulted in dismal failure, and consequently in a darkening of his own mood. Hard work relieved him; still, when the day had passed, his unrest returned. Then he set to deliberate thinking, and there came to him the startling conviction that he must leave Surprise Valley and take Bess with him. As a rider he had taken many chances, and as an adventurer in Deception Pass he had unhesitatingly risked his life; but now he would run no preventable hazard of Bess's safety and happiness, and he was too keen not to see that hazard. It gave him a pang to think of leaving the beautiful valley just when he had the means to establish a permanent and delightful home there. One flashing thought tore in hot temptation through his mind—why not climb up into the gorge, roll Balancing Rock down the trail, and close forever the outlet to Deception Pass? "That was the beast in me—showing his teeth!" muttered Venters, scornfully. "I'll just kill him good and quick! I'll be fair to this girl, if it's the last thing I do on earth!"

Another day went by, in which he worked less and pondered more and all the time covertly watched Bess. Her wistfulness had deepened into downright unhappiness, and that made his task to tell her all the harder. He kept the secret another day, hoping by some chance she might grow less moody, and to his exceeding anxiety she fell into far deeper gloom. Out of his own secret and the torment of it he divined that she, too, had a secret and the keeping of it was torturing her. As yet he had no plan thought out in regard to how or when to leave the valley, but he decided to tell her the necessity of it and to persuade her to go. Furthermore, he hoped his speaking out would induce her to unburden her own mind.

"Bess, what's wrong with you?" he asked.

"Nothing," she answered, with averted face.

Venters took hold of her gently, though masterfully, forced her to meet his eyes.

"You can't look at me and lie," he said. "Now—what's wrong with you? You're keeping something from me. Well, I've got a secret, too, and I intend to tell it presently."

"Oh—I *have* a secret. I was crazy to tell you when you came back. That's why I was so silly about everything. I kept holding my secret back—gloating over it. But when Lassiter came I got an idea—that changed my mind. Then I hated to tell you."

"Are you going to now?"

"Yes—yes. I was coming to it. I tried yesterday, but you were so cold. I was afraid. I couldn't keep it much longer."

"Very well, most mysterious lady, tell your wonderful secret."

"You needn't laugh," she retorted, with a first glimpse of reviving spirit. "I can take the laugh out of you in one second."

"It's a go."

She ran through the spruces to the cave, and returned carrying something which was manifestly heavy. Upon nearer view he saw that whatever she held with such evident importance had been bound up in a black scarf he well remembered. That alone was sufficient to make him tingle with curiosity.

"Have you any idea what I did in your absence?" she asked.

"I imagine you lounged about, waiting and watching for me," he replied, smiling. "I've my share of conceit, you know."

"You're wrong. I worked. Look at my hands." She dropped on her knees close to where he sat, and, carefully depositing the black bundle, she held out her hands. The palms and inside of her fingers were white, puckered, and worn.

"Why, Bess, you've been fooling in the water," he said.

"Fooling? Look here!" With deft fingers she spread open the black scarf, and the bright sun shone upon a dull, glittering heap of gold.

"Gold!" he ejaculated.

"Yes, gold! See, pounds of gold! I found it—washed it out of the stream— picked it out grain by grain, nugget by nugget!"

"Gold!" he cried.

"Yes. Now—now laugh at my secret!"

For a long minute Venters gazed. Then he stretched forth a hand to feel if the gold was real.

"*Gold!*" he almost shouted. "Bess, there are hundreds—thousands of dollars' worth here!"

He leaned over to her, and put his hand, strong and clenching now, on hers.

"Is there more where this came from?" he whispered.

"Plenty of it, all the way up the stream to the cliff. You know I've often washed for gold. Then I've heard the men talk. I think there's no great quantity of gold here, but enough for—for a fortune for *you.*"

"That—was—your—secret!"

"Yes. I hate gold. For it makes men mad. I've seen them drunk with joy and dance and fling themselves around. I've seen them curse and rave. I've seen them fight like dogs and roll in the dust. I've seen them kill each other for gold."

"Is that why you hated to tell me?"

"Not—not altogether." Bess lowered her head. "It was because I knew you'd never stay here long after you found gold."

"You were afraid I'd leave you?"

"Yes."

"Listen! . . . You great, simple child! Listen . . . You sweet, wonderful, wild, blued-eyed girl! I was tortured by my secret. It was that I knew we—*we* must leave the valley. We can't stay here much longer. I couldn't think how we'd get away—out of the country—or how we'd live, if we ever got out. I'm a beggar. That's why I kept my secret. I'm poor. It takes money to make way beyond Sterling. We couldn't ride horses or burros or walk forever. So while I knew we must go, I was distracted over how to go and what to do. *Now!* We've gold! Once beyond Sterling, we'll be safe from rustlers. We've no others to fear.

"Oh! Listen! Bess!" Venters now heard his voice ringing high and sweet, and he felt Bess's cold hands in his crushing grasp as she leaned toward him pale, breathless. "This is how much I'd leave you! You made me live again! I'll take you away—far away from this wild country. You'll begin a new life. You'll be happy. You shall see cities, ships, people. You shall have anything your heart craves. All the shame and sorrow of your life shall be forgotten—as if they had never been. This is how much I'd leave you here alone—you sad-eyed girl. I love you! Didn't you know it? How could you fail to know it? I love you! I'm free! I'm a man—a man you've made—no more a beggar! . . . Kiss me! This is how much I'd leave you here alone—you beautiful, strange, unhappy girl. But I'll make you happy. What—what do I care for—your past! I love you! I'll take you home to Illinois—to my mother. Then I'll take you to far places. I'll make up all you've lost. Oh, I know you love me—knew it before you told me. And it changed my life. And you'll go with me, not as my companion as you are here, nor my sister, but, Bess, darling! . . . *As my wife!*"

CHAPTER SEVENTEEN

Wrangle's Race Run

THE plan eventually decided upon by the lovers was for Venters to go to the village, secure a horse and some kind of a disguise for Bess, or at least less striking apparel than her present garb, and to return post-haste to the valley. Meanwhile, she would add to their store of gold. Then they would strike the long and perilous trail to ride out of Utah. In the event of his inability to fetch back a horse for her, they intended to make the giant sorrel carry double. The gold, a little food, saddle blankets, and Venters's guns were to compose the light outfit with which they would make the start.

"I love this beautiful place," said Bess. "It's hard to think of leaving it."

"Hard! Well, I should think so," replied Venters. "Maybe—in years—" But he did not complete in words his thought that might be possible to return after many years of absence and change.

Once again Bess bade Venters farewell under the shadow of Balancing Rock, and this time it was with whispered hope and tenderness and passionate trust. Long after he had left her, all down through the outlet to the Pass, the clinging clasp of her arms, the sweetness of her lips, and the sense of a new and exquisite birth of character in her remained hauntingly and thrillingly in his mind. The girl who had sadly called herself nameless and nothing had been marvelously transformed in the moment of his avowal of love. It was something to think over, something to warm his heart, but for the present it had absolutely to be forgotten so that all his mind could be addressed to the trip so fraught with danger.

He carried only his rifle, revolver, and a small quantity of bread and meat; and thus lightly burdened, he made swift progress down the slope and out into the valley. Darkness was coming on, and he welcomed it. Stars were blinking when he reached his old hiding-place in the split of cañon wall, and by their aid he slipped through the dense thickets to the grassy enclosure. Wrangle stood in the center of it with his head up, and he appeared black and of gigantic proportions in the dim light. Venters whistled softly, began a slow approach, and then called. The horse snorted and, plunging away with dull, heavy sound of hoofs, he disappeared in the gloom. "Wilder than ever!" muttered Venters. He followed the sorrel into the narrowing split between the walls, and presently had to desist because he could not see a foot in advance. As he went back toward the open Wrangle jumped out of an ebony shadow of cliff and like a thunderbolt shot huge and black past him down into the starlit glade. Deciding that all attempts to catch Wrangle at night would be useless, Venters repaired to the shelving rock where he had hidden saddle and blanket, and there went to sleep.

The first peep of day found him stirring, and as soon as it was light enough to distinguish objects, he took his lasso off his saddle and went out to rope the sorrel. He espied Wrangle at the lower end of the cove and approached him in a perfectly natural manner. When he got near enough, Wrangle evidently recognized him, but was too wild to stand. He ran up the glade and on into the narrow lane between the walls. This favored Venters's speedy capture of the horse, so, coiling his noose ready to throw, he hurried on. Wrangle let Venters get to within a hundred feet and then he broke. But as he plunged by, rapidly getting into his stride, Venters made a perfect throw with the rope. He had time to brace himself for the shock; nevertheless, Wrangle threw him and dragged him several yards before halting.

"You wild devil," said Venters, as he slowly pulled Wrangle up. "Don't you know me? Come now—old fellow—so—so—"

Wrangle yielded to the lasso and then to Venters's strong hand. He was as straggly and wild-looking as a horse left to roam free in the sage. He dropped his long ears and stood readily to be saddled and bridled. But he was exceedingly sensitive, and quivered at every touch and sound. Venters led him to the thicket, and, bending the close saplings to let him squeeze through, at length reached the open. Sharp survey in each direction assured him of the usual lonely nature of the cañon; then he was in the saddle, riding south.

Wrangle's long, swinging canter was a wonderful ground-gainer. His stride was almost twice that of an ordinary horse, and his endurance was equally remarkable. Venters pulled him in occasionally, and walked him up the stretches of rising ground and along the soft washes. Wrangle had never yet shown any indication of distress while Venters rode him. Nevertheless, there was now reason to save the horse; therefore Venters did not resort to the hurry that had characterized his former trip. He camped at the last water in the Pass. What distance that was to Cottonwoods he did not know; he calculated, however, that it was in the neighborhood of fifty miles.

Early in the morning he proceeded on his way, and about the middle of the forenoon reached the constricted gap that marked the southerly end of the Pass, and through which led the trail up to the sage-level. He spied out Lassiter's tracks in the dust, but no others, and dismounting, he straightened out Wrangle's bridle and began to lead him up the trail. The short climb, more severe on beast than on man, necessitated a rest on the level above, and during this he scanned the wide purple reaches of slope.

Wrangle whistled his pleasure at the smell of the sage. Remounting, Venters headed up the white trail with the fragrant wind in his face. He had proceeded for perhaps a couple of miles when Wrangle stopped with a suddenness that threw Venters heavily against the pommel.

"What's wrong, old boy?" called Venters, looking down for a loose shoe or a snake or a foot lamed by a picked-up stone. Unrewarded, he raised himself from his scrutiny. Wrangle stood stiff, head high, with his long ears erect. Thus guided, Venters swiftly gazed ahead to make out a dust-clouded, dark group of horsemen riding down the slope. If they had seen him, it apparently made no difference in their speed or direction.

"Wonder who they are!" exclaimed Venters. He was not disposed to run. His cool mood tightened under grip of excitement as he reflected that, whoever the approaching riders were, they could not be friends. He slipped out of the saddle and led Wrangle behind the tallest sage-brush. It might serve to conceal them until the riders were close enough for him to see who they were; after that he would be indifferent to how soon they discovered him.

After looking to his rifle and ascertaining that it was in working order, he watched, and as he watched, slowly the force of a bitter fierceness, long dormant, gathered ready to flame into life. If those riders were not rustlers he had forgotten how rustlers looked and rode. On they came, a small group, so compact and dark that he could not tell their number. How unusual that their horses did not see Wrangle! But such failure, Venters decided, was owing to the speed with which they were traveling. They moved at a swift canter affected more by rustlers than by riders. Venters grew concerned over the possibility that these horsemen would actually ride down on him before he had a chance to tell what to expect. When they were within three hundred yards he deliberately led Wrangle out into the trail.

Then he heard shouts, and the hard scrape of sliding hoofs, and saw horses rear and plunge back with up-flung heads and flying manes. Several little white puffs of smoke appeared sharply against the black background of riders and horses, and shots rang out. Bullets struck far in front of Venters, and whipped up the dust and then hummed low into the sage. The range was great for revolvers, but whether the shots were meant to kill or merely to check advance, they were enough to fire that waiting ferocity in Venters. Slipping his arm through the bridle, so that Wrangle could not get away, Venters lifted his rifle and pulled the trigger twice.

He saw the first horseman lean sideways and fall. He saw another lurch in his saddle and heard a cry of pain. Then Wrangle, plunging in fright, lifted Venters and nearly threw him. He jerked the horse down with a powerful hand and leaped into the saddle. Wrangle plunged again, dragging his bridle, that Venters had not had time to throw in place. Bending over with a swift movement, he secured it and dropped the loop over the pommel. Then, with grinding teeth, he looked to see what the issue would be.

The band had scattered so as not to afford such a broad mark for bullets. The riders faced Venters, some with red-belching guns. He heard a sharper report, and just as Wrangle plunged again he caught the whizz of a leaden missile that would have hit him but for Wrangle's sudden jump. A swift, hot wave, turning cold, passed over Venters. Deliberately he picked out the one rider with a carbine, and killed him. Wrangle snorted shrilly and bolted into the sage. Venters let him run a few rods, then with iron arm checked him.

Five riders, surely rustlers, were left. One leaped out of the saddle to secure his fallen comrade's carbine. A shot from Venters, which missed the man but sent the dust flying over him, made him run back to his horse. Then they separated. The crippled rider went one way; the one frustrated in his attempt to get the carbine rode another; Venters thought he made out a third rider, carrying a strange-appearing bundle and disappearing in the sage. But in the rapidity of action and vision he could not discern what it was. Two riders with three horses swung out to the right. Afraid of the long rifle—a burdensome weapon seldom carried by rustlers or riders—they had been put to rout.

Suddenly Venters discovered that one of the two men last noted was riding Jane Withersteen's horse Bells—the beautiful bay racer she had given to Lassiter. Venters uttered a savage out-cry. Then the small, wiry, frog-like shape of the second rider, and the ease and grace of his seat in the saddle—things so strikingly incongruous—grew more and more familiar in Venters's sight.

"*Jerry Card!*" cried Venters.

It was indeed Tull's right-hand man. Such a white hot wrath inflamed Venters that he fought himself to see with clearer gaze.

"It's Jerry Card!" he exclaimed, instantly. *"And he's riding Black Star and leading Night!"*

The long-kindling, stormy fire in Venters's heart burst into flame. He spurred Wrangle, and as the horse lengthened his stride Venters slipped cartridges into the magazine of his rifle till it was once again full. Card and his companion were now half a mile or more in advance, riding easily down the slope. Venters marked the smooth gait, and understood it when Wrangle galloped out of the sage into the broad cattle trail, down which Venters had once tracked Jane Withersteen's red herd. This hard-packed trail, from years of use, was as clean and smooth as a road. Venters saw Jerry Card look back over his shoulder; the other rider did likewise. Then the three racers lengthened their stride to the point where the swinging canter was ready to break into a gallop.

"Wrangle, the race's on," said Venters, grimly. "We'll canter with them and gallop with them and run with them. We'll let them set the pace."

Venters knew he bestrode the strongest, swiftest, most tireless horse ever ridden by any rider across the Utah uplands. Recalling Jane Withersteen's devoted assurance that Night could run neck and neck with Wrangle, and Black Star could show his heels to him, Venters wished that Jane were there to see the race to recover her blacks and in the unqualified superiority of the giant sorrel. Then Venters found himself thankful that she was absent, for he meant that race to end in Jerry Card's death. The first flush, the raging of Venters's wrath, passed, to leave him in sullen, almost cold possession of his will. It was a deadly mood, utterly foreign to his nature, engendered, fostered, and released by the wild passions of wild men in a wild country. The strength in him then—the thing rife in him that was not hate, but something as remorseless—might have been the fiery fruition of a whole lifetime of vengeful quest. Nothing could have stopped him.

Venters thought out the race shrewdly. The rider on Bells would probably drop behind and take to the sage. What he did was of little moment to Venters. To stop Jerry Card, his evil hidden career as well as his present flight, and then to catch the blacks—that was all that concerned Venters. The cattle trail wound for miles and miles down the slope. Venters saw with a rider's keen vision ten, fifteen, twenty miles of clear purple sage. There were no on-coming riders or rustlers to aid Card. His only chance to escape lay in abandoning the stolen horses and creeping away in the sage to hide. In ten miles Wrangle could run Black Star and Night off their feet, and in fifteen he could kill them outright. So Venters held the sorrel in, letting Card make the running. It was a long race that would save the blacks.

In a few miles of that swinging canter Wrangle had crept appreciably closer to the three horses. Jerry Card turned again, and when he saw how the sorrel had gained, he put Black Star to a gallop. Night and Bells, on either side of him, swept into his stride.

Venters loosened the rein on Wrangle and let him break into a gallop. The sorrel saw the horses ahead and wanted to run. But Venters restrained him. And in the gallop he gained more than in the canter. Bells was fast in that gait, but Black Star and Night had been trained to run. Slowly Wrangle closed the gap down to a quarter of a mile, and crept closer and closer.

Jerry Card wheeled once more. Venters distinctly saw the red flash of his red face. This time he looked long. Venters laughed. He knew what passed in Card's mind. The rider was trying to make out what horse it happened to be that thus gained on Jane Withersteen's peerless racers. Wrangle had so long been away from the village that not improbably Jerry had forgotten. Besides, whatever Jerry's qualifications for his fame as the greatest rider of the sage, certain it was that his best point was not far-sightedness. He had not recognized Wrangle. After what must have been a searching gaze he got his comrade to face about. This action gave Venters amusement. It spoke so surely of the fact that neither Card nor the rustler actually knew their danger. Yet if they kept to the trail—and the last thing such men would do would be to leave it—they were both doomed.

This comrade of Card's whirled far around in his saddle, and he even shaded his eyes from the sun. He, too, looked long. Then, all at once, he faced ahead again and, bending lower in the saddle, began to fling his right arm up and down. That flinging Venters knew to be the lashing of Bells. Jerry also became active. And the three racers lengthened out into a run.

"Now, Wrangle!" cried Venters. "Run, you big devil! Run!"

Venters laid the reins on Wrangle's neck and dropped the loop over the pommel. The sorrel needed no guiding on that smooth trail. He was surer-footed in a run than at any other fast gait, and his running gave the impression of something devilish. He might now have been actuated by Venters's spirit; undoubtedly his savage running fitted the mood of his rider. Venters bent forward, swinging with the horse, and gripped his rifle. His eye measured the distance between him and Jerry Card.

In less than two miles of running Bells began to drop behind the blacks, and Wrangle began to overhaul him. Venters anticipated that the rustler would soon take to the sage. Yet he did not. Not improbably he reasoned that the powerful sorrel could more easily overtake Bells in the heavier going outside of the trail.

Soon only a few hundred yards lay between Bells and Wrangle. Turning in his saddle, the rustler began to shoot, and the bullets beat up little whiffs of dust. Venters raised his rifle, ready to take snap shots, and waited for favorable opportunity when Bells was out of line with the forward horses. Venters had it in him to kill these men as if they were skunk-bitten coyotes, but also he had restraint enough to keep from shooting one of Jane's beloved Arabians.

No great distance was covered, however, before Bells swerved to the left, out of line with Black Star and Night. Then Venters, aiming high and waiting for the pause between Wrangle's great strides, began to take snap shots at the rustler. The fleeing rider presented a broad target for a rifle, but he was moving swiftly forward and bobbing up and down. Moreover, shooting from Wrangle's back was shooting from a thunderbolt. And added to that was the danger of a low-placed bullet taking effect on Bells. Yet, despite these considerations, making the shot exceedingly difficult, Venters's confidence, like his implacability, saw a speedy and fatal termination of that rustler's race. On the sixth shot the rustler threw up his arms and took a flying tumble off his horse. He rolled over and over, hunched himself to a half-erect position, fell, and then dragged himself into the sage. As Venters went thundering by he peered keenly into the sage, but caught no sign of the man. Bells ran a few hundred yards, slowed up, and had stopped when Wrangle passed him.

Again Venters began slipping fresh cartridges into the magazine of his rifle, and his hand was so sure and steady that he did not drop a single cartridge. With the eye of a rider and the judgment of a marksman he once more measured the distance between him and Jerry Card. Wrangle had gained, bringing him into rifle range. Venters was hard put to it now not to shoot, but thought it better to withhold his fire. Jerry, who, in anticipation of a running fusillade, had huddled himself into a little twisted ball on Black Star's neck, now surmising that this pursuer would make sure of not wounding one of the blacks, rose to his natural seat in the saddle.

In his mind perhaps, as certainly as in Venters's, this moment was the beginning of the real race.

Venters leaned forward to put his hand on Wrangle's neck; then backward to put it on his flank. Under the shaggy, dusty hair trembled and vibrated and rippled a wonderful muscular activity. But Wrangle's flesh was still cold. What a cold-blooded brute, thought Venters, and felt in him a love for the horse he had never given to any other. It would not have been humanly possible for any rider, even though clutched by hate or revenge or a passion to save a loved one or fear of his own life, to be astride the sorrel, to swing with his swing, to see his magnificent stride and hear the rapid thunder of his hoofs, to ride him in that race and not glory in the ride.

So, with his passion to kill still keen and unabated, Venters lived out that ride, and drank a rider's sage-sweet cup of wildness to the dregs.

When Wrangle's long mane, lashing in the wind, stung Venters in the cheek, the sting added a beat to his flying pulse. He bent a downward glance to try to see Wrangle's actual stride, and saw only twinkling, darting streaks and the white rush of the trail. He watched the sorrel's savage head, pointed level, his mouth still closed and dry, but his nostrils distended as if he were snorting unseen fire. Wrangle was the horse for a race with death. Upon each side Venters saw the sage merged into a sailing, colorless wall. In front sloped the lay of ground with its purple breadth split by the white trail. The wind, blowing with heavy, steady blast into his face, sickened him with enduring, sweet odor, and filled his ears with a hollow, rushing roar.

Then for the hundredth time he measured the width of space separating him from Jerry Card. Wrangle had ceased to gain. The blacks were proving their fleetness. Venters watched Jerry Card, admiring the little rider's horsemanship. He had the incomparable seat of the upland rider, born in the saddle. It struck Venters that Card had changed his position, or the position of the horses. Presently Venters remembered positively that Jerry had been leading Night on the right-hand side of the trail. The racer was now on the side to the left. No—it was Black Star. But, Venters argued in amaze, Jerry had been mounted on Black Star. Another clearer, keener gaze assured Venters that Black Star was really riderless. Night now carried Jerry Card.

"He's changed from one to the other!" ejaculated Venters, realizing the astounding feat with unstinted admiration. "Changed at full speed! Jerry Card, that's what you've done unless I'm drunk on the smell of sage. But I've got to see the trick before I believe it."

Thenceforth, while Wrangle sped on, Venters glued his eyes to the little rider. Jerry Card rode as only he could ride. Of all the daring horsemen of the uplands, Jerry was the one rider fitted to bring out the greatness of the blacks in that long race. He had them on a dead run, but not yet at the last strained and killing pace. From time to time he glanced backward, as a wise general in retreat calculating his chances and the power and speed of pursuers, and the moment for the last desperate burst. No doubt, Card, with his life at stake, gloried in that race, perhaps more wildly than Venters. For he had been born to the sage and the saddle and the wild. He was more than half horse. Not until the last call—the sudden up-flashing instinct of self-preservation—would he lose his skill and judgment and nerve and the spirit of that race. Venters seemed to read Jerry's mind. That little crime-stained rider was actually thinking of his horses, husbanding their speed, handling them with knowledge of years, glorying in their beautiful, swift, racing stride, and wanting them to win the race when his own life hung suspended in quivering balance. Again Jerry whirled in his saddle and the sun flashed red on his face. Turning, he drew Black Star closer and closer toward Night, till they ran side by side, as one horse. Then Card raised himself in the saddle, slipped out of the stirrups, and, somehow twisting himself, leaped upon Black Star. He did not even lose the swing of the horse. Like a leech he was there in the other saddle, and as the horses separated, his right foot, that had been apparently doubled under him, shot down to catch the stirrup. The grace and dexterity and daring of that rider's act won something more than admiration from Venters.

For the distance of a mile Jerry rode Black Star and then changed back to Night. But all Jerry's skill and the running of the blacks could avail little more against the sorrel.

Venters peered far ahead, studying the lay of the land. Straight-away for five miles the trail stretched, and then it disappeared in hummocky ground. To the right, some few rods, Venters saw a break in the sage, and this was the rim of Deception Pass. Across the dark cleft gleamed the red of the opposite wall. Venters imagined that the trail went down into the Pass somewhere north of those ridges. And he realized that he must and would overtake Jerry Card in this straight course of five miles.

Cruelly he struck his spurs into Wrangle's flanks. A light touch of spur was sufficient to make Wrangle plunge. And now, with a ringing, wild snort, he seemed to double up in muscular convulsions and to shoot forward with an impetus that almost unseated Venters. The sage blurred by, the trail flashed by, and the wind robbed him of breath and hearing. Jerry Card turned once more. And the way he shifted to Black Star showed he had to make his last desperate running. Venters aimed to the side of the trail and sent a bullet puffing the dust beyond Jerry. Venters hoped to frighten the rider and get him to take to the sage. But Jerry returned the shot, and his ball struck dangerously close in the dust at Wrangle's flying feet. Venters held his fire then, while the rider emptied his revolver. For a mile, with Black Star leaving Night behind and doing his utmost, Wrangle did not gain; for another mile he gained little, if at all. In the third he caught up with the now galloping Night and began to gain rapidly on the other black.

Only a hundred yards now stretched between Black Star and Wrangle. The giant sorrel thundered on—and on—and on. In every yard he gained a foot. He was whistling through his nostrils, wringing wet, flying lather, and as hot as fire. Savage as ever, strong as ever, fast as ever, but each tremendous stride jarred Venters out of the saddle! Wrangle's power and spirit and momentum had begun to run him off his legs. Wrangle's great race was nearly won—and run. Venters seemed to see the expanse before him as a vast, sheeted, purple plain sliding under him. Black Star moved in it as a blur. The rider, Jerry Card, appeared a mere dot bobbing dimly. Wrangle thundered on—on—on! Venters felt the increase in quivering, straining shock after every leap. Flecks of foam flew into Venters's eyes, burning him, making him see all the sage as red. But in that red haze he saw, or seemed to see, Black Star suddenly riderless and with broken gait. Wrangle thundered on to change his pace with a violent break. Then Venters pulled him hard. From run to gallop, gallop to canter, canter to trot, trot to walk, and walk to stop, the great sorrel ended his race.

Venters looked back. Black Star stood riderless in the trail. Jerry Card had taken to the sage. Far up the white trail Night came trotting faithfully down. Venters leaped off, still half blind, reeling dizzily. In a moment he had recovered sufficiently to have a care for Wrangle. Rapidly he took off the saddle and bridle. The sorrel was reeking, heaving, whistling, shaking. But he had still the strength to stand, and for him Venters had no fears.

As Venters ran back to Black Star he saw the horse stagger on shaking legs into the sage and go down in a heap. Upon reaching him Venters removed the saddle and bridle. Black Star had been killed on his legs, Venters thought. He had no hope for the stricken horse. Black Star lay flat, covered with bloody froth, mouth wide, tongue hanging, eyes glaring, and all his beautiful body in convulsions.

Unable to stay there to see Jane's favorite racer die, Venters hurried up the trail to meet the other black. On the way he kept a sharp lookout for Jerry Card. Venters imagined the rider would keep well out of range of the rifle, but, as he would be lost on the sage without a horse, not improbably he would linger in the vicinity on the chance of getting back one of the blacks. Night soon came trotting up, hot and wet and run out. Venters led him down near the others, and unsaddling him, let him loose to rest. Night wearily lay down in the dust and rolled, proving himself not yet spent.

Then Venters sat down to rest and think. Whatever the risk, he was compelled to stay where he was, or comparatively near, for the night. The horses must rest and drink. He must find water. He was now seventy miles from Cottonwoods, and, he believed, close to the cañon where the cattle trail must surely turn off and go down into the Pass. After a while he rose to survey the valley.

He was very near to the ragged edge of a deep cañon into which the trail turned. The ground lay in uneven ridges divided by washes, and these sloped into the cañon. Following the cañon line, he saw where its rim was broken by other intersecting cañons, and farther down red walls and yellow cliffs leading toward a deep blue cleft that he made sure was Deception Pass. Walking out a few rods to a promontory, he found where the trail went down. The descent was gradual, along a stone-walled trail, and Venters felt sure that this was the place where Oldring drove cattle into the Pass. There was, however, no indication at all that he ever had driven cattle out at this point. Oldring had many holes to his burrow.

In searching round in the little hollows Venters, much to his relief, found water. He composed himself to rest and eat some bread and meat, while he waited for a sufficient time to elapse so that he could safely give the horses a drink. He judged the hour to be somewhere around noon. Wrangle lay down to rest and Night followed suit. So long as they were down Venters intended to make no move. The longer they rested the better, and the safer it would be to give them water. By and by he forced himself to go over to where Black Star lay, expecting to find him dead. Instead he found the racer partially if not wholly recovered. There was recognition, even fire, in his big black eyes. Venters was overjoyed. He sat by the black for a long time. Black Star presently labored to his feet with a heave and a groan, shook himself, and snorted for water. Venters repaired to the little pool he had found, filled his sombrero, and gave the racer a drink. Black Star gulped it at one draught, as if it were but a drop, and pushed his nose into the hat and snorted for more. Venters now led Night down to drink, and after a further time Black Star also. Then the blacks began to graze.

The sorrel had wandered off down the sage between the trail and the cañon. Once or twice he disappeared in little swales. Finally Venters concluded Wrangle had grazed far enough, and, taking his lasso, he went to fetch him back. In crossing from one ridge to another he saw where the horse had made muddy a pool of water. It occurred to Venters then that Wrangle had drunk his fill, and did not seem the worse for it, and might be anything but easy to catch. And, true enough, he could not come within roping reach of the sorrel. He tried for an hour, and gave up in disgust. Wrangle did not seem so wild as simply perverse.

In a quandary Venters returned to the other horses, hoping much, yet doubting more, that when Wrangle had grazed to suit himself he might be caught.

As the afternoon wore away Venters's concern diminished, yet he kept close watch on the blacks and the trail and the sage. There was no telling of what Jerry Card might be capable. Venters sullenly acquiesced to the idea that the rider had been too quick and too shrewd for him. Strangely and doggedly, however, Venters clung to his foreboding of Card's downfall.

The wind died away; the red sun topped the far distant western rise of slope; and the long, creeping purple shadows lengthened. The rims of the cañons gleamed crimson and the deep clefts appeared to belch forth blue smoke. Silence enfolded the scene.

It was broken by a horrid, long-drawn scream of a horse and the thudding of heavy hoofs. Venters sprang erect and wheeled south. Along the cañon rim, near the edge, came Wrangle, once more in thundering flight.

Venters gasped in amazement. Had the wild sorrel gone mad? His head was high and twisted, in a most singular position for a running horse. Suddenly Venters descried a frog-like shape clinging to Wrangle's neck. Jerry Card! Somehow he had straddled Wrangle and now stuck like a huge burr. But it was his strange position and the sorrel's wild scream that shook Venters's nerves. Wrangle was pounding toward the turn where the trail went down. He plunged onward like a blind horse. More than one of his leaps took him to the very edge of the precipice.

Jerry Card was bent forward with his teeth fast in the front of Wrangle's nose! Venters saw it, and there flashed over him a memory of this trick of a few desperate riders. He even thought of one rider who had worn off his teeth in this terrible hold to break or control desperate horses. Wrangle had indeed gone mad. The marvel was what guided him. Was it the half-brute, the more than half-horse instinct of Jerry Card? Whatever the mystery, it was true. And in a few more rods Jerry would have the sorrel turning into the trail leading down into the cañon.

"No—Jerry!" whispered Venters, stepping forward and throwing up the rifle. He tried to catch the little humped, frog-like shape over the sights. It was moving too fast; it was too small. Yet Venters shot once . . . twice . . . the third time . . . four times . . . five! All wasted shots and precious seconds!

With a deep-muttered curse Venters caught Wrangle through the sights and pulled the trigger. Plainly he heard the bullet thud. Wrangle uttered a horrible strangling sound. In swift death action he whirled, and with one last splendid leap he cleared the cañon rim. And he whirled downward with the little frog-like shape clinging to his neck!

191

There was a pause which seemed never ending, a shock, and an instant's silence.

Then up rolled a heavy crash, a long roar of sliding rocks dying away in distant echo, then silence unbroken.

Wrangle's race was run.

CHAPTER EIGHTEEN

Oldring's Knell

SOME forty hours or more later Venters created a commotion in Cottonwoods by riding down the main street on Black Star and leading Bells and Night. He had come upon Bells grazing near the body of a dead rustler, the only incident of his quick ride into the village.

Nothing was farther from Venters's mind than bravado. No thought came to him of the defiance and boldness of riding Jane Withersteen's racers straight into the archplotter's stronghold. He wanted men to see the famous Arabians; he wanted men to see them dirty and dusty, bearing all the signs of having been driven to their limit; he wanted men to see and to know that the thieves who had ridden them out into the sage had not ridden them back. Venters had come for that and for more—he wanted to meet Tull face to face; if not Tull, then Dyer; if not Dyer, then anyone in the secret of these master conspirators. Such was Venters's passion. The meeting with the rustlers, the unprovoked attack upon him, the spilling of blood, the recognition of Jerry Card and the horses, the race, and that last plunge of mad Wrangle—all these things, fuel on fuel to the smoldering fire, had kindled and swelled and leaped into living flame. He could have shot Dyer in the midst of his religious services at the altar; he could have killed Tull in front of wives and babes.

He walked the three racers down the broad, green-bordered village road. He heard the murmur of running water from Amber Spring. Bitter waters for Jane Withersteen! Men and women stopped to gaze at him and the horses. All knew him; all knew the blacks and the bay. As well as if it had been spoken, Venters read in the faces of men the intelligence that Jane Withersteen's Arabians had been known to have been stolen. Venters reined in and halted before Dyer's residence. It was a low, long, stone structure resembling Withersteen House. The spacious front yard was green and luxuriant with grass and flowers; gravel walks led to the hugh porch; a well-trimmed hedge of purple sage separated the yard from the church grounds; birds sang in the trees; water flowed musically along the walks; and there were glad, careless shouts of children. For Venters the beauty of this home, and the serenity and its apparent happiness, all turned red and black. For Venters a shade overspread the lawn, the flowers, the old vine-clad stone house. In the music of the singing birds, in the murmur of the running water, he heard an ominous sound. Quiet beauty—sweet music—innocent laughter! By what monstrous abortion of fate did these abide in the shadow of Dyer?

Venters rode on and stopped before Tull's cottage. Women stared at him with white faces and then flew from the porch. Tull himself appeared at the door, bent low, craning his neck. His dark face flashed out of sight; the door banged; a heavy bar dropped with a hollow sound.

Then Venters shook Black Star's bridle, and, sharply trotting, led the other horses to the center of the village. Here at the intersecting streets and in front of the stores he halted once more. The usual lounging atmosphere of that prominent corner was not now in evidence. Riders and ranchers and villagers broke up what must have been absorbing conversation. There was a rush of many feet, and then the walk was lined with faces.

Venters's glance swept down the line of silent stone-faced men. He recognized many riders and villagers, but none of those he had hoped to meet. There was no expression in the faces turned toward him. All of them knew him, most were inimical, but there were few who were not burning with curiosity and wonder in regard to the return of Jane Withersteen's racers. Yet all were silent. Here were the familiar characteristics—masked feeling—strange secretiveness—expressionless expression of mystery and hidden power.

"Has anybody here seen Jerry Card?" queried Venters, in a loud voice.

In reply there came not a word, not a nod or shake of head, not so much as dropping eye or twitching lip—nothing but a quiet, stony stare.

"Been under the knife? You've a fine knife-wielder here—one Tull, I believe! . . . Maybe you've all had your tongues cut out?"

This passionate sarcasm of Venters brought no response, and the stony calm was as oil on the fire within him.

"I see some of you pack guns, too!" he added, in biting scorn. In the long, tense pause, strung keenly as a tight wire, he sat motionless on Black Star. "All right," he went on. "Then let some of you take this message to Tull. Tell him I've seen Jerry Card! . . . Tell him Jerry Card *will never return!*"

Thereupon, in the same dead calm, Venters backed Black Star away from the curb, into the street, and out of range. He was ready now to ride up to Withersteen House and turn the racers over to Jane.

"Hello, Venters!" a familiar voice cried, hoarsely, and he saw a man running toward him. It was the rider Judkins who came up and gripped Venters's hand. "Venters, I could hev dropped when I seen them hosses. But thet sight ain't a marker to the looks of you. What's wrong? Hev you gone crazy? You must be crazy to ride in here this way—with them hosses—talkin' thet way about Tull an' Jerry Card."

"Jud, I'm not crazy—only mad clean through," replied Venters.

"Wal, now, Bern, I'm glad to hear some of your old self in your voice. Fer when you come up you looked like the corpse of a dead rider with fire fer eyes. You hed thet crowd too stiff fer throwin' guns. Come, we've got to hev a talk. Let's go up the lane. We ain't much safe here."

Judkins mounted Bells and rode with Venters up to the cotton-wood grove. Here they dismounted and went among the trees.

"Let's hear from you first," said Judkins. "You fetched back them hosses. Thet *is* the trick. An', of course, you got Jerry the same as you got Horne."

"Horne!"

"Sure. He was found dead yesterday all chewed by coyotes, an' he'd been shot plumb center."

"Where was he found?"

"At the split down the trail—you know where Oldrin's cattle trail runs off north from the trail to the pass."

"That's where I met Jerry and the rustlers. What was Horne doing with them? I thought Horne was an honest cattle-man."

"Lord—Bern, don't ask me thet! I'm all muddled now tryin' to figure things."

Venters told of the fight and the race with Jerry Card and its tragic conclusion.

"I knowed it! I knowed all along that Wrangle was the best hoss!" exclaimed Judkins, with his lean face working and his eyes lighting. "Thet was a race! Lord, I'd like to hev seen Wrangle jump the cliff with Jerry. An' thet was good-by to the grandest hoss an' rider ever on the sage! . . . But, Bern, after you got the hosses why'd you want to bolt right in Tull's face?"

"I want him to know. An' if I can get to him I'll—"

"You can't get near Tull," interrupted Judkins. "Thet vigilante bunch hev taken to bein' bodyguard for Tull an' Dyer, too."

"Hasn't Lassiter made a break yet?" inquired Venters, curiously.

"Naw!" replied Judkins, scornfully. "Jane turned his head. He's mad in love over her—follers her like a dog. He ain't no more Lassiter! He's lost his nerve;

he doesn't look like the same feller. It's village talk. Everybody knows it. He hasn't thrown a gun, an' he won't!"

"Jud, I'll bet he does," replied Venters, earnestly. "Remember what I say. This Lassiter is something more than a gun-man. Jud, he's big—he's great! . . . I feel that in him. God help Tull and Dyer when Lassiter does go after them. For horses and riders and stone walls won't save them."

"Wal, hev it your way, Bern. I hope you're right. Nat'rully I've been some sore on Lassiter fer gittin' soft. But I ain't denyin' his nerve, or whatever's great in him thet sort of paralyzes people. No later 'n this mornin' I seen him saunterin' down the lane, quiet an' slow. An' like his guns he comes black—*black*, thet's Lassiter. Wal, the crowd on the corner never batted an eye, an' I'll gamble my hoss thet there wasn't one who hed a heartbeat till Lassiter got by. He went in Snell's saloon, an' as there wasn't no gun play I had to go in, too. An' there, darn my pictures, if Lassiter wasn't standin' to the bar, drinkin' an' talkin' with Oldrin'."

"*Oldring!*" whispered Venters. His voice, as all fire and pulse within him, seemed to freeze.

"Let go my arm!" exclaimed Judkins. "Thet's my bad arm. Sure it was Oldrin'. What the hell's wrong with you, anyway? Venters, I tell you somethin's wrong. You're whiter 'n a sheet. You can't be *scared* of the rustler. I don't believe you've got a scare in you. Wal, now, jest let me talk. You know I like to talk, an' if I'm slow I allus git there sometime. As I said, Lassiter was talkin' chummy with Oldrin'. There wasn't no hard feelin's. An' the gang wasn't payin' no pertic'lar attention. But like a cat watchin' a mouse I hed my eyes on them two fellers. It was strange to me, thet confab. I'm gittin' to think a lot, fer a feller who doesn't know much. There's been some queer deals lately an' this seemed to me the queerest. These men stood to the bar alone, an' so close their big gun-hilts butted together. I seen Oldrin' was some surprised at first, an' Lassiter was cool as ice. They talked, an' presently at somethin' Lassiter said the rustler bawled out a curse, an' then he jest fell up against the bar, an' sagged there. The gang in the saloon looked around an' laughed, an' thet's about all. Finally Oldrin' turned, and it was easy to see somethin' hed shook him. Yes, sir, thet big rustler—you know he's as broad as he is long, an' the powerfulest build of a man—yes, sir, the nerve had been taken out of him. Then, after a little, he began to talk an' said a lot to Lassiter, an' by an' by it didn't take much of an eye to see thet Lassiter was gittin' hit hard. I never seen him anyway but cooler 'n ice—till then. He seemed to be hit harder 'n Oldrin', only he didn't roar out thet way. He jest kind of sunk in, an' looked an' looked, an' he didn't see a livin' soul in thet saloon. Then he sort of come to, an' shakin' hands—mind you, *shakin' hands* with Oldrin'—he went out. I couldn't help thinkin' how easy even a boy could hev dropped the great gun-man then! . . . Wal, the rustler stood at the bar fer a long time, an' he was seein' things far off, too; then he come to an' roared fer whisky, an' gulped a drink thet was big enough to drown me."

"Is Oldring here now?" whispered Venters. He could not speak above a whisper. Judkins's story had been meaningless to him.

"He's at Snell's yet. Bern, I hevn't told you yet thet the rustlers hev been raisin' hell. They shot up Stone Bridge an' Glaze, an' fer three days they've been here drinkin' an' gamblin' an' throwin' of gold. These rustlers hev a pile of gold. If it was gold dust or nugget gold I'd hev reason to think, but it's new coin gold, as if it had jest come from the United States treasury. An' the coin's genuine. Thet's all been proved. The truth is Oldrin's on a rampage. A while back he lost his Masked Rider, an' they say he's wild about thet. I'm wonderin' if Lassiter could hev told the rustler anythin' about thet little masked, hard-ridin' devil. Ride! He was most as good as Jerry Card. An', Bern, I've been wonderin' if you know—"

"Judkins, you're a good fellow," interrupted Venters. "Some day I'll tell you a story. I've no time now. Take the horses to Jane."

Judkins stared, and then, muttering to himself, he mounted Bells, and stared again at Venters, and then, leading the other horses, he rode into the grove and disappeared.

Once, long before, on the night Venters had carried Bess through the cañon and up into Surprise Valley, he had experienced the strangeness of faculties singularly, tinglingly acute. And now the same sensation recurred. But it was different in that he felt cold, frozen, mechanical, incapable of free thought, and all about him seemed unreal, aloof, remote. He hid his rifle in the sage, marking its exact location with extreme care. Then he faced down the lane and strode toward the center of the village. Perceptions flashed upon him, the faint, cold touch of the breeze, a cold, silvery tinkle of flowing water, a cold sun shining out of a cold sky, song of birds and laugh of children, coldly distant. Cold and intangible were all things in earth and heaven. Colder and tighter stretched the skin over his face; colder and harder grew the polished butts of his guns; colder and steadier became his hands as he wiped the clammy sweat from his face or reached low to his gunsheaths. Men meeting him in the walk gave him wide berth. In front of Bevin's store a crowd melted apart for his passage, and their faces and whispers were faces and whispers of a dream. He turned a corner to meet Tull face to face, eye to eye. As once before he had seen this man pale to a ghastly, livid white, so again he saw the change. Tull stopped in his tracks, with right hand raised and shaking. Suddenly it dropped, and he seemed to glide aside, to pass out of Venters's sight. Next he saw many horses with bridles down—all clean-limbed, dark bays or blacks—rustlers' horses! Loud voices and boisterous laughter, rattle of dice and scrape of chair and clink of gold, burst in mingled din from an open doorway. He stepped inside.

With the sight of smoke-hazed room and drinking, cursing, gambling, dark-visaged men, reality once more dawned upon Venters.

His entrance had been unnoticed, and he bent his gaze upon the drinkers at the bar. Dark-clothed, dark-faced men they all were, burned by the sun, bow-legged as were most riders of the sage, but neither lean nor gaunt. Then Venters's gaze passed to the tables, and swiftly it swept over the hard-featured gamesters, to alight upon the huge, shaggy, black head of the rustler chief.

"*Oldring!*" he cried, and to him his voice seemed to split a bell in his ears. It stilled the din.

That silence suddenly broke to the scrape and crash of Oldring's chair as he rose; and then, while he passed, a great gloomy figure, again the thronged room stilled in silence yet deeper.

"Oldring, a word with you!" continued Venters.

"Ho! What's this?" boomed Oldring, in frowning scrutiny.

"Come outside, alone. A word for you—*from your Masked Rider!*"

Oldring kicked a chair out of his way and lunged forward with a stamp of heavy boot that jarred the floor. He waved down his muttering, rising men.

Venters backed out of the door and waited, hearing, as no sound had ever before struck into his soul, the rapid, heavy steps of the rustler.

Oldring appeared, and Venters had one glimpse of his great breadth and bulk, his gold-buckled belt with hanging guns, his high-top boots with gold spurs. In that moment Venters had a strange, unintelligible curiosity to see Oldring alive. The rustler's broad brow, his large black eyes, his sweeping beard, as dark as the wing of a raven, his enormous width of shoulder and depth of chest, his whole splendid presence so wonderfully charged with vitality and force and strength, seemed to afford Venters an unutterable fiendish joy because for that magnificent manhood and life he meant cold and sudden death.

"*Oldring, Bess is alive! But she's dead to you—dead to the life you made her lead—dead as you will be in one second!*"

Swift as lightning Venters's glance dropped from Oldring's rolling eyes to his hands. One of them, the right, swept out, then toward his gun—and Venters shot him through the heart.

Slowly Oldring sank to his knees, and the hand, dragging at the gun, fell away. Venters's strangely acute faculties grasped the meaning of that limp arm, of the swaying hulk, of the gasp and heave, of the quivering beard. But was that awful spirit in the black eyes only one of vitality?

"*Man—why—didn't—you—wait? Bess—was—*" Oldring's whisper died under his beard, and with a heavy lurch he fell forward.

Bounding swiftly away, Venters fled around the corner, across the street, and, leaping a hedge, he ran through yard, orchard, and garden to the sage. Here, under cover of the tall brush, he turned west and ran on to the place where he had hidden his rifle. Securing that, he again set out into a run, and, circling through the sage, came up behind Jane Withersteen's stable and corrals. With laboring, dripping chest, and pain as of a knife thrust in his side, he stopped to regain his breath, and while resting his eyes roved around in search of a horse. Doors and windows of the stable were open wide and had a deserted look. One dejected, lonely burro stood in the near corral. Strange indeed was the silence brooding over the once happy, noisy home of Jane Withersteen's pets.

He went into the corral, exercising care to leave no tracks, and led the burro to the watering-trough. Venters, though not thirsty, drank till he could drink no more. Then, leading the burro over hard ground, he struck into the sage and down the slope.

He strode swiftly, turning from time to time to scan the slope for riders. His head just topped the level of sage-brush, and the burro could not have been seen at all. Slowly the green of Cottonwoods sank behind the slope, and at last a wavering line of purple sage met the blue of sky.

To avoid being seen, to get away, to hide his trail—these were the sole ideas in his mind as he headed for Deception Pass; and he directed all his acuteness of eye and ear, and the keenness of a rider's judgment for distance and ground, to stern accomplishment of the task. He kept to the sage far to the left of the trail leading into the Pass. He walked ten miles and looked back a thousand times. Always the graceful, purple wave of sage remained wide and lonely, a clear, undotted waste. Coming to a stretch of rocky ground, he took advantage of it to cross the trail and then continued down on the right. At length he persuaded himself that he would be able to see riders mounted on horses before they could see him on the little burro, and he rode bareback.

Hour by hour the tireless burro kept to his faithful, steady trot. The sun sank and the long shadows lengthened down the slope. Moving veils of purple twilight crept out of the hollows and, mustering and forming on the levels, soon merged and shaded into night. Venters guided the burro nearer to the trail, so that he could see its white line from the ridges, and rode on through the hours.

Once down in the Pass without leaving a trail, he would hold himself safe for the time being. When late in the night he reached the break in the sage, he sent the burro down ahead of him, and started an avalanche that all but buried the animal at the bottom of the trail. Bruised and battered as he was, he had a moment's elation, for he had hidden his tracks. Once more he mounted the burro and rode on. The hour was the blackest of the night when he made the thicket which inclosed his old camp. Here he turned the burro loose in the grass near the spring, and then lay down on his old bed of leaves.

He felt only vaguely, as outside things, the ache and burn and throb of the muscles of his body. But a dammed-up torrent of emotion at last burst its bounds, and the hour that saw his release from immediate action was one that confounded him in the reaction of his spirit. He suffered without understanding why. He caught glimpses into himself, into unlit darkness of soul. The fire that had blistered him and the cold which had frozen him now united in one torturing possession of his mind and heart, and like a fiery steed with ice-shod feet, ranged his being, ran rioting through his blood, trampling the resurging good, dragging ever at the evil.

Out of the subsiding chaos came a clear question. What had happened? He had left the valley to go to Cottonwoods. Why? It seemed that he had gone to kill a man—Oldring! The name riveted his consciousness upon the one man of all men upon earth whom he had wanted to meet. He had met the rustler. Venters recalled the smoky haze of the saloon, the dark-visaged men, the huge Oldring. He saw him step out of the door, a splendid specimen of manhood, a handsome giant with purple-black and sweeping beard. He remembered inquisitive gaze of falcon eyes. He heard himself repeating: *"Oldring, Bess is alive! But she's dead to you,"* and he felt himself jerk, and his ears throbbed to the thunder of a gun, and he saw the giant sink slowly to his knees. Was that only the vitality of him— that awful light in the eyes—only the hard-dying life of a tremendously powerful brute? A broken whisper, strange as death: *"Man—why—didn't—you wait! Bess—was—"* And Oldring plunged face forward, dead.

"I killed him," cried Venters, in remembering shock. "But it wasn't *that*. Ah, the look in his eyes and his whisper!"

Herein lay the secret that had clamored to him through all the tumult and stress of his emotions. What a look in the eyes of a man shot through the heart! It had been neither hate nor ferocity nor fear of men nor fear of death. It had been no passionate, glinting spirit of a fearless foe, willing shot for shot, life for life, but lacking physical power. Distinctly recalled now, never to be forgotten, Venters saw in Oldring's magnificent eyes the rolling of great, glad surprise—softness—love! Then came a shadow and the terrible superhuman striving of his spirit to speak. Oldring, shot through the heart, had fought and forced back death, not for a moment in which to shoot or curse, but to whisper strange words.

What words for a dying man to whisper! Why had not Venters waited? For what? That was no plea for life. It was regret that there was not a moment of life left in which to speak. Bess was—Herein lay renewed torture for Venters. What had Bess been to Oldring? The old question, like a specter, stalked from its grave to haunt him. He had overlooked, he had forgiven, he had loved, and he had forgotten; and now, out of the mystery of a dying man's whisper rose again that perverse, unsatisfied, jealous uncertainty. Bess had loved that splendid, black-crowned giant—by her own confession she had loved him; and in Venters's soul again flamed up the jealous hell. Then into the clamoring hell burst the shot that had killed Oldring, and it rang in a wild, fiendish gladness, a hateful, vengeful joy. That passed to the memory of the love and light in Oldring's eyes and the mystery in his whisper. So the changing, swaying emotions fluctuated in Venters's heart.

This was the climax of his year of suffering and the crucial struggle of his life. And when the gray dawn came he rose, a gloomy, almost heartbroken man, but victor over evil passions. He could not change the past; and, even if he had not loved Bess with all his soul, he had grown into a man who would not change the future he had planned for her. Only, and once for all, he must know the truth, know the worst, stifle all these insistent doubts and subtle hopes and jealous fancies, and kill the past by knowing truly what Bess had been to Oldring. For that matter he knew—he had always known, but he must hear it spoken. Then, when they had safely gotten out of that wild country to take up a new and an absorbing life, she would forget, she would be happy, and through that, in the years to come, he could not but find life worth living.

All day he rode slowly and cautiously up the Pass, taking time to peer around corners, to pick out hard ground and grassy patches, and to make sure there was no one in pursuit. In the night sometime he came to the smooth, scrawled rocks dividing the valley, and here set the burro at liberty. He walked beyond, climbed the slope and the dim, starlit gorge. Then, weary to the point of exhaustion, he crept into a shallow cave and fell asleep.

In the morning, when he descended the trail, he found the sun was pouring a golden stream of light through the arch of the great stone bridge. Surprise Valley, like a valley of dreams, lay mystically soft and beautiful, awakening to the golden flood which was rolling away its slumberous bands of mist, brightening its walled faces.

While yet far off he discerned Bess moving under the silver spruces, and soon the barking of the dogs told him that they had seen him. He heard the mocking-birds singing in the trees, and then the twittering of the quail. Ring and Whitie came bounding toward him, and behind them ran Bess, her hands outstretched.

"Bern! You're back! You're back!" she cried, in joy that rang of her loneliness.

"Yes, I'm back," he said, as she rushed to meet him.

She had reached out for him when suddenly, as she saw him closely, something checked her, and as quickly all her joy fled, and with it her color, leaving her pale and trembling.

"Oh! What's happened?"

"A good deal has happened, Bess. I don't need to tell you what. And I'm played out. Worn out in mind more than body."

"Dear—you look strange to me!" faltered Bess.

"Never mind that. I'm all right. There's nothing for you to be scared about. Things are going to turn out just as we have planned. As soon as I'm rested we'll make a break to get out of the country. Only now, right now, I must know the truth about you."

"Truth about me?" echoed Bess, shrinkingly. She seemed to be casting back into her mind for a forgotten key. Venters himself, as he saw her, received a pang.

"Yes—the truth. Bess, don't misunderstand. I haven't changed that way. I love you still. I'll love you more afterward. Life will be just as sweet—sweeter to us. We'll be—be married as soon as ever we can. We'll be happy—but there's a devil in me. A perverse, jealous devil! Then I've queer fancies. I forgot for a long time. Now all those fiendish little whispers of doubt and faith and fear and hope come torturing me again. I've got to kill them with the truth."

"I'll tell you anything you want to know," she replied, frankly.

"Then, by Heaven! we'll have it over and done with! . . . Bess—did Oldring love you?"

"Certainly he did."

"Did—did you love him?"

"Of course. I told you so."

"How can you tell it so lightly?" cried Venters, passionately. "Haven't you any sense of—of—" He choked back speech. He felt the rush of pain and passion. He seized her in rude, strong hands and drew her close. He looked straight into her dark-blue eyes. They were shadowing with the old wistful light, but they were as clear as the limpid water of the spring. They were earnest, solemn in unutterable love and faith and abnegation. Venters shivered. He knew he was looking into her soul. He knew she could not lie in that moment; but that she might tell the truth, looking at him with those eyes, almost killed his belief in purity.

"What are—what were you to—to Oldring?" he panted, fiercely.

"I am his daughter," she replied, instantly.

Venters slowly let go of her. There was a violent break in the force of his feeling—then creeping blankness.

"What—was it—you said?" he asked, in a kind of dull wonder.

"I am his daughter."

"Oldring's daughter?" queried Venters, with life gathering in his voice.

"Yes."

With a passionately awakening start he grasped her hands and drew her close.

"All the time—you've been Oldring's daughter?"

"Yes, of course all the time—always."

"But Bess, you told me—you let me think—I made out you were—a—so—so ashamed."

"It is my shame," she said, with voice deep and full, and now the scarlet fired her cheek. "I told you—I'm nothing—nameless—just Bess, Oldring's girl!"

"I know—I remember. But I never thought—" he went on, hurriedly, huskily. "That time—when you lay dying—you prayed—you—somehow I got the idea you were bad."

"Bad?" she asked, with a little laugh.

She looked up with a faint smile of bewilderment and the absolute unconsciousness of a child. Venters gasped in the gathering might of the truth. She did not understand his meaning.

"Bess! Bess!" He clasped her in his arms, hiding her eyes against his breast. She must not see his face in that moment. And he held her while he looked out across the valley. In his dim and blinded sight, in the blur of golden light and moving mist, he saw Oldring. She was the rustler's nameless daughter. Oldring had loved her. He had so guarded her, so kept her from women and men and knowledge of life that her mind was as a child's. That was part of the secret—part of the mystery. That was the wonderful truth. Not only was she not bad, but good, pure, innocent above all innocence in the world—the innocence of lonely girlhood.

He saw Oldring's magnificent eyes, inquisitive, searching—softening. He saw them flare in amaze, in gladness, with love, then suddenly strain in terrible effort of will. He heard Oldring whisper and saw him sway like a log and fall. Then a million bellowing, thundering voices—gunshots of conscience, thunderbolts of remorse—dinned horribly in his ears. He had killed Bess's father. Then a rushing wind filled his ears like a moan of wind in the cliffs, a knell indeed—Oldring's knell.

He dropped to his knees and hid his face against Bess, and grasped her with the hands of a drowning man.

"My God! . . . My God! . . . Oh, Bess! . . . Forgive me! Never mind what I've done—what I've thought. But forgive me. I'll give you my life. I'll live for you. I'll love you. Oh, I do love you as no man ever loved a woman. I want you to know—to remember that I fought a fight for you—however blind I was. I thought—I thought—never mind what I thought—but I loved you—I asked you to marry me. Let that—let me have that to hug to my heart. Oh, Bess, I was driven! And I might have known! I could not rest nor sleep till I had this mystery solved. God! how things work out!"

"Bern, you're weak—trembling—you talk wildly," cried Bess. "You've overdone your strength. There's nothing to forgive. There's no mystery except your love for me. You have come back to me!"

And she clasped his head tenderly in her arms and pressed it closely to her throbbing breast.

CHAPTER NINETEEN

Fay

A<small>T</small> the home of Jane Withersteen Little Fay was climbing Lassiter's knee. "Does oo love me?" she asked.

Lassiter, who was as serious with Fay as he was gentle and loving, assured her in earnest and elaborate speech that he was her devoted subject. Fay looked thoughtful and appeared to be debating the duplicity of men or searching for a supreme test to prove this cavalier.

"Does oo love my new muvver?" she asked, with bewildering suddenness.

Jane Withersteen laughed, and for the first time in many a day she felt a stir of her pulse and warmth in her cheek.

It was a still drowsy summer of afternoon, and the three were sitting in the shade of the wooded knoll that faced the sage-slope. Little Fay's brief spell of unhappy longing for her mother—the childish, mystic gloom—had passed, and now where Fay was there were prattle and laughter and glee. She had emerged from sorrow to be the incarnation of joy and loveliness. She had grown supernaturally sweet and beautiful. For Jane Withersteen the child was an answer to prayer, a blessing, a possession infinitely more precious than all she had lost. For Lassiter, Jane divined that little Fay had become a religion.

"Does oo love my new muvver?" repeated Fay.

Lassiter's answer to this was a modest and sincere affirmative.

"Why don't oo marry my new muvver an' be my favver?"

Of the thousands of questions put by little Fay to Lassiter that was the first he had been unable to answer.

"Fay—Fay, don't ask questions like that," said Jane.

"Why?"

"Because," replied Jane. And she found it strangely embarrassing to meet the child's gaze. It seemed to her that Fay's violet eyes looked through her with piercing wisdom.

"Oo love him, don't oo?"

"Dear child—run and play," said Jane, "but don't go too far. Don't go from this little hill."

Fay pranced off wildly, joyous over freedom that had not been granted her for weeks.

"Jane, why are children more sincere than grown-up persons?" asked Lassiter.

"Are they?"

"I reckon so. Little Fay there—she sees things as they appear on the face. An Indian does that. So does a dog. An' an Indian an' a dog are most of the time right in what they see. Mebbe a child is always right."

"Well, what does Fay see?" asked Jane.

"I reckon you know. I wonder what goes on in Fay's mind when she sees part of the truth with the wise eyes of a child, an' wantin' to know more, meets with strange falseness from you? Wait! You are false in a way, though you're the best woman I ever knew. What I want to say is this. Fay has taken you're pretendin' to—to care for me for the thing it looks on the face. An' her little formin' mind asks questions. An' the answers she gets are different from the looks of things. So she'll grow up, gradually takin' on that falseness, an' be like the rest of the women, an' men, too. An' the truth of this falseness to life is proved by your appearin' to love me when you don't. Things aren't what they seem."

"Lassiter, you're right. A child should be told the absolute truth. But—is that possible? I haven't been able to do it, and all my life I've loved the truth, and I've prided myself upon being truthful. Maybe that was only egotism. I'm learning much, my friend. Some of those blinding scales have fallen from my eyes. And—and as to caring for you, I think I care a great deal. How much, how little, I couldn't say. My heart is almost broken, Lassiter. So now is not a good time to judge of affection. I can still play and be merry with Fay. I can still dream. But when I attempt serious thought I'm dazed. I don't think. I don't care any more. I don't pray! . . . Think of that, my friend! But in spite of my numb feeling I believe I'll rise out of all this dark agony a better woman, with greater love of man and God. I'm on the rack now; I'm senseless to all but pain, and growing dead to that. Sooner or later I shall rise out of this stupor. I'm waiting the hour."

"It'll soon come, Jane," replied Lassiter, soberly. "Then I'm afraid for you. Years are terrible things, an' for years you've been bound. Habit of years is strong as life itself. Somehow, though, I believe as you—that you'll come out of it all a finer woman. I'm waitin', too. An' I'm wonderin'—I reckon, Jane, that marriage between us is out of all human reason?"

"Lassiter! . . . My dear friend! . . . It's impossible for us to marry."

"Why—as Fay says?" inquired Lassiter, with gentle persistence.

"Why! I never thought why. But it's not possible. I am Jane, daughter of Withersteen. My father would rise out of his grave. I'm of Mormon birth. I'm being broken. But I'm still a Mormon woman. And you—you are Lassiter!"

"Mebbe I'm not so much Lassiter as I used to be."

"What was it you said? Habit of years is strong as life itself! You can't change the one habit—the purpose of your life. For you still pack those black guns! You still nurse your passion for blood."

A smile, like a shadow, flickered across his face.

"No."

"Lassiter, I lied to you. But I beg of you—don't you lie to me. I've great respect for you. I believe you're softened toward most, perhaps all, my people except— But when I speak of your purpose, your hate, your guns, I have only him in mind. I don't believe you've changed.

For answer he unbuckled the heavy cartridge-belt, and laid it with the heavy, swing gun-sheaths in her lap.

"Lassiter!" Jane whispered, as she gazed from him to the black, cold guns. Without them he appeared shorn of strength, defenseless, a smaller man. Was she Delilah? Swiftly, conscious of only one motive—refusal to see this man called craven by his enemies—she rose, and with blundering fingers buckled the belt round his waist where it belonged.

"Lassiter, *I* am a coward."

"Come with me out of Utah—where I can put away my guns an' be a man," he said. "I reckon I'll prove it to you then! Come! You've got Black Star back, an' Night an' Bells. Let's take the racers an' little Fay, an' ride cut of Utah. The hosses an' the child are all you have left. Come!"

"No, no, Lassiter. I'll never leave Utah. What would I do in the world with my broken fortunes and my broken heart? I'll never leave these purple slopes I love so well."

"I reckon I ought to've knowed that. Presently you'll be livin' down here in a hovel, an' presently Jane Withersteen will be a memory. I only wanted to have a chance to show you how a man—*any* man—can be better 'n he was. If we left Utah I could prove—I reckon I could prove this thing you call love. It's strange, an' hell an' heaven at once, Jane Withersteen. 'Pears to me that you've thrown away your big heart on love—love of religion an' duty an' churchmen, an' riders an' poor families an' poor children! Yet you can't see what love is—how it changes a person! . . . Listen, an' in tellin' you Milly Erne's story I'll show you how love changed her.

"Milly an' me was children when our family moved from Missouri to Texas, an' we growed up in Texas ways same as if we'd been born there. We had been poor, an' there we prospered. In time the little village where we went became a town, an' strangers an' new families kept movin' in. Milly was the belle them days. I can see her now, a little girl no bigger 'n a bird, an' as pretty. She had the finest eyes, dark blue-black when she was excited, an' beautiful all the time. You remember Milly's eyes! An' she had light-brown hair with streaks of gold, an' a mouth that every feller wanted to kiss.

"An' about the time Milly was the prettiest an' the sweetest, along came a young minister who began to ride some of a race with the other fellers for Milly. An' he won. Milly had always been strong on religion, an' when she met Frank Erne she went in heart an' soul for the salvation of souls. Fact was, Milly, through study of the Bible an' attendin' church an' revivals, went a little out of her head. It didn't worry the old folks none, an' the only worry to me was Milly's everlastin' prayin' an' workin' to save my soul. She never converted me, but we was the best of comrades, an' I reckon no brother an' sister ever loved each other better. Well, Frank Erne an' me hit up a great friendship. He was a strappin' feller, good to look at, an' had the most pleasin' ways. His religion never bothered me, for he could hunt an' fish an' ride an' be a good feller. After buffalo once, he come pretty near to savin' my life. We got to be thick as brothers, an' he was the only man I ever seen who I thought was good enough for Milly. An' the day they were married I got drunk for the only time in my life.

"Soon after that I left home—it seems Milly was the only one who could keep me home—an' I went to the bad, as to prosperin'. I saw some pretty hard life in the Pan Handle, an' then I went North. In them days Kansas an' Nebraska was as bad, come to think of it, as these days right here on the border of Utah. I got to be pretty handy with guns. An' there wasn't many riders as could beat me ridin'. An' I can say all modest-like that I never seen the white man who could track a hoss or a steer or a man with me. Afore I knowed it two years slipped by, an' all at once I got homesick, an' pulled a bridle south.

"Things at home had changed. I never got over that home-comin'. Mother was dead an' in her grave. Father was a silent, broken man, killed already on his feet. Frank Erne was a ghost of his old self, through with workin', through with preachin', almost through with livin', an' Milly was gone! . . . It was a long time before I got the story. Father had no mind left, an' Frank Erne was *afraid* to talk. So I had to pick up what 'd happened from different people.

"It 'pears that soon after I left home another preacher come to the little town. An' he an' Frank become rivals. This feller was different from Frank. He preached some other kind of religion, and he was quick an' passionate, where Frank was slow an' mild. He went after people, women specially. In looks he couldn't compare to Frank Erne, but he had power over women. He had a voice, an' he talked an' talked an' preached an' preached. Milly fell under his influence. She became mightily interested in his religion. Frank had patience with her, as was his way, an' let her be as interested as she liked. All religions were devoted to one God, he said, an' it wouldn't hurt Milly none to study a different point of view. So the new preacher often called on Milly, an' sometimes in Frank's absence. Frank was a cattle-man between Sundays.

"Along about this time an incident come off that I couldn't get much light on. A stranger come to town, an' was seen with the preacher. This stranger was a big man with an eye like blue ice, an' a beard of gold. He had money, an' he 'peared a man of mystery, an' the town went to buzzin' when he disappeared about the same time as a young woman known to be mightily interested in the new preacher's religion. Then, presently, along comes a man from somewheres in Illinois, an' he up an' spots this preacher as a famous Mormon proselyter. That ri'led Frank Erne as nothin' ever before, an' from rivals they come to be bitter enemies. An' it ended in Frank goin' to the meetin'-house where Milly was listenin', an' before her an' everybody else he called that preacher—called him, well, almost as hard as Venters called Tull here sometime back. An' Frank followed up that call with a hoss-whippin', an' he drove the proselyter out of town.

"People noticed, so 'twas said, that Milly's sweet disposition changed. Some said it was because she would soon become a mother, an' others said she was pinin' after the new religion. An' there was women who said right out that she was pinin' after the Mormon. Anyway, one mornin' Frank rode in from one of his trips, to find Milly gone. He had no real near neighbors—livin' a little out of town—but those who was nearest said a wagon had gone by in the night, an' they though it stopped at her door. Well, tracks always tell, an' there was the wagon tracks an' hoss tracks an' man tracks. The news spread like wildfire that Milly had run off from her husband. Everybody but Frank believed it an' wasn't slow in tellin' why she run off. Mother had always hated that strange streak of Milly's, takin' up with the new religion as she had, an' she believed Milly ran off with the Mormon. That hastened mother's death, an' she died unforgivin'. Father wasn't the kind to bow down under disgrace or misfortune, but he had surpassin' love for Milly, an' the loss of her broke him.

"From the minute I heard of Milly's disappearance I never believed she went off of her own free will. I knew Milly, an' I knew she *couldn't* have done that. I stayed at home awhile, tryin' to make Frank Erne talk. But if he knowed anythin' then he wouldn't tell it. So I set out to find Milly. An' I tried to get on the trail of that proselyter. I knew if I ever struck a town he'd visited that I'd get a trail. I knew, too, that nothin' short of hell would stop his proselytin'. An' I rode from town to town. I had a blind faith that somethin' was guidin' me. An' as the weeks an' months went by I growed into a strange sort of a man, I guess. Anyway, people were afraid of me. Two yars after that, way over in a corner of Texas, I struck a town where my man had been. He'd jest left. People said he came to that town *without* a woman. I back-trailed my man through Arkansas an' Mississippi, an' the old trail got hot again in Texas. I found the town where he first went after leavin' home. An' here I got track of Milly. I found a cabin where she had given birth to her baby. There was no way to tell whether she'd been kept a prisoner or not. The feller who owned the place was a mean, silent sort of a skunk, an' as I was leavin' I jest took a chance an' left my mark on him. Then I went home again.

"It was to find I hadn't any home, no more. Father had been dead a year. Frank Erne still lived in the house where Milly had left him. I stayed with him awhile, an' I grew old watchin' him. His farm had gone to weed, his cattle had strayed or been rustled, his house weathered till it wouldn't keep out rain nor wind. An' Frank set on the porch and whittled sticks, an' day by day wasted away. There was times when he ranted about like a crazy man, but mostly he was always sittin' an' starin' with eyes that made a man curse. I figured Frank had a secret fear that I needed to know. An' when I told him I'd trailed Milly for near three years an' had got trace of her, an' saw where she'd had her baby, I thought he would drop dead at my feet. An' when he'd come round more natural-like he begged me to *give up* the trail. But he wouldn't explain. So I let him alone, an' watched him day an' night.

"An' I found there was one thing still precious to him, an' it was a little drawer where he kept his papers. This was in the room where he slept. An' it 'peared he seldom slept. But after bein' patient I got the contents of that drawer an' found two letters from Milly. One was a long letter written a few months after her disappearance. She had been bound an' gagged an' dragged away from her home by three men, an' she named them—Hurd, Metzger, Slack. They was strangers to her. She was taken to the little town where I found trace of her two years after. But she didn't send the letter from that town. There she was penned in. 'Peared that the proselyter, who had, of course, come on the scene, was not runnin' any risks of losin' her. She went on to say that for a time she was out of her head, an' when she got right again all that kept her alive was the baby. It was a beautiful baby, she said, an' all she thought an' dreamed of was somehow to get baby back to its father, an' then she'd thankfully lay down and die. An' the letter ended abrupt, in the middle of a sentence, an' it wasn't signed.

"The second letter was written more than two years after the first. It was from Salt Lake City. It simply said that Milly had heard her brother was on her trail. She asked Frank to tell her brother to give up the search because if he didn't she would suffer in a way too horrible to tell. She didn't beg. She just stated a fact an' made the simple request. An' she ended that letter by sayin' she would soon leave Salt Lake City with the man she had come to love, an' would never be heard of again.

"I recognized Milly's handwritin', an' I recognized her way of puttin' things. But that second letter told me of some great change in her. Ponderin' over it, I felt at last she'd either come to love that feller an' his religion, or some terrible fear made her lie an' say so. I couldn't be sure which. But, of course, I meant to find out. I'll say here, if I'd known Mormons then as I do now I'd left Milly to her fate. For mebbe she was right about what she'd suffer if I kept on her trail. But I was young an' wild them days. First I went to the town where she'd first been taken, an' I went to the place where she'd been kept. I got that skunk who owned the place, an' took him out in the woods, an' made him tell all he knowed. That wasn't much as to length, but it was pure hell's-fire in substance. This time I left him some incapacitated for any more skunk work short of hell. Then I hit the trail for Utah.

"That was fourteen years ago. I saw the incomin' of most of the Mormons. It was a wild country an' a wild time. I rode from town to town, village to village, ranch to ranch, camp to camp. I never stayed long in one place. I never had but one idea. I never rested. Four years went by, an' I knowed every trail in northern Utah. I kept on an' as time went by, an' I'd begun to grow old in my search, I had firmer, blinder faith in whatever was guidin' me. Once I read about a feller who sailed the seven seas an' traveled the world, an' he had a story to tell, an' whenever he seen the man to whom he must tell that story he knowed him on sight. I was like that, only I had a question to ask. An' always I knew the man of whom I must ask. So I never really lost the trail, though for many years it was the dimmest trail ever followed by any man.

"Then come a change in my luck. Along in Central Utah I rounded up Hurd, an' I whispered somethin' in his ear, an' watched his face, an' then throwed a gun against his bowels. An' he died with his teeth so tight shut I couldn't have pried them open with a knife. Slack an' Metzger that same year both heard me whisper the same question, an' neither would they speak a word when they lay dyin'. Long before I'd learned no man of this breed or class—or God knows what—would give up any secrets! I had to see in a man's fear of death the connections with Milly Erne's fate. An' as the years passed at long intervals I would find such a man.

"So as I drifted on the long trail down into southern Utah my name preceded me, an' I had to meet a people prepared for me, an' ready with guns. They made me a gun-man. An' that suited me. In all this time signs of the proselyter an' the giant with the blue-ice eyes an' the gold beard seemed to fade dimmer out of the trail. Only twice in ten years did I find a trace of that mysterious man who had visited the proselyter at my home village. What he had to do with Milly's fate was beyond all hope for me to learn, unless my guidin' spirit led me to him! As for the other man, I knew, as sure as I breathed an' the stars shone an' the wind blew, that I'd meet him some day.

"Eighteen years I've been on the trail. An' it led me to the last lonely villages of the Utah border. Eighteen years! . . . I feel pretty old now. I was only twenty when I hit that trail. Well, as I told you, back here a ways a Gentile said Jane Withersteen could tell me about Milly Erne an' show me her grave!"

The low voice ceased, and Lassiter slowly turned his sombrero round and round, and appeared to be counting the silver ornaments on the band. Jane, leaning toward him, sat as if petrified, listening intently, waiting to hear more. She could have shrieked, but power of tongue and lips were denied her. She saw only this sad, gray, passion-worn man, and she heard only the faint rustling of the leaves.

"Well, I came to Cottonwoods," went on Lassiter, "an' you showed me Milly's grave. An' though your teeth have been shut tighter 'n them of all the dead men lyin' back along that trail, jest the same you told me the secret I've lived these eighteen years to hear! Jane, I said you'd tell me without ever me askin'. I didn't need to ask my question here. The day, you remember, when that fat party throwed a gun on me in your court, an'—"

"Oh! Hush!" whispered Jane, blindly holding up her hands.

"I seen in your face that Dyer, now a bishop, was the proselyter who ruined Milly Erne!"

For an instant Jane Withersteen's brain was a whirling chaos, and she recovered to find herself grasping at Lassiter like one drowning. And as if by a lightning stroke she sprang from her dull apathy into exquisite torture.

"It's a lie! Lassiter! No, no!" she moaned. "I swear—you're wrong!"

"Stop! You'd perjure yourself! But I'll spare you that. You poor woman! Still blind! Still faithful! . . . Listen. *I know.* Let that settle it. An' I give up my purpose!"

"What is it—you say?"

"I give up my purpose. I've come to see an' feel differently. I can't help poor Milly. An' I've outgrowed revenge. I've come to see I can be no judge for men. I can't kill a man jest for hate. Hate ain't the same with me since I loved you and little Fay."

"Lassiter! You mean you won't kill him?" Jane whispered.

"No."

"For my sake?"

"I reckon. I can't understand, but I'll respect your feelin's."

"Because you—oh, because you love me? . . . Eighteen years! You were that terrible Lassiter! And *now*—because you love me?"

"That's it, Jane."

"Oh, you'll make me love you! How can I help but love you? My heart must be stone. But—oh, Lassiter, wait, wait! Give me time. I'm not what I was. Once it was so easy to love. Now it's easy to hate. Wait! My faith in God—*some* God—still lives. By it I see happier times for you, poor passion-swayed wanderer! For me—a miserable, broken woman. I loved your sister Milly. I *will* love you. I can't have fallen so low—I can't be so abandoned by God—that I've no love left to give you. Wait! Let us forget Milly's sad life. Ah, I knew it as no one else on earth! There's one thing I shall tell you—if you are at my death-bed, but I can't speak now."

"I reckon I don't want to hear no more," said Lassiter.

Jane leaned against him; as if some pent-up force had rent its way out, she fell into a paroxysm of weeping. Lassiter held her in silent sympathy. By degrees she regained composure, and she was rising, sensible of being relieved of a weighty burden, when a sudden start on Lassiter's part alarmed her.

"I heard hosses—hosses with muffled hoofs!" he said; and he got up guardedly.

"Where's Fay?" asked Jane, hurriedly glancing round the shady knoll. The bright-haired child, who had appeared to be close all the time, was not in sight.

"Fay!" called Jane.

No answering shout of glee. No patter of flying feet. Jane saw Lassiter stiffen.

"Fay—oh—Fay!" Jane almost screamed.

The leaves quivered and rustled; a lonesome cricket chirped in the grass; a bee hummed by. The silence of the waning afternoon breathed hateful portent. It terrified Jane. When had silence been so infernal?

"She's—only—strayed—out—of earshot," faltered Jane, looking at Lassiter.

Pale, rigid as a statue, the rider stood, not in listening, searching posture, but in one of doomed certainty. Suddenly he grasped Jane with an iron hand, and, turning his face from her gaze, he strode with her from the knoll.

"See—Fay played here last—a house of stones an' sticks. . . . An' here's a corral of pebbles with leaves for hosses," said Lassiter, stridently, and pointed to the ground. "Back an' forth she trailed here. . . . See, she's buried somethin'—a dead grasshopper—there's a tombstone . . . here she went, chasin' a lizard—see the tiny streaked trail . . . she pulled bark off this cottonwood . . . look in the dust of the path—the letters you taught her—she's drawn pictures of birds an' hosses an' people. . . . Look, a cross! Oh, Jane, *your* cross!"

Lassiter dragged Jane on, and as if from a book read the meaning of little Fay's trail. All the way down the knoll, through the shrubbery, round and round a cottonwood, Fay's vagrant fancy left records of her sweet musings and innocent play. Long had she lingered round a bird-nest to leave therein the gaudy wing of a butterfly. Long had she played beside the running stream, sending adrift vessels freighted with pebbly cargo. Then she had wandered through the deep grass, her tiny feet scarcely turning a fragile blade, and she had dreamed beside some old faded flowers. Thus her steps led her into the broad lane. The little dimpled imprints of her bare feet showed clean-cut in the dust; they went a little way down the lane; and then, at a point where they stopped, the great tracks of a man led out from the shrubbery and returned.

CHAPTER TWENTY

Lassiter's Way

FOOTPRINTS told the story of little Fay's abduction. In anguish Jane Withersteen turned speechlessly to Lassiter, and, confirming her fears, she saw him gray-faced, aged all in a moment, stricken as if by a mortal blow.

Then all her life seemed to fall about her in wreck and ruin.

"It's all over," she heard her voice whisper. "It's ended. I'm going—I'm going—"

"Where?" demanded Lassiter, suddenly looming darkly over her.

"To—to those cruel men—"

"Speak names!" thundered Lassiter.

"To Bishop Dyer—to Tull," went on Jane, shocked into obedience.

"Well—what for?"

"I want little Fay. I can't live without her. They've stolen her as they stole Milly Erne's child. I must have little Fay. I want only her. I give up. I'll go and tell Bishop Dyer—I'm broken. I'll tell him I'm ready for the yoke—only give me back Fay—and—and I'll marry Tull!"

"*Never!*" hissed Lassiter.

His long arm leaped at her. Almost running, he dragged her under the cotton-woods, across the court, into the huge hall of Withersteen House, and he shut the door with a force that jarred the heavy walls. Black Star and Night and Bells, since their return, had been locked in this hall, and now they stamped on the stone floor.

Lassiter released Jane and like a dizzy man swayed from her with a hoarse cry and leaned shaking against a table where he kept his rider's accoutrements. He began to fumble in his saddle-bags. His action brought a clinking, metallic sound—the rattling of gun-cartridges. His fingers trembled as he slipped cartridges into an extra belt. But as he buckled it over the one he habitually wore his hands became steady. This second belt contained two guns, smaller than the black ones swinging low, and he slipped them round so that his coat hid them. Then he fell to swift action. Jane Withersteen watched him, fascinated but uncomprehending;

and she saw him rapidly saddle Black Star and Night. Then he drew her into the light of the huge windows, standing over her, gripping her arm with fingers like cold steel.

"Yes, Jane, it's ended—but you're not goin' to Dyer! . . . *I'm goin' instead!*"

Looking at him—he was so terrible of aspect—she could not comprehend his words. Who was this man with the face gray as death, with eyes that would have made her shriek had she the strength, with the strange, ruthlessly bitter lips? Where was the gentle Lassiter? What was this presence in the hall, about him, about her—this cold, invisible presence?

"Yes, it's ended, Jane," he was saying, so awfully quiet and cool and implacable, "an' I'm goin' to make a little call. I'll lock you in here, an' when I get back have the saddle-bags full of meat an' bread. An' be ready to ride!"

"Lassiter!" cried Jane.

Desperately she tried to meet his gray eyes, in vain; desperately she tried again, fought herself as feeling and thought resurged in torment, and she succeeded; and then she knew.

"No—no—no!" she wailed. "You said you'd foregone your vengeance. You promised not to kill Bishop Dyer."

"If you want to talk to me about him—leave off the Bishop. I don't understand that name, or its use."

"Oh, hadn't you foregone your vengeance on—on Dyer?"

"Yes."

"But—your actions—your words—your guns—your terrible looks! . . . They don't seem foregoing vengeance?"

"Jane, now it's justice."

"You'll—kill him?"

"If God lets me live another hour! If not God—then the devil who drives me!"

"You'll kill him—for yourself—for your vengeful hate?"

"No!"

"For Milly Erne's sake?"

"No."

"For little Fay's?"

"No!"

"Oh—for whose?"

"For yours!"

"His blood on my soul!" whispered Jane, and she fell to her knees. This was the long-pending hour of fruition. And the habit of years—the religious passion of her life—leaped from lethargy, and the long months of gradual drifting to doubt were as if they had never been. "If you spill his blood it'll be on my soul—and on my father's. Listen." And she clasped his knees, and clung there as he tried to raise her. "Listen. Am I nothing to you?"

"Woman—don't trifle at words! I love you! An' I'll soon prove it!"

"I'll give myself to you—I'll ride away with you—marry you, if only you'll spare him?"

His answer was a cold, ringing, terrible laugh.

"Lassiter—I'll love you. Spare him!"

"No!"

She sprang up in despairing, breaking spirit, and encircled his neck with her arms, and held him in an embrace that he strove vainly to loosen. "Lassiter, would you kill me? I'm fighting my last fight for the principles of my youth—love of religion, love of father. You don't know—you can't guess the truth, and I can't speak it! I'm losing all. I'm changing. All I've gone through is nothing to this hour. Pity me—help me in my weakness. You're strong again—oh, so cruelly, coldly strong! You're killing me. I see you—feel you as some other Lassiter! My master, be merciful—spare him!"

His answer was a ruthless smile.

She clung the closer to him, and leaned her panting breast on him, and lifted her face to his. "Lassiter, *I do love you!* It's leaped out of my agony. It comes suddenly with a terrible blow of truth. You are a man! I never knew it till now. Some wonderful change came to me when you buckled on these guns and showed that gray, awful face. I loved you then. All my life I've loved, but never as now. No woman can love like a broken woman. If it were not for one thing—just one thing—and yet! I *can't* speak it—I'd glory in your manhood—the lion in you that means to slay for me. Believe me—and spare Dyer. Be merciful—great as it's in you to be great. . . . Oh, listen and believe—I have nothing, but I'm a woman—a beautiful woman, Lassiter—a passionate, loving woman—and I love you! Take me—hide me in some wild place—and love me and mend my broken heart. Spare him and take me away."

She lifted her face closer and closer to his, until their lips nearly touched, and she hung upon his neck, and with strength almost spent pressed and still pressed her palpitating body to his.

"Kiss me!" she whispered, blindly.

"No—not at your price!" he answered. His voice had changed or she had lost clearness of hearing.

"Kiss me! . . . Are you a man? Kiss me and save me!"

"Jane, you never played fair with me. But now you're blisterin' your lips—blackenin' your soul with lies!"

"By the memory of my mother—by my Bible—no! No, I *have* no Bible! But by my hope of heaven I swear I love you!"

Lassiter's gray lips formed soundless words that meant even her love could not avail to bend his will. As if the hold of her arms was that of a child's he loosened it and stepped away.

"Wait! Don't go! Oh, hear a last word! . . . May a more just and merciful God than the God I was taught to worship judge me—forgive me—save me! For I can no longer keep silent! . . . Lassiter, in pleading for Dyer I've been pleading more for my father. My father was a Mormon master, close to the leaders of the church. It was my father who sent Dyer out to proselyte. It was my father who had the blue-ice eye and the beard of gold. It was my father you got trace of in the past years. Truly, Dyer ruined Milly Erne—dragged her from her home—to Utah—to Cottonwoods. *But it was for my father!* If Milly Erne was ever wife of a Mormon that Mormon was my father! I never knew—never will know whether or not she was a wife. Blind I may be, Lassiter—fanatically faithful to a false religion I may have been, but I know justice, and my father is beyond human justice. Surely he is meeting just punishment—somewhere. Always it has appalled me—the thought of your killing Dyer for my father's sins. So I have prayed!"

"Jane, the past is dead. In my love for you I forgot the past. This thing I'm about to do ain't for myself or Milly or Fay. It's not because of anythin' that ever happened in the past, but for what is happenin' right *now. It's for you!* . . . An' listen. Since I was a boy I've never thanked God for anythin'. If there is a God—an' I've come to believe it—I thank Him now for the years that made me Lassiter! . . . I can reach down an' feel these big guns, an' know what I can do with them. An', Jane, only one of the miracles Dyer professes to believe in can save him!"

Again for Jane Withersteen came the spinning of her brain in darkness, and as she whirled in endless chaos she seemed to be falling at the feet of a luminous figure—a man—Lassiter—who had saved her from herself, who could not be changed, who would slay rightfully. Then she slipped into utter blackness.

When she recovered from her faint she became aware that she was lying on a couch near the window in her sitting-room. Her brow felt damp and cold and wet; some one was chafing her hands; she recognized Judkins, and then saw that his lean, hard face wore the hue and look of excessive agitation.

"Judkins!" Her voice broke weakly.

"Aw, Miss Withersteen, you're comin' round fine. Now jest lay still a little. You're all right; everythin's all right."

"Where is—he?"

"Who?"

"Lassiter!"

"You needn't worry none about him."

"Where is he? Tell me—instantly."

"Wal, he's in the other room patchin' up a few triflin' bullet-holes."

"*Ah! . . . Bishop Dyer?*"

"When I seen him last—a matter of half an hour ago, he was on his knees. He was some busy, *but* he wasn't prayin'!"

"How strangely you talk! I'll sit up. I'm—well, strong again. Tell me. Dyer on his knees! What was he doing?"

"Wal, beggin' your pardon fer blunt talk, Miss Withersteen, Dyer was on his knees an' *not* prayin'. You remember his big, broad hands? You've seen 'em raised in blessin' over old gray men an' little curly-headed children like—like Fay Larkin! Come to think of thet, I disremember ever hearin' of his liftin' his big hands in blessin' over a *woman*. Wal, when I seen him last—jest a little while ago—he was on his knees, *not* prayin', as I remarked—an' he was pressin' his big hands over some bigger wounds."

"Man, you drive me mad! Did Lassiter kill Dyer?"

"Yes."

"Did he kill Tull?"

"No. Tull's out of the village with most of his riders. He's expected back before evenin'. Lassiter will hev to git away before Tull an' his riders come in. It's sure death fer him here. An' wuss fer you, too, Miss Withersteen. There'll be some of an uprisin' when Tull gits back."

"I shall ride away with Lassiter. Judkins, tell me all you saw—all you know about this killing." She realized, without wonder or amaze, how Judkins's one word, affirming the death of Dyer—that the catastrophe had fallen—had completed the change whereby she had been molded or beaten or broken into another woman. She felt calm, slightly cold, strong as she had not been strong since the first shadow fell upon her.

"I jest saw about all of it, Miss Withersteen, an' I'll be glad to tell you if you'll only hev patience with me," said Judkins, earnestly. "You see, I've been pecooliarly interested, an' nat'rully I'm some excited. An' I talk a lot thet mebbe ain't necessary, but I can't help thet.

"I was at the meetin'-house where Dyer was holdin' court. You know he allus acts as magistrate an' judge when Tull's away. An' the trial was fer tryin' what's left of my boy riders—thet helped me hold your cattle—fer a lot of hatched-up things the boys never did. We're used to thet, an' the boys wouldn't hev minded bein' locked up fer a while, or hevin' to dig ditches, or whatever the judge laid down. You see, I divided the gold you give me among all my boys, an' they all hid it, an' they all feel rich. Howsomever, court was adjourned before the judge passed sentence. Yes, ma'm, court was adjourned some strange an' quick, much as if lightnin' hed struck the meetin'-house.

"I hed trouble attendin' the trial, but I got in. There was a good many people there, all my boys, an' Judge Dyer with his several clerks. Also he hed with him the five riders who've been guardin' him pretty close of late. They was Carter, Wright, Jengessen, an' two new riders from Stone Bridge. I didn't hear their names, but I heard they was handy men with guns an' they looked more like rustlers than riders. Anyway, there they was, the five all in a row.

"Judge Dyer was tellin' Willie Kern, one of my best an' steadiest boys—Dyer was tellin' him how there was a ditch opened near Willie's home lettin' water through his lot, where it hadn't ought to go. An' Willie was tryin' to git a word in to prove he wasn't at home all the day it happened—which was true, as I know—but Willie couldn't git a word in, an' then Judge Dyer went on layin' down the law. An' all to onct he happened to look down the long room. An' if ever any man turned to stone he was thet man.

"Nat'rully I looked back to see what hed acted so powerful strange on the judge. An' there, half-way up the room, in the middle of the wide aisle, stood Lassiter! All white an' black he looked, an' I can't think of anythin' he resembled, onless it's death. Venters made thet same room some still an' chilly when he called Tull; but this was different. I give my word, Miss Withersteen, thet I went cold to my very marrow. I don't know why. But Lassiter had a way about him thet's awful. He spoke a word—a name—I couldn't understand it, though he spoke clear as a bell. I was too excited, mebbe. Judge Dyer must hev understood it, an' a lot more thet was mystery to me, for he pitched forrard out of his chair right onto the platform.

"Then them five riders, Dyer's bodyguards, they jumped up an' two of them thet I found out afterward were the stranger from Stone Bridge, they piled right out of a winder, so quick you couldn't catch your breath. It was plain they wasn't Mormons.

"Jengessen, Carter, an' Wright eyed Lassiter, for what must hev been a second an' seemed like an hour, an' they went white an' strung. But they didn't weaken nor lose their nerve.

"I hed a good look at Lassiter. He stood sort of stiff, bendin' a little, an' both his arms were crooked, an' his hands looked like a hawk's claws. But there ain't no tellin' how his eyes looked. I know this, though, an' thet is his eyes could read the mind of any man about to throw a gun. An' in watchin' him, of course, I couldn't see the three men go fer their guns. An' though I was lookin' right at Lassiter—lookin' hard—I couldn't see how he drawed. He was quicker 'n eyesight— thet's all. But I seen the red spurtin' of his guns, an' heard his shots jest the very littlest instant before I heard the shots of the riders. An' when I turned, Wright an' Carter was down, an' Jengessen, who's tough like a steer, was pullin' the trigger of a wabblin' gun. But it was plain he was shot through, plumb center. An' sudden he fell with a crash, an' his gun clattered on the floor.

"Then there was a hell of a silence. Nobody breathed. Sartin I didn't, anyway. I saw Lassiter slip a smokin' gun back in a belt. But he hadn't throwed either of the big black guns, an' I thought thet strange. An' all this was happenin' quick— you can't imagine how quick.

"There come a scrapin' on the floor an' Dyer got up, his face like lead. I wanted to watch Lassiter, but Dyer's face, onct I seen it like thet, glued my eyes. I seen him go fer his gun—why, I could hev done better, quicker—an' then there was a thunderin' shot from Lassiter, an' it hit Dyer's right arm, an' his gun went off as it dropped. He looked at Lassiter like a cornered sage-wolf, an' sort of howled, an' reached down fer his gun. He'd jest picked it off the floor an' was raisin' it when another thunderin' shot almost tore thet arm off—so it seemed to me. The gun dropped again an' he went down on his knees, kind of flounderin' after it. It was some strange an' terrible to see his awful earnestness. Why would such a man cling so to life? Anyway, he got the gun with left hand an' was raisin' it, pullin' trigger in his madness, when the third thunderin' shot hit his left arm, an' he dropped the gun again. But thet left arm wasn't useless yet, fer he grabbed up the gun, an' with a shakin' 'aim thet would hev been pitiful to me—in any other man—he began to shoot. One wild bullet struck a man twenty feet from Lassiter. An' it killed thet man, as I seen afterward. Then come a bunch of thun- derin' shots—nine I calkilated after, fer they come so quick I couldn't count them—an' I knew Lassiter hed turned the black guns loose on Dyer.

"I'm tellin' you straight, Miss Withersteen, fer I want you to know. Afterward you'll git over it. I've seen some soul-rackin' scenes on this Utah border, but this was the awfulest. I remember I closed my eyes, an' fer a minute I thought of the strangest things, out of place there, such as you'd never dream would come to mind. I saw the sage, an' runnin' hosses—an' thet's the beautifulest sight to me—an' I saw dim things in the dark, an' there was a kind of hummin' in my ears. An' I remember distinctly—fer it was what made all these things whirl out of my mind an' opened my eyes—I remember distinctly it was the smell of gunpowder.

"The court had about adjourned fer thet judge. He was on his knees, an' he wasn't prayin'. He was gaspin' an' tryin' to press his big, floppin', crippled hands over his body. Lassiter had sent all those last thunderin' shots through his body. Thet was Lassiter's way.

"An' Lassiter spoke, an' if I ever forgit his words I'll never forgit the sound of his voice.

"'*Proselyter*, I reckon you'd better call quick on thet God who reveals Hisself to you on earth, because He won't be visitin' the place you're goin' to!'

"An' then I seen Dyer look at his big, hangin' hands thet wasn't big enough fer the last work he set them to. An' he looked up at Lassiter. An' then he stared horrible at somethin' thet wasn't Lassiter, nor anyone there, nor the room, nor the branches of purple sage peepin' into the winder. Whatever he seen, it was with the look of a man who *discovers* somethin' too late. Thet's a terrible look! . . . An' with a horrible *understandin'* cry he slid forrard on his face."

Judkins paused in his narrative, breathing heavily while he wiped his perspiring brow.

"Thet's about all," he concluded. "Lassiter left the meetin'-house an' I hurried to catch up with him. He was bleedin' from three gunshots, none of them much to bother him. An' we come right up here. I found you layin' in the hall, an' I hed to work some over you."

Jane Withersteen offered up no prayer for Dyer's soul.

Lassiter's step sounded in the hall—the familiar soft, silver-clinking step—and she heard it with thrilling new emotions in which was a vague joy in her very fear of him. The door opened, and she saw him, the old Lassiter, slow, easy, gentle, cool, yet not exactly the same Lassiter. She rose, and for a moment her eyes blurred and swam in tears.

"Are you—all—all right?" she asked, tremulously.

"I reckon."

"Lassiter, I'll ride away with you. Hide me till danger is past—till we are forgotten—then take me where you will. Your people shall be my people, and your God my God!"

He kissed her hand with the quaint grace and courtesy that came to him in rare moments.

"Black Star an' Night are ready," he said, simply.

His quiet mention of the black racers spurred Jane to action. Hurrying to her room, she changed to her rider's suit, packed her jewelry, and the gold that was left, and all the woman's apparel for which there was space in the saddle-bags, and then returned to the hall. Black Star stamped his iron-shod hoofs and tossed his beautiful head, and eyed her with knowing eyes.

"Judkins, I give Bells to you," said Jane. "I hope you will always keep him and be good to him."

Judkins mumbled thanks that he could not speak fluently, and his eyes flashed.

Lassiter strapped Jane's saddle-bags upon Black Star, and led the racers out into the court.

"Judkins, you ride with Jane out into the sage. If you see any riders comin' shout quick twice. An', Jane, *don't look back!* I'll catch up soon. We'll get to the break into the Pass before midnight, an' then wait until mornin' to go down."

Black Star bent his graceful neck and bowed his noble head, and his broad shoulders yielded as he knelt for Jane to mount.

She rode out of the court beside Judkins, through the grove, across the wide lane into the sage, and she realized that she was leaving Withersteen House forever, and she did not look back. A strange, dreamy, calm peace pervaded her soul. Her doom had fallen upon her, but, instead of finding life no longer worth living she found it doubly significant, full of sweetness as the western breeze, beautiful and unknown as the sage-slope stretching its purple sunset shadows before her. She became aware of Judkins's hand touching hers; she heard him speak a husky good-by; then into the place of Bells shot the dead-black, keen, racy nose of Night, and she knew Lassiter rode beside her.

"*Don't—look—back!*" he said, and his voice, too, was not clear.

Facing straight ahead, seeing only the waving, shadowy sage, Jane held out her gauntleted hand, to feel it enclosed in strong clasp. So she rode on without a backward glance at the beautiful grove of Cottonwoods. She did not seem to think of the past, of what she left forever, but of the color and mystery and wildness of the sage-slope leading down to Deception Pass, and of the future. She watched the shadows lengthen down the slope; she felt the cool west wind sweeping by from the rear; and she wondered at low, yellow clouds sailing swiftly over her and beyond.

"*Don't—look—back!*" said Lassiter.

Thick-driving belts of smoke traveled by on the wind, and with it came a strong, pungent odor of burning wood.

Lassiter had fired Withersteen House! But Jane did not look back.

A misty veil obscured the clear, searching gaze she had kept steadfastly upon the purple slope and the dim lines of cañons. It passed, as passed the rolling clouds of smoke, and she saw the valley deepening into the shades of twilight. Night came on, swift as the fleet racers, and stars peeped out to brighten and grow, and the huge, windy, eastern heave of sage-level paled under a rising moon and turned to silver. Blanched in moonlight, the sage yet seemed to hold its hue of purple and was infinitely more wild and lonely. So the night hours wore on, and Jane Withersteen never once looked back.

Black Star and Night

THE time had come for Venters and Bess to leave their retreat. They were at great pains to choose the few things they would be able to carry with them on the journey out of Utah.

"Bern, whatever kind of a pack's this, anyhow?" questioned Bess, rising from her work with reddened face.

Venters, absorbed in his own task, did not look up at all, and in reply said he had brought so much from Cottonwoods that he did not recollect the half of it.

"A woman packed this!" Bess exclaimed.

He scarcely caught her meaning, but the peculiar tone of her voice caused him instantly to rise, and he saw Bess on her knees before an open pack which he recognized as the one given him by Jane.

"By George!" he ejaculated, guiltily, and then at sight of Bess's face he laughed outright.

"A woman packed this," she repeated, fixing woeful, tragic eyes on him.

"Well, is that a crime?"

"There—there *is* a woman, after all!"

"Now Bess—"

"You've lied to me!"

Then and there Venters found it imperative to postpone work for the present. All her life Bess had been isolated, but she had inherited certain elements of the eternal feminine.

"But there *was* a woman and you *did* lie to me," she kept repeating, after he had explained.

"What of that? Bess, I'll get angry at you in a moment. Remember you've been pent up all your life. I venture to say that if you'd been out in the world you'd have had a dozen sweethearts and have told many a lie before this."

"I wouldn't anything of the kind," declared Bess, indignantly.

"Well—perhaps not lie. But you'd have had the sweethearts. You couldn't have helped that—being so pretty."

This remark appeared to be a very clever and fortunate one; and the work of selecting and then of stowing all the packs in the cave went on without further interruption.

Venters closed up the opening of the cave with a thatch of willows and aspens, so that not even a bird or a rat could get in to the sacks of grain. And this work was in order with the precaution habitually observed by him. He might not be able to get out of Utah, and have to return to the valley. But he owed it to Bess to make the attempt, and in case they were compelled to turn back he wanted to find that fine store of food and grain intact. The outfit of implements and utensils he packed away in another cave.

"Bess, we have enough to live here all our lives," he said once, dreamily.

"Shall I go roll Balancing Rock?" she asked, in light speech, but with deep-blue fire in her eyes.

"No—no."

"Ah, you don't forget the gold and the world," she sighed.

"Child, you forget the beautiful dresses and the travel—and everything."

"Oh, I want to go. But I want to stay!"

"I feel the same way."

They let the eight calves out of the corral, and kept only two of the burros Venters had brought from Cottonwoods. These they intended to ride. Bess freed all her pets—the quail and rabbits and foxes.

The last sunset and twilight and night were both the sweetest and saddest they had ever spent in Surprise Valley. Morning brought keen exhilaration and excitement. When Venters had saddled the two burros, strapped on the light packs and the two canteens, the sunlight was dispersing the lazy shadows from the valley. Taking a last look at the caves and the silver spruces, Venters and Bess made a reluctant start, leading the burros. Ring and Whitie looked keen and knowing. Something seemed to drag at Venters's feet and he noticed Bess lagged behind. Never had the climb from terrace to bridge appeared so long.

Not till they reached the opening of the gorge did they stop to rest and take one last look at the valley. The tremendous arch of stone curved clear and sharp in outline against the morning sky. And through it streaked the golden shaft. The valley seemed an enchanted circle of glorious veils of gold and wraiths of white and silver haze and dim, blue, moving shade—beautiful and wild and unreal as a dream.

"We—we can—th—think of it—always—re—remember," sobbed Bess.

"Hush! Don't cry. Our valley has only fitted us for a better life somewhere. Come!"

They entered the gorge and he closed the willow gate. From rosy, golden morning light they passed into cool, dense gloom. The burros pattered up the trail with little hollow-cracking steps. And the gorge widened to narrow outlet and the gloom lightened to gray. At the divide they halted for another rest. Venters's keen, remembering gaze searched Balancing Rock, and the long incline, and the cracked toppling walls, but failed to note the slightest change.

The dogs led the descent; then came Bess leading her burro; then Venters leading his. Bess kept her eyes bent downward. Venters, however, had an irresistible desire to look upward at Balancing Rock. It had always haunted him, and now he wondered if he were really to get through the outlet before the huge stone thundered down. He fancied that would be a miracle. Every few steps he answered to the strange, nervous fear and turned to make sure the rock still stood like a giant statue. And, as he descended, it grew dimmer in his sight. It changed form; it swayed; it nodded darkly; and at last, in his heightened fancy, he saw it heave and roll. As in a dream when he felt himself falling yet knew he would never fall, so he saw this long-standing thunderbolt of the little stone-men plunge down to close forever the outlet to Deception Pass.

And while he was giving way to unaccountable dread imaginations the descent was accomplished without mishap.

"I'm glad that's over," he said, breathing more freely. "I hope I'm by that hanging rock for good and all. Since almost the moment I first saw it I've had an idea that it was waiting for me. Now, when it does fall, if I'm thousands of miles away, I'll hear it."

With the first glimpses of the smooth slope leading down to the grotesque cedars and out to the Pass, Venters's cool nerve returned. One long survey to the left, then one to the right, satisfied his caution. Leading the burros down to the spur of rock, he halted at the steep incline.

"Bess, here's the bad place, the place I told you about, with the cut steps. You start down, leading your burro. Take your time and hold on to him if you slip. I've got a rope on him and a half-hitch on this point of rock, so I can let him down safely. Coming up here was a killing job. But it'll be easy going down."

Both burros passed down the difficult stairs cut by the cliff-dwellers, and did it without a misstep. After that the descent down the slope and over the mile of scrawled, ripped, and ridged rock required only careful guidance, and Venters got the burros to level ground in a condition that caused him to congratulate himself.

"Oh, if we only had Wrangle!" exclaimed Venters. "But we're lucky. That's the worst of our trail passed. We've only men to fear now. If we get up in the sage we can hide and slip along like coyotes."

They mounted and rode west through the valley and entered the cañon. From time to time Venters walked, leading his burro. When they got by all the cañons and gullies opening into the Pass they went faster and with fewer halts. Venters did not confide in Bess the alarming fact that he had seen horses and smoke less than a mile up one of the intersecting cañons. He did not talk at all. And long after he had passed this cañon and felt secure once more in the certainty that they had been unobserved he never relaxed his watchfulness. But he did not walk any more, and he kept the burros at a steady trot. Night fell before they reached the last water in the Pass and they made camp by starlight. Venters did not want the burros to stray, so he tied them with long halters in the grass near the spring. Bess, tired out and silent, laid her head in a saddle and went to sleep between the two dogs. Venters did not close his eyes. The cañon silence appeared full of the low, continuous hum of insects. He listened until the hum grew into a roar, and then, breaking the spell, once more he heard it low and clear. He watched the stars and the moving shadows, and always his glance returned to the girl's dimly pale face. And he remembered how white and still it had once looked in the starlight. And again stern thought fought his strange fancies. Would all his labor and his love be for naught? Would he lose her, after all? What did the dark shadow around her portend? Did calamity lurk on that long upland trail through the sage? Why should his heart swell and throb with nameless fear? He listened to the silence, and told himself that in the broad light of day he could dispel this leaden-weighted dread.

At the first hint of gray over the eastern rim he awoke Bess, saddled the burros, and began the day's travel. He wanted to get out of the Pass before there was any chance of riders coming down. They gained the break as the first red rays of the rising sun colored the rim.

For once, so eager was he to get up to level ground, he did not send Ring or Whitie in advance. Encouraging Bess to hurry, pulling at his patient, plodding burro, he climbed the soft, steep trail.

Brighter and brighter grew the light. He mounted the last broken edge of rim to have the sun-fired, purple sage-slope burst upon him as a glory. Bess panted up to his side, tugging on the halter of her burro.

"We're up!" he cried, joyously. "There's not a dot on the sage. We're safe. We'll not be seen! Oh, Bess—"

Ring growled and sniffed the keen air and bristled. Venters clutched at his rifle. Whitie sometimes made a mistake, but Ring never. The dull thud of hoofs almost deprived Venters of power to turn and see from where disaster threatened. He felt his eyes dilate as he stared at Lassiter leading Black Star and Night out of the sage, with Jane Withersteen, in rider's costume, close beside them.

For an instant Venters felt himself whirl dizzily in the center of vast circles of sage. He recovered partially, enough to see Lassiter standing with a glad smile and Jane riveted in astonishment.

"Why, Bern!" she exclaimed. "How good it is to see you! We're riding away, you see. The storm burst—and I'm a ruined woman! . . . I thought you were alone."

Venters, unable to speak for consternation, and bewildered out of all sense of what he ought or ought not to do, simply stared at Jane.

"Son, where are you bound for?" asked Lassiter.

"Not safe—where I was. I'm—we're going out of Utah—back East," he found tongue to say.

"I reckon this meetin's the luckiest thing that ever happened to you an' to me—an' to Jane—an' to Bess," said Lassiter, coolly.

"*Bess!*" cried Jane, with a sudden leap of blood to her pale cheek.

It was entirely beyond Venters to see any luck in that meeting.

Jane Withersteen took one flashing, woman's glance at Bess's scarlet face, at her slender, shapely form.

"Venters! is this a girl—a woman?" she questioned, in a voice that stung.

"Yes."

"Did you have her in that wonderful valley?"

"Yes, but Jane—"

"All the time you were gone?"

"Yes, but I couldn't tell—"

"Was it for *her* you asked me to give you supplies? Was it for *her* that you wanted to make your valley a paradise?"

"Oh—Jane—"

"Answer me."

"Yes."

"Oh, you liar!" And with these passionate words Jane Withersteen succumbed to fury. For the second time in her life she fell into the ungovernable rage that had been her father's weakness. And it was worse than his, for she was a jealous woman—jealous even of her friends.

As best he could, he bore the brunt of her anger. It was not only his deceit to her that she visited upon him, but her betrayal by religion, by life itself.

Her passion, like fire at white heat, consumed itself in little time. Her physical strength failed, and still her spirit attempted to go on in magnificent denunciation of those who had wronged her. Like a tree cut deep into its roots, she began to quiver and shake, and her anger weakened into despair. And her ringing voice sank into a broken, husky whisper. Then, spent and pitiable, upheld by Lassiter's arm, she turned and hid her face in Black Star's mane.

Numb as Venters was when at length Jane Withersteen lifted her head and looked at him, he yet suffered a pang.

"Jane, the girl is innocent!" he cried.

"Can you expect me to believe that?" she asked, with weary, bitter eyes.

"I'm not that kind of a liar. And you know it. If I lied—if I kept silent when honor should have made me speak, it was to spare you. I came to Cottonwoods to tell you. But I couldn't add to your pain. I intended to tell you I had come to love this girl. But, Jane, I hadn't forgotten how good you were to me. I haven't changed at all toward you. I prize your friendship as I always have. But, however it may look to you—don't be unjust. The girl is innocent. Ask Lassiter."

"Jane, she's jest as sweet an' innocent as little Fay," said Lassiter. There was a faint smile upon his face and a beautiful light.

Venters saw, and knew that Lassiter saw, how Jane Withersteen's tortured soul wrestled with hate and threw it—with scorn, doubt, suspicion, and overcame all.

"Bern, if in my misery I accused you unjustly, I crave forgiveness," she said. "I'm not what I once was. Tell me—who is this girl?"

"Jane, she is Oldring's daughter, and his Masked Rider. Lassiter will tell you how I shot her for a rustler, saved her life—all the story. It's a strange story, Jane, as wild as the sage. But it's true—true as her innocence. That you must believe!"

"Oldring's Masked Rider! Oldring's daughter!" exclaimed Jane. "And she's innocent! You ask me to believe much. If this girl is—is what you say, how could she be going away with the man who killed her father?"

"Why did you tell that?" cried Venters, passionately.

Jane's question had roused Bess out of stupefaction. Her eyes suddenly darkened and dilated. She stepped toward Venters and held up both hands as if to ward off a blow.

"Did—did you kill Oldring?"

"I did, Bess, and I hate myself for it. But you know I never dreamed he was your father. I thought he'd wronged you. I killed him when I was madly jealous."

For a moment Bess was shocked into silence.

"But he was my father!" she broke out, at last. "And now I must go back—I can't go with you. It's all over—that beautiful dream. Oh, I *knew* it couldn't come true. You can't take me now."

"If you forgive me, Bess, it'll all come right in the end!" implored Venters.

"It can't be right. I'll go back. After all, I loved him. He was good to me. I can't forget that."

"If you go back to Oldring's men I'll follow you, and then they'll kill me," said Venters, hoarsely.

"Oh no, Bern, you'll not come. Let me go. It's best for you to forget me. I've brought you only pain and dishonor."

She did not weep. But the sweet bloom and life died out of her face. She looked haggard and sad, all at once stunted; and her hands dropped listlessly; and her head drooped in slow, final acceptance of a hopeless fate.

"Jane, look there!" cried Venters, in despairing grief. "Need you have told her? Where was all your kindness of heart? This girl has had a wretched, lonely life. And I'd found a way to make her happy. You've killed it. You've killed something sweet and pure and hopeful, just as sure as you breathe."

"Oh, Bern! It was a slip. I never thought—I never thought!" replied Jane. "How could I tell she didn't know?"

Lassiter suddenly moved forward, and with the beautiful light on his face now strangely luminous, he looked at Jane and Venters and then let his soft, bright gaze rest on Bess.

"Well, I reckon you've all had your say, an' now it's Lassiter's turn. Why, I was jest prayin' for this meetin'. Bess, jest look here."

Gently he touched her arm and turned her to face the others, and then outspread his great hand to disclose a shiny, battered gold locket.

"Open it," he said, with a singularly rich voice.

Bess complied, but listlessly.

"Jane—Venters—come closer," went on Lassiter. "Take a look at the picture. Don't you know the woman?"

Jane, after one glance, drew back.

"Milly Erne!" she cried, wonderingly.

Venters, with tingling pulse, with something growing on him, recognized in the faded miniature portrait the eyes of Milly Erne.

"Yes, that's Milly," said Lassiter, softly. "Bess, did you ever see her face—look hard—with all your heart an' soul?"

"The eyes seem to haunt me," whispered Bess. "Oh, I can't remember—they're eyes of my dreams—but—but—"

Lassiter's strong arm went round her and he bent his head.

"Child, I thought you'd remember her eyes. They're the same beautiful eyes you'd see if you looked in a mirror or a clear spring. They're your mother's eyes. You are Milly Erne's child. Your name is Elizabeth Erne. You're not Oldring's daughter. You're the daughter of Frank Erne, a man once my best friend. Look! Here's his picture beside Milly's. He was handsome, an' as fine an' gallant a Southern gentleman as I ever seen. Frank came of an old family. You come of the best of blood, lass, and blood tells."

Bess slipped through his arm to her knees and hugged the locket to her bosom, and lifted wonderful, yearning eyes.

"It—can't—be—true!"

"Thank God, lass, it *is* true," replied Lassiter. "Jane an' Bern here—they both recognize Milly. They see Milly in you. They're so knocked out they can't tell you, that's all."

"Who are you?" whispered Bess.

"I reckon I'm Milly's brother an' your uncle! . . . Uncle Jim! Ain't that fine?"

"Oh, I can't believe—Don't raise me! Bern, let me kneel. I see truth in your face—in Miss Withersteen's. But let me hear it all—all on my knees. Tell me *how* it's true!"

"Well, Elizabeth, listen," said Lassiter. "Before you was born your father made a mortal enemy of a Mormon named Dyer. They was both ministers an' come to be rivals. Dyer stole your mother away from her home. She gave birth to you in Texas eighteen years ago. Then she was taken to Utah, from place to place, an' finally to the last border settlement—Cottonwoods. You was about three years old when you was taken away from Milly. She never knew what had become of you. But she lived a good while hopin' and prayin' to have you again. Then she gave up an' died. An' I may as well put in here your father died ten years ago. Well, I spent my time tracin' Milly, an' some months back I landed in Cottonwoods. An' jest lately I learned all about you. I had a talk with Oldrin' an' told him you was dead, an' he told me what I had so long been wantin' to know. It was Dyer, of course, who stole you from Milly. Part reason he was sore because Milly refused to give you Mormon teachin', but mostly he still hated Frank Erne so infernally that he made a deal with Oldrin' to take you an' bring you up as an infamous rustler an' rustler's girl. The idea was to break Frank Erne's heart if he ever came to Utah—to show him his daughter with a band of low rustlers. Well—Oldrin' took you, brought you up from childhood, an' then made you his Masked Rider. He made you infamous. He kept that part of the contract, but he learned to love you as a daughter an' never let any but his own men know you was a girl. I heard him say that with my own ears, an' I saw his big eyes grow dim. He told me how he had guarded you always, kept you locked up in his absence, was always at your side or near you on those rides that made you famous on the sage. He said he an' an old rustler whom he trusted had taught you how to read an' write. They selected the books for you. Dyer had wanted you brought up the vilest of the vile! An' Oldrin' brought you up the innocentest of the innocent. He said you didn't know what vileness was. I can hear his big voice tremble now as he said it. He told me how the men—rustlers an' outlaws—who from time to time tried to approach you familiarly—he told me how he shot them dead. I'm tellin' you this 'specially because you've showed such shame—sayin' you was nameless an' all that. Nothin' on earth can be wronger than that idea of yours. An' the truth of it is here. Oldrin' swore to me that if Dyer died, releasin' the contract, he intended to hunt up your father an' give you back to him. It seems Oldrin' wasn't all bad, an' he sure loved you."

Venters leaned forward in passionate remorse.

"Oh, Bess! I know Lassiter speaks the truth. For when I shot Oldring he dropped to his knees and fought with unearthly power to speak. And he said: 'Man—why—didn't—you—wait? Bess was—' Then he fell dead. And I've been haunted by his look and words. Oh, Bess, what a strange, splendid thing for Oldring to do! It all seems impossible. But, dear, you really are not what you thought."

"Elizabeth Erne!" cried Jane Withersteen. "I loved your mother and I see her in you!"

What had been incredible from the lips of men became, in the tone, look, and gesture of a woman, a wonderful truth for Bess. With little tremblings of all her slender body she rocked to and fro on her knees. The yearning wistfulness of her eyes changed to solemn splendor of joy. She believed. She was realizing happiness. And as the process of thought was slow, so were the variations of her expression.

Her eyes reflected the transformation of her soul. Dark, brooding, hopeless belief—clouds of gloom—drifted, paled, vanished in glorious light. An exquisite rose flush—a glow—shone from her face as she slowly began to rise from her knees. A spirit uplifted her. All that she had held as base dropped from her.

Venters watched her in joy too deep for words. By it he divined something of what Lassiter's revelation meant to Bess, but he knew he could only faintly understand. That moment when she seemed to be lifted by some spiritual transfiguration was the most beautiful moment of his life. She stood with parted, quivering lips, with hands tightly clasping the locket to her heaving breast. A new conscious pride of worth dignified the old wild, free grace and poise.

"Uncle Jim!" she said, tremulously, with a different smile from any Venters had ever seen on her face.

Lassiter took her into his arms.

"I reckon. It's powerful fine to hear that," replied Lassiter, unsteadily.

Venters, feeling his eyes grow hot and wet, turned away, and found himself looking at Jane Withersteen. He had almost forgotten her presence. Tenderness and sympathy were fast hiding traces of her agitation. Venters read her mind—felt the reaction of her noble heart—saw the joy she was beginning to feel at the happiness of others. And suddenly blinded, choked by his emotions, he turned from her also. He knew what she would do presently; she would make some magnificent amend for her anger; she would give some manifestation of her love; probably all in a moment, as she had loved Milly Erne, so would she love Elizabeth Erne.

"'Pears to me, folks, that we'd better talk a little serious now," remarked Lassiter, at length. "Time flies."

"You're right," replied Venters, instantly. "I'd forgotten time—place—danger. Lassiter, you're riding away. Jane's leaving Withersteen House?"

"Forever," replied Jane.

"I fired Withersteen House," said Lassiter.

"Dyer?" questioned Venters, sharply.

"I reckon where Dyer's gone there won't be any kidnappin' of girls."

"Ah! I knew it. I told Judkins—And Tull?" went on Venters, passionately.

"Tull wasn't around when I broke loose. By now he's likely on our trail with his riders."

"Lassiter, you're going into the Pass to hide till all this storm blows over?"

"I reckon that's Jane's idea. I'm thinkin' the storm'll be a powerful long time blowin' over. I was comin' to join you in Surprise Valley. You'll go back now with me?"

"No. I want to take Bess out of Utah. Lassiter, Bess found gold in the valley. We've a saddle-bag full of gold. If we can reach Sterling—"

"Man! how're you ever goin' to do that? Sterlin' is a hundred miles."

"My plan is to ride on, keeping sharp lookout. Somewhere up the trail we'll take to the sage and go round Cottonwoods and then hit the trail again."

"It's a bad plan. You'll kill the burros in two days."

"Then we'll walk."

"That's more bad an' worse. Better go back down the Pass with me."

"Lassiter, this girl has been hidden all her life in that lonely place," went on Venters. "Oldring's men are hunting me. We'd not be safe there any longer. Even if we would be I'd take this chance to get her out. I want to marry her. She shall have some of the pleasures of life—see cities and people. We've gold—we'll be rich. Why, life opens sweet for both of us. And, by Heaven! I'll get her out or lose my life in the attempt!"

"I reckon if you go on with them burros you'll lose your life all right. Tull will have riders all over this sage. You can't get out on them burros. It's a fool idea. That's not doin' best by the girl. Come with me an' take chances on the rustlers."

Lassiter's cool argument made Venters waver, not in determination to go, but in hope of success.

"Bess, I want you to know. Lassiter says the trip's almost useless now. I'm afraid he's right. We've got about one chance in a hundred to go through. Shall we take it? Shall we go on?"

"We'll go on," replied Bess.

"That settles it, Lassiter."

Lassiter spread wide his hands, as if to signify he could do no more, and his face clouded.

Venters felt a touch on his elbow. Jane stood beside him with a hand on his arm. She was smiling. Something radiated from her, and like an electric current accelerated the motion of his blood.

"Bern, you'd be right to die rather than not take Elizabeth out of Utah—out of this wild country. You must do it. You'll show her the great world, with all its wonders. Think how little she has seen! Think what delight is in store for her! You have gold; you will be free; you will make her happy. What a glorious prospect! I share it with you. I'll think of you—dream of you—pray for you."

"Thank you, Jane," replied Venters, trying to steady his voice. "It does look bright. Oh, if we were only across that wide, open waste of sage!"

"Bern, the trip's as good as made. It'll be safe—easy. It'll be a glorious ride," she said, softly.

Venters stared. Had Jane's troubles made her insane? Lassiter, too, acted queerly, all at once beginning to turn his sombrero round in hands that actually shook.

"You are a rider. She is a rider. This will be the ride of your lives," added Jane, in that same soft undertone, almost as if she were musing to herself.

"Jane!" he cried.

"I give you Black Star and Night!"

"Black Star and Night!" he echoed.

"It's done. Lassiter, put our saddle-bags on the burros."

Only when Lassiter moved swiftly to execute her bidding did Venters's clogged brain grasp at literal meanings. He leaped to catch Lassiter's busy hands.

"No, no! What are you doing?" he demanded, in a kind of fury. "I won't take her racers. What do you think I am? It'd be monstrous. Lassiter! stop it, I say! . . . You've got her to save. You've miles and miles to go. Tull *is* trailing you. There are rustlers in the Pass. Give me back that saddle-bag!"

"Son—cool down," returned Lassiter, in a voice he might have used to a child. But the grip with which he tore away Venters's grasping hands was that of a giant. "Listen—you fool boy! Jane's sized up the situation. The burros'll do for us. We'll sneak along an' hide. I'll take your dogs an' your rifle. Why, it's the trick. The blacks are yours, an' sure as I can throw a gun you're goin' to ride safe out of the sage."

"Jane—stop him—please stop him," gasped Venters. "I've lost my strength. I can't do—anything. This is hell for me! Can't you see that? I've ruined you—it was through me you lost all. You've only Black Star and Night left. You love these horses. Oh! I know how you must love them now! And—you're trying to give them to me. To help me out of Utah! To save the girl I love!"

"That will be my glory."

Then in the white, rapt face, in the unfathomable eyes, Venters saw Jane Withersteen in a supreme moment. This moment was one wherein she reached up to the height for which her noble soul had ever yearned. He, after disrupting the calm tenor of her peace, after bringing down on her head the implacable hostility of her churchmen, after teaching her a bitter lesson of life—he was to be her salvation. And he turned away again, this time shaken to the core of his soul. Jane Withersteen was the incarnation of selflessness. He experienced wonder and terror, exquisite pain and rapture. What were all the shocks life had dealt him compared to the thought of such loyal and generous friendship?

And instantly, as if by some divine insight, he knew himself in the remaking—tried, found wanting; but stronger, better, surer—and he wheeled to Jane Withersteen, eager, joyous, passionate, wild, exalted. He bent to her; he left tears and kisses on her hands.

"Jane, I—I can't find words—now," he said. "I'm beyond words. Only—I understand. And I'll take the blacks."

"Don't be losin' no more time," cut in Lassiter. "I ain't certain, but I think I seen a speck up the sage-slope. Mebbe I was mistaken. But, anyway, we must all be movin'. I've shortened the stirrups on Black Star. Put Bess on him."

Jane Withersteen held out her arms.

"Elizabeth Erne!" she cried, and Bess flew to her.

How inconceivably strange and beautiful it was for Venters to see Bess clasped to Jane Withersteen's breast!

Then he leaped astride Night.

"Venters, ride straight on up the slope," Lassiter was saying, "an' if you don't meet any riders keep on till you're a few miles from the village, then cut off in the sage an' go round to the trail. But you'll most likely meet riders with Tull. Jest keep right on till you're jest out of gunshot an' then make your cut-off into the sage. They'll ride after you, but it won't be no use. You can ride, an' Bess can ride. When you're out of reach turn on round to the west, an' hit the trail somewhere. Save the hosses all you can, but don't be afraid. Black Star and Night are good for a hundred miles before sundown, if you have to push them. You can get to Sterlin' by night if you want. But better make it along about to-morrow mornin'. When you get through the notch on the Glaze trail, swing to the right. You'll be able to see both Glaze an' Stone Bridge. Keep away from them villages. You won't run no risk of meetin' any of Oldrin's rustlers from Sterlin' on. You'll find water in them deep hollows north of the Notch. There's an old trail there, not much used, an' it leads to Sterlin'. That's your trail. An' one thing more. If Tull pushes you—or keeps on persistent-like, for a few miles—jest let the blacks out an' lose him an' his riders."

"Lassiter, may we meet again!" said Venters, in a deep voice.

"Son, it ain't likely—it ain't likely. Well, Bess Oldrin'—Masked Rider—Elizabeth Erne—now you climb on Black Star. I've heard you could ride. Well, every rider loves a good horse. An', lass, there never was but one that could beat Black Star."

"Ah, Lassiter, there never was any horse that could beat Black Star," said Jane, with the old pride.

"I often wondered—mebbe Venters rode out that race when he brought back the blacks. Son, was Wrangle the best hoss?"

"No, Lassiter," replied Venters. For this lie he had his reward in Jane's quick smile.

"Well, well, my hoss-sense ain't always right. An' here I'm talkin' a lot, wastin' time. It ain't so easy to find an' lose a pretty niece all in one hour! Elizabeth—good-by!"

"Oh, Uncle Jim! . . . Good-by!"

"Elizabeth Erne, be happy! Good-by," said Jane.

"Good-by—oh—good-by!"

In lithe, supple action Bess swung up to Black Star's saddle.

"Jane Withersteen! . . . Good-by!" called Venters hoarsely.

"Bern—Bess—riders of the purple sage—good-by!"

CHAPTER TWENTY TWO

Riders of the Purple Sage

Black Star and Night, answering to spur, swept swiftly westward along the white, slow-rising, sage-bordered trail. Venters heard a mournful howl from Ring, but Whitie was silent. The blacks settled into their fleet, long-striding gallop. The wind sweetly fanned Venters's hot face. From the summit of the first low-swelling ridge he looked back. Lassiter waved his hand; Jane waved her scarf. Venters replied by standing in his stirrups and holding high his sombrero. Then the dip of the ridge hid them. From the height of the next he turned once more. Lassiter, Jane, and the burros had disappeared. They had gone down into the Pass. Venters felt a sensation of irreparable loss.

"Bern—look!" called Bess, pointing up the long slope.

A small, dark, moving dot split the line where purple sage met blue sky. That dot was a band of riders.

"Pull the black, Bess."

They slowed from gallop to canter, then to trot. The fresh and eager horses did not like the check.

"Bern, Black Star has great eyesight."

"I wonder if they're Tull's riders. They might be rustlers. But it's all the same to us."

The black dot grew to a dark patch moving under low dust-clouds. It grew all the time, though very slowly. There were long periods when it was in plain sight, and intervals when it dropped behind the sage. The blacks trotted for half an hour, for another half-hour, and still the moving patch appeared to stay on the horizon line. Gradually, however, as time passed, it began to enlarge, to creep down the slope, to encroach upon the intervening distance.

"Bess, what do you make them out?" asked Venters. "I don't think they're rustlers."

"They're sage-riders," replied Bess. "I see a white horse and several grays. Rustlers seldom ride any horses but bays and blacks."

"That white horse is Tull's. Pull the black, Bess. I'll get down and cinch up. We're in for some riding. Are you afraid?"

"Not now," answered the girl, smiling.

"You needn't be. Bess, you don't weigh enough to make Black Star know you're on him. I won't be able to stay with you. You'll leave Tull and his riders as if they were standing still."

"How about you?"

"Never fear. If I can't stay with you I can still laugh at Tull."

"Look, Bern! They've stopped on that ridge. They see us."

"Yes. But we're too far yet for them to make out who we are. They'll recognize the blacks first. We've passed most of the ridges and the thickest sage. Now, when I give the word, let Black Star go and ride!"

Venters calculated that a mile or more still intervened between them and the riders. They were approaching at a swift canter. Soon Venters recognized Tull's white horse, and concluded that the riders had likewise recognized Black Star and Night. But it would be impossible for Tull yet to see that the blacks were not ridden by Lassiter and Jane. Venters noted that Tull and the line of horsemen, perhaps ten or twelve in number, stopped several times and evidently looked hard down the slope. It must have been a puzzling circumstance for Tull. Venters laughed grimly at the thought of what Tull's rage would be when he finally discovered the trick. Venters meant to sheer out into the sage before Tull could possibly be sure who rode the blacks.

The gap closed to a distance to half a mile. Tull halted. His riders came up and formed a dark group around him. Venters thought he saw him wave his arms, and was certain of it when the riders dashed into the sage, to right and left of the trail. Tull had anticipated just the move held in mind by Venters.

"Now Bess!" shouted Venters. "Strike north. Go round those riders and turn west."

Black Star sailed over the low sage, and in a few leaps got into his stride and was running. Venters spurred Night after him. It was hard going in the sage. The horses could run as well there, but keen eyesight and judgment must constantly be used by the riders in choosing ground. And continuous swerving from aisle to aisle between the brush, and leaping little washes and mounds of the pack-rats, and breaking through sage, made rough riding. When Venters had turned into a long aisle he had time to look up at Tull's riders. They were now strung out into an extended line riding northeast. And, as Venters and Bess were holding due north, this meant, if the horses of Tull and his riders had the speed and the staying power, they would head the blacks and turn them back down the slope. Tull's men were not saving their mounts; they were driving them desperately. Venters feared only an accident to Black Star or Night, and skilful riding would mitigate possibility of that. One glance ahead served to show him that Bess could pick a course through the sage as well as he. She looked neither back nor at the running riders, and bent forward over Black Star's neck and studied the ground ahead.

It struck Venters, presently, after he had glanced up from time to time, that Bess was drawing away from him as he had expected. He had, however, only thought of the light weight Black Star was carrying and of his superior speed; he saw now that the black was being ridden as never before, except when Jerry Card lost the race to Wrangle. How easily, gracefully, naturally, Bess sat her saddle! She could ride! Suddenly Venters remembered she had said she could ride. But he had not dreamed she was capable of such superb horsemanship. Then all at once, flashing over him, thrilling him, came the recollection that Bess was Oldring's Masked Rider.

He forgot Tull—the running riders—the race. He let Night have a free rein and felt him lengthen out to suit himself, knowing he would keep to Black Star's course, knowing that he had been chosen by the best rider now on the upland sage. For Jerry Card was dead. And fame had rivaled him with only one rider, and that was the slender girl who now swung so easily with Black Star's stride. Venters had abhorred her notoriety, but now he took passionate pride in her skill, her daring, her power over a horse. And he delved into his memory, recalling famous rides which he had heard related in the villages and round the camp-fires. Oldring's Masked Rider! Many times this strange rider, at once well known and unknown, had escaped pursuers by matchless riding. He had to run the gauntlet of vigilantes down the main street of Stone Bridge, leaving dead horses and dead rustlers behind. He had jumped his horse over the Gerber Wash, a deep, wide ravine separating the fields of Glaze from the wild sage. He had been surrounded north of Sterling; and he had broken through the line. How often had been told the story of day stampedes, of night raids, of pursuit, and then how the Masked Rider, swift as the wind, was gone in the sage! A fleet, dark horse—a slender, dark form—a black mask—a driving run down the slope—a dot on the purple sage—a shadowy, muffled steed disappearing in the night!

And this Masked Rider of the uplands had been Elizabeth Erne!

The sweet sage wind rushed in Venters's face and sang a song in his ears. He heard the dull, rapid beat of Night's hoofs; he saw Black Star drawing away, farther and farther. He realized both horses were swinging to the west. Then gunshots in the rear reminded him of Tull. Venters looked back. Far to the side, dropping behind, trooped the riders. They were shooting. Venters saw no puffs or dust, heard no whistling bullets. He was out of range. When he looked back again Tull's riders had given up pursuit. The best they could do, no doubt, had been to get near enough to recognize who really rode the blacks. Venters saw Tull drooping in his saddle.

Then Venters pulled Night out of his running stride. Those few miles had scarcely warmed the black, but Venters wished to save him. Bess turned, and, though she was far away, Venters caught the white glint of her waving hand. He held Night to a trot and rode on, seeing Bess and Black Star, and the sloping upward stretch of sage, and from time to time the receding black riders behind. Soon they disappeared behind a ridge, and he turned no more. They would go back to Lassiter's trail and follow it, and follow in vain. So Venters rode on, with the wind growing sweeter to taste and smell, and the purple sage richer and the sky bluer in his sight; and the song in his ears ringing. By and by Bess halted to wait for him, and he knew she had come to the trail. When he reached her it was to smile at sight of her standing with arms round Black Star's neck.

"Oh, Bern! I love him!" she cried. "He's beautiful; he knows; and how he can run! I've had fast horses. But Black Star! . . . Wrangle never beat him!"

"I'm wondering if I didn't dream that. Bess, the blacks are grand. What it must have cost Jane—ah!—well, when we get out of this wild country with Star and Night, back to my old home in Illinois, we'll buy a beautiful farm with meadows and springs and cool shade. There we'll turn the horses free—free to roam and browse and drink—never to feel a spur again—never to be ridden!"

"I would like that," said Bess.

They rested. Then, mounting, they rode side by side up the white trail. The sun rose higher behind them. Far to the left a low line of green marked the site of Cottonwoods. Venters looked once and looked no more. Bess gazed only straight ahead. They put the blacks to the long, swinging rider's canter, and at times pulled them to a trot, and occasionally to a walk. The hours passed, the miles slipped behind, and the wall of rock loomed in the fore. The Notch opened wide. It was a rugged, stony pass, but with level and open trail, and Venters and Bess ran the blacks through it. An old trail led off to the right, taking the line of the wall, and this Venters knew to be the trail mentioned by Lassiter.

The little hamlet, Glaze, a white and green patch in the vast waste of purple, lay miles down a slope much like the Cottonwoods slope, only this descended to the west. And miles farther west a faint green spot marked the location of Stone

Bridge. All the rest of that world was seemingly smooth, undulating sage, with no ragged lines of cañons to accentuate its wildness.

"Bess, we're safe—we're free!" said Venters. "We're alone on the sage. We're half way to Sterling."

"Ah! I wonder how it is with Lassiter and Miss Withersteen."

"Never fear, Bess. He'll outwit Tull. He'll get away and hide her safely. He might climb into Surprise Valley, but I don't think he'll go so far."

"Bern, will we ever find any place like our beautiful valley?"

"No. But, dear, listen. We'll go back some day, after years—ten years. Then we'll be forgotten. And our valley will be just as we left it."

"What if Balancing Rock falls and closes the outlet to the Pass?"

"I've thought of that. I'll pack in ropes and ropes. And if the outlet's closed we'll climb up the cliffs and over them to the valley and go down on rope ladders. It could be done. I know just where to make the climb, and I'll never forget."

"Oh yes, let us go back!"

"It's something sweet to look forward to. Bess, it's like all the future looks to me."

"Call me—Elizabeth," she said, shyly.

"Elizabeth Erne! It's a beautiful name. But I'll never forget Bess. Do you know—have you thought that very soon—by this time to-morrow—you will be Elizabeth Venters?"

So they rode on down the old trail. And the sun sloped to the west, and a golden sheen lay on the sage. The hours sped now; the afternoon waned. Often they rested the horses. The glisten of a pool of water in a hollow caught Venters's eye, and here he unsaddled the blacks and let them roll and drink and browse. When he and Bess rode up out of the hollow the sun was low, a crimson ball, and the valley seemed veiled in purple fire and smoke. It was that short time when the sun appeared to rest before setting, and silence, like a cloak of invisible life, lay heavy on all that shimmering world of sage.

They watched the sun begin to bury its red curve under the dark horizon.

"We'll ride on till late," he said. "Then you can sleep a little, while I watch and graze the horses. And we'll ride into Sterling early to-morrow. We'll be married! . . . We'll be in time to catch the stage. We'll tie Black Star and Night behind—and then—for a country not wild and terrible like this!"

"Oh, Bern! . . . But look! The sun is setting on the sage—the last time for us till we dare come again to the Utah border. Ten years! Oh, Bern, look, so you will never forget!"

Slumbering, fading purple fire burned over the undulating sage ridges. Long streaks and bars and shafts and spears fringed the far western slope. Drifting, golden veils mingled with low, purple shadows. Colors and shades changed in slow, wondrous transformation.

Suddenly Venters was startled by a low, rumbling roar—so low that it was like the roar in a sea-shell.

"Bess, did you hear anything?" he whispered.

"No."

"Listen! . . . Maybe I only imagined—*Ah!*"

Out of the east or north, from remote distance, breathed an infinitely low, continuously long sound—deep, weird, detonating, thundering, deadening—dying.

CHAPTER TWENTY THREE

The Fall of Balancing Rock

THROUGH tear-blurred sight Jane Withersteen watched Venters and Elizabeth Erne and the black racers disappear over the ridge of sage.

"They're gone!" said Lassiter. "An' they're safe now. An' there'll never be a day of their comin' happy lives but what they'll remember Jane Withersteen an'—an' Uncle Jim! . . . I reckon, Jane, we'd better be on our way."

The burros obediently wheeled and started down the break with little, cautious steps, but Lassiter had to leash the whining dogs and lead them. Jane felt herself bound in a feeling that was neither listlessness nor indifference, yet which rendered her incapable of interest. She was still strong in body, but emotionally tired. That hour at the entrance to Deception Pass had been the climax of her suffering—the flood of her wrath—the last of her sacrifice—the supremy of her love—and the attainment of peace. She thought that if she had little Fay she would not ask any more of life.

Like an automaton she followed Lassiter down the steep trail of dust and bits of weathered stone; and when the little slides moved with her or piled around her knees she experienced no alarm. Vague relief came to her in the sense of being enclosed between dark stone walls, deep hidden from the glare of sun, from the glistening sage. Lassiter lengthened the stirrup straps on one of the burros and bade her mount and ride close to him. She was to keep the burro from cracking his little hard hoofs on stones. Then she was riding on between dark, gleaming walls. There were quiet and rest and coolness in this cañon. She noted indifferently that they passed close under shady, bulging shelves of cliff, through patches of grass and sage and thicket and groves of slender trees, and over white, pebbly washes, and around masses of broken rock. The burros trotted tirelessly; the dogs, once more free, pattered tirelessly; and Lassiter led on with never a stop, and at every open place he looked back. The shade under the walls gave place to sunlight. And presently they came to a dense thicket of slender trees, through which they passed to rich, green grass and water. Here Lassiter rested the burros for a little while, but he was restless, uneasy, silent, always listening, peering under the trees.

She dully reflected that enemies were behind them—before them; still the thought awakened no dread or concern or interest.

At his bidding she mounted and rode on close to the heels of his burro. The cañon narrowed; the walls lifted their rugged rims higher; and the sun shone down hot from the center of the blue stream of sky above. Lassiter traveled slower, with more exceeding care as to the ground he chose, and he kept speaking low to the dogs. They were now hunting-dogs—keen, alert, suspicious, sniffing the warm breeze. The monotony of the yellow walls broke in change of color and smooth surface, and the rugged outline of rims grew craggy. Splits appeared in deep breaks, and gorges running at right angles, and then the Pass opened wide at a junction of intersecting cañons.

Lassiter dismounted, led his burro, called the dogs close, and proceeded at snail pace through dark masses of rock and dense thickets under the left wall. Long he watched and listened before venturing to cross the mouths of side cañons. At length he halted, tied his burro, lifted a warning hand to Jane, and then slipped away among the boulders, and, followed by the stealthy dogs, disappeared from sight. The time he remained absent was neither short nor long to Jane Withersteen.

When he reached her side again he was pale, and his lips were set in a hard line, and his gray eyes glittered coldly. Bidding her dismount, he led the burros into a covert of stones and cedars, and tied them.

"Jane, I've run into the fellers I've been lookin' for, an' I'm goin' after them," he said.

"Why?" she asked.

"I reckon I won't take time to tell you."

"Couldn't we slip by without being seen?"

"Likely enough. But that ain't my game. An' I'd like to know, in case I don't come back, what you'll do."

"What can I do?"

"I reckon you can go back to Tull. Or stay in the Pass an' be taken off by rustlers. Which'll you do?"

"I don't know. I can't think very well. But I believe I'd rather be taken off by rustlers."

Lassiter sat down, put his head in his hands, and remained for a few moments in what appeared to be deep and painful thought. When he lifted his face it was haggard, lined, cold as sculptured marble.

"I'll go. I only mentioned that chance of my not comin' back. I'm pretty sure to come."

"Need you risk so much? Must you fight more? Haven't you shed enough blood?"

"I'd like to tell you why I'm goin'," he continued, in coldness he had seldom used to her. She remarked it, but it was the same to her as if he had spoken with his old gentle warmth. "But I reckon I won't. Only, I'll say that mercy an' goodness, such as is in you, though they're the grand things in human nature, can't be lived up to on this Utah border. Life's hell out here. You think—or you used to think—that your religion made this life heaven. Mebbe them scales on your eyes has dropped now. Jane, I wouldn't have you no different, an' that's why I'm going to try to hide you somewhere in this Pass. I'd like to hide many more women, for I've come to see there are more like you among your people. An' I'd like you to see jest how hard an' cruel this border life is. It's bloody. You'd think churches an' churchmen would make it better. They make it worse. You give names to things—bishops, elders, ministers, Mormonism, duty, faith, glory. You dream—or you're driven mad. I'm a man, an' I know. I name fanatics, followers, blind women, oppressors, thieves, ranchers, rustlers, riders. An' we have—what you've lived through these last months. It can't be helped. But it can't last always. An' remember this—some day the border'll be better, cleaner, for the ways of men like Lassiter!"

She saw him shake his tall form erect, look at her strangely and steadfastly, and then, noiselessly, stealthily slip away amid the rocks and trees. Ring and Whitie, not being bidden to follow, remained with Jane. She felt extreme weariness, yet somehow it did not seem to be of her body. And she sat down in the shade and tried to think. She saw a creeping lizard, cactus flowers, the drooping burros, the resting dogs, an eagle high over a yellow crag. Once the meanest flower, a color, the flight of the bee, or any living thing had given her deepest joy. Lassiter had gone off, yielding to his incurable blood lust, probably to his own death; and she was sorry, but there was no feeling in her sorrow.

Suddenly from the mouth of the cañon just beyond her rang out a clear, sharp report of a rifle. Echoes clapped. Then followed a piercingly high yell of anguish, quickly breaking. Again echoes clapped, in grim imitation. Dull revolver shots—hoarse yells—pound of hoofs—shrill neighs of horses—commingling of echoes—and again silence! Lassiter must be busily engaged, thought Jane, and no chill trembled over her, no blanching tightened her skin. Yes, the border was a bloody place. But life had always been bloody. Men were blood-spillers. Phases of the history of the world flashed through her mind—Greek and Roman wars, dark, mediaeval times, the crimes in the name of religion. On sea, on land, everywhere—shooting, stabbing, cursing, clashing, fighting men! Greed, power, oppression, fanaticism, love, hate, revenge, justice, freedom—for these, men killed one another.

She lay there under the cedars, gazing up through the delicate lacelike foliage at the blue sky, and she thought and wondered and did not care.

More rattling shots disturbed the noonday quiet. She heard a sliding of weathered rock, a hoarse shout of warning, a yell of alarm, again the clear, sharp crack of the rifle, and another cry that was a cry of death. Then rifle reports pierced a dull volley of revolver shots. Bullets whizzed over Jane's hiding-place; one struck a stone and whined away in the air. After that, for a time, succeeded desultory shots; and then they ceased under long, thundering fire from heavier guns.

Sooner or later, then, Jane heard the cracking of horses' hoofs on the stones, and the sound came nearer and nearer. Silence intervened until Lassiter's soft, jingling step assured her of his approach. When he appeared he was covered with blood.

"All right, Jane," he said. "I come back. An' don't worry."

With water from a canteen he washed the blood from his face and hands.

"Jane, hurry now. Tear my scarf in two, an' tie up these places. That hole through my hand is some inconvenient, worse'n this cut over my ear. There—you're doin' fine! Not a bit nervous—no tremblin'. I reckon I ain't done your courage justice. I'm glad you're brave jest now—you'll need to be. Well, I was hid pretty good, enough to keep them from shootin' me deep, but they was slingin' lead close all the time. I used up all the rifle shells, an' then I went after them. Mebbe you heard. It was then I got hit. I had to use up every shell in my own gun, an' they did, too, as I seen. Rustlers an' Mormons, Jane! An' now I'm packin' five bullet holes in my carcass, an' guns without shells. Hurry, now."

He unstrapped the saddle-bags from the burros, slipped the saddles and let them lie, turned the burros loose, and, calling the dogs, led the way through stones and cedars to an open where two horses stood.

"Jane, are you strong?" he asked.

"I think so. I'm not tired," Jane replied.

"I don't mean that way. Can you bear up?"

"I think I can bear anything."

"I reckon you look a little cold an' thick. So I'm preparin' you."

"For what?"

"I didn't tell you why I jest had to go after them fellers. I couldn't tell you. I believe you'd have died. But I can tell you now—if you'll bear up under a shock?"

"Go on, my friend."

"*I've got little Fay!* Alive—bad hurt—but she'll live!"

Jane Withersteen's dead-locked feeling, rent by Lassiter's deep, quivering voice, leaped into an agony of sensitive life.

"Here," he added, and showed her where little Fay lay on the grass.

Unable to speak, unable to stand, Jane dropped on her knees. By that long, beautiful golden hair Jane recognized the beloved Fay. But Fay's loveliness was gone. Her face was drawn and looked old with grief. But she was not dead—her heart beat—and Jane Withersteen gathered strength and lived again.

"You see I jest had to go after Fay," Lassiter was saying, as he knelt to bathe her little pale face. "But I reckon I don't want no more choices like the one I had to make. There was a crippled feller in that bunch, Jane. Mebbe Venters crippled him. Anyway, that's why they were holdin' up here. I seen little Fay first thing, an' was hard put to it to figure out a way to get her. An' I wanted hosses, too. I had to take chances. So I crawled close to their camp. One feller jumped a hoss with little Fay, an' when I shot him, of course she dropped. She's stunned an' bruised—she fell right on her head. Jane, she's comin' to! She ain't bad hurt!"

Fay's long lashes fluttered; her eyes opened. At first they seemed glazed over. They looked dazed by pain. Then they quickened, darkened, to shine with intelligence—bewilderment—memory—and sudden wonderful joy.

"Muvver—Jane!" she whispered.

"Oh, little Fay, little Fay!" cried Jane, lifting, clasping the child to her.

"*Now*, we've got to rustle!" said Lassiter, in grim coolness. "Jane, look down the Pass!"

Across the mounds of rock and sage Jane caught sight of a band of riders filing out of the narrow neck of the Pass; and in the lead was a white horse, which, even at a distance of a mile or more, she knew.

"Tull!" she almost screamed.

"I reckon. But, Jane, we've still got the game in our hands. They're ridin' tired hosses. Venters likely give them a chase. He wouldn't forget that. An' we've fresh hosses."

Hurriedly he strapped on the saddle-bags, gave quick glance to girths and cinches and stirrups, then leaped astride.

"Lift little Fay up," he said.

With shaking arms Jane complied.

"Get back your nerve, woman! This's life or death now. Mind that. Climb up! Keep your wits. Stick close to me. Watch where your hoss's goin' an' ride!"

Somehow Jane mounted; somehow found strength to hold the reins, to spur, to cling on, to ride. A horrible quaking, craven fear possessed her soul. Lassiter led the swift flight across the wide space, over washes, through sage, into a narrow cañon where the rapid clatter of hoofs rapped sharply from the walls. The wind roared in her ears; the gleaming cliffs swept by; trail and sage and grass moved under her. Lassiter's bandaged, blood-stained face turned to her; he shouted encouragement; he looked back down the Pass; he spurred his horse. Jane clung on, spurring likewise. And the horses settled from hard, furious gallop into a long-striding, driving run. She had never ridden at anything like that pace; desperately she tried to get the swing of the horse, to be of some help to him in that race, to see the best of the ground and guide him into it. But she failed of everything except to keep her seat in the saddle, and to spur and spur. At times she closed her eyes, unable to bear sight of Fay's golden curls streaming in the wind. She could not pray; she could not rail; she no longer cared for herself. All of life, of good, of use in the world, of hope in heaven centered in Lassiter's ride with little Fay to safety. She would have tried to turn the iron-jawed brute she rode; she would have given herself to that relentless, dark-browed Tull. But she knew Lassiter would turn with her, so she rode on and on.

Whether that run was of moments or hours Jane Withersteen could not tell. Lassiter's horse covered her with froth that blew back in white streams. Both horses ran their limit, were allowed to slow down in time to save them, and went on dripping, heaving, staggering.

"Oh, Lassiter, we must run—we must run!"

He looked back, saying nothing. The bandage had blown from his head, and blood trickled down his face. He was bowing under the strain of injuries, of the ride, of his burden. Yet how cool and gray he looked—how intrepid!

The horses walked, trotted, galloped, ran, to fall again to walk. Hours sped or dragged. Time was an instant—an eternity. Jane Withersteen felt hell pursuing her, and dared not look back for fear she would fall from her horse.

"Oh, Lassiter! Is he coming?"

The grim rider looked over his shoulder, but said no word. Little Fay's golden hair floated on the breeze. The sun shone; the walls gleamed; the sage glistened. And then it seemed the sun vanished, the walls shaded, the sage paled. The horses walked—trotted—galloped—ran—to fall again to walk. Shadows gathered under shelving cliffs. The cañon turned, brightened, opened into long, wide, wall-enclosed valley. Again the sun, lowering in the west, reddened the sage. Far ahead round, scrawled stone appeared to block the Pass.

"Bear up, Jane, bear up!" called Lassiter. "It's our game, if you don't weaken."

"Lassiter! Go on—*alone!* Save little Fay!"

"Only with you!"

"Oh!—I'm a coward—a miserable coward! I can't fight or think or hope or pray! I'm lost! Oh, Lassiter, look back! Is he coming? I'll not—hold out—"

"Keep your breath, woman, an' ride not for yourself or for me, but for Fay!"

A last breaking run across the sage brought Lassiter's horse to a walk.

"He's done," said the rider.

"Oh, no—no!" moaned Jane.

"Look back, Jane, look back. Three—four miles we've come across this valley, an' no Tull yet in sight. Only a few more miles!"

Jane looked back over the long stretch of sage, and found the narrow gap in the wall, out of which came a file of dark horses with a white horse in the lead. Sight of the riders acted upon Jane as a stimulant. The weight of cold, horrible terror lessened. And, gazing forward at the dogs, at Lassiter's limping horse, at the blood on his face, at the rocks growing nearer, last at Fay's golden hair, the ice left her veins, and slowly, strangely, she gained hold of strength that she believed would see her to the safety Lassiter promised. And, as she gazed, Lassiter's horse stumbled and fell.

He swung his leg and slipped from the saddle.

"Jane, take the child," he said, and lifted Fay up. Jane clasped her arms suddenly strong. "They're gainin'," went on Lassiter, as he watched the pursuing riders. "But we'll beat 'em yet."

Turning with Jane's bridle in his hand, he was about to start when he saw the saddle-bag on the fallen horse.

"I've jest about got time," he muttered, and with swift fingers that did not blunder or fumble he loosened the bag and threw it over his shoulder. Then he started to run, leading Jane's horse, and he ran, and trotted, and walked, and ran again. Close ahead now Jane saw a rise of bare rock. Lassiter reached it, searched along the base, and, finding a low place, dragged the weary horse up and over round, smooth stone. Looking backward, Jane saw Tull's white horse not a mile distant, with riders strung out in a long line behind him. Looking forward, she saw more valley to the right, and to the left a towering cliff. Lassiter pulled the horse and kept on.

Little Fay lay in her arms with wide-open eyes—eyes which were still shadowed by pain, but no longer fixed, glazed in terror. The golden curls blew across Jane's lips; the little hands feebly clasped her arm; a ghost of a troubled, trustful smile hovered round the sweet lips. And Jane Withersteen awoke to the spirit of a lioness.

Lassiter was leading the horse up a smooth slope toward cedar-trees of twisted and bleached appearance. Among these he halted.

"Jane, give me the girl an' get down," he said. As if it wrenched him he unbuckled the empty black guns with a strange air of finality. He then received Fay in his arms and stood a moment looking backward. Tull's white horse mounted the ridge of round stone, and several bays or blacks followed. "I wonder what he'll think when he sees them empty guns. Jane, bring your saddle-bag and climb after me."

A glistening, wonderful bare slope, with little holes, swelled up and up to lose itself in a frowning yellow cliff. Jane closely watched her steps and climbed behind Lassiter. He moved slowly. Perhaps he was only husbanding his strength. But she saw drops of blood on the stone, and then she knew. They climbed and climbed without looking back. Her breast labored; she began to feel as if little points of fiery steel were penetrating her side into her lungs. She heard the panting of Lassiter and the quicker panting of the dogs.

"Wait—here," he said.

Before her rose a bulge of stone, nicked with little cut steps, and above that a corner of yellow wall, and overhanging that a vast, ponderous cliff.

The dogs pattered up, disappeared round the corner. Lassiter mounted the steps with Fay, and he swayed like a drunken man, and he too disappeared. But instantly he returned alone, and half ran, half slipped down to her.

Then from below pealed up hoarse shouts of angry men. Tull and several of his riders had reached the spot where Lassiter had parted with his guns.

"You'll need that breath—mebbe!" said Lassiter, facing downward, with glittering eyes.

"Now, Jane, the last pull," he went on. "Walk up them little steps. I'll follow an' steady you. Don't think. Jest go. Little Fay's above. Her eyes are open. She jest said to me, 'Where's muvver Jane?' "

Without a fear or a tremor or a slip or a touch of Lassiter's hand Jane Withersteen walked up that ladder of cut steps.

He pushed her round the corner of the wall. Fay lay, with wide staring eyes, in the shade of a gloomy wall. The dogs waited. Lassiter picked up the child and turned into a dark cleft. It zigzagged. It widened. It opened. Jane was amazed at a wonderfully smooth and steep incline leading up between ruined, splintered, toppling walls. A red haze from the setting sun filled this passage. Lassiter climbed with slow, measured steps, and blood dripped from him to make splotches on the white stone. Jane tried not to step in his blood, but was compelled, for she found no other footing. The saddle-bag began to drag her down; she gasped for breath; she thought her heart was bursting. Slower, slower yet the rider climbed, whistling as he breathed. The incline widened. Huge pinnacles and monuments of stone stood alone, leaning fearfully. Red sunset haze shone through cracks where the wall had split. Jane did not look high, but she felt the overshadowing of broken rims above. She felt that it was a fearful, menacing place. And she climbed on in heartrending effort. And she fell beside Lassiter and Fay at the top of the incline in a narrow, smooth divide.

He staggered to his feet—staggered to a huge, leaning rock that rested on a small pedestal. He put his hand on it—the hand that had been shot through—and Jane saw blood drip from the ragged hole. Then he fell.

"Jane—I—can't—do—it!" he whispered.

"What?"

"Roll the—stone! . . . All my—life I've loved—to roll stones—an' now I—can't!"

"What of it? You talk strangely. Why roll that stone?"

"I planned to—fetch you here—to roll this stone. See! It'll smash the crags— loosen the walls—close the outlet!"

As Jane Withersteen gazed down that long incline, walled in by crumbling cliffs, awaiting only the slightest jar to make them fall asunder, she saw Tull appear at the bottom and begin to climb. A rider followed him—another—and another.

"See! Tull! The riders!"

"Yes—they'll get us—now."

"Why? Haven't you strength left to roll the stone?"

"Jane—it ain't that—I've lost my nerve!"

"*You!* . . . Lassiter!"

"I wanted to roll it—meant to—but I—can't. Venters's valley is down behind here. We could—live there. But if I roll the stone—we're shut in for always. I don't dare. I'm thinkin' of you!"

"Lassiter! Roll the stone!" she cried.

He arose, tottering, but with set face, and again he placed the bloody hand on the Balancing Rock. Jane Withersteen gazed from him down the passageway.

Tull was climbing. Almost, she thought, she saw his dark, relentless face. Behind him more riders climbed. What did they mean for Fay—for Lassiter—for herself?

"Roll the stone! . . . Lassiter, I love you!"

Under all his deathly pallor, and the blood, and the iron of seared cheek and lined brow, worked a great change. He placed both hands on the rock and then leaned his shoulder there and braced his powerful body.

"ROLL THE STONE!"

It stirred, it groaned, it grated, it moved; and with a slow grinding, as of wrathful relief, began to lean. It had waited ages to fall, and now was slow in starting. Then, as if suddenly instinct with life, it leaped hurtlingly down to alight on the steep incline, to bound more swiftly into the air, to gather momentum, to plunge into the lofty leaning crag below. The crag thundered into atoms. A wave of air—a splitting shock! Dust shrouded the sunset red of shaking rims; dust shrouded Tull as he fell on his knees with up-lifted arms. Shafts and monuments and sections of wall fell majestically.

From the depths there rose a long-drawn rumbling roar. The outlet to Deception Pass closed forever.

THE TRAIL DRIVER

CHAPTER ONE

THAT hot summer day in June the Texas town of San Antonio was humming like a drowsy beehive. The year 1871 appeared destined to be the greatest for cattle-drives north since the first one inaugurated by Jesse Chisholm in 1868. During the Civil War cattle had multiplied on the vast Texas ranges by the hundreds of thousands. There was no market. Ranches were few and far between, and the inhabitants very poor. Chisholm conceived the daring idea of driving a herd north to find a market. Despite the interminable distance, the hardships and perils, his venture turned out a success. It changed the history of Texas.

By the spring of 1871 the Chisholm Trail had become a deciding factor in the recovery of Texas. The hoofs of Texas long-horns and Spanish mustangs had worn a mile-wide trail across the undulating steppes of the Lone Star State.

Adam Brite had already made one trip this year. Starting in March with twenty-five hundred head of cattle and seven drivers, he had beaten the Indians and floods in his most profitable venture. He had started too early for both. The misfortunes of trail drivers following him that year could not dampen his ardour for a second drive. Perhaps he might make three drives this auspicious year. Buying cattle right and left for cash, he had in sight a herd of four thousand five hundred. This would be by far the largest number of long-horns ever collected, let alone driven north. And Brite's immediate and vital problem was trail drivers.

Five boys were on the way to San Antonio from Uvalde Ranch with a herd, and their services had been secured in the sale. Brite did not care to undertake so big a job without at least ten of the hardest-riding and hardest-shooting drivers on the ranges. To this end he had been a busy man for the single day that he had been back in San Antonio. At Dodge his seven drivers had seemed to vanish as if by magic in the smoke and dust of that wildest of frontier posts. But Brite felt himself particularly fortunate in having secured one of Chisholm's right-hand drivers for his foreman.

Brite waited for this man, eager and hopeful. His life-long friend, the cattleman Colonel Eb Blanchard, had recommended Texas Joe Shipman, and promised to find him and fetch him around. The afternoon was waning now. Lines of dusty riders were off to the range; the lobby of the Alamo Hotel was thinning out of its booted, spurred, and belted cattlemen; the saloon inside had lost something of its roar. Sloe-eyed Mexicans in colourful garb passed down the street. Brite was about to give up waiting when Colonel Blanchard entered with a young man who would have stood out paramount even among a host of rangy, still-faced, clear-eyed Texans.

"Heah yu air, Adam," called out Blanchard cheerily, as he dragged up the tall rider. "Tex, meet my old partner, Adam Brite, the whitest stockman in this State.... Adam, this is Joe Shipman. He rode on my ootfit longer than I can recollect, an' has made two trips up the Trail. Little the wuss for likker at this time. But never yu mind thet. I vouch for Tex."

"How do, Shipman," replied Brite, shortly, extending his hand. This rider was tall, wide-shouldered, small-hipped, lithe, and erect. His boldly cut features were handsome. He had tawny hair, eyes of clear amber, singularly direct, and a lazy, cool, little smile. He looked about twenty-four years old.

"Howdy, Mistah Brite," he replied. "I'm shore sorry I'm drunk. Yu shee, I met old pard—Less Holden—an' dog-gone him—he hawg-tied me an' poured aboot a barrel of applejack down me."

Brite knew Texans. He required no second look at this stalwart rider to like him, to accept him even without Colonel Blanchard's recommendation.

"I'll leave yu to talk it over," went on Blanchard. "Reckon yu'd do wal to take Tex on right heah."

"All right, Colonel. Much obliged," replied Brite. "Come, Shipman, let's set down.... Have a cigar.... What wages do yu want to be foreman for me on my next drive?"

"Wal, what'll yu pay?" inquired Shipman, and it was easy to see that he did not care what he got.

"Forty a month, considerin' we'll drive forty-five hundred haid."

"Whew!... An' how many drivers, boss?"

"Ten, at least, an' fifteen if we can get them."

"Wal, we cain't never make it with only ten. There'll be hell shore up the Trail this summer."

"Will yu take the job?"

"I reckon so," drawled the rider. "Shore swore I'd never go again. I've been up three times. Had a Comanche arrer in my shoulder. An' I'm packin' lead in my hip."

"I seen yu walked with a limp. Hurt yore ridin' any?"

"Wal, nobody ever said nothin' aboot it if it did."

"Ahuh. Do yu know any riders yu can hire?"

"I might get my old pard, Less Holden," replied Shipman, brightening. "No better ever forked a hawse. But Less is the wildest hombre."

"Thet's no matter. Get him, an' half a dozen more. Also a cook. I'll go oot an' buy a new chuck-wagon. The last one went to pieces on us. We lost time. I'll buy supplies, too."

"When yu aim to hit the Trail, boss?"

"Soon as thet Uvalde ootfit comes in. Expect them to-day. We ought to get away day after to-morrow."

"Dog-gone! I had a gurl somewhere heah in this town. I cain't find her. . . . Wal, it's a dog's life. . . . Reckon with such a big herd yu'll want a real ootfit."

"Hardest riders on the range."

"Wal, thet ain't a-goin' to be easy. Drivers shore as scarce as hen teeth. Boss, there's fifty thousand haid due to leave this month."

"All the more reason for us to get the jump on them."

"Wal, I'd just as lief there was half a dozen herds ahaid of us."

"Shipman, grass an' water good only in spots this spring."

"All right, boss. I'll do my best," replied the rider, rising.

"Report to me heah after supper," concluded Brite, and watched the Texan move leisurely away. His limp was not pronounced and it did not detract from his striking appearance. Brite thought that he would have liked to call him son. After all, he was a lonely old cattleman. And more than once he had felt a strange melancholy, almost a presentiment in regard to this trail driving. It had developed into a dangerous business. Storm, flood, drought and cold, lightning, and the extremely strenuous nature of the work, were bad enough. But of late the Comanches and Kiowas had gone on the warpath. There had always been Indian depredations in Texas; however, nothing so serious as threatened now. Brite concluded the buffalo meat and hide hunters were responsible. The time would come when the Indians would no longer stand for the slaughter of the buffalo. And when that time arrived all the hunters and trail drivers as well as settlers would be forced to unite for war against the redskin. The wild young Texans scouted this idea, but all the old timers like Brite knew its truth.

Brite had to shoulder his way into Hitwell's merchandise store. Three months before he had bought supplies here and had the place to himself. A motley horde of *vaqueros,* soldiers, cattlemen, drivers, Indians, and loungers now filled the big place. Brite finally got Hitwell's ear. They had been in the cattle business together before the war. "Sam, what's all this aboot?"

"Wal, it's shore a rush," replied Hitwell, rubbing his hands. "If old Jesse Chisholm had foreseen this he'd have gone in the supply business."

"Reckon yu better duplicate thet order I gave yu in March an' add a third more to it."

"When yu leavin', Adam?"

"Day after to-morrow."

"Be all packed for yu. Fresh supplies just in from New Orleans."

"How aboot a chuck-wagon?"

"Sold oot, Adam. Haven't got any kind of a wagon left."

"Cain't yu get me one?"

"Wal, I'll try, Adam, but chances air slim."

"Hell! I'd better go rustlin' aboot."

He visited other stores without avail. It was long after sunset when he got back to the hotel. Brite had supper and then went out to look for Shipman. The heat of day had passed and it was pleasant sitting out in front. Across the street stood a saloon which evidently rivalled the merchandise store for visitors. A tall gambler leaned against the door. He wore a long black coat and a flowered vest and a wide-brimmed black sombrero. Booted, spurred, gun-packing trail drivers passed in and out, noisy and gay. Riders passed to and fro against the lighted windows.

Soft steps and clinking spurs behind Brite drew his attention.

"Wal, boss, I shore been lucky," drawled the voice of Shipman.

Brite turned to see the trail driver, accompanied by a flaming-faced youth under twenty. He had eyes of blue fire and an air of reckless insouciance.

"Hullo, Shipman. Shore glad yu had some luck. It's more than I had. Couldn't buy any kind of a wagon."

"Boss, this heah's my pard, Less Holden. . . . Less, shake with Mr. Brite."

"Where yu hail from?" queried Brite, after the introduction, bending keen eyes on the stripling.

"Dallas. I was born there."

"Wal, yu didn't need to tell me yu was a Texan. Who yu been ridin' for?"

"Dave Slaughter. Goin' on three years. But I've never been up the Trail."

"Holden, if yu've rode for Dave Slaughter yu're good enough for me. . . . Shipman, what's the other good luck?"

"Boss, I corralled a boy named Whittaker. Couldn't be no better. An' I talked with a chap from Pennsylvania. Tenderfoot, all right, but husky. Says he can ride. Reckon yu better let me hire him, boss. Santone is shore full of riders, but they've got jobs."

"Yes, by all means," replied Brite. "Looks like we'll be delayed findin' an ootfit. I'm stumped aboot a chuck-wagon, too."

"Wal, Less an' me will look around for a second-hand wagon."

"Don't overlook a cook. . . . Hullo! did I heah my name called?"

"Shore did. That boy who just limped off his hawse there," returned Shipman, pointing.

Turning, Brite espied a mustang and rider that had arrived in front of the hotel. He was in the act of dropping his bridle and evidently had just addressed one of the men present.

"Brite? Shore, he's around somewheres."

"Heah I am," called Brite, stepping along the kerb, followed by the two drivers. The rider was young, dark as a Mexican, ragged and soiled, and he smelled of dust.

"Air you Mr. Adam Brite?" he asked, when Brite strode up.

"Yes, I'm Brite. Yu must be one of my boys with the Uvalde herd?"

"Shore am, boss, an' glad to report we got in without losin' a steer."

"What's yore name?"

"Ackerman, sir."

"Meet my foreman, Shipman, an' his pard, Holden."

"Howdy, Deuce," drawled Shipman, extending a hand.

"Dog-gone if it ain't Texas Joe," burst out the rider, with a delighted grin. They gripped hands warmly.

"Whar yu beddin' the herd, Deuce?" asked Shipman, when the greetings were over.

"Aboot five miles oot in the creek bottom. Not much grass, but plenty of water. Stock all fine an' fat as pigeons. We mozeyed along slow."

"Have yu got a wagon?"

"Shore, an' a good cook. He's a niggah, but he shore is a white one. An' how he can cook!"

"Wal, Mr. Brite, this sounds like music to me," said Shipman, turning to his employer. "Whar's the stock yu had heah already?"

"I've two thousand haid in three pastures just oot of town. We can bunch them on the Trail in no time an' work along slow while Ackerman catches up."

"Shore, boss, but we gotta have drivers," protested the foreman.

"There's eight of us now, includin' myself. I'd risk it with two more good men."

"Wal, we'll find them, somewhares. . . . An', boss, how aboot grub?"

"Ordered at Hitwell's. . . . Let's see, Ackerman. Send yore wagon in early mawnin' to-morrow. An' after loadin' supplies have it catch up oot on the trail."

"Deuce, cain't yu stay in town an' see the sights?" queried Shipman, his eyes kindly on the weary, dusty rider.

"Wisht I could. But two of the boys air all in, an' I gotta rustle back." With that he stepped astride, and bidding them good-bye he trotted away.

"Wal, boss, we'll comb Santone for a couple of drivers. An' in the mawnin' I'll be heah to help load thet chuck-wagon."

"All right. I'll meet yu oot at the pastures. Good night."

Brite headed back toward the lobby of the hotel to be confronted by a man he well knew, yet on the moment could not place. The blond, cold-faced, tight-lipped, gimlet-eyed Texan certainly recognized him. "Howdy, Brite. Don't yu-all know me?" he drawled.

"Shore I know yu. But I don't recollect yore handle," replied Brite, slowly drawing back his half-extended hand.

"Wal, stick a pan on thet handle an' yu'll have me pat."

"Hell yes! Pan Handle Smith!" exclaimed Brite, and this time shot out his hand. The other met it with his, and the steely grip of that soft ungloved member thrilled Brite to his marrow. "How'd yu turn up heah?"

"Just rode in. From the river. An' I'm rustlin' north pronto."

"Wal, Pan Handle, yu always was on the move. I hope it's not the same old——"

"Shore is, Brite. By ——! I cain't have any peace. I dropped into a little game of draw below an' got fleeced. Thet riled me. I hung on an' caught a cairdsharp at his tricks. Wal, I called him an' his pard. They'd been workin' the buffalo camps. Didn't know me. Drawed on me—settin' at table at thet—the damn fools! I had to shoot my way oot, which is why I left my money. Been ridin' hard an' just got in. I'm hungry, Brite, an' haven't a dollar."

"Easy. Glad yu bumped into me," replied Brite, handing him a greenback. An idea flashed into his mind simultaneously with the action. And it chased away the cold little chill Smith's story had given him. "On the dodge, eh?"

"Wal, it might be hot for me heah till thet fracas is forgotten."

CHAPTER ONE

"Pan Handle, if I recollect right, yu used to drive cattle?"

"Wal, I reckon," replied Smith, with a far-away look in his eyes and a wistful smile.

"How'd yu like to help me drive a big herd north to Dodge?"

"Brite, I'd like it a heap. I don't want no wages. I can get a stake at Dodge," returned the other keenly.

"Yu're on. For wages, of course. What ootfit have yu?"

"Not much. A fine hawse. But he needs a rest. A saddle, blanket, an' Winchester. An' all the rest of my worldly goods is on my back."

"An' on yore hips, too, I notice," drawled Brite, his glance taking in the grey travel-worn figure and the gun butts, protruding from sheaths, significantly low. "Go get a good feed, Smith. Yu shore look peaked. An' meet me heah in an hour or so. Yu'll need to stock up heavy on ammunition. An' yu'll need a change of duds."

"Wal, I appreciate this more than I can say, Brite," replied Smith, and strode away.

Brite watched him out of sight. And not until then did he realize what he had done. Hired one of the most notorious of Texas gun-fighters to be a trail driver! The fact was that he was actually harbouring an outlaw on the dodge. It shocked Brite a little—the bare fact. But on second thought he laughed. This was frontier Texas. And every community had a gunman of whom it was inordinately proud. Wess Hardin, Buck Duane, King Fisher, and a host of lesser lights were as representative of Texas as Crockett and Travis and Bowie. On the other hand, there were men noted for fast and deadly trigger work who put themselves outside the pale. They were robbers, bandits, desperadoes, sheriffs with an itch to kill instead of arrest, cowboys on the rampage, gamblers who shot to hide their cheating. Pan Handle Smith had been outlawed, but he had really been more sinned against than sinning. Brite concluded that he was fortunate to engage the outlaw for his second drive north. Something presaged a tremendous ordeal. Forty-five hundred long-horns! Too late now to undo this rash deal! He would go through with it. Still, old Texan that he was, he experienced a cold tight contraction of skin at the thought of possibilities. Many a driver had failed to reach the end of the long Trail.

CHAPTER TWO

BRITE's first camp was Pecan Swale, some twelve or more miles out of San Antonio. Grass had been scarce until the drivers reached this creek bottom. The gigantic herd had drifted faster than usual, arriving at the Swale before sunset.

Shipman with the chuck-wagon, and Ackerman with the second herd, rolled in together.

"Any drive close behind?" called Brite, from his resting-spot in the shade. He was tired. Tough as he was, it took several days to break him in to saddle and trail.

"Nope, boss. Henderson is startin' next with two herds. But he won't be ready for days. Then the herds will come a-whoopin'," returned the rider.

"Wal, thet's good. Shipman, I reckon yu better take charge now."

"Then we'll all lay off till after supper. Looks like a mighty good place for cattle to hang."

The location was a most satisfactory one, and would be hard to leave, at least for those drivers who had been up the Trail. A grove of pecan and walnut trees and blackberry bushes choked the upper end of the valley with green and yellow verdure. Below it a lazy shallow stream meandered between its borders of willow. Grass grew luxuriantly all through the bottom-lands, and up the gentle slopes. Dust clouds were lifting here and there where the mustangs were rolling. The drivers threw saddles, blankets, and bridles to the ground, and flopped down after them. Gloves, sombreros, chaps, and boots likewise went flying. The boys were disposed to be merry and to look each other over and take stock of the whistling cook. Alabama Moze, they called him, and he was a prepossessing negro, baffling as to age. His chuck-wagon was a huge affair, with hoops for canvas, and a boarded contraption at the rear. Moze was in the act of letting down a wide door which served as a table. He reached for an axe and sallied forth for firewood. That article appeared scarce, except for the green standing trees.

From his lounging-spot Brite studied his outfit of men, including his cook. Shipman had not been able to secure any more drivers. Brite thought it well indeed that he had taken on Pan Handle Smith. That worthy followed Moze out into the grove. Divested of coat and chaps, he made a fine figure of a man. Even on the Texas border, where striking men were common, Smith would have drawn more than one glance. In fact, he earned more than that from Joe Shipman. But no remarks were made about Smith.

Bender, the tenderfoot from Pennsylvania, appeared to be a hulking youth, good natured and friendly, though rather shy before these still-faced, intent-eyed Texans. He had heavy, stolid features that fitted his bulky shoulders. His hair was the colour of tow and resembled a mop. He had frank, eager blue eyes. Whittaker was a red-faced, sleepy-eyed young rider of twenty-two, notable for his superb physique.

The Uvalde quintet mostly interested Brite. In a land where young, fierce, rollicking devils were the rule rather than the exception this aggregation would not have attracted any particular attention in a crowd of drivers. But Adam Brite loved Texas and Texans, and as he studied these boys he conceived the impression that they had a shade on the average trail driver. Not one of them had yet reached twenty years of age. The dark, slim, bow-legged Deuce Ackerman appeared to be the most forceful personality. The youth who answered to the name San Sabe had Indian or Mexican blood, and his lean shape wore the stamp of *vaquero*. Rolly Little's name suited him. He was small and round. He had yellow hair, a freckled face, and flashing brown eyes, as sharp as daggers. Ben Chandler was a typical Texas youth, long, rangy, loose-jointed, of sandy complexion and hair, and eyes of clear, light blue. The last of the five, Roy Hallett, seemed just to be a member of the group—a quiet, sombre, negative youth.

Preparations for supper proceeded leisurely. Brite marked that Pan Handle helped the negro in more ways than packing in firewood. The drivers noted it, too, with significant stares. On the trail it was not usual for any rider to share the tasks of a negro. Manifestly Pan Handle Smith was a law unto himself. The interest in him increased, but it did not seem likely that anyone would question his pleasure.

Texas Joe left camp to climb the ridge from which he surveyed the valley. Evidently he was satisfied with what he saw. Brite's opinion was that the cattle would not stray. It was unusual, however, to leave them unguarded for even a moment. Presently Smith appeared to be studying the land to the north. Upon his return to camp he announced:

"Trail riders haided for Santone. An' there's a lone hawseman ridin' in from cross country."

"Wal, Shipman, we'll shore see more riders than we want on this trip," said Brite.

"Ahuh, I reckon."

"Boss, yu mean painted riders?" spoke up Ackerman.

"Not particular, if we're lucky. I had to feed a lot of Comanches last trip. But they made no trouble. I reckon the riders thet bother me most are the drifters an' trail dodgers."

"Boss, mebbe we'll be an ootfit thet breed had better pass up," drawled Shipman.

"Wal, I hope so. Yu cain't never tell what yore ootfit is until it's tried."

"Tried by what, Mr. Brite?" asked the tenderfoot Bender, with great curiosity.

The boss laughed at this query. Before he could reply Shipman spoke up: "Boy, it's jest what happens along."

"Nothing happened to-day in all that nice long ride. I've an idea these trail dangers are exaggerated."

Suddenly one of Ackerman's boys let out a stentorian: "*Haw! Haw!*" This would probably have started something but for the cook's yell following and almost as loud. "Yo-all come an' git it!"

There ensued a merry scramble, and then a sudden silence. Hungry boys seldom wasted time to talk. Brite called for Moze to fetch his dinner over under the tree. It took no second glance for the boss to be assured that this cook was a treasure.

The sun set in a cloudless, golden sky. An occasional bawl of a cow from the stream bottom broke the silence. A cooling zephyr of wind came through the grove, rustling the leaves, wafting the camp-fire smoke away. Brite had a sense of satisfaction at being on the Trail again and out in the open. Much of his life had been spent that way.

"Moze, where yu from?" asked Shipman, as he arose.

"Ise a Alabama niggah, sah," replied Moze, with a grin. "Thet's what they calls me. Alabama."

"Wal, so long's yu feed me like this I'll shore keep the redskins from scalpin' you."

"Den I'll be awful sho to feed yu dat way."

"Wal, boys, I hate to say it, but we gotta get on guard," went on Shipman, addressing the outfit. "There's ten of us. Four on till midnight, three till three o'clock, an' three till mawnin'. Who goes on duty with me now?"

They all united in a choice of this early-night duty.

"Shipman, I'll take my turn," added Brite.

"Wall, I'll be dog-goned," drawled the foreman. "What kind of an ootfit is this heah? Yu all want to work. An' the boss, too!"

"Fust night oot," said someone.

"I reckon I gotta make myself disliked," returned Shipman resignedly. "Bender, yu saddle yore hawse. Lester, same for yu. An', Smith, I reckon I'd feel kinda safe with yu oot there."

"Suits me fine. I never sleep, anyhow," replied the outlaw, rising with alacrity.

"Deuce, I'll wake yu at midnight or thereaboots. Yu pick yore two guards. . . . An' say, boss, I 'most forgot. Who's gonna wrangle the hawses? Thet's a big drove we got."

"Shore, but they're not wild. Herd them on good grass with the cattle."

"All right, we'll round them up. But we ought to have someone regular on thet job. . . . Wal, so long. It's a lucky start."

Brite agreed with this last statement of his foreman, despite the strange presentiment that came vaguely at odd moments. The Brite herd of forty-five hundred head, trail-branded with three brands before they had been bought, had a good start on the herds behind, and full three weeks after the last one that had gone north. Grass and water should be abundant, except in spots. Cattle could go days without grass, if they had plenty of water. It had been rather a backward spring, retarding the buffalo on their annual migration north. Brite concluded they would run into buffalo somewhere north of the Red River.

"Moze, couldya use some fresh meat?" called Deuce Ackerman.

"Ise got a whole quarter of beef," replied Moze. "An' yo knows, Mars Ackerman, Ise a economical cook."

"I saw a bunch of deer. Some venison shore would go good. Come on, Ben. We've a half-hour more of daylight yet."

The two drivers secured rifles and disappeared in the grove. Hallett impressively acquainted Little with the fact that he was going to take a bath. That worthy expressed amaze and consternation. "My Gawd! Roy, what ails yu? We'll be fordin' rivers an' creeks every day pronto. Ain't thet so, boss?"

"It shore is, an' if they're high an' cold yu'll get all the water yu want for ten years," returned Brite.

"I'm gonna, anyway," said Hallett.

"Roy, I'll go if yu'll pull off my boots. They ain't been off for a week."

"Shore. Come on."

Soon the camp was deserted save for the whistling Moze and Brite, who took pains about unrolling his canvas and spreading his blanket. A good bed was what a trail driver yearned for and seldom got. At least, mostly he did not get to lie in it long at a stretch. That done, Brite filled his pipe for a smoke. The afterglow burned in the west and against that gold a solitary rider on a black horse stood silhouetted dark and wild. A second glance assured Brite that it was not an Indian. Presently he headed the horse down into the Swale and disappeared among the trees. Brite expected this stranger to ride into camp. Strangers, unfortunately many of them undesirable, were common along the Chisholm Trail. This one emerged from the brush, having evidently crossed the stream farther above, and rode up, heading for the chuck-wagon. Before the rider stopped Brite answered to a presagement not at all rare in him—that there were meetings and meetings along the trail. This one was an event.

"Howdy, cook. Will yu give me a bite of grub before yu throw it oot?" the rider asked, in a youthful, resonant voice.

"Sho I will, boy. But Ise tellin' yo nuthin' ever gits throwed away wid dis chile cookin'. Jus' yo git down an' come in."

Brite observed that the horse was not a mustang, but a larger and finer breed than the tough little Spanish species. Moreover, he was a magnificent animal, black as coal, clean-limbed and heavy-chested, with the head of a racer. His rider appeared to be a mere boy, who, when he wearily slid off, showed to be slight of stature, though evidently round and strong of limb. He sat down cross-legged with the pan of food Moze gave him. Brite strolled over with the hope that he might secure another trail driver.

"Howdy, cowboy. All alone?" he said genially.

"Yes, sir," replied the boy, looking up and as quickly looking down again. The act, however, gave Brite time to see a handsome face, tanned darkly gold, and big, dark, deep eyes that had a furtive, if not a hunted, look.

"Whar yu from?"

"Nowhere, I reckon."

"Lone cowboy, eh? Wal, thet's interestin' to me. I'm short on riders. Do yu want a job? My name's Brite an' I'm drivin' forty-five hundred haid north to Dodge. Ever do any trail drivin'?"

"No, sir. But I've rode cattle all my life."

"Ahuh. Wal, thet cain't be a very long while, son. Aboot how old air yu?"

"Sixteen. But I feel a hundred."

"Whar's yore home?"

"I haven't any."

"No? Wal, yu don't say? Whar's yore folks, then?"

"I haven't any, Mr. Brite. . . . My dad an' mom were killed by Indians when I was a kid."

"Aw, too bad, son. Thet's happened to so many Texas lads. . . . What yu been doin' since?"

"Ridin' from one ranch to another. I cain't hold a job long."

"Why not? Yu're a likely-lookin' youngster."

"Reckon I don't stand up good under the hardest ridin'. . . . An' there's other reasons."

"How aboot hawse-wranglin'?"

"Thet'd suit me fine. . . . Would yu give me a job?"

"Wal, I don't see why not. Finish yore supper, lad. Then come have a talk with me."

All this while Brite stood gazing down at the youth, changing from curiosity to sympathy and interest. Not once after the first time did the boy look up. There were holes in his battered old black sombrero, through one of which peeped a short curl of red-gold hair. He had shapely brown hands, rather small, but supple and strong. The end of a heavy gun-sheath protruded from his jacket on the left side. He wore overalls, high-top Mexican boots, and huge spurs, all the worse for long service.

Brite went back to his comfortable seat under the pecan tree. From there his second glance at the horse discovered a canvas pack behind the saddle. The old cattleman mused that it was only necessary to get out over this wild, broad Texas range to meet with sad and strange and tragic experiences. How many, many Texas sons were like this youth! The vast range exacted a hard and bloody toll from the pioneers.

Dusk had fallen when the boy came over to present himself before the cattleman.

"My name is Bayne—Reddie Bayne," he announced, almost shyly.

"Red-haided, eh?"

"Not exactly. But I wasn't named for my hair. Reddie is my real given name."

"Wal, no matter. Any handle is good enough in Texas. Did yu ever heah of Liver-eatin' Kennedy or Dirty-face Jones or Pan Handle Smith?"

"I've heahed of the last, shore."

"Wal, yu'll see him pronto. He's riding for me this trip. . . . Air yu goin' to accept my offer?"

"I'll take the job. Yes, sir. Thanks."

"What wages?"

"Mr. Brite, I'll ride for my keep."

"No, I cain't take yu up on thet. It's a tough job up the Trail. Say thirty dollars a month?"

"Thet's more than I ever earned. . . . When do I begin?"

"Mawnin' will be time enough, son. Shipman an' the boys have bunched the hawses for the night."

"How many haid in yore *remuda*?"

"Nigh on to two hundred. More'n we need, shore. But they're all broke an' won't give much trouble. Yu see, when we get to Dodge I sell cattle, hawses, wagon, everythin'."

"I've heahed so much aboot this Chisholm Trail. I rode 'cross country clear from Bendera, hopin' to catch on with a trail-drive."

"Wal, yu've ketched on, Reddie, an' I shore hope yu don't regret it."

"Gosh, I'm glad. . . . An' if I have, I'd better unsaddle Sam."

Bayne led the black under an adjoining pecan, and slipping saddle, bridle, and pack, turned him loose. Presently the lad returned to sit down in the shadow.

"How many in yore ootfit, Mr. Brite?"

"An even dozen now, countin' yu."

"Regular Texas ootfit?"

"Shore. It's Texas, all right. But new to me. I've got a hunch it'll turn oot regular Texas an' then some. Texas Joe Shipman is my Trail boss. He's been up three times, an' thet shore makes him an old-stager. Lucky for me. The rest is a mixed bunch except five Uvalde boys. Fire-eatin' kids, I'll bet! There's a tenderfoot from Pennsylvania, Bender by name. Shipman's pard, Less Holden. A Carolinian named Whittaker. If he's as good as he looks he couldn't be no better. An' last Pan Handle Smith. He's a gunman an' outlaw, Bayne. But like some of his class he's shore salt of the earth."

"Ten. Countin' yu an' me an' the cook makes thirteen. Thet's unlucky, Mr. Brite."

"Thirteen. So 'tis."

"Perhaps I'd better ride on. I don't want to bring yu bad luck."

"Boy, yu'll be good luck."

"Oh, I hope so. I've been bad luck to so many ootfits," replied the youth, with a sigh.

Brite was struck at the oddity of that reply, but thought better of added curiosity. Then Deuce Ackerman and Chandler came rustling out of the shadow, coincident with the return of Little and Hallett.

"Boss, I seen a dog-gone fine black hawse oot heah. No pony. Big thoroughbred. I didn't see him in our *remuda*," declared Ackerman.

"Belongs to Reddie Bayne heah. He just rode up an' threw in with us. . . . Bayne, heah's four of the Uvalde boys."

"Howdy, all," rejoined the rider.

"Howdy yoreself, cowboy," said Ackerman, stepping forward to peer down. "I cain't see yu, but I'm dog-gone glad to meet you. . . . Boys, Reddie Bayne sounds like a Texas handle."

The other Uvalde boys called welcome greetings. Someone threw brush on the fire, which blazed up cheerily. It was noticeable, however, that Bayne did not approach the camp fire.

"Boss, did yu heah me shoot?" queried Ackerman.

"No. Did you?"

"I shore did. Had an easy shot at a buck. But the light was bad an' I missed. I'll plug one in the mawnin'."

"Deuce, if yu'd let me have the rifle we'd got the deer meat all right," declared Ben.

"Is thet so? I'll bet yu I can beat yu any old day!"

"What'll yu bet?"

"Wal, I hate to take yore money, but——"

"Sssh! Riders comin'," interrupted Ackerman, in a sharp whisper.

Brite heard the thud of hoofs off under the trees. Horses were descending the road from above.

"Cain't be any of our ootfit," went on Ackerman, peering into the darkness. "Fellars, we may as wal be ready for anythin'."

Dark forms of horses and riders loomed in the outer circle of camp-fire light. They halted.

"Who comes?" called out Ackerman, and his young voice had a steely ring.

"Friends," came a gruff reply.

"Wal, advance, friends, an' let's see yu."

Just then a hard little hand clutched Brite's arm. He turned to see Reddie

Bayne kneeling beside him. The lad's sombrero was off, exposing his face. It was pale, and the big dark eyes burned.

"Wallen! He's after me," whispered Bayne, hoarsely. "Don't let him——"

Brite gripped the lad and gave him a little shake. "Keep still."

The riders approached the camp fire, but did not come close enough to be seen distinctly. The leader appeared to be of stalwart frame, dark of face, somehow forceful and forbidding. Brite had seen a hundred men like him ride into Texas camps.

"Trail drivers, huh?" he queried, with gleaming eyes taking in the boys round the camp fire.

"Wal, we ain't Comanche Injuns," retorted Deuce curtly.

"Who's ootfit?"

"Brite, of Santone. We got four thousand haid an' twenty drivers. Any more yu want to know?"

"Reckon yu took on a new rider lately, huh?"

"Wal, if we did——"

Brite rose to stride out into the firelight.

"Who're yu an' what's yore business heah?"

"My name's Wallen. From Braseda. We tracked a—a young—wal, a fellar whose handle was Reddie Bayne."

"Reddie Bayne. So thet was thet rider's name? What yu trackin' him for?"

"Thet's my business. Is he heah?"

"No, he isn't."

"Wal, then, he was heah, Brite."

"Shore. Had supper with us. An' then he cut oot for Santone. Reckon he's there by now. What yu say, Deuce?"

"Reddie was forkin' a fast hawse," replied Ackerman casually.

"Any camps between heah an' Santone?" went on the rider.

"Not when we passed along. May be by this time."

"Brite, if yu don't mind we'll spend the night heah," said Wallen speculatively.

"Waal, stranger, I'm sorry. One of my rules is not to be too hospitable on the old Trail," drawled Brite. "Yu see thet sort of thing has cost me too much."

"Air yu handin' me a slap?" queried Wallen roughly.

"No offence. Just my rule, thet's all."

"Ahuh. Wal, it's a damn pore rule for a Texan."

"Shore," agreed Brite coolly.

The rider wheeled, cursing under his breath, and, accompanied by his silent companion, thudded off into the darkness. Brite waited until he could make sure they took the road, then he returned to the spot where he had left the lad. Bayne sat against the tree. By the dim light Brite saw the gleam of a gun in his hand.

"Wal, I steered them off, Bayne," said Brite. "Hope I did yu a good turn."

"Yu bet yu did. . . . Thank yu—Mr. Brite," replied the lad in a low voice.

Deuce Ackerman had followed Brite under the tree. "Boss, thet Wallen shore didn't get nowheres with me. Strikes me I'd seen him some place."

"Who is Wallen, son?"

"Rancher I rode for over Braseda way."

"What's he got against you?"

There was no reply. Ackerman bent over to peer down. "Throwed yore hardware, hey, Reddie? Wal, I don't blame yu. Now, cowboy, come clean if yu want to, or keep mum. It's all the same to us."

"Thank you. . . . I'm no rustler—or thief—or anythin' bad. . . . It was just . . . Oh, I cain't tell yu," replied the lad, with emotion.

"Ahuh. Wal, then it must be somethin' to do aboot a gurl?"

"Yes. . . . Somethin' aboot a gurl," hurriedly replied Bayne.

"I've been there, cowboy. . . . But I hope thet hombre wasn't her dad. 'Cause she's liable to be an orphan."

Ackerman returned to the camp fire, calling out: "Roll in, fellars. Yu're a-gonna need sleep this heah trip."

"Bayne, I'm shore glad it wasn't anythin' bad," said Brite in a kindly tone.

One of the boys rekindled the fire, which burned up brightly. By its light the old cattleman had a better view of young Bayne's face. The hard and bitter expression appeared softening. He made a forlorn little figure that touched Brite.

"I—I'll tell yu—sometime—if yu won't give me away," whispered the lad, and then hurried off into the darkness.

Brite sought his own blankets and lay thinking of the lad's confession—something about a girl! That had been true of him once, long ago, and to it could be traced the fact of his lonely years. He warmed to this orphaned lad. The old Trail was a tough and bloody proposition; but anything might be met upon it.

CHAPTER THREE

BRITE opened his eyes to grey dawn. A rifle-shot had awakened him. Moze was singing about darkies and cotton, which argued that the camp had not been attacked by Indians. Brite crawled out of his blankets, stiff and sore, to pull on his boots and don his vest, which simple actions left him dressed for the day. He rolled his bed. Then, securing a towel, he made through camp for the creek. Texas Joe was in the act of getting up. Three other boys lay prone, quiet, youthful, hard faces clear in the grey light.

"Boss, it's sho turrible gittin' oot in de mawnin'," was Moze's laconic greeting.

"Moze, I reckon I'm not so young as I was."

Down by the stream Brite encountered Reddie Bayne busy with his ablutions. "Howdy, son. I see yu're up an' doin'."

"Mawnin', Mr. Brite," replied the youth as he turned on his knees to show a wet and shining face as comely as a girl's. Brite thought the lad rather hurriedly got into his jacket and covered his red-gold curly hair with the battered old sombrero. Then he wiped face and hands with his scarf.

"I'll rustle my hawse before breakfast."

The water was cold and clear. Brite drank and washed with the pleasure of a trail driver who valued this privilege. At most places the water was muddy, or stinking and warm, or there was none at all. Upon his return up to the level bank he heard the lowing of cattle. Daylight had come. The eastern sky was ruddy. Mocking birds were making melody in the grove. Rabbits scurried away into the willows. Across the wide shallow stream deer stood on the opposite bank, with long ears erect. A fragrance of wood smoke assailed Brite's keen nostrils. There seemed to be something singularly full and rich in the moment.

Brite got back to camp in time to hear an interesting colloquy.

"Say, boy, who'n hell air yu?" Texas Joe was asking in genuine surprise. "I cain't recollect seein' yu before."

"My name's Reddie Bayne," replied the lad. "I rode in last night. The boss gave me a job."

"He did? Packin' water, or what?" went on Shipman.

"Hawse-wranglin'," said Reddie shortly.

"Humph! You're pretty much of a kid, ain't yu?"

"I cain't help it if I'm not an old geezer like——"

"Like who?—Me!—Say, youngster, I'm cantankerous early in the mawnin'."

"So it would seem," dryly responded Bayne.

"What yu packin' thet big gun on yore left hip for?"

"Kind of a protection against mean cusses."

"Heah, I didn't mean was yu wearin' it ornamental. But what for on the left side?"

"I'm left-handed."

"Aw, I see. Gun-slinger from the left hip, huh? Wal, I reckon yu got a lot of notches on the handle."

Bayne did not deign to make a reply to this, but it was evident that he was a little upset by the cool and sarcastic foreman. As Brite came on he saw the lad's fine eyes flash.

"Mawnin', boss. I see yu have gone an' hired another gunman," drawled Texas Joe.

"Who? Reddie Bayne, heah?"

"Shore. No one else. What's Texas comin' to thet boys who ought to be home a-milkin' cows rustle oot on bloody trails packin' big guns?"

"I haven't any home," retorted Bayne, with spirit.

"Reddie, shake hands with my foreman, Texas Joe Shipman," said Brite.

"Howdy, Mr. Shipman," rejoined Bayne resentfully, with emphasis on the prefix, and he did not offer his hand.

"Howdy, Girlie Boy," drawled Joe. "Suppose yu rustle yore hawse an' let me see him an' yore ootfit."

Bayne's face flamed red and he trotted off into the grove, whereupon Brite took occasion to acquaint Shipman with the incident that had made Bayne one of the outfit.

"Hell yu say! Wal!—Pore kid! . . . Wallen, now I just wonder where I've heahed thet name. Odd sort of handle. I'll bet my spurs he's no good. It's the no-good fellars' names thet stick in yore craw."

"Yu cow-tail twisters, come an' git it," sang out Moze.

San Sabe romped into camp with a string of mustangs which the men had to dodge or catch.

"Boots an' saddles heah, my tenderfoot Hal from Pennsylvania," yelled Texas Joe to the slow-moving Bender. "Thet's for all of yu. Rustle. An' get ootside some chuck. This's our busy day, mixin' a wild herd of long-horns with a tame one."

Strong brown hands flashed and tugged. As if by magic the restless ponies were bridled and saddled. The trail drivers ate standing. Texas Joe was the first to mount.

"Fork yore hawses, boys," he called vibrantly. "Boss, I'll point the herd, then send Ackerman in with his guard to eat. Follow along, an' don't forget yore new hawse-wrangler, young Bayne."

In a few moments Brite was left alone with Moze. The red sun peeped over the eastern rim and the world of rolling ranges changed. The grove appeared full of bird melody. Far out the bawl of new-born calves attested to the night's addition to the herd. A black steed came flashing under the pecans. Bayne rode into camp and leaped off.

"All bunched an' ready, boss," he said, in keen pleasure. "Gee! thet's a *remuda*. Finest I ever seen. I can wrangle thet ootfit all by myself."

"Wal, son, if yu do yu'll earn Texas Joe's praise," returned Brite.

"Pooh for thet cowboy! I'd like to earn yores, though, Mr. Brite."

"Fall to, son, an' eat."

Brite bestrode his horse on the top of the slope and watched the riders point the herd and start the drive up out of the creek bottom.

Used as he was to all things pertaining to cattle, he could not but admit to himself that this was a magnificent spectacle. The sun had just come up red and glorious, spreading a wonderful light over the leagues of range; the air was cool, fresh, sweet, with a promise of warmth for midday; flocks of blackbirds rose like clouds over the cattle, and from the grove of pecans a chorus of mocking-bird melody floated to his ears; the shining creek was blocked by a mile-wide bar of massed cattle, splashing and ploughing across; shots pealed above the bawl and trample, attesting to the fact that the drivers were shooting new-born calves that could not keep up with their mothers.

Like a colossal triangle the wedge-shaped herd, with the apex to the fore, laboriously worked up out of the valley. Ackerman's Uvalde herd had the lead, and that appeared well, for they had become used to the Trail, and Brite's second and third herds, massing in behind, were as wild a bunch of long-horns as he had ever seen. Their wide-spread horns, grey and white and black, resembled an endless mass of uprooted stumps of trees, milling, eddying, streaming across the flat and up the green slope. The movement was processional, rhythmic, steady as a whole, though irregular in spots, and gave an impression of irresistible power. To Brite it represented the great cattle movement now in full momentum, the swing of Texas toward an Empire, the epic of the herds and the trail drivers that was to make history of the West. Never before had the old cattleman realized the tremendous significance of the colourful scene he was watching. Behind it seemed to ride and yell and sing all the stalwart sons of Texas. It was their chance after the Civil War that had left so many of them orphaned and all of them penniless. Brite's heart thrilled and swelled to those lithe riders. He alone had a thought of the true nature of this undertaking, and the uplift of his heart was followed by a pang. They had no thought of the morrow. The moment sufficed for them. To drive the herd, to stick to the task, to reach their objective—that was an unalterable obligation assumed when they started. Right then Brite conceived his ultimate appreciation of the trail driver.

At last the wide base of the herd cleared the stream bed, leaving it like a wet ploughed field. Then the *remuda* in orderly bunch crossed behind. Brite recognized Reddie Bayne on his spirited black mount. The lad was at home with horses. Moze, driving the chuck-wagon, passed up the road behind Brite and out on the level range.

Then the sharp point of the herd, with Texas Joe on the left and Less Holden on the right, passed out of sight over the hill. Farther down the widening wedge, two other riders performed a like guard. The rest held no stable position. They flanked the sides and flashed along the rear wherever an outcropping of unruly longhorns raised a trampling roar and a cloud of dust. Each rider appeared to have his own yell, which Brite felt assured he would learn to recognize in time. And those yells rang out like bells or shrilled aloft or pealed across the valley.

Brite watched the dashing drivers, the puffs of dust rising pink in the sunrise flush, the surging body of long-horns crowding up the slope. A forest of spear-pointed horns pierced the sky line. And when the last third of the herd got up out of the valley, on the wide slope, the effect was something to daunt even old Adam Brite. Half that number of cattle, without the wilder element, would have been more than enough to drive to Dodge. Brite realized this now. But there could not be any turning back. He wondered how many head of stock, and how many drivers, would never get to Dodge.

Brite turned away to ride to the highest ridge above the valley, from which he scanned the Trail to the south. For a trail drive what was coming behind was as important almost as what lay to the fore. To mix a herd with that of a following trail driver's was bad business. It made extra toil and lost cattle. To his relief, the road and the range southward were barren of moving objects. A haze of dust marked where San Antonio lay. To the north the purple, rolling prairie-land spread for leagues, marked in the distance by black dots and patches and dark lines of trees. It resembled an undulating sea of rosy grass. Only the unknown dim horizon held any menace.

The great herd had topped the slope below and now showed in its entirety, an arrow-headed mass assuming proper perspective. It had looked too big for the valley; here up on the range it seemed to lengthen and spread and find room. The herd began its slow, easy, grazing march northward, at the most eight or ten miles a day. In fine weather and if nothing molested the cattle, this leisurely travel was joy for the drivers. The infernal paradox of the trail driver's life was that a herd might be driven north wholly under such comfortable circumstances, and again the journey might be fraught with terrific hardship and peril. Brite had never experienced one of the extreme adventures, such as he had heard of, but the ordinary trip had been strenuous and hazardous enough for him.

Brite caught up with the chuck-wagon and walked his horse alongside it for a while, conversing with the genial negro. From queries about the Rio Grande country and the Uvalde cattlemen, Brite progressed to interest in the quintet of riders who had brought the southern herd up. Moze was loquacious and soon divulged all his knowledge of Deuce Ackerman and his comrades. "Yas, suh, dey's de finest an' fightenest boys I ever seen, dat's shore," concluded Moze. "I ben cookin' fer two-t'ree years fer de U-V ootfit. Kurnel Miller run dat ootfit fust, an' den sold oot to Jones. An' yo bet Jones was sho glad to get rid of dem five boys. What wid shootin' up de towns every pay day an' sparkin' Miss Molly, de Kurnel's dotter, why, dat gennelman led a turrible life."

"Wal, I reckon they weren't no different from other boys where a pretty girl was concerned."

"Yas, suh, dere wuz a difference, 'cause dese boys wuz like twin brothers, an' Miss Molly jes' couldn't choose among 'em. She sho wanted 'em all, so Mars Jones had to sell 'em to yo along wid de cattle."

"Wal, Moze, we shore might run into anythin' along the old Trail," replied Brite, with a laugh. "But it's reasonable to hope there won't be any girls till we reach Dodge."

"Dat's a hot ole town dese days, I heah, boss."

"Haw! Haw! Just you wait, Moze. . . . Wal, we're catchin' up with the herd, an' from now it'll be lazy driftin' along."

Soon Brite came up with the uneven, mile-wide rear of the herd. Four riders were in sight, and the first he reached was Hallett, who sat cross-legged in his saddle and let his pony graze along.

"How're yu boys makin' oot, Roy?"

"Jes' like pie, boss, since we got up on the range," was the reply. "There's some mean old mossy-horns an' some twisters in thet second herd of yores. Texas Joe shot two bulls before we got 'em leavin' thet valley."

"Bad luck to shoot cattle," replied Brite seriously.

"Wal, we're short-handed an' we gotta get there, which I think we never will."

"Shore we will. . . . Where's Reddie Bayne with the *remuda*?"

"Aboot a half over, I reckon. Thet's Rolly next in line. He's been helpin' the kid with the *remuda*."

"Ahuh. How's Reddie drivin'?"

"Fine, boss. But thet's a sight of hawses for one boy. Reckon he could wrangle them alone but fer them damn old mossy-horns."

Brite passed along. Rolly Little was the next rider in line, and he appeared to be raising the dust after some refractory steers. Cows were bellowing and charging back, evidently wanting to return to calves left behind.

"Hey, boss, we got some ornery old drags in this herd," he sang out.

"Wal, have patience, Little, but don't wear it oot," called Brite.

The horses were grazing along in a wide straggling drove, some hundred yards or more behind the herd. Reddie Bayne on the moment was bending over the neck of his black, letting him graze. Brite trotted over to join him.

"Howdy, Reddie."

"Howdy, Mr. Brite."

"Wal, I'll ride along with yu an' do my share. Everythin' goin' good?"

"Oh yes, sir. I'm havin' the time of my life," rejoined the youth. He looked the truth of that enthusiastic assertion. What a singularly handsome lad! He looked younger than the sixteen years he had confessed to. His cheeks were not full, by any means, but they glowed rosily through the tan. In the broad sunlight his face shone clear cut, fresh and winning. Perhaps his lips were too red and curved for a boy. But his eyes were his most marked feature—a keen, flashing purple, indicative of an intense and vital personality.

"Thet's good. I was some worried aboot yu last night," returned the cattleman, conscious of gladness at having befriended this lonely lad. "Have my boys been friendly?"

"Shore they have, sir. I feel more at home. They're the—the nicest boys I ever rode with. . . . All except Texas Joe."

"Wal, now, thet's better. But what's Joe done?"

"Oh, he—he just took a—a dislike to me," replied the lad hurriedly, with a marked contrast to his former tone. "It always happens, Mr. Brite, wherever I go. Somebody—usually the rancher or trail boss or foreman—has to dislike me—an' run me off."

"But why, Reddie? Air yu shore yu're reasonable? Texas Joe is aboot as wonderful a fellar as they come."

"Is he?—I hadn't noticed it. . . . He—he cussed me oot this mawnin'."

"He did? Wal, thet's nothin', boy. He's my Trail boss, an' shore it's a responsibility. What'd he cuss yu aboot?"

"Not a thing. I can wrangle these hawses as good as he can. He's just taken a dislike to me."

"Reddie, he may be teasin' yu. Don't forget yu're the kid of the ootfit. Yu'll shore catch hell."

"Oh, Mr. Brite, I don't mind atall—so long's they're decent. An' I do so want to keep this job. I'll love it. I'm shore I can fill the bill."

"Wal, yu'll keep the job, Reddie, if thet's what's worryin' yu. I'll guarantee it."

"Thank yu. . . . An', Mr. Brite, since yu are so good I—I think I ought to confess——"

"Now see heah, lad," interrupted Brite. "Yu needn't make no more confessions. I reckon yu're all right an' thet's enough."

"But I—I'm not all right," returned the lad bravely, turning away his face. They were now walking their mounts some rods behind the *remuda*.

"Not all right? . . . Nonsense!" replied Brite sharply. He had caught a glimpse of quivering lips, and that jarred him.

"Somethin' tells me I ought to trust yu—before——"

"Before what?" queried Brite curiously.

"Before they find me oot."

"Lad, yu got me buffaloed. I'll say, though, thet yu can trust me. I dare say yu're makin' a mountain oot of a mole hill. So come on, lad, an' get it over."

"Mr. Brite, I—I'm not what I—I look—atall."

"No?—Wal, as yu're a likely-lookin' youngster, I'm sorry to heah it.—Why ain't yu?"

"Because I'm a girl."

Brite wheeled so suddenly that his horse jumped. He thought he had not heard the lad correctly. But Bayne's face was turned and his head drooped.

"Wha-at?" he exclaimed, startled out of his usual composure.

Bayne faced him then, snatching the old sombrero off. Brite found himself gazing into dark, violet, troubled eyes.

"I'm a girl," confessed Reddie hurriedly. "Everywhere I've worked I've tried to keep my secret. But always it was found oot. Then I suffered worse. So I'm tellin' yu, trustin' yu—an' if—or when I *am* found oot—maybe yu'll be my friend."

"Wal, I'm a son-of-a-gun!" burst out Brite. "Yu're a girl! . . . Shore I see thet now. . . . Why, Reddie, yu pore kid—yu can just bet yore life I'll keep yore secret, an' be yore friend, too, if it's found oot."

"Oh, I felt yu would," replied Reddie, and replaced the wide sombrero. With the sunlight off those big eyes and the flushed face, and especially the rebellious red-gold curls she reverted again to her disguise. "Somehow yu remind me of my dad."

"Wal, now, lass, thet's sweet for me to heah. I never had a girl, or a boy, either, an' God knows I've missed a lot. . . . Won't yu tell me yore story?"

"Yes, sometime. It's a pretty long an' sad one."

"Reddie, how long have yu been masqueradin' as a boy rider?"

"Three years an' more. Yu see, I had to earn my livin'. An' bein' a girl made it hard. I tried everythin' an' I shore hated bein' a servant. But when I grew up—then it was worse. 'Most always boys an' men treated me fine—as yu know Texans do. There was always some, though, who—who wanted me. An' they wouldn't leave me free an' alone. So I'd ride on. An' I got the idee pretendin' to be a boy would make it easier. Thet helped a lot. But I'd always get found out. An' I'm scared to death thet hawk-eyed Texas Joe suspects me already."

"Aw no—no! Reddie, I'm shore an' certain not."

"But he calls me Girlie Boy!" ejaculated Reddie tragically.

"Thet's only 'cause yu're so—so nice-lookin'. Land sakes! If Texas really suspected he'd act different. All these boys would. They'd be as shy as sheep. . . . Come to think of thet, Reddie, wouldn't it be better to tell Texas Joe an' all of them?"

"Oh, for Heaven's sake!—please—please don't, Mr. Brite. . . . Honest, we'd never get to Dodge!"

Brite greeted this appeal with a hearty laugh. Then he recalled Moze's talk about the Uvalde boys. "Wal, maybe yu're right. . . . Reddie, I've a hunch now thet hombre Wallen knows yu air a girl."

"Yu bet he does. Thet's the trouble."

"In love with yu?"

"Him! . . . Why, Wallen's too low to love anyone, even his own kin, if he ever had any. . . . He hails from the Big Bend country, an' I've heahed it said he wasn't liked around Braseda. He claims he bought me with a bunch of cattle. Same as a nigger slave! I was ridin' for John Clay, an' he did let me go with the deal. Wallen made thet deal 'cause he'd found oot I was a girl. So I ran off an' he trailed me."

"Reddie, he'd better not follow yore trail up this way."

"Would yu save me?" asked the girl softly.

"Wal, I reckon, but Texas Joe or Pan Handle would have thet hombre shot before I could wink," declared the cattleman, in grim humour.

The girl turned an agitated face to him. "Mr. Brite, yu make me hope my dream'll come true—some day."

"An' how, Reddie?"

"I've dreamed some good rancher—some real Texan—would adopt me—so I could wear girl's clothes once more an' have a home an'—an'——"

Her voice trailed away and broke.

"Wal, wal! Stranger things than thet have happened, Reddie," replied Brite, strangely stirred. On the moment he might have committed himself to much but for an interruption in the way of distant gun shots.

"Rumpus over there, Mr. Brite," suddenly called Reddie, pointing to a huge cloud of dust over the west end of the herd. "Yu better ride over. I'll take care of the hawses."

Putting spurs to his mount, Brite galloped in the direction indicated. Hallett and Little were not in sight, and probably had been obscured by the dust. A low roar of trampling hoofs filled his ears. The great body of the herd appeared intact, although there were twisting *mêlées* of cattle over toward the left on the edge of the dust line. Brite got around the left wing to see a stream of long-horns pouring out of the main herd at right angles. The spur was nearly a mile long, and bore the ear-marks of a stampede. With too few drivers the danger lay in the possibility of the main herd bolting in the opposite direction. Except in spots, however, they were acting rationally. Then Brite observed that already the forward drivers had the stream curving back to the north. He became conscious of relief, and slowed up to take his place behind the most exposed section of the herd. All across the line the cattle were moving too fast. A restlessness had passed through the mass. It was like a wave. Gradually they returned to the former leisurely gait and all appeared well again. Little rode past at a gallop and yelled something which Brite did not distinguish.

The drive proceeded then in its slow, orderly procession, a time-swallower, if no more. Hours passed. The warm sun began its westering slant, which grew apace, as did all the details of driving, the rest and walk and jog, the incessant stir of cattle, the murmur of hoofs, the bawl of cows, the never-failing smell of dust, manure, and heated bodies, and ever the solemn sky above and the beckoning hills, the dim purple in the north.

In another hour the great herd had surrounded a little lake in the centre of an immense shallow bowl of range land. Trees were conspicuous for their absence. Moze had wisely hauled firewood, otherwise he would have had to burn buffalo chips for fuel. Brite walked his horse a mile along the left flank before he reached the chuck-wagon and camp. These were at the head of the lake, from which slight eminence the whole centre of the depression could be seen. Gramma grass was fair, though not abundant. The cattle would need to be herded this night.

Reddie Bayne came along swinging on the beautiful black, always a delight to a rider's eye. Reddie reined in to accommodate Brite's pace.

"Heah we air, the long day gone an' camp once more. Oh, Mr. Brite, I am almost happy," declared Reddie.

"There shore is somethin' sweet aboot it. Make the best of it, Reddie, for God only knows what'll come."

"Ah! There's thet Texas Joe!" exclaimed Reddie as they neared camp. "Looks mighty pert now. I reckon he's pleased with himself for turnin' thet break back. . . . Boss, what'll I do when he—he gets after me again?"

"Reddie, don't be mealy-mouthed," advised Brite, low-voiced and earnest. "Talk back. Be spunky. An' if yu could manage a cuss word or two it'd help a lot."

"Lord knows I've heahed enough," replied Reddie.

They rode into camp. Texas Joe had thrown off sombrero, vest, and chaps, and gun-belt as well. It occurred to Brite that the tall, amber-eyed, tawny-haired young giant might well play havoc with the heart of any fancy-free girl.

"Wal, heah yu air, boss," he drawled, with his winning smile. "Fust I've seen yu since mawnin'. Reckoned yu'd rode back to Santone. . . . It shore was a good drive. Fifteen miles, an' the herd will bed down heah fine."

"Texas, I got sort of nervous back there," replied Brite as he dismounted.

"Nothin' atall, boss, nothin' atall. I'd like to inform yu, though, thet this heah Pan Handle Smith might have rode up this Trail with Jesse Chisholm an' been doin' it ever since."

"Thanks, Joe. I hardly deserve thet," rejoined the outlaw, who appeared to be getting rid of the dust and dirt of the ride.

Lester Holden was the only other driver present, and he squatted on a stone, loading his gun.

"I had fo' shots at thet slate-coloured old mossy-horn. Bullets jest bounced off his haid."

"Boys, don't shoot the devils, no matter how mean they air. Save yore lead for Comanches."

"Wal, if there ain't our Reddie," drawled Texas Joe, with a dancing devil in his eye. "How many hawses did yu lose, kid?"

"I didn't count 'em," replied Reddie sarcastically.

"Wal, I'll count 'em, an' if there's not jest one hundred an' eighty-nine yu're gonna ride some more."

"Ahuh. Then I'll ride, 'cause yu couldn't count more'n up to ten."

"Say, yu're powerful pert this evenin'. I reckon I'll have to give yu night guard."

"Shore. I'd like thet. But no more'n my turn, Mister Texas Jack."

"Right. I'm mister to yu. But it's Joe, not Jack."

"Same thing to me," returned Reddie, who on the moment was brushing the dust off his horse.

"Fellars, look how the kid babies that hawse," declared Shipman. "No wonder the animal is pretty. . . . Dog-gone me, I'll shore have to ride him to-morrow."

"Like bob yu will," retorted Reddie.

"Say, I was only foolin', yu darned little pepper-pot. Nobody but a hawse thief ever takes another fellar's hawse."

"I don't know yu very well, Mister Shipman."

"Wal, yu're durned liable to before this drive is much older."

Somehow, Brite reflected, these two young people rubbed each other the wrong way. Reddie was quite a match for Texas Joe in quick retort, but she was careful to keep her face half averted or her head lowered.

"Reckon we'll all know each other before we get to Dodge."

"Ahuh. An' thet's a dig at me," replied Texas Joe peevishly. "Dog-gone yu, anyhow."

"Wal, haven't yu been diggin' me?" demanded Reddie spiritedly.

"Sonny, I'm Brite's Trail boss an' yu're the water-boy."

"I am nothin' of the sort. I'm the hawse-wrangler of this outfit."

"Aw, yu couldn't wrangle a bunch of hawg-tied suckin' pigs. Yu shore got powerful testy aboot yoreself, all of a sudden. Yu was meek enough this mawnin'."

"Go to hell, Texas Jack!" sang out Reddie, with most exasperating flippancy.

"What'd yu say?" blustered Texas, passing from jest to earnest.

"I said yu was a great big, sore-haided, conceited giraffe of a trail-drivin' bully," declared Reddie, in a very clear voice.

"Aw! Is thet all?" queried Texas, suddenly cool and devilish. Quick as a cat he leaped to snatch Reddie's gun and pitch it away. Reddie, who was kneeling with his back turned, felt the action and let out a strange little cry. Then Texas fastened a powerful hand in the back of Reddie's blouse, at the neck, and lifted him off his feet. Whereupon Texas plumped down to draw Reddie over his knees.

"Boss, yu heahed this disrespectful kid," drawled Texas. "Somethin' shore has got to be done aboot it."

CHAPTER FOUR

THE astounding thing to the startled Brite was the way Reddie lay motionless over the knees of the cowboy, stiff as a bent poker. No doubt poor Reddie was petrified with expectation and horror. Brite tried to blurt out with a command for Texas to stop. But sight of that worthy's face of fiendish glee completely robbed that cattleman of vocal powers.

"Pan Handle, do you approve of chastisement for unruly youngsters?" queried Texas.

"Shore, on general principles," drawled Smith. "But I reckon I cain't see thet Reddie has been more than sassy."

"Wal, thet's it. If we don't nip him in the bud we jest won't be able to drive cattle with him babblin' aboot."

"Lam him a couple, Tex," spoke up Lester. "Reddie's all right, I reckon, only turrible spoiled."

Texas raised high a broad, brown, powerful hand.

"Shipman—don't yu—dare—smack me!" cried Reddie, in a strangled voice.

But the blow fell with a resounding whack. Dust puffed up from Reddie's trousers. Both her head and feet jerked up with the force of the blow. She let out a piercing yell of rage and pain, then began to wrestle like a lassoed wildcat. But Texas Joe got in three more sounding smacks before his victim tore free to roll over and bound erect. If Brite had been petrified before, he was now electrified. Reddie personified a fury that was beautiful and thrilling to see. It seemed to Brite that anyone but these thick-headed, haw-hawing drivers would have seen that Reddie Bayne was an outraged girl.

"Oh-h-h! Yu devil!" she screamed, and jerked for the gun that had been on her hip. But it was gone, and Lester had discreetly picked it up.

"Ump-umm, kid. No gun-play. This heah is fun," said Lester.

"Fun—hell!" Then quick as a flash Reddie leaped to deal the mirth-convulsed Texas a tremendous kick on the shin. That was a horse of another colour.

"Aggh-gh-gh!" roared Texas, clasping his leg and writhing in agony. "Aw, my Gawd! . . . My sore laig!"

Reddie poised a wicked boot for another onslaught. But she desisted and slowly settled back on both feet.

"Huh! So *yu* got feelin's?"

"Feelin's?—Say, I'll—be—daid in a minnit," groaned Texas. "Kid, thet laig's full of lead bullets."

"If yu ever touch me again I'll—I'll fill the rest of yore carcass with lead."

"Cain't yu take a little joke? . . . Shore I was only in fun. The youngest driver always gets joked."

"Wal, Texas Jack, if thet's a sample of yore trail-drivin' jokes, I pass for the rest of the trip."

"But, say, yu ain't no better than anybody else," protested Texas, in a grieved tone. "Ask the boss. Yu wasn't a good fellar—to get so mad."

Reddie appealed voicelessly to the old cattleman.

"Wal, yu're both right," declared Brite, anxious to conciliate. "Tex, yu hit too darned hard for it to be fun. Yu see, Reddie's no big, husky, raw-boned man."

"So I noticed. He certainly felt soft for a rider. . . . Kid, do you want to shake an' call it square? I reckon I got the wust of it at thet. Right this minnit I've sixteen jumpin' toothaches in my laig."

"I'd die before I'd shake hands with yu," rejoined Reddie, and snatching up her sombrero, and taking her gun from the reluctant Lester, she flounced away.

"Dog-gone!" ejaculated Texas ruefully. "Who'd took thet kid for such a spit-fire? Now I've gone an' made another enemy."

"Tex, yu shore was rough," admonished Brite.

"Rough? Why, I got mine from a pair of cowhide hobbles," growled Texas, and getting up he limped about his tasks.

Presently Moze called them to supper, after which they rode out on fresh horses to relieve the guard. Deuce Ackerman reported an uneasy herd, owing to the presence of a pack of wolves. Brite went on guard, taking a rifle with him. He passed Bayne's black horse. The *remuda* had bunched some distance from the herd. It was still warm, though the fiery-red sun had gone down behind the range. Brite took up his post between the horses and cattle, and settled to a task he had never liked.

The long-horns had not quieted down for the night. Distant rumblings attested to restlessness at the other end of the herd. Brite patrolled a long beat, rifle across his pommel, keeping a sharp lookout for wolves. He saw coyotes, jack-rabbits, and far away over the grass, a few scattered deer. Before dusk settled thick Reddie Bayne appeared with the *remuda*, working them off to the eastward, toward a sheltered cove half a mile beyond Brite. Twilight stole on them down in the bowl, and over the western horizon gold rays flushed and faded.

Before dark Reddie rode up to Brite.

"Hawses all right, boss. I reckon I'll hang around yore end. We all got orders to stand guard till called off."

"Maybe somethin brewin'. Maybe not. *Quien sabe?*"

"I reckon what's brewin' is in thet hombre's mind."

"Which hombre, Reddie?"

"Yu know. . . . Wasn't it perfectly awful—what he did to me, Mr. Brite?"

"Wal, it was kinda tough," agreed Brite. "Tex got in action so quick I was just too flabbergasted."

"Yu shore wasn't very chivalrous," rejoined Reddie dubiously. "I've my doubts aboot *yu* now."

"It sort of paralysed me 'cause I knowed yu was a girl."

"I'll bet *thet* would paralyse him, too," retorted Reddie, darkly. "Boss, I could get even with Texas by tellin' him thet he had insulted a lady."

"By thunder! yu could. But don't do it, Reddie. He might shake the ootfit."

"I'd hate to have *him* know I—I'm a girl," replied Reddie, musingly.

"Let's hope none of them will find oot."

"Mr. Brite, I'd never forgive myself if I brought yu bad luck."

"Yu won't, Reddie."

"Listen," she whispered, suddenly.

A weird chanting music came on the warm air, from the darkness. Brite recognized the Spanish song of a *vaquero*.

"San Sabe singin' to the herd, Reddie."

"Oh—how pretty! He shore can sing."

Then from another quarter came a quaint cowboy song, and when that ceased a faint mellow voice pealed from far over the herd. The rumblings of hoofs ceased, and only an occasional bawl of a cow broke the silence. San Sabe began again his haunting love song, and then all around the herd pealed out the melancholy refrains. That was the magic by which the trail drivers soothed the restless longhorns.

The moon came up and silvered the vast bowl, lending enchantment to the hour. Reddie passed to and fro, lilting a Dixie tune, lost in the beauty and serenity of the night. From a ridge pealed forth the long, desolate, blood-curdling moan

of a prairie wolf. That brought the ghastly reminder that this moment was real—
that there was death waiting just beyond.

The cowboys smoked and sang, the cattle slept or rested, the balmy night
wind rustled the grass, the ducks whirred to and fro over the lake. The stars paled
before the full moon.

Texas Joe came trotting up. "Boss, yu an' Reddie go to bed. Two hours off
an' then two on, for five of us. I ain't shore yet thet all is wal."

Reddie never stopped singing the sweet ditty.

"Gosh, Tex, it cain't be midnight yet!" exclaimed Brite.

"It cain't be, but it shore is. Go along with you. . . . Reddie, yu got a sweet
voice for a boy. I shore am a-wonderin' aboot you."

"Boss, yu see?" whispered Reddie, fiercely, clutching Brite's arm. "Thet hombre
suspects me."

"Let him—the son-of-a-gun! Then if he finds yu oot it'll be all the wuss."

"For him or me?"

"For him, shore."

"How yu mean, boss, wuss?"

"Wall, it'd serve him right to fall so dinged in love with yu thet——"

"O my Gawd!" cried Reddie, in faint, wild tones, and spurred ahead to vanish
in the shadows.

"Wal!" quoth Brite, amazed. It was evident that he had said something amiss.
"Thet was an idee. Didn't she fly up an' vamoose?"

Brite made his way slowly into camp. Hallett and Ackerman were already
in by the fire, drinking coffee. San Sabe came riding up, still with the remnants
of song on his lips. Reddie's horse was haltered out in the moonlight and something prone and dark showed beside a low bush. Brite sought his own blankets.

Next morning, when Brite presented himself for breakfast, Whittaker and Pan
Handle were the only drivers in camp. They were eating in a hurry.

"Herd movin' boss," announced Smith. "We been called."

Brite answered their greetings, while his ears attuned themselves to the distant
sound of hoofs. The hour was early, as the sun had not yet risen. A cloudless sky
and balmy air attested to promising weather.

"Where's Reddie?"

"Off with the hawses. When he heahed Joe yell he quit eatin' like a scared
jack rabbit. I called for fresh hawses."

"Must be somethin' up," muttered Brite. "Wal, it's aboot time."

"I don't care much aboot this heah trail drivin'," drawled Whittaker. "Too slow. I hired oot for action."

"Humph! Son, yu'll get yore belly full of action," declared Brite grimly.

"Heah comes Red with hawses," announced Pan Handle. "Boss, I shore like thet kid. Nice quiet lad. Rides like a *vaquero* an' shore knows hawses."

"Hey, men, ketch yore ponies," shrilled Reddie, and flashed away out of sight.

It was everybody for himself. Fortunately, a rope corral aided the drivers in catching the fresh, unwilling horses. Brite haltered his, a ragged little bay, and returned to finish his meal. Soon the others were off.

"Moze, what started the herd so pronto?" queried Brite.

"I dunno, boss. Jes' started themselves, I reckon. Cattle is sho pustiferous annimiles. De Law Hisself nebber knows what dey'll do."

"Right. . . . Pack without washin' up, Moze. An' move right along."

"Ise a-movin', sah."

Brite climbed aboard the little bay. He, like all the drivers, had to ride what horses Reddie could fetch in promptly, and in this case he realized at once that he was in for tricks. The bay showed every indication of bucking, but by spurring him off over the prairie Brite wore off his mean edge. A red disc of sun peeped up over the eastern rim. The day had begun. Flocks of black birds wheeled from the water in the direction of the cattle. A distant low cloud of dust moved to the northward. Brite caught up with it to find the cattle slowing down and spreading out. Bayne had the *remuda* in order on the right, and half a mile behind.

Ackerman sat his mustang, waiting for Brite, whom evidently he had seen following.

"Boss, did yu run acrost thet daid steer back a ways?" he queried.

"No, I didn't."

"Wal, I did. An' I had to shoot it."

"What for?"

"Somebody had crippled it. Laig broke by a needle-gun slug."

"Yu don't say! We haven't any buffalo guns in this ootfit."

"Looks queer to me. Must have been done jest before daylight."

"Does Texas know aboot it?"

"Cain't say. Reckon not. He was off guard. Went on at dawn. Same for me. But one of the boys must have heahed thet big gun."

"Ahuh. Plenty of thick brush around thet lake. There might have been a camp somewhere. Somebody wantin' beef, mebbe."

CHAPTER FOUR

Brite rode on to fill in a wide breach behind the herd, and there he walked his horse, and rested, and watched the horizon to the rear, and found the long hours pleasant. By mid-afternoon the endless, long slope, almost imperceptible until it had been surmounted, lay behind the herd and in front the land dropped to a creek bottom. Wide white bars of sand hemmed in a winding sheet of water. Across on the far bank green groves of timber and light green levels of grass invited camp and rest for that night. Four drivers, one after the other, pealed back the foreman's order: "Cross above. Keep movin'. Push the drags."

Brite saw the head of the great herd swerve to the west along the bank. Seven riders congregated on that side. The cattle wanted to drink, and after drinking they would cross. The danger evidently lay in stragglers working off the bars into bad places. Gunshots attested to hard practice in turning stock. Brite could not recall just where the trail did cross, but he calculated anywhere along there. Smith waved a red scarf from a high bank. He alone rode on the west of the herd. Then he disappeared, and the cattle appeared to roll in a bobbing stream down the incline. The after mass of long-horns crowded those in front, and the knocking of horns and bellowing of cows grew incessant. Brite saw that he was needed more around on the right flank, to help keep the stragglers in line, and the slow ones from dropping back. When the red and white front of the herd appeared wading and wallowing across, then the difficulty of holding back the rear grew greater, and passed from hard riding to hazardous toil. Seven riders on that side had their work cut out for them. Reddie Bayne got the *remuda* in line to the left, then joined the drivers on the right. Brite yelled for the youngster to keep out from in front of those ugly old mossy-horns. Some of these charged, kicked their heels like mules, and wickedly shook their heads. When at length the wide ragged rear end of the herd passed on into the shallow water they left a number mired in the quicksand. These were mostly the unruly cattle that had run too soon off the bank. Some of them were floundering; some were sinking; all were bellowing lustily.

Texas Joe came galloping back from upstream.

"Reddie, what'n hell yu mean layin' off yore *remuda*?" he shouted, his amber eyes flashing. "Git oot of heah!"

Reddie took to the shallow water with his horse on the run. Then Joe sent Whittaker, Bender, and Smith across.

"Boss, yu ain't needed heah. Go along," he concluded.

"Let 'em alone, Tex. There's only twenty-one haid," replied Brite.

"Hell no!" rang out the foreman, untying his lasso. "We ain't lettin' nuthin'

291

go. . . . Pile in, boys, an' stretch hemp. Keep away from thet ooze an' drag 'em upstream."

Whereupon Shipman rode off the bar, swinging the loop of his rope around his head. His horse sank up to his fetlocks, but kept moving. Texas cast a long loop and snared a bull that had only horns and head above the mire. Then spurring and yelling, the driver set to the task of dragging the long-horn out. The other boys followed suit, and there ensued a scene of strenuous noisy activity. They all got fast to a cow or steer, and put spurs to their mounts. Some of the cattle were dragged out easily. Others came but slowly and by dint of tremendous effort on the part of horse and rider. Texas could not budge the big bull, and Brite yelled to let that one go. Then the foreman's horse bogged down to his flanks. Like a flash Texas was off to loosen his cinch and tear his saddle free. Thus encumbered, with the rope still fast to the pommel and the bull at the other end, he bogged down himself. His horse floundered out to safety, but Texas had to yell for help. Ackerman and San Sabe rode to his assistance.

"Cut free," yelled Ackerman as he pitched an open loop to Texas.

"San, go below an' sling yore rope over thet damn bull," ordered Texas, and catching Ackerman's rope he fastened it over the pommel of his saddle. He was half-way up to his thighs in the quicksand and perceptibly sinking.

"I'm fast, Deuce," called out San Sabe, wheeling his horse. "Now drag 'em oot!"

The horses plunged, the ropes twanged. Texas was pulled over on his side, but clinging to the rope he held on. The two riders broke the bull loose from the anchoring mire and began to drag him upstream. Presently he let go and found his footing, to crawl out like a giant mud-turtle. A third rider swung in to catch the bull, and then with three ropes on him he was literally dragged out of the quicksand. Texas cursed the old mossy-horn as if he were human.

Brite revelled in this scene, and only once thought it necessary to lend a hand, and then he was not wanted. Like Comanche Indians these young riders yelled and rode, with fierce flashing eyes and many a ringing shout. Their profanity and grim humour seemed to fit their actions—all so hard, primitive, and inevitable.

The last unfortunate cow appeared to be too far out and too deeply sunk to be extricated. But these boys laboured on. They did all save get off and wade. The lassoes were too short. Only one caught over a horn and it slipped off.

"Boys, she's gone. Stranglin' now," called Brite. "Come off an' let well enough alone."

"Aw, put her oot of her misery," called one of them.

Guns boomed. One bullet whizzed off the skull of the cow.

"Hey, I thought yu fellars from down Uvalde way could shoot," drawled Texas, pulling his gun. He took deliberate aim. There was a significance in his posture. At the discharge the rolling eye of the animal went out. She laid her head over, and it sank until only the top of a long horn stuck up.

"Aw, hell!" laughed Deuce Ackerman, sheathing his gun.

"Tex, I shore hope yu hit plumb centre like thet when some redskin is about to peel my hair," said Less Holden.

Texas made no further comment. Dragging his saddle out of the mud, he shook the blanket and flopped it over his horse. The saddle went on, dripping water and sand. Soon Texas mounted to ride after the boys, now splashing across the shallow stream. Brite followed, careful to go briskly and let his horse pick the way. He had been in quicksand before.

They drove the twenty rescued cattle across the broadly marked sand bar and up into the timber. Beyond the strip of trees the great herd had stopped to graze on the green level, now contented with their lot.

"Right heah is good enough," said Texas wearily. "Deuce, keep an eye open for Moze. He'll need some direction an' mebbe help comin' across. . . . Gosh! I'm as tired as if I'd done a day's work. An' wet. Sand in my boots! —— the luck! Nice new boots! . . . Heah, Red, pull 'em off for me. Thet's a good kid."

"Who was yore nigger this time last year?" asked Reddie coolly.

"Never mind who, darn yu. . . ." Then Texas subtly changed. "Say, I asked yu a favour. My hands air all skinned."

"Shore," agreed Reddie hastily, and with good grace he pulled off Shipman's boots.

Deuce Ackerman sat his horse, peering back through the thin strip of trees to the river.

"Tex, did yu see thet crippled steer this mawnin'?" he asked.

"No. How crippled?"

"By a big buffalo gun. Laig broke. I shot it."

"Buffalo gun! Who's got one in this ootfit?"

"Nobody."

"Deuce, air yu shore?" queried Texas, suddenly interested.

"Shore. I know needle guns. An' the holes they make."

"What's on yore mind? . . . Hey, boss, yu heah him?"

"Yes. He told me this mawnin'," replied Brite.

Pan Handle Smith knelt on one knee, after the manner of riders, and he looked keenly at Ackerman.

"Somebody not in our ootfit shot thet steer this mawnin' aboot daylight," returned the rider.

"Texas I heahed thet gun," put in Smith. "It woke me up."

"Ahuh. There was a camp near us, then. I reckoned I smelled smoke when we rode down to the lake."

"Shore. I seen smoke way down to the west. Made a little stringy cloud ag'in thet gold sunset."

"Campers wantin' meat, I reckon," spoke up Brite. He suggested what he wanted to believe.

"Ump-umm," responded Deuce, pondering. "Thet was a tough old steer. An' he'd been shot from far off. Somebody took a pot shot at thet herd. But not for meat."

"What for, then?" demanded Texas sharply.

Nobody replied to that. Brite knew that the three men were thinking the same as he was, and did not readily voice their suspicions.

"Wal, heah comes Moze," went on Ackerman. "Come on, Reddie. Yu got a big hawse. We'll lend Moze a drag."

The two rode off under the trees out upon the bar. Moze had halted the chuck-wagon on the opposite bank, where evidently he was looking for a safe place to drive across.

Texas looked from Pan Handle to Brite, and the curious, cold, little gleam in his amber eyes was something to see.

"Do you reckon we're bein' follered?" he queried.

"Like as not," returned Brite.

"What'd the idee be, if we was?" asked Smith. "We're a dozen strong. Thet'd be a fool trick."

"Smith, it looks bad. Tex has been up the Trail before. He knows an' I know thet the chances air stampeders air on our track. My herd is too big. An' my ootfit too small."

"Stampeders, eh? I sabe."

"Never had any trouble before," went on Brite. "Fact is I've been amazin' lucky. But I've heahed of the hell other herd-owners have had. There's a regular drain on herds. Most of it comes from two-bit stampeders who collect a few haid heah an' there an' finally get enough to drive to Dodge on their own hook. An' again jealous drivers hire some of the trail-dodgers to stampede the herd ahaid of them. It's a dirty bizness."

"Say, it's a shootin' bizness," declared Texas, with fire in his eyes. "Boss, will we do a little scoutin' back to-night, or wait an' see if——?"

"Let's wait," interrupted Brite. "If we air trailed we'll shore find it oot soon enough. An' if we're not it's no matter. . . . Ask Moze if he seen any riders back along the Trail."

During the night Brite was awakened by he knew not what. The three belted stars he knew were sloping to the west, so the hour was late. It was also very still. No sound from the herd! No sing-song of lonely cowboys on duty! The insects had thinned down their melancholy dirge to a faint ghost of its earlier strength. The fire had burned down low. Coyotes wailed piercingly off to the north, no doubt on the edge of the herd.

Then a ringing shot cracked the silence. Brite sat up, fully awake.

"Forty-five," he soliloquized, and peered around in the darkness to see who lay near him. Three sleeping drivers never stirred. Then heavier shots boomed out, reports that Brite recognized as belonging to buffalo guns. One of the cowboys stalked erect like a spectre. Texas Joe! He turned his ear to the south. The biting ring of a 45 brought a sharp command from Shipman.

"Out of heah, men! Grab yore rifles an' rustle!"

Two of the drivers moved in concert. They sat up, looked, dove for rifles, to leap up and follow the stalking Texas, now already in shadow. The third rider awoke slowly, bewildered. It was Hal Bender.

"Get up, Bender," called Brite, rising himself.

"What's up, boss?" queried the tenderfoot, aghast, as he pulled on his boots.

"Somethin', I don't know what. Heahed shootin' oot there. Fetch yore guns."

"Ah!—What's that?"

A low rolling rumble off to the south smote Brite's keen ears.

"Hawses. Rustlers after our *remuda*, I'll bet," declared Brite, quickening his stride to a trot. His gun barrel clinked on a sapling. He had to go slower or risk knocking himself on trees in the darkness. Bender panted closely behind him. Twice Brite halted to listen, each time getting the direction by sound. Then they emerged from the timber into the open—a grey level under the wan stars. Sharp voices drew Brite farther to the left. He ran, careful not to trip in the grass, holding his rifle forward and peering keenly ahead.

"Who comes?" rasped from the opaque gloom. That was Texas' voice.

"Brite. Where air yu?"

"This way. Look oot for a hole."

Brite and Bender soon joined a group of four, one of whom was mounted. This rider was talking: "... don't know nothin' 'cept what I heahed. Hawses runnin' wild. Then shots. Two big buffalo guns an' a forty-five."

"Ahuh. Which way, Sans?"

The *vaquero* stretched his arm to the south.

"Everybody listen," ordered Texas, and he for one got down to lay his ear to the ground.

The silence was vibrant, intense. Nothing disturbed it. Texas stood up.

"Hawses movin' somewhere. Just restless. No more runnin'. . . . Now, listen some more."

Texas cupped his hands around his mouth. A whistling intake of air attested to his purpose. Suddenly he exploded: "HEY REDDIE!"

The stentorian yell split the silence and rolled away across the level, strange and wild. At once came an answer, faint but unmistakable, from the south.

"There! Sounds like . . ."

"Ssshh! Listen hard," interrupted Texas. Another reply came from the opposite direction, and then a very distant cry from the west. Lastly a nearer voice concluded the location of the herd.

"Spread oot, fellars, an' run this way," ordered Texas. "Stop every hundred yards or so, an' look sharp for the hawses. Hell to pay, I reckon."

San Sabe took the lead on his horse and was soon out of sight. Brite worked to the right and obeyed orders. He must have halted a dozen times before he was rewarded by any sound, and then he heard horses that he could not see. After this he walked, out of breath, and strung with eagerness. Texas Joe had not reacted quietly to this midnight disturbance. Shrill neigh of horses swerved Brite back to the left. Soon a compact black patch stood out against the grey.

"Where'n hell air yu, Reddie?" called Shipman.

"Heah, I'm comin'," came in the high-pitched voice Brite had learned to know. Presently he ran into the waiting group just as Reddie Bayne's big black loomed out of the grey.

"What yu doin' oot heah at this hour?" demanded Texas peremptorily.

"I didn't go to camp," replied Bayne.

"Ahuh. An' why didn't yu obey orders?"

"I got suspicious, Shipman. An' I stayed with the hawses. I heahed voices an' I seen lights. Then I bunched the *remuda* an' worked them toward camp away from the herd. Pretty soon I heahed poundin' hoofs. Then a string of riders showed comin' fast. I shot at the leader an' hit him or his hawse. But he kept right on. He an' the riders with him piled right into my *remuda*. When they began to shoot I savvied what they were up to. They cut oot some of my hawses an' drove them away. I shot at them an' they shot back. . . . Reckon thet's aboot all."

"Stampeders! . . . Wal, Deuce had it figgered," declared Texas.

"Let's fork our hawses an' hunt 'em up," suggested Holden.

Brite did not think this advisable, but he held his tongue.

"How many'd they run off, Reddie?" queried Texas.

"I cain't tell. Not many, though."

"Wal, we'll wait till mawnin' anyhow. . . . Reddie, go to camp an' get some sleep. It's most daybreak."

"If yu don't mind, I'd as lief hang oot heah," returned Bayne.

"Mebbe thet's just as wal. . . . Spread oot, boys, an' surround the *remuda* loose like. Yell if yu heah any hawses comin'."

Silence once more settled down over the prairie. The riders vanished one by one. Brite patrolled a beat that eventually fetched him close to Texas Joe.

"What yu make of this, Joe?"

"Wal, we oughta expected it. I reckon we're in for rough sleddin'. Too many haid of stock an' too few drivers."

"Thet's how I figger it," rejoined the boss thoughtfully. "But I'll tell yu, Shipman. If we get to Dodge with half our stock I'll still make a big stake. An' shore I won't forget yu boys."

"Boss, I ain't carin' a damn how many haid we lose. But I won't give up one single damn old long-horn without a fight. But hawse-stealin'! Thet riles me. . . . Say, Brite, did it strike yu—how game thet kid Bayne was, stayin' oot heah all alone? Dog-gone him! He rubs me the wrong way, but somehow I gotta like him."

"So do I.—Tex, I wish yu'd treat Reddie a—a bit better."

"Ahuh. I seen thet. Wal, I ain't a-goin' to have any favourites this drive. Why, the whole ootfit will hate my guts before we reach Dodge! . . . At thet, the whole ootfit never will make it, Brite."

"Got a hunch, hey?" queried the boss gloomily.

"So bad it hurts. . . . Wal, the east is greyin'. Wonder what this *heah* day will bring forth."

Brite plodded back to his beat, and watched the stars pale and die, the east kindle, the grey steal away as if by magic, and the horses and cattle and land take shape.

Presently Texas Joe waved him campward. The herd appeared to be up and on the slow move north. And again the day promised fine. As Brite trudged into camp he espied San Sabe, Bender, and Ackerman, standing, cups in hand, around Alabama Moze.

Then Texas came striding in on foot, his hawk eyes narrowed and his handsome lips tight.

"Deuce, yu point the herd an' get goin'," he said tersely. "Send Pan Handle back shore with the others."

"Air yu goin' to rustle?"

"Yu bet. Reddie's drivin' in some hawses. I reckon I'll take a look at them tracks south. . . . Boss, we lost upward of twenty-five haid of hawses."

"Small loss, if it ends there."

"Ahuh. Say, for an old Texan yu're nice disposed toward these stampeders."

"Tex, I'll bet he'll rave one of these days," laughed Deuce.

Reddie came loping in behind half a dozen ragged mustangs. The drivers spread and waved arms and ropes to corral them in a corner. Soon, then, only Brite, Texas Joe, Reddie, and the negro were left in camp. Texas appeared taciturn, as well as hungry. He was in a hurry, too. Reddie received his pan of food and cup from Moze, and repaired to an improvised seat, where he devoted himself assiduously to his meal.

The sun peeped up red over the purple horizon, and all the range land took on a rosy sheen. Even the birds heralded that transformation. Brite paused to take in the fresh radiance of the dawn. The long gramma grass shone bright as silver, and the flowers stood up with pale beautiful faces toward the east.

All of a sudden Texas Joe got up, cursing inaudibly. His lean head stuck out like that of a hawk as he peered to the south.

"What yu heah, Tex?" queried Brite sharply.

"Hawses."

Brite soon had to confess that Texas was correct.

"What of thet?" went on the boss.

"Wal, nothin'. Only couplin' it with what come off this mawnin' it ain't so good."

Presently a group of riders appeared at the far corner of timber. Brite counted seven or eight, all dark figures, coming at a brisk trot. Texas gave one long look, then turned to Brite.

"Boss, thet bunch has been watchin' us," he said, his eyes gleaming. "Timed us nice. Our boys just left an' the guard not in sight."

Suddenly Reddie Bayne leaped up, letting his pan clang to the ground.

"Wallen an' his ootfit!" cried Reddie, startled.

"Shore aboot thet, boy?" asked Texas darkly.

"Yes, shore. I know *him*. . . . I'll bet they stampeded my *remuda*. . . . An' now they're after me."

"Wal, keep back an' be careful what yu say. . . . Brite, have yore Winchester handy. Let me do the talkin'. . . . This heah's a time we may need yore Pan Handle Smith."

The dark compact bunch of riders closed the gap quickly and drew up in a semicircle just opposite the fire and chuck-wagon. Brite did not need to question their character and intent—not this time! He recognized the swarthy Wallen, whose big bold eyes swept the camp, and the range beyond. Foremost of the other riders was a more striking individual even than Wallen—a man of about fifty years, with a visage like a bleak stone bluff and eyes like fiery cracks. Brite had seen this same man somewhere. The five others were a likely crew for these leaders—all young, lean, unkempt cowboys.

"Wal, heah's our Reddie Bayne," spoke up Wallen, gruffly, pointing a heavy hand at Reddie.

"Shore an' proper, Wal," replied his lieutenant, in a dry, crisp voice.

Whereupon Wallen turned his rolling eyes upon Brite. "Lied to me back on the trail a ways—hey, Brite?"

"If I did I'll stick to it," retorted Brite, his blood leaping.

Texas Joe strode forward and to one side, getting out of line of the chuck-wagon with a significance that no Texan could have mistaken.

"Wallen, I see some of yore outfit packin' needle guns on their saddles," he said, with biting sarcasm.

"What if they air? We're huntin' buffalo."

"Ahuh. Thet's what *yu* say."

"I'll talk to Brite, an' not to yu, cowboy," declared Wallen aggressively.

"Yu talk to Texas Joe," interposed Brite caustically.

"Brite, we want thet youngster yu kidnapped. Reddie Bayne," declared the leader of the visitors.

"Wallen, I ain't used to palaverin' with men like yu," rejoined Texas bitingly. It struck Brite that his foreman was playing for time to let Pan Handle Smith and the others reach camp. Brite flashed a furtive glance across the rosy grassland. No sign of a rider! This was serious, for there surely would be violence here promptly.

"Who the hell air yu?" shouted Wallen hoarsely.

"Wal, I know this hombre," said Wallen's partner. "It's Texas Shipman."

"That means nothin' to me."

"Then yu do the talkin', pard," returned his companion, in cool hard voice that told Brite much. This lieutenant was the more dangerous man.

"I shore don't need yu, Ross Hite, to do my talkin'," snorted Wallen.

Ross Hite! Brite responded to that name well known to trail drivers. Hite had run the gamut of all Texas occupations known to the range.

"Wal, *talk* then, damn yu, an' make it short," shot out Texas. "What yu want?"

"We're drivin' our stock on ahaid," replied Wallen bluntly. "Yu travel too slow, an' they're crowdin' us. . . . I want this rider, Reddie Bayne. He come to me in a deal I made with Jones at Braseda."

"Ahuh. Does Bayne owe yu his services?"

"He shore does."

"What yu say, Reddie?"

Reddie leaped forward. "He's a damn liar, Texas," shrilled Reddie passionately. "I've run off from three ranches to get away from him."

"Shet up or it'll be the wuss for yu," replied Wallen stridently.

"Slow there, Wallen," rang out Texas. "This heah is a free country. The day of slaves, white or black, is over."

"Reddie, tell *why* Wallen wants yu," spoke up Brite cunningly. His Texan blood was not proof against this evasion. Besides, out on a far ridge top he descried a dark rider coming fast. Pan Handle!

"Oh—Tex," burst out Reddie poignantly, "he's after me because—'cause I'm—a—I'm not what yu—think."

Texas stiffened slightly, but never turned the breadth of a hair from the rider he was facing. Wallen's face turned a dirty grey.

"What air yu—Reddie?" queried Texas, low and cool.

"I—I'm a girl, Texas. . . . An' thet's why," replied Reddie huskily.

"*Look oot!*" shouted Ross Hite, piercingly.

Wallen clapped his hand to his hip. Texas appeared to blur in Brite's strained sight. A gun belched red, and with the loud crack Wallen jerked up with terrible sudden rigidity. His dark face changed from hideous rage to an awful ghastliness, and he pitched from the saddle to fall with a sodden crash. His horse lunged away. The other horse reared and snorted.

"Haid aboot or I'll bore yu!" yelled Texas, his gun outstretched. "Brite, back me up with yore rifle. Reddie, line oot heah!"

Brite had scarcely needed the ringing order, for his rifle was levelled before Texas had finished. Likewise Reddie leaped forward, fearless and menacing.

All the riders except Ross Hite had wheeled abruptly. Several were walking their horses away. Hite showed no fear in his lean sallow face as he peered from Texas to the prostrate Wallen, and then back across the camp. Brite heard the thud of flying hoofs, and farther back the violent cries of riding cowboys.

"Brite, do yu want us to pack Wallen away?" queried Hite.

"No, thanks, we'll 'tend to him," retorted Brite sarcastically.

Just then a horse plunged by the chuck-wagon and, being pulled up short, slid to a halt, scattering dust and gravel everywhere. Pan Handle Smith leaped off in their midst, a gun magically appearing in each hand. It was then Brite's tension relaxed.

"What's the deal?" asked Smith quietly.

Ross Hite stared hard at Smith and then laughed harshly.

"Wal, Brite, yu air a trail driver thet goes heeled. Texas Shipman an' now Pan Handle Smith!"

"Rustle oot of heah!" ordered Texas.

"Men, this was Wallen's deal, not mine," returned Hite, and turning his horse he drove his companions ahead of him, quickly breaking into a gallop. Soon they passed round the corner of timber whence they had come.

Only then did Texas Joe move. He gave a quick glance at the dead Wallen and then wheeled with pale face and glittering eyes.

"Heah yu, Reddie Bayne," he called, and in two long strides he confronted Reddie. "Did yu say yu was a girl?"

"Yes, Texas Joe—I—I am," replied Reddie, and took off her sombrero to prove it. Her face was ashen and her eyes darkly dilated with receding terror. Texas fastened his left hand in her blouse and drew her up on her toes, close under his piercing gaze. His tawny hair stood up like the mane of a lion. But his cold fury was waning. Bewilderment hung close upon his passion.

"Yu—yu . . . all the time—yu've been a—a girl?" he broke out hoarsely.

"Yes, Texas, all the time," she whispered, sagging in his iron grasp. "I—I didn't mean to fool yu. I told the boss. . . . I—I wanted to tell you, but he wouldn't let me. . . . I'm sorry."

301

CHAPTER FIVE

TEXAS Joe appeared to shrink. He released Reddie so suddenly that she sagged and almost sank down, her hand at the neck of her blouse.

"Ootrag-eous of yu!" panted Texas as his pallid face grew red. "Makin' oot yu was a boy—before us all! . . . An' lettin' me spank yu—an'——"

"Let yu!" flashed Reddie, her face flaming worse than his. "Why, yu darn big brute, I couldn't help myself!"

"An' all thet camp cussin' of ours—an' dirty talk before a girl! . . . My Gawd! Yu done a turrible thing, Miss Reddie Bayne!"

"I reckon, but it was these damn hombres like *him*—thet drove me to it," declared Reddie passionately, pointing a shaking finger at the ghastly, quiet Wallen.

With that Texas Joe seemed to realize the tragic side of what had happened. Wheeling abruptly away from the girl, he sheathed his gun and bent a grim, strange look upon the dead man.

"Search him, some of yu," he said, sharp and cold. "Drag him oot an' throw him in thet wash. . . . Come a-rustlin' now, all of yu. Let's get oot of this."

"Where yu goin', Tex?" called Brite, as the driver strode away.

"Take my hawse," cried Reddie, after him.

But Texas Joe paid no heed to either. Soon he passed out of sight in the low brush. Then the strain among those around the camp fire relaxed. Reddie sat down as if her legs had grown weak.

"I've seen men shot before—but *never* for *me*," she whispered. "I feel like a—murderer."

"Nonsense, Reddie," spoke up Brite brusquely. "I'd have bored Wallen myself if Texas hadn't. . . . Pan Handle, did yu see thet one of Wallen's ootfit forked a hawse of mine?"

"No, boss, I didn't. Fact is I had eyes only for Ross Hite."

"Wal, it's true. When I bought thet bunch of stock I happened to take notice of a little bay mustang with a white face. I don't mistake hawses I've once looked over. Wallen's ootfit stampeded some of our *remuda* this mawnin'."

"Boss, I don't know Wallen, but he shore was ridin' in bad company," said Pan Handle.

"Ahuh. Yu know this Ross Hite?" rejoined Brite.

"Wal, rather. He was a cattle-buyer at Abilene. But he got into shady deals an' found Abilene too hot for him. Surprises me, though, to find him stampedin' a few hawses. I reckon thet was just by the way. Or else he's goin' to work somethin' big on this Chisholm Trail."

"Humph! Mebbe Hite is at the haid of this new game," declared the boss seriously. "Cattle-drivers sometimes lose half their stock from stampeders. I've heahed of one whole herd bein' stole."

"Texas Joe ought to have done for Hite same as Wallen. Hite will give us trouble on the way up," said Smith darkly.

Meanwhile Ackerman, with Whittaker and San Sabe, had dragged the dead Wallen out of camp. They returned presently packing gun and belt, spurs, a huge silver watch, and a heavy, fat wallet.

"Boss, I opened this," said Ackerman, handing over the wallet. "He shore was heeled."

Brite found the greasy wallet stuffed full of greenbacks.

"Say, he must have robbed a bank," declared the boss, in amaze. "Boys, hundreds of dollars heah. What'll we do with it?"

"What yu think?" queried Deuce Ackerman sarcastically. "Yu want me to ride after Wallen's ootfit an' give thet money to his pards?"

"No. I was only figgerin'. . . . I'll keep this an' divide it among yu boys at the end of the drive. It'll be a big bonus."

The drivers gave vent to great appreciation of this decision. Brite stowed the money away in his saddle-bag, and put the other articles of Wallen's in the chuck-wagon.

"Boys, did yu look where Texas Joe hit thet Wallen?" asked Pan Handle Smith curiously.

"Sure. Right in the middle of Wallen's left vest pocket. Bullet went through his tobacco-pouch."

"Pretty daid-centre shot for such a quick throw," went on Smith ponderingly. "Thet Texas Joe must be there on the draw."

Brite was familiar with this peculiar interest of the gunman in regard to the proficiency of others. He replied that the cattleman who had recommended Shipman had made significant mention of the fact.

"Hurry an' eat, boys," went on Brite. "We want to be on the prod."

All but Reddie Bayne answered to that suggestion with alacrity. Reddie sat with her face in her hands, her red-gold curls exposed. She made a pretty and a pathetic little figure, which Brite observed was not lost upon the shy cowboys. Deuce Ackerman looked at her several times, and finally conquered his evident embarrassment.

"Come on, Reddie. Don't take it so hard," he said gallantly. "Shore if *we* can stand it, yu can. We know yu're a girl now an' if yu can only overlook our—our——"

Deuce broke off there, manifestly unable to find words to express his shame for their talk and behaviour before a girl. Reddie answered to that instantly, arising to come to the wagon, a blush dyeing her pale cheek.

"Thank yu, Deuce," she replied, bravely conquering her confusion. "But none of yu boys need feel bad about it. . . . Texas was the only one who hurt my feelin's. . . . I'm shore glad not to be ridin' under false colours no more."

Whittaker gave her a smile. "I doan mind tellin' yu thet I knowed aboot yu all the time," he drawled.

"Wha-at?" faltered Reddie, in alarm.

"Reddie, he's a durned liar," spoke up Deuce forcibly. "Whit, yu cain't come none of thet on her. Can he, Sabe?"

But San Sabe was not vouchsafing for anyone, or else he was tongue-tied. Moze rolled his great ox eyes at Reddie.

"Yo done fool us all, Miss Reddie, an' dat's no mistake," he said, wagging his head. "An' so youse a gal! Wal, Ise doag-goned glad to have a lady in de ootfit."

"Air we all supposed to go on callin' yu Reddie?" queried Pan Handle dryly, as he fixed his keen eyes upon her.

"Why—of course."

Soon they had finished their hasty breakfast, and saddling up were off for the day's drive. As Brite rode down to head the wash, he saw where the boys had tumbled Wallen. They had not taken the trouble even to crumble some of the soft bank of earth over upon him. Perhaps they thought that Wallen's gang would return, and Brite himself concluded that was likely. This was the first tragic happening on any drive Brite had made. It augured ill for this one. But he could not expect always to have phenomenal luck. Many a story of trail drivers had been harrowing. Brite fortified himself anew. And this morning there was a subtle change to the thrill and zest of trail driving. He looked out over the vast rose-

and-purple expanse with hard eyes, quickening to more than the beauty of nature.

The herd was well pointed and moving perceptibly some miles ahead. Reddie and Pan Handle were off to the eastward with the *remuda,* catching up. Brite rode to the highest knoll available and then took his morning survey. The air was clear. Far to the south, perhaps twenty miles, a low black line pencilled the grey expanse. Buffalo or cattle, Brite could not decide which. He hoped they were buffalo. Forward the purple range billowed, and to the west skeleton shadows of hills pierced the haze. Deer and rabbits and coyotes appeared to be numerous this morning.

Finally Brite set off at a trot after the riders, who had caught up with the herd. One of them had been leading a saddled but rider-less horse, undoubtedly meant for Texas Joe, who was on foot. Not for hours did Brite get a glimpse of his foreman, and by that time he was astride again.

The slow miles passed to the rear, and the westering sun had sunk low and dusky red before Shipman halted for the night. This day's drive would total fifteen miles, a long journey for grazing cattle. Water had been crossed about mid-afternoon, which was well for the stock, because this was a dry camp. Grass was luxuriant, and buffalo chips abundant. Moze halted his chuck-wagon in the lee of an outcrop of rock, which was the only obstruction on the level land. Brite finished his own chores and then packed in chips for the camp fire. Not until a dusky haze had mantled the range did he stop gazing back to the southward.

Texas Joe did not ride in until after the night shift had gone on guard. He was silent and taciturn, aloof as Brite had seen other men who had lately snuffed out human life. Texas ate alone, kneeling beside the fire. More than once Brite caught him kneeling there, cup in hand, motionless, his thoughts far from the moment. Presently he slipped away in the darkness and Brite saw him no more. Rolly Little, Ben Chandler, and Roy Hallett betrayed their knowledge of the marvellous fact that the Brite outfit had a young girl in it now, and not only a very pretty one, but also romantic and appealing. They were a changed trio. Excited, gay, decidedly on their good behaviour, they amused Brite. Not once did Brite hear them mention the killing of Wallen. That seemed far past. Rolly was the only one of the trio who had the courage to speak directly to Reddie. Ben took his attention out in covert glances, while Roy talked loudly, almost boast-fully, a singular transformation in this boy.

The most noticeable change, however, and a pleasing one, appeared to be in Reddie Bayne. She seemed natural for the first time, and no longer slunk in and out of camp hurriedly, with her old sombrero pulled down over her eyes. In fact, she did not have it on at all, and only one glance at her pretty head was needed to ascertain that she had brushed her golden curls. Where had she done that, Brite wondered? After supper she helped Moze at his tasks, apparently not heeding the noisy trio around the fire, although a sharp observer might have detected that she heard every word. More than once she flashed a furtive glance off in the direction in which Texas Joe had disappeared. Next she tipped her bedroll off the wagon, and was about to shoulder it when the three cowboys piled over each other to get it. Rolly was the quickest.

"Whar yu want it unrolled, Re . . . Miss Reddie?" he asked.

"Thanks. But give it to me," returned Reddie, bluntly. "Say, I've been totin' this roll every night, haven't I? Why not to-night?"

"Wal, yu se, Miss Reddie, yu—we—it ain't jest the same now."

"Oh, ain't it? What ain't?"

"Yu know. The situation heah. . . . We boys have talked it over. Ridin' *remuda* is enough for yu. No more packin' saddles, bedrolls, firewood, water, an' sich chores. We'll do all thet for yu."

"Yu're awfully good, Rolly. But please wait till I drop, will yu?"

Whereupon she lifted the roll of canvas and carried it over significantly close to where Brite had unrolled his. When she had finished a like task for herself she came over to sit beside Brite.

"I'm still sick to my stomach," she confided. "An' I have thet queer heavy feelin' up heah." She put her hands to her breast, high up, and pressed them there.

"I savvy, Reddie. All thet this mawnin'. . . . Wal, it sort of faded for me. So much to think aboot!"

"Gee! I've thought 'til my pore haid aches," declared Reddie. "Mr. Brite, these cowboys air funny now. Have yu noticed it—since I been found oot?"

"Reckon I have. Shore it's funny," replied Brite. "It's unusual to have a girl on a trail drive. Shore it's goin' to be somethin' beside funny, Reddie."

"I'm afraid so. What do *yu* think?"

"Wal, yu're an awful pretty girl, an' thet's goin' to make complications."

"Oh dear! . . . I reckoned so. But, Mr. Brite, they're nice boys. I—I like them. I'm not afraid. I'll be able to sleep. This is the nicest ootfit of men I ever rode with."

"Wal, thet's a compliment to all of us, Reddie. Thank yu for it. I'll bet the boys would like to heah thet. I'll tell them."

"Oh, I cain't get this mawnin' off my chest," she whispered. "Wasn't he terrible?"

"Who? Wallen?"

"Wallen!—No, he was just low down. . . . I mean Texas Joe. . . . Wasn't he fierce? I could have dropped in my tracks when he shot Wallen. . . . Just as quick as thet! Just the moment I confessed I was a girl—an'—Wallen was after me. . . . Oh! He *killed* him! I prayed for some rider to do thet very thing. But when it was done I was sick. My blood curdled. . . . Yet even thet wasn't as bad as when Texas grabbed me by the throat an' nearly jerked me oot of my boots. . . . 'All the time yu was a girl—*all* the time,' he barked at me. I'll never forget thet."

"Aw, yes, yu will, Reddie," replied Brite soothingly. "Tex took the sap oot of me, too. Gawd! how quick he bored thet skunk! Why, even Pan Handle remarked aboot it. . . . Just forget it, Reddie. We've lots more comin', I reckon, this trip."

"But, Mr. Brite," she faltered. "I—I got the idee Texas Joe thought Wallen had—thet I was a—a hussy."

"Reddie! I'm shore he's thought nothin' of the kind," replied Brite hastily.

"Oh, yes he did. He looked at me so! I could have sunk in my boots. . . . Mr. Brite, I—I just couldn't go on with yore ootfit if he thought I was a bad girl."

"Tex was only shocked. Same as me—an' all of us. It doesn't happen every day, Reddie—a pretty kid of a girl droppin' in on us oot of the sky. Yu see, Tex had swore at yu, an' spanked yu that time, an' otherwise put familiar hands on yu without the least idee yu was anythin' but a boy. He's so ashamed he cain't come aboot."

"It's very kind of you to say thet, Mr. Brite," rejoined Reddie. "I wish I could believe yu. But I cain't. An' I cain't *ask* him—dammit!"

"Ask him what?"

"If he thinks I'm bad."

"Wal, I reckon Tex would be hurt to find oot yu believed he could so insult yu in his mind. But ask him. Thet'll settle it."

"But I cain't, Mr. Brite. I cain't be mad at him—no matter what he believed me. 'Cause he killed a man for my sake! 'Cause he saved me from wuss'n hell—an' from spillin' my own blood."

"Reddie, yu're all upset," replied Brite, moved at the convulsed pale face and the dark eyes. "Yu go to bed. In the mawnin' yu'll feel better."

"Sleep! What's to keep thet man Hite from sneakin' in heah with his ootfit, knifin' yu all, an' makin' off with me?"

The startling query acquainted Brite with the fact that there was not very much to oppose such a catastrophe. Too many drivers were required on guard. That left the camp force weak.

"Reddie, thet's sort of far fetched," said Brite.

"It's been done over Braseda way. I heahed aboot it."

"I'm a light sleeper, Reddie. No Comanches, even, could surprise me."

Reddie shook her curly head as if she were unconvinced. "It's tough enough to be a girl in town," she said. "Oot heah on the trail it's hell."

"No one but Wallen's ootfit knows. An' shore they won't come bracin' us again. Go to bed, Reddie, an' sleep."

Brite lay awake, thinking. This waif of the ranges had disrupted a certain tenor of the trail drivers' life. Having her with them was a drawback, a risk. But Brite could not entertain any idea of not keeping her. The fact that Reddie was a strong, skilful, enduring rider, as good a horse wrangler as any boy, did not alter the case. She was a girl, and growing more every minute a decidedly attractive girl. Impossible was it to keep the cowboys from realizing that alluring fact in a way characteristic of Texan youths in particular, and all youths in general. They would fall in love with her. They would quarrel over her. Nevertheless, suppose they did! Brite would not surrender to dismay. He refused to admit that youth, beauty, romance might detract from the efficiency of a group of trail drivers. On the other hand, they would rise to the occasion. That free, wild spirit to do and dare would burn more fiercely and make them all the more invincible. No, Reddie Bayne was not a liability to this enterprise, but an asset. Brite satisfied himself on that score, and when that conclusion had been reached he realized that the orphan girl had found a place in his heart which had ever been empty.

The events of the day had not been conducive to undisturbed sleep. Brite was awake on and off until the guard changed at midnight. Reddie Bayne was also awakened.

"Boss," she said, "I'm going to have a look at my *remuda*."

"Come along. I'll go up with yu."

Ackerman brought in the relief horses and reported that all was quiet, with the herd bedded down. The moon in its last quarter was low on the horizon. Sheet lightning flaring behind dark, stringy clouds in the west told of heat and storm.

As they rode out together Texas Joe swept by on a lope and hailed them gruffly. "Hang close together, yu!"

Brite heard Reddie mutter something under her breath. How she watched that dark rider across the moonlit plain! They found the horses resting, with only a few grazing. The grass was knee high. Out beyond, a great, black square defaced the silvery prairie, and this was the herd of long-horns. San Sabe's voice doled out a cowboy refrain. The other guards were silent. Brite and Reddie rode around the herd twice, and finally edging the horses into a closer unit they turned campward. Reddie appeared prone to silence. Several times Brite tried conversation, which elicited only monosyllables from the youngster. They went to bed, and Brite slept until sunrise.

That day turned out uneventful. Shipman drove at least twelve miles. Brite observed that his foreman often faced the south to gaze long and steadily. But nothing happened and the night also proved quiet. Another day saw a lessening of anxiety. Ross Hite had not passed them in daylight, that was a certainty. A mild thunderstorm overtook the drivers on the following day, and the wet, shiny horns of the cattle and the fresh, dank odour of thirsty earth were pleasant.

Coon Creek and Buffalo Wallow, Hackberry Flat, The Meadows, and night after night at unnamed camps took the drivers well on into June. Buffalo began to show in straggly lines on the rise of prairie to the west. A few unfriendly riders passed at a distance. Brite began to think that good luck attended his trail again, and forgot the days and camps.

Meanwhile, except for the aloof Texas Joe and Pan Handle, the outfit had grown into a happy family. Reddie Bayne had been a good influence so far. Rivalry for her favour, for who should wait upon her in any conceivable way that she would permit, lacked not friendly spirit, for all its keenness. Smiles grew frequent upon her pretty face. She improved visibly under such pleasant contact. And Brite came to the day when he decided he would adopt her as a daughter, if one of these cowboys did not win her for a wife. Still, Brite, sharp watch and guardianship as he kept over her, found no serious courting. No one of them ever had a chance to get her alone. It just happened that way, or else Reddie was clever enough to bring it about.

Nevertheless, where Texas Joe was concerned there appeared to be smouldering fire. He watched Reddie from afar with telltale eyes. And Reddie, when she imagined she was unobserved, let her dreamy gaze stray in Joe's direction. As foreman he had the responsibility of the herd, and day and night that was his passion. All the same he followed imperceptibly in the footsteps of his riders. Seldom did Joe address Reddie; never did he give her another order. Sometimes he would tell Brite to have her do this or that with the *remuda*. In camp he avoided her when that was possible. He seemed a weary, melancholy rider, pondering to himself.

Brite saw how this aloofness worked upon Reddie. She had come into her own, and his indifference piqued her. Reddie never lost a chance to fret and fume to Brite about his foreman. Pride and vanity had come with the championship of the cowboys. Despite her ragged male attire, she no longer could have been taken for other than a girl. Some kind of climax was imminent. Brite had his choice of a suitor for Reddie, but he liked all his boys. They had warmed to her influence. Perhaps if she had shown any preference then there might have been jealousy. But so far they were all her brothers and she was happy, except at such times as Texas Joe projected his forceful personality and disturbing presence upon the scene.

One early evening camp at Blanco River all the drivers but three were in, and Texas Joe was among the former. It had been an easy day until the crossing of the wide stream, where some blunders, particularly with the *remuda*, had ruffled the foreman. He gave Ackerman one of his round-about orders for Reddie. They were through supper and Joe about ready to take the night guard out. Suddenly Reddie flashed a resentful face in Joe's direction.

"Deuce, I cain't heah yu," she said, quite piercingly. "If Mister Shipman has any orders for me, let him tell them to *me*."

Ackerman was not slow in translating this into his own words, for the benefit of Joe and all. But it really had not been necessary.

"I'll give orders any way I like, Miss Bayne," said Texas.

"Shore. But if yu got anythin' for *me* to do yu'll say so, an' not through somebody else."

"Wal, I'll fire yu when we get to Fort Worth," rejoined Joe coolly.

"Fire me!" cried Reddie, astounded and furious.

"Yu heahed me, Miss."

"Then yu'll fire the whole damn ootfit," declared Reddie hotly. "The idee! When I've not done a single thing wrong. . . . Tell him, boys. Deuce, Roy, Whit, Rolly—tell him."

There were nonchalant and amiable remarks tending to the veracity of Reddie's declaration.

"My Gawd! what a mean ootfit!" ejaculated Joe, in disgust. "Less Holden—my pard—air yu in cahoots with her?"

"Shore, Tex," replied Lester, with a laugh. "We jest couldn't drive cattle withoot Reddie."

"Yu, too!" burst out Texas, deeply chagrined and amazed.

"Say, what kind of a foreman air yu—givin' orders to yore hawse-wrangler through a third person?" flashed Reddie scornfully. "I'm on this ootfit. I'm gettin' wages. Yu cain't ignore me."

"Cain't I?" queried Texas in helpless rage. It was evident that he could not. More than evident was it that something inexplicable and infuriating was at work upon him.

"No, yu cain't—not no more," continued Reddie, carried beyond reserve. "Not withoot insultin' me, Texas Jack Shipman."

"Stop callin' me Texas Jack," shouted the driver.

"I'll call yu wuss'n thet pronto. An' I'll say right now of all the conceited, stuck-up cowboys I ever seen yu're the damnedest. Yu're too proud to speak to poor white trash like me. So yu order me aboot through the boss or one of the boys, or even Moze. An' I'm callin' for a show-down, Tex Shipman."

"Boss, do I have to stand heah an' take all this?" appealed Joe, turning shame-facedly to Brite.

"Wal, Tex, I don't reckon yu have to, but I'd take it if I was yu an' get it over," advised Brite conciliatingly.

Thus championed by her employer, Reddie gave way utterly to whatever complicated emotions were driving her. Like a cat she sprang close to Texas and glared up at him, her eyes blazing, her breast heaving.

"Yu can tell me right heah an' now, in front of the ootfit, why yu treat me like dirt under yore feet," demanded she huskily.

"Wrong again, Miss Bayne," drawled Texas. "Yu flatter yoreself. I jest didn't think aboot yu atall."

This seemed to be a monstrous lie to all except the pale-faced girl to whom it was directed.

"Tex Shipman, yu killed a man to save me, but it wasn't for *me* particularly? Yu'd do thet for any girl, good or—or bad?"

"Why, shore I would."

"An' yu had yore doubts aboot me then, didn't yu, cowboy?"

"Wal, I reckon so. An' I—still got—them," rejoined Texas haltingly. He had doubts about himself, too, and altogether the situation must have been galling to him.

"Yu bet yu have!" flashed Reddie, scarlet of face. "Come oot with them, then—if yu're not yellow! . . . First—yu think I—I'm bad, don't yu?"

"Wal, if yu're keen aboot thet, I don't think yu're so—so damn good!"

"Oh-h!" cried the girl poignantly. Then she gave him a stinging slap with her right hand and another with her left.

"Heah! Yu got me wrong!" yelled Texas, suddenly horrified at the way she took his scathing reply; and he backed away from her flaming assault. But it was too late. Reddie was too violently outraged to comprehend what seemed clear to Brite, and no doubt all the gaping listeners.

"I ought to kill yu for thet," whispered Reddie. "An' I would, by Gawd! but for Mr. Brite! . . . Oh, I've knowed all along yu thought I was a hussy. . . . Thet Wallen had. . . . Damn yu, Tex Shipman. Yu don't know a decent girl when yu meet one! Yu gotta be told. An' I'm tellin' yu. . . . Wallen was a dirty skunk. An' he wasn't the only one who hounded me oot of a job. All because I wanted to be decent. . . . An' I *am* decent—an' as good as yore own sister, Tex Shipman—or any other boy's sister! . . . To think I—I have to *tell yu*!—I ought to do thet—with a gun—or a hawsewhip."

Suddenly she broke down and began to sob. "Now—yu can go to hell—Tex Shipman—with yore orders—an' with what—yu think aboot me! Yu're dirt—under—*my* feet!"

CHAPTER SIX

REDDIE plunged away into the gathering dusk as if she meant to leave the camp forever. Brite decided he would not let her go far, but before following her he took note of the group at the camp fire. Texas Joe stared after Reddie. The boys began to upbraid him in no friendly terms, when Pan Handle silenced them with a gesture.

"Tex, this is liable to split our ootfit," he said, putting a hand on the cowboy's shoulder. "It won't do. We all know yu didn't think Reddie's no good. But *she* doesn't know. Square thet pronto."

Brite hastened after Reddie, and coming up with her just out of the camp-fire light he detained her with a gentle hand.

"Lass, yu mustn't go runnin' off."

"Oh, I—I could run right—into the river," she cried, miserable. "I—I was so—so happy."

"Wal, it'll all come right," returned the cattleman, and put a kindly arm around her and led her to a seat on a nearby rock. Reddie was not proof against sympathy and she sank on his shoulder.

"Tell me yu don't—believe it," she begged.

"Believe what, lass?"

"What Texas thinks—aboot me."

"Wal, I should smile not. None of the boys do. An' I reckon Tex himself . . . Heah he comes, Reddie."

She stiffened in his arms and appeared to hold her breath. Texas strode up to them, bareheaded in the dusk. Only his eyes could be seen, and they gleamed darkly.

"Reddie Bayne, yu listen to me," he began sternly. "If yu wasn't such a darned little spitfire yu'd never disgraced me before the ootfit. I——"

"Disgraced *yu*?" she interrupted.

"Yes, me. . . . I swear to Gawd I had no idee atall thet yu wasn't as honest an'—an' good as any girl. I meant yu was a queer, contrary, temperish, spiteful little devil. But only thet. Sabe? . . . An' I'm sorry I upset yu an' I want to apologize."

"Yu're aboot six days too late, Texas Jack," she burst out defiantly. "An'—an' yu can go to hell, anyhow."

He gave her a slow, strange glance as she lay with her head on Brite's shoulder.

"Wal, I'll have company, for thet's where this ootfit is haided," he replied coldly, and stalked away.

Reddie raised to peer over Brite's shoulder after the cowboy. She was not aware how she clung to Brite. But he felt the strong, little hands on his vest. Slowly then she dropped back, head and breast against him, where she all but collapsed.

"There! . . . I've—done—it—now," she whispered, as if to herself. "I should have—acted the—the lady. . . . But I—I hate him so."

Brite formed his own conclusion about how she hated Texas Joe. It also came to him, and stronger than formerly, how he had come to feel toward Reddie. This was the time to tell it.

"Lass, I reckon folks oot on the Chisholm Trail can have feelin's the same as when they're home safe an' sound. Mebbe stronger an' deeper an' better feelin's. Anyway, I'm goin' to ask yu somethin' particular. I'm alone in the world. No near kin. An' I'd like to have yu for a daughter. How aboot it?"

"Oh, it'd be my dream come true," she cried ecstatically. "Oh, if only I'm worthy!"

"Let me be the judge of thet," he replied happily. "I have a ranch ootside Santone. An' yu can make it yore home. All I ask is thet yu care a little for me."

"I love you now, Mr. Brite," she whispered generously and hugged him. "Oh, it's too good to be true."

"Wal, then, do you accept me as yore adopted dad?"

"I cain't thank God enough," she murmured.

"It's settled an' I reckon I'm doin' some thankin' on my own hook."

"Yu air so good an' kind. . . . Oh, this ootfit is different. . . . I wonder what *he* will say when he finds oot."

"Who?"

"Thet cowboy."

"Aw, he'll have me to reckon with now. But, Reddie, we'll keep it secret till we get to Dodge."

Brite was unrolling his bed when he felt something fine and cold touch his cheek. Rain! He had been so preoccupied that he had not observed any change in weather conditions. The stars had greyed over. All the north appeared gloomy and black. Storms were the bane of the trail drivers. Texas was noted for storms, from the *del norte* of the Mexicans to the Pan Handle cyclone.

"Reddie, it's goin' to rain," he called. "Fetch yore bed over under the wagon."

But Reddie was in the land of dreams. Brite took his long slicker and, stepping across to where Reddie lay, spread it over her bed. Brite experienced a new sensation—a warm wave of joy at realization of his new responsibility. Hearing voices, he went over to the wagon. The boys were moving their beds under it. The wind had quickened, blowing a fine, chilly mist in Brite's face.

"Wal, boss, our luck has changed," spoke up Texas grimly. "We've shore been too damn lucky. Now it's comin'."

"What's comin', yu gloomy geezer?"

"A norther, first off. I don't know what after thet."

"It's a late spring. We could have a norther even this late," replied Brite ponderingly.

"Moze, where'n hell air yu?" called Joe.

"I wuz under de wagon, Mars Joe, till I got rolled oot," answered Moze.

"Wal, yu roll oot farther an' pack all the dry wood yu got in the caboose."

"Yes, suh. Ise done on de way."

"Where's yore axe? I'll split some more wood. Boss, we might as wal use thet extra tarp for a wind an' rain break. Moze has one over the wagon. Lawd! I do hate the wet an' cold. . . . Hadn't yu better wake Reddie an' call her oot heah?"

"I spread my slicker over her," replied Brite, pleased with the solicitude in Shipman's voice. "She'll be all right unless it pours."

Texas went off, muttering to himself. Soon the ring of the axe attested to his occupation. Moze was having his troubles putting wood in the canvas that had been stretched under the wagon for such purpose. The cowboys were in his way.

"Moze, let 'em sleep," suggested Brite. "We'll put up the extra tarp. Yu can lay the wood under thet till mawnin'. . . . Heah. Tie one end of the tarp to the hoops of the wagon an' peg down the other."

"Reckon dat'll save dis black chile's life."

Texas came up staggering under a load of wood which he deposited very considerately without making a noise.

"Boss," he said, "if thet wind comes stronger with rain we'll have a driftin' herd. An' I'd shore hate to have them drift south. Bad for us."

"It's kind of north-west, Tex," replied Brite, holding his hand up.

"Jest as bad, 'cept a norther lasts three days. Mebbe it's nothin' much. We'll know in a couple of hours. Which I'm gonna use sleepin'."

They rolled in their blankets in the shelter of the stretched tarpaulin. Texas dropped off into slumber by the magic of youth. Soon Moze snored like a sawmill. Brite did not feel sleepy. The warmth of his blankets told him just how cold the air had grown. He lay there resting and listening. The wind moaned steadily, weirdly, and whipped in chilly gusts under the wagon, flopped the canvas, and swept away mournfully. Coyotes barked about the camp. Somewhere out there in the black, windy void the great herd would be stirring uneasily in their beds. The old mossy-horns would be bawling. And the guards would be singing to them. What a singular and tremendous movement this was—the driving of cattle herds north! Lying there, Brite seemed to have a vision of what magnitude this business would attain, how it would save Texas and pave the way for an empire. No doubt old Jesse Chisholm had seen that vision first of all the pioneers. These cowboys who were driving up the Trail by hundreds—or those of them who survived the hardships and perils—would see the day their prosperous ranches owed all to this heroic beginning.

These pondering thoughts might have merged into dreams, for all Brite knew, but they were disrupted sooner or later by the thud of plunging hoofs and a ringing voice.

"All oot. Herd driftin'."

When Brite sat up, Texas Joe was on his knees rolling his bed.

"What time, Deuce?" he called.

"After midnight. Cain't see my watch. Colder'n hell!"

"Rainin' much?"

"Not yet. Mixed with sleet."

"Sleet in June! Wal, I forgot aboot it bein' Texas."

"Tex, we'll need lanterns. Cain't see yore hand before yore face."

"Moze, air yu awake?"

"Yas, suh, I reckon I is."

"Air the lanterns filled? An' where'll I find them?"

"All ready, boss. Settin' inside the front wheels where I keeps them every night."

Brite got his heavy coat which had served as a pillow, and while putting it on he advised the drivers to don their warmest.

"Reddie Bayne!" yelled Texas.

No answer! Joe yelled again, with unnecessary peevishness, Brite thought. Still no sound came from Reddie.

"Must be daid. Never knowed Reddie to be hard to wake."

"I heah hawses," spoke up Deuce.

Soon Brite followed the others out from under the shelter into the yellow light of the lanterns. Brite was about to go over to awaken Reddie when a pounding of hoofs preceded a dark, ragged bunch of horses coming into camp.

"Heah she is! Dog-gone!" Deuce Ackerman called.

In the windy gloom Brite espied Reddie on foot, leading half a dozen horses by halters. The long slicker glistened wet in the lantern-light.

"Where'd yu get them hawses?" queried Texas.

"I had them tied oot heah."

"Ahuh. So yu can see in the dark, same as a cat?"

"Yes, sir," replied Reddie meekly.

"Wal, I shore hate to admit it, but yu beat holler any hawse-wrangler I ever seen," concluded Texas gruffly.

"Thanks, Jack," returned Reddie sweetly.

They bridled and saddled the horses. Texas mounted, and calling for one of the lanterns he headed away from the wind.

"Deuce, yu fetch the other lantern," he called. "Moze, hang right heah till we come back. Have a fire an' hot drinks, for we'll shore need 'em."

Brite and the others followed, soon to catch up with Texas. The horses were unwilling to go and rubbed close together. Texas lifted his lantern.

"Thet's Reddie's black, ain't it?" he queried sharply.

"Yes, I'm heah," replied Reddie.

"Wal, yu go back to camp. This won't be no job for little girls."

"Jack, yu go where it's hot. I can stand the cold."

"Stop callin' me Jack," he retorted testily. "Or I—I'll box yore ears. An' I tell yu to stay in camp."

"But, Texas, I'd be afraid in camp withoot yu-all," she returned seriously.

317

"Wal, come to think of thet, I reckon yu're right. . . . Deuce, where'n hell air we haidin'?"

"Darned if I know. I shore had a time findin' camp. Took me half an hour."

"How far oot was the herd?"

"Coupla miles, I reckon."

"Spread oot to the right, Deuce. An' go till yu can just see my light. Rest on you hang in between. . . . Hell, but it's nasty!"

A stiff wind was blowing at their backs. It carried fine rain and sleet, that could be distinctly heard by the impact and the rustling in the grass. The darkness appeared inky black. And Texas' lantern shone fitfully upon weird spectral figures of horses and riders. When they had covered a distance of two or three miles Texas and Deuce began to yell to locate the guards with the herd. No answering yells rewarded them. They went a couple of miles farther, and then the line, with Texas at one end and Deuce at the other, began to sweep in a circle. The situation grew serious. If the herd took to drifting badly, the few guards could not hold them, and they might stampede, or at least travel many miles. Mossy-horns were as limber and enduring as horses when they wanted to go.

"Hold on, fellars," ordered Texas, at last. "I heahed somethin'. Mebbe it was only a coyote. But I'll pile off an' get away so I can heah shore."

Leaping off, he stalked apart from the horses, his light swinging to and fro in his hand. Then he pealed out a stentorian yell. Brite listened, but could hear nothing. After a short silence Texas called: "Yep, I was right. I got an answer."

He hurried back to his horse, and mounting, led somewhat to the left. "Reckon I cain't keep thet direction long. But we'll stop an' yell till we locate them."

By this method Texas Joe found the other guards and the herd at last. But the guards were on the far side of the herd, which was drifting with the wind. Texas called for Brite and Reddie to follow him, and for the others to follow Deuce, who would circle the herd from his end. Time and time again Texas' light fell upon stragglers of the herd, evidently far behind the main body.

"Wal, the drags air good for somethin'," said Texas. "An' thet in a storm."

Answering yells became frequent and louder. Soon Texas led his followers round in front of the herd, where they encountered Pan Handle and Rolly Little.

"How about yu, Pan?" shouted Texas.

"They're driftin', Tex, but not bad," came the reply.

"Where are the other boys?"

"Sometimes near, sometimes far. Now I can heah them an' again I can't."

"Oh, ho, ho! Oh, ho, hell!" sang out Texas. "Line up all. Take yore medicine, boss. Yu will buy cattle at twelve bits a haid. Reddie, heah is where we make a man oot of yu."

The drivers faced the wind and the oncoming herd. A bawling mass of cattle showed a square front to Texas' lantern. They were not ugly and probably could have been wholly halted but for the crowding from behind. Back a hundred yards, the light and the yells and singing of the drivers had little effect. So there was no hope of stopping them. The best that could be done was to retard their advance, to prevent a possible stampede, and give way before them.

Fortunately they had bunched closely, which fact became manifest when Deuce's welcome light showed up half a mile distant. Between these two lights ranged all the other drivers, shouting and singing. They had to rely absolutely on the sight of their horses, for only near the lights could they see anything. They could hear, however, and often located the front line that way. At intervals Deuce would ride across the front with his light and Texas would pass him going the other way. Thus they kept some semblance to a straight line.

It was slow, tedious, discouraging work, not without considerable risk, and wearing to weariness and pain. The wind blew harder and colder; the sleet cut like tiny blades. Brite had always been susceptible to cold. The hour came when his heavy gloves and coat appeared to afford no protection to the storm. He could scarcely endure to face the sleet, yet he had to do it or be run over by cattle. Necessarily the action of his horse had to be slow, seldom more than a walk, and this was not conducive to active blood circulation. Reddie Bayne stayed with him, so near that they could locate each other without yelling. When Texas or Deuce passed with the lanterns they established their positions again.

"Hang on, drivers," Texas shouted cheerily. "It ain't gettin' no wuss an' we shore air lucky."

Brite knew that if the storm increased he and no doubt others of the drivers, certainly Bender and Reddie, would find themselves in desperate straits. The cold, tooth-edged wind grew harder to bear, but evidently it did not increase in volume. Monotonously Brite beat his gloved hands, and thrust his one ear and then the other under the collar of his coat.

"Cheer up, Reddie; the mawnin's aboot to bust," yelled Ackerman, the last time he rode by.

"It shore better come soon or I'll bust," replied Reddie.

Brite peered with tear-dimmed eyes away from the herd. The blackness had grown faintly grey in that direction. He watched it, turning often. How slowly it lightened! The hour dragged with hateful slowness. But almost imperceptibly the dawn came, until all the black void changed to grey, and the grey to pale, obscured stretches of prairie and the dark wall of twisted horns and heads and legs. Soon Brite could distinguish Reddie on her horse, and then the other riders, one by one. The lanterns were extinguished, and the drivers, aided by light enough to see, made far better success of their job. They could ride at a trot, and an occasional lope, from one pressing point to another. Horses as well as riders benefited by this brisker exercise.

Slowly the front line yielded. The mossy-horns would stop and try to graze a bit, only to be pushed on again by the surging from behind.

Brite made sure that but for the sleet turning to rain and the wind lessening a bit the herd would have had to be abandoned until the riders could thaw out and get fresh horses.

Daylight came broadly at last, revealing a dreary range land, and a dragging herd under a low-sailing bank of clouds, and bowed and sodden riders, stuck in their wet saddles. To turn the herd back became imperative. A day lost might mean loss of hundreds, even thousands, of cattle. Texas drove the weary riders to incredible exertions, concentrated at one end; and by hard riding, shooting to take the place of voices gone, he turned that end and the rest followed, like sheep follow a leader. Cattle and drivers then faced the north. The reluctant herd could not be driven faster than a plodding walk. Heads down, weary and hungry, the mossy-horns covered ground like snails. The horses, except Reddie Bayne's black, were spent, and would be useless the remainder of that drive.

Some time during the afternoon Brite recognized landmarks near camp. He saw the *remuda* apparently intact and none the worse for the storm. Texas Joe and Ackerman left the herd bunched on a square of rich grass, and cutting out some horses they drove them into camp.

Brite was not the last by two to ride in. Pan Handle, haggard and drawn, came after him, and finally Bender, who sagged in his saddle. He had to be lifted off his horse. Brite was not so badly frozen, but he did not recall when he had been in such a plight.

"Wal, boss, yu rode in," said Texas, his voice low and hoarse. He stood steaming before a hot fire. Moze was dealing out hot drinks. Brite wondered what would have been the outcome if no fire or reviving whisky had been available.

Reddie Bayne was the only one not wet to the skin. The long slicker had saved her, and though she looked peaked and wan, she had evidently finished better than some of them.

"Coffee—not whisky," she whispered huskily, as she smelled the cup Moze forced upon her.

"Reddie, yu're shore there," remarked Deuce, admiringly.

"Where?"

"I should have said heah. Shore was plumb worried aboot yu."

"Wal, I gotta hunch she's a man, after all," growled Texas, at which sally Reddie joined in the laugh on her.

"Boys, the herd's shiftin' a little south," remarked Texas anxiously. "But I reckon we can hang them heah. Sabe, yu come with me. Deuce, send oot two men in an hour, an' we'll come back for grub. After thet regular guard, an' we'll bed down heah to-night."

"Wonder if any herd's gained on us to-day?" asked Brite, speaking with difficulty.

"Reckon all the drivers back lost as much as us, boss. . . . On second thought, dose Bender up good an' put him to bed." As another afterthought Texas halted as he passed Reddie beside the fire and queried, "Say, kid, yu want any orders from me?"

"Kid—Who air yu addressin', Mister Jack?" retorted Reddie.

He fixed piercing hawk eyes upon her ruddy face. "Don't call me Jack no more."

"All right—Jack."

"I hate thet name. It reminds me of a girl who used to call me by it. She was 'most as uppish as yu, Reddie Bayne."

"I just cain't remember to say Joe—thet is, if I *would* get so familiar."

"Aw, indeed. So familiar? Yu call the rest of this ootfit by their given names. I even heahed yu call the boss Daddy."

"So I did . . . but I'd no idee I was heahed," replied Reddie, blushing.

"Wal, if yu cain't be so awful familiar as to call me Joe or Tex, yu can call me Mister Shipman," returned Texas sarcastically.

"Ump-umm! I like Jack best," said Reddie, with a roguish look in her eye. Still she did not look at Texas.

"Listen. Thet settles yu," he flashed, with something of the ringing note in which he had addressed Wallen. "I cain't spank yu any more, much as yu deserve it. I ain't hankerin' for any more lead. But yu'll shore call me Jack somethin' or other before this drive ends."

"Somethin' or other! What?" exclaimed Reddie very curiously.

"Wal, it might be Jack darlin'," replied Texas, and wheeled away.

The boys howled merrily. Reddie for once looked squelched. It was not the heat of the fire that added the crimson to her face. Brite caught a glimpse of her eyes before she lowered them, and they had a look of startled surprise. But her dishevelled head did not long stay drooping; it bobbed up with a toss of curls, the action of a spirited girl strange to see in one wearing rough and muddy male attire.

"Never on this heah green earth!"

The night was long and comfortable, both in camp and out on guard. But the morning brought slowly clearing weather, and by the time the herd was pointed there was promise of sunshine. Wet grass and frequent pools of water made an easy day for the stock, a fact Shipman took advantage of with a long drive until dark. No droll repartee around the camp fire that night!

Two more uneventful drives brought the outfit to Austin, the first settlement on the Trail. Brite halted to see a rancher who lived three miles or less out of town, and got disturbing news about conditions to the north. The usual run of disasters multiplied! But particularly the Colorado River, which ran by Austin, was flooded to its banks, and there would be a necessity of waiting to use the customary ford or go up the river and swim the herd. When Brite passed this information on to Texas Joe he received a reply to his liking:

"Wal, we shore won't hang aboot thet burg."

Austin, like other settlements along the Chisholm Trail, was subject to fluctuations of populace, and sometimes it was just as well for a driver not to be sociable. In the second place, cowboys usually looked upon red liquor at such places, always a deterring and uncertain factor.

Texas gave the place a wide berth, and aimed to strike the river five miles west, where Brite's rancher informant claimed there was a good gradual slope to point the herd across. Brite rode into Austin alone. He ate supper at a lodging-house where he had stopped before, and then went down the street to call at Miller's store. In the darkness, where so few lights flickered here and there, it was difficult to tell whether Austin was full of men or not. It appeared quiet and lonely enough. Miller, a gaunt Missourian, greeted Brite cordially, as became him toward a customer.

"Been lookin' for you," he said. "How close are the herds behind?"

"Wal, there's one a day or so," replied Brite. "In a week they'll be comin' like buffalo."

"So Ross Hite reckoned."

"Hite. Is he heah?" asked Brite casually.

"Yes. He rode in a few days back," returned Miller. "Had a bunch of mustangs he's been sellin' around."

"How many in Hite's ootfit?"

"Can't say. Only a couple of men, strangers to me, with him when he came in here. Didn't he pass you on the way up?"

"There was some ootfit went by. Aboot seven or eight, I reckon. Somebody said it was Wallen's."

"Wallen? Don't know him. Well, the more outfits comin' the better I like it. And I ain't curious or particular. Ha! Ha!"

Brite left orders for a pack of supplies, tobacco for the riders and sundries for Moze, and while these were being filled he strolled out to enter Snell's saloon. It was a big barnlike place full of yellow light, blue smoke, odour of rum, and noise. He had been in Snell's on each drive north, and all the other times together had not totalled the number of inmates present on this occasion. Gambling games were in progress, and at one of the rude tables sat Ross Hite with other gamesters, all obsessed in their play. Brite gazed sharply to see if he recognized any of the other faces. But the light was poor and many faces were in shadow. He had not a doubt, however, that all of Wallen's outfit were there. Cowboys, as Brite knew them, were conspicuous for their absence. The majority consisted of rugged, matured men; the minority, Mexicans and a few negroes. Brite gravitated to a corner where he was in shadow and could watch all of the gamblers and one corner of the bar. He was just curious and thought he might happen on some chance talk. Ranchers, as a rule, did not spend their evenings in gambling-halls. Nevertheless, Brite thought he knew the inveterate cattlemen well enough to identify a few present. He had been there scarcely longer than a half-hour when he was chagrined to see Roy Hallett and Ben Chandler jostling to get room at the bar. Possibly Shipman had let them off, but the probabilities were that they had ridden in without permission and expected to ride back without discovery. That was the cowboy of it.

Chandler was red-faced and manifestly jocose, but Hallett looked more than usually sombre. Drink, instead of changing him, augmented his peculiar characteristics. But he was not drunk. He had to drag Chandler away from the bar. That worthy was out to make the most of this opportunity. Hallett, however, evidently had other designs. At least he did not show the usual disposition of a cowboy free to indulge. Brite concluded that Hallett had something on his mind. They sat down at an empty table, where Hallett began a low and earnest talk with his partner. It was not pleasing for Ben to listen. More than once he essayed good-humouredly to get up, but could not escape. Then he showed indications of sullenness. Hallett was plainly trying to persuade him into something. It might have been more drinking, or gambling, or staying in town all night, but somehow Brite leaned to none of these. Presently Ben spoke out quite clearly: "I'm —— if I'm gonna go through with it!"

There was that in his hard look, his angry tone, which warned Brite to interrupt this colloquy. Only on the very moment he saw Ross Hite give Hallett a meaning glance, dominant and bold, though unobtrusive. Brite jerked up, transfixed and thrilling. What was this?

Two of the gamblers left their chairs, at a significant word from Hite, and approached the bar. Whereupon the leader called to Hallett: "Want to sit in for a spell? Two-bit limit."

"Don't care if I do," replied Hallett. "Come on, Ben, let's skin 'em."

"I'm rustlin' back to camp," declared Ben, rising.

Hallett seized him, and pushing a fierce red face close to Ben's he hissed something inaudible but that was none the less forceful to Brite for that. Chandler reacted with like fierceness, which led, after a short tussle, to free himself, to a lunge and a swing. He knocked Hallett flat, and then crouched, his hand on his gun. But his caution appeared needless. Hallett was not senseless, though he recovered slowly. Chandler glared from him to the gaping Hite, then wheeling, he hurried out of the saloon. Hite spoke in a low tone to one of his associates, a thick-necked, heavy-visaged man, who arose and hurried out after Chandler.

Hallett got up and joined Hite at the gaming-table, with his hand to his face. He glowered malignantly at the door, as if he expected Chandler to come back. Hite sat shuffling the cards and talked low to Hallett. They had conversed before. Hite dealt cards all around, as if a game were in progress. But the watchful Brite saw that this was only a blind. It ended presently with Hite and Hallett going to the bar, where they drank and left the saloon.

Brite was in a quandary. Some devilry was stirring. He wanted to hurry out and warn Chandler that he was being followed. On the other hand, he did not care to risk encountering Hite and Hallett. Uncertainty chained him for a few moments, then, realizing that he must get out of the place, he pulled his sombrero down and made a break for it. The street appeared dark and empty. The few lights accentuated the blackness. Upon walking down toward the store to call for his purchases, he caught a glimpse of Hite and Hallett crossing the flare from the open doorway. Brite slunk into the shadow off the road. The two men went by, talking low. The listener could not distinguish their words; nevertheless, their tone was subtle, calculating.

When they had re-entered the saloon Brite went on to the hitching-rail to find his horse. He did not feel safe until he was astride in the middle of the road, headed for the up-river trail. He kept keen lookout for Chandler, to no avail. Once he thought he heard the beat of hoofs. Soon he had gained the open range out under the starlight. He had much to ponder over on the way to camp.

CHAPTER SEVEN

THE road out of Austin ended at the river, from which point a trail ran along the bank to the west. The old Colorado was in flood and at that hour a magnificent sight, broadly gleaming under the stars, and rolling on in low, sullen roar. Brite had not yet in his several drives encountered such a flood as this. The herd would have to be put across, if that were humanly possible. The trail drivers' habit was to take any risk rather than have several herds bunch together. More cattle were lost in that kind of a mix-up than in even the big stampedes. There had been instances, however, where stampedes had spelled loss of the whole herds.

Brite had no hope of coming up with Ben Chandler. If that cowboy had gotten to his horse he would be far on the way to camp by this time. Brite had an uneasy conviction that Chandler would be late if he got there at all. And as for Hallett, the chances were that if he showed up in camp it would be at dawn. Brite was keen to impart his information to Shipman and get his angle. At the very least Hallett was capable of extreme disloyalty. On the face of it his action looked suspicious.

Brite rode on, slowly over uneven places, at a trot on the long stretches. At the end of an hour or so he began to attend to the lie of the land. Camp ought to be somewhere within a mile. He had no idea where it would be, but the herd could scarcely be missed. And so it proved. He located the cattle by the bawling of cows. They were out of sight back in the grey gloom some distance from the river. A little further on Brite's roving gaze caught the flicker of a camp fire. He rode toward that and soon reached it, to recognize the chuck-wagon.

No one was astir. He sighted several sleepers lying dark and quiet near the wagon. On second thought he decided not to wake any of them. If he was asleep when the guard changed, it would be time enough in the morning. Brite unsaddled and let his horse go. Then finding his bed, he crawled into it and went to sleep.

Brite awoke with a start. It seemed he had not lain there more than a moment. Daylight had come. He heard the ring of an axe. But that hardly had awakened him. Rolling over to face camp, he sat up.

Hallett sat astride his horse, his sullen countenance betraying recent signs of dissipation. Pan Handle and Deuce Ackerman stood by the fire, facing the others. Then Brite espied Texas Joe glaring at the rider. Evidently words had already been exchanged.

"An' where the hell have yu been?" queried Joe.

"Rode to town last night. Didn't mean to stay all night, but I did," replied Hallett coolly.

"You didn't ask me if yu could get off."

"Nope. I just went."

"Ahuh. So I see. Wal, it'll aboot cost yu yore job," drawled Texas.

"Shipman, I don't take much store in this job nohow."

Ackerman made a passionate gesture and stepped forward. "Roy, what's got into yu lately?" he demanded.

"Nothin' 'cept a little rye. I'm fed up on this job, Deuce. Too many steers an' too few drivers."

"Why'n hell didn't yu *say* so? I'm responsible for yu. I picked yu oot for this drive."

"Wal, yu ain't responsible for me no more," replied Hallett rudely.

"By thunder! I had a hunch yu'd——"

"Shet up, Deuce," interposed Texas curtly. "I don't hold yu responsible for Hallett. An' I'll do the talkin'."

"Aw, talk an' be damned. Yu're pretty windy, Shipman," returned Hallett sarcastically, as he lighted a cigarette.

"Shore. An' I may blow on yu if yu keep slingin' yore gab so free. Looks like yu want to quit this job."

"I'd just as leave."

"Wal, you're off. An' now I'll tell yu somethin'. It's a dirty mean deal yu're givin' Mr. Brite. We're short of hands. An' yore deal has a queer look."

"Has it? Yu ought to know Texas is the place for queer deals."

"Yes, an' for yellow cowhands, I'm ashamed to say," rejoined Shipman, his gaze fixed in piercing intensity upon the rider.

Hallett responded to that significantly. Brite's sharp eyes followed the rider's sweeping survey of Texas Joe. The latter had just rolled out of his blankets. He had one boot on and the other in his hand; he had not buckled on his gun-belt. Hallett slid off his horse to step clear. His face was lowering and his eyes shone like dull coals.

"There's more'n one yellow cowhand in this ootfit," declared Hallett. "An'

I'm gonna tell yu what'll make yu take water. It was Ben Chandler who got me to go in town last night. He had some queer deal on. But I didn't know thet then. I went just for fun. An' I stayed to keep Ben from double-crossin' this ootfit. An' I couldn't do it."

"Ahuh," ejaculated Texas, unconvinced, but certainly checked.

Brite meanwhile had pulled on his boots, and now he arose, meaning to inter-ject a few pertinent words into this argument. But he did not get very far. Ben Chandler stalked into their midst, wearing a bloody scarf round his head.

"Tex, he's a —— liar!" he announced.

"Where yu come from?" queried Texas astounded.

"My bed's over there in the bushes, Tex. I just crawled oot an' happened to heah this confab."

"Wal, by gum! yu aboot got heah in time."

Hallett's appearance and demeanour underwent a drastic change. He first showed complete astonishment and incredulity. These gave way to deeper emotions, sudden anger and fear and hate.

"So *yu* turned up, hey?" he queried scornfully. "I'll bet yu don't remember yu was drunk last night?"

"Not me, Hallett."

"Huh. I reckon yu'll say yu wasn't in a fight, either."

"I wasn't. Somebody bounced lead off my haid, all right. I rode oot to camp, as you see, an' now, by Gawd! I'm gonna come clean with what I done an' what I know."

"Shipman, this cowhand was so drunk last night thet he cain't remember shootin' up Snell's place."

"So yu say, Hallett. But Ben has called yu a —— liar. If I know Texans thet calls for a show-down."

Brite stepped out from behind the group.

"Tex, I was in Snell's last night. I saw Hallett an' Chandler there. Ben was not drunk."

During the moment of silence that ensued Hallett's face turned a pale, livid hue. He crouched a little, as if about to spring, and with a hand at each hip he slowly edged toward his horse. His mask was off. His motive was to escape. But he looked venomous.

"Shipman, yu squawk again an' I'll bore yu," he rasped, his eyes deadly.

Texas swallowed hard, but he kept a cool silence.

"Bah, yu wouldn't bore nobody," shouted Ben Chandler passionately. "You're a bluff an' a liar. Yu cain't lay this on to me, Hallett."

"Shet up, yu —— fool!" rejoined the rider, backing toward his horse.

"Ben, don't say any more," advised Brite, recognizing what seemed so plain to Shipman.

"But, Mr. Brite, I'm ashamed of what I've done," protested Ben, his face flaming. "An' I want to confess it an' call this lyin' four-flush cowhand to his face before yu all."

"*Wait!*" came in cold, sharp exclamation from Pan Handle Smith.

"Lend me a gun, somebody," hurriedly broke out Chandler.

"Don't nobody move," ordered Hallett darkly. Evidently he thought he had the situation in hand.

"Hallett, I'm gonna give yu away right heah," shouted Chandler stridently. "I don't stand for yore dirty deal bein' laid on me."

"Hold yore chin, Chandler," hissed Hallett.

"Hold nothin'. I'm givin' away yore deal with Ross Hite. I'm——"

"*Take it then!*" As Hallett rang out those words he jerked at his guns. Out they leaped and were flashing up when a heavy shot cracked from behind Brite. Smoke and fire burned his cheek. Hallett's intense action ceased as if he had been struck by lightning. His left eye and temple appeared blotted out in blood. He sank down as if his legs had telescoped under him, his face rooting in the dust, his hands sliding forward, lax and nerveless, to release the guns.

"Boss, I cain't stand around an' see yore good boys bored," Smith's cool, vibrant drawl broke the strained silence.

"So help me—Gawd!" burst out Ackerman excitedly. "He got it. I was leary aboot him."

"Pan Handle, I'd forgotten yu were aboot," declared Brite, in excited relief. "Thet was wal done. . . . I saw Hallett with Ross Hite last night."

"Ben, come clean with yore story," ordered Texas Joe. "Yu damn near got yore everlastin' then."

"Texas, yu were in line, too. I saw thet in his eye," said Smith dryly.

"Hah! Mebbe *I* didn't see it," replied Texas huskily. "Pan, thet's one I owe you. . . . An' if I ever get caught ag'in withoot my gun!"

"Come on, Ben, get it off your chest," interposed Brite.

Chandler sagged on a pack and dropped his head into his hands.

"Boss, there ain't much to tell," he replied, in a low voice. "Hallett got around me. Persuaded me to go in with him on a deal with Hite. One night back on the Trail Hite got hold of Hallett when he was standin' guard. Offered him five hundred to leave a breach in the line so Hite an' his ootfit could cut oot a big bunch of stock. . . . First, I—I agreed. I shore was yellow. But it rode me day an' night—thet low-down deal. . . . An' when it come to the scratch I—I weakened. I couldn't go through with it. . . . Thet's all, sir."

"My Gawd, Ben. . . . To think yu'd double-cross us like thet!" exclaimed Deuce Ackerman, wringing his hands. "I never knowed Hallett very good. But *yu*, Ben—why, we've rode together—slept together for years."

"It's done. I've told yu. I'm making no excuses—only Roy always had likker to feed me," replied Ben miserably.

"Ben, in thet case I forgive you," spoke up Brite feelingly. "An' I hope to heaven yu never fall down thet way again."

"Thanks, Mr. Brite. I promise yu—I won't," returned Chandler brokenly.

"Ben, what yu suppose Reddie Bayne will say to this?" queried Texas Joe, in ringing scorn. "She sort of cottoned to yu most of all."

"I've no idee, Tex. But I'll tell her myself."

"Heah she comes with the *remuda*," added Deuce.

"Wonder why Reddie's rustlin' in so pert with all them hawses?" inquired Texas.

"Somebody cover up thet daid man," said Ackerman.

"Not so yu'd notice it, cowboy. Let the little lady take her medicine. Wasn't she kinda sweet on Hallett?" rejoined Tex.

"Not so yu'd notice it, Tex."

No more was said directly. Reddie circled the *remuda* about a hundred yards outside of camp, and came tearing on, her big black horse swinging with his beautiful action. She made the drivers jump before she pulled him to a halt.

"Mr. Brite—Texas—Pan Handle," she panted, her eyes wide with excitement. "I've shore got news. Nichols with his herd of two thousand odd haid is right on our heels. An' following him close is Horton in charge of a big herd for Dave Slaughter."

"Thunderation!" ejaculated Brite, throwing up his hands.

Texas Joe used language equally expressive, but hardly for a young girl's ears. Then he pulled on his boot, a task that made him struggle.

"Both drivers sent a man over to tell us to hop the river pronto or they'd be on our heels," went on Reddie, her cheeks aglow. "Oh! Look at the river! It was dark when I went oot. . . . Mr. Brite, it cain't be possible to swim our ootfit across thet flood."

"Reddie, it may not be possible, but we must make the attempt," replied Brite.

"Ah-h!" screamed Reddie, suddenly espying the bloody-faced Hallett on the ground. "What's—happened? Isn't thet Roy?"

"I reckon 'tis, lass."

"Oh!—He's daid!"

"So it would seem."

"*Who?*" flashed Reddie, plainly stirred to righteous wrath.

"Reddie, I'm the bad hombre," drawled Pan Handle.

"Yu—yu wicked gunman! Why on earth did yu shoot thet poor boy?"

Pan Handle turned away; Texas dropped his head; Brite watched, but spoke no word. Then Ben looked up.

"Why, Ben! Yu shot too?"

"Only a scratch, Reddie. Yu see it was this way," he began, and bravely outlined his part in the tragedy, scoring Hallett mercilessly, but not sparing himself.

"Ben Chandler!" she cried, in shocked voice. Then, as the realization dawned on her and she gazed from Texas to Brite, to the ghastly Hallett, and back with blazing eyes to Ben, the enormity of such an offence seemed to mount prodigiously.

"Yu agreed to double-cross our boss!" she burst out, in withering scorn. "To steal from the hand thet paid yu! Lawd! but thet's a low-down trick!"

"But, Reddie, give the devil his due," interrupted Texas sharply. "Ben was easy'-goin'. He cottoned to Hallett. An' his weakness was the bottle. An' after all he didn't—he couldn't go through with it."

"I don't care a damn," cried Reddie, the very embodiment of ruthlessness. "I'd never forgive him in a million years. . . . Why, the dirty sneakin' cowhand was coaxin' me for a kiss—only two nights ago!"

"Wal, in thet case, it's plumb important to know if Ben got it," drawled Texas.

"Yu bet yore life he didn't," retorted Reddie, her face on fire. "If he had I'd jump in the river this minute."

"Reddie, I've overlooked Ben's break," interrupted Brite.

"Ahuh. Wal, all I say is yu're a lot of soft melon haids," replied Reddie, with passion. "I'll never overlook it. An' I'll never speak to him again or stand guard near him or——"

"Come an' git it while it's hot," sang Moze.

Texas Joe was studying the river. It was two hundred yards wide at that point, a swirling, muddy, swift flood, carrying logs and trees and driftwood of all descriptions. The current had to be reckoned with. If it carried the stock below a certain point there would almost certainly be a disaster. For two miles below on the opposite side the bank was steep and straight up as far as the eye could see.

"Boss, I swear I don't know aboot it," said Texas. "But we cain't turn back now. The boys have their orders an' heah comes the herd in sight."

"We'll try it, win or lose," replied Brite grimly, stirred with the gamble.

"Hey, Reddie," yelled Texas, waving his hands. "Come on."

Reddie sent back a pealing cry and wheeled to ride behind the *remuda*. They came on in a bunch, restless and scared, though not wild. Pan Handle rode below the taking-off slope while Texas rode on the up-stream side. Reddie drove her mustangs down the slope on a run. Some sheered aside below and above, only to be driven back by Pan Handle and Texas. In a moment more the leaders were pointed and with shrill snorts they plunged into the shallow river. The others followed in good order. Texas rode out with them until the water deepened perceptibly. He was yelling at the top of his voice. Pan Handle shot in front of mustangs leading out of line. Reddie, with her wild cries, drove them off the land, and when her black splashed the water high the leaders had gone off the bar and were swimming.

"WHOOPEE KID!" yelled Texas, brandishing his sombrero. "Keep up-stream yoreself an' let 'em go."

When Texas got back to the shore the rear and broad end of the *remuda* was well out, and the leaders about to hit the swift current.

"Tex, we ought to have gone with her," expostulated Pan Handle seriously.

"Thet's a grand hawse she's forkin'," said Brite hopefully.

Texas Joe did not voice his fears or hopes, but he fixed his hawk eyes intently on that marvellous scene of action. Brite's last count had totalled one hundred and seventy-nine mustangs in the *remuda*. The doughty little Spanish stock had no dislike for water. Whistling and rearing, the thickly bunched body of ponies went off into deep water with the intrepid girl close behind, waving her sombrero and pealing her shrill cry to the skies. How her red-gold head shone in the sunlight! Once the black horse struck out into deeper water, Brite got rid of his fright. He could swim like a duck.

Reddie kept him up-stream to the left end of the bobbing line. Trees and logs floated into their midst, hampering the mustangs. Here and there one would fetch up to paw over the obstruction, slide off, go under, and come up to go on. Down-river swept those in the current, swiftly leaving those in the still water. But they kept on swimming, and they had plenty of leeway to clear the steep bank far below. Soon the whole *remuda* was in the current, and then the spectacle seemed moving and splendid to Brite. If his heart had not gone out to this orphaned girl long before she braved the flood as a part of her job and scorning help, it would have yielded to her then. The long black patch of lean heads disintegrated and lengthened and curved away down-river, a wild and beautiful sight.

A mile below where Brite and his men watched breathlessly the leaders waded out into shallow water, and the long string curved faithfully toward that point. One by one, in twos and threes, and then in bunches, the mustangs struck the bar, to bob up and heave wet shoulders out, to flounder and splash ashore. Soon the wedge-shaped line thickened as the ponies passed the swift current; and it was only a matter of a few minutes before the last horse was wading out. And Reddie Bayne bestrode him!

"Dog-gone! Thet was great," breathed Texas.

"Shore was a pretty sight," agreed Pan Handle.

"Wal, I reckon we had our fears for nothin'," added Brite.

"Boss, we ought to stop her. It's different comin' this way. Not enough room to allow for thet current," replied Pan Handle anxiously.

"By Gawd, can yu beat thet!" exclaimed Texas, and whipping out his gun he shot twice. Then he waved his sombrero and yelled in stentorian tones: "GO BACK! GO BACK!"

Reddie heard, for she waved her hand in reply, and she kept coming on. In another moment her horse would be in over his depth, and the swift current, with big, muddy waves, right ahead of her. Texas shot all the remaining charges left in his gun, and he aimed so the bullets would hit the water not a great way below Reddie. Then he roared like a giant:

"TURN ABOOT!—Reddie, it ain't the same . . . DAMN YU—I'M GIVIN' ORDERS!"

Reddie's high-pitched, pealing cry came sweet and wild on the wind.

"Too late, Tex. She's in now."

"Thet's a hawse, Brite. I say let her come," put in Pan Handle. Texas Joe became as an equestrian statue in bronze. The big muddy waves curled over the neck and head of the black, and up to the shoulders of the girl. They were swept down-stream with a rush. But in a hundred yards the powerful horse had left the high waves and was entering the swirling, lesser current. Brite saw the girl check him to let a log pass, and again turn him down-stream to avoid a huge mass of green foliage. That horse and rider knew what they were doing. Again he breasted the current with power and worked across. But he would never make the point of bar where the *remuda* had taken off. This worried Brite. Only so few rods below where the high bank began! Already Pan Handle was riding down to head her off. The black, however, was coming faster than the watchers had figured. His lean head jerked high, his wet shoulders followed and with a lunge he was out of the depths into the shallows. He had made it with room to spare. Reddie came trotting ashore.

Here Texas got off his horse, and in the very extreme of rage or exasperation or something, he slammed his sombrero down, he stamped to and fro, he cursed like a drunken cowhand. Plain it was to Brite that his foreman had surrendered to the release of pent-up agony.

"Come back, Pan," Reddie was calling gaily. "Shore had fun. What yu think of my hawse?"

"He's grand, but yu took a big chance, all for nothin'."

"Yu'll need me an' don't overlook thet," declared Reddie. Then as she joined Pan Handle she espied Texas going through remarkable actions. "Gee! Our Trail boss is riled aboot somethin'."

Soon Reddie rode up to rein in before Texas and Brite. She was something to gaze at. Pale with suppressed excitement, her eyes large and dark and daring, she sat awaiting sentence to fall. She was wringing wet to her neck. Her blouse no longer hid the swelling contour of her breast.

"Sorry I scared you, gentlemen," she said, a little feafully. "But yu need me over heah an' I had to come."

"Reddie Bayne, I yelled to yu," began Texas sternly.

"Shore. I heahed yu."

"I ordered yu back. Did yu heah thet?"

"Course I did. Laws! yu'd woke the daid."

"Wal, then, yu have no respect for me as Trail boss of this drive?"

"I wouldn't of turned back for Mr. Brite himself," retorted Reddie spiritedly. But her face had paled and her eyes were dilating.

"Yu disobeyed me again?" thundered Texas.

"Yes, I did—dammit."

"Not only thet—yu scared us oot of our wits, just to be smart. Yu're a spoiled girl. But yu cain't disorganize this ootfit no more."

"Cain't I?" echoed Reddie weakly.

"Reddie Bayne, yu listen. Just 'cause yu've got the boss eatin' oot of yore hand—an' cause yu're the distractinest pretty girl—an' 'cause I happen to be turrible in love with yu, don't make no damn bit of difference. Yu're wearin' driver's pants, yu're takin' driver's wages, yu're pullin' driver's tricks."

Texas stepped over to her horse, and flashing a lean, brown hand up, like a striking smoke, he clutched the front of her blouse high up and jerked her sliding out of her saddle.

"Oh-h!" cried Reddie, in a strangled voice. "How dare . . . Let me go!—Texas, wha—what air yu goin' to——"

"I cain't slug yu one as I would a man—an' I cain't spank yu no more as I once did," said Texas deliberately. "But I'm shore gonna shake the daylight oot of yu."

Then he grasped her shoulders and began to make good his threat. Reddie offered no resistance whatever. She was as one struck dumb and hopeless. Brite grasped that Texas' betrayal of his love had had more to do with this collapse than any threat of corporal punishment. She gazed up with eyes that Texas must have found hard to look into. But soon she could not see, for he shook her until she resembled an image of jelly under some tremendous vibrating force. When from sheer exhaustion he let her go she sank down upon the sand, still shaking.

"There—Miss Bayne," he panted.

"Where—Texas Jack?" she gasped flippantly.

"Gawd only knows," he burst out helplessly, and began to tear his hair.

"Heah comes the herd!" sang out the thrilling word from Pan Handle.

CHAPTER EIGHT

THE old bull Mossy-horns, huge and fierce, with his massive horns held high, led the spear-shaped mass of cattle over the brow of the long slope. Densely packed, resistless in slow advance, they rolled like a flood of uprooted stumps into sight.

"By all thet's lucky!" yelled Texas, in elation. "Pointed already! If they hit the river in a wedge like thet they'll make Moses crossin' the Red Sea only a two-bit procession."

"Orders, Texas, orders," replied Brite uneasily. "It won't be long till they roll down on us."

"Got no orders, 'cept keep on the up-river side. For Gawd's sake don't ride in below 'em. The boys have been warned. . . . Ben, yu ride on the wagon. We'll come back an' float it across."

"I will like hell," shouted Ben derisively, and he ran for a horse to saddle. Brite did likewise, and while he was at the task he heard Texas cursing Chandler for not obeying orders. When he was in the saddle the magnificent herd, a moving colourful triangle of living beasts, had cleared the ridge, and the leaders were close. Drivers on each side of the wedge rode frantically forward and back, yelling, shooting, waving. But the noise they made came faintly through the din of brawls.

"Reddie," called Texas earnestly, turning a stern, tight-lipped face and falcon eyes upon the girl, "this heah's new to yu. Yore hawse is a duck, I know, but thet won't save yu if yu get in bad. Will yu stick close to me, so I can tell yu if yu start wrong?"

"I shore will," replied Reddie, with surprising complaisance.

"Boss, yu hang to their heels," concluded Texas curtly. "Pan, yu drop back aboot halfway. Above all, don't drift into the herd. . . . Come on, Reddie!"

Bad rivers had no terrors for old Mossy-horns. A rod ahead of his herd he ran, nimble as a calf, down the sandy slope, roaring like a buffalo. All sound was deadened in the trampling thunder of the cattle as they yielded to the grade

336

and came on pell-mell. The ground shook under Brite. Nearly five thousand head of stock in a triangular mass sweeping like stampeding buffalo down a long hill! Certain it was that Brite's sombrero stood up on his stiff hair. No daring, no management, no good luck could ever prevent some kind of a catastrophe here.

Texas plunged his horse into the river ahead of Mossy-horns, swinging his lasso round his head and purple in the face from yelling. But Brite could not hear him. Reddie's big black lashed the muddy water into sheets as she headed him after Texas. Then the great wedge, like an avalanche, hit the shallow water with a tremendous sound. Hundreds of cows and steers had reared to ride on the haunches of those ahead, and the mass behind pushed all in a cracking, inextricable mass. But those to the front, once in the water, spread to find room. Herein lay the peril of the drivers, and the dire necessity of keeping the herd pointed as long as possible. Such a feat seemed utterly futile to Brite.

Across the backs and horns Brite espied Ben Chandler on the down-stream side of the herd, close to the leaders, and oblivious or careless of danger. Bent on retrieving his fatal error, he had no fear. Soon Brite lost sight of Ben's bloody, bandaged head in the flying yellow spray. Try as he might, he could not see the reckless driver again. San Sabe and Ackerman, both on the down-river side, slowly gave ground toward the rear of the herd, intending to fall in behind as soon as the end passed. Rolly Little, Holden, and Whittaker passed Brite in order, fire-eyed and gaunt with excitement.

When next Brite cast his racing glance out ahead he was in time to see old Mossy-horns heave into deep water. He went clear under, to bob up like a duck and sail into the current. Like sheep the sharply pointed head of the herd piled in after him. Texas went off the bar far up-stream, and Reddie still farther. As Brite gazed spellbound the wide rear of the herd, in crashing momentum, rolled past his position. It was time for him to join the drivers. He spurred ahead, and the mustang, excited and fiery, his blood up, would have gone anywhere. Brite had one last look out into the current, where a thousand wide-horned heads swept in a curve down the middle of the river. Then he leaped off the bank and into the water, just even with the up-river end of the herd. Thunder would not have done justice to the volume of sound. It was a strange, seething, hissing, bone-cracking roar. But that seemed to be diminishing as the cattle, hundreds after hundreds, took to the deeper water. Texas and then Reddie passed out of sight. The great herd curved abruptly. Next Ackerman disappeared round the corner, and then Holden. That left only Whittaker in sight and he was sweeping down.

Behind the herd Brite espied Bender, who was nearest to him, and certainly a scared young man if Brite had ever seen one.

In a maelstrom of swishing water and twisting bodies the broad rear of the herd smashed off the bar. Magically then all sound ceased. There was left only a low, menacing swish and gurgle of current against Brite's horse. Easily he took to deep water, and Brite felt at once that he had drawn a river horse. What wonderful little animals were those Spanish mustangs of Arabian blood!

The scene had immeasurably changed. No white splashes now! A mile of black horned heads, like a swarm of shining bees, sweeping down the river! The terror, the fury of the onslaught upon the flood were no longer evident. There was left only the brilliance, the action, the beauty of this crossing. Brite had never seen anything in his life to compare with it; and once he had seen a million buffalo cross the Brazos River. But they just blotted out the river. Here the wide flood held the mastery. The sun shone down on an endless curve of wet, shiny horns and heads; the sky bent its azure blue down over the yellow river; the green trees of the opposite bank beckoned and seemed to grow imperceptibly closer.

Then Brite's mustang met the swift centre current of the river. Here there were smooth waves that rolled over the horse and wet Brite to his shoulders. And he saw that he was going down-stream, scarcely quartering at all. The long head of the curve appeared far towards the opposite shore.

To Brite's right the three drivers were working their horses away from the herd, or so it appeared to him. Then Brite saw San Sabe point up the river. A mass of driftwood was coming down on the crest of a rise. What execrable luck to be met by a heavy swell of flood and current in the middle of the river at the most critical time! Brite reined his mustang to avoid the big onrush of driftwood. With hands and feet he pushed aside logs and branches. A whole tree, green and full-foliaged, surrounded by a thick barrage of logs, drifted right into the middle of the swimming herd. This the drivers were unable to prevent. They could only save themselves, which, in the case of two of them, at least, was far from easy.

The swift-floating island of débris split the herd, turned the rear half down-stream, and heralded certain disaster. Brite saw the broad lane between the two halves, one quartering away toward the north shore, the other swimming with the current. If it kept on down-river it was doomed.

Brite came near to becoming entangled in heavy brush, which he had not seen because his attention was fixed on the separated half of his herd. He owed it to the clever mustang that he was not engulfed. Thereafter he looked out for himself and his horse. All the while they were sweeping down, at the same time gaining toward the shore. Looking back, Brite was surprised to see the chuck-wagon, a dot on the horizon line, a mile back up the river. Ahead and below, somewhat less of a distance, began the cutting edge of the steep bank Texas had warned all they must not pass. Standing in his stirrups, Brite made out the head of the herd now beyond the current, well toward the shore. There! A horse and rider had struck shallow water again. That must be Texas.

An eddy caught the mustang and whirled him around and around. Brite was about to slide off and ease the burden, but the horse tore out of the treacherous whirlpool and, thoroughly frightened, he redoubled his efforts. Brite's next discovery was sight of the vanguard of cattle wading out on the wide bar below. Already two of the riders were out. Grateful indeed for so much, Brite turned to see what had become of the endangered half of the herd. They were milling back toward the centre of the river. This amazed Brite until he heard the boom-boom-boom of a heavy gun. Chandler, the dare-devil, must be on the other side there, driving the cattle again into the current.

The milling circle of horned heads struck into the swift current, to be swept on down the river, past the wading vanguard, surely to slide by that steep corner of bank, beyond which could lie only death. Brite could stand the loss of stock. But a rider sacrificed hurt him deeply. He had never lost one until this drive. Still he clung to hope. Somewhere down around the bend, on one bank or the other, there might be a place for Chandler to climb out.

At this juncture Brite saw another rider, one of the three ahead of him, wade his horse out and go across the bar at a gallop, to mount the bank and ride swiftly along its edge, the mane and tail of the mustang flying wildly in the wind. He did not recognize either Texas' or Pan Handle's horse, so that rider must have been Ackerman, speeding to give aid to Chandler.

When Brite at last waded out on the bar there were only a few hundred head of stock behind and below him. They were wearied, but safe, as all had found footing. Three riders were waiting. Texas and Reddie had vanished. Bender, Pan Handle, and San Sabe were working out behind the cattle, and all three were facing down-river, no doubt watching the cattle that had been swept away.

Presently Brite joined the six drivers on the bar and surely encountered a disheartened group of cowboys. Pan Handle was the only one to present anything but a sad countenance.

"Mr. Brite, we had bad luck," he said. "The herd split in the middle an' the back half went down-river taking Chandler with it. Our good luck is thet more of us might have been with him."

"Hell with—the cattle!" panted Brite. "Any hope for Chandler?"

"Shore. He's a gamblin' chance to get oot somewhere. But I wouldn't give two-bits for the cattle. Ackerman is ahaid, keepin' up with them. Texas followed with Reddie."

"What'll we do?"

"Make camp heah on the bank in the grove. Plenty of grass. The stock shore won't move to-night."

"Thet chuck-wagon's to be got over. An' I wouldn't give much for it."

"Boss, thet wagon was made to float," said San Sabe. "It's got a double bottom of heavy planks. Don't worry none aboot our grub."

They rode up the sandy slope to a level bank of timber and grass, an ideal place to camp. The horses were heaving after their prolonged exertions. "Get off an' throw yore saddles, boys," said Brite, suiting action to his words. "Somebody light a fire so we can dry oot."

A little later, while Brite was standing in his shirt sleeves before a fire, Texas Joe and Reddie rode into camp.

"We cain't send good money after what's lost," he said philosophically. "I reckon Ben is gone, an' there's only one chance in a thousand for thet bunch of cattle. We gotta look after what's left an' fetch Moze across. . . . Reddie, yore hawse ain't even tired. Wal, I never seen his beat. But yu don't weigh more'n a grasshopper. Let San Sabe have him to help me with the wagon."

"Shore. But I'd like to go," replied Reddie eagerly.

"My Gawd! air yu still wantin' more of thet river?" queried Texas incredulously.

"Oh, I was havin' a grand time until the herd split. . . . Poor Ben! If he's lost I'll never forgive myself. I—I was mad an' I said too much."

"Wal, yu shore said a heap," drawled Texas. "If yu'd said as much to me I'd drowned myself pronto."

"Don't—don't say it—it might be my fault," wailed Reddie, almost weeping.

"No, kid. I was only foolin'. Ben was just makin' up for the wrong he did us. An' he's shore square with me."

"Oh, I hope an' pray he got oot," rejoined Reddie as she dismounted.

San Sabe removed her saddle and put his own on the black. Then he followed Texas, who was already far up the bar, making for the bend of the river, from which point they would head across. It was a sombre group that stood drying out around the blazing fire. Reddie looked sick and wretched. Her gaze ever strayed down the stream, where the muddy current swept out of sight.

Texas and San Sabe gave their comrades some bad moments when even their heads disappeared in the waves, but it turned out they crossed safely. Meanwhile Moze had driven the chuck-wagon down to meet them. It was too far for Brite to see distinctly, but he knew that the riders would tie on to the wagon with their ropes and encourage and help the team. With little ado they were off and soon in the water. Great furrows splashed up as the wagon ploughed in. Brite had his doubts about that venture, and when horses and wagon struck off the bar into deep water, to be swept down by the current, he expected it was but a forerunner of more misfortune. The wagon floated so high that part of the bed and all the canvas showed above the water. It sailed down like a boat and gradually neared the shore, at last to cross out of the current, into the slack water, and eventually to the bar. He had suffered qualms for nothing. Moze, however, although he was a black man, looked a little pale about the gills. The usual banter did not appear to be forthcoming from the dejected drivers, an omission Moze was quick to catch.

"Men, I reckon yo-all will hev to dry yo beds," he said, his big eyes rolling. "I packed them under de grub."

"Aw, my tobacco!" wailed Deuce.

"Niggah, I ought to petasterize you," added Whittaker severely. "I had my only extra shirt in my bed."

"What is dis petasterizin'?" asked Moze, beginning to throw off his packs. "Yo-all is a glum ootfit."

"Moze, we lost half my stock an' Ben Chandler, too," replied Brite.

"Lawd Amighty! I done reckoned trubble when I seen dis ribber."

That was the end of jocularities, as well as other conversation. The hour was approaching noonday, an astounding fact to Brite. If it had been at all possible for the stock to move on for several hours more, he would have ordered it. But cattle and horses alike were spent.

The herd following Brite's would bed down that night on the south shore, and cross in the morning. It was too close for comfort. But the cattleman could not see how that might be avoided. Presently the silent drivers stirred to the advent of Deuce Ackerman riding into sight up the river bank. His posture and the gait of his horse were significant of what had happened. Deuce rode into camp, haggard of face, his garb mud from head to foot, and he all but fell out of the saddle.

"Come to the fire, Deuce. I'll throw yore leather," said Little solicitously.

"Mr. Brite, I have to report thet Chandler was drowned," he said.

"So we all reckoned," returned Brite resignedly.

"Stake me to a drink, if yu want to heah aboot it."

But Ackerman did not soon begin his narrative. Finally he began: "Wal, I rode along the bank an' ketched up with the cattle. An' there was thet idjit Chandler hangin' along the leads, slappin' his rope ahaid of him. He hadn't given up pointin' thet bunch of long-horns to this shore. I yelled an' yelled my lungs oot, but he never heahed me. After a while, though, he seen me. I waved him oot of the river an' he paid no attention. He kept on, the herd kept on, an' so did I. I'd run a coupla miles, I reckon, before I ketched up. An' we wasn't long travellin' another mile or so. Then I seen far ahaid on my side a wide break in the bank. Dam' if Chandler hadn't seen it, too. An' he lashed them lead cattle like a fiend from hell. He beat them farther an' farther to this side. An' I'm a son-of-a-gun if he didn't work 'em over to shore just when the current had carried 'em to this break. The water close in was shallow, too. Once the leads hit bottom they come to life, an' my! how they swarmed off thet bar!"

"Yu mean to tell us Ben drove them cattle oot on dry land?" demanded Texas incredulously.

"Dam' if he didn't! But his hawse was all in, an' on account of the cattle blockin' his way he couldn't get oot of deep water. So he was carried on down-river, past the break. I rode on for all I was worth, yellin' to Ben to hang on. By this time he was on his hawse's neck. But for the current thet little dogie would have sunk. He could hardly swim a lick. I seen where the swift water run close under the bank, an' I made for thet place. Shore enough Ben swept in close, an' I leaped off with my rope. Fust throw I hit Ben clean with my loop. But it was too small. It didn't ketch, an' he missed it. I kept runnin' an' throwin', but no good. The bank was awful steep an' crumbly. Then I broke off a section an' damn near fell in myself. Seein' thet wasn't gettin' us nowhere, I run ahaid a good ways an' waited for Ben to float by a likely place. . . . But jest as they was aboot to come within reach of my rope the game little pony sunk. Ben made a feeble effort to stay up. He seen me. He opened his mouth to call. . . . Only a gurgle! His mouth filled—an' the water come up over his bloody face. My Gawd! There he floated, a hand up, then his back, his haid onct more—an' thet was the last."

Reddie burst into tears and ran from the camp fire. Texas knelt to throw bits of wood upon the coals.

"Ross Hite or no—Ben shore paid for his fling," he muttered to himself.

"Ackerman, thet was a terrible thing," declared Brite, badly upset.

"'Most as tough on me as Ben," said the cowboy huskily. "I'll never forget his eyes. At the last he wanted to be saved. I seen thet. When I first come up to him he didn't care a dam'. All he wanted was to get the haid of thet string of cattle pointed to land. An' he done it. Never did I see the like of thet."

Texas rose dark and stern. "I'll get me a hawse an' ride down to locate thet bunch. How far, Deuce, aboot?"

"I don't know. Four miles, mebbe."

Shipman trudged wearily away, despite Brite's call for him to rest awhile longer. Perhaps Texas wanted to be alone, a disposition more than one of the drivers soon manifested. Reddie had evidently hidden in the green brush. Being a woman, she would take this tragedy hardest to heart, believing she had been partly to blame.

"Then, judgin' from what I've heahed at Dodge an' Abilene, we're just gettin' a taste of real trail drivin'," said Pan Handle. "It's a gamble an' the cairds air against us."

"I take the blame," spoke up Brite feelingly. "It was my hawgishness. Half my herd would have been plenty to start with."

"We doan' know how things ever will come oot," declared Whittaker, in his quaint drawl.

Moze called them to eat, to which they answered eagerly, if not quickly. Reddie Bayne did not come in. And Brite decided he would let her alone awhile longer, until the drivers had gone. But even after eating they remained in camp, still damped by the misfortune, no doubt waiting for Texas to return with orders.

"He ought to be back," complained Deuce. "Hadn't I better have a look?"

"Wal, yu'd likely miss him, Deuce."

They conjectured as to the probable movements of the separated halves of the herd, gradually gathering conviction among themselves that all was well. The hot fire dried Brite's clothes and made him drowsy. Lying down in the sand under a tree he fell from rest to slumber. Upon awakening Brite was chagrined to note that the sun was westering. Pan Handle, Reddie Bayne, Rolly Little, and Texas were in camp, a stone-faced quartet. The other drivers were gone.

"Ha, Tex, yu back?" queried Brite, sitting up with stiffened joints.

"Yeh, boss, I'm back," replied the cowboy wearily.

"How far's the split half of the herd?"

"Wal, countin' the half-hour I been heah, I'd say aboot ten miles to the northard."

"Wha—at?"

"Shore, an' travellin' to beat hell!"

Brite sensed more tragedy, and braced himself to continue coolly: "How come?"

"Boss, I plumb hate to tell yu," rejoined Texas miserably. "Reddie, clap yore hands over yore ears. I gotta let go! . . . Of all the —— —— —— luck any —— ootfit ever had we've had the wust. I'm seein' red. I'm madder'n any rattler-bitten coyote yu ever seen. I gotta get pizen drunk or kill——"

"Hell! yu're not *tellin'* me anythin'," interrupted Brite testily.

"Tell him, Pan."

"Mr. Brite, it's an unheahed-of deal an' I'm not agreed with Texas aboot its bein' so bad as he reckons," complied Pan Handle. "Texas rode oot to get a line on thet split herd an' couldn't see it nowhere. So he rode up a high ridge an' soon spotted yore cattle. They was travellin' north at a good lick in front of aboot ten drivers."

"Ross Hite!" thundered Brite, in a sudden rage, leaping up.

"So Tex reckoned. An' as was right an' proper he rode back to tell us. We been havin' a pow-wow aboot it. Tex was riled somethin' fierce. He wanted to take fresh hawses an' ride oot to shoot up thet stampedin' gang of Hite's. So did all the boys except me. I was against thet an' the more I reckon the stronger I am set."

"I agree with yu, Pan Handle," rejoined Brite at once. "We air let down. If we chase Hite an' pick a fight, win or lose, some of us air goin' to get killed. An' we leave what's left of my herd heah to mix in with the herds comin' behind. No! Let's stick with the bird in the hand."

"By all means," agreed Pan Handle, with satisfaction. "Now, if yu follow me on thet maybe yu'll see what I see. Ross Hite cain't get so far ahaid thet we cain't ride him down in a day. Let him go. Keep close on his trail aboot a day behind. He's drivin' our cattle for us. But he's the damdest fool in this range. There's no sale for cattle short of Dodge. He'll take thet branch of the Chisholm Trail, because it's much farther to Abilene. An' the night before we expect him to ride into Dodge I'll take a fast hawse, cut off the trail, an' be there to meet him."

"Boss, it's a good idee, except Pan wants to go it alone, an' I won't stand for thet," interposed Texas.

"Meet Hite?" echoed Brite.

"Thet's what I said," concluded Pan Handle tersely.

"Wal, Pan, on the face of it, thet's hardly fair to yu," replied Brite ponderingly. He understood perfectly. Pan Handle Smith chose to attempt this single-handed.

CHAPTER EIGHT

It was the way of the real gunman to seek the dramatic, to take advantage of the element of surprise, to subject no other to risk than himself.

"Boss, on second thought I stand by Pan," spoke up Texas. "But thet's the last way to get our cattle back. Shorer'n Gawd made little apples somethin' else will turn up. We got a dozen more rivers to cross, an' redskins to meet, an' buffalo. Buffalo by the million! This hombre Hite is no trail driver. His ootfit air a lot of hawse thieves, some of them grey-haided. They cain't drive cattle. Hite is plumb loco. He reckons he'll clean up aboot thirty thousand dollars. An' thet'll hold him to the trail an' the herd. He's got no more chance to get thet money than a snowball has in hell!"

CHAPTER NINE

THE night fell warm, with a hint of summer in its balmy sweetness; the stars shone white through the foliage of the trees; the river gurgled and murmured along the shore, without any of the menace that it had seemed to have by day; the frogs trilled lonesome music. And all the vast range was locked in silence and slumber. Yet even then thieves and death were at work.

Brite felt all this while trying to woo sleep. But it would not come. Reddie had made her bed near him in the shadow of the heavy bushes. Presently a tall, dark form stalked between Brite and the pale starlight. Texas Joe was roaming around camp, as usual, in the dead of night, perhaps about to call change of guards. But he stealthily went around Brite to halt beside Reddie, where, after a moment, he knelt.

There followed a moment of silence, then Reddie murmured drowsily: "Huh? . . . Who is it?"

"Ssssch! Not so loud. Yu'll wake the boss up. . . . It's only Tex."

"Yu again! My Gawd! man, cain't yu even let me sleep?" returned Reddie in a disgusted whisper.

"I heahed yu cryin' an' I wanted to come then. But I waited till everybody was sunk."

"What yu want?"

"I'd like to talk to yu a bit. Never have no chance in daytime. An' since I run into Ben sittin' beside yore bed thet night I haven't had no nerve."

"I hadn't noticed thet," whispered Reddie, with faint sarcasm. "Wal, if yu *must* talk, move over a little. Yu're settin' aboot on top of me."

"Ben was turrible in love with yu, too, wasn't he?"

"Texas, I don't know aboot him bein' *too*, as yu call it, but I reckon he was. Anyway he swore it. I don't trust no cowboys."

"So I seen. Reddie, they ain't all bad. . . . Was yu sweet on Ben?"

"No, of course not."

"But yu let him kiss yu!"

346

"I did nothin' of the sort. Thet night yu caught him it wasn't no fault of mine. He grabbed me. At thet he never kissed my mouth."

"Aw! I reckoned different. I'm sorry."

A long silence followed. Brite had a desire to cough or roll over, or do something to acquaint the young couple that he was awake. He had also a stronger desire, however, not to do it. The river murmured on, the frogs trilled, the leaves rustled. There seemed to be something big and alive and wonderful abroad in the night.

"Wal, thet all yu wanted to say?" resumed Reddie.

"No. I always have a lot to say. An' I cain't say it," whispered Texas sadly. "I feel awful sorry aboot Ben. He was no good, Reddie. I've knowed thet for some time. But he shore died grand."

"Don't make me cry again."

"Wal, did Ben ask yu to marry him?"

"Lands sake, no!" exclaimed Reddie, with an embarrassed little laugh.

"It's not so funny. Haven't any of this ootfit asked yu?"

"Not thet I heahed, Texas," replied Reddie, almost with a titter.

"Funny!"

"Thet's not so funny. They shore ought to have."

"Wal, I'm gonna ask yu some day."

"Texas, yu're oot of yore head!"

"Shore I reckon I am. But it's the first time—aboot a girl."

"Taffy! What do yu think I am?"

"Honest Injun, kid. Since I growed up I've been too busy ridin' range an' dodgin' gun-slingers to get moony over girls."

"Wal, I'll bet yu've mixed up with bad women, like Mr. Brite tells me Dodge is full of."

"Ump-umm, Reddie. If I ever did I was so drunk I never knowed it. But I won't believe I ever did, 'cause somebody would have told me."

"I'd like to believe yu, Texas."

"Wal, yu can. I wouldn't lie to any girl, much less yu."

"But yu lied to me when yu swore yu knowed I was a girl. All the time yu swore yu knowed."

"Reddie, I wasn't lyin'."

"Shore yu was. All yu wanted was to pretend to have the edge on the other boys. I was on to yu, Texas."

"Wal, I'll tell yu, if yu swear yu'll forgive me."

"Forgive yu!—Say, cowboy, yu're talkin' strange."

"Wal, I feel strange. But I reckon I better confess."

"Texas Jack, don't confess anythin' thet'll make me hate yu."

"Yu're forgettin' aboot thet Texas Jack handle. I've warned yu. . . . Reddie, since way back on the trail I've knowed yu was a girl. Before I killed Wallen. Do yu reckon I could have shot him so quick—if I hadn't known?"

"Damn yu! I'm scared. . . . How'd yu know?"

"Reddie, yu remember thet creek bottom where we camped. Prettiest camp so far. Willows an' pecans an' blackberries an' flowers hangin' over thet clear creek. It was aboot sunset, I'd been below an' took a short cut to camp. The brush was awful thick. I heahed a floppin' aboot in the water an' I sneaked up to peep through the green."

"Yu—yu. . . . Tex Shipman!" she cried, in a low, strangled voice.

"Yes. I seen yu bathin'. . . . Only seen the—the upper part of yu. . . . Don't be so awful ashamed, Reddie. . . . Just one peep—then I fell down an' lay there as if I was shot. Then I crawled away. . . . After thet I was never the same."

"I—I should think not. . . . But why did yu ever tell me? . . . Yu're no gentleman. . . . An' I do hate yu now!"

"Wal, I cain't help thet. But I don't believe yu, Reddie. There's no sense or justice in hatin' me. For Gawd's sake, why?"

"Yu've been so mean to me."

"Mean! Say, I had to fool everybody. I had to keep yu an' all our ootfit from findin' oot I'd gone plumb, starin', stark mad aboot yu. So I picked on yu."

"Tex Shipman—thet time yu spanked me—did yu know I was a girl then?"

"So help me Gawd—I did."

"Now! I'll never look at yu again."

"But, Reddie, don't yu want a man to be honest?"

"Not—not when he knows too much."

"I had to tell yu thet before I could ask yu to marry me. An' I'm doin' thet now."

"Doin' what?" she flashed, in a full, thrilling whisper.

"Askin' yu to marry me."

"Oh, indeed! Yu think I'm a poor waif of the range. No kin, no home, no friends. Just an outcast."

"You come to us a pretty lonely kid, if I recollect. Reckon yu've had a tough time. I shore wonder how yu got through so good an' fine a girl."

"Yes, it is a wonder, Texas. But I did, thank Gawd. An' now I'm the happiest girl alive."

"Reddie!—Has my askin' yu to—to be my wife—has thet anythin' to do with how yu feel?"

"Wal, it's a satisfaction, Tex," she replied demurely. "Cowboy, yu don't know how high yu're aspirin'. I *was* a waif but *now* I'm an heiress!"

"What? . . . Yu're a locoed kid."

"Texas, I'm Mr. Brite's adopted daughter!'" she announced proudly.

"*Aw!* . . . Honest, Reddie?"

"Cross my heart. I don't know how it all come aboot. I don't care. I only know I'm happy—the first time in my whole life!"

"Dog-gone!—I'm shore glad. It's aboot the best thet could happen to yu. The boss is a fine old Southern gentleman. A real Texan. He owns a big ranch ootside Santone. . . . Yu'll have a home. Yu'll be rich some day. Yu'll have all the hawses any girl could set her heart on. . . . An' beaus, too, Reddie!"

"Beaus?—Oh, dear! How—how funny! Me, Reddie Bayne, heah sleepin' in my overalls!"

"Yep, an' them beaus mean Tex Shipman an' all his gun-totin' breed can go hang. But no one of them will ever love yu so turrible as Tex Shipman."

"Faint heart never won fair lady, Texas Jack," she taunted.

Then followed a sudden low thump, a convulsive wrestling, and the soft sound of a kiss.

"Oh!—Don't—yu—yu——"

"I *told* yu," he whispered passionately. "I warned yu. . . . An' now I'll get even. I swore once thet if yu didn't quit callin' me Texas Jack I'd make yu call me Jack darlin'. An' I'm shore goin' to."

"Yu *air* not," flashed Reddie, with heat. But she was frightened.

"I shore am."

"If yu try thet again I—I'll scream."

"I'll bet yu won't. I'll risk it, anyway."

"Texas, yu're hurtin' me, yu big brute. . . . Don't press me down so hard. . . . Yore hands. . . . Ah-h!"

"There!—Now say Jack darlin'—or I'll kiss you again."

"I—won't—I won't—I——"

A tense interval elapsed significant with faint straining sounds.

"Wal, I had to take two—then. . . . My Gawd! I'm ruined! . . . I never knowed what a kiss was. . . . Now yu can hold off saying Jack darlin' as long as yu want."

Evidently she fought fiercely for a moment, to judge by the commotion, then she gasped and gave up.

"Please, Tex. . . . This is no way to treat a girl. . . . Oh! . . ."

"I can do thet all night," replied Texas, his full whisper poignant and rich. "Air yu goin' to say Jack darlin'?"

"But, man, thet won't mean nothin'!" she exclaimed wildly.

"Very wal." And he kissed her again and again. Brite heard the slight, sibilant, thrilling contacts of lips, and he was living this romance with them both.

"Oh—yes—yes—I give—in," she found voice to say. "Let me—breathe!"

"Not till yu say it. Pronto now, unless——"

"Devil! . . . Jack—dar-lin'!"

"Thanks, Reddie. An' heah's for givin' in! . . . Next time yu'll ask *me*."

Evidently he released her and sat up, breathing hard.

"I'm sorry to offend yu. Yet I'm glad, too," he said, no longer in a whisper. "'Cause yu're oot of a pore trail driver's reach now, Miss Reddie Bayne Brite. Yu been kissed an' yu called me darlin'. Thet'll have to do me all my life."

He stood up. His tall, dark form crossed the pale starlight glow under the trees.

"But I didn't mean it—Texas Jack!" she ended, in a whisper that was not comprehensible to Brite. Manifestly it was no more comprehensible to Texas, and vastly provocative, for he rushed away like the wind into the darkness.

After he had gone Reddie sighed and sighed, and rolled restlessly in her bed, and murmured to herself. Then she quieted down. Brite knew when she dropped to sleep again. The moan of the river and lament of the coyotes and the song of insects once again became unbroken. He lay there amused and stirred at the eternal feminine that had so easily cropped out in Reddie Bayne. She might be a waif, used to male attire for years, and accustomed to the uncouth and rough life of the range, but she had a woman's heart, a woman's subtlety and secretiveness. Brite could not tell now whether she was in love with Shipman or not. He was sure of one thing, however, and that was that she would make Texas the most wretched cowboy on all the plains before she capitulated.

At last Brite slept. Call to breakfast awakened him. San Sabe, Whit, and Less Holden were sitting cross-legged on the ground, eating. Reddie was gone and her bed had been rolled, and was now leaning on the hub of the front wagon-wheel.

The morning was fine, but the cowboys appeared oblivious to that. While Brite ate Reddie rode in bareback, driving some fresh mounts.

"Boys, where's the trail from heah?" queried Brite, remembering the drive had crossed the river above the town.

"Deuce said aboot four below," replied Holden. "Fact is, it come across where Ben haided the cattle. An' Mr. Brite, it's shore interestin' to know Deuce forgot to tell us aboot the boat."

"Boat?" echoed the boss.

"Yes. He seen a boat across the river, on the town side. An' he an' Tex reckon whoever stole our cattle came over in thet boat an' swum their hawses."

Brite felt an eagerness to be on the move again. He had resigned himself to a loss of half his herd; nevertheless, the deal rankled in him, and no doubt would grow into a bitter defeat. It was one thing to decide upon a wise and reasonable course after being robbed, and an entirely different one to follow it. These cowboys would obey orders, but they would never accept such a loss. Texas Joe and Pan Handle were the wrong men to rob.

By sun-up the drivers were on the trail again, with the cattle stepping along around two miles an hour. Moze had caught up and had stopped to let his horses graze.

That day passed without any of the drivers catching a glimpse of the half of the herd which had been driven on ahead.

"Wal, if I know cow tracks, thet ootfit lost instead of gained on us last night," said Texas. "They cain't drive a herd. Funny thing, boys. Yu know we had aboot all the mean old mossy-horns in thet back half. An' Ross Hite had the bad luck to get them. Pan's got the deal straight. The d—— stampeder will do our work for us an' get shot full of holes for his pains."

Camp had lost its jollity. A different spirit prevailed. These drivers reacted visibly to betrayal by two of their number, to the death of the traitor, to the ordeal of the flood, and Chandler's fate. Loss of half their herd had made them grim and stern. Excepting Texas Joe, who had changed most overnight, they all lent a hand to Reddie wherever possible, but the fun, the sentiment, the approach to love-making, had vanished. Texas had scarcely ever a word for Reddie, or anybody else. Instinctively they all began to save themselves, as if what had happened was little compared with what was to come.

But Round Top and Brushy Creek camps, and Cornhill, Noland Creek, Loon River, Bosque River, were reached and passed with only minor mishaps. Once from a swell of the vast prairie, which had taken them all day to surmount, San

Sabe pointed out the stolen half of Brite's herd, only a long day ahead. They knew for a certainty now that Ross Hite was driving those cattle. At Belton, a little ranch settlement on Noland Creek, Hite had left behind enough to identify him.

Rains had been few and far between, but enough to keep the creeks fresh and the water holes from drying up. Much anticipation attended their arrival at the great Brazos River. Here Brite expected another flood and strenuous crossing, but was agreeably disappointed. The Brazos had been up recently, but now offered no obstacle. They camped on the north shore, where a fine creek came in, and struck again, for the first time in days, an abundance of game. Turkeys and deer were so tame they scarcely moved out of the way of horse or man. The young turkeys were now the size of a hen chicken, and made a most toothsome dish.

Brite calculated that at this rate of travel they would drive the distance in ninety days. A third of that time had passed, and more. But he had lost track of the date. Four more days brought them half-way to Fort Worth from the Brazos; and it was noticeable that the drivers began to respond to the absence of the evil that had dogged their trail.

Fort Worth at last! It might have been a metropolis for the importance it held for the drivers. But there were only a few buildings, a store and saloon, and not many inhabitants. Texas Joe bedded down the herd outside the town, wholly unaware that the other half of Brite's cattle were not far away this night. That news was brought to camp by San Sabe, who was the only one of the four boys sober enough to tell anything straight. That was some time before midnight. In the morning Texas Joe hauled these recalcitrants out for what Brite anticipated would be dire punishment.

"Fellars, yu laid down on me last night," said Texas soberly, with not a trace of rancour. "Yu got drunk. If yu hadn't an' had rustled back heah pronto with this news aboot our cattle—why, we'd all sneaked over while Hite's ootfit was in town, an' drove 'em back. I found oot this mawnin' thet Hite drove away early in the evenin'. He got wind of us."

All the cowboys, one of whom was Less Holden, showed shame and consternation at their delinquency.

"Wal, it's too late now for this chance," went on Texas. "But I'm askin' yu to let this be the last till we get to Dodge. There we can get awful drunk. I shore wanted some drinks. I'd like to forget, same as yu. When we cross Red River, then we'll have hell. Them infernal lightnin' storms thet play bob with cattle. An' the buffalo. We'll shore meet up with them. So, even if we miss the Comanches, we'll shore have hell enough."

"Tex, we won't take another drink till the drive's over," announced Ackerman. "I promise yu. I'll cowhide any fellar who tries to break thet."

"Fine, Deuce. I couldn't ask no more," replied Texas, satisfied.

Before the drivers broke camp that morning a company of soldiers passed, and a sergeant halted for a chat with Brite. Disturbing information was elicited from this soldier. The detachment was under Lieutenant Coleman of the Fourth Cavalry, and was on the way to Fort Richardson, where a massacre of settlers had been perpetrated by Comanches not long before. Comanches and Kiowas were on the warpath again and raiding all the wide territory between the Brazos and Red Rivers. Buffalo herds were to be encountered frequently south of the Red, and north of it, according to Coleman, were packed almost solid clear to the Canadian River. Beef and hide hunters, rustlers and horse thieves, were also following the buffalo.

"Lieutenant Coleman advises you stay at the fort for a while," concluded the sergeant. "There's only one herd ahead of yours. An' that outfit wouldn't listen to reason."

"Ross Hite's ootfit?"

"Didn't get the name. Tall sandy-complexioned Texan with deep slopin' lines in his face an' narrow eyes."

"Thet's Hite," confirmed Pan Handle.

"He'll run plump into everything this range can dig up. You'd better hold up for a spell."

"Impossible, Sergeant," replied Brite. "There air two big herds right behind us. One an' two days. An' then six days or so more there's no end of them. Two hundred thousand haid of stock will pass heah this summer."

"My word! Is it possible? Well, a good many of them will never get to Kansas. . . . Good-bye and good luck."

"Same to yu," called Texas, and then turned to his outfit with fire in his eyes. "Yu all heahed, so there's nothin' to say. We'll go through shootin'. Boss, I reckon we'd better load up with all the grub an' ammunition we can pack. No store till we get to Doan's, an' they're always oot of everythin'."

Brite's outfit of drivers went on, prepared for the worst. And again they had days of uneventful driving. At Bolivar, a buffalo camp, the Chisholm Trail split, the right fork heading straight north to Abilene, and the left cutting sharply to the northwest. The Abilene branch was the longer and safer; the Dodge branch was shorter, harder and more hazardous, but ended in the most profitable market for cattle and horses.

"Brite, do yu reckon yu can find oot which fork Hite took? A coupla drinks will do it. Shore this ootfit heah might be just as bad as Hite's. All the rustlers an' hawse thieves call themselves hide-hunters."

"Yu go, Tex. I'll lend yu my flask," replied the boss.

"All right. Come with me, Pan Handle," replied Texas.

"Let me go, too," spoke up Reddie.

"What!—Why yu want to go?"

"I'd like to see somebody. I'm tired of all yu cross men."

"Ahuh. Yu want to meet some new men? Wal, it's nix on thet. The Brite ootfit wants to hang on to yu, seein' we done it so far."

The afternoon was not far spent and camp had been selected on a stream that ran on into Bolivar, some little distance east. There was a beautiful big swale for the stock to graze on without strict guarding. It was the second best site so far on the drive. The stream was lined with trees that hid the camp from the little settlement. Brite proposed to Reddie that they go fishing. This brought smiles to the girl's discontented face. Whereupon Brite procured fishing lines and hooks from his bag, and cutting poles, proceeded to rig them while Moze was instructed to get grubs, worms, or grasshoppers for bait.

Then followed a happy and a successful hour for Brite. Reddie was a novice, but wildly enthusiastic and excruciatingly funny. The climax of this little adventure came when Reddie hooked a heavy catfish which not only could she not hold, but that was surely pulling her down the bank on the stout line and pole. She was thoroughbred enough not to let go, but she yelled lustily for help. It was one of Brite's rules never to aid a fisherman; in this instance, however, he broke it and helped Reddie hold the big fish until it became exhausted. They landed it, and adding it to their already respectable string, hurried back to camp in triumph. Moze was delighted. "I sho's glad of dis. Yu-all beat the niggahs fishin'. Mebbe a change from dat meat will be good."

Before supper was ready Texas Joe and Pan Handle returned, to Brite's great relief.

"Wal, boss, Hite took the Dodge trail yestiddy aboot noonday," said Texas cheerfully. "He's ahaid of us right smart, but accordin' to them buff hunters he'll be stuck in no time."

"Wal, thet's good news, I guess," replied Brite dubiously. "What yu mean— stuck?"

"Wal, if nuthin' else stops Hite the buffalo shore will."

"Then they'll stop us, too."

"We don't give a damn so long's we get our cattle back. Thet Hite deal shore went against the grain for me."

"A rest wouldn't hurt us none," rejoined Brite.

"Reckon this'll be the last peaceful rest in camp we'll get," drawled Texas. Then he espied Moze cleaning the fish. "Dog-gone! Where'd yu get them?"

"Miss Reddie an' the boss snaked them oot of de crick dere."

"Did yu ketch any?" Texas asked Reddie.

"Shore. I got three—an' thet big one."

"No! Yu never pulled thet oot."

"I had to have help. Took us both. Gee! it was fun. Thet darn catfish nearly pulled me in. I yelled an' yelled for Mr. Brite. But he only laughed an' never came till I was shore slidin' in."

"Ahuh. You like to fish?"

"Like it. I *love* it. Nobody ever took me before. Oh, I've missed so much. But I'll learn or die."

Texas Joe nodded his head gloomily over what seemed a fatalistic, inevitable fact.

"Who ever heahed of a girl lovin' to fish? Dog-gone yu, Reddie Bayne, yu're just the natural undoin' of Tex Shipman. Of all things I love in this turrible Texas it's to set in the shade along the bank of a creek an' fish, an' listen to the birds an' all, an' watch the minnows, an'—an'——"

"Gosh! Mr. Brite, our Texas Jack is a poet," burst out Reddie gleefully.

There were indications, for a moment, of a cessation of hostilities between Reddie and Texas. They looked at each other with absorbing eyes.

"Tex, I thought yu'd stopped her Texas Jackin' yu," drawled Brite, with a sly glance at Reddie. She blushed for the first time in many days.

"Reckoned I had. Wal, I'll have to see aboot it," replied Texas, leaving no doubt in Reddie's mind what he meant. Wherefore the truce was ended.

Toward the close of their supper two strangers approached in the dusk. Texas greeted them, thereby relieving Brite's concern. The visitors proved to be hide-hunters stationed at Bolivar.

"We been lookin' over yore herd," announced the taller of the two, undoubtedly a Texan. "An' we want to inform yu thet Hite's cattle wore two of yore brands."

"No news to us. But yore tellin' us makes a difference. Much obliged. It happened this way," rejoined Texas, and related the circumstances of the fording of the Colorado and loss of half the herd.

"Then yu needn't be told no more aboot Ross Hite?" queried the hide-hunter, in a dry tone.

"Nope. Nary no more."

"Wal, thet's good. Now heah's what Pete an' me come over to propose. We want to move our ootfit up somewheres between the Little Wichita an' the Red, whar we heah thar's a million buffs. An' we'd like to go with yu thet fer."

Texas turned to interrogate his boss with a keen look.

"Men, thet depends upon Shipman," returned Brite. "We shore could use more hands, if it comes to a mess of any kind."

"Wal, I'd like to have yu, first rate," said Texas frankly. "But we don't know yu. How can we tell yu ain't in with Hite or have some deal of yore own?"

"Hell no, yu cain't tell," laughed the hunter. "But yu've got guns."

"Shore, an' yu might spike 'em. . . . Tell yu what I'll do, fellars." Texas proceeded leisurely to replenish the fire, so that it blazed up brightly in the gathering dusk. Standing in its glare the two visitors showed to advantage.

"Reddie, come heah," called Texas. The girl was not slow in complying. She had moved away into the shadow.

"What yu want?" she replied, slowly coming forth.

"Reddie, these two men want to throw in with us, far as the Little Wichita. If yu was Trail boss of this ootfit what would yu say?"

"Gee! give me somethin' easy," retorted Reddie, but she came readily closer, sensing an importance in the event. And certainly no two strangers ever received any sharper, shrewder survey than they got then.

"Howdy, Lady. Do yu know Texans when yu see them?" queried one quizzically.

The shorter of the two removed his sombrero to bow with all Southern politeness. The act exposed a ruddy, genial face.

"Evenin', miss. If it's left to yu I'm shore we'll pass," he said frankly.

"Texas, I've seen a heap of bad hombres, but never none thet I couldn't size up pronto. Guess it got on my mind. If I was foreman I'd be glad to have these men."

"Wal, thet was my idee," drawled Texas. "I only wanted to see what yu'd say."

"What yu got in yore ootfit?" asked Brite.

"Two wagons an' eight hawses, some hides an' grub. An' a box of needle-gun ammunition."

"Thet last may come in handy. . . . But I understood from my foreman thet there was six in yore ootfit."

"Thet's correct. But Pete an' me want to pull leather away from them, an' not answer any questions, either."

"All right. Yu're welcome. Be heah at daybreak. . . . An' say, what's yore handles?"

"Wal, my pard goes by the name of Smilin' Pete. An' mine's Hash Williams. Much obliged for lettin' us throw in with you. Good night. See yu in the mawnin'."

When they left, considerable speculation was indulged in by some of the drivers. Pan Handle settled the argument by claiming he would not be afraid to sleep without his guns that night. The guard changed early, leaving Brite, Reddie, and Texas in camp, the very first time that combination had been effected.

For once Texas stayed in camp beside the fire, and appeared more than amenable. He and Brite discussed the proximity of Hite's outfit and the certainty that a clash would intervene before they reached the Canadian. However, when the conversation drifted to the late Indian depredations Reddie vigorously rebelled.

"Cain't yu talk aboot somethin' else?" she demanded. "I always had a horror of bein' scalped."

"Wal, kid, yore red curls would shore take the eye of a Comanche buck," drawled Texas. "But yu'd never be scalped. Yu'd be taken captive to be made a squaw."

"I'd be a daid squaw, then," said Reddie, shuddering.

"Wal, to change the subject, Brite, we'll shore have a party when we get to Dodge."

"I'm in for it. What kind of a party, Tex?"

"Darn if I know. But it wants to come off quick before yu pay us hands. 'Cause then we'll soon be mighty drunk."

"Why do yu have to drink?" queried Reddie, in unconcealed disgust.

"Dog-gone! I often wondered aboot thet. I don't hanker much for likker. But after a long spell oot on the prairie, 'specially one of these turrible trail drives, I reckon it's a relief to bust oot."

"If yu had a woman, would yu go get stinkin' drunk?" queried Reddie.

"A—a woman!" blustered Texas, taken aback. "Reddie Bayne, I told yu I never mixed up with thet sort of woman, drunk or sober."

"I didn't mean a painted dance-hall woman, like Mr. Brite told me aboot. . . . I mean a—a nice woman."

"Ahuh. For instance?" went on Texas curiously, as he poked the red coals with a stick.

"Wal, for instance—one like me."

"Lawd's sake! . . . I shore couldn't imagine such a wonderful girl as *yu* carin' aboot me."

"Cain't yu answer a civil question just for sake of argument?"

"Wal, yes. If I had a nice wife yu can bet yore sweet life I'd not disgust her by gettin' stinkin' drunk."

A silence ensued. Brite smoked contentedly. He felt that these two were scarcely aware of his presence. Some fatal leaven was at work on them. Sooner or later they would rush into each other's arms, which probability had Brite's heartfelt approval. Still, he had an idea that since Reddie had refused once to accept Texas, if she ever wanted him, she would have to take the bit in her teeth.

"Thanks, Tex," replied Reddie finally. "I sort of had a hunch yu'd be thet sort."

Texas betrayed that he realized he had been paid a high tribute from this waif of the ranges. But all he said was: "Dog-gone! Did Reddie Bayne say somethin' good aboot me?"

"Tex, it's only three hours till we go on guard," spoke up Brite.

"Yu're talkin'. I'm gonna turn in right now an' heah." Whereupon Texas unrolled his bed close to the fire, threw the blankets over him so that his spurred boots stuck out, and was asleep almost as soon as he stretched out.

Reddie gazed at him a long time, then she shook her curly head and said: "No hope. . . . Dad, yu can make my bed an' roll me in it, if yu want to."

"Wal, I'll do the first, shore an' certain," replied Brite, with alacrity. And he proceeded to pack their bed-rolls in under the trees close to camp.

"Not so far away, Dad," objected Reddie. "I may be wearin' men's pants an' packing a gun, but I'm growin' all queer an' loose inside. I'm gettin' scared."

"So am I, dear," admitted Brite. "I've got some funny feelin's myself."

"We're darn lucky to have Texas an' Pan Handle with us," replied Reddie, and rolling her bed so close to Brite that she could reach out to touch him, she bade him good-night.

Next morning, two hours after the start, a dust-devil, whirling down into the herd, stampeded them. Fortunately it was toward the north. The drivers had nothing much to do save ride alongside and keep the herd bunched. They ran ten miles or more, in a rolling cloud of dust and thunder, before they slowed up. It was the first stampede for Brite that trip, and was unfavourable in that it gave the herd a predisposition to stampede again.

Texas Joe drove on until the chuck-wagon and the two hide-hunters caught up, which was late in the day.

That night at the camp fire the trail drivers compared notes. San Sabe had seen smoke columns rising above the western hills; Ackerman and Little reported buffalo in the distance; Brite thought he noted an uneasy disposition on the part of all game encountered; Reddie had sighted a bunch of wild horses; Pan Handle averred he had spotted a camp far down a wooded creek bottom.

Texas apparently had nothing to impart, until Reddie tartly said: "Wal, Hawkeye, what're yu haid of this ootfit for, if yu cain't see?"

"I wasn't goin' to tell. I shore hate to do it. . . . I seen two bunches of redskins to-day."

"No!" they chorused, starting up.

"Shore did. Both times when I was way up front, an' had first crack at the hill tops. Country gettin' rough off to the west. We're nearin' the Wichita Mountains. I shore had to peel my eyes, but I seen two bunches of Injuns, aboot two miles apart. They come oot on the hill tops. Might have been only one bunch. They was watchin' us, yu bet, an' got back oot of sight pronto."

"*Comanches!*" cried Reddie, aghast.

"I don't know, kid. But what's the difference? Comanches, Kiowas, Apaches, Cheyennes, Arapahoes, it's all the same."

"No, Tex. I'll take all the last on to pass up the Comanches."

"Men, it's nothin' to be seen by Indians," spoke up Pan Handle coolly. "From now on we'll probably see redskins every day. We'll get visits from them, an' like as not we'll get a brush with some bunch before we're through."

Smiling Pete and Hash Williams had listened quietly, as became late additions to the outfit. Whatever apprehensions Brite may have entertained toward them were rapidly disseminating. When they were asked, however, they readily added further reason for speculation. Both had seen Indian riders so near at hand that they recognized them as Comanches.

"Reckon yu've seen some Indian-fightin'?" queried Brite.

"Wal, I reckon. But not so much this spring an' summer as last. Our camp was only raided once this trip out."

Later council developed the fact that these hunters were a valuable addition to Brite's outfit. They advised that the *remuda* be kept close to camp and strongly guarded. Comanches were fond of making raids on the horses of the trail drivers. Seldom did they bother with cattle, except to kill a steer for meat when it suited them.

A couple of hours' sleep for each driver was all he got that night. The herd was pointed at dawn. This day the range land grew wilder and rougher, making travel slow. Buffalo showed in every swale and hollow; wolves and coyotes trotted the ridge tops too numerous to count. Their presence in any force attested to the proximity of the buffalo herd. That night these prairie beasts made the welkin ring with their mourns and yelps. The coyotes boldly ventured right into camp, and sometimes sat on their haunches, circling the camp fire, and yelped until driven away. But the night passed without any other untoward event.

CHAPTER TEN

Every day's travel was fraught with increasing suspense. Tracks of Indian ponies, old camp fires in the creek bottoms, smoke signals from the hill tops, and lean wild mustangs with half-naked riders vanishing like spectres in the distance—these kept the Brite contingent vigilant and worried all the way to the Little Wichita.

Ordinarily it was a small river, easily forded by stock. But now it was a raging torrent, impassable until the freshet had gone by. That might take a day or longer. A short consultation resulted in a decision to find a protected swale or valley where grass would hold the cattle and timber would afford cover for the trail drivers in case of attack.

The drivers of the herd ahead of them, presumably the one stolen by Ross Hite, could not have crossed, and no doubt had gone up the river with the same idea Texas Joe had decided upon. Buffalo were everywhere, though only in scattered bunches in the river bottom and along the grassy slopes. Up on the range it was probably black with them.

Texas sent San Sabe down the river to reconnoitre and he proceeded up the stream for a like purpose, leaving the rest of the drivers to tend to the stock.

The hour was about midday, hot and humid down in the protected valley. The stock rested after days of hard travel. All the drivers had to do was sit their horses and keep sharp lookout. Most of the attention was directed to the low brushy rims of the slopes. Texas had driven off the trail half a mile to halt in the likeliest place, which was good for the cattle, but not so good for the drivers, as they could be reached by rifle-shot from the hills. The three wagons were hauled into the thickest clump of trees. It looked like a deadlock until the river went down. Smiling Pete and Hash Williams, the hide-hunters, climbed under cover of the brush to scout from the hill tops. The trail drivers held their rifles across their saddles. Brite had two, the lighter of which he lent to Reddie. Armed to the teeth, alert and determined, the drivers awaited events.

Reddie called to Brite that she heard a horse running. Brite made signs to the closest rider and then listened intently. Indeed, Reddie's youthful ears had been right. Soon Brite caught a rhythmic beat of swift hoofs on a hard trail. It came from down-river and therefore must be San Sabe. Also Brite heard shouts from the slope. These proved to come from the hide-hunters. Pan Handle and Ackerman evidently heard, for they rode around to join more of the drivers. Then in a bunch they galloped to a point outside the grove where Brite and Reddie were stationed.

"It's San Sabe," shrilled Reddie, pointing. "Look at him ride!"

"Injuns after him, I'll bet," added Brite. "We want to be huntin' cover."

Soon they were surrounded by Pan Handle and the others. San Sabe reached them only a moment later.

"Injuns!" he shouted hoarsely, and he reined in. "But they ain't after me. They didn't see me. Haven't yu heahed the shootin'?"

No one in Brite's company had heard shots. "Wal, it's down around thet bend, farther than I reckoned. . . . I was goin' along when I heahed yellin' an' then guns. So I hid my hawse in the brush an' sneaked on foot. Come to a place where hawses had just rid up the bank oot of the river. Sand all wet. They was Injun ponies. I follered the tracks till I seen them in an open spot. Heahed more shots an' wild yells. The timber got pretty thick. Takin' to the hillside, I sneaked along under cover till I seen what the deal was. Some settlers had made camp in a shady place, no doubt waitin' to cross the river. I seen three wagons, anyhow, an' some men behind them shootin' from under. An' I seen Injun arrows flashin' like swallows, an' I heahed them hit the wagons. Then I sneaked back to my hawse an' come a-rarin'."

"Brite, we'll have to go to their assistance," replied Pan Handle grimly.

"Shore we will. Heah comes the hunters. Let's get their angle on what's best to do while we're waitin' for Tex."

The hunters came running under the trees, and reaching the drivers they confirmed San Sabe's story in a few blunt words. Whereupon Brite repeated briefly what San Sabe had told them.

"How many redskin ponies?" queried Hash Williams, in businesslike tones.

"No more'n twenty—probably less."

"How far?"

"Half mile aboot below the bend."

"Pile off, cowboy, an' draw us a map heah in the sand."

San Sabe hopped off with alacrity, and kneeling he picked up a stick and began to trace lines. In a twinkling all the drivers were off, bending over to peer down with intense interest. Brite heard a horse coming down the trail.

"Must be Tex comin' back."

"Heah's the bend in the river," San Sabe was saying. "Injun hawses trail aboot heah, aboot half a mile below. Anyway to make shore there's a big daid tree all bleached white. We can risk ridin' thet far. . . . Heah's the open spot where the redskins took to the woods. Thet's aboot even with a big crag like an eagle's haid on the rim. The wagons air not more'n a quarter below thet. On the level ground in a nice grove of trees with heavy timbered slope on three sides. The reddys air in thet cover, low down."

"Boys, halter a couple of hawses for Pete an' me. Don't take time to saddle."

"What's all the confab aboot?" queried a cool voice. Texas Joe had come up behind them to dismount, holding his bridle in one hand, rifle in the other. San Sabe gave him the facts in few words. Then Hash Williams spoke up: "Shipman, I'm takin' it yu'll go pronto to the rescue?"

"Hell yes!—Have yu any plan? Yu're used to redskins."

"We'll split, soon as we leave the hawses. Come on. We might get there too late."

San Sabe led off down the trail at a canter, followed by the drivers, except Texas, who waited a moment for the hunters to mount bareback. One mustang threatened to buck, but a sharp blow from Texas changed his mind. Soon the trio overtook the others, and then San Sabe spurred his horse into a run. Brite did not forget Reddie in the excitement. She was pale, but given over to the thrill of the adventure rather than to the peril. Brite would not have considered leaving her behind with Moze. The cavalcade rounded the river bend, stringing out, with Brite and Bender in the rear. San Sabe soon halted, and leaping off led into the timber on the right of the trail. Brite and Bender came up just as Reddie was following Texas on foot into the woods. They tied their horses in the thick brush at the foot of the slope. Heavy booms of buffalo guns, and the strange, wild staccato yells of Indians, soon sounded close.

"Comanches," said Williams grimly.

Presently San Sabe parted the bushes. "Heah's their ponies."

"Less'n twenty. Wal, they're our meat, boys," replied Hash Williams as his dark eyes surveyed the restless, ragged mustangs, the river bottom beyond, the densely wooded slope, and lastly the rugged rim, with its prominent crag standing up like a sentinel. The place was small and restricted. To Brite the slope appeared to curve below into a bluff sheer over the river.

"Shipman, keep Pete heah with yu, an' choose five men to go with me," said Williams swiftly.

"What's yore idee?" flashed Texas, his hawk eyes roving all around, then back to the hunter.

"If I can git above these red devils they're our meat," replied Williams. "Most of them will have only bows an' arrers. They'll crawl under the brush an' be low along the slope.... Strikes me there ain't enough shootin'. Hope we're not too late.... When we locate them an' let go, it's a shore bet they'll run for their hawses. Yu'll be hid heah."

"Ahuh. Thet suits me. I see where we can crawl within fifty feet of them Injun mustangs an' be wal hid.... All right. Yu take San Sabe, Ackerman, Whittaker, an' Little."

"Boys, throw off spurs an' chaps, an' follow me quiet."

In another moment the five men had disappeared and only soft steps and rustling could be heard. Texas peered keenly all around the glade where the mustangs had been left.

"Come on, an' don't make no noise," he whispered, and slipped away under the brush. Holden followed, then Smiling Pete, then Bender and Pan Handle, after which went Brite with Reddie at his heels. Shrill yells occasionally and an answered boom of a needle gun augmented the excitement. Texas led to a little higher ground, at the foot of the slope, and on the edge of the glade, where broken rock and thick brush afforded ideal cover.

"Heah we air," whispered Texas, to his panting followers. "Couldn't be better. We'll shore raise hell with them redskins. Spread along this ledge an' get where yu can see all in front. When yu see them wait till we give the word. Thet's all. Keep mighty still."

In the rustling silence that ensued Brite took care to choose a place where it was hardly possible for Reddie to be hit. He stationed her between him and Texas, behind a long, low rock over which the hackberry bushes bent. Pan Handle knelt beyond Texas with a gun in each hand. He was the only one of the party without a rifle. Bender, showing evidence of great perturbation, was being held back by Smiling Pete. Holden crawled to an even more advantageous position.

"All set. Now let 'em come," whispered Texas. "I shore hope to Gawd the other fellars get there in time. Not enough shootin' to suit me."

"It ain't begun yet or it's aboot over," replied Pan Handle. "But we couldn't do no more. Tex, heah's Reddie to think of."

"Dog-gone if I didn't forget our Reddie.... Hey, kid, air yu all right?"

"Me? Shore I am," replied Reddie.

"Scared?"

"I reckon. Feel queer. But yu can bet I'll be heah when it comes off."

"Think yu can do as yu're told once in yore life?"

"Yes. I'll obey."

"Good.... Now everybody lay low an' listen."

Brite had been in several Indian skirmishes, but never when the life of a woman had to be taken into consideration. He had to persuade himself of the fact that little peril threatened Reddie Bayne. Perhaps there were women folk with these settlers, and surely terrible danger faced them.

The Indian mustangs were haltered to the saplings at the edge of the glade. What a ragged, wild-eyed bunch! They had nothing but halters. These they strained against at every rifle-shot. And more than a few of them faced the covert where the drivers lay in ambush. They had caught a scent of the whites. Heads were pointed, ears high, nostrils quivering.

"Fellars, I smell smoke, an' not burned powder, either," said Texas Joe, presently, in a low voice. "Pete, what yu make of thet?"

"Camp fire, mebbe."

Suddenly the noonday silence broke to the boom of guns. Fast shooting, growing long drawn out, then desultory. Brite saw Texas shake his head. Next came a series of blood-curdling yells, the hideous war-cry of the Comanches. Brite had been told about this—one of the famed facts of the frontier—but he had never heard a Comanche yell till now.

"By Gawd! They've charged thet wagon train," ejaculated Pete hoarsely. "Williams mustn't hev located them."

"He can do it now," replied Texas.

Reddie lay flat, except that she held head and shoulders up, resting on her elbows. The stock of her rifle lay between them. She was quite white now and her eyes were big, dark, staring.

"Looks bad for them, Reddie," whispered Brite.

"Yu mean our men?"

"No. For whoever's corralled there."

"Oh-h! What awful yells!"

"No more shots from them needle guns!" said Pete. "Reckon we've come only at the fag end of thet massacre. Another tally for these Comanches! But our turn'll come. Williams an' his men will be on thet bunch pronto."

All at once the whoops and piercing yells were drowned in a crash of firearms.

"Ho! Ho! Listen to thet. . . . Gawd! I hope they were in time! . . . Now, men, lay low an' watch. It'll be short now. The Comanches will be comin' in a jiffy, draggin' their wounded. They won't stop to pick up their daid—not in the face of thet blast."

The shooting ceased as suddenly as it had commenced. Hoarse yells of white men took the place of the Comanche war-cry. Cracklings of dead snags came faintly to Brite's ears.

"Oh—Dad!—I heah 'em runnin'," whispered Reddie.

"Men, they're comin'," said the hunter, low and hard. "Wait now—mind yu—wait till they get out in the open!"

Swift oncoming footfalls, rustlings of the brush, snapping of twigs, all affirmed Reddie and the hunter. Brite cocked his rifle and whispered to Reddie: "Aim deliberate, Reddie. Yu want to count heah."

"I'm—gonna—kill one!" panted the girl, her eyes wild, as she cocked her rifle and raised to one knee while she thrust the barrel over the rock.

"Reddie, after yu paste one be shore to duck," advised Texas, who must have had eyes in the back of his head. "Pan, look! I see 'em comin' hell-bent."

"Shore. An' some way far back in the woods. They're draggin' cripples. Don't shoot, men, till they're all oot."

Brite gripped his rifle and attended to the far side of the glade and the shadowy forms under the trees. The foremost ones flitted from tree to tree, hiding, peering back. Lean, bronze devils—how wild they seemed! Four or five flashed into plain sight, then disappeared again. Swift footfalls, soft as those of a panther, sounded quite a little closer to the ambushers. Brite espied a naked savage stepping forward, his dark face turned over his shoulder, his long, black hair flying with his swift movements. Reddie's gasp proved that she saw him, too. Then farther down the edge of the woods other Indians emerged into the sunlight. Two carried rifles, most of them had bows, but Brite saw no arrows. They made for the mustangs, peering back, making signs to others coming, uttering low, guttural calls. In a moment more, when several bucks had mounted their ponies, four or five couples emerged from the woods, dragging and supporting wounded comrades.

A warrior let out a screeching cry. No doubt he had seen or heard something of the ambushers. Next instant Reddie had fired at the nearest Comanche, halfway across the glade, facing back from the direction he had come. He let out a mortal yell of agony and stumbled backward, step after step, his dark face like a ghastly mask of death, until he fell. Simultaneously then with fierce shouts the ambushers began to fire. The shots blended in a roar. Brite downed the Comanche he aimed at, then strove to pick out among the falling, leaping, plunging Indians another to shoot at. Out of the tail of his eye he saw Pan Handle flip one gun out, aim and shoot, and then the other, alternately. He was swift yet deliberate. No doubt every bullet he sent found its mark. The wounded and terrorized mustangs tore away their halters, and scattered in every direction. The firing thinning out, then ceased, after which there followed a dreadful silence.

"Reckon thet's aboot all," drawled Texas Joe, with a little cold laugh. "Load up quick. All down an' most daid."

"Thet first buck who yelled got away," replied Pete. "I missed him. But I didn't see no more. We shore dropped them pronto. I know I only bored one. Yu must have some daid shots in this outfit."

"One I know of, anyway."

"Let's charge 'em, an' baste the cripples," said the hunter, and he plunged up to burst out of the brush. Texas and Pan Handle followed, as evidently had Holden and Bender. Brite lay a restraining hand upon the agitated girl, who appeared about to rush after the others.

"Yu stay heah, lass," he said. "It's all over so far as we're concerned. An' there'll be a mess oot there."

"Oh-h!" cried Reddie, breathing hard. She pushed the rifle before her and sank face down on the stone, beginning to shake like a leaf in the wind.

"Reddie, yu shore conducted yoreself in a way to make me proud," said Brite, patting her shoulder. "Don't give way now."

"Listen!—Oh, that's terrible."

The drivers were cracking the skulls of the crippled Comanches, accompanying every whack from a rifle butt with a demon-like yell. Brite did not look in that direction. He heard halloes from the vicinity of the wagons and also answers from Texas' men.

"Come, Reddie, let's get oot in the open," suggested Brite, dragging at her. "But we won't go near thet shambles."

She picked up her rifle and followed him out into the glade. A curtain of smoke was drifting away. It disclosed the first victim of the ambush—the Comanche who had backed away from the grove, to fall at Reddie's shot.

Texas Joe stalked back toward them, bareheaded, his hair disheveled, and halted beside the prostrate Comanche.

"Boss, yu didn't plug this buck," he asserted.

"Shore I did."

"Yu're a liar. Thet gun yu had is a needle gun. It was Reddie who done it. . . . Dog-gone! Right plumb through his middle!" He came up to them, hard-faced and tremendously forceful, his slits of amber eyes upon Reddie.

"Wal, yu opened the bawl pronto," he said.

"Texas, I—I couldn't wait. I had to shoot thet Indian," she faltered.

"Wal, Miss Bayne, allow me to congratulate yu on bein' a real shore-enough Texas pioneer's daughter."

"I—I feel like a murderer. But I'm not sorry. How cruel they looked—like lean, bloody wolves."

"Boss, if I go to ranchin' soon, I'd like a wife after Reddie's breed," concluded Texas, with a little satire in his flattery.

"Tex, heah comes Williams an' our boys," shouted someone.

The hunter could be seen approaching hurriedly, yet warily, with several men at his heels.

"Hash, only one got away," called Smiling Pete. "We done 'em up quick an' brown."

"Good! But we was too late. —— our souls!" boomed the hunter stridently. "Come along heah back with us."

Texas Joe and the others rushed after Williams, who had turned to follow the drivers with him. Brite and Reddie fell behind. The strip of woodland grew more open until it let sunshine into a little park where a camp had been established. Three wagons had been lined up to enclose a triangular space. The wheels had been barricaded in places with packs and beds. Indian arrows stuck out with ominous significance. In the foreground lay a white man on his face. An arrow head protruded from his back. His scalp had been half torn off.

"Pete, we slipped up as fast as we could," Williams was explaining. "But too late. I reckon we was in only at the finish."

Brite bade Reddie remain behind while he followed the hunters. He had seen gruesome sights before, yet it was a shock to renew such experiences. Williams dragged two dead men from under the wagons, and then a third who was still alive. Evidently he had been shot, for no arrow showed in him. They tore open his shirt and found a bad wound high up, just about missing the lung. The bullet had gone clear through.

"Reckon this fellar will live," said Williams practically. "One of yu tie a scarf tight over this hole an' under his arm. . . . Search everywhar, fellars. This has been a pretty long scrap. Yu see the blood has dried on thet man."

"I know I seen a girl just as we bust loose on 'em," said Ackerman, sweaty and grimy, his face working. "There was two redskins chasin' her. I crippled one. Seen him go down an' crawl. Then the other grabbed him into the brush."

"Heah's a daid woman," called Texas Joe, from the back of the third wagon. His comrades hurried to confirm this statement. Brite shuddered to see a woman, half stripped, hanging scalpless and gory half out of the wagon.

"Thet's not the girl I seen," shouted Ackerman. "I swear it, men. She was runnin'. She had light hair. She wore a plaid skirt."

"Wal, spread out, some of yu, an' search," ordered Texas Joe.

"Three daid men, one daid woman, this heah man thet's still alive," Hash Williams was counting. "Thet makes five. An' the girl yore cowboy swears he seen—thet makes six. There may be more. 'Cause when we cut loose on the red devils it'd be natural for anyone alive to run, if he was able."

Deuce Ackerman went rushing around in a frenzy, calling aloud: "Come oot, girl, wherever yu air. Yu're saved."

But neither the wagons, nor the brush, nor the clumps of trees rewarded their hasty search. Deuce strode to the river bank, which was not far away, and thickly covered by willows. Here he called again. Suddenly he gave a wild shout and leaped off the bank out of sight. Texas Joe and other drivers ran in that direction. Before they could reach the bank Deuce appeared, half supporting a light-haired girl. They all ran then to meet Deuce, and Reddie flew after them.

"There, little lady, don't be scared," Ackerman was saying as he halted with the girl. "We're friends. We've killed the Indians. Yu're all right."

He helped her to a log, where she sank down, and her head fell against his shoulder. She appeared to be about sixteen years old. Wide horror-stricken blue eyes gazed at the men. Freckles shone on her deathly white face.

"Lass, air yu hurted?" queried Williams anxiously.

"I don't—know. . . . I guess—not," she answered faintly.

"How many in yore party?"

"Six," she whispered.

"There's one man alive. He has a black beard. Reckon he'll live."

"My father!—Oh, thank God!"

"What's yore name?"

"Ann Hardy. My father is—John Hardy. We were on oor way to Fort Sill—to join a wagon-train there. . . . The Indians had attacked us—for days—then left us. . . . We had to stop—on account of the high water. . . . They came back to-day."

"Is the woman yore mother?"

"No, sir."

"Wal, that's all now," concluded Williams. "Men, we better not lose any time gettin' this girl an' her father up to our camp. Some of yu rustle now. Take the girl. I'll stay with Pete, an', say, three more of yu. We'll do what we can for Hardy an' fetch him along. Then if all's well we can come back heah, bury the daid, an' look over this ootfit."

"I'll put her on my hawse," said Ackerman. "Come, Miss Hardy.... Lean on me."

"You saved my life," she replied, and fixed strained eyes upon him. "I was just—about to jump into the river."

"All's wal thet ends wal," rejoined Deuce, with a nervous little laugh. "You an' yore dad air lucky, I'll tell you.... Come. We have a girl in our ootfit. Heah she is.... Reddie Bayne"

"Oh, yu poor dear!" cried Reddie, putting her arm around the girl. "But yu're safe now with us. This is Brite's ootfit. An' there's some hard fighters an' gunmen in it. Texas Jack an' Pan Handle Smith an' Deuce Ackerman heah. All bad hombres, lady, but shore good to have around when stampeders an' redskins come."

Deuce and Reddie led the girl up the trail, followed by Brite, Texas Joe, and the other drivers who were not going to stay with Williams. The trail ran between the river and the spot where the Comanches had met their doom. Texas and Holden forged ahead to get the horses. Deuce put the girl up on his saddle and mounted behind her. In a few minutes after that they reached a familiar grove of trees. But Brite did not recognize it.

"Wal, I'll be——!" vociferated Texas Joe, suddenly halting. To curse so formidably under the circumstances could mean only disaster.

"What ails yu, Tex?"

"Look about yu, boss. Heah's camp an' our chuck-wagon. But where's Moze— an' where's our hawses an' cattle?"

"*Gone!*" screamed Reddie.

CHAPTER ELEVEN

Bᴿɪᴛᴇ scratched his stubby chin. His two thousand odd cattle, less than half the original number he started with, had disappeared as if by magic.

"Wal, I'm not surprised," snorted Texas. "Boss, when I rode back from up-river awhile ago, San Sabe had just come in holler-in' Injuns. So I had no time to tell yu thet Ross Hite's ootfit was up there with the other half of yore herd."

"Damnation!" swore Brite. "Did they have the nerve to steal the rest of them? Right under our eyes!"

"Mebbe not. Long-horns air queer brutes. They might have just sloped off an' then again they might have stampeded. Shore they didn't come down-river."

"Where's Moze?"

"Heah, yu Alabama coon!" yelled Texas.

"I'se heah, boss," came from the thick clump of trees, high up among the branches. "Heah I is."

Presently they heard his feet thud on the soft turf and soon he appeared, shuffling toward them at a great rate.

"Moze, what's become of our cattle?" demanded Brite.

"I dunno, suh. Jest after yu-all left I seen some riders comin' down the ribber. An' dis chile perambulated up de tree. Pretty soon I heahed them close, an' I seen dat long lean Hite man. I sho did. They dess rode behind de cattle an' chased dem at a run up de ribber. An' dey missed our hawses."

"Ahuh. Now, boss, we have no more trouble atall," drawled Texas. "Pile off an' soon as the rest of our ootfit gets heah we'll put our haids together."

"Moze, we've got a visitor, Miss Hardy," announced Ackerman, as he leaped off to help the girl down. "All her ootfit except her dad got killed by the Comanches."

"Yu may as wal start a fire, Moze," added Texas. "We're stuck heah for I don't know how long. Heat water, get oot some clean bandages. We'll have a cripple heah pronto."

"Lawd, but dis Chissum Trail is waxin' hot," exploded Moze, showing the whites of his eyes.

Deuce unrolled a bed for the Hardy girl, and he and Reddie made her comfortable in the shade. Brite had the same thought he divined was passing in Reddie's mind—that the Uvalde cowboy had been shot through the heart by something vastly different from a bullet.

The girl was more than pretty, now that the ghastliness was fading from her face and the horror from her eyes. She was about medium height, slender, but strong and well-rounded of form. Reddie sat beside her and held her hand while Deuce made a show of serious attention.

"Shut yore eyes an' don't think," advised Reddie. "Let our men folks do thet."

Brite's survey of Texas, Pan Handle, and the others convinced him that never before had they cudgelled their brains so fiercely. Moreover, they were silent. Brite paced to and fro, under the trees, doing his own thinking. It was inconceivable that Ross Hite should ultimately succeed in this second outrage. The fight that had been deferred must now be hastened. A grave risk for the two girls! Brite was in a quandary whether to permit it or not. But he reasoned that men of the stamp of Texas Joe and Pan Handle could not be held back any longer. The two hide-hunters had materially added to the strength of the outfit. Hite, now encumbered by all the cattle, was in a tight hole.

"Wal, they must have been drunk," declared Texas suddenly.

"Who?" queried one of the drivers.

"Hite's ootfit. Onless they got a lot more hands then they had when Wallen braced us, they're just committin' suicide."

"Tex, would it do for me to scout up the river? On foot, of course, an' keepin' to cover?" asked San Sabe.

"Wal, no. Thet idee come to me. But it's no good. We're shore Hite drove the cattle an' they cain't be far. He cain't cross the river anyway neah heah."

"So far so good. What're we gonna do?"

"Dam' if I know, San," replied Texas gloomily. "We're saddled with two girls now, an' a crippled man, besides. Mebbe thet Hash Williams will have an idee. He 'pears to be an old-timer."

Texas walked out a few rods to look down the river. "They're comin'," he announced, with satisfaction. "Now we'll soon see where we air."

While still some distance from camp, Williams, evidently missing the cattle, came on at a gallop.

"Whar's our long-horns?" he roared.

"Hite drove them off while we was fightin' the Comanches," replied Texas.

"Whole hawg or none, huh? I'd a-reckoned he'd be smarter than to do thet."

"Williams, is it better or wuss for us?"

"Two times better, easy," declared the hunter. "I jest wonder what led to thet trick. Sort of stumps me."

"What'll we do?"

"Wal, we'll talk it over," returned Williams, dismounting. "But sight unseen I'd say let Hite go with the cattle. Foller him across the Red, anyway. He cain't dodge us. He cain't sell the stock. He cain't make a deal with the Injuns, for he couldn't get nothin' from them. An' they won't drive cattle."

Presently the approaching horsemen reached camp, two of them supporting the wounded settler, Hardy. He was conscious, but unable to sit up. They lifted him off the horse and carried him to a place beside his daughter.

"Oh, Daddy, say yu're not bad hurt," she cried.

"I'm all—right—Ann, so they tell me," he replied weakly.

"Dig up some whisky an' fix him a bed," ordered Texas.

"Brite, what'll we do aboot them wagons? I reckon we ought to take one of them an' a load of supplies. We seen two hawses, anyway. We could haul Hardy an' his girl as far as Doan's store. What yu say?"

"I say yes, of course. Send two men back to fetch one wagon an' a load. We can cross this river with wagons as soon as the cattle can."

"Thet'll be to-morrer. River's goin' down fast. An' we'll camp right heah to-night. Thet'll give us time to bury them poor folks."

"Williams, don't yu reckon Hite will ambush the trail, thinkin' we'll be fools enough to chase him?" asked Texas.

"He'll do thet, shore. We ain't goin' to chase him. Mister Hite stole our herd too quick. We'll let him look oot for them an' we'll look oot for ourselves."

"Would yu advise me to scout up the river?"

"No, I wouldn't. But yu might send thet little chap, Sabe," replied Williams. "Heah, cowboy, yu climb the hill, keepin' oot of sight all the time. Work along the rim an' see if yu can locate thet ootfit. An' come to think of it, Shipman, let's hold off on sendin' anyone down after thet wagon ontil Sabe gets back with his report."

Pan Handle sat apart, cleaning his guns. They glinted in the sunlight like polished steel. The gunman appeared absorbed in his task. His brow was corded and dark, the line of his cheek tight and grey. Brite calculated for a certainty that Smith had done away with half the bunch of Comanches. He gathered solace from that and pondered on the doubtful future of one Ross Hite.

Reddie and Ackerman were trying to induce Ann to drink something. Texas sat idle, his narrow eyes upon Reddie. Moze was busy about the fire. Williams and Smiling Pete were dressing Hardy's wound. The other drivers were resting and whispering together. San Sabe had vanished in the brush on the slope, where he made no more noise than a bird.

Brite sought a seat himself. The exertion and excitement had tired him out. He pondered upon the day and gave thanks to God for having been spared the catastrophe which had befallen Hardy's outfit. What a common thing such massacres had come to be! Wagon-trains without scouts or Indian-hunters or a large force for defence fell easy prey to these marauding bands of savages. He thought of rumours he had heard at Fort Dodge last trip. Santana, a chief of Kiowas, and a merciless fiend, had been reported to be in league with a band of white desperadoes whose speciality was to seek and waylay small caravans, and massacre every man, woman, and child, steal horses and supplies, and make away with the wagons so that not a single vestige of the caravan was ever discovered or heard of again.

Such terrible things seemed no longer incredible. Hundreds of wagon-trains crossed the plains; thousands of trail drivers rode up the vast stretches of Texas. And if a few were lost the tragedy scarcely came home to the many. But Brite saw it now. If he got out of this drive with his life, and this dear child he had adopted, he would let well enough alone. Yet how peaceful, even pastoral, that valley scene! The river glided on yellow as corn; the summer breeze waved the grass and willows; flowers bloomed along the banks and birds sang; the sky spread a blue canopy overhead, accentuated by white cloud-sails. Across the river, on the high bluff, a huge buffalo bull came out to stand gazing, silhouetted black against the sky, magnificently wild in aspect, and symbolic of that nature dominant for the hour.

Hours passed. Still San Sabe did not return. Toward sunset Williams deemed it advisable to get Hardy's wagon, horses, personal effects, and supplies up to Brite's camp before night. To this end he went himself, taking two men.

San Sabe hailed them from the bluff just as Moze called the outfit to supper. His call evidently was only to assure them of his safety, a fact Brite gave audible thanks for. He could not afford to lose any more drivers. In due time San Sabe burst out of the brush to approach the expectant group. His garb attested to rough work in this brush and his dark face was caked with sweat and dust.

"Had to haid a lot of canyons," he explained. "Thet accounts for me takin' so long. . . . Hite is drivin' the cattle, all one big herd again, up the river. He——"

"How far's he got?" interrupted Texas.

"Aboot five miles from heah."

"Did yu get near enough to count his ootfit?"

"Shore. Seven drivers with the herd. An' one with their hawses. They're shy of saddle hawses. I counted six pack animals."

"Travellin' light. No chuck-wagon. San, don't yu reckon they'll bed down thet herd pronto?"

"Lawd only knows. What does Hite care aboot cattle? He'll lose ten per cent, withoot accidents."

"He'll lose more'n thet," replied Texas thoughtfully. "Boss, what yu say to havin' the ootfit somewhere close when Hite drives that herd into the river?"

"I say I'd like it," returned Brite emphatically.

"Wal, we all would. We'll plan to move pronto. But not go against Williams' advice, if he says not."

"Tex, I've got confidence in thet buffalo-hunter, too."

"We all have. He's a real Texan. I'm ashamed I didn't see thet right off. But Texas Joe ain't himself these days. . . . Finish yore supper, boys, an' girls, too. Gee! We got another beauty in the ootfit."

Ann heard this from her seat under the tree, where Reddie was persuading her to eat, and she blushed prettily.

"Don't pay no attention to these trail drivers, Ann," said Reddie, quite seriously and loud enough for all to hear. "Thet is, when they're talkin' sweet. They're shore a fine fightin' bunch thet yu feel safe with. But don't let any of them get around yu."

"Aw, Reddie, thet's not kind of yu," expostulated Deuce, quite offended.

"Wal, Ann, to be honest, Deuce Ackerman—he's the boy who saved yore life—he's the best of a bad ootfit. But thet soft-voiced Whittaker with his sheep's eyes—look oot for him. An' the handsome one—he's never to be trusted."

"But there appear to be several handsome ones," replied Ann, with a hint of roguishness that showed she would be dangerous under happy circumstances.

This reply fetched the first hearty laugh for many long hours. They were young and easily stirred to pleasure. Brite laughed with them. Watching Reddie, he discerned that she had more up her sleeve.

"Shore, Ann. Our boys air all nice-lookin', an' some of them air what yu could call handsome. But I meant particular thet tall one, with the wide shoulders an' small hips—thet tawny-haided, amber-eyed devil who limps when he walks."

A shout greeted this elaborate description of Texas Joe. He did not participate in it. Blushing like a girl, he rose to doff his sombrero and make a low bow.

"Thanks, Miss Bayne. Thet's shore the first time this whole trip yu done me justice." Then with another bow, this time to Ann, he added: "Miss Hardy, there's folks who could tell yu thet the lead bullet in my laig was received in the interest of a young lady 'most as pretty as yu. An' the hombre who shot it there got mine in his haid."

Ann looked mightily impressed and embarrassed; Reddie dropped her eyes, defeated; while the riders grew silent. Texas had taken offence. Brite eased the situation by ordering Moze to hurry at his tasks and pack up ready to start at a moment's notice.

"Fetch in the team, somebody. An' round up the *remuda*. Tex, I reckon Williams will think of packin' the new wagon so Hardy can ride comfortable. An' the girl can ride on the front seat. Who'll volunteer to drive thet wagon?"

"I will," flashed Deuce Ackerman, before the other boys could get in their vociferations.

Here Texas Joe interposed, cool and authoritative, his sombrero pulled well down. Perhaps only Brite saw the michievousness in his eyes.

"Deuce, if yu don't mind, I'll drive thet wagon. Yu see, we haven't any herd to point."

"But, Tex, yu cain't drive a team," burst out Deuce, almost in a wail.

"I cain't?"

"Yu told me so. Wal, I've drove teams all my life, since I was thet high. Besides, I'm not so—so darn well, an' I'm saddle sore, an' off my feed—an'——"

"My Gawd! Deuce, yu need a doctor!" ejaculated Texas solicitously. "I hadn't seen how seedy yu look till now. Shore yu can drive the Hardy wagon."

This effected a remarkable transformation in Deuce. He grew radiant. The boys gazed at him in slow-dawning realization at his perfidy.

"Miss Ann, air yu able to ride hawseback?" asked Texas.

"Oh yes—I can ride anything," she replied earnestly. "Really, Mister Texas, I'm not hurt or sick. I'm getting over my scare."

"Wal, thet's fine. Then yu can ride hawseback with me. I have just the pony for you. A pinto thet come from Uvalde. He's Arabian if I ever seen one."

Deuce's face fell. He was wholly unconscious of the sincerity and depth of his emotions. Brite detected another reaction to this innocent fun Texas was having. Reddie betrayed signs of the green-eyed monster.

"An Arabian? Oh, I shall love to ride him," Ann replied, with enthusiasm. "But I'd rather go on the wagon to be close to Daddy."

"Yu win, lady," retorted Texas, with dry humour. Manifestly the fair sex was beyond him. Brite made certain that the girl had spoken the simple, natural truth. But that Texas cowboy had a suspicion that Ann wanted to ride beside her rescuer.

After that all hands became busy, except the new members of the outfit. Ann rested with closed eyes. Her father lay still, as he had been advised, suffering patiently. Brite thought that the settler had a good chance to recover. The bullet had missed his lung. Blood poisoning was the only complication to fear. That very often set in from a dirty slug of lead, tearing through the flesh. Evidently Williams was no poor hand at dressing gun-shot wounds, and the medicine Brite had packed for just such a contingency was a sure preventive if applied in time.

Just about sundown the cowboys rode in from down-river, leading two saddle horses, and following them came a wagon with Williams and Smiling Pete on the seat.

Texas lost no time acquainting the hunters with his eagerness to start at once up the river, so that they could be on hand when Hite drove the herd across the river.

"Texas, great minds run the same," boomed Williams. "I had thet idee myself. What did San Sabe report?"

When this information had been briefly imparted he said: "Good! Send Sabe an' another rider up the trail pronto. An' we'll foller as soon as we can start."

Pan Handle, Texas Joe, and Smiling Pete rode at the head of that caravan. Reddie Bayne and Brite drove the *remuda* next. Ackerman, at the reins of the Hardy wagon, with Ann on the seat beside him, came next. Whittaker was prevailed upon by vast argument and some anger to handle the third wagon. Moze followed with his chuck-wagon, and Hash Williams, accompanied by Less Holden and Bender, brought up the rear.

The wagon-drivers had orders to keep close together on the tail of the *remuda*. If there had ever been a road up this river-bottom, the herd had ploughed it out. The ground was sandy and therefore made hard pulling for the horses. It was so dark that the drivers had difficulty in keeping to the most level ground.

After an hour's travelling Brite noted a brightening of the sky and paling of the stars. The moon had risen. But it was behind the high bluff to their left and for the time being did not materially help the progress. Presently the rim of the opposite bluff turned silver, and this shiny line slowly worked downward. The time came when the far shore grew bright and then the river shone like silver. Eventually the blackness under the cliff yielded to the rising moon, until all was clear and blanched.

Better progress was made then. The valley narrowed until there appeared to be scarcely a quarter mile of land between the river and the bluff. It was brushy, too, and often dotted by clumps of trees. These did not offer any obstacles to Brite's caravan, but it would certainly slow down the herd of cattle.

The hours passed. It was comfortable travel for the trail men, except for the menace that gradually grew with their progress toward an inevitable climax. Suspense always wore upon Brite. Texas Joe, no doubt, chafed under it. Probably Pan Handle and the hunters were the only ones in the outfit who were not affected one way or another.

Some time long after midnight Texas rode back to halt the *remuda*, and then the wagons as they came up.

"We heahed cows bawlin' ahaid," he said. "An' I reckon we're just aboot too close for comfort now. What yu say, Williams?"

"Wal, let's haul up heah while some of yu sneak ahaid on foot. I'll go along. Texas, it ain't so long till mawnin'. An' we shore want to be around when Hite's ootfit drives the herd across."

"Hash, we *want* the cattle to get over," replied Texas forcibly. "Thet'll save us work. An' we oughtn't begin hostilities until the rear end is half-way across."

"Ahuh. Ha! Ha! Kinda hot for the drivers at the tail, huh?"

"Miss Ann, how yu ridin'?" queried Texas as he passed the Hardy wagon.

"All right, but I'll be glad to lie down," she replied.

"Deuce, have yu made a bed for her in the wagon?"

"Not yet. But I have a roll of blankets handy. I'll take care of her," returned Deuce, too casually. He was obsessed with his importance.

"Wal, so long. Some of yu boys stand guard, so the girl an' the boss can sleep."

Reddie bunched the *remuda* on the best available space, fortunately large and grassy enough to hold it, and then unrolled her bed as usual next to Brite's.

"Yu awake, Dad?"

"Yes, lass. Anythin' troublin' you?"

"Lawd, yes. But I only wanted to ask if yu don't think there'll be hell to pay before long?"

"Reddie, I don't see how we can avoid it," replied Brite gloomily. "Some of our ponies gone, all our cattle gone. Two riders daid! An' not even to the Red River yet. It's between the Red an' the Canadian thet the trail drivers ketch hell."

"Oh, it'd just be my luck!" she exclaimed, disheartened, as she kicked off her boots.

"What'd be?"

"To get stole by stampeders or scalped by redskins or drowned, or lose *yu*, just when I've begun to be happy."

"Wal, Reddie, don't give up. Hang on like a Texan. Remember the Alamo!"

"Dog-gone it, Mr. Brite, them Texans shore never gave up. They hung on till they was all daid."

"I meant their spirit, honey. Now yu go to sleep."

Brite was pulled out by Texas Joe in the grey of dawn. "Boss, I just rode back with the news. Hite is crossin' the herd," he whispered. "If yu don't want to miss the fun, come on. Don't wake Reddie. We're leavin' five men heah. An' we'll be back before sun-up."

"Don't wake Reddie!" spoke up that young person derisively. "Fine chance yu have of keepin' me from seein' the fun, Texas Jack."

"Say, yu must want to be kissed some more," drawled Texas coolly.

"Shore do. But not by the same gentleman—I mean hombre—who kissed me last."

"Gosh! Who was thet lucky hombre?" laughed Texas, and went his way.

Brite had been swift to comply with his foreman's suggestion, and had only to snatch up his rifle. Texas waited in the grey gloom with Pan Handle, San Sabe, and Williams. Reddie joined them there, rifle in hand.

"Listen," whispered Texas. "Foller me an' keep still. Do what I do. The idee is to break up Hite's ootfit before it gets across the river. Most of his drivers, yu know, will be behind the herd. When they get all in the river then we gotta do some tall shootin'. Thet's all."

He set off up the trail at a swift stride. The others followed in single file. San Sabe brought up the rear. Texas did not stop until he got around a bend in the river. He listened.

The bawl of cattle arose on the still, warm air. Brite calculated that they could scarcely be more than a mile—two at the most—from the crossing Hite had chosen. The valley had widened. On the opposite side of the river the rim of the bluff sloped down to a distant break. Soon Texas led off the trail into the woods. Here going was impeded by brush until they emerged upon the sandy bank of the river. It was wide here and shallow, flowing on with a gurgle and murmur. Judging by the wet sand and weeds, the water had dropped several feet during the night. By this time broad daylight had come, but not under a clear sky as usual. Hazy clouds presaged rain.

Texas hurried along, keeping in the lee of willows, halting to listen every hundred paces or so. At length he turned a corner to stop with a low: "Hist! . . . Look!"

Half a mile beyond, the wide river space presented a wonderful spectacle. It appeared to be blotted out by a great mass of moving cattle that extended across, and out on the opposite bank, and up under the trees. The herd had not been pointed by expert trail drivers. Brite did not see a rider. They would be, of course, on the up-stream side, if the water was swift and deep. All the cattle were wading, which ensured a safe, though slow, crossing.

"Wal, pards, this heah is shore low-down Comanche work we're goin' to do, but Hite's ootfit ain't worth us riskin' a scratch. Careful now. Watch me an' not the river. It'll come off soon enough!"

He took to the willows, and glided through them, scarcely moving a leaf. Brite could see the water and hear its soft flow, but had no clear view. Meanwhile the intermittent bawling of cattle grew closer. Texas led on slower and slower. In places the willows became almost impenetrable, whereupon he had to worm a way through, but he always worked toward the river and not inshore.

Yells of the drivers halted Texas. He sank down on one knee and beckoned his followers to come close. They stooped and crawled to surround him.

"Reckon a—hundred yards—more will fetch us," he panted low. "Get yore breath. A winded man cain't shoot. Wait heah."

He crawled out to the sandbar, where he could just be made out through the willows. Soon he came back.

"In aboot five minutes—the brawl will open," he whispered. The beads of sweat dropped off his dark, stern face. "They're quarterin' across current. Thet'll fetch the men in range, if we can—work up a little—farther."

He rose to a stooping posture and glided on, this time without any apparent caution, probably because he had ascertained that they could not be detected. Brite kept close to Reddie's heels, marvelling the more at her all the time. Every few steps she would turn her head, like an alert bird, to see if he was close to her. At such moments she smiled. Her eyes were dark and daring, and only the pearly hue of her cheek indicated that her blood had receded. Faint whistling pants issued from her lips.

The cattle were now close. They made a stamping, splashing roar, above which neither the bawls of cows nor yells of drivers could be heard. Brite could smell the herd, and through interstices in the foliage he could see moving red and white.

Texas' steps grew shorter and slower, until they ceased. He knelt, and all followed suit. His eyes acquainted his comrades with the issue close at hand, and if that was not sufficient, the way he tapped his rifle and pointed surely spoke volumes. Then he listened intently to the clattering, splashing roar. It appeared to pass by their covert, working out.

"We gotta rustle," he whispered fiercely. "We didn't get far enough up an' they're quarterin' away from us. Spread oot an' crawl to the edge."

Before Brite, who encountered a tangle of willows, could reach the open the thundering boom of needle guns dinned in his ears. He rushed ahead, split the willows with his rifle, and peered out. Reddie slipped in a few feet to his right.

The wide rear of the herd was a full hundred yards out. Half a dozen riders were beating and spurring their horses in a mad haste to escape. Brite saw horses down and one man pitching in and out of the water.

"Aim low an' shoot, Reddie," he called harshly, yielding to the fight lust of the moment. Then he tried to cover the rider of a plunging horse, and fired. In vain! Guns were banging on each side of him, until his ears appeared to crack. The last rider, whose horse was crippled, threw up his arms and lunged out of his saddle into the water. He did not come up.

Puffs of white smoke from the retreating drivers told of a return fire. Bullets began to splatter on the water and sand, and to whistle by into the willows. But the danger for Brite's men appeared negligible, owing to the fact that the thieves were shooting with small arms from plunging horses. Only a chance bullet could find its mark. The swift water came up to the flanks of the horses, hindering progress on foot. It was not deep enough for them to swim. Nevertheless, the riders drew nearer the shore in a hail of bullets. This pursuing fusillade ceased almost as suddenly as it had begun, because Brite's men had exhausted all the loads in both rifles and revolvers.

The yelling, frantic robbers reached the land, five of them, where they joined one who had crossed ahead of them, and they surrounded him like a pack of wolves, no doubt cursing him for this attack. They pointed to three horses down, and one man floating, face up. Texas, having reloaded his buffalo gun, took a long shot at them by way of farewell. The big bullet splashed water and sand in their faces, making them beat a hasty retreat into the willows.

"Wal, dog-gone!" ejaculated Texas, pleased as a child. "It turned oot better'n I hoped when we got heah. What yu say, Hash?"

"Not so good as I was hankerin' for. But not bad, either," replied Williams. "Thar's three hawses down, an' yu bet I didn't see no fellar wade ashore."

"There's a crippled man in thet bunch," averred Texas. "I hit him myself."

"Mr. Brite, we'll be drivin' yore herd again before we cross the Red," said the hunter. "We'll have these robbers buffaloed from now on. They'll have to leave the herd or croak, thet's all. Reckon thet tall fellar on the bay horse was Hite, reckonin' from the way they ranted at him."

"Load up, everybody. We mustn't forget we're now in Comanche country," advised Texas. "Boss, who's the young fellar with burnt powder on his nose?"

"This heah?—Oh, this is Red Bayne," replied Brite, eager for some fun now the tension was removed. "Did yore rifle kick?"

"Did it? Wuss than a mule. I forgot to hold the darn thing tight," replied Reddie, in rueful disgust.

"Let's rustle back to camp, eat, an' get goin' 'cross this river," said Texas. "It'll shore be little sleep or rest Ross Hite will get from now on."

CHAPTER TWELVE

I F it were needed, Texas' coup inspirited the drivers who had not shared it. Deuce Ackerman let out one long wild whoop.

"Hip, hip, thet's great! Look what we missed, Rolly. But some of us had to stay behind. . . . Tex, we'll get goin' yet an' then Gawd help 'em!"

In an hour they were on the move, and soon after that halted at the crossing where Hite's men had been routed. The three dead horses had floated down-stream some distance to lodge in shallower water. Williams had sent a scout back in the trail, another put on the bluff, and a third ahead. They met the outfit at the ford to report nothing in sight but buffalo.

"How aboot us bein' ambushed?" queried Texas.

"Wal, strikes me Hite would pick oot a better place than thet over there," replied Williams. "Mr. Brite, suppose yu hand up yore glass to young Ackerman, so he can have a look. . . . Stand up on the seat, son."

After a long survey Ackerman shook his head decisively. "Nope. I can see all under the trees an' right through thet thin skift of brush."

"Wal, just to make shore, some of us'll ride over ahaid," said Texas. "Come, San, an' yu Bender, an' Less. . . . Look sharp, an' if yu see puffs of smoke wheel an' ride for dear life."

These riders crossed in good order, proving the validity of Ackerman's judgment. Reddie crossed next with the *remuda*, and then Moze made it without going over his wagon wheels. The Hardy vehicle had to have help, stalling a little beyond the middle.

"Rustle before she mires down," yelled Texas, who had ridden out. "Come, Miss Ann. I'll pack yu ashore. Yu'll get all wet there."

Ackerman's face was a study while Ann Hardy readily leaned out to be taken in Texas Joe's arms and carried ashore. Then the riders, hitching on with their ropes, aided the team to pull the wagon out. Williams drove the third wagon across without mishap. But the fourth and last stuck in the mud about half-way over.

This accident held up the caravan. It was the largest wagon, half-full of buffalo hides, and it sank deeper in the mire after every effort to dislodge it. The drivers broke their ropes. Then they got off in water up to their waists and performed all manner of strenuous labour, to no avail.

Finally, Williams waded in and, unhitching the team, drove them ashore.

"Wagon's no good, anyhow, an' never mind the hides. Thar's ten million of 'em loose oot heah."

They went on with two teams hitched to the Hardy wagon, which held the heaviest load. And soon they were up out of the bottom land upon the vast heave of the range. The cattle herd had been driven almost due east. Williams said that had been done to strike the Chisholm Trail. Before long this proved to be a correct surmise.

The day was sultry and brooded storm. Bands of buffalo grazed on all sides, attended by droves of wolves and coyotes and flocks of birds. By noon Ackerman, who still retained Brite's glass, reported the herd in sight ahead less than ten miles. All afternoon the caravan gained, which fact probably was known to the Hite outfit. At sunset Hite halted the herd on the open range, where not a tree or a bush could be picked up with the glass. A little swale well watered and wooded appealed to Texas Joe, who turned off here and selected a camp site. Scarcely half a dozen miles separated the two outfits.

The sun set in a red flare and dusk trooped up from the west, sultry and ominous. Dull rumbles of thunder heralded an approaching storm, and flashes of sheet lightning flared along the dark horizon. The silence, the absence of even a slightest movement of air, the brooding wait of nature, were not propitious to the caravan caught out upon the open range. Brite told the girls how the electric storms prevalent in that latitude of Texas were the bane of trail drivers, actually more dreaded than redskins or buffalo.

"But why?" asked Ann Hardy wonderingly.

"Wal, they're just naturally fearful in the first place, an' they drive hawses an' cattle crazy. Fred Bell, a trail driver I know, said he got caught once in a storm near the Canadian an' had thirty-seven haid of cattle an' one driver struck daid by lightnin'."

Reddie was no less shocked than Ann and vowed she would surely pray that they miss such a storm as that.

"I been in a coupla electric storms," spoke up Texas, who had paused in his walk to listen. "Been in hundreds of plain lightnin'-an'-thunder storms. Only two of these darn floods of electricity thet cover the earth an' everythin' on it.

I've seen balls of fire on the tops of all the cows' horns. I've seen fire run along a hawse's mane, an' heahed it too. Yes, sir, bad storms air hell for cowhands."

Later, when the girls had walked away, Texas spoke low and seriously to Brite.

"Boss, any kind of a storm to-night, if it'll only flash lightnin' enough, will shore suit me an' Pan Handle."

"Tex!—What's in yore mind?" queried Brite hastily.

"We're gonna get back our herd to-night."

"Yu an' Pan? Alone?"

"Shore alone. Thet's the way to do it. Pan wanted to tackle it by hisself, an' so did I. But we compromised by joinin' forces. We're goin' together."

"Shipman, I—I don't know thet I'll permit it," rejoined Brite gravely.

"Shore yu will. I'd hate to disobey yu, Mr. Brite. But I'm Trail boss. An' as for Pan Handle, hell! Thet fellar cain't be bossed."

"What's yore idee, Tex? I hope to heaven it ain't crazy. Yu an' Pan air grown men. An' yu shore know yore responsibility heah. Two young girls to protect now, an' a crippled man."

"Wal, the idee strikes yu worse than it really is," went on Texas. "Pan an' me plan to strike the herd in the thickest of the thunder an' lightnin'. When we do I'll circle it one way an' he'll circle the other. If the cattle stampede, as is likely, we'll ride along an' wait till they begin to mill or stop. Now Hite's ootfit will be havin' their hands full. They'll be separatin', naturally, tryin' to keep the herd bunched an' stopped. An' in a flash of lightnin', when any one of them seen us, he wouldn't know us from Adam. Savvy, boss?"

"I cain't say thet I do," replied Brite, puzzled.

"Wal, yu're gettin' thick-haided in yore old age. Kinda gettin' dotty adoptin' this pretty kid, huh?"

"Tex, don't rile me. Shore I'm dotty, aboot her anyway. But I don't get yore hunch. Now, for instance, when yu 'an Pan circle thet herd, goin' in opposite directions, when yu meet how'n hell will yu know each other? Shootin' by lightnin' flash had ought to be as quick as lightnin', I'd say. How'n hell would yu keep from shootin' each other?"

"Wal, thet's got me stumped, I'll admit. Let's put our haids together after supper. Mebbe one of us will hit on just the idee. If we think up somethin' shore— wal, it's all day with Hite an' his ootfit."

Moze rolled out his familiar clarion blast.

"Gosh! this's fine, all heah together, first time," exclaimed Ackerman, whose spirits ran high. He had just seated Ann on a pack beside him.

"Wal, it may be the last, so make the most of it," drawled Texas, his dark, piercing eyes upon Reddie. Brite saw her catch her breath. Then silence fell.

Dusk deepened into night, still close, humid, threatening, with the rumbles sounding closer and more frequent. In the western sky all the stars disappeared. The moon was not yet up.

"Chuck on some firewood an' gather aboot me heah," said Texas, after the meal ended. "It's shore gonna storm pronto. An' me an' Pan have a job on."

"What?" bluntly jerked out Holden.

"Thought yu was kinda glum," added San Sabe.

"Reddie, yu're in on this," called Texas. "An' Ann, too, if she likes. Shore no one ever seen an idee come oot of a pretty girl's haid. But I'm sorta desperate to-night."

In the bright light of the replenished fire they all surrounded their foreman, curious and expectant.

"Wal, heah's at yu. Me an' Pan air ridin' oot to round up Hite. Soon as the storm's aboot to break we'll ride up on the herd an' the guards. I've got them located. We plan to circle the herd in different directions, an' we want to know ab-so-loot-lee when we meet each other. How we goin' to do thet?"

"Yu mean recognize each other by lightnin' flashes?" queried Less.

"Shore."

"It cain't be did."

"Aw, yes it can. A lightnin' flash lasts a second—sometimes a good deal longer. How much time do I need to see to throw a gun—or not?"

"Oh-h! Thet's the idee!"

"Lemme go along."

"No, it's a two man job. . . . Use yore grey matter now, pards."

"It'll be rainin', most likely, an' the herd will be driftin', mebbe movin' fast. An' of course, Hite's ootfit will be surroundin' it, all separated. It's a grand idee, Tex, if yu don't plug each other."

"Wal, let's see," put in another driver. "When yu separate yu'll know for shore yu cain't meet very soon. It'll take most a quarter or mebbe half an hour to trot around a big herd, guidin' by lightnin' flashes."

"Boys," drawled Pan Handle, in amusement, "yore minds work slow. What we want to know is what to wear thet can be seen quick. Somethin' shore to identify each other. Remember we'll both be holdin' cocked guns."

One by one the male contingent came forward with suggestions, each of which was summarily dismissed.

"If it storms, the wind will blow, shore?" interposed Reddie.

"Breeze blowin' already. There'll be a stiff wind with the rain," replied Texas.

"Tie somethin' white aboot yore sombreros an' leave the ends long so they'll flap in the wind."

"White?" responded Pan Handle sharply.

"Dog-gone!" added Texas.

"Men, thet is a splendid idee," interposed Brite earnestly. "Somethin' white streakin' oot! It couldn't be beat."

"Where'll we get this heah somethin' white?" asked Texas. "In this dirty ootfit it'd be huntin' a needle in a haystack."

"Ann has a clean white towel," replied Reddie.

"Yes, I have," said the girl eagerly. "I'll get it."

When the article was produced and placed in Texas' hands he began to tear it into strips. "Wal, Reddie, yu've saved my life. I shore want this Pan Handle galoot to make quick an' shore thet I'm Tex Shipman. . . . Heah, we'll knot two strips together, an' then tie the double piece round our hats. . . . Come, Reddie, take it."

She complied, and when he bent his head she clumsily wound the long streamer around the crown of his sombrero. The firelight showed her face white as the towel.

"What yu' shakin' for?" demanded Texas. "Anyone would get the halloocin-nation yu reckoned I was gonna be killed an' yu felt bad."

"I would feel—very bad—Tex," she faltered.

"Wal, thet makes up for a lot. . . . Tie it tighter, so the wind cain't blow it off. . . . There. I reckon that'll do. How aboot yu, Pan?"

"I'm decorated, too."

"Wal, I could 'most see thet in the dark. . . . Now, fellars, listen. Like as not we won't come back to-night, onless our plan fails. If it works we'll be with the herd, yu bet. So yu rout Moze oot early, grab some grub, an' ride oot soon as it's light. The wagons can foller on the road. Yu'll find us somewhere."

In utter silence, then, the two mounted their horses, that had been kept haltered close by, and rode away into the sulphurous, melancholy night.

"Thet's a new wrinkle on Hash Williams," ejaculated that worthy. "What them gun-throwers cain't think of would beat hell!"

His caustic remark broke the tensity of the moment. Reddie had stood like a statue, her face in shadow, gazing into the blackness where Texas Joe had vanished. Brite did not need this time to see her eyes; her form, rigid with speechless protest, betrayed her.

The wind swept in from the range with a moan, blowing a stream of red sparks aloft. Thunder boomed. And a flare of lightning showed inky black clouds swooping down from the west.

"We better think aboot keepin' ourselves an' beds dry," advised Brite. "Deuce, see thet Ann an' her father will be protected. Moze, get oot our tarp. Come, Reddie, we'll bunk under the chuck-wagon an' say we like it."

"Dad, I wonder if my *remuda* will hang in a storm?" inquired Reddie, undecided what to do.

"Wal, thet bunch of dogies can go hang if they want."

"Reddie, I'll have a look at 'em before the storm busts," said San Sabe.

"Yu'll have to rustle, then."

"Thet's only wind. It ain't rainin' yet."

By the time Moze, Brite, and Reddie had tied and stoned the ends of the tarpaulin so that it could not blow away the rain was coming in big scattered drops. Brite felt them cool and fresh upon his face. He and Reddie rushed for shelter, and had made it fast when the pitch blackness blazed into an intense blue-white brilliance which lighted camp, wagons, horses, and all the vicinity into a supernatural silvery clearness. A thunderbolt followed that seemed to rend the earth.

The succeeding blackness appeared an intensified medium impenetrable and pitchy. Then the thunder reverberated away in terrific concussions.

"Where air yu, Dad?" shouted Reddie.

"I'm right heah," Brite replied. "Listen to the roar of thet rain comin'."

"Gosh! I better say my prayers pronto, or the good Lawd'll never heah me," cried Reddie.

"Lass, it might be a good idee," replied Brite. "Let's don't unroll our beds till this storm is over."

Reddie answered something to that, but in the pressing fury of the deluge he could not distinguish what it was. With a rippling onslaught upon their canvas shield, rain and wind enveloped the wagon. Then the pitch black split to a weird white light that quivered all around them, showing the torrent of rain, the flooded land, the horses bunched, heads down, together. Thunder burst like disrupted mountains. Again the black mantle fell. But before that reverberation rolled away another zigzag rope of lightning divided the dense cloud, letting loose an all-embracing supernatural glow, silver-green, that lent unreality to everything. White flash after white flash followed until for moments there appeared scarcely a dark interval between, and the tremendous boom and peal of thunder was continuous.

Reddie sat huddled under the wagon, covered with the long slicker. Brite could see her pale face and dark eyes in the lightning flare. Fear shone there, but it did not seem to be for herself. Reddie was gazing out over the blaze-swept range with the terrible consciousness of what was taking place out there.

That, too, obsessed Brite's mind. He reclined on his elbow close beside Reddie and not far from Moze, who had also sought shelter under the wagon. Reddie appeared to be fairly shielded from the deluge that beat in everywhere. But Brite needed the old canvas with which he covered himself. The other drivers had huddled under the other wagons, and could be seen, a dark mass, inside the wheels.

Brite was not at all fond of Texas storms, even of the ordinary kind. He had a wholesome fear of the real electric storm, which this one did not appear to be. At this time, however, he scarcely thought of the fact that lightning struck camp frequently.

His thoughts dwelt on the unparalleled action of Texas Joe and Pan Handle, riding forth in that storm to mete dire justice to the stampeders. It must have been an original idea—stalking Hite's outfit in face of the furious rain and deafening thunder and scintillating flashes. For sheer iron nerve it had no equal in Brite's memory of cold, hard deeds. These men would be drenched to the skin by now, blinded by piercing rain and lightning, almost blown from their saddles, in imminent peril of being run down by a stampeding herd, and lastly of being shot by the men they had set out to kill.

By the strange green light Brite calculated whether or not he could shoot accurately under such conditions. The flashes lasted long enough for a swift eye and hand. All the same he would not have cared to match wits and faculties with hunted desperadoes on a night like this.

It took an hour or longer for the heavy centre of the storm to pass, after which rain and wind, and an occasional flare, diminished in volume. Perceptibly the storm boomed and roared and flashed away. Whatever had been fated to happen out there was over. Brite had no doubt of its deadly outcome. Still, that might be over-confidence in his gunmen. He had nothing sure to go by. Ross Hite was a crafty desperado, and for all Brite knew he might be the equal of Texas Joe.

But not of Pan Handle Smith! Pan Handle could only be compared to the great Texas killers of that decade.

Reddie had rolled in her blankets and was asleep, as Brite dimly made out by the receding flares. He sought his own bed, weary, strangely calm, somehow fixed in his sense of victory.

It was still dark when noise aroused him from slumber. A grey-ness, however, betrayed the east and was the harbinger of day. He reached over to give Reddie a shake, but the dark object he had taken for her was her bed. Moze was out, too, splitting wood. Brite hurried out to lend a hand.

Gruff voices sounded toward the other wagons. Dark forms of men strode to and fro against that grey light. "Pete, we got to grease the wagon," Williams called gruffly. Reddie's clean, high-pitched call came floating in. She had the *remuda* moving. One by one the cowboys appeared at the brightening camp fire, cold, cramped, wet, silent, and morose. Ackerman was not present, wherefore Brite concluded that he had gone with Reddie to round up the *remuda*. This surmise proved correct. When the mustangs got in there followed the sharp whistle of wet ropes, the stamp of little hoofs, the grind of hard heels, and an occasional low growl or curse from a cowhand. That task done, the riders flocked around Moze to snatch at something to eat.

The dawn lightened. Ackerman called at the Hardy wagon: "Miss Ann, air yu awake?"

"I should smile I am," came the reply.

"How air yu?"

"All right, I reckon, Mr. Deuce, but pretty wet."

"How's yore father?"

"Son, I'm still alive an' kickin'," replied Hardy, for himself.

"Good. . . . Miss Ann, better come oot an' dry yoreself an' have a hot drink. We'll be on the move pronto."

Hash Williams stamped up to the fire, spreading his huge hands.

"Cleared off fine. Gonna be best kind of a day for travel."

"Do yu reckon we'll travel?" inquired Brite.

"I'll bet we do," replied the hunter gruffly.

"Williams, what's yore idee aboot startin'?" queried Ackerman sharply.

"Pronto. Yu drive Hardy same as yestiddy. Pete will drive our wagon. I'll go with the boys. Let's see, thet'd be six of us. Suppose yu keep one rider back with yu."

"All right. Rolly, yu're stuck heah with us."

In a moment more the five were mounted on restive mustangs, a formidable quintet in the pale morning light.

"Take the trail an' keep comin' till yu ketch us. We'll shore bear yu all in mind."

They were off swiftly, and close together, a sight that betrayed to Brite the uncertainty of their errand and the mood in which it was undertaken.

"Mawnin', Ann," greeted Reddie to the settler girl as she appeared, dishevelled and wet, but bright-eyed and cheerful. "Did yu heah the storm?"

"Good morning. Oh, wasn't it terrible? . . . An' to think of those two who rode out. I could not sleep."

"It wasn't a very comfortable night, Miss Ann," said Brite. "Come to the fire. . . . Moze, rustle our breakfast. We must not lose any time."

They were on the trail at daylight, when the range had just awakened, and all the distant landmarks were shrouded in mist. But the sky was clear, the east reddening, the air fresh and cool.

Rolly Little took the lead to scout the way; the wagons followed close together, and the *remuda* brought up the rear, with Brite and Reddie driving them. All horses were fresh. They trotted over the hard ground and splashed through the little pools. Meanwhile the red in the east deepened to rose, and then the rose burst into glorious sunrise, before which the shadows and mists, the mysteries of distance and obscurity of draw and swale dissolved and vanished.

Five miles out Rolly Little rode off the trail and appeared to search. When the *remuda* came even with this point Brite swerved off to have a look. He found where Ross Hite had camped. Packs and saddles, utensils left beside a sodden bed of ashes, attested to the hasty departure of the stampeders. A long yell pierced Brite's ears, startling him. Little, some distance ahead, was waving. But his action seemed the result of excitement rather than alarm. Brite, curious and thrilled, galloped to join him; before he got there, however, Little pointed to an object on the ground and rode on.

Brite soon gazed down upon a dead man, flat on his back, his arms spread, gun on the ground, a telling spectacle, emphatic of the law of that range. Brite rode an imaginary circle then, soon to come upon another of Hite's outfit, still and horrible, half his face shot away and his open shirt bloody. Farther on in the lengthy curve Brite espied a dead horse and two dead men, lying in a group. Brite did not go close, and he sheered off that circle and made for the *remuda*.

Reddie gave him a flashing, fearful glance.

"Boy, would yu believe it?—Four of Hite's ootfit lyin' along the trail, in a circle. I only rode the half."

Reddie swallowed hard and had no answer. They rode on, eyes now glued ahead to the wavering, deceiving prairie. Buffalo showed in spots, dark patches on the green, off the trail. The purple hills beckoned, and beyond them the Wichita Mountains loomed dimly in the clear air. To the right the range sloped away to merge into sky. And what seemed hours of watchful suspense passed while the wheels rolled, the horses trotted, the drivers urged the lagging *remuda* on.

"Look ahaid!" called Reddie shrilly.

Smiling Pete stood on top of his wagon, waving his hat. His energetic actions could be assigned to either joy or alarm.

"Reddie! . . . Pete sees our boys with the herd—or else a bunch of Comanches. Which?"

"I cain't say, Dad, but I'm prayin' hard," she cried.

CHAPTER THIRTEEN

From the summit of an endless slope Brite and Reddie espied far ahead that which elicited shouts of joy. Miles down in the green valley an immense wedge-shaped patch of colour crawled over the prairie. It was the great herd together once more, sharp end pointed north, and the wide rear spread far to the east and west.

"*Thet cowboy!*" cried Reddie, in awesome wonder. She did not need to say any more.

Brite found silence his best tribute. The wagons and *remuda* quickened to a downhill grade. Soon the freshness of morning gave way to the heat of noonday, and when they reached the rolling floor of the valley, to encounter reflection from the dragging sand, horses and riders alike suffered severely.

Beyond that arid spot a gradual slope waved on toward the horizon where dim hills showed. Grass became abundant again, and toward late afternoon the herd appeared to be halted at the head of a swale where a fringe of willow signified the presence of water.

Brite's end of the cavalcade caught up eventually. The cattle had bunched in a meadow that surely would hold them all night, but at this hour they were weary and only a few were grazing.

Reddie swung the *remuda* off to a bend in the creek. Brite rode on up to the head of the swale, where Moze had halted. Only two drivers remained with the herd, each solitary on opposite sides of it. They drooped in their saddles. A scattering of low trees afforded a fairly good site for camp. All the other drivers were dismounted. Brite got off, and stumbled around on cramped legs until he located Pan Handle and Texas Joe off to one side under a tree.

Brite's heart contracted when he espied Joe lying with a bloody bandage round his head. He heard Pan Handle say: "Tex, it's kinda low down of yu."

"All's fair in love an' war. I'm crazy aboot her an' I reckon she doesn't care a damn——"

"Heah comes the boss," interrupted Pan Handle warningly. Brite had heard enough, however, to get an inkling of what the wily cowboy was up to. He decided he would hide his suspicion.

"Tex, old man, I shore hope yu ain't bad hurt," he burst out, in alarm, as he hurried up.

"Aboot goin' to cash, boss."

"My Gawd!—Man, this is terrible. Let me see."

"Rustle Reddie over heah," replied Texas, in an awful voice.

Reddie was unsaddling her black on the other side of camp. She heard Brite's call, but showed no inclination to hurry. Her face flashed in their direction.

"Reckon I'd better go prepare her, Tex," said Brite, conceiving a loyal idea in the girl's behalf.

"Fetch her pronto," called Texas, after him.

Brite lost no time reaching Reddie, and when she turned he was amazed to find her white and shaking.

"Dad—I saw! Tex has—been shot!" she whispered, with a gasp. "For pity's sake—don't tell me——"

"Reddie, the damn cowboy ain't hurt atall," retorted Brite. "He 'pears bloodied up some. But I've a hunch he wants to scare yu."

Reddie's face warmed, and slow comprehension drove the horror from her telltale eyes.

"Honest Injun, Dad?" she asked hoarsely.

"I'll swear it."

She pondered a moment, then jerked up, all spirit. "Thanks, Dad. But for yore hunch I'd shore have given myself away."

"Lass, yu turn the tables on thet tricky hombre," suggested Brite.

"Watch me!—Come a-runnin'," she replied, and fled toward where Texas lay. Brite thumped after her as best he could, arriving just in time to see Reddie fall on her knees with a poignant cry.

"Oh, Pan—he's been shot," she cried, in horrified tones.

Pan Handle confirmed that with a gloomy nod. Texas lay with the bloody yellow scarf across his forehead, just shading his eyes. Devil as he was, perhaps he could not risk exposing them to her perception.

"Wal, I should smile I have, Reddie," he drawled, in a husky whisper. "But no matter. Pan an' me got the herd back."

"But, Jack!—Jack—Yu're not—not——" she wailed in accents that must have tricked the lover into ecstasy.

"Reckon—I'm gonna—cash."

"*Not die!*—Jack?—Oh, my heaven!"

"Yes, girl. I'm gonna die—oot heah on the lone prairie."

"Jack, darlin'!" she sobbed, covering her face with her hands and rocking to and fro over him.

"Aw! . . . Then yu'll be sorry?" asked Texas, in a tender voice.

"My heart will break. . . . It will kill me!"

Texas Joe manifested, a peculiar reaction for a man about to depart from life at such a harrowing moment. Reddie, too, appeared about to go into convulsions.

"Kiss me—good-bye," whispered the villain, determined to carry the subterfuge as far as possible.

Suddenly Reddie uncovered her face, which was rosy, and convulsed, too, but in smiles. She snatched the scarf off Texas' forehead, exposing the superficial scalp wound over his temple.

"Yu deceitful, lyin' cowboy!" she burst out. "Yu may have fooled a lot of pore girls in yore day. But yu cain't fool this one."

"Dog-gone!" ejaculated Texas, his eyes popping. "Yu air smart!"

"The minute I seen yu I was on to yu," she replied mockingly, as she arose.

"Yeah? . . . All right, Miss Reddie," he replied, in grim discomfiture. "Pan said it was a low-down trick. An' it was, I reckon, but next time there won't be no foolin'."

Always, at the last, Texas Joe was not only a match for Reddie, but a master at finesse. Her dark eyes changed startlingly. It was indeed easy to see when this complex range-rider was in earnest. Reddie sobered instantly, and drooping her head she hastened away.

"Boss, did yu double-cross me?" demanded Texas, with those piercing eyes shifting to Brite.

"Lands sake! How could I?" ejaculated the boss.

"Wal, you're a pretty smart old hombre," growled Texas. Then he brightened. "Dog-gone! She had me most oot of my haid. Pan, ain't Reddie just the wonderfullest girl thet ever was?"

"I haven't seen 'em all," drawled Pan Handle. "But she shore would be hard to beat. . . . Tex, I don't believe she gives a dam' aboot yu."

"Aw!"

"No girl could have come thet with yu lyin' there all bloody. An' yu're a natural liar an' actor. My idee is thet yu found oot what yu wanted to know so powerful bad."

"Wal, thet's some good, anyhow," rejoined Texas, sitting up with a change of manner. "Boss, did yu take a look oot there?"

He pointed with a long arm and his gesture had impressiveness.

"Boy, I been lookin' my eyes oot," responded Brite. "Shore don't know how to thank yu an' Pan. Or what to say. I'll wait till yu tell me aboot it."

"There, Pan, what yu make of thet? He's an old Texas cattleman, too."

"Mr. Brite, if yu had looked the herd over carefully yu'd have seen thet we have fifteen hundred haid of long-horns more'n when we started."

"What!" ejaculated Brite, astounded.

"It's a fact, boss," added Texas. "Our good luck is matchin' our bad. Thet Hite ootfit had a herd of their own, stole, I reckon, from other drivers. Must have had them just this side of the Little Wichita."

"Wal, I'm stumped. What's the brand?"

"We saw a lot of X Two Bar and some Circle H. Do yu know them brands?"

"Reckon I don't."

"New branded over an old mark, we figger. Wilder'n hell, too. As if we hadn't had enough hard work. . . . Get Pan to tell yu aboot last night."

Texas strode off, muttering to himself, and went down toward the creek, evidently to wash his blood-stained scarf, which he carried in his hand. Brite waited for the sombre-faced gunman to speak, but was disappointed. Whereupon Brite, pretending tasks to do, moved about the camp fire, where the trail drivers were congregated, talking low. The advent of Reddie and Ann entirely silenced them. If Brite had expected his boys to be elated, he made a mistake. Perhaps they were keeping something from him and the girls. Mr. Hardy was holding his own, considering the serious nature of his wound, but he had developed a fever and was a pretty sick man. Williams said if they could get him to Doan's Post on the Red River that he had a fighting chance for his life. Presently Moze called them to supper, which turned out to be a more than usually silent meal.

San Sabe and Little rode in, after being relieved, and reported Indians with the buffalo several miles to the west.

"Thet bunch been keepin' along with us all day," said Williams. "But it ain't a very big one, so I reckon we needn't set up huggin' ourselves all night. Howsomever, we won't keep no fire burnin'."

"I gotta get some sleep," complained Texas Joe. "Pan Handle is an owl. But if I don't get sleep I'm a daid one."

Just before dark Texas called Brite aside, out of earshot of camp.

"Gimme a smoke, boss. Funny, me bein' nervous. . . . Did Pan tell yu what come off last night?"

"Not a word."

"Humph! Dam' these gunmen, anyhow," growled Texas. "Yu just cain't make one of 'em talk. I'll say Pan talked last night, though, with his gun. . . . Boss, thet was the strangest deal I was ever up against. If we'd known there was ten or eleven men instead of six we might have been a little leary."

"Tell me as much as yu like, Texas," replied Brite quietly. "It's enough for me to know yu're safe an' we got our cattle back."

"Ahuh. . . . Wal, Hite wasn't standin' guard, so we reckoned after it was over. . . . Luck was with us, boss. We rode oot an' located before the storm busted. So when the lightnin' began to flash we didn't have far to go. As we worked up on the herd we seen one guard ride off hell bent for election. He'd seen us shore. Just after thet the rain hit us somethin' fierce. We split as planned an' started round the herd. They was millin' around in a bunch, lowin' an' crackin' their horns, an' gettin' restless. Wind an' rain, an' lightnin' too, were all at my back. An' thet shore was lucky. I hadn't gone far when I heahed a shot. The wind was comin' off an' on, so when it lulled a bit I could heah. Thet was how I come to heah one of Hite's guards yell: 'Thet yu, Bill?—Yu heah a shot?' . . . I yelled yes an' kept on ridin'. It was black as coal 'cept when the flashes came. I got close to this guard when all the sky 'peared to blaze. He yelled: *Hell!—Who!* . . . An' thet was all he had time for. I rode on, sort of feelin' my way, bumpin' into cattle off an' on. If they'd stampeded then they'd run me down. It didn't rain. It just came down in bucketsful. I couldn't see more'n twenty steps, an' could heah nothin' but wind an' rain an' thunder. Then I seen another guard. Seen him clear. But the next flash was short an' when I shot it was in the dark. When it lighten'd again I seen a hawse down an' the guard gettin' to his feet. It went dark again quick just as I shot. An' he shot back, for I saw the flash an' heahed his gun. He missed, though. An' so did I. Couldn't see him next time, so I rode on ahaid. . . . Wal, after thet I had it most as light as day, for seconds at a time. But I didn't meet no more guards. A long time after I expected to I seen the white flag wavin' from Pan's hat, an' I was shore glad. We met an' yelled at each other, then the long-horns took it in their haids to run. Right at us! We had to ride to get oot of the way. But the lightnin' kept flashin', an' the rain slowin' up, so we kept tab on them easy. They must have run ten miles. The storm passed an' they quit to settle down."

"How'd yu get thet bullet crease in yore haid?" queried Brite.

"Thet was this mawnin' a little after daybreak," concluded Texas. "We hung around the herd, watchin' an' listenin'. But nobody come. In the mawnin', however, four hawsemen charged us. They had only one rifle. An' we had our buffalo guns. So we stopped them an' held them off. I got this cut first thing. So far as we could tell we didn't hit one of them. Finally they rode off over the ridge. Pan an' me both recognized Ross Hite. He had the rifle, an' he was the one who bloodied me up. Hope I run into him again."

"I hope yu don't," returned Brite bluntly.

"Wal, so does Pan Handle," drawled Texas. "Do yu know, boss, I reckon Pan an' Hite have crossed trails before. Because Pan said I didn't want to be meetin' Hite before he did. An' after thet I needn't never look for him again. What yu make of thet?"

"Humph," was all Brite replied. His brevity was particularly actuated by the approach of Reddie and Ann.

"Better go to bed, girls," advised Texas. "Thet's shore what I'm aboot to do."

"Won't you let us bandage your head?" asked Ann solicitously. "Reddie says you had a terrible wound."

"Shore. But thet's not in my haid, Ann," drawled Texas. "I got a scratch heah. It's stopped bleedin'."

"Texas, air yu goin' to tell us aboot last night?" queried Reddie curiously. "Pan Handle seems all strange an' froze. We shore left him pronto."

"Nothin' much happened, Reddie," replied Texas. "We scared thet Hite ootfit an' stampeded the herd. An' heah we air."

"Scared my eye!" quoth Reddie. "Do yu reckon me an' Ann air kids to give guff to?"

"Wal, if guff is taffy, I say shore."

"Yu shot some of Hite's men," declared Reddie, with force. "I saw some daid——"

"Aw, yu mean them guards thet was struck by lightnin' last night," went on Texas coolly. "Talk aboot retribushun! Why, girls, the Lawd was on oor side last night. It's common enough for lightnin' to kill a trail driver or cowhand now an' then. But to strike three or four men in one storm an' all close together—thet's somethin' supernatural."

In the gathering dusk the girls regarded the nonchalant cowboy with different glances—Ann's wide-eyed and awed—Reddie's with dark disdain.

"Wal, there's shore a lot supernatural aboot yu, Texas Jack," she drawled.

Brite slept with one eye open that night, which passed at length without any disruption of the quiet camp. The trail drivers got off slowly and not until the sun burst red over the ridge top.

Orders were for the wagons and *remuda* to keep close to the herd. Watchful eyes circled the horizon that day. Far over on each side of the trail black lines of buffalo showed against the grey. Their movement was imperceptible. Brite often turned his glass upon them, but more often on the distant knolls and high points, seeking for Indian signs.

Eight or ten miles a day was all the trail drivers risked for their herds. Even this could not always be adhered to, especially with the obstacles of flooded rivers ahead, buffalo all around, and the menace of the savages, if not sight of them, ever present. Brite had begun to feel the strain of suspense, but had not noted it in any of his men.

At length, about mid-afternoon, it was almost a relief actually to sight a band of mounted Indians on a high top back from the trail. Uncertainty ceased for Brite, at least. By trying he ascertained that he could not make out this band with his naked eye. Perhaps the blurred figures might be clearer to his keen-sighted scouts. With the glass, however, Brite could see well enough to recognize the Indians as Comanches, and in sufficient force to cause more than apprehension.

Whereupon he rode forward to acquaint Hash Williams with his discovery. The hunter halted his team, and, taking up the glasses without a word, he searched the horizon line.

"Ahuh, I see 'em. About forty, or so," he said, and cursed under his breath. "Looks like Comanches to me. If thet's Nigger Hawse we're shore flirtin' with the undertaker. Ride on ahaid and tell Shipman to keep on goin' till he finds a place where we'd have some chance if attacked."

Brite was to learn that Texas had already espied the Indians.

"Up to deviltry, I reckon," he said. "I was thinkin' thet very thing Williams advises. Don't tell the girls, boss."

When Brite dropped back behind the *remuda* again he was accosted by Reddie, who suspected that something was amiss. Brite told her, but advised not letting Ann know.

"Gosh! I don't know what good bein' an heiress would be if I lost my hair!" she exclaimed.

"Lass, yu wouldn't be anythin' but a good daid girl," replied Brite.

At last, at almost dusk, the herd was halted out on a flat near which a thread of water ran down a shallow gully. Camp was selected on the north bank in the shelter of rocks. Moze was ordered to make his fire in a niche where it would be unseen. The riders came and went, silent, watchful, sombre. Night fell. The wolves mourned. The warm summer air seemed to settle down over the camp as if it bore no tidings of ill. But the shadows in the rock cracks and caverns harboured menace.

Three guards kept continual watch around camp all night and six guards stayed with the herd. Two of the drivers were allowed to sleep at one time. So the night passed and the grey dawn—always the perilous hour for Indian attack— and the morning broke without incident.

But that day was beset with trials—barren ground for the cattle, hard going on the horses, ceaseless dread on the part of the trail drivers for the two girls and the injured man in their party. Several times during the day the Comanches were sighted watching them, riding along even with their position, keeping to the slow pace of the herd. How sinister that seemed to Brite! The red devils knew the trail; they were waiting for a certain place, or for something to happen, when they would attack.

Buffalo increased in numbers on all sides, still distant, but gradually closing up grey gaps in their line. That black line extended north as far as eye could see. The fact became evident that Brite's outfit was driving into the vast herd, leisurely grazing along. The situation grew hourly more nerve-racking. To swerve to either side was impossible, to stop or go back meant signal failure, defeat, and loss. The drivers absolutely had to stick to the trail and keep going.

The Chisholm Trail had again taken a decided slant to the north-west. And probably somewhere ahead, perhaps across the Red River, it would bisect the vast herd of buffalo. The alarming discovery was made that the following herd of long-horns had come up in plain sight, and ten miles behind it another wavered, a long, dark line on the grey. Brite asked his men why these pursuing trail drivers were pressing him so hard. And the answer was Indians, buffalo, and the two hundred thousand head of cattle that had started and must keep on. To turn or slow down meant to fall by the wayside.

Texas Joe drove late that day and made dry camp. All night the guards sang and rode to keep the herd bedded down. Morning disclosed the endless stream of buffalo closer. But Indians were not in sight. Smoke signals, however, arose from two distant hills, one on each side of the trail.

Loss of sleep and ceaseless vigilance by night, and the slow march by day, wore upon the drivers. Brite had ceased to count the camps. Every hour was fraught with dread expectation. Yet at last they reached the Red River. The buffalo were crossing some miles above the trail, but a spur of the prodigious herd kept swinging in behind. Texas Joe pointed the cattle across and took the lead himself, magnificent in his dauntlessness.

The Red was midway between high and low water stages—its most treacherous condition. Four hours were consumed in the drive across and more than a hundred long-horns were lost. All the drivers were needed to get the wagons over, a desperate task which only such heedless young men would have undertaken.

Night found them in camp, some of them spent, all of them wearied, yet cheered by the fact that Doan's Post was within striking distance on the morrow.

Texas Joe drove the remaining ten miles to Doan's before noon of the next day. All the drivers wanted to get a few hours' release from the herd, to drink, to talk, to get rid of one danger by hearing of another. But when Brite called for volunteers to stand guard with the herd for a few hours they all voiced their willingness to stay.

"Wal, I'll have to settle it," said Brite. "Ackerman, yu drive the Hardys in. Tex, yu an' Pan Handle come with me. . . . Boys, we'll be back pronto to give yu a chance to ride in."

Doan's Post gave evidence of having more than its usual number of inhabitants and visitors. Horses were numerous on the grass plain around the post. Half a dozen wagons were drawn up before the grey, squat, weather-beaten houses. A sign, Doan's Store, in large black letters, showed on the south side of the largest house. This place, run by Tom Doan, was a trading-post for Indians and cattlemen, and was in the heyday of its useful and hazardous existence.

Mounted men, riders with unsaddled horses, Indians lounging and squatting before the doors, watched the newcomers with interest. Arriving travellers were the life of Doan's Post. But the way Pan Handle and Texas Joe dismounted a goodly distance from these bearded watchers, and proceeded forward on foot, surely had as much significance for them as it had for Brite. The crowd of a dozen or more spread to let the two slow visitors approach the door. Then Brite came on beside the Hardy wagon. Reddie, disobedient as usual, had joined them.

"Howdy, Tom," called Brite to the stalwart man in the door.

"Howdy yoreself," came the hearty response. "Wal, damme if it ain't Adam Brite. Git right down an' come in."

"Tom, yu ought to remember my foreman, Texas Joe. An' this is Pan Handle Smith. We've got a sick man in the wagon heah. Hardy, by name. Thet's his daughter on the seat. They're all thet's left of a wagon-train bound for California.

Can yu take care of them for a while, till Hardy is able to join another train?"

"Yu bet I can," replied the genial Doan. Willing hands lifted Hardy out of the wagon and carried him into the Post. Ann sat on the wagon seat, her pretty face worn and thin, her eyes full of tears, perhaps of deliverance, perhaps of something else, as she gazed down upon the bareheaded cowboy.

"We've come to the partin' of the trail, Miss Ann," Deuce was saying, in a strong and vibrant voice, "Yu're safe heah, thank God. An' yore dad will come around. I'm shore hopin' we'll make it through to Dodge. An'—I'm askin' yu—will it be all right for me to wait there till yu come?"

"Oh yes—I—I'd be so glad," she murmured shyly.

"An' go on to California with yu?" he concluded boldly.

"If yu will," she replied; and for a moment time and place were naught to these two.

"Aw, thet's good of yu," he burst out at last. "It's just been wonderful—knowin' yu. . . . Good-bye. . . . I must go back to the boys."

"Good-bye," she faltered, and gave him her hand. Deuce kissed it right gallantly, and then fled out across the prairie toward the herd.

CHAPTER FOURTEEN

REDDIE jumped off her horse beside the Hardy wagon, on the seat of which Ann sat still as a stone, watching the cowboy. Ackerman turned once to hold his sombrero high. Then she waved her handkerchief. He wheeled and did not look back again.

"Ann, it's pretty tough—this sayin' good-bye," spoke up Reddie. "Let's go in the Post, away from these men. I'm shore gonna bawl."

"Oh, Reddie, I—I'm bawling now," cried Ann, as she clambered down, not sure of her sight. "He was so—so good—so fine. . . . Oh, will we ever meet—again?"

Arm in arm the girls went toward the door of the Post, where Brite observed Ann shrink visibly from two sloe-eyed, gaunt, and sombre Indians.

"Let's get this over pronto, Tex," said Brite. "I'll buy what supplies Doan can furnish."

"All right, boss, Pan an' I will come in presently," replied Texas. "We want to ask some questions thet mebbe Doan wouldn't answer."

Brite hurried into the Post. It was a picturesque, crowded, odorous place with its colourful Indian trappings, its formidable arsenal, its full shelves and burdened counters. When Doan returned from the other quarters, where evidently he had seen to Hardy's comfort, Brite wrote with a stub of a lead pencil the supplies he needed.

"What you think? This ain't Santone or Abilene," he said gruffly. "But I can let you have flour, beans, coffee, tobacco, an' mebbe——"

"Do yore best, Tom," interrupted Brite hastily. "I'm no robber. Can yu haul the stuff oot to camp?"

"Shore, inside an hour."

"Thet's all, then, an' much obliged. . . . Any trail drivers ahead of me?"

"Not lately. You've got the trail all to yourself. An' thet's damn bad."

Brite was perfectly well aware of this.

"Comanches an' Kiowas particular bad lately," went on Doan. "Both Nigger

403

Horse an' Santana are on the rampage. Let me give you a hunch. If thet old Comanche devil rides into camp, you parley with him, argue with him, but in the end you give him what he wants. An' for thet reason take grub to spare an' particular coffee an' tobacco. But if thet Kiowa chief stops you don't give him a thing 'cept a piece of your mind. Santana is dangerous to weak outfits. But he's a coward an' he can be bluffed. Don't stand any monkey business from the Kiowas. Show them you are heavily armed an' will shoot at the drop of a hat."

"Much obliged, Doan. I'll remember your advice."

"You're goin' to be blocked by buffalo, unless you can break through. I'll bet ten million buffalo have passed heah this month."

"What month an' day is it, anyhow?"

"Wal, you have been trail-drivin'. . . . Let's see. It's the sixteenth of July."

"Yu don't say? Time shore flies on the trail. . . . I'd like to know if Ross Hite an' three of his ootfit have passed this way lately?"

"Been several little outfits by this week," replied the trader evasively. "Travellin' light an' fast. . . . I don't know Hite personally. Heard of him, shore. I don't ask questions of my customers, Brite."

"Yu know yore business, Doan," returned Brite shortly. "For yore benefit, though, I'll tell yu Hite's ootfit raided us twice. He had all of my herd at one time."

"Hell you say!" ejaculated Doan sharply, pulling his beard. "What come of it?"

"Wal, we got the stock back an' left some of Hite's ootfit along the trail."

Reddie Bayne came stumbling along, wiping her eyes.

"Wait, Reddie. I'll go with you," called Brite. "Where can I say good-bye to the Hardys?"

She pointed to the open door through which she had emerged. Brite went in quickly and got that painful interview over.

"Just a minute, Brite," called Doan, as the cattleman hurried out. "I'm not so particular aboot Indians as I am aboot men of my own colour. But I have to preserve friendly relations with all the tribes. They trade with me. I am goin' to tell you, though, that the two bucks standin' outside are scouts for some Comanche outfit, an' they've been waitin' for the first trail herd to come along. You know what all you trail drivers do. Pack the bucks back to the next herd, if you can. It's a mistaken policy. But the hunch I want to give you is to stop those two Comanches."

"Stop them?"

"Shore. Don't let them come out an' look over your outfit—then ride to report to their chief. Like as not it's Nigger Horse, himself."

"That *is* a hunch. I'll tell Texas," replied Brite, pondering, and went out with Reddie.

"Gee!" she whispered, with round eyes. "He's givin' us a hunch to shoot some more Comanches."

"'Pears thet way. Yet he shore didn't give us any hunch aboot Ross Hite."

Texas Joe and Pan Handle appeared to be in a colloquy with two men, and Williams and Smiling Pete were engaged with the remainder of the white men present.

"Williams, yu'll ride over to say good-bye?" queried Brite.

"Shore we will. For two bits I'd go on all the way with yu," he replied.

"Wal, I'll give yu a lot more than thet. . . . Yu've been mighty helpful. I couldn't begin to thank yu."

"Pete wants to hunt buffalo," rejoined Williams. "An' thet sticks us heah."

Brite got on his horse. "Tex, we're goin'. Come heah."

Texas strode over, and giving Reddie a gentle shove as she mounted, he came close to Brite.

"Texas," whispered Brite, bending over. "Those two Comanches there are scouts for a raidin' bunch, so says Doan. Dam' if he didn't hint we ought to do somethin' aboot it. He cain't, 'cause he has to keep on friendly terms with all the reddies."

"Wal, boss, we got thet hunch, too, an' heahed somethin' aboot Hite. I'll tell yu when we come back to camp."

Reddie had put her black to a canter, and had covered half the distance back to camp before Brite caught up with her.

"Save yore hawse, girl. What's yore hurry?"

"Dad, I just get sick inside when I see thet look come to Texas Jack's eyes," she replied.

"What look?"

"I don't know what to call it. I saw it first thet day just before he drawed on Wallen. Like thet queer lightnin' flash we saw durin' the storm the other night."

"Reddie, yu ought to be used to hard looks of trail drivers by now. It's a hard life."

"But I want Texas Jack to quit throwin' guns!" she cried, with surprisingly poignant passion.

"Wal! Wal!" exclaimed Brite. "An' why, lass?"

"Pretty soon he'll be another gunman like Pan Handle. An' then, sooner or later, he'll get killed!"

"I reckon thet's true enough," replied Brite. "Come to think aboot thet, I feel the same way. What air we goin' to do to stop him?"

"Stop Tex? It cain't be done, Dad."

"Wal, mebbe not oot heah on the trail. But if we ever end this drive—then it could be done. *Yu* could stop Tex, lass."

She spurred the black and drew away swift as the wind. Brite gathered that she had realized how she could put an end to the wildness of Joe Shipman.

The cattle were grazing and in good order. Westward along the river, clouds of dust rolled aloft, and at intervals a low roar of hoofs came on the still hot air. The buffalo were crossing the Red River. Brite and Reddie took the places of San Sabe and Rolly Little at guard, and the two cowboys were like youngsters just released from school. They raced for town. Several slow dragging hours passed by. The herd did not move half a mile; the *remuda* covered less ground. Brite did not relish the sight of a mounted Indian who rode out from the Post and from a distance watched the camp.

A little later Brite was startled out of his rest by gunshots. He leaped up in time to see the Indian spy riding like a streak across the plain. Texas and Pan Handle, two hundred yards to the left, were shooting at the Comanche as fast as they could pull triggers. Probably their idea was to frighten him, thought Brite, in which case they succeeded amply. No Indian could ride so well as a Comanche and this one broke all records for a short race. It chanced that he took down the plain in a direction which evidently brought him close to the far end of the herd, where one of the cowboys was on guard. This fellow, either Holden or Bender, saw the Indian and opened up on him with a buffalo gun. From that instant until the Comanche was out of sight he rode hidden on the far side of his mustang.

Texas Joe was using forceful range language when he rode in, and manifestly had been irritated by something.

"What ails yu, Tex?" asked Brite. "I'm feelin' cheerful, myself."

"Yu're loco. Do yu know what we did?—We hired them cowhands to hawg-tie the two Comanches an' to keep 'em in Doan's storehouse for a couple of days. Great idee! But all for nothin'. This buck we was shootin' at had counted our wagons, hawses, cattle, an' drivers. We was shore shootin' at thet redskin to kill. But he was oot of range. What'n hell was eatin' yu men thet yu didn't see him long ago?"

Brite maintained a discreet silence.

"Boss, the supplies will be oot pronto," went on Texas as he dismounted. "Reddie, if yu have another hawse handy I'll relieve one of the boys."

"Same heah," spoke up Pan Handle.

"Throw some grub pronto, Moze. . . . Boss, our man Hite rode through heah day before yestiddy mawnin'. He had three fellars with him, one crippled up serious an' had to be tied in the saddle. Hite was spittin' fire, an' they all was ugly."

"Did they stop at Doan's?"

"Shore, accordin' to Bud. They was oot of grub an' ammunition. Had only two pack hawses. We shore won't see no more of Hite till we get to Dodge. He hangs oot at Hays City, so Bud said, an' comes often to Dodge."

"Let Hite go, boys. No sense huntin' up trouble," advised Brite tersely.

"Boss, yu're a forgivin' cuss," drawled Texas admiringly. "Now I just cain't be thet way. An' Pan, heah, why, he'll ride a thousand miles to meet thet Ross Hite again. An' I'm goin' with him."

"Yu air not," spoke up Reddie tartly, a red spot in each cheek.

"Wal, dog-gone! There's the kid, bossy as ever. Brite, if I get plugged on the way up yu let Reddie boss the ootfit."

Texas Joe had found a way to make Reddie wince, and he was working it on every possible occasion. The chances were surely even that the daring cowboy would lose his life one way or another before the end of the trail, and Reddie simply could not stand a hint of it without betraying her fear. Probably, to judge from her flashing eyes, she would have made a strong retort had it not been for the arrival of Williams and Smiling Pete.

"Wal, heah we air to set in our last supper on Moze," said Williams genially. "I shore hate to say good-bye to this outfit. Folks get awful close on such drives as we had comin' up."

"Reddie Bayne, don't yu want to stay behind with us?" asked Smiling Pete teasingly. "We shore won't boss yu about like thet Texas fellar."

"Ump-umm. I like yu, Smilin' Pete," replied Reddie, in the same spirit. "But I'm strong for Santone an' Dad's ranch."

"Dad?" echoed the hunters, in unison.

"Shore. I've adopted Mr. Brite as my dad."

"Haw! Haw! The lucky son-of-a-gun. He ain't so old, neither. Mebbe Hash an' me will have to send our cairds to yore——"

But Reddie ran away behind the chuck-wagon.

"Come heah, yu men, and be serious," said Brite. "We want all the hunches yu can give us for the rest of this drive north."

Brite's outfit left Doan's Post before sunrise next morning with just short of six-thousand long-horn cattle. The buffalo herd had apparently kept along the Red River.

In the afternoon of that day a band of Comanches rode out from a pass between two hills and held up the cavalcade. Brite galloped ahead in some trepidation, yelling for Reddie to leave the *remuda* and follow him. When he arrived at the head of the herd he found Texas Joe and Pan Handle, with the other drivers, lined up before about thirty squat, pointed-faced, long-haired Indians.

"Boss, meet Nigger Hawse an' his ootfit," was Texas's laconic greeting.

"Howdy, Chief," returned Brite, facing Nigger Horse. This Comanche did not look his fame, but appeared to be an ordinary redskin, stolid and unofficious. He did not altogether lack dignity. To Brite he was a surprise and a relief. But his basilisk eyes might have hid much. Brite wished the buffalo hunters had come on with them.

"How," replied Nigger Horse, raising a slow hand.

"What yu want, Chief?"

"Beef."

Brite waved a magnanimous hand toward the herd.

"Help yoreself."

The Comanche spoke in low grunts to his redmen.

"Tobac," he went on, his dark, inscrutable eyes again fixing on Brite.

"Plenty. Wagon come," replied Brite, pointing to Moze, who had the team approaching at a trot. Nigger Horse gazed in the direction of the chuck-wagon, then back at the vast herd, and lastly at the formidably armed drivers solidly arrayed in a line.

"Flour," resumed the chief. His English required a practised ear to distinguish, but Brite understood him and nodded his willingness.

"Coffee."

Brite held up five fingers to designate the number of sacks he was willing to donate.

"Beans."

"Heap big bag," replied Brite.

Manifestly this generosity from a trail driver had not been the accustomed thing.

"Boss, the old devil wants us to refuse somethin'," put in Texas.

"An' he'll keep on askin' till yu have to refuse," added Pan Handle.

Moze arrived with the chuck-wagon, behind which the Comanches rode in a half-circle, greedy-eyed and jabbering. Moze's black face could not turn pale, but it looked mighty strange.

"Pile oot, Moze," ordered Brite. "Open up yore box, an' get oot the goods we selected for this missionary business."

"Yas s-suh—y-yas, suh," replied the negro, scared out of his wits.

"Sack of flour first, Moze," said Brite. "An' throw it up on his hawse. Make oot it's heavy."

Obviously this last was not necessary. Either the sack was heavy or Moze had grown weak, for he laboured with it and almost knocked Nigger Horse off his mustang. The Indian let out what sounded like: "Yah! Yah!" But he surely held on to the flour. Then Brite ordered Moze to burden the Comanche further with the generous donation of tobacco, coffee, and beans.

"There yu air, Chief," called out Brite, making a show of friendliness.

"Flour," said Nigger Horse.

"Yu got it," replied Brite, pointing to the large sack.

The Indian emphatically shook his head.

"Greasy old robber!" ejaculated Texas. "He wants more. Boss, heah's where yu stand fast. If yu give in he'll take all our grub."

"Brite, don't give him any more. We'd better fight than starve," said Pan Handle.

Whereupon Brite, just as emphatically, shook his head and said: "No more, Chief."

The Comanche yelled something in his own tongue. Its content was not reassuring.

"Heap powder—bullet," added Nigger Horse.

"No," declared Brite.

The Indian thundered his demand. This had the effect of rousing Brite's ire, not a particularly difficult task. Brite shook his head in slow and positive refusal.

"Give Injun all!" yelled the chief.

"Give INJUN HELL!" roared Brite, suddenly furious.

"Thet's the talk, boss," shouted Texas. "Yu can bluff the old geezer."

"Brite, stick to thet," broke in Pan Handle, in ringing voice. "Listen, all of yu. If it comes to a fight, Tex an' I air good for Nigger Hawse an' four or five on each side of him. Yu boys look after the ends."

"Reddie, yu duck back behind the wagon an' do yore shootin' from there," ordered Texas.

Then ensued the deadlock. It was a critical moment, with life or death quivering on a hair balance. How hideously that savage's lineaments changed! The wily old Comanche had made his bluff and it had been called. Probably he understood more of the white man's language than he pretended. Certainly he comprehended the cold front of those frowning trail drivers.

"Boys, yu got time to get on the ground," called the practical Texas, slipping out of his saddle and stepping out in front of his horse. In another moment all the men, except Brite, had followed suit. Texas and Pan Handle held a gun in each hand. At such close range they would do deadly work before the Comanches could level a rifle or draw a bow. Nigger Horse undoubtedly saw this—that he had bluffed the wrong outfit. Still, he did not waver in his savage dominance.

Brite had an inspiration.

"Chief," he burst out, "we do good by yu. We give heaps. But no more. If yu want fight, we fight. . . . Two trail herds to-morrow." Here Brite held up two fingers, and indicating his cattle, made signs that more were coming up the trail. "Heap more. So many like buffalo. White men with herds come all time. Two moons." And with both hands up he opened each to spread his fingers, and repeated this time and again.

"Ugh!" ejaculated Nigger Horse. He understood, and that tactful persuasion of Brite's was the deciding factor. He let out sharp guttural sentences. Two of his followers wheeled their ponies toward the herd, fitting arrows to their bows. Then Nigger Horse, burdened with his possessions, not one parcel of which would he relinquish to eager hands, rode back without another word, followed by his band.

"Close shave!" breathed Brite, in intense relief.

"Shore. But closer for thet bull-haided Comanche an' his ootfit," declared Texas. "He made a mistake an' got in too close. We'd cleaned them oot in ten seconds. Hey, Pan?"

"I'd like to have broke loose," replied Pan Handle, in a queer voice.

"Let wal enough alone, yu fire-eaters," yelled Brite.

"Boss, we'll hang together till the *remuda* passes," returned Texas.

"Whoopee! We're a hot ootfit!" shouted Deuce Ackerman lustily, his head thrown back, his jaw corded. The relaxation of other drivers showed in yell or similar wild statement.

"I doan' know aboot this heah ootrageous luck," observed Whittaker softly, as if to himself. He was the quietest of the drivers.

"Somebody'd had to shoot quick to beat me borin' thet dirty old redskin," spoke up Reddie coolly.

"My Gawd! The girl's ruined!" ejaculated Texas.

"Haw! Haw! Haw!" roared the tenderfoot Bender. But a second look at the hulking, fierce-eyed, black-faced young Pennsylvanian convinced the cattleman that Bender's tenderfoot days were passed. He himself felt the cold, hard, wild spirit rise.

"On, boys," he ordered. "Once across the Canadian we'll be half-way an' more to Dodge."

"We'll drive 'em, boss," replied Texas Joe grimly. "No more lazy, loafin', fattenin', mossy-horns this trip!"

They made ten miles before night, ending the longest drive since they had left San Antonio. The night fell dark, with rumble of thunder and sheet lightning in the distance. The tired cattle bedded down early and held well all night. Morning came, lowering and threatening, with a chill wind that swept over the herd from the north. Soon the light failed until day was almost as dark as night. A terrific hailstorm burst upon the luckless herd and drivers. The hailstones grew larger and larger as the storm swept on, until the pellets of grey ice were as large as walnuts. The drivers from suffering a severe pounding passed to extreme risk of their lives. They had been forced to protect heads and faces with whatever was available. Reddie Bayne was knocked off her horse and carried senseless to the wagon; San Sabe swayed in his saddle like a drunken man; Texas Joe tied his coat round his sombrero and yelled when the big hailstones bounced off his head; bloody and bruised, the other drivers resembled men who had engaged in fierce fistic encounters.

When this queer freak of nature passed, the ground was covered half a foot deep with hailstones. Dead rabbits and antelope littered the plain, and all the way, as far as Brite could see to the rear, stunned and beaten cattle lay on the ground or staggered along.

"I told yu-all things were gonna happen," yelled Texas to his followers as they made camp that night, sore and beaten of body. "But I'm not carin', if only the buffalo will pass us by."

Next day they were visited by members of a tribe of Kiowas supposed to be friendly with the whites. They had held "heap big peace talk" with Uncle Sam. Brite did not give so much as he had in the case of the Comanches, yet he did well by them.

During the night these savages stampeded the south end of the herd. How it was done did not appear until next day, when among the scattered cattle was found a long-horn here and there with an arrow embedded in his hide. Some of these had to be shot. The herd was held over until all the stampeded steers and cows could be rounded up. It took three days of strenuous riding by day and guarding by night. Texas Joe and his trail drivers passed into what San Sabe described as being "poison-fightin' mad!"

Bitter as gall to them was it to see two trail herds pass them by and forge to the front. After seven weeks or more of leadership! But Brite did not take it so hard. Other herds now, and both together not so large as his, would bear the brunt of what lay ahead.

That fourth day, when they were off again, buffalo once more made their appearance. Soldiers from Fort Cobb, a post forty miles off the trail to the east, informed Brite that they had been turned back by the enormous, impenetrable mass of buffalo some miles westward. They had been trailing a marauding bunch of Apaches from the Staked Plain.

Brite's men drove on, and their difficulties multiplied. Stampedes became frequent; storms and swollen creeks further impeded their progress; the chuck-wagon, springing leaks in its boat-like bottom, had almost to be carried across the North Fork of the Red. Sometimes it became necessary to build pontoons, and riders had to swim their horses alongside, holding the pontoons in place. But they kept on doggedly, their foreman cool and resourceful, all bound to this seemingly impossible drive.

Pond Creek, which headed sixty miles north-west of Fort Cobb, was an objective Texas Joe spoke of for twenty-four hours and drove hard one long day to reach.

Brite had his misgivings when at sunset of that day he rode to the top of a slope and saw the herd gaining momentum on the down grade, drawn by sight and scent of water after a hot, dry drive.

This creek, usually only a shallow run, appeared bank-full, a swift, narrow river extremely dangerous at that stage for beast and man. There had been no rain that day anywhere near the region the herd had traversed. Texas Joe had been justified in thinking Pond Creek was at normal height, and he had let the herd go over the ridge without first scouting ahead, as was his custom. It was too late now unless the herd could be stopped.

Brite spurred his horse down the slope, yelling over his shoulder for Reddie to hurry. Drivers on each side of the herd were forging to the front, inspired, no doubt, by the fiercely riding Texas Joe. It was bad going, as Brite found out to his sorrow, when he was thrown over the head of his falling horse, thus sustaining a mean fall. Reddie was quick to leap off and go to his side.

"Oh, Dad! Thet was a tumble!" she cried. "I thought yu'd break yore neck.... Set up. Air yu all heah? Let me feel."

"I reckon—nothin' busted," groaned the cattleman, getting up laboriously. "If thet ground hadn't been soft—wal, yu'd——"

"My Gawd, Dad! Look!" cried Reddie frantically, leaping on her horse. "They're stampedin' down this hill."

Brite got up to stand a moment surveying the scene. A tremendous trampling, tussling, cracking roar, permeated by a shrill bawling sound, dinned in his ears.

"Red, it's only the back end thet's stampedin'," he shouted.

"Yes. But they're rushin' the front down."

"Rustle. We can help some, but don't take chances."

They galloped down along the flank of the jostling cattle to the short quarter of a mile of slope between the point of the herd and the river. The drivers were here in a bunch, yelling, riding, shooting, plunging their mounts at the foremost old mossy-horns. Brite and Reddie rode in to help, keeping close to the outside.

Then followed a hot-pressed, swift and desperate charge on the part of the trail drivers to hold the front of the herd. It was hazardous work. Texas Joe yelled orders through pale lips, but no driver at any distance heard them. The bulls and steers had been halted, but as pressure was exerted in the rear they began to toss their great, horned heads, and to bawl and tear up the ground. The mass of the herd, up on the steeper slope, maddened now to get to the water, could not be bolstered back by the front line.

"BACK!" yelled Texas, in stentorian voice, waving wide his arms to the drivers. All save San Sabe heard or saw, and ran their horses to either side. Deuce, Texas, Reddie, Whittaker, and Bender reached the open behind Brite just as a terrible groan ran through the herd.

Texas Joe's frantic yells and actions actuated all to join in the effort to make San Sabe hear. His position was extremely perilous, being exactly in the centre of the straining herd. His horse was rearing. San Sabe, gun in each hand, shot fire and smoke into the very faces of the leaders. Pan Handle, Holden, and Little, flashing by on terrorized horses, failed to attract him. How passionate and fierce his actions! Hatless and coatless, his hair flying, this half-breed *vaquero* fronted the maddened herd with an instinct of a thousand years of cattle mastery.

The line of horned heads curved at each end, as if a dam had burst where it

413

joined the banks. Suddenly then the centre gave way with that peculiar grinding roar of hoofs, horns, and bodies. Like a flood it spilled down upon San Sabe. His horse gave a magnificent leap back and to the side, just escaping the rolling juggernaut. The horse saw, if San Sabe did not, that escape to either side was impossible. On the very horns of the running bulls he plunged for the river.

But he did not gain a yard on those fleet long-horns, propelled forward by thousands of rushing bodies behind. To Brite's horror it appeared that the limber cattle actually gained on San Sabe. His horse tripped at the brink of the bank and plunged down. The rider was pitched headlong. Next instant a live wall of beasts poured over the brink with a resounding hollow splash, and as if by magic the river bank became obliterated.

CHAPTER FIFTEEN

SPELLBOUND, Brite gazed at the thrilling and frightful spectacle. A gigantic wave rose and swelled across the creek to crash over the opposite bank. In another moment the narrow strip of muddy water vanished, and in its place was a river of bristling horns, packed solid, twisting, bobbing under and up again, and sweeping down with the current. But for that current of deep water the stream bed would have been filled with cattle from bank to bank, and the mass of the herd would have plunged across over hundreds of dead bodies.

In an incredibly short space the whole herd had rolled into the river, line after line taking the place of the beasts that were swept away in the current. From plunging pell-mell the cattle changed abruptly to swimming pell-mell. And when the last line had gone overboard the front line, far down the stream, was wading out on the other side.

The change from sodden, wrestling crash to strange silence seemed as miraculous as the escape of the herd. Momentum and current forced the crazy animals across the river. Two hundred yards down all the opposite shelving shore was blotted out by cattle, and as hundreds waded out other hundreds took their places, so that there was no blocking of the on-sweeping tide of heads and horns. It was the most remarkable sight Brite had ever seen in connection with cattle.

Texas Joe was the first to break out of his trance.

"——thet fool!" he thundered, with a mighty curse and with convulsed face, eyes shut tight, and tears streaming from under the lids, with lips drawn and cheeks set in rigid holes, he seemed to gaze up blindly at the sky, invoking help where there was no help, surrendering in that tragic moment to the inevitable and ruthless calling of the trail driver.

Pan Handle rode down to the scored bank where San Sabe had disappeared. His comrade Holden followed slowly. Rolly Little bestrode his horse as if stunned.

Brite remembered Reddie, and hastened to her side. With bowed head and shaking shoulders she bent over, hanging to the pommel of her saddle.

"Brace up, Red," said Brite hoarsely, though deeply shaken himself. "We got to go through."

"Oh—we'd grown—like one family," cried the girl, raising her face.

"Reddie, drive yore *remuda* in," shouted Texas, in strident voice. "Deuce, take Holden an' foller the herd. Rest of yu help me with the wagon."

Night settled down again, silent except for the rush of the sliding river and the strange back-lashes of sand-laden water. Moze bustled silently around the camp fire. Several of the drivers were eating as if that task, like the others, had to be done. Texas, Pan Handle, Deuce, and Rolly were out on guard, hungry and wet and miserable. Reddie had gone supperless to bed. Brite sat drying his legs, fighting his conscience. Three young faces appeared spectrally in the white embers of the fire!

Next day it was as if the trail drivers had never weakened and almost cracked. Obstacles heightened their spirits and deadened their memories. Deer Creek was bone dry. The stock got through the following day without water. A third drive over miles of wasteland and dragging sand put horses as well as cattle in a precarious condition. All night long the herd milled like the ceaseless eddy of a river, bawling and lowing. No sleep or rest that night for any of Brite's outfit! If next morning they found a branch of the South Canadian dusty and dry, that would be the end.

Indians stopped with Moze that night. "No water!" they said. Buffalo had ranged to the West.

At dawn the drivers pointed the herd and goaded them on ruthlessly. The sun rose red in a copper sky. The heat veils floated up from the sand. Miles from the branch of the Canadian the old mossy-horns scented water. The riders could not hold them. Nothing could stop the thirst-maddened brutes. When the leaders launched out, the whole herd stampeded as one. The trail drivers had a wild run, but without hope of checking the stampede. They rolled on, a sweeping, thundering clatter, shaking the earth and sending aloft a great yellow cloud of dust.

The river checked that stampede and saved Brite incalculable loss. Once across the South Branch into grassy level range again, the trail drivers forgot the past and looked only ahead. Day after day passed. At Wolf Creek they encountered the long-looked-for buffalo herd, the ragged strings of which reached out to the east. Texas Joe rested his outfit and stock a day at this good camp site.

A sultry night presaged storm. But the interminable hours wore to dawn, and the torrid day passed without rain. Texas Joe, sensing another storm, drove the herd into the head of a narrow valley, steep-walled and easy to guard.

"I doan' like this heah weather," said Whittaker, breaking a sombre silence around the camp fire.

"Wal, who does?" rejoined Texas wearily. "But a good soakin' rain would help us oot."

"Shore, if it rained rain."

"My hair cracks too much to suit me," said another.

"Reddie, how's the *remuda*?"

"Actin' queer," she replied. "Sniffin' the air, poundin' the ground, quiverin' all over."

Brite feared that the peculiar condition of earth, atmosphere, and sky presaged one of the rare, awe-inspiring, and devastating electric storms that this region was noted for. He recalled what trail drivers had told which seemed too incredible to believe. But here was the strange red sunset, the absolutely still and sultry dusk, the overcast sky that yet did not wholly hide the pale stars, the ghastliness of the unreal earth.

"World comin' to an end!" ejaculated Texas Joe. Like all men of the open, used to the phenomena of the elements, he was superstitious and acknowledged a mysterious omniscience in nature.

"Fine night to be home sparkin' my girl," joked Rolly Little.

"Rolly, boy, yu'll never see home no more, nor thet flirtin' little redhaid," taunted Deuce Ackerman fatalistically.

"Come to think of thet, all redhaids are flirty an' fickle," philosophized Texas.

Reddie heard, but for once had no audacious retort. She was obsessed with gravity.

"Tex—Dad—it ain't natural," she said nervously.

"Wal, lass, whatever it is, it'll come an' pass, an' spare us mebbe, please God," rejoined the cattleman.

"Boss, is it gonna be one of them storms when electricity runs like water?" queried Texas.

"I don't know, Tex, I swear to goodness I don't. But I've heahed when the sky looks like a great white globe of glass with a light burnin' inside thet it'll burst presently an' let down a million jumpin' stars an' balls an' ropes an' sparks."

Texas got to his feet, dark and stern. "Fork yore hawses, everybody. If we're goin' to hell we'll go together."

They rode out to join the four guards already on duty.

"What's comin' off?" yelled Less Holden, as the others came within earshot.

"We're gamblin' with death, cowboy," returned Texas Joe.

So indeed it seemed to Brite. The weird conditions imperceptibly increased. It became so light that the faces of the drivers shone like marble in moonlight. There were no shadows. Darkness of night had been eliminated, yet no moon showed, and the stars had vanished in the globe overhead.

"We can hold 'em in heah onless they stampede," said Texas. "What's the stock doin', Less?"

"Not grazin', thet's shore. An' the *remuda* is plumb loco."

Brite followed Reddie over to the dark patch of mustangs, huddled in a compact drove under the west wall. This embankment was just steep and high enough to keep the mustangs from climbing. A restless nickering ran through the mass. They trooped with low roar of hoofs away from the approaching riders.

"Just a little fussy, Dad," said Reddie hopefully.

"Cain't yu sing them quiet, Reddie?" asked Brite.

"I'll try, but I shore don't feel like no nightingale to-night," replied Reddie. "I haven't heahed any of the boys."

In low and quavering tones Reddie began "La Paloma," and as she progressed with the song, her sweet and plaintive voice grew stronger. The strange atmosphere appeared to intensify it, until toward the close she was singing with a power and beauty that entranced the listening cattlemen. When she finished, Texas Joe, who seldom sang, burst out with his wild and piercing tenor, and then the others chimed in to ring a wonderful medley down that lonely valley. The *remuda* quieted down, and at length the great herd appeared chained to music.

The trail drivers sang in chorus and in quartets, duets, and singly, until they had repeated their limited stock of songs, and had exhausted their vocal powers.

When they had no more to give, the hour was late, and as if in answer, from far down the range rumbled and mumbled low thunder, while pale flashes of lightning shone all over the sky.

The drivers sat their horses and waited. That they were uneasy, that they did not smoke or sit still, proved the abnormality of the hour. They kept close together and spoke often. Brite observed that Reddie seldom let her restless black move a rod away.

The rumble of thunder and the queer flashes might have presaged a storm, but apparently it did not come closer. Brite observed that the singular sheen became enhanced, if anything. The sultry, drowsy air grew thicker. It had weight. It appeared to settle down over stock and men like a transparent blanket.

Suddenly the sky ripped across with terrific bars of lightning that gave forth a tearing, cracking sound. Rain began to fall, but not in any quantity. Brite waited for the expected clap of thunder. It did not materialize. Then he recognized for a certainty the symptoms of an electrical storm such as had been described to him.

"Boys, we're in for a galvanizin'," he called. "We're as safe heah as anywheres. We cain't do nothin' but take our chance an' try to hold the cattle. But if what's been told me is true they'll be scared still."

"We're heah, boss," boomed Texas, and a reassuring shout came from Pan Handle.

"Oh, Dad!" cried Reddie. "Run yore hand through yore hawse's mane!"

Brite did as bidden, to be startled at a cracking, sizzling sweep of sparks clear to the ears of his horse. He jumped as if he had been shot. Brite did not attempt that again. But he watched Reddie. Electric fluid appeared to play and burn with greenish fire through the black's mane, and run out on the tips of his ears and burst. The obedient horse did not like this, but he held firm, just prancing a little.

"Lass, the air is charged," said Brite fearfully.

"Yes, Dad, an' it's gonna bust!" screamed Reddie as the whole range land blazed under the white dome.

Hoarse shouts from the drivers sounded as if wrenched from them. But after that one outburst they kept mute. Brite had involuntarily closed his eyes at the intense flare. Even with his lids tightly shut he saw the lightning flashes. He opened them upon an appalling display across the heavens. Flash after flash illumined the sky, and if thunder followed it was faint and far off. The flashes rose on all sides to and across the zenith, where, fusing in one terrible blaze, they appeared to set fire to the roof of the heavens.

The *remuda* shrank in a shuddering, densely packed mass, too paralysed to bolt. The cattle froze in their tracks, heads down, lowing piteously.

No longer was there any darkness anywhere. No shadow under the wall! No shadow of horse and rider on the ground! Suddenly the flash lightning shifted to forked lightning—magnificent branched streaks of white fire that ribbed the sky. These were as suddenly succeeded by long, single ropes or chains of lightning.

Gradually the horses drew closer together, if not at the instigation of their riders, then at their own. They rubbed flanks; they hid their heads against each other.

"My Gawd! it's turrible!" Texas cried hoarsely. "We gotta get oot of the way. When this hell's over, thet herd will run mad."

"Tex, they're struck by lightnin'," yelled Holden. "I see cattle down."

"Oot of the narrow place heah, men," shouted Brite.

They moved out into the open valley beyond the constricted neck, and strange to see, the *remuda* followed, the whole drove moving as one horse. They had their heads turned in, so that they really backed away from the wall.

The chain lightnings increased in number, in brilliance, in length and breadth until all in a marvellous instant they coalesced into a sky-wide canopy of intensest blue too burning for the gaze of man. How long that terrifying phenomenon lasted Brite could not tell, but when, at the husky yells of his men, he opened his eyes, the terrific blue blaze of heaven had changed to balls of lightning.

Here was the moment Brite believed he was demented. And these fearless cowhands shared the emotion which beset him. They gaped with protruding eyes at the yellow balls appearing from nowhere, to roll down the walls, to bounce off and burst into crackling sparks. It appeared that balls of fire were shooting in every direction to the prolonged screams of horses in terror.

Brite took the almost fainting Reddie into his arms, and held her tight. He expected death at any instant. Zigzag balls of lightning grew in size and number and rapidity until the ground was criss-crossed with them. They ran together to burst into bits or swell into a larger ball. Then to Brite's horror, to what seemed his distorted vision, these fiendish balls ran over the horses, to hang on their ears, to drop off their noses, to roll back and forth along the reins, to leap and poise upon the rim of his sombrero. Yet he was not struck dead, as seemed inevitable.

All at once Brite became aware of heat, intense sulphurous heat, encompassing him like a hot blanket. Coincident with that the rolling, flying balls, like the chains of lightning before them, coalesced with strange sputtering sound into a transparent white fog.

The air reeked with burnt sulphur and contained scarcely enough oxygen to keep men and beasts alive. By dint of extreme will power Brite kept from falling off his horse with Reddie unconscious in his arms. The men coughed as if half strangled. They were bewildered. The herd had been swallowed up in this pale mysterious medium. The hissing, crackling sound of sparks had ceased.

Slowly that fog lifted like a curtain to disclose to Brite's eyes the dark forms of horses and riders. Cooler air took the place of the heat. A vast trampling stir ran through the herd. It seemed likewise to revivify the trail drivers.

"Pards, air we in hell?" shouted Texas huskily. "Or air we oot? . . . Boys, it's passed away. We're alive to tell the tale. . . . Ho! Ho! Brite's ootfit on the Canadian! . . . The herd's millin', boys!—Bear in!—Ride 'em, cowboys! . . . By Gawd! our luck is great!—Not bad, but great! . . . An' shore we're drivin' on to Dodge. . . . Ride 'em, men!—Charge an' shoot to kill! . . . The night's gone an' the day's busted."

"*Hi! Hi! Hi! Hi!*" screamed the drivers as they drove the leaders back.

In the grey of dawn Brite supported the swaying Reddie in her saddle back to camp.

"Oh, Dad—my *remuda*!—where air they?" she sobbed.

"Inside, lass, inside thet line of fire-eaters," replied the old cattleman. "An' they'll hold!"

Only the reality of the sunrise, the calm morning with its sweet clarified air, the solid earth under their feet and the grazing stock, could ever have dispelled the nightmare of those hours of brimstone.

Texas Joe rode in to fall off his horse and limp to the camp fire. He stretched wide his long arms, as if to embrace the fresh sweetness of the dawn.

"On our way, men! The herd's pointed," he called, his voice thick and shaky. "Gimme aboot a gallon of coffee if there ain't any likker." He fell on a pack, favouring his lame leg. "Wal, my sins air shore wiped oot. All the hell I ever deserved I got last night."

Five watchful, strenuous, endless days later Brite's outfit drove across the North Fork of the Canadian River to camp on Rabbit Ear Creek.

The day before they had passed Camp Supply in the middle of the morning. Texas Joe was too wise to make a halt. Brite rode in with the chuck-wagon.

This camp was teeming with soldiers, Indians, cowhands, and bearded men of no apparent occupation. It was also teeming with rumour of massacre of the wagon-train Hardy had hoped to join at Fort Sill, of trail herds north and south, of bands of rustlers operating in Kansas and rendezvousing in the Indian Territory, of twenty million buffalo between the Canadian and Arkansas rivers, of hell itself let loose in Dodge and Abilene. Brite had kept all this to himself. The boys were sombre enough, and somehow they might make the drive through.

"Aboot what time is it?" asked Whittaker, dreamily, as some of them sat in camp.

"Sundown, yu locoed galoot," retorted Ackerman.

"Shore. But I mean the month an' day."

"Gawd only knows.... An' *I* don't care."

"I'll bet my spurs Holden can figger it oot. He's a queer duck. But I like him heaps. Don't yu?"

"Cain't say thet I do," returned Deuce gruffly. Brite had noted more than once how devoted the Uvalde cowboys had been to each other, and how Ackerman appeared jealous of his partner Little, now that the others were gone. Loss of San Sabe had been hard on Deuce.

"Wal, I'll ask him, anyhow," went on Whittaker. "Less," he shouted, "can yu figger oot what day this is?"

"Shore. I'm a walkin' calendar," rejoined Holden, with self-satisfied air, as he pulled a tobacco-pouch from his pocket. "But don't tell Tex. He says to hell with when an' where it is." He emptied a handful of pebbles out of the bag and began carefully to count them. When he had concluded he said: "Gosh, but they add up! Fifty-six.... Fifty-six days oot an' to-day makes fifty-seven. Boys, we're just three days shy of bein' two months on the trail."

"Is thet all!" ejaculated Whittaker.

"Then it's near August?" queried Ackerman ponderingly. "We ought to make Dodge by the end of August.... I wonder aboot thet Fort Sill wagon-train.... Boss, I forgot to ask yu. Did yu heah any word of thet wagon-train Doan expected from Fort Sill?"

Brite could not look into the lad's dark, eager eyes and tell the truth.

Next day, half-way to Sand Creek, Texas Joe stood up in his stirrups and signalled the news of buffalo. Day after day this had been expected. Somewhere north of the Canadian the great herd would swing across the Chisholm Train.

Soon Brite saw the dark, ragged, broken lines of buffalo. They appeared scarcely to move, yet after an interval, when he looked again, the struggling ends were closer. Texas Joe halted for dry camp early in the day. What little conversation prevailed around the fire centred on the buffalo.

"Nothin' to fear drivin' along with the buffs," vouchsafed Bender.

"Thet's all yu know."

"Wal, mebbe they'll work back west by mawnin'."

"But s'pose they keep on workin' east—acrost our trail?"

"Trail drivers never turn back."

"An' we could be swallered up by miles of buffalo—cattle, hawses, chuck-wagon, riders an' all?"

"I reckon we could.... Boss, did yu ever heah of thet?"

"Of what?" asked Brite, though he had heard plainly enough.

"Ootfit gettin' surrounded by buffalo."

"Shore I have. Thet happens often. Stock grazin' right along with the buffalo."

"Ahuh. Wal, what'd happen if the buffalo stampeded? . . . Thirty million buffalo all movin' at once?"

"Hell, cowboy! It ain't conceivable."

"I'll bet my last cigarette it happens."

So they talked, some of them optimistically, others the opposite, all of them reckless, unafraid, and unchangeable. Morning disclosed long black strings of buffalo crossing the trail ahead.

All day Brite's herd had shaggy monsters for company, short lines, long thin strings, bunches and groups, hundreds and twos and fours of buffalo, leisurely grazing along, contented and indifferent. Sand Creek offered a fine camp site and range for cattle. The mossy-horns appeared as satisfied as their shaggy brothers. They bedded down early and offered no trouble. The guards slept in their saddles.

All next day the trail followed Sand Creek. The drivers were concerned about the booming of needle guns to the east and south. Hunters on the outskirts of the herd or trail drivers coming! That day a long, black, thick line of buffalo crossed behind Brite's herd, and turning north crept along parallel with it. This line had no break. Behind and to the west the black wave, like a tide of broken lava, rolling imperceptibly, slowly augmented and encroached upon the cattle herd. How insignificant and puny that herd of six thousand long-horns now! It was but a drop in the bucket of the Great Plains.

But the west and north remained open, at least as far as eye could see. Brite thought he had crossed directly in front of the mass of buffalo. They might travel that tranquil way for days; and again the whirl of a dust-devil, the whip of a swallow on the wing, might stampede them into a stupendous, rolling avalanche.

Sand Creek merged into Buffalo Creek, a deep, cool, willow-bordered stream where all the luxuriant foliage of the prairie bloomed. Texas made camp at the point where the creeks met.

"We'll rest up heah a day or two," he said. "Somebody knock over a buffalo. Rump steak would shore go great. . . . Reddie, do yu want to kill a buff?"

"No. I'm too tender-hearted," she replied musingly. "I see so many cute little buffalo calves. I might shoot one's mother."

"Tender-hearted?—Wal, I'm dog-goned!" drawled Texas mildly. He had greatly sobered these late days of the drive and seldom returned to his old raillery. "We-all had it figgered yu was a killer."

"Aw, I don't count redskins, greasers, stampeders—an' now an' then an occasional cowhand."

"I savvy. But I meant a killer with yore gun—not yore red curls, yore snappin' eyes, yore shape thet no boys' pants could hide."

Reddie promptly vanished physically and vocally into the empty air. That was all the pleasantry in camp on this night.

"I wish thet Hash Williams had stuck with us," Texas mused.

"But, Tex, what the hell difference does it make now?"

"Wal, a lot, if we knowed what the pesky buffs would do."

"Ump-umm! I say, since we gotta drive on, to keep goin'."

"But mebbe the buffalo might drift by."

"What? Thet herd? Never this summer. They are as many as the tufts of gramma grass."

"What yu think, boss?" queried the foreman, showing that he needed partisanship to bolster up any of his judgments.

"Wait till mawnin'," advised the cattle-owner.

Certainly the morning brought to light fewer buffalo and wider space, yet to east and south and west the black lines encroached upon the green. Only the north was clear.

"Point the herd!" ordered Brite, driven by fears and hopes.

"I was gonna do thet, anyhow," drawled Texas Joe. "We can only die once, an' if we have to die let's get it over. This dyin' by days an' hours is like tryin' to win a woman's love."

If Joe had but known it—if he could have seen the light in Reddie's eyes as Brite saw it—he would have learned that that could be attained by the very things he thought so little of.

So they drove on and the buffalo closed in black all around them. Herd, *remuda*, and riders occupied the centre of a green island surrounded by rugged, unbroken waves. This island was a couple of miles long by about the same in width, almost a circle. It kept that way for hours of suspense to the drivers.

Long-horns had no fear of buffalo. Brite remembered how the mossy-horned old bulls bawled and tossed their mighty horns at sight of buffalo coming close. But to the vast herd these cattle and horses were grains of dust under their feet.

About noon there came a change. Something quickened the buffalo. Brite felt it, saw it, but could give no solution. Buffalo were beyond understanding.

"Oh, Dad, I heah somethin' behind!" called Reddie fearfully.

"What?"

"I don't know. It's like the wind in the pines."

Brite strained his ears to hear. In vain! The noonday hour was silent, oppressive, warm with the breath of midsummer. But he saw Texas halt his horse, to turn and stand in his stirrups, gazing back. He, too, had heard something. Brite looked behind him. The buffalo were a mile in the rear, ambling along, no longer nipping the grass. The shaggy line bobbed almost imperceptibly.

"Dad, I heah it again," cried Reddie.

Pan Handle rode around the rear of the cattle, to gallop ahead and join Texas. They watched. Other cowboys turned their faces back. Something was amiss. The cattle grazed along as if buffalo were not encompassing them. But the little Spanish mustangs evinced uneasiness. They trotted to and fro, stood with pointed ears, heads to the south. They had the heritage of two hundred years of prairie life. At sight of them Brite's heart sank. He tried to stem the stream of his consciousness and not think.

"There it comes, stronger," declared Reddie, who had ridden to Brite's side.

"What yu make of it, lass?"

"Like low thunder now.... Mebbe a storm brewin'."

The sky, however, was cloudless, a serene azure vault, solemn and austere, keeping its secrets. Miles back, low down over the black horizon of shaggy, uneven line, a peculiar yellow, billowy smoke was rising. Dust clouds! Brite would rather have been blind than have been compelled to see that.

"Look! Dust risin'!" cried Reddie, startled. She pointed with shaking hand.

"Mebbe it's nothin' to worry aboot," said Brite, averting his eyes.

"An' heah comes Tex. Look at thet hawse!"

The foreman swerved in round the rear of the herd to meet the three riders who rode toward him. After a short consultation one of these galloped off to the east, to round the herd on that side. Texas then came on at a run.

He reined in before Brite and Reddie, who had stopped involuntarily. Texas Joe's face was a bronze mask. His amber eyes were narrow slits of fire.

"Heah anythin' boss?" he queried sharply.

"Nope. But Reddie does. I see some dust rollin' up behind."

"*Stampede!*" flashed the cowboy, confirming Brite's suspicion.

"Oh, my Gawd!" burst out Reddie, suddenly realizing. "We're trapped in a circle.... Jack, what will we do?"

"It's been comin' to us all this drive," replied Texas. "An' I reckon now it's heah. If thet stampede back there spreads through the whole herd we've got about one chance in a thousand. An' thet chance is for our cattle to run bunched as they air now, square an' broad across the rear. Ride behind thet, Mr. Brite, an' good luck to yu. . . . Reddie, if the buffs close in on yu, take to the wagon. A big white heavy wagon like ours might split a herd thet'd trample over the hawses."

"Oh, Jack—don't go—till I——" she flung after him. But Texas only turned to wave good-bye, then he rode on to meet Moze. That worthy was coming at a stiff trot. They met, and Texas must have imparted alarming orders, for the negro put the team to a lope that promised shortly to overtake the *remuda*. Texas wheeled back to the left.

Brite and Reddie drove the *remuda* to the rear of the herd, just back of the riders. Soon Moze came lumbering up. Then all accommodated their paces to the movement of the cattle and maintained their position. All of the seven guards now rode at the rear of the herd.

As soon as this change was established Brite took stock of the buffalo. Apparently the immense green oval inside the herd was just as big as ever. But had it narrowed or shortened? He could not be sure. Yet there was a difference. On all sides the buffalo line bobbed at a slow walk. All still seemed well. Brite tried to get his nerve back. But it had been shaken. A terrible peril hung over them. At the last word he did not care particularly about himself, though the idea of being ridden down and pounded by millions of hoofs into a bloody pulp was horrible, but he suffered poignantly for Reddie, and her lover, and these tried and true men who had stood by him so loyally. But God disposed of all. Brite framed a prayer for them, and then like a true Texan prepared to fight to the last bitter gasp.

This enabled him to look back to make out what to expect and how soon. No change in the buffalo. But that yellow, rolling cloud had arisen high, to blot out the sky half-way to the zenith.

All of a sudden Brite realized that for a moment or perhaps longer he had been aware of a filling of his ears with distant sound.

"Reddie!" he yelled. "I heah it!"

To his amazement, the girl had gravitated toward Texas Joe, who had ridden around the *remuda* to approach her. They met, and his forceful gesture sent Reddie back alongside the wagon.

There was no more need for words. Still Brite's stubbornness refused to yield to the worst. Had not some vital, unforeseen chance saved them more than once on this fatal drive? *"Quien sabe?"* he muttered through his teeth.

On each flank the buffalo had markedly changed in aspect. Where before they had wagged along, now they bobbed. Far ahead the forward mass had not yet caught this acceleration. From behind, the low roar gradually increased. Brite's mustang snorted and baulked. He had to be spurred. All the horses betrayed a will to bolt. The *remuda* pranced at the heels of the herd, held in on each flank by the riders.

That state of action and sound stayed the same for moments. It was Texas' strange throwing up of his hands that acquainted Brite with a transformation. The buffalo had broken into a lope. An instant later that low roar perished in an engulfing sound that would have struck terror to the stoutest heart. The gap between the rear of the herd and the oncoming buffalo began rapidly to close. Louder grew the roar. On each side of the cattle, far ahead, the buffalo closed in, so that the shape of a great triangle was maintained. It would be impossible for the cattle to mix with the buffalo. An impenetrable, shaggy wall moved on all sides.

Before the advancing mass behind had caught up to Brite the nimble-footed long-horns broke into a swinging lope. That seemed well. It evened matters. The *remuda* appeared less likely to bolt. Moze kept the chuck-wagon rolling at their heels.

Above the steady roar of hoofs all around swelled a sound that swallowed it—the deafening thunder of the stampede in the rear. It had started the herd into action. But now its momentum forced the buffalo ahead again to break their pace. Like a wave rolling onward in the sea it caught up with the cattle, passed through the buffalo on each flank and raced forward to the leaders.

Brite realized the terrible instant when the stampede spirit claimed the whole mass. He felt the ground shake with his horse and his ears cracked to an awful rumble. It ceased as suddenly. He could no longer hear. And as if of one accord, the long-horns and the horses broke into a run.

Brite looked back. A thousand hideously horned and haired heads close-pressed together formed the advance line fifty yards or less behind him. Only gradually did they gain now. Before this moment the pursuing buffalo had split to go on each side of the cattle herd.

For miles the fleet long-horns evened pace with the shaggy monsters of the plains. And in that short while the circle closed. Buffalo raced cows and did not win. The wicked long-horned bulls charged the black wall of woolly hides, to be bowled over and trampled underfoot.

The conformation of the land must have changed from level to up-grade.

Brite's distended eyes saw a vast sea of black ahead, a sweeping tide, like a flood of fur covering the whole prairie. No doubt it was the same on each side of him and for miles behind. Even in that harrowing moment he was staggered by the magnificence of the spectacle. Nature had staged a fitting end for his heroic riders. Texas Joe, on one side of the chuck-wagon, Pan Handle on the other, rode with guns belching fire and smoke into the faces of bulls that charged perilously close. Moze's team was running away, the *remuda* was running away, the six thousand cattle were running away. But where? They were lost in that horde of bison. They were as a few grains of sand on the sea shore.

When the buffalo filled all the gaps, dust obscured Brite's vision. He could see only indistinctly and not far. Yet he never lost sight of Reddie or the wagon. Any moment he expected the wagon to lurch over or to lose a wheel in one of its bounces, and to see Moze go down to his death. But that would be the fate of them all.

Only the *remuda* hung together. Except Pan Handle, Texas, and Reddie all the riders were surrounded by buffalo. Brite's stirrups rubbed the hump-backed monsters; they bumped his mustang on one side, then on the other.

Bender on his white horse was a conspicuous mark. Brite saw him forced to one side—saw the white horse go down and black bodies cover the place. Brite could feel no more. He closed his eyes. He could not see Reddie sacrificed to such a ghastly fate and care to endure himself.

The hellish stampede went on—a catastrophe which perhaps a gopher had started. A violent jolt all but unseated Brite. He opened his eyes to see a giant bull passing. Yielding to furious fright, Brite shot the brute. It rolled on the ground and the huge beasts leaped over or aside. Sometimes Brite could see patches of ground. But all was yellow, infernal haze, obscuring shadows, and ceaseless appalling motion. It must have an end. The cattle could run all day, but the terrorized horses would fall as had Bender's.

Yet there were Reddie and Texas, sweeping along beside the wagon, with buffalo only on the outside. Farther on, through the yellow pale, Brite made out white and grey against the black. A magenta sun burned through the dust. Sick and dizzy and reeling, Brite clung to his saddle-horn, sure that his end was near. He had lived long. Cattle had been his Nemesis. If it had not been for Reddie——

Suddenly his clogged ears appeared to open—to fill again with sound. He could hear once more. His dazed brain answered to the revivifying suggestion. If he was no longer deaf, the roar of stampede had diminished. The mustang broke his gait to allow for down-grade. Rifts of sky shone through the yellow curtain.

A gleam of river! Heart and sense leaped. They had reached the Cimarron. All went dark before Brite's eyes. But consciousness rallied. The terrible trampling roar was still about him. His horse dragged in sand. A rude arm clasped him and a man bawled in his ear.

Brite gazed stupidly out upon the broad river where strings of cattle were wading out upon an island. To right and left black moving bands crossed the water. The stampede had ended at the Cimarron where the buffalo had split around an island.

"How—aboot—Reddie?" whispered the cattleman as they lifted him out of the saddle.

"Heah, Dad, safe an' sound. Don't yu feel me?" came as if from a distance.

"An'—everybody?"

"All heah but Bender an' Whittaker. They were lost."

"Aw! . . . I seen Bender—go down."

"Boss, it could have been wuss," said Texas gratefully.

"Oh, Dad!—Did yu see me go down?" cried Reddie. "I got pitched ahaid— over my hawse. . . . Thet cowboy snatched me up—as if I'd been his scarf."

"Which cowboy?" queried Brite.

"Texas—Jack. . . . Thet's the second time—shore."

"Boss, we're stuck," reported the practical Texas, brushing Reddie aside. "Some of our cattle went with the buffalo. The rest is scattered. Our *remuda* half gone. . . . But, by Gawd! we're heah on the Cimarron! When these cussed buffs get by we'll round up our stock an' drive on."

Before dark the last straggling ends of the buffalo herd loped by. Meanwhile camp had been made on high ground. Two of the riders were repairing the wagon. Moze was cooking rump steak. Pan Handle laboured zealously at cleaning his guns. Texas Joe strode here and there, his restless eyes ever seeking Reddie, who lay on the green grass beside Brite. The outfit had weathered another vicissitude of the Trail.

It took Brite's remaining riders four days to round up five thousand head of cattle. The rest were lost, and a hundred head of the *remuda*. And the unbeatable cowboys kept telling Brite that he had still five hundred more long-horns than the number with which he had started.

Trail herds crossed the Cimarron every day, never less than two, and often more, and once five herds. The rush was on. Good luck had attended most of the drivers. A brush with Nigger Horse, a few stampedes, a bad electrical storm that caused delay, hailstones that killed yearling calves—these were reports given by the passing drivers.

A huge cowhand, red of face and ragged of garb, hailed the members of Brite's outfit in camp.

"On the last laig to Dodge! I'll be drunker'n hell soon," he yelled, and waved his hand.

Brite got going again on the fifth day, with cattle and *remuda* rested, but with his cowboys ragged as scarecrows, gaunt and haggard, wearing out in all except their unquenchable spirit.

They had company at every camp. Snake Creek, Salt Creek, Bear Creek, Bluff Creek, and at last Mulberry Creek only a few miles out of Dodge.

That night the sun went down gloriously golden and red over the vast, level prairie. Ranchers called on the trail drivers.

"Dodge is shore a-hummin' these days," said one. "Shootin', drinkin', gamblin'!—They're waitin' for yu boys—them painted women an' black-coated caird sharps."

"WHOOPEE!" yelled the cowboys, in lusty passion. But Deuce Ackerman was silent. Texas Joe took a sly look at the downcast Reddie, and with a wink at Brite he drawled:

"Gosh! I'm glad I'm free. Just a no-good cowhand in off the Trail with all the hell behind! Boss, I want my pay pronto. I'll buck the tiger. I'll stay sober till I bore thet rustler Hite. Then me for one of them hawk-eyed gurls with a pale face an' painted lips an' bare arms an'——"

"Yes, yu *air* a no-good cowhand," blazed Reddie furiously. "Oh, I—I'm ashamed of yu. I—I hate yu! . . . To give in to the bottle—to some vile hussy—when—when all the time our boys—our comrades lay daid oot there on the prairie. How can yu—do—it?"

"Thet's why, Reddie," replied Texas Joe, suddenly flayed. "It shore takes a hell of a lot to make a man forget the pards who died for him. . . . An' I have nothin' else but likker an' a painted——"

"Oh, but yu have!" she cried, in ringing passion. "Yu fool! Yu fool!"

CHAPTER SIXTEEN

DODGE City was indeed roaring. Brite likened the traffic in the wide street, the dust, the noise, the tramp of the throng to a stampede of cattle on the trail.

After the drive in to the pastures, and the count, Brite had left the cowboys and the wagon, and had ridden to town with Reddie. He had left her asleep in her room at the hotel, where she had succumbed at sight of a bed. He hurried to the office of Hall and Stevens, with whom he had had dealings before. He was welcomed with the eagerness of men who smelled a huge deal with like profit.

"Brite, you're a ragamuffin," declared the senior member of the firm. "Why didn't you rid yourself of that beard? And those trail togs?"

"To-morrow is time enough for thet. I want to sell an' go to bed. What're yu payin' this month?"

"We're offerin' twelve dollars," replied the cattle-buyer warily.

"Not enough. My count is five thousand an' eighty-eight. Call it eighty even. Fine stock an' fairly fat."

"What do you want?"

"Fifteen dollars."

"Won't pay it. Brite, there are eighty thousand head of cattle in."

"Nothin' to me, Mr. Hall. I have the best stock."

"Thirteen dollars."

"Nope. I'll run over to see Blackwell," replied Brite, moving to the door.

"Fourteen. That's my highest. Will you sell?"

"Done. I'll call to-morrow sometime for a certified check. Meanwhile send yore cowhands down to take charge."

"Thanks, Brite. I'm satisfied if you are. Cattle movin' brisk. How many head will come up the Trail before the snow flies?"

"Two hundred thousand."

Hall rubbed his hands. "Dodge will be wide open about the end of August."

"What is it now? I'm goin' to get oot quick."

"Won't you need some cash to pay off?"

"Shore. I forgot. Make it about two thousand five hundred. Good-day."

Brite wrestled his way back to the hotel, landing there out of breath and ready to drop. He paid a negro porter five dollars to pack up a tub of water. Then he took a bath, shaved, and went to bed, asleep before he hit the pillow.

What seemed but a moment later a knocking at his door awakened him.

"Dad, air yu daid?" called a voice that thrilled him.

"Come in."

Reddie entered, pale, with hollow eyes and strained cheeks, but sweet to gaze upon. She sat down upon the bed beside him.

"Yu handsome man! All clean shaved an' nice. Did yu buy new clothes?"

"Not yet. I left thet till this mawnin'."

"It's ten o'clock. When did yu go to bed?"

"At four. Sixteen hours! Oh, I was daid to the world."

"Where is—air the boys?"

"Also daid asleep. Don't worry. They'll straggle in late to-day, lookin' for money."

"Dad, do me a favour?"

"Shore. Anythin' yu want."

"Don't give the cowboys—at least Texas Jack—a-any money right away."

"But, honey, I can't get oot of it," protested Brite, puzzled. "Soon as he comes heah."

"Will he want to—to get drunk—as he bragged an'—an'——"

She dropped her head to the pillow beside Brite's.

"Shore. They'll all get drunk."

"Could I keep Jack from thet?" she whispered.

"I reckon yu could. But it'll cost a lot. Do yu care enough aboot him, lass?"

"Oh! . . . I—I love him!"

"Wal, then, it'll be easy, for thet fire-eatin' hombre loves the ground yu ride on."

"Have I yore consent?"

"Why, child!"

"But yu're my Dad. I cain't remember my real one."

"Yu have my blessin', dear. An' I think the world of Texas Joe. He's the salt of the earth."

"Could yu let him quit trail drivin'? Because if he drove I'd have to go, too."

"Reddie, I got a fortune for thet herd. Which reminds me I still have ninety-two hawses to sell."

"But yu caint sell mine."

"We'll leave him with Selton, to be sent south with the first ootfit."

She leaped up, flushed and happy, with tears like pearls on her tanned cheeks and eyes of sweet, thoughtful shadows.

"Hurry. Get up an' dress. Take me oot to buy things. A girl's! Oh, I will not know what to buy. It's like a dream. . . . Hurry, Dad. I wouldn't dare go alone."

"I should smile yu wouldn't."

When she ran out Brite made short work of getting into his torn and trail-stained rags. Soon they were on their way down the main street of Dodge. It presented a busy scene, but the roar was missing. Too early in the day! Reddie was all eyes. She missed nothing. Cowboys, gamblers, teamsters, negroes, Mexicans, Indians, lined the street, waiting for something to begin.

Brite took Reddie into Denman's big merchandise store, where he turned her over to a woman clerk to give her the best of everything and not consider expense. Then he hastened to purchase an outfit for himself. That did not require long, but he encountered a trail driver, Lewis by name, and in exchanging experiences time flew by. Hurrying back, he found Reddie dazed and happy, sitting amid a circle of parcels. They had a merry and a toilsome job packing their purchases back to the hotel. Reddie barred herself in with her precious possessions.

Some time later a tap on Brite's door interrupted the finishing-touches of his dressing.

"Come in," he answered.

Texas Joe entered, his lean handsome face shining despite its havoc.

"Mawnin' boss," he drawled. "My, but yu're spruced up fine."

"Yes, an' yu'll be feelin' like me pronto. How's the boys?"

"I don't know. Asleep I reckon. They come in town to go to bed. I'll find them some place."

"Where's Pan Handle?"

"Sleepin' to quiet his nerves. Boss, he'll be lookin' for Hite before the day's oot."

"Tex, if I asked yu as a particular favour, would yu give up goin' on a debauch an' take first stage with me an' Reddie?"

"Boss, yu're askin' too much. Somethin' turrible, or mebbe wonderful, has gotta come between me an' thet hell-rattlin' drive."

"I understand. But do this for me. Go with me to Hall's office, then to the bank. An' I'll take yu to the store where I bought this ootfit."

"Thet's easy. I'll stick to yu shore till I get my money. Clean broke, boss. Not a two-bit piece. An' I had some money when we left Santone. My Gawd! will I ever see thet town again?"

"Shore yu will. Come on."

They went out into the street. "Boss, would yu mind walkin' on my left side. I might have to clear for action, yu know. If we meet Hite—wal! our pard Pan is gonna be left."

But nothing happened on their several errands. Upon returning to the hotel, Texas engaged a room and proceeded to get rid of the stains and rags of the Chisholm Trail. Brite went to Blackwell, where he sold the *remuda* for twenty dollars a head. He was treading the clouds when he got back to the hotel. Cattlemen he knew engaged him in spirited inquiry about the resourcefulness of Texas. Men and women, some of them flashily dressed, passed through the lobby to the dining-room. Brite noted a very pretty young lady, in gaily colourful array, pass to and fro as if on parade. He observed that she had attracted the attention of a frock-coated gambler. And when he accosted her, Brite decided he had better make sure the girl wanted this kind of attention. When he strode over, what was his amaze and consternation to hear the girl say in a sharp familiar voice: "Heah, Mr. Flowery Vest, if I was packin' my gun I'd shoot yore laig off!"

"*Reddie!*" burst out Brite, beside himself.

"Hello, Dad. An' yu didn't know me! Lend me yore gun."

The gambler fled. Brite gazed speechless at his adopted daughter, unable to believe his own sight.

"Reddie, darlin', is it yu?"

"Shore it's me. Thet is, I think an' feel it is 'cept when I look in thet mirror. . . . Oh, Dad! I feel so strange—so tormented—so *happy*. Thet woman was smart. She picked oot all these things for me. . . . Do I look—nice?"

"Nice! Reddie, yu air the sweetest thing I ever seen. I am knocked flat. I am so glad I could bust. An' to think yu're my lass."

"I'd hug yu—if we was anywhere else. . . . Dad, will *he* like me—this way?"

"He!—Who?"

"Texas Jack, of course."

"Like yu? He'll fall on his knees if yu give him a chance."

"Oh!" She started, with dark bright eyes widening. "There's Texas now. Oh, I hardly knew him. . . . Dad, stand by me now. I wouldn't say my happiness is at stake—or all of it—but my love is. . . . If I've only got—the nerve——"

"Remember Wallen, honey, an' thet day of the stampede," was all Brite had time to say, when Texas Joe transfixed him and Reddie in one lightning flash of falcon eyes.

"Boss!—Who—who——"

"Jack, don't yu know me?" Reddie asked roguishly. Brite marvelled at the woman of her—so swift to gain mastery over her weakness.

"For Gawd's sake!" gasped Texas.

"Come, Jack," she cried, clasping his arm and then Brite's, and dragging them away. "We'll go up to Dad's room. I've somethin' to say—to yu."

All the way up the stairs and down the hall Texas Joe seemed in a trance. But Reddie talked about the town, the people, the joy of their deliverance from the bondage of the Trail. Then they were in Brite's room with the door shut.

Reddie subtly changed. She tossed her dainty bonnet on the bed as if she had been used to such finery all her life.

"Jack, do yu like me?" she asked sweetly, facing him with great dark eyes aglow, and she turned round for his benefit.

"Yu're staggerin' lovely, Reddie," he replied. "I'd never have knowed yu."

"This ootfit is better then them tight pants I used to wear?"

"Better! Child, yu're a boy no more," he said wistfully. "Yu're a girl—a lady. An' no one who knowed yu would want to see yu go back now."

"Yu'd never dare spank me in this dress, would yu?"

Texas flushed red to the roots of his tawny hair. "Gawd, no! An' I never did spank yu as a girl."

"Yes, yu did. Yu knew me. Yu saw me bathin' in the creek thet day. . . . Naked! Don't yu dare deny thet."

It was a torturing moment for Texas and he seemed on the rack. "Never mind. I forgive yu. Who knows? Mebbe but for thet . . . Jack, heah is what I want to say—Will yu give up goin' on a drunk?"

"Sorry, Miss Bayne, but I cain't. Thet's a trail driver's privilege. An' any human bein' wouldn't ask him not to drown it all."

"Not even for me?"

"I reckon—not even for yu."

She slowly drew close to him, as white as if sun and wind had never tanned her face, and her dark purple eyes shone wondrously.

"If I kiss yu—will yu give it up? . . . Once yu begged for a kiss."

Texas laughed mirthlessly. "Funny, thet idee. *Yu* kissin' *me*!"

"Not so funny, Jack," she flashed, and seizing his coat in strong hands she almost leaped at his lips. Then she fell back, released him, sank momentarily against him, and stepped back. Texas Joe, with corded jaw in restraint, bent eyes of amber fire upon her. They had forgotten Brite or were indifferent to his presence.

"Wal, yu did it. Yu kissed me. An' I'm ashamed of yu for it. . . . Reddie Bayne, yu cain't buy my freedom with a kiss."

"Oh, Jack, it's not yore freedom I want to buy. It's yore salvation."

"Bah! What's life to me?" he retorted, stern-lipped and sombre-eyed. "I want to carouse, to fight, to kill, to sleep drunk—drunk—drunk."

"I know, Jack. Oh, I think I understand. Wasn't I a trail driver, too? An' do I want these awful things? No! No! An' I want to save yu from them. . . . Yu madden me with yore cold. . . . Jack, spare me an' end it—quick."

"I'm sparin' yu more'n yu know, little lady," he replied, darkly passionate.

"Shore *somethin'* will coax yu oot of this hell-givin' idee. . . . What? I'll do anythin'—anythin'——"

He seized her in strong arms and lifted her off her feet against his breast.

"Yu'd marry me?"

"Oh yes—yes—yes!"

"But why, girl? *Why?*" he demanded in a frenzy of doubt.

Reddie flung her arms around his neck and strained to reach and kiss his quivering cheek. "'Cause I love yu, Jack—so turrible!"

"Yu love me, Reddie Bayne?"

"I do. I do."

"Since—when?" he whispered, playing with his joy.

"Thet day—when Wallen came—an' yu—saved me."

He kissed her hair, her brow, her scarlet cheek, and at last the uplifted mouth.

"Aw, Reddie—Aw! It was worth goin' through—all thet hell—for this. . . . Girl, yu've got to kill the devil in me. . . . When will yu marry me?"

"To-day—if yu—must have me," she whispered faintly. "But I—I'd rather wait—till we get back to Dad's—to Santone, my home."

"Then we'll wait," he rang out passionately. "But we must leave to-day, darlin' . . . This Dodge town is brewin' blood for me."

"Oh, let's hurry," she cried, and slipping out of his arms she turned appealingly to Brite. "Dad, it's all settled. We've made up. When can yu take us away?"

"To-day, an' pronto, by thunder," replied Brite heartily. "Pack yore old duds an' go to the stage office at the east end of the street. We've got plenty of time. But go there pronto. It's a safer place to wait. I will pay off an' rustle to meet yu there."

Brite spent a fruitless hour trying to locate the cowboys. Upon returning to the hotel, with the intention of leaving their wages, as well as their share of the money found on the stampeder Wallen, he encountered Pan Handle, vastly changed in garb and face, though not in demeanour.

"Hullo, Pan. Lookin' for yu. Heah's yore wages as a trail driver an' yore share—"

"Brite, yu don't owe me anythin'," returned the gunman, smiling.

"Heah! None of thet or we're not friends," retorted Brite, forcing the money upon him. "I'm leavin' in an hour by stage with Tex an' Reddie. They made it up, an' we're all happy."

"Fine!—I'm shore glad. I'll go to the stage to see yu off."

"Pan, hadn't yu better go with us, far as Abilene, anyway?"

"Wal, no, much as I'd like to. I've somebody to see heah yet."

"Wal, I'm sorry. Will yu take this wad of bills an' pay off those fire-eaters of mine?"

"Shore will. But they're heah, just round on the side porch."

"Let's get thet over, pronto," said Brite fervently. Strange how he wanted to see the last of these faithful boys!

Holden sat on the porch steps, while Ackerman and Little leaned arm in arm on the rail. They still wore their ragged trail garb, minus the chaps, but their faces were clean and bright from recent contact with razor and soap.

"Howdy, boss. Got any money?" asked Rolly lazily, with a grin.

"Shore. I have it heah waitin' for yu—wages, an' bonus, too. Thet share of Wallen's money amounts to more'n all yore wages."

"Boss, I'm gonna take ten to blow in, an' want yu to put the rest in somebody's hands to keep for me," said Ackerman keenly. "Yu know I'm not trailin' back to Texas."

"We'll miss yu, Deuce."

Less Holden stood up, lithe and clean cut, with warm glance on the money about to be handed to him.

"Dog-gone yu! Rolly, gimme thet quirt," drawled Deuce mildly.

"Darn if I will," rejoined Little, holding the quirt behind his back.

"It's mine, yu son-of-a-gun!" They wrestled like boys in play, but before Deuce could obtain the quirt from his friend, Holden snatched it.

"I reckon findin's keepin's," he laughed.

With a shout the two cowboys flung themselves upon him. Brite sat down to watch the fun. Pan Handle looked on dubiously. The boys were sober. They had not had a drink. They were just full of lazy glee. As the three of them tugged at the quirt their warm young faces flashed into sight, one after the other. And they grunted and laughed and tugged.

"Aw, Less, thet hurt. Don't be so gol-durned rough," complained Rolly as Holden wrenched the quirt away from the other two. Little looked askance at the blood on his hand. But he was too good-natured to take offence. Deuce, however, suddenly changing from jest to earnest, wrenched the quirt in turn from Holden.

"Heah, Rolly. It's yores. Let's quit foolin'," said Deuce.

But Holden leaped for the quirt, and securing a grip he tore at it. He flung Rolly off his balance. Like a cat, however, the agile cowboy came down on his feet. The playful violence succeeded to something else. Holden, failing to secure the quirt, let go with his right and struck Rolly in the face.

"*Aw!*" cried Rolly, aghast. Then as fierce wild spirit mounted he slashed at Holden's darkening face with the quirt. Blood squirted.

"Heah, boys! Stop!" yelled Pan Handle.

But too late. Holden threw his gun and shot. Rolly doubled up, his face convulsed in dark dismay, and fell. Like tigers then Holden and Ackerman leaped to face one another, guns spouting. Holden plunged on his face, his gun beating a tattoo on the hard ground. Brite sat paralysed with horror as Deuce sank down, his back to the porch.

The demoniac expression faded from his dark face. His gun slipped from his hand to clatter on the steps, blue smoke rising from the barrel. His other hand sought his breast and clutched there, with blood gushing out between his fingers. He never wasted a glance upon the prostrate Holden, but upon his beloved comrade Rolly he bent a pitying, all-possessing look. Then his handsome head fell back.

Pan Handle rushed to kneel beside him. And Brite, dragging up out of his stupor, bent over the dying boy. He smiled a little wearily. "Wal, old—trail driver, we pay," he whispered feebly. "I reckon—I cain't—wait for—little grey-eyed—Ann!"

His whisper failed, his eyes faded. And with a gasp he died.

An hour later Brite met Pan Handle and with him left the hotel.

"Pan, I'll never drive the trail again," he said.

"Small wonder. But you're a Texan, Brite, an' these air border times."

"Poor, wild, fire-hearted boys!" exclaimed Brite, still shaken to his depths. "All in less than a minute! My God! . . . We must keep this from Reddie. . . . I'll never forget Deuce's eyes—his words. 'Old trail driver, we pay!' . . . I know an'

God knows he paid. They all paid. Oh, the pity of it, Pan! To think thet the grand game spirit of these cowboys—the soul thet made them deathless on the trail—was the cause of such a tragedy!"

Dodge was not concerned with auditing a few more deaths. It was four in the afternoon and the hum of the cattle metropolis resembled that of a hive of angry bees.

Saddle horses lined the hitching-rails as far as Brite could see. Canvas-covered wagons, chuck-wagons, buckboards, vehicles of all Western types, stood outside the saddle horses. And up one side and down the other a procession ambled in the dust. On the wide sidewalk a throng of booted, belted, spurred men wended their way up or down. The saloons roared. Black-sombreroed, pale-faced, tight-lipped men stood beside the wide portals of the gaming-dens. Beautiful wrecks of womanhood, girls with havoc in their faces and the look of birds of prey in their eyes, waited in bare-armed splendour to be accosted. Laughter without mirth ran down the walk. The stores were full. Cowboys in twos and threes and sixes trooped by, young, lithe, keen of eye, bold of aspect, gay and reckless. Hundreds of cowboys passed Brite in that long block from the hotel to the intersecting street. And every boy gave him a pang. These were the toll of the trail and of Dodge. It might have been in the march of empire, the tragedy of progress, but it was heinous to Brite. He would never send another boy to his death.

They crossed the intersecting street and went on. Brite finally noticed that Pan Handle walked on the inside and quite apart. He spoke briefly when addressed. Brite let him be, cold and sick with these gunmen—with their eternal watchfulness—their gravitating toward the violence they loved.

Dodge roared on, though with lesser volume, toward the end of the main thoroughfare. Brite gazed with strange earnestness into the eyes of passers-by. So many intent, quiet, light eyes of grey or blue! Indians padded along in that stream, straight, dusky-eyed, aloof, yet prostituted by the whites. No more of the gaudy butterfly girls! Young men and old who had to do with cattle! The parasites were back in that block of saloons and dance-halls and gambling-dens.

They passed Beatty and Kelly's store, out from under an awning into the light. A dark-garbed man strode out of the barber's shop.

"*Jump!*" hissed Pan Handle.

Even as Brite acted upon that trenchant word his swift eye swept to the man in front of the door. Sallow face, baleful eyes, crouching form—Ross Hite reaching for his gun!

Then Brite's dive took him out of vision. As he plunged off the sidewalk two shots boomed out, almost together. A heavy bullet spanged off the gravel in the street.

Lunging up, Brite leaped forward. Then he saw Pan Handle standing erect, his smoking gun high, while Hite stretched across the threshold of the barber's shop door.

A rush of feet, excited cries, a loud laugh, then Pan Handle bent a little, wrenching his gaze from his fallen adversary. He sheathed his gun and strode on to join Brite. They split the gathering crowd and hurried down the street. Dodge roared on, but in lessening volume.

Breathless with haste and agitation, Brite reached the stage office.

"Waitin' for yu, boss," drawled Texas Joe from inside the big stage-coach. "Wal, yu're all winded. Yu needn't have rustled. I'd kept this stage-driver heah."

"Oh, Dad, I was afraid," cried Reddie, leaning out with fair face flushed.

"Dog-gone! Heah's Pan Handle, too," exclaimed Texas. "Shore was fine of yu to come down to say good-bye."

Pan Handle coolly lighted a cigarette with fingers as steady as a rock. He smiled up at Reddie.

"Lass, I shore had to wish yu all the joy an' happiness there is in this hard old West."

"Thank you, Pan," she replied shyly. "I wish——"

"All aboard thet's goin'," yelled the stage-driver from his seat.

Brite threw his bag in and followed, tripping as he entered. The strong hand that had assisted him belonged to Pan Handle, who stepped in after him. Then the stage-coach lurched and rolled away.

"Wal now, Pan, where's yore baggage?" drawled Texas Joe, his falcon eyes narrowing.

"Tex, I reckon all I've got is on my hip," replied Pan Handle, his glance meeting that of Texas Joe.

"Ahuh. . . . Wal, I'm darn glad yu're travellin' with us."

"Oh, Dad, yu didn't forget to say good-bye to the boys for me, especially to Deuce, who'll never come back to Texas?"

"No, Reddie, I didn't forget," replied Brite.

"I hope Ann can coax Deuce never again to be a trail driver," concluded Reddie happily, as she smiled up at Texas Joe. "I'd shore like to tell her how."

RANGERS OF THE LONE STAR

CHAPTER ONE

The Future of the Service

"UNITED States Deputy Marshal Sittell to see Captain MacNeal of the Texas Rangers." I spoke with more force than politeness, and I flashed my shield at the block-headed attendant who had denied me admittance to the adjutant general's office.

In Texas, where nearly every man was such a giant that he had to lower his head to enter a door, it was exasperating to be only five feet six. As my business was to impress a class of men exceedingly hard to impress, and as I, despite my size, had some little reason for pride, I was naturally nettled by the manner of the attendant. Mildness of disposition was not one of my strong characteristics.

"Marshal Sittell, excuse me!" the attendant quickly replied with a vast change of demeanor that somewhat assuaged my wounded vanity.

He led me into an anteroom from which I could see into Adjutant General Weed's office. Motioning me to a chair, he passed into the office, evidently to announce my arrival. Voices sounded from within. Directly the attendant returned and now approached me with a show of respect.

"Captain MacNeal will see you presently. He is about to leave an interview with Adjutant General Weed and Governor Stone. You are to listen, hear what you can."

Then he went out, closing the door behind him.

I sat down, decidedly interested. There was something in the wind. Captain MacNeal's summons had been urgent, much in the nature of an appeal. I had been one of his rangers for three years before my service had earned me a higher post. Our relationship had been something more than that of ranger to captain, and my respect and admiration for him were great.

Since MacNeal had been leader of the rangers, he had not only been fighting the horde of outlaws, west of the Colorado, but a political faction at Austin that opposed the ranger system. MacNeal had so far accomplished wonders, making sections of that wild and vast Southwest habitable for pioneers and ranchmen. I

443

did not doubt that he had some unusual task in the accomplishment of which he hoped to enlist my aid.

The door to the inner office was open and I overheard the earnest voice of the adjutant general, whom I knew.

"Governor Stone, this is Captain MacNeal of the Texas Rangers."

Both men courteously acknowledged the introduction, and the governor said that, of course, he was familiar with MacNeal's splendid record, won during the Rebellion. "And Captain MacNeal," he added, "I shall be pleased to hear what you have to say."

"Governor Stone," replied MacNeal earnestly, "I sought this interview to try to show you what a great . . . a fatal error it would be now to discontinue the ranger service. I have no axe to grind. I'm independent of salary, and I'm not seeking anything for myself. I love the great Lone Star state. Although I am doing a great deal, I want to do something more for it.

"When I heard about the possibility of abolishing the ranger system, I scarcely credited the rumor. But, now that there seems reason to believe it, I am here to place my case and make a fight. Governor Stone, I want to ask bluntly . . . do you know anything about the ranger system . . . about the rangers? You are from eastern Texas. We needn't beat about the bush. It's well known that between east and west Texas there's differences of opinion . . . political and otherwise. Eastern Texas has no need of a ranger service. But as for the western . . . the wild Panhandle, the Staked Plains, the Rio Grande . . . that's a different matter. Will you be kind enough to give me your idea of the Texas Rangers?"

That certainly was blunt. It brought back to me strong recollections of MacNeal's personality. He was a man. I warmed to his side of what I sensed might be more than an argument.

"Captain MacNeal, since you ask me directly, you are welcome to my opinion," replied the governor coldly. "Personally, I know nothing of the rangers. But I've been told by good authorities that as a whole they are a lot of swashbuckling adventurers and gunfighters, looking for somebody to kill. The sentiment in certain parts of the state makes heroes out of them, a fact which they are not slow to take advantage of. They have too much power. They are too much a law unto themselves. The sheriffs ought to be able to cope with any lawless element in western Texas, as they do in the eastern part of the state. There is a bill pending in the legislature now for the abolishment of this ranger service, and unless very strong evidence is put before me . . . great enough to change my mind . . . I shall sign the bill."

"Thank you for plain speaking," replied MacNeal, and the tone of his voice told me how cool and tense he could be when feeling anger or resentment. "You will remember, Governor, that the original bill provided for a ranger service operating only west of the Colorado River. If you are not familiar with the conditions in the remote and wild sections of the border, it is time you were availing yourself of reports sent monthly to Adjutant General Weed.

"I have this to say, pointblank. Sheriffs cannot deal with the situation as it stands today. There's a horde of criminals along the Rio Grande. I have a record of three thousand. The Panhandle and Staked Plains are also overrun by outlaws and desperadoes. There are honest communities . . . towns . . . whole counties under the dominance of clever, unscrupulous rustlers. A band of militia could not clean up these places. If it is to be done, the rangers must do it. As to my men . . . well, some of them *are* gunfighters. I have tried to find that class of men. I have rangers who have been outlaws. A reformed outlaw who has been a famous gunfighter makes the best kind of ranger. His fame is as much help as his actual work.

"You will not understand this, because you know nothing of the class of men who harass the border. I think a careful study of the reports sent in by my rangers will open the eyes of any unprejudiced person."

"Let us see one of these reports," suggested the governor.

"Adjutant, get that last one of Vaughn Steele's I sent in. It's a case in point, and, besides, I'll have something else to say about Steele."

I heard the opening of a drawer and rustling of papers.

"Here it is. Steele certainly does things. You can see that by what he leaves out in his report," replied the adjutant general.

"Read it to me," said Governor Stone.

"Please take note that this is the report of one ranger's work for one month," put in Captain MacNeal.

The adjutant began by naming the town of Del Rio, where evidently the report had been written, and the date; then, after a pause, he read:

El Paso to Valentine to Del Rio. Arrested three Mexicans . . . cattle thieves. In absence of sheriff guarded them till his return. To Ensign. Called by attack of schoolteacher. School house burned in fight. No arrests. Brought teacher to Del Rio. Prevented lynching of Negro. Arrested sheriff in getting Negro to safe place. Traced down rumor of Mexican raiders operating on this side border. Unfounded. Arrested white man named Jinks with boatload of stolen goods. Chased the outlaw, Mott, across into Mexico. Killed my horse. No arrest. Assisted rancher. Found bunch of cattle hidden in brush along river. Enlisted cowboys. Drove herd to owner. Nursed maltreated Mexican. Got him home over river. Arrested four Negroes for attacking him. Shot two ... not fatally. Called to Ensign. No arrest. To Del Rio. Arrested rioters in gambler's resort. Chased them with posse. No arrests. To Ensign, to Cargo, to Junction, to Del Rio after the outlaw and murderer ... Chick Owens. Was shot making arrest. Jail torn down by Owens's pals. Wounded again in fight. Had to kill Owens. . . .

"There! That's quite sufficient," interrupted Governor Stone. "I don't want to hear any bloody details."

"The half is not told here," said Captain MacNeal. "But I can read between the lines. This ranger rode seven hundred miles last month. He simply states ... To El Paso, to Valentine, to Del Rio, *et cetera*. But that means the hardest kind of riding over desert country. He merely states he was wounded twice. No particulars. He ... "

"I gather the report must have been a chronicle of a most remarkable month's work. But is it ... er ... true?"

For a moment, following the governor's cold question, there was silence in the other room.

"Governor Stone, I believe you can rely on these reports," replied the adjutant.

"He must be an able fellow. Where is he now?"

Here I pricked up my ears and listened a little harder. I had never met this magnificent ranger, but I, like every other outdoor man in western Texas, had heard all about him. Some of Steele's jobs had given me jealous qualms, yet thrilled me through and through.

"I have just sent Steele upon the most difficult and, perhaps, dangerous service he ever undertook. Certainly it is the most important one. It is one I would have undertaken myself, had I had the confidence and ability needed."

"What is the service?" inquired the governor.

"Have you ever heard of Fairdale, Pecos County?"

"Let me see ... Fairdale? Why, yes, indeed, I've read things in the papers. Somebody has spoken to me about Fairdale. A remote town or settlement, rich but exceedingly lawless."

"Lawless!" Captain MacNeal uttered a short, grim laugh. "Fairdale is far to the southwest. I've never been there. It's a good-sized town, located west of the Pecos River. Pecos County is merely a name for a great wild barren. Fairdale is favorably located in a rich, well-watered valley, and the ranchers are prosperous in spite of the raiders.

"For a year now, from time to time, I've been receiving anonymous letters. They are from persons afraid to sign names . . . persons whose friends and families have been robbed, assaulted, murdered. In every case I was importuned to send a company of rangers there. I sent an unknown ranger to make an investigation . . . to be careful and secret . . . and to return with a report.

"He did so. Used as I am to reports of lawlessness, this one amazed me. All the deviltry common to the border goes on there by day and night. More than that, and more interesting, was the ranger's report that Fairdale must be a center for the most secret, powerful, mysterious, and dangerous band of criminals operating in the Southwest. I decided to send Steele there, to ferret out this lawless gang and break it up."

"Sir, you don't mean to tell me you've given one single ranger such a job as that?" queried the governor incredulously.

"I expect to send him another ranger . . . that's all," replied MacNeal.

"But, man alive, it's absurd! What you ought to send is a company of militia!"

"That would entail great expense, and that is what this new legislative bill is aiming to cut down, isn't it?"

"That is the aim . . . yes."

"Well, anyway, soldiers would be powerless, even if you did send them. So also would a whole company of rangers. What this job needs is a couple of keen, resourceful, implacable, dangerous men!"

"But how can they . . . alone . . . break up a powerful gang of ruffians?"

"Perhaps they're not all ruffians. I've known respected and intelligent citizens to be mixed up in shady deals. I have detailed Steele to go to Fairdale, openly as a ranger, and to begin work. I'll send another ranger to help him. If they are not killed, they will clean up the town. My men have made more than one town safe for the decent people to live in. Of course, not such places as Fairdale, but bad enough to show their capacity for dangerous work."

"Captain, your confidence is beyond me," commented the governor. "Frankly, this is the most extraordinary undertaking I've ever heard of."

"If you knew the ranger, it wouldn't seem so strange," went on Captain

MacNeal. "I expect, of course, to lend them every assistance possible. Steele asked for a nervy and clever man to be sent to Fairdale as a secret aid. I've had the man in mind, and he's now waiting outside."

"Another ranger?"

"No, not now. Formerly he was with my service. But at present he is a special officer, United States deputy marshal."

"Call him in," said the governor.

It was the adjutant general who came into the anteroom for me. His greeting made me believe he sided with MacNeal in this matter. I went with him.

MacNeal seemed the same slim, erect, and soldierly officer I remembered so well, and his dark face surely expressed welcome and pleasure at sight of me. We shook hands as we greeted each other.

Then Adjutant General Weed introduced me to the governor. I saw a tall, pale man with a pointed beard and an aristocratic bearing that reminded me of a rich Louisiana planter. The way the governor looked me over with his cold, blue eyes was not especially to my liking. He did not offer his hand, though from habit I had made a move to extend mine.

"Does the ... er ... the marshal know yet of the dangerous mission upon which you would send him?" asked Governor Stone of MacNeal.

"I heard your conversation," I replied bluntly.

"Will you care to accept Captain MacNeal's proposition?"

"I'll be glad to go. Adjutant General Weed can authorize me, if he sees fit."

"You, of course, appreciate the danger of this work?" queried the governor.

"The more the danger, the better I'll like it," I rejoined.

My tongue sometimes was swifter than it ought to have been, and I had a hankering for the governor to take me for one of those swashbucklers that had so disgusted him.

"Do you know this Ranger Steele?"

"Only by reputation."

"And what is that reputation?"

"Steele's known on the border from El Paso to the mouth of the Rio Grande. He is feared."

"Do you entertain any conviction of his success in this service?"

"He'll clean up Fairdale."

I put it strongly, without a shadow of doubt. I was eager to help MacNeal's argument.

"Ah! Indeed! You seem to share the captain's confidence. I see you wear a gun there, under your coat. How is that . . . carrying a weapon here in the capital?"

"I always pack a gun. Any minute I might run into men."

"Men you want to arrest, I presume?"

"No. Men who are hankering to kill me!"

"Indeed? May I ask what for?"

"Because I did arrest them once, and now that one thing or another . . . perhaps political influence . . . has helped them out of jail, they'll be looking for me."

Plain it was that Governor Stone was impressed with me, but scarcely favorably.

"No doubt you've had victims . . . er . . . you've killed men?"

"Only a few. I never counted."

That sickened the aristocratic governor from eastern Texas, and he turned to the others. "Gentlemen, manifestly the United States deputy marshal will be an able lieutenant for Ranger Steele." He turned his face to MacNeal. "Have you anything further to say to me about the matter?"

"Only this, Governor Stone," replied MacNeal quickly. "Will you make a test case of this? Will you wait till Steele has succeeded or failed in his attempt to make Fairdale a law-abiding town? I shall find means to furnish you with authentic details of his work. Will you hold off signing this bill for a while?"

"Captain MacNeal, that is a most fair and reasonable request," replied the governor with some warmth. "If you are satisfied to make this a test of the ranger service, I shall be glad to wait, even a year or more. I remind you, I am open to conviction. You have made some remarkable statements in regard to your rangers. For the welfare of Texas I hope and pray they are true."

Governor Stone bowed to the captain, then to me, and in company with the adjutant general he left the office.

When Captain MacNeal turned to me he was white, and his jaw was working. "Russ!" he exclaimed passionately, calling me by the familiar name once common among my ranger comrades, "Russ, the future of the service depends on you and Vaughn Steele!"

CHAPTER TWO

Two Fair Ladies

THERE never lived a more indomitable man than MacNeal. His agitation showed me not only the apparent hopelessness of this ranger venture, but also how his whole heart was in the service. It made me glad the captain had appealed to me. Right there, I conceived a strong desire to help him. And at the same time I had a strange feeling — something amounting to a premonition — that this undertaking with Vaughn Steele was to be a significant and fateful one in my life. So from the start I found the spirit that would encourage MacNeal.

"Well, Cap, if the future of the ranger service depends on Steele and me, it's in good hands."

He brightened at that and began to pace the room. "Yes, yes. You're right. I know him, and I know you. If it were only an ordinary job! But that report my ranger brought from Fairdale . . . here, read it at your leisure. It'll make you cold in the pit of your stomach."

"Not me, Cap. I never get sick that way." Then I grew earnest. "MacNeal, I like the job. I know I'll be proud to help Steele. I always wanted to work with him. This is a big thing, aside from what political move may hang upon it. But I have only one concern. Will Steele like me? I've heard of his patience, his forbearance, his reluctance to fight. You know, I've a temper. And I'm quick to pull a gun. My only concern is . . . will I suit Steele?"

The captain laughed and dived into his pocket to produce a paper. "Rather," he said. "Here are the names he asked me to pick from. The number of men named shows how difficult he expected it to be to get a man to tackle this job with him. And what he thinks of their fitness shows in the order he named them."

Russ Sittell was the first name on the list. That gave me a warm thrill, and more than a little surprise. Steele did not know me. To be sure, I had served the state, but as a ranger I had never been in Steele's class. However, as he was in a class by himself, and as he had chosen to elevate me to it, I gathered considerable pride from the fact and suddenly found myself bound to him by strong ties.

"Good!" exclaimed MacNeal, who evidently had been watching my face. "Russ, it's settled. The adjutant is glad to let me send you."

"Sure is good," I replied. "So, I'm to go in my capacity as United States deputy marshal, taking orders from Steele?"

"Absolutely. You're to obey him, trust him implicitly, help him all you can. Steele has a free hand. You both have free hands. You will never get a single order from this office. You have all the authority the adjutant can give and papers to prove it. You can arrest anybody without warrants. You can search any house or place without warrants. You can swear in any men as deputies and give them orders. You can . . . and you *must* . . . shoot when it's necessary.

"I'm glad you're quick with your gun. For Steele, with his damned stony nerve, risks his life too much. You'll obey him, yes. But tell him that in one sense I'm giving you a free hand with a gun. See?"

"Cap, the job grows on me," I said. "How about letters, reports, money?"

MacNeal went into his pocket again, but this time I made note that his hand dragged a little. No wonder, for it came forth with a huge bundle of greenbacks. I did not need to be told that it was his own money.

"Here's five thousand dollars. Take it to Steele. Tell him to exercise care in spending but not to hamper developments by stinginess. There's more money, if it's needed.

"Now as to letters and reports, I think Steele will decide how and when they are to be sent to me. I gathered that he wanted you to be a secret aid. You will have no open relation with him. You'll not be known as an officer at first. Probably Steele will want you to pretend you're a cowboy or gambler or rustler . . . to make yourself known to mingle with this or that crowd. It seems to me, Russ, you're in for an adventure. I remember you always liked to be detailed on a job that promised adventure. Perhaps you'll get enough now, for once."

"Cap, I can stand a lot," I replied cheerfully. "This promises a lot, too. I'm eager to start. When?"

"At once. Wait a moment till Adjutant General Weed returns. Just a matter of form."

The adjutant general entered the office at that moment. He carried a card in his extended hand, and his face wore an expression of interest and expectancy. "Gentlemen, look here," he said, laying the card down upon a desk before us.

The captain and I bent over. Cards were not frequent in those days, and I had never had my name on one. Upon this one I read:

COL. GRANGER LONGSTRETH
Mayor of Fairdale,
Pecos County, Texas

Both MacNeal and I were too surprised to speak. Straightening up, we looked at the adjutant.

"Quite a coincidence, isn't it? This man, Longstreth, is waiting. I haven't seen him. His card was brought to me. He wants to call on Governor Stone. The name Fairdale caught my eye, and it struck me that you gentlemen might be interested in the mayor of Fairdale, Pecos County, Texas."

"By George, this's luck!" exclaimed MacNeal. "Russ, I knew you'd bring luck. You always were the luckiest fellow. Here, let me have the report I gave you."

I returned it, and the captain, hurriedly turning over closely written pages, found the place he sought.

"Listen to this. 'The biggest man in Fairdale is Longstreth. He's rancher, cattle buyer, merchant. Of all the rich men about Fairdale he's the richest. He owns the inn. Rumored that he owns the biggest gambling resort. Couldn't substantiate rumor. He lives at his magnificent ranch, the finest in southwest Texas. Is often absent from home. He is the mayor. A splendid man, esteemed by his townsfolk. The only reason he has been given space in this report is because he's mayor of Fairdale, and Fairdale is wide open for all kinds of crime.' "

MacNeal closed the report and, returning it to me straightway, became thoughtful. Finally he added: "Steele hasn't reached Fairdale yet, so, of course, he knows nothing of this Mayor Longstreth. Equally sure it is that Longstreth knows nothing of Steele. I imagine that we can get some kind of interesting point of view from the mayor of the town we expect to clean up. He may be as honorable as any man and worthy of the esteem mentioned in the report. But . . . Fairdale is wide open. That sticks in my craw.

"Now, Adjutant, I'll suggest something. Let Sittell and me hide somewhere. I'll go behind that screen. Sittell will go into the closet and leave the door open an inch or so. You have Mayor Longstreth shown in here. Receive him cordially. Draw him out. That is, help him to talk.

"He has some motive for coming. Perhaps it's only to make a social call . . . to go home and be able to say he called on the governor. Whatever it is, you lead him to talk about Fairdale. If he admits Fairdale is wide open, overrun by a bad lot, and that he can do nothing, why he'll be honest, and it won't hurt our case to favor his desire to meet the governor. But, if he laughs at any casual query of yours . . . if he makes light of your repetition of rumors regarding the viciousness of Fairdale, steer him off . . . don't let him meet Governor Stone. We know positively that Fairdale is a nest of secret and dangerous criminals. Now, Adjutant, what do you say?"

Weed entered readily into the little scheme. After MacNeal was placed behind the screen and I was in the closet, he rang for his clerk and bade him to show in the waiting gentleman.

I placed my eye to the narrow slit in the nearly closed door and had a good view of the larger part of the office. Presently the clerk entered and, to my surprise, was followed by two girls, one tall and dark, the other petite and fair. I wanted to bestow a second glance on them, but the entrance of a striking-looking man drew all my attention.

"Adjutant General Weed?" he asked, stepping forward.

"Yes. You are Colonel Granger Longstreth? Mayor Longstreth, I am pleased to meet you," replied the adjutant courteously.

"That honor is mine," said Longstreth, bowing. "Permit me to introduce my daughter, Ray, and my niece, Ruth Herbert."

My gaze leaped swiftly back and forth from this handsome, dark man to the daughter that resembled him and then to the niece, who, as she blushed at the adjutant's greeting, appeared to me to be about the prettiest girl I had ever seen.

"Will Governor Stone receive me?" asked Longstreth.

"I shall see. He is exceedingly busy. But, perhaps, I can arrange it. Please be seated." As he spoke, the adjutant brought chairs for the ladies. "Let me have the pleasure of a little chat. It is seldom, indeed, that I meet anyone, especially ladies, from so remote a corner of our great state as Fairdale. I have heard, too, that Fairdale was such a wild, uncivilized place. That must be a mistake."

The adjutant general smiled winningly. He was, indeed, very pleasant and likable in that mood, and his glance more than his words implied a compliment. For my part I would certainly not have expected these girls to belong to western Texas.

"I've never been to Fairdale," said Miss Ray Longstreth. Her voice surprised me. It was low, sweet, deep, like that of a singer who had thrilled me once. "Papa says it's a terrible place. But it's his home and is going to be my home."

Granger Longstreth laughed, and that laugh broke up a certain hardness of face I had been studying. "Adjutant Weed, my home town is the worst corner of Texas," he said. "There's no place on the Rio Grande that can hold a candle to it. No place for my daughter and niece. But they will go out.

"You see, I am a Louisianian by birth. Went West years ago, after the death of my wife. Have succeeded out there. My daughter has lived with relatives, except the last few years, which have been spent at school in Atlanta. I occasionally visited her, and, upon this last visit, she calmly announced her intention of going home with me. I stormed and pleaded. It was of no use. She's her father's daughter. She's going out to the ranch."

"Very commendable, I think," replied the adjutant. "And you, Miss Herbert, are also going out for a visit?"

"Yes. I'm crazy to ride broncos and meet cowboys," she said.

She had a lazy, Southern drawl, altogether charming to hear, but it was what she said, rather than her tone, that most interested me. I looked closer at her. She had chestnut hair, curly and unruly, gray or hazel eyes, a sweet, red mouth, and altogether a saucy arch kind of prettiness that made me feel I would not soon forget her.

"I envy the lucky cowboys," remarked Adjutant Weed with smile and bow. "If Fairdale is such a wild and dangerous place, there may be opportunities for cowboys to play the gallant." Then the adjutant turned to Longstreth. "Seriously, Mayor, what kind of a . . . a country is this you live in? We are very ignorant of life on the frontier of Texas. I have heard a rumor now and then about Fairdale and its lawlessness. But rumors only, very vague. We hear so much authentic news about places famous for rustlers and gunfighters that we have no time to trace rumors."

"Well, sir," replied Longstreth, "Fairdale is unique. I know Texas. And there's no town like it. We have about twenty-five hundred people. We have a rich country and are prosperous. There were a hundred thousand head of cattle in the valley when I left home. Then, we are close to the great ranges south of the Pecos. Naturally we attract the vicious element. But every isolated town does that. The queer thing about Fairdale is that every man looks askance at his neighbor. Each one personally is honest, it seems, but doubts the other. However, there is no open doubt. That wouldn't be healthy. When I was elected to office, there was no law. I have maintained a little. If I didn't, there would be no law at all. I have a county judge, a justice of the peace, and two sheriffs."

"Well, I suppose conditions, such as you mention, are certain to arise in the development of wild ranges," observed Weed.

"They are indeed. But I take a hopeful view of prospects. We are slowly progressing. The pioneer can't be stopped. Meanwhile, the gunmen are killing each other. And in time the outlaws and rustlers must go."

"I hope so . . . soon. While they're passing, it's hard on the honest pioneer."

The adjutant paused a moment and played with a paper-knife upon his desk. Then he looked at Longstreth rather intently. "Colonel Longstreth, do you imagine a company of Texas Rangers would be of any use to you out there on the frontier?"

"Hardly. One of two things would happen. Either the lawless element would leave the country temporarily, until the rangers had left, then return to make us suffer all the more, or they would band together and annihilate the rangers."

The adjutant general raised his eyebrows in surprise. "Is there a large enough force to do that?"

"I believe there are a thousand badmen in Pecos County."

"Well, we can't spare a whole company of rangers, even if there were a chance to clean up Fairdale. I wonder how it would do to send . . . say, *one* ranger?"

Weed gazed with innocent, clear eyes straight at the mayor, and for his pains he received an incredulous stare, then a mellow laugh. While Longstreth's head lay back, as he was shaken with mirth, the adjutant turned away from his visitors, and I was sure some kind of signal passed between him and MacNeal.

"But, Colonel," rejoined Weed in expostulation, "you don't know rangers. Let me read a report from one ranger about another ranger's work. Miss Longstreth, and you, Miss Herbert, will surely find this interesting."

The adjutant picked over some papers, and, selecting one, he began to read. He had not progressed far before I realized that he was fabricating such a report as was never in the world written by any ranger. The adjutant showed a quick mind, and he was clever. As he read, the color came to Miss Herbert's cheeks, and Miss Longstreth listened with mounting interest.

What purpose Weed had in mind, I could not divine, but he detailed accounts of hard riding, arrests, rescues, and fights, with a series of remarkable doings entirely new to me as a ranger. As far as these details were concerned, what puzzled me most was how he ever made them up. As he concluded and carefully replaced the papers on his desk, there was a significant silence.

"How splendid!" exclaimed Miss Longstreth. "What a noble fellow."

Her deep voice, sweet like a bell, made me look closer at her. I had at first noted her pale face and dark eyes and hair, but that was all. I had not really looked at her. This time I saw pride, fire, passion in her, and something that made me sure she had French blood. She had beauty, as I had never seen it in another woman. Then my gaze shifted to Miss Herbert, and the expression on her arch face gave me a feeling that was new to me. I must have been jealous of the adjutant's fictitious ranger.

"A ranger! I want to meet a man like that," she burst out. "I think I'd prefer him to the cowboys."

Somehow I gathered from Miss Herbert's tone that generally she attached persons she liked to her train, and I did not wonder at that.

"A remarkable report . . . almost inconceivable, unless you know character west of the Colorado," said Colonel Longstreth. "Is that the ranger's name, Steele . . . Vaughn Steele?"

The adjutant general showed surprise, but I was not surprised. I knew something of Steele's fame on the border. What did surprise me was to see Weed nod his head. "Yes, Steele's the ranger," he said. Probably he wanted Longstreth to carry back to Fairdale as strong an impression of the ranger as it was possible to give.

"I've heard of Steele," the colonel mused. "He's called the Lone Wolf Ranger. No, it's the Lone Star Ranger. That report about him is a remarkable document."

"Vaughn Steele. Lone Star Ranger," said Miss Longstreth dreamily. "Truly, I know little about the state and the country where my father lives. I'm to make my home where such a man as Vaughn Steele is needed. It's very strange. What is he like?" She asked the question suddenly.

"Steele? Oh, he's a magnificent fellow, Miss Longstreth," replied the adjutant, and it was evident to me that he meant to impress the daughter further, if possible. "Why, he'd have to stoop and almost turn sidewise to come in that door. I think you ladies would find him too somber-faced, too stern to be handsome. He can talk, for he is well educated and has a fine mind, but he seldom talks unless it has to do with his work. He does strange, chivalric things. He is gentle, kind. Captain MacNeal tells me Steele's the best nurse among the rangers. He's brave as a lion. In fact, he's a composite of many traits. I suppose, more than anything else, his fame rests upon his marvelous quickness with a gun. That's his best asset as a ranger, and quite naturally the one least calculated to interest you ladies."

"Then he has killed men?" Miss Longstreth asked, shrinking, yet fascinated.

"Yes."

Weed let the single word stand with all its force. I would have liked to tell Miss Longstreth what MacNeal had said about Steele's reluctance to kill a man. But obviously the adjutant's purpose was to let the ranger appear, apart from his noble attributes, as a stern, ruthless, wonderful officer.

"Don't send Steele to Fairdale," interposed the colonel with a little laugh that made me start. "He's too valuable to your ranger service. Adjutant Weed, I thank you for your courtesy. Will you ask Governor Stone to receive us now?"

"I'll have you taken in at once," replied the adjutant, rising. "I've enjoyed meeting you. May I ask when you leave?"

"By first stage tomorrow . . . to San Antonio."

The adjutant shook hands with Colonel Longstreth, then turned to the ladies. "Miss Longstreth, I wish you a pleasant journey and hope that you will like your new home. Miss Herbert, I'm sure you'll have your desire fulfilled. You'll ride broncos and work sad havoc among the cowboys. And you may meet the Lone Star Ranger. ¿Quien sabe? Good bye."

He rang for his clerk, who led the party out. When they were gone, Weed closed the door, and MacNeal came forth from behind his screen and I out of the closet.

"What did you make of Longstreth, mayor of Fairdale?" queried Weed of the captain.

"He's not much of a mayor. Lax, I'd call him," replied MacNeal.

"He certainly wasn't backward about admitting the lawlessness at Fairdale. Say, but that must be a place! Russ, what did you think of Longstreth?"

I was non-committal on that score, but I said I was willing to tell what I thought about the colonel's daughter and his niece.

"You'll be on that stage tomorrow?"

"I sure will."

"Well, Marshal," said Weed, with his engaging smile, "your lot appears to begin pleasantly. Make the most of it."

CHAPTER THREE

Nearly a Hold-Up

I<small>T</small> did not take me long to show the wary captain that I could take the stage ride to San Antonio without danger of being recognized as a United States deputy marshal. I seldom visited the capital, always riding to and fro on horseback, and had few acquaintances. Having allayed his fears on this point, I talked to him a little more about our plan, asked his advice on this and that procedure, received it in good measure, and a stern parting reminder not to be backward in pulling my gun on behalf of my own and Steele's life, and then we said farewell.

Never had I faced a ranger assignment or any other kind with such a stir of blood and speculative mind. First, I sold my horse, pack, and trappings, keeping out from my old outfit only a few articles that I used in disguising myself. In my official capacity a disguise was often necessary—and healthy, to use Longstreth's expression — and I imagined the Fairdale enterprise might call for all manner of strategy.

I bought another gun, a small one, easily carried in a coat pocket, and that done I thought I had completed my preparation. But it developed, somewhat to my surprise, that I had a sudden and unaccountable dissatisfaction with my clothes and, for that matter, with my whole personal appearance. Not until I had purchased new suit, sombrero, boots, and other necessary articles, did I discover that I had been prompted by a strange desire to look well in the eyes of Miss Ruth Herbert whom I expected to meet on the stage ride to San Antonio.

The interest I felt in her was not amazing. I had observed similar symptoms, often before, but not lately. What amazed me was the realization that this time, and before I really thought about it, I was doing unprecedented things. At first it seemed funny. A man old in hardened experience, an adventurer, ranger, marshal of the wildest state in the Union — a gun-thrower without scruples—a fighter whose softer side must long ago have become blunted to finer feelings — an outlaw-hunter almost as alien as those he hunted — what business on earth had *I* to want to appear well in the eyes of a charming, arch-faced girl? After all, it was not in the least funny, and I experienced a depression unusual to my buoyant spirit. But I did not remain cast down for long.

The remainder of that day I kept to myself at the inn where I stayed and went to bed early. Next morning I was up with the sun, ready and eager for the ride, and what was to come after. My mind was strangely fertile with possibility and conjecture.

The stagecoach started from another inn, across town, and, when I got there, I found all the inside seats reserved, but I might ride on top of the coach with the driver. This did not please me, still, I had to make the best of it. Even in my disappointment I felt a little relief, the reason of which was not clear to me.

The stagecoach was a huge, lumbering affair, littered with baggage on top and tied behind, and already was nearly full of passengers. I imagined that, when the Longstreth party arrived, they would find it a tight squeeze in the coach.

I took my little pack of luggage and climbed up in front. It was the loftiest vehicle I had ever been on, and the seat was wide and comfortable, with a back rest. A rifle lay on the seat, and it reminded me that not by any means was it beyond the bounds of probability for the stage to be held up by highwaymen. The eighty-mile ride to San Antonio might be interesting for me from various points of view.

Four splendid horses were being hitched to the coach by stablemen. The stage driver, however, had not put in an appearance. Naturally I presumed, after the nature of stagecoach drivers, he was in at the bar, taking long odds against a future thirst. I was curious to see this driver I had to ride with, for I wanted to get along well with him. How pleasant it would have been if my old friend Joel Harkness, most noted of Texas stagecoach drivers, had been the one to handle the reins on this ride.

Scarcely had I had the thought when a grizzled and bronzed Texan in corduroys, high boots, and black sombrero full of holes strode from the inn. He wore a six-shooter and a belt full of cartridges, and he carried a long whip in his hand. It *was* Joel Harkness, and I remembered what MacNeal had said about my luck. Turning my head aside so Joel could not recognize me, I awaited developments.

"Say, who's thet up there on top?" I heard him ask somebody.

He was told that it was a passenger for San Antonio.

"Wal, he shore 'pears like one of these heah flash Mississippi River gamblers . . . all spick an' span," remarked Joel, not exactly in an undertone.

I was considerably crestfallen at the impression he had gathered from my new attire. The arrival of the Longstreth party, however, made me forget myself. They alighted from a hack. While the colonel went into the inn, probably for the same reason that made all stagecoach drivers and passengers late in starting, the ladies, both wearing long, gray ulsters and veils, got into the stage.

Joel clambered up on the seat, gave me a shove that was as unnecessary as it was powerful, and then he gathered up the reins, grumbling to himself. By dint of some strength of hand and no little dexterity, I regained my balance without falling off the stage. Then I turned to Joel, swore softly into his ear, and prodded him in the side with the gun I had in my coat pocket.

"Wal, dog-gone me!" he ejaculated. "If it ain't Russ . . . "

"My name's Russ . . . just Russ, on this ride," I whispered.

"And I'm a tenderfoot or a cowboy, whichever you like. Savvy, Joel?"

He crushed my hand with his great paw. "Heah in Austin. Wal, I shore am surprised an' glad," he said. "Say, it was down Brownsville way I run into you last. I like this new job better, Russ. Shore there ain't so much dodgin' of bullets. Wal, what air you doin', Russ? Never seen you so togged out. Ain't been an' gone an' done took a pardner for life?"

"No. Same old job, Joel."

"Chasin' some o' the poor homeless cusses. I was on the dodge once."

"Well, Joel, I'm after some cusses, sure, but they're not poor or homeless. They're rich and own a whole town."

"Wal, I shore seen thet kind of a bunch more'n once in this heah Lone Star state. Say, who's the tall gent? Is he a passenger?"

Joel had caught sight of Colonel Longstreth who appeared, walking briskly toward the stage. He carried something in his hand.

"Hello, the new driver," he said, looking up. "You're Harkness, eh? Glad to make your acquaintance. My name's Longstreth. From Pecos."

He shook hands with Joel and gave him a flask, which the driver took beamingly. Then Longstreth, waving his hand, stepped up into the coach.

"Uncle, I want to ride outside . . . on top of the coach," spoke up a voice that made me start.

"Ruth, you'd better not," replied Miss Longstreth. "It'll be dusty and sunny up there."

"But Ray, I can't breathe in here," protested Ruth. "It was bad enough before Uncle got in. Now, I'm squeezed to death. Uncle, won't you ask if I may ride outside?"

"Ray, it's pretty crowded. Let Ruth go up. She likes that kind of thing," said the colonel. Then he raised his voice. "Hello, driver, will you make room up there for my niece?"

"Now, Mister Longstreth, I'm shore dee-lighted," replied Joel. "There's room for her an' a nice easy seat."

Miss Ruth lightly leaped out.

"Wait, Ruth, I'll give you a lift," said the colonel.

But she did not need any. She gathered up the long ulster, disclosing little feet and shapely ankles, and climbed like a boy. It was my hand that caught and steadied her, and I moved over toward Joel, leaving my seat for her.

"Thank you," she said, and she looked at me.

"Wal, we're off," called Joel cheerily, and he cracked his whip.

The horses started, the coach rattled, and presently we were going at a trot down a good road toward the open country.

I had faced the open on many a ride but never with the sensations that beset me now. The close proximity of this girl had a strange effect on me. At every jolt of the coach her arm touched mine, and sometimes we bumped shoulder to shoulder. I could see out of the corner of my eye that she had tucked the veil back from her face. I wanted to look directly at her, but, as I thought that would be imprudent, I refrained.

"Miss Longstreth . . . ," began Joel.

"Herbert . . . Ruth Herbert," corrected the girl. "I'm Colonel Longstreth's niece."

"Aw. Wal, now, Miss Ruth, it's shore powerful fine to hev you up heah. This gentleman's name's . . . Russ. He's an ole acquaintance . . . a cowboy . . . an' I'm shore sorry to say, out of a job. Reckon he's as glad as me to hev company."

My vanity suffered a little shock at Joel's naïve manner of introducing me, but it was forgotten when I looked at Miss Herbert.

"Mister Russ," she said demurely, and bowed.

I bowed, too, spoke, and with sound of my voice suddenly lost all stiffness and embarrassment. If ever I had met a born flirt, it was then. Her eyes were hazel, clear, roguish, with a devil in the deeps of them. Her face was round, but not plump, with a fine skin, just a little tanned by sun and wind. Her lips were red, sweet, extremely thought-provoking. She had a good, square little chin, denoting a will of her own. This close sight of her made me think she was less pretty than I at first had believed, but it gave me a feeling of spirit more attractive than any prettiness.

After an interchange of commonplaces usually incident to an introduction, Miss Ruth gave me a theme for conversation by expressing fervent admiration for Joel's splendid horses. I knew horses almost as well as if I had really been the cowboy Joel had pretended I was. So I talked about horses. However, the talk was not one-sided, because Miss Ruth loved horses, had owned and ridden many, and was gifted with what a cowboy called horse sense.

We began to get pretty well acquainted, although I did not see that there was any change in a certain subtle something that I had before encountered in Southern girls of quality. There was a considerable difference between the niece of a rich rancher, who evidently belonged to a family of blooded Louisiana planters, and a cowboy out of a job. Time and again I caught Miss Ruth looking at me, neither hiding her interest nor something that puzzled her. This occasioned me to redouble my efforts to be worthy of such attention.

Joel put in his big voice occasionally, telling things about the road and the country, sometimes sandwiching in a little anecdote. There was no doubt that, between the two of us, Miss Ruth passed a morning far from dull.

At noon Joel pulled up at a water hole and called all hands to get down for a rest in the shade and lunch while the horses were feeding. Nobody lost any time complying. Besides Colonel Longstreth and his daughter there had been five other passengers inside the coach — one woman and four men. These last were not interesting.

Miss Ruth introduced me to her cousin and her uncle. I was aware of a keen scrutiny from the genial rancher. The girls laid aside ulsters, veils, and hats, and appeared to be more comfortable. Certainly they looked better. When Miss Ruth went to the little brook and began to bathe her face, I ventured to say that alkali water was decidedly not good for the complexion.

"I don't care. It's cool," she replied, and I liked her the better for it.

It appeared, presently, that everybody except myself had brought lunch. Miss Ruth called her cousin's attention to my lack of lunch, and I was promptly asked to share theirs. The opportunity thus presented itself for me to take a good and unobtrusive look at Miss Ray Longstreth.

She was slender, but the womanly development of her figure made me think she was twenty years old, at the least. She had the most exquisite hands I had ever seen, and her wrists and arms were molded in like symmetry. Close by, she did not resemble her father so much. She looked tired, quiet, even melancholy, yet that did not detract from her beauty. A finely chiseled oval face, clear, olive-tinted skin, long eyes set wide apart and black as coal, beautiful to look into, a slender, straight nose that had something nervous and delicate about it which made me think of a Thoroughbred, a mouth by no means small but perfectly curved, and hair like jet. All these features proclaimed her loveliness to me and confirmed my first impression. She was a descendant of one of the old French families that had settled Louisiana.

She was gracious to me, and there was not any of the aloofness that I had felt or imagined I had felt in her cousin. Strange to me was this quality I sensed in Miss Ruth, who I believed was ready to flirt with me. Somehow, Ray Longstreth made me feel how a man could fight for a woman. I liked her. And thinking of that, I was surprised to find that I disliked her father. There seemed absolutely no cause for it.

My instincts were queer, and, though I had not learned to understand them, I had lived to find out they rarely directed me wrong. After lunch I went over to where Joel sat and talked with him. There was to be an hour of rest. The month was April, and in the middle of the day it was sultry, hot, without a breath of wind.

While I was with Joel, I heard Miss Ruth tell her cousin that I was a cowboy out of a job and that she had supposed cowboys were all illiterate, ignorant. I thought she said something more about me, but in too low a voice for me to hear. Most shamelessly would I have listened. When Joel finished his pipe, he appeared inclined to a little nap, so I left him and found for myself a comfortable seat located under a mesquite, where I could see, yet not readily be seen.

How interested I was in this Longstreth party! It occurred to me that I ought to tell them I was on the way to Fairdale. But whenever I met ladies the worst of my job manifested itself — I had to be the deputy marshal, the hounder of criminals, before I could be the gentleman. That keen instinct of mine told me I would have more to do with the mayor of Fairdale and his daughter and niece, but I had no inkling whether that relation would be friendly or otherwise.

I had taken him at his face value — a fine, genial, Southern rancher, good-natured and apparently lax in certain principles. I imagined he. cared more for mint juleps and horses than he cared for his family. But that might have been imagination only, in line with my instinctive dislike.

What did he intend to do away out there in the Pecos country with this beautiful daughter? Probably, as he had intimated, he had no choice in the matter of her going. The cousin, I supposed, would visit them for a while, then return to Louisiana. But Ray Longstreth struck me as a girl close to womanhood — one who had strong ideas of duty and who would be hard to change. She would stay in her father's home, if it lay in the middle of the Staked Plains.

Again there came over me that subtle and unintelligible promise of the future. In a way, like nearly all men used to lonely lives, I was a dreamer. Dreaming never interfered with my practical duties, and it often enabled me to forget much that I did not want to remember. If Vaughn Steele and I were ever to be mixed up with this party I had so strangely fallen in with, what kind of a relation would it be?

For myself, I admitted straight out that I could not very long resist the demure Miss Ruth. She had a petiteness, a fragility, a prettiness that appealed to me, and I believed she had a temper as well as a coquetry that would tantalize my heart out of me in a day. For Steele, I could not speak, though I could dream. He was young. I had heard that he never approached women except when his ranger duty demanded. Still, I imagined that one look at Ray Longstreth would be his undoing.

Even while this dream conjecture held me, I thought that it was silly and sentimental. Likewise, I thought it might just as well be my prophetic sense of things to come. Anyway, dreams aside, the situation at Fairdale was bound to be absorbing. Here was Steele, a wonderful instrument for the subjugation of criminals, let foot loose on the most vicious settlement in the wilds of Texas. Here was myself, confessedly an adventurer, yet one who could love his comrade. Here was Colonel Longstreth, a lax mayor, sure to oppose ranger interference in the law and order of his town. Here was Ray Longstreth, a beautiful girl, bordering on womanhood, proud, fiery, surely passionate in her devotion to her kin, surely gentle and noble, surely one who would hate any form of wickedness. Lastly, here was Ruth Herbert, a piquant little disturber of man's peace. Verily that was a combination of characters and possibilities calculated to make even me draw a deep, full breath of pure joy and face the future with all my spirit aflame, yet with a graver something, an earnestness never before felt, knocking at my heart.

Joel's call roused me out of my reverie. I helped him hitch up. The passengers betook themselves to the coach and settled themselves for a long ride. Miss Ruth patted the horses. I awaited her pleasure while Joel climbed to his seat.

When she did get ready to climb, I offered to assist her, but she shook her head. As my luck would have it, she slipped on the second step and fell into my arms. There was laughter then, and embarrassment, and no further refusal of my help up to the driver's seat. Miss Ruth had more color in her cheeks, too.

This time she took the middle seat next to Joel, and, for all the attention she paid to me, I might not have been on the coach. Her manner occasioned some reflection on my part. What I had done on the spur of the moment, when she fell into my arms, I had no idea, unless it was that I might have held her just a moment too long. I made one or two unsuccessful attempts to enlist her attention again, or a little of it, and then I gave up trying. I threw a robe back on top of the coach, and, climbing over the seat, I lay down.

My intention was to go to sleep, but it was frustrated by a rather active mind, so to carry out my idea of indifference, I pretended to sleep. Under the edge of my silk scarf, with which I had covered my face, I saw Miss Ruth turn twice to look at me and heard her tell Joel something.

"Wal, he's all in, poor boy, no wonder," said that worthy with a most amazing solicitude. "Grand boy, Russ is, Miss Ruth, but he's jest onable to hold a job."

"Why?"

"Because he's plumb wild."

"Wild? Why, he seemed so . . . nice," she said. "My cousin thought so, too."

"Nice? Wal, reckon Russ's the nicest boy thet ever punched a steer. Comes from good family, Russ does. But he's jest wild. Why, if I'd tell you some of his cowboy stunts, you'd think Joel Harkness shore an ole liar."

"Tell me some," she said.

Joel was noted for his loquacity and his stories. He began to talk, and he made me the hero of more fights, more conquests of fair ladies, of more rescues and wild rides and strange adventures than could possibly have been the experience of a dozen cowboys.

"But if only Russ'd fall in love with a nice girl, one as could boss him an' put a cinch on his wildness, wal, he'd shore be saved," said the old villain in conclusion.

"Maybe," returned Miss Ruth, with a glance back at me. "But wouldn't it be risky for the girl?"

At this juncture I quickly lifted the scarf and met her gaze full. Disconcerted and flushing, she whirled away. Then the shaking of her shoulders and a sound like smothered mirth furnished more food for reflection.

That roused me to an Homeric mood. She would probably laugh at me more, unless I did something to justify to some little degree the reputation Joel had given me. So I resumed my seat beside her and, if anything, sat a little closer.

"Didn't you say you were crazy to meet cowboys?" I asked abruptly.

"Sir!" she exclaimed with a start.

"Now, honest, didn't you ever say that?"

The pink cheeks shaded to red, and she turned to me stiffly, yet she was not far from laughing. "Yes, I said that," she replied. "How on earth you know, I can't imagine. You guessed it! Well, I *was* crazy to meet cowboys."

The emphasis on the past tense was not lost upon me.

"You don't seem to be making the best of your opportunity," I retorted.

At that she faced straight ahead and made no reply. But she looked anything except dangerous.

Leaning a little nearer to her, I said in a low tone: "Do you believe in love at first sight?"

"No," she replied with stinging coldness. Then she turned her back upon me and engaged Joel's attention.

I had made her angry and was glad of it. The remainder of the ride apparently would be lonely for me. It certainly was monotonous, so far as scenery was concerned. The road was level and smooth. The horses kept at a steady trot. On each side spread a scant growth of brush, with occasional mesquites, and far into the distance stretched the green and yellow plain to merge into dim hills or clouds on the horizon. There was not a living creature to be seen. I looked and mused, tried to be oblivious of the girl so close to me, tried not to hear her vivacious talk and occasional merry laugh.

After a while two dark specks appeared against the green, far down the road. They were horses. I spoke to Joel and pointed.

"Jest seen them," he replied, "but wasn't shore what they was. My eyes ain't sharp fer distance any more."

"Do you meet any travelers between Austin and San Antonio?" asked Miss Ruth.

"Shore. Allus meetin' some. That's the wust of this trip. You jest never can pick out the road agents."

"Road agents. What are they?" queried Miss Ruth.

"Highwaymen! Robbers!"

"Oh, you never meet any?" she said with eyes wide.

"Lots of them. I've been held up twice this side of San Antonio."

"How dreadful! What do road agents usually do when they . . . hold you up?"

"Wal, they jump out from the brush or drop out of the clouds, so to say, an' surprise me before I can pull a gun. One feller holds the hosses an' the others make the passengers git out an' line up an' deliver. I've met some pretty decent road agents . . . fellers thet wouldn't rob a lady."

"Joel, those horses have gone out of sight," I interposed quietly.

"So they hev. Mebbe hid by a bend in the road or dropped behind a hill."

"Perhaps. But the road looks straight and level, far as I can see."

"Them horses was all of five miles off, wasn't they, Russ?"

"More than that."

He said nothing further, and I made no other comment. Miss Ruth looked from Joel to me, with something of alarm in her glance. Then I gazed ahead, trying to espy the horses that had disappeared.

The incident might not have any significance, and then again it could mean a great deal. There was an even chance. So I would have been relieved to see the horses show up again. They didn't. When we had covered two miles, I began to consider the disappearance unusual, and another mile brought misgivings. From the lay of the land ahead there did not appear to be any good reason why travelers should turn off the road out of sight.

"Stop the stage, Joel," I said.

"Reckon that'll be about the deal," replied Joel gruffly, as he hauled on the reins. Presently he brought the stage to a halt.

"Miss Herbert, would you mind hiding my money somewhere about you?" I asked her, producing my roll of greenbacks. "If we're held up, there's a chance they won't search such a demure and innocent little maid as you are."

She missed entirely the satire in my remark, and I felt a little ashamed. As she took the money, there was fire in her eye. "I'll hide it all right," she said.

Then with swift directness, and as absolutely unabashed as if I had been her brother, she lifted her skirt. Swiftly, as I tried to turn away my eyes, I could not help seeing the little foot and shapely leg thrust out. I jumped down off the coach.

"What's up?" asked the colonel sharply.

"Reckon we ain't shore," replied Joel. "But we want Miss Ruth to go inside. If you heah me yell, put the women down between the seats, an' them of you as has guns git busy."

That was all from Joel. Colonel Longstreth laughed, which fact struck me as odd. His daughter murmured plaintively. Some of the other men muttered. I helped Miss Ruth down and into the coach. Then I climbed back. Joel cracked his long whip, and we resumed our journey.

Joel had his rifle across his knees and his gun by his side on the seat. I held both my guns in readiness. We were just as liable to be held up as we were not. The fact was that travelers usually were wary about carrying considerable money or valuables. That five thousand dollars of MacNeal's suddenly became a white elephant on my hands.

Joel kept the horses at a steady trot, and we covered another couple of miles. Just ahead the road turned slightly at a point where the brush grew thick and straggly clumps of mesquite marked lower ground.

"Hit the pace now, Joel," I said. "If we're jumped, it'll be hereabouts."

"Keep your eye peeled, boy," replied Joel as he put the horses to a brisker trot.

Fortunately, here the road ran somewhat down hill, and the sharp gait of the horses might appear natural. It would never have done to race by that dangerous point. For, if there were robbers awaiting our approach, they would shoot the leaders of a running team.

I peered ahead from side to side of the road, looking low down between the trees and bushes, trying to spy out dark figures or the legs of horses. At the same time I had a sharp eye sweeping the side of the road. Just before we reached the bend, I discovered fresh horse tracks leading into the brush. Joel, too, saw them. But no riders or horses were in sight.

We bowled along, turned the curve down into a little swale where water ran in wet season. Here, if anywhere, would be the place. Certainly I expected to hear the harsh "Halt!" ring out, and I meant to shoot at the voice. But nothing happened, and we trotted out of the swale to level ground once more.

"Looked us over an' shore lost their nerve or rid ahaid to make a stand somewheres," said Joel.

We agreed on that. However, the situation was less critical. We entered upon another long level stretch, bordered by both dense patches and open places. After we had passed the first few thickets, we began to feel easier. Joel drew the horses to a less wearing gait. Still we did not lack vigilance, and for me, what with the excitement of keen watching, the afternoon passed swiftly.

It was just sunset when we made out a cluster of adobe houses that marked the half way point between Austin and San Antonio. Here was stationed a comfortable inn for wayfarers and the home of an acquaintance, with whom I had stayed once. This place was the last where I had any reason to fear being recognized before the Longstreth party, and, accordingly, I made my plans.

It developed, when I questioned Joel about my acquaintance, that I need fear no risk at all, for he had moved to Austin. Presently we drew up before the inn, where the landlord and his family and a number of loungers awaited the stage with that interest common to isolated people upon the arrival of the one daily event of consequence. I entered the inn without waiting for the Longstreth party.

Supper was soon ready, and at table I found myself next to Miss Herbert. She appeared to be looking for me — apparently she had forgotten her annoyance. I did not mention the money she had of mine, and I divined she wanted to speak of it, but found the matter a little difficult to approach.

Supper was usually merry when it was eaten in a wild country, half way between civilized points. Joel Harkness was at his best. I had to kick him in the shin to shut off further encomiums calculated to bring me into notice. Miss Ruth heard me kick him, and it made her thoughtful. Colonel Longstreth was inclined to joke about the incident of the afternoon.

Miss Longstreth enjoyed her supper and was evidently excited about the journey. It was something to hear her low laugh. She appeared interested in me and asked me what way my path led beyond San Antonio.

I replied that I was out of work and did not know what I was going to do or where I would head for.

She looked sympathetic, and so did her father. Manifestly I had given an impression somewhat at variance with the one Miss Ruth had. For I caught her grave questioning look and suddenly remembered again the huge roll of money I had given her for safekeeping.

After supper we all assembled in a big sitting room where an open fireplace with blazing mesquite sticks gave out warmth and cheery glow. I had gotten hold of a paper and was reading at a table in one corner of the room when Miss Ruth came up to me. She had something in her hand wrapped in a handkerchief.

"Haven't you forgotten your money?" she asked.

"Why, so I had. But it was in a safe . . . in safekeeping."

She blushed. "Isn't this an awful lot of money for a poor cowboy, out of a job, to be carrying around?" she asked severely.

"It's all I have in the world," I replied, as if it were two dollars. "I'd rather no one but you knew about it. Please don't tell."

"Certainly not," she replied. "Mister Russ, I don't know about you," she went on dubiously.

"If you hadn't been so cold, you'd have known all . . . "

"Here's your money," she interrupted.

Hastily I took off the handkerchief and put the bills in my pocket. "Thank you," I said. "But I almost wish we'd been held up and robbed."

"Why?" she asked blankly.

"Because I'll treasure this money now. I can't ever spend it. How could I? And I'll always think of . . . "

She silenced me with a look and turned away.

As I glanced after her, I saw two dark-faced men, strangers who had not appeared before, and they were watching me from a doorway. As I caught a glimpse of them, they stepped back out of sight.

CHAPTER FOUR

Floyd Lawson

IT flashed over me that the strangers had seen the roll of greenbacks pass from Miss Ruth's hand to mine. This fact disturbed me. In Texas in the 'Seventies it was always bad policy to let strangers see any considerable sum of money. If it had been my own, however, its possession might not have given me so much uneasiness. I pondered a moment. Then, with an assurance that was my nature as much as it was the habitual sense of my authority, I went to look over these two men.

The doorway opened onto a patio and across from that was a little dingy, dim-lighted barroom. Here I found the innkeeper dispensing drinks to the two strangers. They glanced up when I entered, and fell to whispering.

I imagined I had seen one of them before. In Texas, where outdoor men were so rough, bronzed, bold, and sometimes grim of aspect, it was no easy task to pick out the crooked ones. But my years of ranger and marshal service had augmented a natural instinct or gift to read character, or at least to sense the evil in men — and I knew at once that these strangers were dishonest.

"Hev somethin'?" one of them asked, leering.

Both looked me up and down. Probably they were puzzled to understand why my clothes gave an impression that did not fit my face.

"No, thanks ... I don't drink," I replied, and returned their scrutiny with interest. "How's tricks in the Big Bend?"

Both men stared. It had taken only a close glance for me to recognize a type of ruffian most frequently met in the Big Bend of the Rio Grande, an outlaw-infested region. These strangers had that stamp, and their surprise proved I was right.

Here the innkeeper showed signs of uneasiness and seconded the surprise of his customers. No more was said at the instant, and the two rather hurriedly went out.

"Say, boss, do you know those fellows?" I asked the innkeeper.

"Nope."

"Which way did they come?"

"Now I think of it, them fellers rid in from both corners today," he replied, and he put his hands on the bar and looked at me. "They nooned heah, comin' from Santone, they said, an' by Josh! they trailed in after the stage."

If I needed to know any more, that was enough. These fellows had met the stage, which for some reason or other they had not halted, and they had followed us back with evil intent' that waited upon opportunity.

Might I have been mistaken? In my ranger days I had acquired the habit of always anticipating violent action, dark deeds. But that was not unnatural. I knew Texas. I gravitated toward criminals. I had knowledge. A resident of eastern Texas would have found in me a cheerful presager of fights, hold-ups, assaults, and killings, and he would have been aghast, possibly disgusted, as had been Governor Stone. The truth was, I seldom made mistakes, and I did not intend to give these dark-faced strangers the benefit of a doubt.

When I returned to the sitting room, Colonel Longstreth was absent — also several of the other passengers. Miss Ruth sat in the chair I had vacated, and across the table from her sat Miss Longstreth. I went directly to them.

"Miss Herbert, I was rude today," I said in a low, earnest voice. "But only teasing. I ask your pardon now, because I want you to take me seriously."

I paused, while Miss Ruth looked up in amazement, and her cousin leaned forward in sudden interest.

"The men whom we expected to hold up the stage today have followed us here. I've just seen them. They mean evil. I want to warn you to be careful. Lock your door . . . bar your window tonight."

"Oh!" cried Miss Ruth, very low.

"Thank you, we'll be careful," said her cousin gratefully. The rich color had faded in her cheek. "I saw those men watching you from that door. They had such bright black eyes. Is there really danger . . . here?"

"I think so," was my reply.

Soft, swift steps behind me preceded a harsh voice.

"Hands up!"

No man quicker than I to recognize the intent in those words! My hands shot up. Miss Ruth uttered a little frightened cry and sank into her chair. Miss Longstreth turned white, and her eyes dilated. Both girls had glances riveted behind me.

"Turn around," ordered the harsh voice.

Like a soldier I pivoted. The big, dark stranger, the bearded one who had whispered to his comrade in the barroom and asked me to drink, had me covered with a cocked gun.

He strode forward, his eyes gleaming, pressed the gun against me, and with his other hand dived into my inside coat pocket and tore out my roll of bills. Then he reached low at my hip, felt my gun, and took it. Then he slapped my other hip, evidently in search of another weapon.

That done, he backed away, wearing an expression of fiendish satisfaction that made me think he was only a common thief — a novice at this kind of game.

His comrade stood in the door with a gun leveled at the other two men, who stood frightened, speechless. "Git a move on, Bill," called this fellow, and he took a hasty glance backward.

A stamp of hoofs came from outside. Of course, the robbers had horses waiting. The one called Bill strode across the room and with brutal, careless haste began to prod the two men with his weapon and to search them.

The robber in the doorway called: "Rustle!" and disappeared.

I wondered where the innkeeper was and Colonel Longstreth and the other two passengers who had ridden with us. The bearded robber quickly got through with his searching, and from his growls I gathered he had not been well remunerated.

Then he wheeled to us once more. I had not moved a muscle, stood perfectly calm, with my arms high. He strode back with his bloodshot eyes fastened upon the girls. Miss Longstreth never flinched, but her little cousin appeared about to faint.

"Don't yap there!" he said, low and hard. He had thrust the gun close to Ruth.

Then I knew for sure that he was no knight of the road, but a plain cutthroat robber. Danger always acted strangely upon me, made me exult in a kind of cold glow. But now something hot worked within me. I had the little gun in my pocket. The robber had missed it. And I began to calculate chances.

"Any money, jewelry, diamonds?" ordered the ruffian fiercely.

Miss Ruth had collapsed, so he made at Miss Longstreth. She stood with her hands at her breast. Evidently the robber took this position to mean that she had valuables concealed there. But I fancied she had instinctively pressed her hands against a throbbing heart.

"Come out with it!" he said harshly, reaching for her.

"Don't dare touch me!" she cried, her eyes ablaze. She did not move. She had nerve. It made me thrill.

I saw I was going to get my chance, if I could only wait. Waiting has been a science with me. But here it was hard. Miss Ruth had fainted, and that was well.

Miss Longstreth had fight in her, which fact helped my chance, yet made injury possible to her.

She eluded two lunges he made at her. Then his rough hand caught her waist and with one pull ripped it asunder, exposing her beautiful shoulder white as snow.

"Mister Russ!" she wildly appealed.

The prospect of being robbed or even killed had not shaken Miss Longstreth's nerve as had this brutal tearing off of half her waist. My icy control seemed to crack as if with heat. The ruffian was only turned partially away from me. For myself, I could have waited longer. But for her!

His gun was still held dangerously upward, close to her. I watched only that. Then a bellow made me jerk my head.

Colonel Longstreth stood in the doorway in a magnificent rage. He had no weapon. Strange how he showed no fear!

He bellowed something again.

My shifting glance caught the robber's sudden movement. It was a kind of start. He seemed stricken. I expected him to shoot Longstreth. Instead, the hand that clutched Miss Longstreth's torn waist loosened its hold. The other hand, with its cocked weapon, slowly dropped till it pointed to the floor. That was my chance. Swift as a flash I drew my gun and fired.

Thud! went my bullet, and I could not tell on the instant whether it hit him or went into the ceiling. Then the robber's gun boomed harmlessly. He fell, with blood spurting over his face. I realized I had hit him, but the small bullet had glanced.

Miss Longstreth reeled and might have fallen had I not supported her. It was only a few steps to a couch, to which I half led, half carried her. Then I rushed out of the room, across the patio, through the bar to the yard. Nevertheless, I was cautious.

In the gloom stood a saddled horse, probably the one belonging to the fellow I had shot. His comrade had escaped. Returning to the sitting room, I found a condition approaching pandemonium.

The innkeeper rushed in, pitchfork in hands. Evidently he had been out at the barn. He was now shouting to find out what happened. Joel Harkness was trying to quiet the men who had been robbed. The woman, wife of one of the men, had come in, and she had hysterics. The girls were still and white.

Bill lay where he had fallen, and I guessed I had made a fair shot, after all. And, lastly, the thing that struck me strangest of all was Longstreth's rage. I never saw such passion. Like a caged lion he stalked and roared, and I saw him bestow a kick on the prostrate robber. I had no time then to think of his actions, but as was my habit I missed nothing that occurred.

There came a quieter moment in which the innkeeper shrilly protested. "Man! what'er you ravin' aboot? Nobody's hurt, an' that's lucky. I swear to God I hadn't nothin' to do with them fellers!"

"I ought to kill you, anyhow!" replied Longstreth, and his voice now astounded me. I saw that he had a gun, and I was about to remonstrate with him when he put it in his pocket.

When I turned, I realized that he was recovering from passion which had transformed him. Here I sensed a power incalculable at the moment.

"Russ, is this thug dead?" he asked.

Upon examination we found that my bullet had furrowed the robber's temple, torn a great piece out of his scalp, and, as I had guessed, had glanced. He was not seriously injured and already showed signs of returning consciousness.

"Drag him out of here," ordered Longstreth, and he turned to his daughter.

Before the innkeeper reached me, I had secured the money and gun taken from me. Presently we recovered the property of the other men. Joel helped the innkeeper carry the injured man somewhere outside.

Miss Longstreth was sitting, white but composed, upon the couch where lay Miss Ruth, who evidently had been carried there by the colonel. I did not believe she had wholly lost consciousness, and now she lay very still, with eyes dark and shadowy, her face pallid and wet. The colonel, now that he finally remembered his womenfolk, seemed to be gentle and kind. He talked soothingly to Miss Ruth, made light of the adventure, and said she must learn to have nerve out here where such things happened.

"Can I be of any service?" I asked solicitously.

"Thanks, Russ . . . guess there's nothing you can do," replied the colonel. "Talk to these frightened girls while I go see what's to be done with that thick-skulled robber." Then, telling the girls that there was no more danger, he went out.

Miss Longstreth sat with one hand holding her torn waist in place, while she extended the other to me. I took it awkwardly, I fear, but she was so wonderful then that I was embarrassed. She pressed my hand.

"You saved my life," she said in grave, sweet seriousness.

"No, no!" I exclaimed. "He might have struck you, hurt you . . . but no more."

"I saw murder in his eyes. He thought I had jewels under my dress. I couldn't bear his touch. The beast! I'd have fought. Surely my life was in peril!"

"Did you kill him?" asked Miss Ruth who lay, listening.

"Oh, no. He's not badly hurt," I returned.

"I'm very glad he's alive," said Miss Longstreth, shuddering.

"My intention was bad enough," I went on. "It was a ticklish place for me. You see . . . he was half drunk, and I was afraid his gun might go off. Fool careless he was!"

"Yet you say you didn't save me!" Miss Longstreth returned quickly.

"Well, let it go at that," I responded. "I saved you something, and I'm proud."

"Tell me about it?" asked Miss Herbert, who was fast recovering.

So, happy to have a chance to talk to her, I told the incident from my point of view.

"Then you stood there all the time with your hands up, thinking of nothing . . . watching for nothing except a little moment when you might draw your gun?" asked Miss Ruth.

"I guess that's about it," I replied.

There was no occasion for me to regret that I had wanted to appear well in Miss Ruth's eyes.

"Ruth," said Miss Longstreth thoughtfully, "we're fortunate to have Mister Russ for a traveling companion on part of this wild journey. Papa scouts . . . laughs at danger. He seemed to think there was no danger. Yet he raved after it came."

"Go with us all the way to Fairdale . . . please?" asked Miss Ruth, sweetly offering her hand.

"Glad to go," I burst out, taking the proffered hand. What I lacked in speech I made up in pressure.

"But, Ruth, you should not ask so much," protested Miss Longstreth. "It may not suit Mister Russ. Did you not say he was . . . out of work?"

"Yes, out of a job. Poor . . . no money," she replied, and the demure little devil came back to her eyes. "I tell you what, Ray. Give Mister Russ a job! Your horses are coming. You'll buy more out here. Mister Russ is a cowboy. He knows horses. *I* can recommend him."

"Indeed, that's worth thinking of," replied Miss Longstreth. "Would you consider an offer from me, Mister Russ?"

"Consider it! Well, I think . . . I will," I replied, half bewildered by the idea and by Miss Ruth's little hand squeezing mine. "Wouldn't you need to consult your father?"

"Not at all. I've long had my own horses to take care of. And, when you see them, you'll understand why I am particular."

"What would be my duties?" I inquired, prolonging the pleasure of this startling new proposition.

"Merely to take care of my horses. Of course, you can have a boy or man to help you. Then I would expect you to ride with me and Ruth. We love riding. Papa made strenuous objections to the idea of taking my horses out to Fairdale. You know, he expects I'll last there only a few months. But I'm going for good."

"Miss Longstreth, I admire your pluck," I said. "Do you know . . . Fairdale is wild?"

"Yes, I've heard, but I don't pay much heed to warnings. I understand more . . . now . . . after tonight. I don't fear, but then it makes me a little sick. His home should be my home. I don't really know my father. I . . . " She broke off here and I respected her emotion.

"Shall you need references as to my character?" I asked.

"No," she replied.

"Well . . . let Miss Herbert decide it," I replied. "She made the suggestion. Let her say whether I go or not."

Miss Longstreth showed surprise.

"Yes," replied Miss Ruth instantly.

Colonel Longstreth returned then and, after bidding me what I thought a rather curt good night, which perhaps seemed so by contrast to the graciousness of the girls, he led them away.

Before going to bed I went outside to take a look at the injured robber, and perhaps to ask him a few questions. To my surprise he was gone and so was his horse. The innkeeper was dumbfounded. He said that he had left the fellow on the floor in the barroom.

"Had he come to?" I inquired.

"Sure. He asked me for whiskey."

"Did he say anything else?"

"Not to me. I heard him talkin' to the father of them girls."

"You mean Colonel Longstreth?"

"I reckon. He sure was some riled, wasn't he? Jest as if I was to blame fer thet two-bit hold-up!"

"What did you make of the old gent's rage?" I asked, watching the innkeeper.

He scratched his head dubiously. He was sincere, and I believed in his honesty.

"Wal, I'm dog-goned if I know what to make of it. But I reckon he's either crazy or got more nerve than most Texans."

"More nerve, maybe," I replied. "Show me a bed now, innkeeper."

Once in bed in the dark I composed myself to think over the several events of the evening. I called up the details of the hold-up and carefully revolved them in my mind. I approved of my own course of action — could not see how it could have been improved upon. The colonel's wrath, under circumstances where most any Texan would have been cool, nonplused me, and I put it down to a choleric temperament. I pondered long on the action of the robber when Longstreth's bellow of rage burst in upon us. This ruffian, as bold and mean a type as I had ever encountered, had for some reason or other been startled. From whatever point I viewed his strange indecision, I could come to only one conclusion — his start, his check, his fear had been that of recognition.

I compared this effect with the suddenly acquired sense I had gotten of Colonel Longstreth's powerful personality. Why had that desperate robber lowered his gun and stood paralyzed at sight and sound of the mayor of Fairdale? This was not answerable. There might have been a number of reasons, all to Colonel Longstreth's credit, but I could not harbor one of them in mind. Longstreth had not appeared to see danger for his daughter, even though she had been roughly handled and had struggled right in front of a cocked gun.

I probed deep into this singular fact, and I brought to bear on the thing all my knowledge and experience of violent Texas life. And I found that the instant Colonel Longstreth had appeared on the scene there *was* no further danger threatening his daughter. Why? That, likewise, I could not answer.

Then his rage, I concluded, had been solely at the idea of *his* daughter being assaulted by a robber. This deduction was indeed disturbing, but I put it aside to crystallize after far more careful consideration. I passed to thought of my relation to Miss Longstreth and her cousin. If my conscience had not begun to prick, I should have found the prospect most pleasant. But I was thrilled and fascinated even while I was ashamed.

Miss Longstreth was gracious, kind — too fine a woman to deceive. Miss Ruth was a most lovable little rogue, full of the devil, and perhaps, as I had imagined, a natural-born flirt, yet her trust should not have been requited with deceit. It often had been my business to sail under false colors, and the fact seldom disturbed me. Here, however, it was different.

Evidently I had, with my usual luck, made a favorable impression upon Miss Longstreth, and somehow I desired to be worthy of it. She was the kind of a woman to make a fellow want to be a man. In Miss Ruth's case I was all the deeper at sea because, if in one day I could so far fall victim to her charms, in a week I would be hopelessly in love. That was all the more reason why I needed to be myself. Thought of MacNeal came, then of Vaughn Steele, and the work cut out for me in Fairdale. They must be first because they had come first, and I kept my promises. I did not need to accept Miss Longstreth's kind offer — to have any relation with her at all. But to give up the prospects of riding with her, and especially with her cousin, to turn my back on something which beckoned smilingly and sweetly — that was hard.

It began to be so hard to consider that I thought there need be no hurry to tell them I could not accept the position. That was temptation assailing me — a rather new experience. Suddenly I conceived the idea that Steele might favor my working for Miss Longstreth. It might fall into line with his plans for my secret aid to him. Was I justified in being a liar for his sake and the ultimate good of Fairdale? Perhaps — but I hated the thought of being untrue to the beautiful woman who had looked straight into my eyes and said she needed no references as to my good character.

Finally I decided to put aside the tormenting problem until Steele had solved it for me. Then I went to sleep.

Evidently I had lain awake a long time thinking for, when I did fall asleep, I slept so soundly that I had to be called in the morning. I began the day in amusement with myself, for I found the new and natty suit distasteful, and I put on my rough clothes. Then I was late for breakfast and had to rush to catch the stage. Joel and Miss Ruth were up on the seat, and I received a hearty greeting from the one and a bright smile and appraising glance from the other. She liked me better — or she liked me — in the boots and corduroys and sombrero.

Miss Longstreth appeared no worse for the incident of the preceding night. She was glad to see me, and right then my conscience again awakened to what bade fair to be considerable activity. Her father, however, was gruff, and did not invite sociability. I wondered if she had told him and decided that she had. Then I climbed up in front.

Joel cracked his long whip and called cheerily to his horses. A smooth, open road strung out ahead as far as eye could see and then melted into a bright green haze. The morning was beautiful. We had a northeast wind at our backs with prospects of a cool day.

The horses struck out eagerly, and Joel had to hold them in. Song of lark and mockingbird filled the fresh morning air. There had been a little rain during the night, so now there was no dust, and the mesquite glistened in the sunlight.

Disquieting and sweet was the unmistakable fact that this morning I stood upon a different footing with Miss Ruth Herbert. The difference was impossible to describe, yet it was there. I saw a most enjoyable day before me, and with a feeling of shame I smothered the still, small voice that cried to be heard and prepared to enjoy myself.

"What became of the robber you shot?" was one of Miss Ruth's first questions.

"I remembered him as I came out," was my reply. "Haven't any idea. Of course, though, he rode away last night."

"Ray and I were . . . a little afraid you might have . . . "

"What?" I interrupted.

"Well, you see . . . Mister Harkness here told me you were such a terrible man with guns and things . . . and Ray and I feared . . . "

"Miss Herbert, Joel is an old liar," I declared. "And I never saw the robber after he was carried out. I'm glad I didn't hurt him much."

"Honest Injun?" she asked archly, but with thoughtful eyes.

"Yes," I answered, and returned her glance.

Then she besieged me with a thousand questions about horses, saddles, rides, about Fairdale and Pecos County and outlaws — every kind of question prompted by the alluring prospects of her visit to the wild ranges of Texas.

Not improbably I was a mine of information regarding all that pertained to the outdoors, ranges, and wildlife of the frontier, and I felt an unqualified pleasure in talking. The fact that my personal feelings of the moment did not lead me into any such rash speech as had offended her yesterday was further indication of how earnestly I desired to be liked by Miss Herbert. I could not help it. We were far on the road of acquaintance that morning.

At noon, Joel halted in a shady corner where, however, there was no water, and for that reason our midday rest was shorter than that of the day before. Colonel Longstreth's taciturnity made me rather avoid his presence, and, as I wandered aimlessly around under the mesquite, I did not give any chance to offer me lunch.

Again I was the last one to go aboard the stage. To my surprise, Miss Ruth drew a napkin from under her coat and gave it to me. It contained two sandwiches.

"Thank you. How good of you to think of me!" I said warmly.

"We'd have called you," she replied, "but Uncle's grouchy today. He isn't . . . just nice when he's that way."

"Grouchy? I hope it's not about . . . because Miss Longstreth offered me a job?"

"Oh, no. He didn't mind that. He said she could hire whom she likes. But I imagine he's put out or worried because Ray insists that she *will* make Fairdale her home. Uncle says he's happy to have her for a visit, but that the frontier is no place for a girl raised as Ray has been."

That afternoon I had deep insight into Miss Ruth Herbert's charming personality, and the deeper I saw, the more danger menaced my peace of mind. There had never been the real girl for me yet. Suppose Miss Ruth should be the one? I had a feeling of alarm before I persuaded myself that I was only caught for the moment.

One thing she did pleased Joel as much as it pleased me, and that was she drove his four horses at a bracing trot and did it beautifully. No small feat for a slip of a girl with those leaders pulling hard on the reins. I had always liked coy, roguish girls, but never until now had I met one who added to this doubtful charm the strength and spirit to do red-blooded things.

It was dark when we reached San Antonio, and I left the party at the inn where Joel hauled up. I said that I could continue the journey with them — they expected to stay a day in town — and would catch up with them by the time they reached Del Rio. Miss Ruth looked surprised, and, if my eyes did not deceive me in the dusk, she was disappointed.

A little thought after I had left her vicinity showed me that it would be an unwise move for me to be seen with Colonel Longstreth's party this side of Del Rio on the Rio Grande. I was well known in San Antonio and all along the stage route to the river. Fine predicament for me to have some outspoken Texan call me by name and ask what particular outlaw I was chasing. No, it would never do to risk so much. I spent the evening with friends and tried my best to appreciate their hospitable kindness, when all the time my mind was full of that hazel-eyed girl and the adventure which loomed strangely about her and Fairdale.

Next morning I took the stage for Uvalde where they were due to arrive the following night. The first day was wearisome, for a stage ride without any distraction was much harder on me than horseback, but the time passed quickly because I had much to think of. Similar was the next day — but, if anything, it passed even more quickly.

Upon reaching Uvalde, I wavered, wanting to wait there so as to see Miss Ruth all the sooner; and then somewhat in disgust at my vacillation I dismissed the temptation and next day continued on my journey to Del Rio. That day was long, and the next longer yet. At last, however, I reached the river town.

I passed the hours in a casual and unobtrusive questioning of ranchers and cowboys in regard to Fairdale, and I learned very little for my pains. It lay somewhere in the wilds of Pecos County, and from Sanderson could be reached by horseback or wagon.

The following evening I watched with eager eyes for the stage to roll in from Uvalde. Finally it came. To my satisfaction I saw the Longstreth party alight and go into the little hotel. Perhaps it was imagination, but I thought Miss Ruth had peered around at the loungers lined up before the stage.

Next morning, when the Longstreth party came out to resume their journey, I was sitting on top of the stage. Ruth espied me, and her quick smile made me happy. Then Miss Longstreth bowed, as if right pleased to see me, and her father spoke civilly enough. I had forfeited my seat inside, and, before Miss Ruth expressed any desire to ride outside, a huge individual clambered up beside me, taking all the available room.

She laughed at something in my face and stepped into the stage with all the other passengers. Then we started on the long ride, this time traveling northwest. My state of mind was one of unprecedented content, while at the same time I had an unreasonable resentment toward the fat man beside me.

At midday we halted for a rest and lunch at a small village, where I at once joined Miss Longstreth and her cousin, and, if my usual hard-headed judgment had not succumbed to a softening vanity, both girls were glad to have me with them. Here, at this place, I discovered that Colonel Longstreth was addicted to drink, and under its influence his genial manner suffered.

When the stage driver made ready to start for the afternoon's travel, I outmaneuvered the stout gentleman and got Miss Ruth up on the front seat. Miss Longstreth said she would also like to ride outside, so we made room for her. Once the mountain of flesh came waddling toward the coach, Ruth giggled, and I endeavored to look grave. He did not see us at all. Laboriously he began to climb.

"Gracious!" whispered Ruth. "He's coming up. Where on earth will he sit?"

"Comrade, I'm afraid there's no room left," I said politely.

He looked up, saw us, and burst out with an *"Ah!"* like a huge puff, then he fell off clumsily. When he clambered inside, someone among the passengers uttered an audible groan, and then there came a squeezing kind of sound, followed by a growl, this last quite unmistakably from Colonel Longstreth.

Miss Longstreth did not succeed in suppressing a smile, and Miss Ruth's eyes clearly showed the little dancing devil. That incident started us off merrily, and straightway I found myself pleasantly engaged. The time sped by. I enjoyed that afternoon all the more because, despite the innumerable questions concerning myself I answered, I did not have to tell one lie.

With the passing of the afternoon, the sun set over the bleak low mountains in the west, and darkness came on. The air was cool at night, for we had climbed to a higher altitude that day. For hours we had not passed a house or shack or range — anything to indicate the nearness of a settlement. It was, indeed, wild country, and now in the darkness with the mesquite so gloomy and the road shadowy and mysterious ahead, the ride could not longer have been pleasant for the girls. No doubt their silence told of both weariness and anxiety.

When the moon came up over a dark broken line of hills, the wildness of the place seemed all the more notable. We were high on a slope from which the rolling land stretched away in night haze. Patches of dense mesquite seemed to be harboring robbers; shadows hanging over the road resembled waiting, hiding horsemen; rustlings in the brush made the girls start. Yet, there came a moment when this part of the ride was beautiful to me.

"I'm afraid," whispered Ruth.

"What of?" I asked.

"Nothing," she replied. That, perhaps, was the trouble — the feeling of nothingness roused by that weird moon and the vast, pale, barren land, stretching away under the sky.

Then an owl or a hawk tore out of a mesquite along the road. The sound startled Ruth. I caught the gleam of her eyes, now dark in the moonlight. The stage lurched a little and my hand touched hers, and then, but not from any action, her hand was in mine. I clasped it warmly. I understood. But I could scarcely believe. If it had not been a warm, soft, clinging hand, glad to be held, I never could have realized it was real.

So I sat there, tingling, afraid to look at her, with my gaze on the dark breaks in the slope and the moon-blanched ridges, wondering what on earth this adventure would lead to and conscious that with the clinging pressure of this little hand something strange and troublesome and sweet had birth within my breast. Sooner or later the coach swung around the slope and lights of a town twinkled below us, not far away. When Ruth slipped her hand from mine, the rest of the ride lacked something.

Sanderson was a much larger town than I had expected to see. The main street appeared to be one of stores and saloons, all ablaze with lights and busy. A good many Mexicans mingled in the crowd before the hotel where our driver brought us to a halt.

"It'd be jolly, if I wasn't scared," said Miss Ruth, looking down at the growing circle of curious bronzed faces. Miss Longstreth made no comment, but her look was scarcely flattering to Sanderson.

While I was assisting the girls to the ground, I distinctly heard Colonel Longstreth utter an exclamation. Then I saw him shake hands with a tall, dark, striking-looking fellow. Longstreth looked surprised and angry, and he spoke with force, but I could not hear what it was he said. The fellow laughed, yet somehow he struck me as sullen, until suddenly he spied Miss Longstreth. Then his face changed, and he removed his sombrero.

"Floyd, did you come with the teams?" asked Longstreth sharply.

"Not me. I rode a horse, good and hard," was the reply.

"*Humph!* I'll have a word to say to you later." Then Longstreth turned to his daughter. "Ray, here's the cousin I've told you about. You used to play with him ten years ago . . . Floyd Lawson. Floyd, my daughter . . . and my niece, Ruth Herbert."

Straightway I seemed to be forgotten. Naturally I did not perceive this fact with any considerable degree of pleasure.

Taking my baggage, I turned away, entered the hotel, and asked for accommodations. I did not hurry to go in to supper, and, when I did, the Longstreth party had preceded me.

There were two tables, one large and one small. I seated myself at the smaller, because it was unoccupied. Miss Herbert was not so absorbed with the presence of this handsome cousin that she had not a smile for me, a fact for which I was grateful entirely beyond any reason. Miss Longstreth, however, did not see me at all. Her eyes were sparkling, and her cheeks were red.

Any man of my pursuits, who always scrutinizes everyone he meets, would have studied this stranger attentively, and I with a new and dangerous game to play, with a consciousness of Longstreth's unusual and significant personality, with a little jealousy sharpening my edge, assuredly bent a keen and searching glance upon this Floyd Lawson. He was under thirty, yet gray at his temples — dark, smooth-shaven, with lines left by wildness, dissipation, shadows under dark eyes, a mouth strong and bitter, and a square chin — a reckless, careless, handsome, sinister face, strangely losing the hardness when he smiled.

The grace of a gentleman clung around him and seemed like an echo in his mellow voice. I did not doubt that he, like many a young man I had known, had drifted out to the frontier where rough and wild life had wrought sternly but had not quite effaced the mark of a good family. Colonel Longstreth apparently did not share the pleasure of his daughter and his niece in the advent of this cousin. I recalled what he had said to Lawson and pondered its import. Something hinged on this meeting.

After supper, they all went into the hall that did duty as parlor, office, and what not, and I imagined the girls, at Colonel Longstreth's suggestion, bade the newly found cousin a reluctant good night before they went to their room. The colonel and Lawson turned with voiceless but tacit intention toward the bar.

I followed, saw them seated at a table near an open door. It was dark outside. I went out the other exit and found my way around the corner to a porch upon which the door opened. I tiptoed as close as I dared, and, leaning against the wall in as careless a position as I could assume, I listened.

I heard the clink of glasses, the striking of a match, the scraping of a boot. I saw the red end of the burning match fall outside the door where it had been flung.

"Who's the little guy with the sharp eyes?" asked Lawson presently. "He was on the stage. I saw him help the girls off."

"Cowboy named Russ," replied Longstreth. "Ray hired him to come on. Wants him to handle her horses."

There was a long pause, fraught with more than interest for me. "Better drop him here," added Lawson.

"Easier said than done."

"Why?"

"Ray took a liking to him. She hired him. She'll want a good reason to fire him. The fellow's a cool hand. I'd just as lief let him go along. Ray and Ruth will need someone like him if they ride around much out here."

"I'll take care of them."

"Floyd, you've got work of mine to attend to, and, if you'd been doing it right, you wouldn't be here."

"Wait till you know why I'm here, will you?" replied Lawson impatiently. "As for this cowboy, Russ, I didn't like his sharp eye. I'll see that he goes in the morning."

"Have it your own way," replied Longstreth in a worried tone. "Now I want to know what you're doing here."

"I came to Sanderson to get Joe and Brick out of jail."

"What!" ejaculated Longstreth.

Lawson repeated his statement.

"What jail?"

"A jail put into use here in Sanderson," replied Lawson with grim, ironic humor. "You've been away for some time, Mayor Longstreth. Things have happened."

"What were my cowboys arrested for?"

"There's a difference of opinion. The boys say for nothing. The officer who made the arrest couldn't find anybody to appear against them. So I got them released. They're around town, wild and roaring for trouble."

"Officer? What officer?" Longstreth asked in amazement.

"Vaughn Steele, the ranger."

A blank silence ensued.

"Steele! Here in Pecos?"

"I should smile. About six feet four of him, and wide in proportion."

"Alone?"

"He always goes alone, they say. He certainly was alone when he collared Joe and Brick. And didn't need help."

"It happened here, then?"

"Yes. Nelson rode over to the ranch and hurried me here. The boys were drunk and deserved arrest, he said. The town's divided, half on Steele's side, half on the other side. Steele had the boys red-handed. But the rancher whom they fleeced . . . a fellow from El Paso . . . hadn't the nerve to appear against them, though he accused them to Steele."

"Law and order on the frontier! One ranger!" exclaimed Longstreth.

"It looks funny. But law and order and Steele went right into Sancho's saloon. The usual gang was there, a gang that ought to scare one ordinary man out of his skin. Steele didn't know Joe and Brick. He yelled at them . . . that they were wanted by law. Both boys rose to that. And Steele arrested them without even showing a gun."

There was another long pause.

"I'll speak to the boys," said Longstreth in a constrained voice. "Where is this Steele now?"

CHAPTER FIVE

Vaughn Steele

"GONE to Fairdale," replied Lawson with a short, expressive laugh.

"What?" roared Longstreth.

"Gone to Fairdale on extended ranger service . . . so I hear."

"He won't last a day!" bellowed the mayor.

"Wait till you see him," was the curt reply.

My burning curiosity was no further gratified. Both men left the bar, probably to go to bed, and I saw them no more. However, I had sufficient to think about for one night. So Vaughn Steele had passed through Sanderson, and already the frontier town was divided against itself. How glad that made me. How much I would have liked to get the news to MacNeal. *Wait till you see him!* That curt speech of Floyd Lawson's gave me a thrill. I had heard something of the kind before regarding Vaughn Steele. For my part, I could not curb my impatience to see the ranger.

Much as I had heard about Steele, he was a stranger to me. I wanted to see him, judge him, form my own estimate of this singular man. It was just as well, perhaps, that Floyd Lawson intended to have Miss Longstreth let me go. But his disposal of me was the kind of bitter pill that was hard for me to swallow. If Lawson had otherwise impressed me favorably, this move would not have earned my resentment, but most assuredly I had not liked him. How much of this fact was owing to jealousy and how much to my instinct, I had no means to tell, but I gave him at least a benefit of my weakness. Conclusive estimate of Lawson must wait in all fairness till time proved what he was, and I had an intimation that this course would be just as fair in Colonel Longstreth's case.

I was a little off my balance, probably because I wanted to think well of Ray Longstreth's father and cousin. But without going any further and not in the least blindly, I knew there was something about these men that made me dubious. Naturally the mayor of Fairdale and his kin would resent any action that reflected upon Longstreth's ability to preserve what law and order were possible in the frontier town. If his honor were impeached, there would be a fight.

I tried to see the situation from the Longstreth side of the fence — tried not to be unduly influenced by the impression at that meeting in the adjutant general's office and by the significance of what had occurred at the road house. Moreover, I remembered two or three occasions in my service to the state where my suspicions proved to be unfounded and unjust.

Then I went to bed.

In the morning, after breakfasting early, I took a turn up and down the main street of Sanderson, made observations, got information likely to serve me at some future day, and then returned to the hotel ready for what might happen. The stage-coach was there and already full of passengers. This stage did not go to Fairdale, but I had found that another one left for that point three days in a week.

Several cowboy broncos stood hitched to a railing, and farther down were two buckboards with horses that took my eye. These probably were the teams Colonel Longstreth had spoken of to Lawson. As I strolled up, both men came out of the hotel. Lawson saw me, and, making an almost imperceptible sign to Longstreth, he walked toward me.

"You're the cowboy, Russ?" he asked.

I nodded and looked him over. By day he made as striking a figure as I had noted by night, but the light was not generous to his dark face.

"Here's pay," he said, handing me some bills. "Miss Longstreth won't need you out at the ranch."

I counted the money and with deliberation put it into my pocket.

"Is Miss Longstreth discharging me . . . or are you?" I asked coolly.

Perhaps at my tone, perhaps at my look, he gave me closer attention, as if meeting with something unexpected in a cowboy. Plainly he showed that he was intolerant of any opposition.

"She gave me the money . . . told me to pay you off," he replied coldly. "You needn't bother to speak with her."

He might as well have said, just as politely, that my seeing her, even to say good bye, was undesirable. As my luck would have it, the girls appeared at that moment, and I went directly up to them to be greeted in a manner I was glad Floyd Lawson could not help but see.

In Miss Longstreth's smile and "Good morning, Russ," there was not the slightest discoverable sign that I was not to serve her indefinitely. It was as I expected — she knew nothing of Lawson's discharging me in her name.

"Miss Longstreth," I said in dismay, "what have I done? Why did you let me go?"

She looked astonished. "Russ, I don't understand you."

"Why did you discharge me?" I went on, trying to look heart-broken. "I haven't had a chance yet. I wanted so much to work for you . . . Miss Ruth, what have I done? Why did she discharge me?"

"I did not," declared Miss Longstreth, her dark eyes lighting.

"But . . . look here . . . here's my pay," I went on, exhibiting the money. "Mister Lawson just came to me . . . said you sent this money . . . that you wouldn't need me out at the ranch."

It was Miss Ruth, then, who uttered a little exclamation. Miss Longstreth seemed scarcely to have believed what she had heard.

"My cousin . . . Mister Lawson . . . said that?"

I nodded vehemently.

At this juncture Lawson strode before me, practically thrusting me aside. "Come, girls, let's walk a little before we start," he said gaily. "I'll show you Sanderson."

"Wait, please," Miss Longstreth replied, looking directly at him. "Cousin Floyd, I think there's a misunderstanding. Here's the cowboy I've engaged . . . Mister Russ. He declares you gave him money . . . told him I discharged him."

"Yes, Cousin, I did," he replied, his voice rising a little. There was a tinge of red in his cheeks. "We . . . you don't need him out at the ranch. We've any number of boys. I just told him that . . . let him down easy . . . didn't want you to be bothered."

Certain it was that Floyd Lawson had made a poor reckoning. First she showed utter amaze, followed by distinct disappointment, and then she lifted her head with a kind of haughty grace. She would have addressed him again had not Colonel Longstreth come up.

"Papa, did you instruct Cousin Floyd to discharge Russ?" she asked.

"I sure didn't," declared the colonel with a laugh. "Floyd took that upon his own hands."

"Indeed! I'd like my cousin to understand that I'm my own mistress. I've been accustomed to attending to my own affairs and shall continue doing so. Russ, I'm sorry you've been treated this way. Please, in future, take your orders only from me."

"Then . . . I'm to go to Fairdale with you?" I asked.

"Assuredly. Ride with Ruth and me today, please."

She turned away with Ruth, and they walked toward the first buckboard.

Colonel Longstreth found a grim enjoyment in Lawson's discomfiture. "Ray's like her mother was, Floyd," he said. "You've made a bad start with the girl."

Here Lawson showed manifestation of the Longstreth temper, and I took him to be a dangerous man with unbridled passions. "Russ, here's my own talk to you," he said, hard and dark, leaning toward me. "Don't go to Fairdale."

"Say . . . Mister Lawson," I blustered, for all the world like a young and frightened cowboy, "if you threaten me, I'll have you put in jail."

Both men seemed to have encountered a slight shock.

Then Colonel Longstreth roared.

Lawson hardly knew what to make of my boyish speech. "Are you going to Fairdale?" he asked thickly.

I eyed him with an entirely different glance from my other fearful one. "I should smile" was my reply, as caustic as the most reckless cowboy's, and I saw him shake.

Colonel Longstreth laid a restraining hand on Lawson. Then they both regarded me with undisguised interest. I sauntered away.

"Floyd, your temper'll do for you some day," I heard the colonel say. "You'll get in bad with the wrong man some time. Here are Joe and Brick."

Mention of these fellows engaged my attention once more. I saw two cowboys, one evidently getting his name from his brick-red hair. They were the roistering type, hard drinkers, devil-may-care fellows, packing guns and wearing bold fronts — a kind that the rangers always called four-flushes.

However, as the rangers' standard of nerve was high, there was room left for cowboys like these to be dangerous to ordinary men. The little one was Joe, and, directly Lawson spoke to him, he turned to look at me, and his thin mouth slanted down as he looked. Brick eyed me, too, and I saw that he was heavy, not a hard-riding cowboy. Here, right at the start, were three enemies for me — Lawson and his cowboys. But it did not matter. Under any circumstances there would have been friction between such men and me.

I believed there might have been friction right then had not Miss Longstreth called me.

"Get our baggage, Russ," she said.

I hurried to comply, and, when I had fetched it, Lawson and the cowboys had mounted their horses. Colonel Longstreth was in the one buckboard with two men I had not before observed, and the girls were in the other.

The driver of this one was a tall, lanky, tow-headed youth, growing like a Texas weed. We had not any too much room in the buckboard, but that fact was not going to spoil the ride for me. We followed the leaders through the main street, out into the open, onto a wide, hard-packed road, showing years of travel. It headed northwest.

To our left rose the range of low, bleak mountains I had noted yesterday, and to our right sloped the mesquite-patched sweep of ridge and flat. The driver pushed his team to a fast trot, which gait surely covered ground rapidly. We were close behind Colonel Longstreth who, from his vehement gestures, must have been engaged in very earnest colloquy with his companions.

The girls behind me, now that they were nearing the end of the journey, manifested less interest in the ride and were speculating upon Fairdale and what it would be like. Occasionally I asked the driver a question, and sometimes the girls did likewise, but to my disappointment the ride seemed not to be the same as that of yesterday.

Every half mile or so we passed a ranch house, and, as we traveled on, these ranches grew farther apart until, twelve or fifteen miles out of Sanderson, they were so widely separated that each appeared alone on the wild range. We came to a stream that ran north, and I was surprised to see a goodly volume of water. It evidently flowed down from the mountain far to the west. Tufts of grass were well scattered over the sandy ground, but it was high and thick, and, considering the immense area in sight, there was grazing for a million head of stock.

We made three stops in the forenoon, one at a likely place to water the horses, the second at a chuck wagon belonging to cowboys who were riding after stock, and the third at a small cluster of adobe and stone houses, constituting a hamlet the driver called Longstreth, named after the colonel. From that point on to Fairdale there were only a few ranches, each one controlling great acreage.

Early in the afternoon from a ridge top we sighted Fairdale, a green patch in the mass of gray. For the barrens of Texas it was indeed a fair sight. But I was more concerned with its remoteness from civilization than its beauty. At that time in the early 'Seventies, when the vast western third of Texas was a wilderness, perhaps the pioneer had done wonders to settle there and establish places like Fairdale.

As we rolled swiftly along, the whole sweeping range was dotted with cattle, and farther on, within a few miles of town, there were droves of horses that brought enthusiastic praise from Miss Longstreth and her cousin.

"Plenty of room here for the long rides," I said, waving a hand at the gray-green expanse. "Your horses won't suffer on this range."

"Isn't it glorious? The open is so different . . . there's no end. And the air!"

She was delighted, and her cousin for once seemed speechless.

"That's the ranch," said the driver, pointing with his whip.

It needed only a glance for me to see that Colonel Longstreth's ranch was on a scale fitting the country. The house was situated on the only elevation around Fairdale, and it was not high or more than a few minutes' walk from the edge of town. It was a low, flat-roofed structure made of red adobe bricks and covered what appeared to be fully an acre of ground. All was green about it except where the fenced corrals and numerous barns or sheds showed gray and red.

Lawson and the cowboys disappeared ahead of us in the cottonwood trees. Colonel Longstreth got out of the buckboard and waited for us. His face wore the best expression I had seen upon it yet. There was warmth and love, and something that approached sorrow or regret.

His daughter was agitated, too. I got out and offered my seat, which Colonel Longstreth took. It was scarcely a time for me to be required, or even noticed at all, and I took advantage of it and turned toward the town. Ten minutes of leisurely walking brought me to the shady outskirts of Fairdale, and I entered the town with mingled feelings of curiosity, eagerness, and expectation.

The street I walked down was not a main one. There were small, red houses among oaks and cottonwoods. I went clear through to the other side, probably more than half a mile. I crossed a number of intersecting streets, met children, nice-looking women, and more than one dusty-booted man.

Half way back on this street I turned at right angles and walked up several blocks till I came to a tree-bordered plaza. On the far side opened a broad street which for all its horses and people had a sleepy look. I walked on, alert, trying to take in everything, wondering if I would meet Steele, wondering how I would know him if we did meet. But I believed I could have picked that ranger out of a thousand strangers, though I had never seen him.

Presently the residences gave place to buildings, fronting right upon the stone sidewalk. I passed a grain store, a hardware store, a grocery store, then several unoccupied buildings and a vacant corner. The next block, aside from the rough fronts of the crude structures, would have done credit to a small town even in eastern Texas. Here was evidence of business consistent with any prosperous community of two thousand inhabitants.

The next block, on both sides of the street, was a solid row of saloons, resorts, hotels. Saddled horses stood hitched all along the sidewalk in two long lines with a buckboard and team here and there, breaking the continuity. This block was busy and noisy. From all outside appearances Fairdale was no different from other frontier towns, and my expectations were scarcely realized.

As the afternoon was waning, I retraced my steps and returned to the ranch. The driver boy, whom I had heard called Dick, was looking for me, evidently at Miss Longstreth's order, and he led me up to the house. It was even bigger than I had conceived from a distance, and so old that the adobe bricks were worn smooth by rain and wind. I had a glimpse in at several doors as we passed by. There was comfort here that spoke eloquently of many a freighter's trip from Del Rio. For the sake of the young ladies I was glad to see things little short of luxurious for that part of the country.

At the far end of the house Dick conducted me to a little room, very satisfactory, indeed, to me. I asked about bunk-houses for the cowboys, and he said they were full to overflowing.

"Colonel Longstreth has a big outfit, eh?"

"Reckon he has," replied Dick. "Doan' know how many cowboys. They're always comin' an' goin'. I ain't acquainted with half of them."

"Much movement of stock these days?"

"Stock's always movin'," he replied with a queer look.

"Rustlers?"

But he did not follow up that look with the affirmative I expected.

"Lively place, I hear . . . Fairdale is?"

"Ain't so lively as Sanderson, but it's bigger."

"Yes, I heard it was. Fellow down there was talking about two cowboys who were arrested."

"Sure. I heerd all about thet. Joe Bean an' Brick Higgins . . . they belong heah, but they ain't heah much."

I did not want Dick to think me overly inquisitive, so I turned the talk into other channels. It appeared that Miss Longstreth had not left any instructions for me, so I was glad to go with Dick to supper, which we had in the kitchen.

Dick informed me that the cowboys prepared their own meals down at the bunkhouses. As I had been given a room at the ranch house, he supposed I would get my meals there, too.

After supper I walked all over the grounds, had a look at the horses in the corrals, and came to the conclusion that it would be strange if Miss Longstreth did not love her new home and if her cousin did not enjoy her sojourn there. From a distance I saw the girls approaching with Lawson, and, not wishing to meet them, I sheered off.

When the sun had set, I went down to the town with the intention of finding

Steele. This task, considering I dare not make inquiries and must approach him secretly, might turn out to be anything but easy. While it was still light, I strolled up and down the main street. When darkness set in, I went into a hotel, bought cigars, sat around, and watched without any clue.

Then I left and went into the next place. This was of rough, crude exterior, but the inside was comparatively pretentious and ablaze with lights. It was full of men, coming and going — a dusty-booted crowd that smelled of horses and smoke. I sat down for a while with wide eyes and open ears. Then I hunted up the bar, where most of the guests had been or were going. I found a great square room lighted by six huge lamps, a bar at one side, and all the floor space taken up by tables and chairs.

This must have been the gambling resort mentioned in the ranger's letter to Captain MacNeal, and the one rumored to be owned by the mayor of Fairdale. This was the only gambling place of any size in southern Texas in which I had noted the absence of Mexicans. There was some card playing going on at this moment. I stayed in there for a spell and knew that strangers were too common in Fairdale to be conspicuous. But I saw no man whom I could have taken for Steele. Then I went out.

It had often been a boast of mine that I could not spend an hour in a strange town, or walk a block along a dark street, without having something happen out of the ordinary. Mine was an experiencing nature. MacNeal had always called this luck. But it was my private opinion that things gravitated my way because I looked and listened for them. However, upon the occasion of my first day and evening in Fairdale it appeared, despite my vigilance and inquisitiveness, that here was to be an exception.

This thought came to me just before I reached the last lighted place in the block, a little dingy restaurant out of which, at the moment, a tall, dark form passed. It disappeared in the gloom. I saw a man sitting on the low steps and another standing in the door.

"That was the fellow the whole town's talkin' about . . . the ranger," said one man.

Like a shot I halted in the shadow, where I had not been seen.

"Sho! ain't boardin' heah, is he?" said the other.

"Yes."

"Reckon he'll hurt your business, Jim."

The fellow called Jim emitted a mirthless laugh. "Wal, he's been all my business these two days. An' he's offered to rent that old 'dobe of mine just out of town. You know . . . where I lived before movin' in heah. He's goin' to look at it tomorrow."

"Lord! does he expect to *stay?*"

"Say so. An', if he ain't a stayer, I never see one. Nice, quiet, easy chap, but he looks deep. I don't know his game, but he says he was heah for a while. An' he impressed me some. Just now he says . . . 'Where does Longstreth live?' I asked him if he was goin' to make a call on our mayor, an' he says, yes. Then I told him how to go out to the ranch. He went out, headed that way."

"The hell he did!"

I gathered from this fellow's exclamation that he was divided between amaze and mirth. Then he got up from the steps, went into the restaurant, and was followed by the man called Jim. Before the door was closed, he made another remark, but it was unintelligible to me.

As I passed on, I decided I would scrape acquaintance with this restaurant keeper. The thing of most moment was that I had gotten track of Steele. I hurried ahead. While I had been listening back there, moments had elapsed, and evidently he had walked swiftly.

I came to the plaza, crossed it, and then did not know which direction to take. Concluding that it did not matter, I hurried on in an endeavor to reach the ranch before Steele. Although I was not sure, I believed I had succeeded.

The moon shone brightly. I heard a banjo in the distance and a cowboy song. There was not a person in sight in the wide courts or on the porch. I did not yet have a well defined idea about the inside of the house.

Peeping in at the first lighted window, I saw a large room. Miss Longstreth and Ruth were there alone. Evidently this was a parlor or a sitting room, and it had clean, white walls, a blanketed floor, an open fireplace with a cheery blazing log, and a large table upon which were lamp, books, papers. Backing away, I saw that this corner room had a door opening on the porch and two other windows.

I listened, hoping to hear Steele's footsteps coming up the road. But I heard only Ruth's merry laugh and her cousin's mellow voice. Then I saw lighted windows down at the other end of the front part of the house. I walked down. A door stood open, and through it I saw a room identical with that at the other corner. Here were Colonel Longstreth, Lawson, and several other men, all smoking and talking.

It might have been interesting to tarry there within earshot, but I wanted to get back to the road to intercept Steele. Scarcely had I retraced my steps and seated myself on the porch steps when a very tall, dark figure loomed up in the moonlit road.

Steele! I wanted to yell like a boy.

He came on slowly, looking all around, halted some twenty paces distant, surveyed the house, then evidently espying me, came on again. My first feeling was — *what a giant!* But his face was hidden in the shadow of a sombrero.

I had intended, of course, upon first sight to blurt out my identity. Yet I didn't. He affected me strangely, or perhaps it was my emotion at the thought that we rangers, with so much in common and at stake, had come together.

"Is Longstreth at home?" he asked abruptly.

I said yes.

"Ask him if he'll see Vaughn Steele, ranger."

"Wait here," I replied. I did not want to take up any time then, explaining my presence there.

Deliberately and noisily I strode down the porch and entered the room with the smoking men. I went in farther than was necessary for me to state my errand. But I wanted to see Longstreth's face, to see into his eyes. As I entered, the talking ceased. I saw no face except his, and that seemed blank.

"Vaughn Steele, ranger . . . come to see you, sir," I announced.

Did Longstreth start? — did his eyes show a fleeting glint? — did his face almost imperceptibly blanch? I could not have sworn to any. But there was a change — maybe from surprise. The first sure effect of my announcement came in a quick exclamation from Lawson — a sibilant intake of breath that, strange to me, did not seem to denote surprise so much as certainty. Lawson might have emitted a curse with less force.

Longstreth moved his hand significantly, and the action was a voiceless command for silence as well as an assertion that he would attend to this matter. I read him clearly so far. He had authority, and again I felt his power.

"Steele to see me. Did he state his business?"

"No, sir," I replied.

"Russ, say I'm not at home," said Longstreth presently, bending over to relight his pipe.

I went out. Someone slammed the door behind me.

As I strode back across the porch, my mind worked swiftly. The machinery had been idle for a while and was now started.

"Mister Steele," I said, "Colonel Longstreth says he's not at home. Tell your business to his daughter."

Without waiting to see the effect of my taking up so much upon myself, I knocked upon the parlor door. Miss Longstreth opened it. She wore white. Looking at her, I thought it would be strange if Steele's well-known indifference to women did not suffer an eclipse.

"Miss Longstreth, here is Vaughn Steele to see you," I said.

"Vaughn Steele?" she echoed. "The ranger! Why . . . ?"

Then she saw Steele, looming behind me, and in some degree hid her astonishment. "Won't . . . you come in?" she said graciously.

Steele had to bend his head to enter the door. I went in with him, an intrusion, perhaps, that in the interest of the moment she appeared not to notice. Steele seemed to fill the room with his giant form. His face was fine, stern, clear cut, with blue or gray eyes, strangely penetrating. He was coatless, vestless. He wore a gray flannel shirt, corduroys, a big gun swinging low, and top boots, reaching to his knees. He was the most stalwart son of Texas I had ever seen in many a day, but neither his great stature nor his striking face accounted for something I felt — something spiritual, vital, compelling that drew me.

"Mister Steele, I'm pleased to meet you," said Miss Longstreth. "This is my cousin, Ruth Herbert. We just arrived . . . I, to make this my home . . . she to visit me."

Steele smiled as he bowed to Ruth. He was easy with a kind of rude grace and showed no sign of embarrassment or that beautiful girls were unusual to him.

"Mister Steele, we heard of you in Austin," said Ruth with her eyes misbehaving.

I hoped I would not have to be jealous of Steele. But this girl was a little minx if not altogether a flirt.

"I did not expect to be received by ladies," replied Steele.

"I called upon Mister Longstreth. He would not see me. I was to tell my business to his daughter. I'm glad to know you, Miss Longstreth, and your cousin, but sorry you've come to Fairdale now."

"Why?" queried both girls in unison.

"Because it's . . . oh, pretty rough . . . no place for girls to walk and ride."

"Ah! I see. And your business has to do with rough places," said Miss Longstreth. "Strange that Papa would not see you. Stranger that he should want me to hear your business. Either he's joking or wants to impress me. Papa tried to persuade me not to come. He tried to frighten me with tales of this . . . this roughness out here. He knows I'm in earnest, how I'd like to help somehow . . . do some little good. Pray, tell me this business."

"I wished to get your father's co-operation in my work."

"Your work? You mean your ranger duty . . . the arresting of rough characters?"

"That, yes. But that's only a detail. Fairdale is bad internally. My job is to make it good."

"A splendid and worthy task," replied Miss Longstreth warmly. "I wish you success. But, Mister Steele, aren't you exaggerating Fairdale's wickedness?"

"No," he answered forcibly.

"Indeed! And Papa refused to see you . . . presumably refused to co-operate with you?" she asked thoughtfully.

"I take it that way."

"Mister Steele, pray tell me what is the matter with Fairdale and just what the work is you're called upon to do?" she asked seriously. "I heard Papa say that he was the law in Fairdale. Perhaps he resents interference. I know he'll not tolerate any opposition to his will. Please tell me. I may be able to influence him."

I listened to Steele's deep voice as he talked about Fairdale. What he said was old to me, and I gave heed only to its effect. Miss Longstreth's expression, that at first had been earnest and grave, turned into one of incredulous amaze. She, and Ruth, too, watched Steele's face in fascinated attention.

When it came to telling what he wanted to do, the ranger warmed with his subject. He talked beautifully, convincingly, with a certain strange, persuasive power that betrayed how he worked his way. His fine face, losing its stern, hard lines, seemed to glow and give forth a spirit austere, yet noble, almost gentle, assuredly something vastly different from what might have been expected in the expression of a gunfighting ranger. I sensed that Miss Longstreth felt this, just as I did.

"Papa said you were a hounder of outlaws . . . a man who'd rather kill than save!" she exclaimed.

The old stern cast returned to Steele's face. It was as if he had suddenly remembered himself. "My name is infamous, I am sorry to say," he replied.

"You *have* killed men?" she asked, her dark eyes dilating.

Had any one ever dared ask Steele that before? His face became a mask. It told the truth to me, but she could not see, and he did not answer.

"Oh, you are above that! Don't . . . don't kill anyone here!"

"Miss Longstreth, I hope I won't."

His voice seemed to check her. I had been right in my estimate of her character — young, untried, but all pride, fire, passion. She was white then, and certainly beautiful.

Steele watched her, could scarcely have failed to see the white gleam of her beauty, and all that evidence of a quick and noble heart.

"Pardon me, please, Mister Steele," she said, recovering her composure. "I am . . . just a little overexcited. I didn't mean to be inquisitive. Thank you for your confidence. I've enjoyed your call, though your news did distress me. You may rely on me to talk to Papa."

That appeared to be a dismissal, and, bowing to her and Ruth, the ranger went out. I followed, not having spoken.

At the end of the porch I caught up with Steele and walked out into the moonlight beside him. Just why I did not now reveal my identity, I could not say, for certainly I was bursting with the desire to surprise him, to earn his approval. He loomed dark above me, appearing not to be aware of my presence. What a cold, strange proposition this ranger was.

Still, remembering the earnestness of his talk to Miss Longstreth, I could not think him cold — but I thought him just that when it came to any attraction to those charming girls. Suddenly we passed under the shade of cottonwoods. He clamped a big hand on my shoulder.

"My God, Russ, isn't she lovely!"

In spite of my being dumbfounded I had to hug him. He knew me. "Thought you didn't swear!" I gasped.

Ridiculously those were my first words to Vaughn Steele.

"Old son, I saw you parading up and down the street, looking for me," he said. "I intended to help you find me tomorrow."

We gripped hands, and that strong feel and clasp meant much.

"Yes, she's lovely, Steele," I said. "But did you look at the cousin, the little girl with the eyes?"

Then we laughed and loosed hands.

"Come on," I said, "let's get out somewhere. I've a million things to tell you."

We went off into the open where some stones gleamed white in the sand. With our backs against a rest and all quiet about us, we settled down for a long conference. I began with Mac-Neal's urgent message to me, then told of my going to the capital — what I had overheard when Governor Stone was in the adjutant's office — of my interview with them — of the spying on Colonel Longstreth — MacNeal's directions, advice, and command — the ride toward San Antonio — the hold-up, and my being engaged as a cowboy by Miss Longstreth — of the further ride on to Sanderson and the incident there — and finally how I had approached Longstreth and then had thought it well to get his daughter into the scheme of things. It was a long talk, even for me, and my voice sounded husky.

"I told MacNeal I'd be lucky to get you," said Steele, after a silence.

That was the only comment on my actions, the only praise, but the quiet way he spoke it made me feel like a boy, undeserving of so much.

"Here, I forgot the money MacNeal sent," I went on, glad to be rid of the huge roll of bills.

The ranger showed surprise, but he was also very pleased.

"The captain loves the service," said Steele. "He alone knows the worth of the rangers. And the work he's given his life to . . . the *good* that service really does . . . all depends on you and me, Russ."

I assented, gloomily enough. Then I waited while he pondered.

The moon soared clear. There was a cool wind, rustling the greasewood. A dog bayed at a barking coyote. Lights twinkled down in the town. I looked back up at the dark hill and thought of Ruth Herbert. Getting here to Fairdale, meeting Steele, had not changed my feelings toward her, only somehow they had removed me far off in thought, out of possible touch, it seemed.

"Well, old son, listen," began Steele. His calling me that was a joke, yet I didn't feel it. "You've made a better start than I could have figured. MacNeal said you were lucky. Perhaps. But you've got brains.

"Now, here's your cue for the present. Work for Miss Longstreth. Do your best for her, as long as you last. I don't suppose you'll last long. You have got to get in with this gang in town. Be a flash cowboy. You don't need to get drunk, but you're to pretend it. Gamble. Be a good fellow. Hang round the barrooms. I don't care how you play the part, just so you make friends, learn the ropes. We can meet out here at night to talk and plan. You're to take sides with those who're against me. I'll furnish you the money. You'd better appear to be a winning gambler, even if you're not. How's this plan strike you?"

"Great . . . except for one thing," I replied. "I hate to lie to Miss Longstreth. She's true blue, Steele."

"Old son, you haven't gone soft on her?"

"Not a bit. Maybe I'm soft on the little cousin. But I just like Miss

499

Longstreth . . . think she's fine . . . could look up to her. And I hate to be different from what she thinks."

"I understand, Russ," he replied in his deep voice that had such quality to influence a man. "It's no decent job. You'll be ashamed before her. So would I. But here's our work, the hardest ever cut out for rangers. Think of what depends upon it. And . . . "

"I hope Longstreth turns out to be on the square," I said. "He might be a lax mayor, too good-natured to uphold law in a wild country. And his Southern pride would fire at interference. I don't like him, but for his daughter's sake I hope we're wrong."

Steele's eyes, deep and gleaming in the moonlight, searched my face. "Old son, sure you're not in love with her . . . you'll not fall in love with her?"

"No. I'm positive. Why?"

"Because, in either case, I'd likely have need of a new man in your place," he said.

"Steele, you know something about Longstreth . . . something more!" I exclaimed swiftly.

"No more than you. When I meet Longstreth face to face, I may know more. Russ, when a fellow has been years at this game, he has a sixth sense. Mine seldom fails me. I never yet faced a criminal who didn't somehow betray fear . . . not so much fear of me, but fear of himself . . . his life . . . his deeds. That's conscience or, if not that, just realization of fate."

Had that been the thing I imagined I had seen in Longstreth's face?

"I'm sorry Ray Longstreth came out here," I said impulsively.

Steele did not say he shared that feeling. He was looking out upon the moon-blanched plain. Some subtle thing in his face made me divine that he was thinking of the beautiful girl to whom he might bring disgrace and unhappiness.

CHAPTER SIX

A Kiss and an Arrest

A MONTH had passed, a swiftly flying time full of new life. Wonderful it was for me to think that I was still in Ray Longstreth's employ.

It was the early morning hour of a day in May. The sun had not yet grown hot. Dew like diamond drops sparkled on the leaves and grass. The gentle breeze was clear, sweet, with the song of larks upon it. And the range, a sea of gray-green growing greener, swept away westward in rolling ridges and hollows, like waves, to meet the dark low hills that notched the horizon line of blue.

I was sitting on the top bar of the corral fence, and before me stood three saddled horses that would have gladdened any eye. I was waiting to take the young ladies on their usual morning ride. Once upon a time, in what seemed the distant past to this eventful month, I had flattered myself that there had been occasions for thought, but scornfully I soliloquized that in those days I had no cue for thought such as I had now. This was one of the moments when my real self seemed to stand off and skeptically regard the fictitious cowboy. This gentleman of the range wore a huge sombrero with an ornamented silver band, a silken scarf of red, a black velvet shirt, much affected by the Indians, an embroidered buck-skin vest, corduroys, and fringed chaps with silver buttons, a big blue gun swinging low, high heeled boots, and long spurs with silver rowels. A flash cowboy! Steele vowed I was a born actor, but I never divulged the fact that, had it not been for my infatuation with Ruth Herbert, I never could have carried on that part, not to save the ranger service or the whole state of Texas.

The hardest part had not been the establishing of a reputation. The scorn of cowboys, the ridicule of gamblers, the badinage of the young bucks of the settlement — these I had soon made dangerous procedures for anyone. I was quick with tongue and fist and gun. There had been fights and respect was quickly earned, though the constant advent of strangers in Fairdale always had me in hot water. Moreover, instead of being difficult, it was fun to spend all the time I could in the hotels and resorts, shamming a weakness for drink, gambling, lounging, making friends among the rough set, when all the time I was a cool, keenly registering machine. The hard thing was the lie I lived in the eyes of Ray Longstreth and Ruth Herbert.

I had, indeed, won the sincere regard of my employer. Her father, her cousin, Floyd, and new-made friends in town had come to her with tales of my reckless doings and had urged my dismissal. But she had kept me and all the time pleaded like a sister to have me mend my vicious ways. She believed what was told about me, but had faith in me despite that.

As for Ruth, I had fallen hopelessly in love with her. By turns, Ruth was indifferent to me, cold, friendly like a comrade, and dangerously sweet. Somehow she saw through me, knew I was not just what I pretended to be. But she never breathed her conviction. She championed me. I wanted to tell her the truth about myself, because I believed the doubt of me alone stood in the way of my winning her. Still, that might have been my vanity. She had never said she cared for me, although she had looked it.

This tangle of my personal life, however, had not in the least affected my loyalty and duty to Vaughn Steele. Day by day I had grown more attached to him, keener in the interest of our work. It had been a busy month — a month of foundation building. My vigilance and my stealthy efforts had not been rewarded by anything calculated to strengthen our suspicions of Longstreth. But, then, he had been absent from home very often and was difficult to watch even when he was at home.

Floyd Lawson came and went, too, presumably upon stock business. I could not yet see that he was anything but an honest rancher, deeply involved with Longstreth and other men in stock deals. Nevertheless, as a man he had earned my contempt. He was a hard drinker, cruel to horses, a gambler not above stacking the cards, a quick-tempered, passionate Southerner. He had fallen in love with Ray Longstreth, was like her shadow when at home. He hated me and treated me as if I were the scum of the earth. If he had to address me for something, which was seldom, he did it harshly, like ordering a dog. Whenever I saw his sinister, handsome face, with its dark eyes always half shut, my hand itched for my gun, and I would go my way with something thick and hot inside my breast.

In my talks with Steele we spent time studying Floyd Lawson's character and actions. He was Longstreth's partner and at the head of a small group of Fairdale ranchers who were rich in cattle and property, if not in money. Steele and I had seen fit to wait before we made any thorough investigation into their business methods. Ours was a waiting game, anyway.

Right at the start Fairdale had apparently risen in resentment at the presence of Vaughn Steele. But it was my opinion that there were men in Fairdale secretly glad of the ranger's presence. What he intended to do was food for great speculation. His fame, of course, had preceded him. A company of militia could not have had the effect upon the wild element of Fairdale that Steele's presence had. A thousand stories went from lip to lip, most of which were false. He was lightning swift on the draw. It was death to face him. He had killed thirty men — wildest rumor of all! He had the gun skill of Buck Duane, the craft of Cheseldine, the deviltry of King Fisher, these most notorious of Texas desperadoes. His nerve, his lack of fear — these made him stand out alone even among a horde of bold men.

At first there had not only been great conjecture among the vicious element, with which I had begun to affiliate myself, but also a very decided checking of all kinds of action calculated to attract a keen-eyed ranger. Steele did not hide, but, during these opening days of his stay in Fairdale, he was not often seen in town. At the tables, at the bars and lounging places remarks went the rounds: "Who's thet ranger after? What'll he do fust off? Is he waitin' fer somebody? Who's goin' to draw on him fust . . . an' go to hell? Jest about how soon will he be found somewhere full of lead?"

Those whom it was my interest to cultivate grew more curious, more speculative and impatient as time went by. When it leaked out somewhere that Steele was openly cultivating the honest stay-at-home citizens, to array them in time against the other element, then Fairdale showed those wolf teeth hinted at in the letters to Captain MacNeal.

Several times Steele was shot at in the dark and once slightly injured. Rumor had it that Jack Blome, the gunman of those parts, was coming in to meet Steele. Part of Fairdale awakened, and another part, much smaller, became quieter, more secluded. Strangers, upon whom we could get no line, mysteriously came and went. The drinking, gambling, fighting in the resorts seemed to gather renewed life. Abundance of money floated in circulation. And rumors, vague and unfounded, crept in from Sanderson and other points, rumors of a gang of rustlers off here, a hold-up of the stage off there, robbery of a rancher at this distant point, and murder done at another.

This was Texas and New Mexico life in these frontier days, but, strangely, neither Steele nor I had yet been able to associate any rumor or act with a possible gang of rustlers in Fairdale. Nevertheless, we had not been discouraged. After three weeks of waiting, we had become alive to activity around us, and, though it was unseen, we believed we would soon be on its track.

My task was the busier and the easier. Steele had to have a care for his life. I never failed to caution him of this. My long reflection on the month's happenings and possibilities was brought to any end by the appearance of Miss Longstreth and Ruth. My employer looked worried. Ruth was in regular cow-girl riding costume, in which her trim, shapely figure showed at its best, and her face was saucy, sparkling, daring.

"Good morning, Russ," said Miss Longstreth, and she gazed searchingly at me.

I had dropped off the fence, sombrero in hand. I knew I was in for a lecture, and I put on a brazen, innocent air.

"Did you break your promise to me?" she asked reproachfully.

"Which one?" I asked. It was Ruth's bright eyes upon me, rather than Miss Longstreth's reproach, that bothered me.

"About getting drunk again," she said.

"I didn't break that one."

"My cousin, Floyd, saw you in the Hope So gambling place last night . . . drunk, staggering, mixing with that riffraff, on the verge of a brawl."

"Miss Longstreth, with all due respect to Mister Lawson, I want to say that he has a strange wish to lower me in the eyes of you ladies," I protested with a fine show of spirit.

"Russ, were you drunk?" she demanded.

"No. I should think you needn't ask me that. Didn't you ever see a man the morning after a carouse?"

Evidently she had. And there I knew I stood, fresh, clean-shaven, clear-eyed as the morning.

Ruth's saucy face grew thoughtful, too. The only thing she had ever asked of me was not to drink. The habit had gone hard with the Longstreth family.

"Russ, you look just as . . . as nice as I'd want you to," Miss Longstreth replied. "I don't know what to think. They tell me things. You deny them. Whom shall I believe? Floyd swore he *saw* you."

"Miss Longstreth, did I ever lie to you?"

"Not to my knowledge."

Then I looked at her, and she understood what I meant.

"Floyd has lied to me. That day at Sanderson. And since, too, I fear. Do *you* say he lies?"

"Miss Longstreth, I would not call your cousin a liar."

Here Ruth edged closer, with the bridle rein of her horse over her arm. "Russ, Cousin Floyd isn't the only one who saw you. Burt Waters told me the same," she said nervously. I believe Ruth hoped I was telling the truth.

"Waters! So he runs me down behind my back. All right, I won't say a word about him. But do you believe I was drunk when I say no?"

"I'm afraid I do, Russ," she replied with reluctance. Was she testing me?

"See here, Miss Longstreth," I burst out. "Why don't you discharge me? Please let me go. I'm not claiming much for myself, but you don't believe even that. I'm pretty bad. I never denied the scraps, the gambling . . . all that. But I did do as Miss Ruth asked me . . . I did keep my promise to you. Now, discharge me. Then I'll be free to call on Mister Burt Waters."

Miss Longstreth looked alarmed, and Ruth, to my extreme joy, turned pale. Those girls believed I was a desperate devil of a cowboy, who had been held back from spilling blood solely through their kind relation to me.

"Oh, no!" exclaimed Ruth. "Ray, don't let him go."

"Russ . . . pray don't get angry," replied Miss Longstreth, and she put a soft hand on my arm that thrilled me, while it made me feel like a villain. "I won't discharge you. I need you. Ruth needs you. After all, it's none of my business what you do away from here. But, I hoped . . . I would be so happy to . . . to reclaim you from . . . Didn't you ever have a sister, Russ?"

I kept silent for fear that I would perjure myself anew. Yet this situation was delicious, and suddenly I conceived a wild idea. "Miss . . . Longstreth," I began haltingly, but with a brave front, "I've been wild in the past. But I've been tolerably straight here . . . trying to please you. Lately I *have* been going to the bad again. Not drunk, but leaning that way. Lord knows what I'll do soon if . . . if my trouble isn't cured."

"Russ! What trouble?"

"You know what's the matter with me," I went on hurriedly. "Anybody could see that."

Ruth turned a flaming scarlet. Miss Longstreth made it easier for me then by reason of her quick glance of divination.

"I've fallen in love with Miss Ruth. I'm crazy about her. Here I've got to see these fellows flirting with her. And it's killing me. I've . . . "

"If you *are* crazy about me, you don't have to tell!" cried Ruth, red and white by turns.

"I want to stop your flirting one way or another. I've been in earnest. I wasn't flirting. I begged you to . . . to . . . "

"You never did," interrupted Ruth furiously. That hint had been a spark.

"I couldn't have dreamed it," I protested in a passion to be earnest, yet tingling with the fun of it. "That day when I . . . didn't I ask . . . ?"

"If my memory serves me correctly, you didn't ask anything," she replied with anger and scorn now struggling with mirth.

"But, Ruth, I meant to. You understood me? Say, you don't believe I could take that liberty without honorable intentions."

That was too much for Ruth. She jumped at her horse, made the quickest kind of a mount, and was off like a flash. "Stop me if you can," she called back over her shoulder, her face alight and saucy.

"Russ, go after her," said Miss Longstreth. "In that mood she'll ride to Sanderson. My dear fellow, don't stare so. I understand many things now. Ruth *is* a flirt. She would drive any man mad. Russ, I've grown in a short time to like you. If you'll be a man . . . give up drinking and gambling . . . maybe you'll have a chance with Ruth. Hurry now . . . go after her."

I mounted and spurred my horse after Ruth's. She was down on the level now, out in the open, and giving her mount his head. Even had I wanted to overhaul her at once, the matter would have been difficult, well-nigh impossible under five miles. Ruth had as fast a horse as there was on the range. She made no weight in the saddle, and she could ride. From time to time she looked back over her shoulder.

I gained enough to make her think I was trying to catch her. Ruth loved a horse. She loved a race. She lived to win. My good fortune had given me more than one ride alone with Ruth. Miss Longstreth enjoyed riding, too, but she was not a madcap. When she accompanied us, there was never any race. If Ruth got out alone with me, she made me ride to keep her from disappearing somewhere on the horizon. This morning I wanted her to enjoy to the fullest her utter freedom and to feel that, for once, I could not catch her.

Perhaps my declaration to Miss Longstreth had liberated my strongest emotions. However that might be, the fact was that no ride before had ever been like this one — no sky so blue — no scene so open, free, and enchanting as that beautiful, gray-green range — no wind so sweet. The breeze that rushed at me might have been laden with the perfume of Ruth's hair.

I sailed along on what seemed a strange ride. Grazing horses pranced and whistled as I went by. Jackrabbits bounded away to hide in the longer clumps of grass. A prowling wolf trotted from his covert near a herd of cattle. Far to the west rose the low, dark lines of bleak mountains, always mysterious to me, as if holding a secret I needed to know.

It was a strange ride because in the back of my head worked a haunting consciousness of the deadly nature of my business here on the frontier — a business in such contrast with this dreaming and dallying, this longing for what surely was futile. Any moment I might be stripped of my disguise. Any moment I might have to be the ranger.

Ruth kept the lead across the wide plain and mounted to the top of a ridge where, tired out and satisfied with her victory, she awaited me. I was in no hurry to reach the summit of the long, slow-sloping ridge, and I let my horse walk.

Just how would Ruth Herbert meet me now, after my regretted exhibition before her cousin? There was no use to conjecture, but I was not hopeful. When I got there to find her in her sweetest mood, with some little difference never before noted — a touch of shyness — I concealed my surprise.

"Russ, I gave you a run that time," she said. "Ten miles and you never caught me!"

"But look at the start you had. I've had my troubles beating you with an even break." Ruth was susceptible to flattery in regard to her riding, a fact that I made subtle use of.

"But in a long race I was afraid you'd beat me. Russ, I've learned to ride out here. Back home, I never had room to ride a horse. Just look! Miles and miles of level, of green. Little hills with black bunches of trees. Not a soul in sight. Even the town hidden in the green. All wild and lonely. Isn't it glorious, Russ?"

"Lately it's been getting into me," I replied soberly.

We both gazed out over the sea of gray-green, at the undulating waves of ground in the distance. On these rides with her I had learned to appreciate the beauty of the lonely reaches of plain. But, when I could look at her, I seldom wasted time on scenery. Looking at her now, I tried to get again that impression of a difference in her. It eluded me.

Just now with the rose in her brown cheeks, her hair flying, her eyes with grave instead of mocking light, she seemed only prettier than usual. I got down, ostensibly to tighten the saddle girth on her horse, but I lingered over the task. Presently, when she looked down at me, I received that subtle impression of change and read it as her soft mood, the dangerous sweetness that came so seldom, mingled with something deeper, more of character and womanliness than I had ever sensed in her.

"Russ, it wasn't . . . nice to tell Ray," she said.

"Nice! It was . . . oh, I'd like to swear," I ejaculated. "But now I understand my miserable feeling. I was jealous, Ruth. I'm sorry. I apologize."

She had drawn off her gloves, and one little hand, brown, shapely, rested upon her knee very near to me. I took it in mine. She let it stay, though she looked away from me, the color richer in her cheeks.

"I can forgive that," she murmured. "But the lie. Jealousy doesn't excuse a lie."

"You mean . . . what I intimated to your cousin," I said, trying to make her look at me. "That was the devil in me. Only it's true, Ruth."

"How can it be true when you never asked . . . said . . . a word you hinted of?" she queried. "Ray believed what you said. I know she thinks me horrid."

"No, she doesn't. As for what I said, or meant to say, which's the same thing, how'd you take my actions? I hope not the same as you take Lawson's or the other fellows'."

Ruth was silent, a little pale now, and I saw that I did not need to say any more about the other fellows. The change, the difference was now marked. It drove me to give in wholly to this earnest and passionate side of myself.

"Ruth, I do love you. I don't know how you took my actions. Anyway, now I'll make them plain. I was beside myself with love and jealousy. Will you marry me?"

She did not answer. But the old willful Ruth was not in evidence. Watching her face, I gave her a slow and gentle pull, one she could easily resist if she cared to, and she leaned from her saddle into my arms.

Then there was one wildly sweet moment in which I had the blissful certainty that she kissed me of her own accord. She was abashed, yet yielding. She let herself go, yet seemed not utterly unstrung. Perhaps I was rough, held her too hard, for she cried out a little.

"Russ! Let me go. Help me . . . back."

I righted her in the saddle, although not entirely releasing her. "But, Ruth, you haven't told me anything," I remonstrated tenderly. "Do you love me?"

"I think so," she whispered.

"Ruth, will you marry me?"

She disengaged herself then, sat erect, and faced away from me, with her breast heaving. "No, Russ," she presently said, once more calm.

"But Ruth . . . if you love me . . . ?" I burst out, and then stopped, stilled by something in her face.

"I can't help . . . loving you, Russ," she said. "But to promise to marry you, that's different. Why, Russ, I know nothing about you, not even your first name. You're not a . . . a steady fellow. You drink, gamble, fight. You'll kill somebody yet, I fear. *Then* I'll not love you. Besides, I've always felt you're not just what you seemed. I can't trust you. There's something wrong about you."

I knew my face darkened, and perhaps hope and happiness died in it. Swiftly she placed a kind hand on my shoulder.

"Now I've hurt you. Oh, I'm sorry! Your asking me makes such a difference. The *others* are not in earnest. But, Russ, I had to tell you why I couldn't be engaged to you."

"I'm not good enough for you. I'd no right to ask you to marry me," I replied abjectly.

"Russ, don't think me . . . proud," she faltered. "I wouldn't care who you were if I could only . . . only respect you. Some things about you are splendid . . . you're such a man . . . that's why I cared. But you gamble. You drink . . . and I *hate* that. You're dangerous, they say . . . and I'd be . . . I am in constant dread you'll kill somebody. Remember, Russ, I'm no Texan."

This regret of Ruth's, this faltering distress at giving me pain, was such sweet assurance that she did love me better than she knew, that I was divided between extremes of emotion.

"Will you wait? Will you trust me a little? Will you give me a chance? After all . . . maybe I'm not so bad as I seem."

"Oh, if you weren't! Russ, are you asking me to trust you?"

"I beg you to . . . dearest. Trust me, and wait."

"Wait? What for? Are you really on the square, Russ? Or are you what Floyd calls you . . . a drunken cowboy, a gambler, sharp with the cards, a gunfighter?"

My face grew cold as I felt the blood leave it. At that moment mention of Floyd Lawson fixed once for all my hate of him. Bitter, indeed, was it that I dared not give him the lie. But what could I do? The character Lawson gave me was scarcely worse than what I had chosen to represent. I had to acknowledge the justice of his claim, but, nevertheless, I hated him.

"Ruth, I ask you to trust me . . . in spite of my reputation."

"You ask a great deal," she replied.

"Yes, it's too much. Let it be only this, then . . . you'll wait. And, while you wait, promise not to flirt with Lawson and Waters."

"Russ, I'll not let Floyd or any of them as much as dare touch me," she declared in girlish earnestness, her voice rising. "I'll promise, if you'll promise me not to go into those saloons any more."

One word would have brought her into my arms for good and all. The better side of Ruth Herbert showed then in her appeal. That appeal was as strong as the drawing power of her little face, all eloquent with its light, eyes dark with tears, and lips wanting to smile.

My response should have been instantaneous. How I yearned to give it and win the reward I imagined I saw on her tremulous lips! But I was bound. The grim, dark nature of my enterprise there in Fairdale returned to stultify my eagerness, dispel my illusion, shatter my dream. For one moment it flashed through my mind to tell Ruth who I was, what my errand was, all the truth, but the secret was not mine to tell. And I kept my pledge.

The hopeful glow left Ruth's face. Her disappointment seemed keen. Then a little scorn of certainty was the bitterest of all for me to bear.

"That's too much to promise all at once," I protested lamely, and I knew I would have done better to keep silent.

"Russ, a promise like that is nothing if a man loves a girl," she retorted. "Don't make any more love to me, please, unless you want me to laugh at you. And don't feel so terribly hurt if you happen to see me flirting occasionally."

She ended with a little mocking laugh. That was the perverse side of her, the cat using her claws. I tried not to be angry, but failed.

"All right, I'll take my medicine," I replied bitterly. "I'll certainly never make love to you again. And I'll stand it, if I happen to see Waters kiss you, or any other decent fellow. But look out how you let that damned backbiter Lawson fool around you!"

I spoke to her as I had never spoken before, in quick, fierce meaning, with eyes holding hers. She paled. But even my scarcely veiled hint did not chill her anger. Tossing her head, she wheeled and rode away.

I followed at a little distance, and thus we traveled the ten miles back to the ranch. When we reached the corrals, she dismounted, and, turning her horse over to Dick, she went off toward the house without so much as a nod or good-bye to me.

I went down to town for once in a mood to live up to what had been heretofore only a sham character. But, turning a corner into the main street, I instantly forgot myself at sight of a crowd congregated before the town hall. There was a babel of voices and an air of excitement that I immediately associated with Longstreth who, as mayor of Fairdale, once in a month of moons held court in this hall.

It took slipping and elbowing to get through the crowd. Once inside the door I saw that the crowd was mostly outside and evidently not so desirous as I was to enter. The first man I saw was Steele, looming up. The next was Longstreth, chewing his mustache — the third, Lawson, whose dark and sinister face told much. Something was up in Fairdale. Steele had opened the ball.

There were other men in the hall, a dozen or more, and all seemed shouting excitedly in unison with the crowd outside. I did not try to hear what was said. I edged closer in among the men to the front.

Longstreth sat at a table up on a platform. Near him sat a thick-set grizzled man, with deep eyes. This was Hanford Owens, county judge. To the right stood a tall, angular, yellow-faced fellow with a drooping sandy mustache. Conspicuous on his vest was a huge silver shield. This was Gorsech, one of Longstreth's sheriffs. There were four other men whom I knew, several whose faces were familiar, and half a dozen strangers, all dusty horsemen.

Steele stood apart from them, a little to one side, so that he faced them all. His hair was disheveled, and his shirt open at the neck. He looked cool and hard. When I caught his eye, I realized in an instant that the long-deferred action — the beginning of our real fight in Fairdale — was at hand.

Longstreth pounded hard on the table to be heard. Mayor or not, he was unable at once to quell the excitement. Gradually, however, it subsided. From the last few utterances before quiet was restored, I gathered that Steele had intruded upon some kind of a meeting in the hall.

"Steele, what'd you break in here for?" demanded Longstreth.

"Isn't this the court? Aren't you the mayor of Fairdale?" interrogated Steele. His voice was so clear and loud, almost piercing, that I saw at once that he wanted all those outside to hear.

"Yes," replied Longstreth. Like flint he seemed, yet I felt his intense interest.

I had no doubt then that Steele intended to make him stand out before the crowd as the real mayor of Fairdale, or as a man whose office was a sham.

"I've arrested a criminal," said Steele. "Bud Snell. I charge him with assault on Laramie and attempted robbery . . . if not murder. Snell has a shady past here, as the court will know if it keeps a record."

Then I saw Snell, hunching down on a bench, a nerveless and shaken man if there ever was one. He had been a hanger-on around the gambling dens — the kind of sneak I never turned my back to.

Jim Laramie, the restaurant keeper, was present also, and on second glance I saw that he was pale. There was blood on his face. I knew Jim, liked him, had tried to make a friend of him.

I was not dead to the stinging interrogation in the concluding sentence of Steele's speech. Then I felt sure I had correctly judged Steele's motive. I began to warm to the situation.

"What's this I hear about you, Bud? Get up and speak for yourself," said Longstreth gruffly.

Snell got up, not without a furtive glance at Steele, and he shuffled forward a few steps toward the mayor. He had an evil front, but not the boldness even of a rustler.

"It ain't so, Longstreth," he began loudly. "I went in Laramie's place fer grub. Some feller I never seen before come in from the hall . . . an' hit Laramie an' wrastled him on the floor. Then this big ranger grabbed me an' fetched me here. I didn't do nothin'. This ranger's hankerin' to arrest somebody. Thet's my hunch, Longstreth."

"What do you have to say about this, Laramie?" sharply queried Longstreth. "I call to your mind the fact that you once testified falsely in court, and got punished for it."

Why did my sharpened and experienced wits interpret a hint of threat or menace in Longstreth's reminder? Laramie rose from the bench and with an unsteady hand reached down to support himself. He was no longer young, and he seemed broken in health and spirit. He had been hurt somewhat about the head.

"I haven't much to say," he replied. "The ranger dragged me here. I told him I didn't take my troubles to court. Besides, I can't swear it was Snell who hit me."

Longstreth said something in an undertone to Judge Owens, and that worthy nodded his great, bushy head.

"Bud, you're discharged," said Longstreth bluntly. "Now, the rest of you clear out of here."

He absolutely ignored the ranger. That was his rebuff to Steele's advances — his slap in the face to an interfering ranger service.

If Longstreth was crooked, he certainly had magnificent nerve. I almost decided he was above suspicion. But his non-chalance, his air of finality, his authoritative assurance — these to my keen and practiced eyes were in significant contrast to a certain tenseness of line about his mouth and a slow paling of his olive skin. He had crossed the path of Vaughn Steele. He had blocked the way of this Lone Star ranger. If he had intelligence, which surely he had, and remembered Steele's fame, then he had some appreciation of what he had undertaken.

In that momentary lull my scrutiny of Longstreth gathered an impression of the man's intense curiosity. Then the prisoner, Bud Snell, with a cough that broke the spell of silence, shuffled a couple of steps toward the door.

"Hold on!" called Steele.

It was a bugle call. It halted Snell as if it had been a bullet. He seemed to shrink.

"Longstreth, I saw Snell attack Laramie," said Steele, his voice still ringing. "What has the court to say to that?"

The moment for open rupture between ranger service and Longstreth's idea of law was at hand. Longstreth showed not the slightest hesitation.

"The court has this to say . . . west of the Pecos we'll not aid or abet or accept any ranger service. Steele, we don't want you out here. Fairdale doesn't need you."

"That's a lie, Longstreth," retorted Steele. "I've a pocket full of letters from Fairdale citizens, all begging for ranger service."

Longstreth turned white. The veins corded at his temples. He appeared about to burst into rage. He was at a loss for a quick reply.

Steele shook a long arm at the mayor. "I asked your help. You refuse. Now, I'll work alone. This man, Snell, goes to Del Rio in irons."

Floyd Lawson rushed up to the table. The blood showed black and thick in his face. His utterance was incoherent, and his uncontrollable outbreak of temper seemed out of all proportion to any cause he should reasonably have had for anger. Longstreth shoved him back with a curse and a warning glare.

"Where's your warrant to arrest Snell?" shouted Longstreth to Vaughn. "I won't give you one. You can't take him without a warrant."

"I don't need warrants to make arrests. Longstreth, you're ignorant of the power of the Texas Rangers."

"You'll take Snell without papers?" bellowed Longstreth.

"He goes to Del Rio to jail," answered Steele grimly.

"He won't. You'll pull none of your damned ranger stunts out here. I'll block you, Steele."

That passionate reply of Longstreth's appeared to be the signal Steele had been waiting for. He had helped on the crisis. I believe I saw how he wanted to force Longstreth's hand and show the town his stand.

Steele backed clear of everybody, and like two swift flashes of light his guns leaped forth. He was transformed. My wish was fulfilled. Here was Steele, the ranger, in one of his lone lion stands. Not exactly alone, either, for my hand itched for my gun.

"Men! I call on you all!" cried Steele piercingly. "I call on you to witness the arrest of a criminal opposed by Longstreth, mayor of Fairdale. It will be recorded in the report sent to the adjutant general at Austin. Longstreth, I warn you . . . don't follow up your threat."

Longstreth sat white with working jaw.

"Snell, come here," ordered Steele. The man went, as if drawn, and appeared to slink out of line with the guns. Steele's cold gray glance held every eye in the hall. "Take the handcuffs out of my pocket. This side. Go over to Gorsech with them. Gorsech, snap those irons on Snell's wrists. Now, Snell, back here to the right of me."

No wonder was it to me to see how instantly Steele was obeyed. He might have seen more danger in that moment than was manifest to me. On the other hand, he might have wanted to drive home hard what he meant.

It was a critical moment for those who opposed him. There was death in the balance. This ranger, whose last resort was gun play, had instantly taken the initiative, and his nerve chilled even me. Perhaps, though, he read this crowd differently from me and saw that intimidation was his cue. I forgot I was not a spectator, but an ally.

"Longstreth, you've shown your hand," said Steele in the deep voice that carried so far and held those who heard. "Any honest citizen of Fairdale can now see what's plain . . . yours is a damn' poor hand! You're going to hear me call a spade a spade. Your office is a farce. In the two years you've been mayor you've never arrested one rustler. Strange . . . when Fairdale's a nest for rustlers! You've never sent a prisoner to Del Rio, let alone to Austin. You have no jail. There have been nine murders during your office . . . innumerable street fights and hold-ups. Not one arrest! But you have ordered arrests for trivial offenses and have punished these out of all proportion.

"There have been lawsuits in your court . . . suits over water rights, cattle deals, property lines. Strange how in these lawsuits you or Lawson or other men close to you were always involved . . . stranger how it seems the law was stretched to favor your interests."

Steele paused in his cold, ringing speech. In the silence, both outside and inside the hall, could be heard the deep breathing of agitated men. I did not need to fear that any man might draw on Steele. Never had I seen a crowd so cold, so stiff, so held. I would have liked to search for possible satisfaction on the faces of any present, but I was concerned only with Longstreth, and Longstreth was indeed a study. Yet, did he betray anything but rage at this interloper?

"Longstreth, here's plain talk for you and Fairdale to digest," went on Steele. "I don't accuse you and your court of dishonesty. I say . . . *strange!* Law here has been a farce. The motive behind all this laxity isn't plain to me . . . yet. But I call your hand."

CHAPTER SEVEN

Sounding the Timber

WHEN Steele left the hall, pushing Snell before him, making a lane through the crowd, it was not any longer possible to watch everybody. Yet, now, he seemed to ignore the men behind him. Any friend of Snell's among the vicious element might have pulled a gun. I wondered if Steele knew how I watched those men at his back — how fatal it would have been for any of them to make a significant move. No. I decided that Steele trusted to the effect his boldness had created. It was this power to cow ordinary men that explained so many of his feats — just the same as it was his keenness to read desperate men, his nerve to confront them, that made him great.

The crowd followed Steele and his captive down the middle of the main street, watched him secure a team and buckboard, and drive off on the road to Sanderson. Only then did the crowd appear to realize what had happened.

Then my long-awaited opportunity arrived. In the expression of silent men I found something which I had sought. From the hurried departure of others homeward I gathered import. On the husky, whispering lips of yet others I read words I needed to hear. The other part of that crowd — to my surprise, the smaller part — was the roaring, threatening, complaining one. Thus, I segregated those in Fairdale who were lawless from those in Fairdale who wanted law, but for some reason not yet clear the latter did not dare to voice their choice. How could Steele and I win them openly to our cause? If that could be done long before the year was up, Fairdale would be free of violence and Captain MacNeal's ranger service saved in the state.

I went from place to place, corner to corner, bar to bar, watching, listening, recording. It was not until long after sunset that I went back out to the ranch. The excitement had preceded me and speculation was rife. Hurrying through my supper, to get away from questions and to go on with my spying, I went out to the front of the house.

The evening was warm. The doors were open, and in the twilight the only lamps that had been lit were in Longstreth's big sitting room at the far end of the house. Neither Longstreth nor Lawson had come home to supper. I would have given much to hear their talk right then and certainly intended to try to hear it when they did come home. When the buckboard drove up, and they alighted, I was well hidden in the bushes, so well screened that I could get but a fleeting glimpse of Longstreth as he went in. For all I could see, he appeared to be a calm and quiet man, intense beneath the surface, with an air of dignity under insult. My chance to observe Lawson was lost. They went into the house without speaking, and closed the door.

At the other end of the porch, close under a window, was an offset between step and wall, and there in the shadow I hid. If Longstreth or Lawson visited the girls that evening, I wanted to hear what was said about Steele. It seemed to me that it might be a good clue for me — the circumstance whether or not Ray Longstreth was told the truth. So I waited there in the darkness with patience born of many hours of similar watches.

Presently the small lamp was lit — I could tell the difference in light when the big one was burning — and I heard the swish of skirts.

"Something's happened surely, Ruth," I heard Miss Longstreth say anxiously. "Papa just met me in the hall and didn't speak. He seemed pale, worried."

"Cousin Floyd looked like a thundercloud," said Ruth. "For once, he didn't try to kiss me. Something's happened. Well, Ray . . . this has been a bad day for me, too."

Plainly I heard Ruth sigh, and the little pathetic sound brought me vividly out of my sordid business of suspicion and speculation. So she was sorry.

"Bad for you, too?" replied Ray in amused surprise. "Oh, I see . . . I forgot. You and Russ had it out."

"Out? We fought like the very deuce. I'll never speak to him again."

"So your little . . . affair with Russ is all over?"

"Yes." Here she sighed again.

"Well, Ruth, it began swiftly and it's just as well short," said Ray earnestly. "We know nothing at all of Russ . . ."

"Ray, after today I respect him in . . . in spite of things . . . even though he seems no good. I . . . I cared a lot, too."

"My dear, your loves are like the summer flowers. I thought maybe your flirting with Russ might amount to something. Yet, he seems so different now from what he was at first. It's only occasionally I get the impression I had of him after that night he saved me from violence. He's strange. Perhaps it all comes of his infatuation with you. He *is* in love with you. I'm afraid of what may come of it."

"Ray, he'll do something dreadful to Floyd, mark my words," whispered Ruth. "He swore he would if Floyd fooled around me any more."

"Oh, dear! Ruth, what can we do? These are wild men. Floyd makes life miserable for me. And he teases you unmer . . . "

"I don't call it teasing. Floyd wants to spoon," declared Ruth emphatically. "He'd run after any woman."

"A fine compliment to me, Cousin Ruth," laughed Ray.

"I don't care," replied Ruth stubbornly. "It's so. He's spoony. And when he's been drinking and tries to kiss me . . . I hate him!"

"Ruth, you look as if you'd rather like Russ to do something dreadful to Floyd," said Ray with a laugh that this time was only half mirth.

"Half of me would and half of me wouldn't," returned Ruth. "But all of me would if I weren't afraid of Russ. I've got a feeling . . . I don't know what . . . something will happen between Floyd and Russ some day."

There were quick steps on the hall floor, steps I thought I recognized.

"Hello, girls!" sounded Lawson's voice, minus its usual gaiety.

Then ensued a pause that made me bring to mind a picture of Lawson's glum face.

"Floyd, what's the matter?" asked Ray presently. "I never saw Papa as he is tonight, nor you so . . . so worried. Tell me . . . what has happened?"

"Well, Ray, we had a jar today," replied Lawson with a blunt, expressive laugh.

"Jar?" echoed the girls curiously.

"Jar? We had to submit to a damnable outrage," added Lawson passionately, as if the sound of his voice augmented his feeling. "Listen, girls. I'll tell you all about it."

He coughed, clearing his throat in a way that betrayed he had been drinking. I sank deeper in the shadow of my covert and, stiffening my muscles for a protracted spell of rigidity, prepared to listen with all acuteness and intensity. Just one word from this Lawson, inadvertently uttered in a moment of passion, might be the word Steele needed to provide his clue.

"It happened at the town hall," began Lawson rapidly. "Your father and Judge Owens and I were there in consultation with three ranchers from out of town. First we were disturbed by gunshots from somewhere, but not close at hand. Then we heard the loud voices outside.

"A crowd was coming down the street. It stopped before the hall. Men came running in, yelling. We thought there was a fire. Then that damned ranger, Vaughn

Steele, stalked in, dragging a fellow by the name of Snell. We couldn't tell what was wanted because of the uproar. Finally your father restored order.

"Steele had arrested Snell for alleged assault on a restaurant keeper named Laramie. It developed that Laramie didn't accuse anybody, didn't know who attacked him. Snell, being obviously innocent, was discharged. Then this . . . this gun-fighting ranger pulled his guns on the court and halted the proceedings."

When Lawson paused, I plainly heard his intake of breath. Far, indeed, was he from calm.

"Steele held everybody in that hall in fear of death, and he began shouting his insults. Law was a farce in Fairdale. The court was a farce. There was no law. Your father's office as mayor should be impeached. He made arrests only for petty offenses. He was afraid of the rustlers, highwaymen, murderers. He was afraid or . . . he just let them alone. He used his office to cheat ranchers and cattlemen in lawsuits. All this Steele yelled for everyone to hear. A damnable outrage! Your father, Ray, insulted in his own court by a rowdy ranger! Not only insulted, but threatened with death . . . two big guns thrust almost in his face."

"Oh, how horrible!" cried Ray Longstreth in mingled distress and anger.

"Steele's a ranger. The ranger service wants to rule western Texas," went on Lawson. "These rangers are all a low set, many of them worse than the outlaws they hunt. Some of them were outlaws and gunfighters before they became rangers. This Steele is one of the worst of the lot. He's keen, intelligent, smooth, and that makes him more to be feared. For he is to be feared. He wanted to kill. He meant to kill. If your father had made the least move, Steele would have shot him. He's a cold-nerved devil . . . the born gunman. My God, any instant I expected to see your father fall dead at my feet!"

"Oh, Floyd! The . . . the unspeakable ruffian!" cried Ray Longstreth passionately.

"You see, Ray, this fellow Steele has failed here in Fairdale. He's been here weeks and done nothing. He must have got desperate. He's infamous, and he loves his name. He seeks notoriety. He made that play with Snell just for a chance to rant against your father. He tried to inflame all Fairdale against him. That about lawsuits was the worst. Damn him. He'll make us enemies."

"What do you care for the insinuations of such a man?" said Ray Longstreth, her voice now deep and rich with feeling. "After a moment's thought no one will be influenced by them. Do not worry, Floyd. Tell Papa not to worry. Surely, after all these years he can't be injured in reputation by . . . by an adventurer."

"Yes, he can be injured," replied Floyd quickly. "The frontier is a queer place.

There are many bitter men here . . . men who have failed at ranching. And your father has been wonderfully successful. Steele has dropped some poison, and it'll spread."

Then followed a silence during which, evidently, the worried Lawson bestrode the floor.

"Cousin Floyd, what became of Steele and his prisoner?" asked Ruth suddenly.

How like her it was, with her inquisitive bent of mind and shifting points of view, to ask a question of which the answering would be gall and wormwood to Lawson. It amused while it thrilled me. Ruth might be a flirt, but she was no fool.

"What became of them? Ha! Steele bluffed the whole town . . . at least all of it who had heard the mayor's order to discharge Snell," growled Lawson. "He took Snell . . . rode off for Del Rio to jail him there."

"Floyd!" exclaimed Ray. "Then, after all, this ranger was able to arrest Snell, the innocent man father discharged, and take him off to jail?"

"Exactly. That's the toughest part . . . " — Lawson stopped abruptly, and then broke out fiercely — "but, by God, he'll never come back!"

Lawson's slow pacing quickened, and he strode from the parlor, leaving behind him a silence eloquent of the effect of his sinister prediction.

"Ruth, what did he mean?" asked Ray in a low voice.

"Steele will be killed," replied Ruth, just as low-pitched.

"Killed! That magnificent fellow! Ah, I forgot. Ruth, my wits are sadly mixed. I ought to be glad if somebody kills my father's defamer. But, oh, I can't be. This bloody frontier makes me sick. Papa doesn't want me to stay for good. And no wonder! Shall I go back? I hate to show a white feather. Do you know, Ruth, I was . . . a little taken with this Lone Star ranger. Miserably, I confess. He seemed so like in spirit to the good stature of him. How can so splendid a man be so bloody, so base at heart? It's hideous. How little we know of men. I had my dream about Vaughn Steele. I confess because it shames me . . . because I hate myself."

Next morning I awakened with a feeling that I was more like my old self. In the experience of activity of body and mind, with a prospect that this was merely the forerunner of great events, I came around to my own again. Ruth was not forgotten. She just had become a sorrow. So, perhaps, my downfall as a lover was a precursor of better results as an officer.

I held in abeyance my last conclusion regarding Longstreth and Lawson, and only awaited Steele's return to have fixed in mind what these men were. Lawson's remark about Steele's not returning did not worry me. I had heard many such dark sayings in reference to rangers. Rangers had a trick of coming back. I did not see any man or men on the present horizon of Fairdale equal to the killing of Vaughn Steele.

As Miss Longstreth and Ruth had no inclination to ride, I had even more freedom. I went down to the town and burst, cheerily whistling, into Jim Laramie's place. Jim always made me welcome there, as much for my society as for the money I spent, and I never neglected being free with both. I bought a handful of cigars and shoved some of them in Jim's pocket.

"How's tricks, Jim?" I asked.

"Reckon I'm feelin' as well as could be expected," replied Jim. His head was circled by a bandage that did not conceal the lump where he had been struck. He looked a little pale, but he was bright enough.

"That was a hell of a biff Snell gave you, the skunk!" I remarked with nonchalant assurance.

"Russ, I ain't accusin' Snell," remonstrated Laramie with eyes that made me thoughtful.

"Sure, I know you're too good a sport to send a fellow up. But Snell deserved what he got. I saw his face when he made his talk to Longstreth. Snell lied. And I'll tell you what, Jim, if it'd been me instead of that ranger, Bud Snell would have got settled."

Laramie appeared to be agitated by my forcible intimation of friendship.

"Jim, that's between ourselves," I went on. "I'm no fool. And much as I blab when I'm hunky, it's all air. Maybe you've noticed that about me. In some parts of Texas it's policy to be close-mouthed. Policy and health-preserving! Between ourselves, as friends, I want you to know I lean some on Steele's side of the fence."

As I lighted a cigar, I saw, out of the corner of my eye, how Laramie gave a quick start. I expected some kind of a startling idea to flash into his mind. Presently I turned and frankly met his gaze. I had startled him out of his habitual set taciturnity, but, even as I looked, the light that might have been amaze and joy faded out of his face, leaving it the same old mask. Still I had seen enough. Like a bloodhound, I had a scent.

"Thet's funny, Russ, seein' as you drift with the gang Steele's bound to fight," remarked Laramie.

"Sure. I'm a sport. If I can't gamble with gentlemen, I'll gamble with ... rustlers."

Again he gave a slight start, and this time he hid his eyes. "Wal, Russ, I've heard you was slick," he said.

"You tumble, Jim. I'm a little better on the draw."

"On the draw? With cards, an' gun, too, eh?"

"Now, Jim, that last follows natural. I haven't had much chance to show how good I am on the draw with a gun. But that'll come soon."

"Reckon thet talk's a little air," said Laramie with his dry laugh. "Same as you leanin' a little on the ranger's side of the fence."

"But Jim, wasn't he game? What'd you think of that stand? Bluffed the whole gang! The way he called Longstreth . . . why, it was great. The justice of that call doesn't bother me. It was Steele's nerve that got me. That'd warm any man's blood."

There was a little red in Laramie's pale cheeks, and I saw him swallow hard. I had struck deeply again.

"Say, don't you work for Longstreth?" he queried.

"Me? I *guess* not. I'm Miss Longstreth's man. He and Lawson have tried to fire me many a time."

"Thet so?" he said curiously. "What for?"

"Too many silver trimmings on me, Jim. And . . . I pack my gun low down."

"Wal, them two don't go much together out here," replied Laramie. "But I ain't seen thet anybody has shot off the trimmin's."

"Maybe it'll commence, Jim, as soon as I stop buying drinks. Talking about work . . . who'd you say Snell worked for?"

"When he works at all, which sure ain't often, he rides for Longstreth."

"*Humph!* Seems to me, Jim, that Longstreth's the whole circus 'round Fairdale. I was some sore the other day to find I was losing good money at Longstreth's faro game. Sure, if I'd won, I wouldn't have been sore, eh? But I was surprised to hear some cully say Longstreth owned the Hope So dive."

"I've heard he owned considerable property hereabouts," replied Jim constrainedly.

"*Humph* again! Why, Jim, you know it . . . only like every other cully I meet in this town, you're afraid to open your mug about Longstreth. Get me straight, Jim Laramie. I don't care a damn for Colonel Mayor Longstreth. And for cause I'd throw a gun on him just as quick as on any rustler in Pecos."

"Talk's cheap, my boy," replied Laramie, making light of my bluster, but the red was deeper in his face.

"Sure. I know that," I said, calming down. "My temper gets up, Jim. Then it's not well known that Longstreth owns the Hope So?"

"Reckon it's known in Pecos, all right. But Longstreth's name isn't connected with the Hope So. Blandy runs the place."

"That Blandy . . . I've no use for him. His faro game's crooked, or I'm a locoed bronc'. Not that we don't have lots of crooked faro dealers. A fellow can stand for them. But Blandy's mean, back-handed, never looks you in the eyes. That Hope So place ought to be run by a good fellow like you, Laramie."

"Thanks, Russ," he replied, and I imagined his voice a little husky. "Didn't you ever hear I used to . . . run it?"

"No. Did you?" I said quickly.

"I reckon. I built the place, made additions twice, owned it for eleven years."

"Well, I'll be dog-goned." It was indeed my turn to be surprised, and with the surprise came a glimmering. "I'm sorry you're not there now. Jim, did you sell out?"

"No. Just lost the place."

Laramie was bursting for relief now — to talk — to tell. Sympathy had made him soft. I did not need to ask another question.

"It was two years ago . . . two years last March," he went on. "I was in a big cattle deal with Longstreth. We got the stock . . . an' my share . . . eighteen hundred head . . . was rustled off. I owed Longstreth. He pressed me. It come to a lawsuit . . . an' I . . . was ruined."

It hurt me to look at Laramie. He was white, and tears rolled down his cheeks. I saw the bitterness, the defeat, the agony of the man. He had failed to meet his obligation because he had been swindled. All that he suppressed, all that would have been passion, had the man's spirit not been broken, lay bare for me to see. I had now the secret of his bitterness. But the reason he did not openly accuse Longstreth, the secret of his reticence and fear — these I thought best to try to learn at some later time, after I had consulted with Steele.

"Hard luck. Jim, it certainly was tough," I said. "But you're a good loser. And the wheel turns. Now, Jim, here's what I come particular to see you for. I need your advice. I've got a little money. Between you and me, as friends, I've been adding some to that roll all the time. But, before I lose it, I want to invest some. Buy some stock or buy an interest in some rancher's herd. What I want you to steer me on is a good, square rancher. Or maybe a couple of ranchers, if there happen to be two honest ones in Pecos. Eh? No deals with ranchers who ride in the dark with rustlers. I've got a hunch Fairdale is full of them. Now, Jim, you've been here for years. Sure you must know a couple of men above suspicion."

"Thank God I do, Russ," he replied feelingly. "Frank Morton an' Si Zimmer, my friends an' neighbors all my prosperous days. An' friends still. You can gamble on Frank an' Si. But, Russ, if you want advice from me, don't invest money in stock now."

"Why?"

"Because any new feller buyin' stock in Pecos these days will be rustled faster an' quicker'n he can say Jack Robinson. The pioneers, the cattlemen . . . these are easy enough pickin'. But the new fellers have to learn the ropes. They don't know anythin' or anybody. An' the old ranchers are wise an' sore. They'd fight if they . . . "

"What?" I put in as he paused. "If they knew who was rustling the stock?"

"Nope."

"If they had the nerve?"

"Not that so much."

"What then? What'd make them fight?"

"A leader."

I went out of Laramie's with that word ringing in my ears.

A leader. In my mind's eye I saw a horde of dark-faced, dusty-booted cattlemen, riding grim and armed behind Vaughn Steele. More thoughtful than usual I walked on, passing some of my old haunts, and was about to turn in front of a feed and grain store when a hearty slap on my back disturbed my reflection.

"Howdy thar, cowboy," boomed a big voice.

It was Morton, the rancher whom Jim had mentioned and whose acquaintance I had made. He was a man of great bulk with a ruddy, merry face.

"Hello, Morton. Let's have a drink," I suggested.

"Gotta rustle home," he said. "Young feller, I've a ranch to work."

"Sell it to me, Morton."

He laughed and said he wished he could. His buckboard stood at the rail, the horses stamping impatiently. "Cards must be runnin' lucky," he went on with another hearty laugh.

"Can't kick on the luck. But I'm afraid it will change. Morton, my friend, Laramie, gave me a hunch you'd be a good man to tie to. Now, I've a little money, and, before I lose it, I'd like to invest it in stock."

He smiled broadly, but for all his doubt of me he took definite interest.

"I'm not drunk, and I'm on the square," I continued bluntly. "You've taken me for a no-good cowpuncher without any brains. Wake up, Morton. If you never size up your neighbors any better than you have me . . . well, you won't get any richer."

It was sheer enjoyment for me to make my remarks to this man pregnant with meaning. Morton showed his pleasure, his interest, but his faith remained aloof.

"I've got some money. I had some. The cards have run lucky. Will you let me in on some kind of deal? Will you start me up as a stockman with a little herd all my own?"

"Russ, this's durn strange, comin' from Longstreth's cowboy," he said bluntly.

"I'm not in his outfit. My job's with Miss Longstreth. She's fine. But the old man? Nit! He's been after me for weeks. I won't last long. That's one reason why I want to start up for myself."

"Laramie sent you to me, did he? Poor ole Jim! Wal, Russ, to come out flat-footed, you'd be foolish to buy cattle now. I don't want to take your money an' see you lose out. Better go back across the Pecos where the rustlers ain't so strong. I haven't had more'n twenty-five hundred head of stock for ten years. The rustlers let me hang on to a breedin' herd. Kind of them, ain't it?"

"Sort of kind. All I hear is rustlers, Morton," I replied with impatience. "You see, I haven't ever lived long in a rustler-run county. Who heads the gang, anyway?"

Frank Morton looked at me with a curiously amused smile.

"I hear a lot about Jack Blome and Snecker," I continued. "Everybody calls them out-and-out bad. Do they head this mysterious gang?"

"Russ, I opine Blome an' Snecker parade themselves as boss rustlers, same as gun-throwers. But thet's the love such men have for bein' thought hell. Thar's brains headin' the rustler gang hereabouts."

"Maybe Blome and Snecker are blinds. Savvy what I mean, Morton? Maybe there's more in the parade than just the fame of it."

Morton snapped his big jaw as if to shut in impulsive words.

"Look here, Morton. I'm not so young in years even if I am young west of the Pecos. I can figure ahead. It stands to reason, no matter how damn' strong these rustlers are, how hidden their work, however involved with supposedly honest men . . . they can't last."

"They come with the pioneers, an' they'll last while thar's a single steer left," he declared.

"Well, if you take that view of circumstances, I just figure you as one of the rustlers."

Morton looked as if he were about to brain me with the butt of his whip. His anger flashed by then as unworthy of him, and something striking him as funny caused him to boom out a laugh.

"It's not so amusin'," I went on. "If you're not going to pretend a yellow streak, what else will I think?"

"Pretend?" he repeated.

"Sure. You can't fool me, Morton. I know men of nerve. And here in Pecos they're not any different from those in other places. I say, if you show anything like a lack of sand, it's all bluff. By nature, you've got nerve. There are a lot of men round Fairdale who're afraid of their shadows . . . afraid to open their mouths. But you're not one. So I say, if you claim these rustlers will last, you're pretending lack of nerve just to help the popular side along. For they can't last. Morton, I don't want to be a hard-riding cowboy all my days. Do you think I'd let fear of a gang of rustlers keep me from going in business with a rancher? Nit. What you need out here in Pecos is some new blood . . . a few youngsters like me to get you old guys started. Savvy what I mean?"

"Wal, I reckon I do," he replied, looking as if a storm had blown over him. I gauged the hold the rustler gang had on Fairdale by the difficult job it was to stir this really courageous old cattleman. He had grown up with the evil. To him it must have been a necessary one, the same as dry seasons and cyclones. "Russ, I'll look you up the next time I come to town," he said soberly.

We parted, and I, more than content with the meeting, retraced my steps downstreet to the Hope So saloon. Here I entered, bent on tasks as sincere as the ones just finished, but displeasing, because I had to mix with a low, profane set to cultivate them, to drink occasionally despite my deftness at emptying glasses on the floor, to gamble with them and strangers, always playing the part of a flush and flashy cowboy, half drunk, ready to laugh or fight.

On the night of the fifth day after Steele's departure I went, as was my habit, to the rendezvous we maintained at the pile of rocks out in the open. The night was clear, with bright starlight but no moon, and for this latter fact safer to be abroad. Often from my covert I had seen dark figures, skulking in and out of Fairdale. It would have been interesting to hold up these mysterious travelers. So far, however, this had not been our game. I had enough to keep my own tracks hidden, and my own comings and goings.

I liked to be out in the night, with the darkness close down to the earth, and the feeling of a limitless open all around. Not only did I listen for Steele's soft step, but for any sound — the yelp of coyote or mourn of wolf, the creak of wind in the dead brush, the distant clatter of hoofs, a woman's singing voice, faintly from the town.

This time, just when I was about to give up for that evening, Steele came looming like a black giant long before I heard his soft step. It was good to feel his grip, even if it hurt, because after five days I had begun to worry. We sat down close together, he, facing one direction, and I, the other.

"Well, boy, how've you been?" he asked easily.

"Well, old man, did you land that son-of-a-gun in jail?" I mimicked.

"You bet I did. And he'll stay there for a while. Del Rio rather liked the idea, Russ. All right there. I sidestepped Sanderson on the way back. But over here at the little village . . . Longstreth they call it . . . I was held up. Couldn't help it, because there wasn't any road around."

"Held up?" I queried.

"That is, the buckboard was held up. I got into the brush in time to save my bacon. They began to shoot too soon."

"Did you get any of them?"

"Didn't stay to see," he chuckled. "Had to hoof it to Fairdale, and it's a good long walk."

"Been to your 'dobe yet tonight?"

"I slipped in at the back. Russ, it bothered me some to make sure no one was laying for me in the dark."

"You'll have to get a safer place. Why not take to the open every night?"

"Russ, that's well enough on a trail. But I need grub, and I've got to have a few comforts. I'll risk the 'dobe yet a little."

Then I narrated all that I had seen, done, and heard during his absence, holding back one thing. What I did tell him sobered him at once, brought the quiet, somber mood, the thoughtful air.

"So that's all. Well, it's enough."

"All pertaining to our job, Vaughn," I replied. "The rest is sentiment, perhaps. I had a pretty bad case of moons over the little Herbert girl. But we quarreled. And it's ended now. Just as well, too, because if she'd . . . "

"Russ, did you honestly care for her? The real thing, I mean?"

"I . . . I'm afraid so, Vaughn. I'm sort of hurt inside. But, hell! There's one thing sure, a love affair might have hindered me, made me soft. I'm glad it's over."

He said no more, but his big hand pressing on my knee told me of his sympathy — another indication that there was nothing wanting in this ranger.

"The other thing concerns you," I went on, somehow reluctant now to tell this. "You remember how I heard Lawson making you out as vile to Miss Longstreth. Swore you'd never come back? Well, after he'd gone, when Ruth said he'd meant you'd be killed, Miss Longstreth felt bad about it. She said she ought to be glad if someone killed you, but she couldn't be. She called you a bloody ruffian, yet she didn't want you shot. She said some things about the difference between your hideous character and your splendid stature. Called you a magnificent fellow . . . that was it. Well, then she choked up and confessed to Ruth in shame and disgrace."

"Shame . . . disgrace?" he echoed, greatly interested. "What was it?"

"She confessed she had been taken with you . . . had her little dream about you. And she hated herself for it."

Never, I thought, would I forget Vaughn Steele's eyes. It did not matter that it was dark. I saw the fixed gleam, then the leaping, shadowy light.

"Did she . . . say that?" His voice was not quite steady. "Wonderful! Even if it only . . . lasted a minute. She might . . . we might . . . if it wasn't for this hellish job! Russ, has it dawned on you yet . . . what I've got to do to Ray Longstreth?"

"Yes," I replied. "Vaughn, you haven't . . . gone sweet on her?"

What else could I make of that terrible thing in his eyes? He did not reply to that at all. I thought my arm would break in his clutch.

"You said you knew what I've got to do to Ray Longstreth," he repeated hoarsely.

"Yes. You've got to ruin her happiness, if not her life."

"Why? Speak out, Russ. All this comes like a blow. There, for a little, I hoped you had worked out things . . . differently from me. No hope. Ruin her life. Why?"

I could explain this strange agitation in Steele in no other way except that realization had brought keen suffering as incomprehensible as it was painful. I could not tell if it came from suddenly divined love for Ray Longstreth equally with a poignant conviction that his fate was to wreck her. But I did see that he needed me to speak the brutal truth.

"Steele, old man, you'll ruin Ray Longstreth because . . . as arrest looks improbable to me . . . you'll have to kill her father."

"My God! Why, why? Say it."

"Because Longstreth is the leader of the Fairdale gang of rustlers."

* * *

That night, before we parted, we had gone rather deeply into the plan of action for the immediate future. First I gave Steele my earnest counsel and then as stiff an argument I knew how to put up, all anent the absolute necessity of his eternal vigilance. If he got shot in a fair encounter with his enemies — well, that was a ranger's risk and no disgrace. But to be massacred in bed, knifed in the dark, shot in the back, ambushed in any manner — not one of these miserable ends must be the last record of Vaughn Steele.

He promised me to remain vigilant in a way that made me wonder if he would ever sleep or turn his back on anyone — made me wonder, too, at the menace in his voice. Steele seemed likely to be torn in two ways, and already there was a hint of future desperation.

It was agreed that I make cautious advances to Laramie and Morton and, when I could satisfy myself of their trustworthiness, reveal my identity to them. Through this I was to cultivate Zimmer, and then other ranchers whom we should decide could be let into the secret. It was not only imperative that we learn from them clues by which we might eventually fix guilt on the rustler gang, but also just as imperative that we develop a band of deputies to help us when the fight began.

Steele, now that he was back in Fairdale, would have the center of the stage, with all eyes upon him. We agreed, moreover, that the bolder the front now, the better chance of ultimate success. The more nerve he showed, the less danger of being ambushed, the less peril in facing vicious men.

But we needed a jail. Prisoners had to be corralled after arrest, or the work would be useless, almost a farce, and there was no possibility of repeated trips to Del Rio. We could not use an adobe house for a jail because that could be easily cut out of or torn down. Finally I remembered an old stone house near the end of the main street. It had one window and one door, and had been long in disuse. Steele would rent it, hire men to guard and feed his prisoners. If these prisoners bribed or fought their way to freedom, that would not injure the great principle for which he stood.

Both Steele and I simultaneously, from different angles of reasoning, had arrived at a conviction of Longstreth's guilt. It was not so strong as realization, rather a divination. Long experience in detecting, in feeling the sudden guilt of men, had sharpened our senses for that particular thing. Steele acknowledged a few mistakes in his day, but I, allowing for the same strength of conviction, had never made a single mistake. But conviction was one thing — and proof vastly another. Furthermore, when proof was secured, then came the crowning task — that of taking desperate men in a wild country they dominated.

Verily, Steele and I had our work cut out for us. However, we were prepared to go at it with infinite patience and implacable reserve. Steele and I differed only in the driving incentive, of course, outside of that one binding vow to save the ranger service. He had a strange passion, almost an obsession, to represent the law of Texas, and by so doing render something of safety and happiness to the honest pioneers. Beside Steele, I knew, I shrunk to a shadow. I was not exactly a heathen, and certainly I wanted to help harassed people, especially women and children, but mainly with me it was the zest, the thrill, the hazard, the matching of wits — in a word, the adventure of the game.

Next morning I rode with the young ladies. In the light of Ruth's persistently flagrant advances, to which I was apparently blind, I saw that my hard-won victory over self was likely to be short-lived. That possibility made me outwardly like ice. I was an attentive, careful, reliable, and respectful attendant, seeing to the safety of my charges, but the one-time gay and debonair cowboy was a thing of the past.

Ruth, womanlike, had been a little — a very little — repentant. She had showed it. My indifference had piqued her. She made advances, and then my coldness aroused her spirit. She was the kind of girl to value most what she had lost, and to throw consequences to the winds in winning it back.

When I divined this, I saw my revenge. To be sure, when I thought of it, I had no reason to want revenge. She had been most gracious to me. But there was the catty thing she had said about being kissed again by her admirers. Then, in all seriousness, sentiment aside, I dared not make up with her.

We halted out on the ridge and dismounted for the usual little rest. Mine I took in the shade of a scrubby mesquite. The girls strolled away out of sight. It was a drowsy day, and I nearly fell asleep.

Something roused me — a patter of footsteps or a rustle of skirts. Then a soft thud behind me gave me at once a start and a thrill. First, I saw Ruth's little brown hands on my shoulders. Then her head, with hair all shiny and flying and fragrant, came around over my shoulder, softly smoothing my cheek, until her sweet, saucy, heated face was right under my eyes.

"Russ, don't you love me any more?" she whispered.

CHAPTER EIGHT

He Loves You

THE little devil! She did not have the grace to wear a blush of shame. She was brazenly sure — and all the prettier for it. Some latent dignity gave me power to regard her with silent scorn.

"Russ, no one has kissed me for seven days . . . seven long days."

She sighed. Her implied faithfulness to me was balm to wounded love and vanity, even if it were only a hinted ruse to soften me.

My great trial, however, lay in the dewy, red, coaxing lips so near my own. How I ever held back from them was strange, indeed. Perhaps I could not have held back a moment longer had not Miss Longstreth's steps alarmed Ruth.

Like a bent branch she sprang erect. Her eyes darted clear flames down at me. Under them I preserved a melancholy dignity that was not all pretense. Miss Longstreth returned and said we had better be starting for home.

All the way Ruth seemed to become more and more thoughtful, as if the significance of the repulse to her presented varying aspects, each of which mitigated her anger. Assuredly she was over her temper by the time we reached the ranch, and, when she turned over her horse to me, it was with a sweet, appealing smile.

Longstreth remained at home, invisible most of the time. When I did get a glimpse of him, it was to see him moody, irascible, and altogether out of sorts. I heard a scrap of conversation between him and his daughter, in which he was urging her to go back to Louisiana, and she was replying with a will of her own. For my part, I hoped she would go away, and Ruth, too, before the trouble began.

In view of Longstreth's state of mind, I was somewhat surprised to learn that he had consented to allow his daughter to give a party, to which all Fairdale was to be invited. Miss Longstreth was delighted, immediately fixed the date, and put us all to various tasks. As I had imagined, a party was Ruth Herbert's especial weakness, and she appeared quite beside herself with rapture. Ruth's emotion was always sincere while it lasted. She waylaid me at my work and might have hugged me, I dare say, if someone had not been near.

"Russ, I've a dress you never saw. All white . . . low neck . . . short sleeves."

It was impossible not to respond to her pleasure, but I did not let show any outward satisfaction. "Fine feathers make fine birds," I said.

"Russ, will you dance with me?" she whispered, undaunted.

"Miss Herbert, I'll dance at your wedding . . . soon, I hope."

"My wedding with whom, Mister Russ?" she replied with tilted chin and fire beginning to kindle in her eyes.

"Oh, I suppose one of these fortunate young bucks . . . the one who has the most wool pulled over his eyes . . . and who doesn't drink."

She gazed down upon me, suddenly furious, and I was ready to dodge to save my ears. "Very well, my one-time cowboy cavalier," she said with more force than elegance. "I'll bet I make you sick Thursday night."

Then she flounced away, as if my presence breathed contagion. I had not the slightest doubt that she would succeed in her threat, but I did not intend to let her find that out. My lack of responsiveness to her friendly and then more intimate advances had discovered to me the fact that of all routes to Miss Herbert's affections this one was likely to be the surest. She simply could not stand indifference. She was like a spoiled child.

Then, perhaps, my iron and callous front, so suddenly following upon my abject adoration, was something calculated to rouse even a less coquettish girl than she. Although the situation for me began to be vexatiously irresistible, the possibilities it opened up were bewildering.

Up to Wednesday I was so busily engaged helping with a multiplicity of tasks that I found no time to get away to go to town. That night, however, I saw Steele at our meeting place. We compared notes and pondered details of our problem.

Steele had rented the stone house to be used as a jail. While the blacksmith was putting up a door and window calculated to withstand many onslaughts, all the idlers and strangers in town had gone to see the sight. Manifestly it was an occasion for Fairdale. When Steele had let it be known that he wanted to hire a jailer and a guard, this caustically humorous element had offered itself *en masse*. The men had made a joke out of it. Steele said dryly that it would not be much of a joke after a week.

When Steele and I were about to separate, I remembered the party to be given by Miss Longstreth, and I told him about it. He shook his head sadly, almost doubtfully. Was it possible that Longstreth could be a deep-eyed, cunning scoundrel, yet keep that beautiful and innocent girl out on the frontier and let her give parties to sons and daughters of a community he had robbed? To any but remorseless rangers the idea was incredible.

Thursday evening came in spite of what the girls must have regarded as an interminably dragging day. It was easy to differentiate their attitudes toward this party. Ruth wanted to look beautiful, to excel all the young ladies who were to attend, to attach to her train all the young men and have them fighting to dance with her. Miss Longstreth had an earnest desire to open her father's house to the people of Fairdale, to show that a daughter had come into his long-cheerless home, to make the evening one of pleasure and entertainment.

I happened to be present in the parlor and was carrying in some flowers for final decoration when Miss Longstreth learned that her father had just ridden off with three horsemen Dick, who brought the news, had not recognized. In her keen disappointment she scarcely heard Dick's concluding remark about the hurry of the colonel. My sharp ears, however, took this in, and it was thought-provoking. Longstreth was known to ride off at all hours, yet this incident seemed unusual.

At eight o'clock the house and porch and patio were ablaze with lights. Every lantern and lamp on the place, together with all that could be bought and borrowed, had been brought into requisition. The cowboys arrived first, all dressed in their best, clean-shaven, red-faced, bright-eyed, eager for the fun to commence. Then the young people from town, and a good sprinkling of older people, came in a steady stream. Miss Longstreth received them graciously, excused her father's absence, and bade them be at home.

The music, or the discordance that went by the name, was furnished by two cowboys with banjos and an antediluvian gentleman with a fiddle. Nevertheless, it was music that could be danced to, and there was no lack of enthusiasm.

I went from porch to parlor and thence to patio, watching and amused. The lights and the decorations of flowers, the bright dresses and the flashy scarves of the cowboys furnished a gay enough scene to a man of lonesome and stern life like mine. During the dance there was a steady, continuous shuffling of boots and, during the interval following, a steady low hum of merry talk and laughter.

My wandering from place to place, apart from my usual careful observation, was an unobtrusive but, to me, a sneaking pursuit of Ruth Herbert. She had on the white dress I had never seen, with the low neck and the short sleeves, and she looked so sweet, so dainty, so altogether desirable, that I groaned a hundred times in my jealousy — because, manifestly, Ruth did not intend to run any risk of my not seeing her in her glory, no matter where my eyes looked. A couple of times, in promenading, I passed her on the arm of some proud cowboy or gallant young buck from town, and on these occasions she favored her escort with a languishing glance that probably did as much damage to him as to me.

Presently she caught me red-handed in my careless, sauntering pursuit of her, and then, whether by intent or from indifference, she apparently deigned me no more notice. But, quick to feel a difference in her, I marked that from that moment her gaiety gradually merged into coquettishness and soon into flirtation. Then, just to see how far she would go, perhaps desperately hoping she would make me hate her, I followed her shamelessly from patio to parlor, porch to court, even into the waltz.

To her credit, she always weakened when some young fellow got her in a corner and tried to push the flirting to extremes. Young Waters was the only one lucky enough to kiss her, and there was more of strength in his conquest of her than any decent fellow could be proud of.

When Floyd Lawson sought Ruth out, there was added to my jealousy a real anxiety. I had brushed against Lawson more than once that evening. He was not drunk, yet under the influence of liquor. Ruth, however, evidently did not discover this, because, knowing her abhorrence of drink, I believe she would not have walked out with him had she known. Anyway, I followed them, close in the shadow.

Lawson was unusually gay. I saw him put his arm around her without remonstrance. When the music recommenced, they went back to the house. Lawson danced with Ruth, not ungracefully for a man who rode a horse as much as he. After the dance he waved aside Ruth's many partners, not so gaily as would have been consistent with good feeling, and led her away. I followed. They ended that walk at the extreme corner of the patio, where, under gaily colored lights, a little arbor had been made among the flowers and vines.

Ruth seemed to have lost something of her vivacity. They had not been out of my sight for a moment before Ruth cried out. It was a cry of impatience or remonstrance, rather than alarm, but I decided that it would serve me an excuse. I dashed back, leaped to the door of the arbor, my hand on my gun.

Lawson was holding Ruth. When he heard me, he let her go. Then she uttered a cry that was one of alarm. Her face blanched; her eyes grew strained. One hand went to her breast. She thought I meant to kill Lawson.

"Excuse *me*," I burst out frankly, turning to Lawson. I never saw a hyena, but he looked like one. "I heard a squeal. Thought a girl was hurt . . . or something. Miss Longstreth gave me orders to watch out for accident, fire, anything. So, excuse me, Lawson."

As I stepped back, to my amaze, Ruth, excusing herself to the scowling Lawson, hurriedly joined me.

"Oh, it's our dance, Russ!" She took my arm, and we walked through the patio. "I'm afraid of him, Russ," she whispered. "You frightened me worse, though. You didn't mean to . . . to . . . ?"

"I made a bluff. Saw he'd been drinking, so I kept near you."

"You return good for evil," she replied, squeezing my arm. "Russ, let me tell you . . . whenever anything frightens me, since we got here, I think of you. If you're only near, I feel safe."

We paused at the door, leading into the big parlor. Couples were passing. Here I could scarcely distinguish the last words she said. She stood before me, eyes downcast, face flushed, as sweet and pretty a lass as any man could want to see, and with her hand she twisted around and around a silver button on my buckskin vest.

"Dance with me . . . the rest of this," she said. "Floyd shooed away my partners. I'm glad for the chance. Dance with me, Russ . . . not gallantly or dutifully, because I ask you, but because you *want* to. Else not at all."

There was a limit to my endurance. There would hardly be another evening like this — at least, for me — in that country. I capitulated with what grace I could express.

We went into the parlor, and, as we joined the dancers, despite all that confusion I heard her whisper, "I've been a little beast to you."

That dance, seemingly, lasted only a moment — a moment while she was all airy grace, radiant, and alluring, floating close to me, with our hands clasped. Then it appeared the music had ceased, the couples were passing out and finding seats, and Ruth and I were laughingly accosted by Miss Longstreth. She said we made a graceful couple in the dance. And Ruth said she did not have to reach up a mile to me — I was not so awfully tall. And I, tongue-tied for once, said nothing.

Lawson had returned and was now standing, cigarette between lips, in the door leading out to the patio. At the same moment that I heard a heavy tramp of boots from the porch side, I saw Lawson's face change remarkably, expressing amaze, consternation, then fear. I wheeled in time to see Vaughn Steele bend his head to enter the door on that side. The dancers fell back.

At sight of him I was again the ranger — his ally. Steele was pale, yet heated. He panted. He wore no hat. He had his coat turned up, and with left hand he held the lapels together.

In a quick ensuing silence Miss Longstreth rose, white as her dress. The young women present stared in astonishment, and their partners showed excitement.

"Miss Longstreth . . . I came to search . . . your house!" panted Steele, courteous yet with authority.

I disengaged myself from Ruth, who was clinging to my hands, and stepped forward out of the corner. Steele had been running. Why did he hold his coat like that? I sensed action, and the cold thrill animated me.

Miss Longstreth's astonishment was succeeded by anger difficult to control. "In the absence of my father I am mistress here. I will not permit you to search my house."

"Then . . . I regret to say . . . I must do so without your permission," he said sternly.

"Do not dare!" she flashed. She stood erect, her bosom swelling, her eyes magnificently black with passion. "How dare you intrude here? Have you not insulted us enough? To search my house tonight . . . to break up my party . . . oh, it's worse than outrage. Why on earth do you want to search here? Ah, for the same reason you dragged a poor innocent man into my father's court. Sir, I forbid you to take another step into this house."

Steele's face was bloodless now, and I wondered if it had to do with her scathing scorn — or with something having to do with his hand, closing his coat that way.

"Miss Longstreth, I don't need warrants to search houses," he said. "But this time I'll respect your command. It would be . . . too bad . . . to spoil your party. Let me add . . . perhaps you do me a . . . little wrong. God knows, I hope so. I was shot by a rustler. He fled. I chased him here. He has taken refuge here . . . in your father's house. He's hidden somewhere."

Steele spread wide his coat lapel. He wore a light shirt, the color of which in places was white. The rest was all a bloody mass — from which dark red drops fell to the floor.

"Oh!" cried Miss Longstreth.

Scorn and passion vanished in the horror, the pity of a woman who imagined she saw a man mortally wounded. It was a hard sight for a woman's eyes — that crimson, heaving breast.

"Surely I didn't seek that," went on Steele, closing his coat. "You used unforgettable words, Miss Longstreth. From you . . . they hurt. For I stand alone. My fight is to make Fairdale safer, cleaner, a better home for women and children. Some day you will remember what you just said."

How splendid he looked — how strong against odds — how simple a dignity fitted his words — and a woman, far blinder than Ray Longstreth was, could have seen that here stood a man. Steele bowed, turned on his heel, and strode out to vanish in the dark.

Then, while she stood bewildered, still shocked, I elected to do some rapid thinking. How seriously was Steele injured? An instant's thought was enough to tell me that, if he had sustained any more than a flesh wound, he would not have chased his assailant — not with so much at stake in the future. I concerned myself with a cold grip of desire to get near the rustler who had wounded Steele. As I started forward, however, Miss Longstreth detained me, Ruth once more clung to my hands, and directly we were surrounded by an excited circle. It took a moment or two to calm them.

"Then there's a rustler . . . here . . . hiding?" repeated Miss Longstreth. "What shall I do? We can't go on with the dance."

"Miss Longstreth, I'll find him . . . I'll rout him out," I said.

"Yes, yes, find him Russ, but don't use violence," she replied. "Send him away . . . no, give him over to . . . "

"Nothing of the kind," interrupted Floyd Lawson, loudvoiced. "Cousin, go on with your dance. I'll take a couple of cowboys. I'll find this . . . this rustler, if there's one here. But I think it's only another bluff of Steele's."

This from Lawson angered me deeply, and I strode right for the door.

"Where are you going?" he demanded.

"I've Miss Longstreth's orders. She wants me to find this hidden man. She trusts me not to allow any violence."

"Didn't I say I'd see to that?" he snarled.

"Lawson, I don't care what you say," I retorted. "But I'm thinking you might not want me to find this . . . rustler."

Lawson turned black in the face. Verily, if he had worn a gun, he would have pulled it on me. As it was, Miss Longstreth's interference probably prevented more words, if no worse.

"Don't quarrel," she said. "Floyd, you go with Russ. Please hurry. I'll be nervous till . . . the rustler's found or you're sure there's not one."

We started with several cowboys to ransack the house. We went through the rooms, searching, calling out, flashing our lanterns in dark places. It struck me more than forcibly that Lawson did all the calling. He was hurried, too, trying to keep in the lead. I wondered if he knew his voice would be recognized by the hiding man.

Be that as it might, it was I who peered into a dark corner — and then, with a cocked gun leveled, I said: "Come out!"

He came forth into the flare of lanterns, a tall, slim, darkfaced youth, wearing dark sombrero, blouse, and trousers. I collared him before any of the others could move, and I held the gun close enough to make him shrink. He did not impress me as being frightened just then. Nevertheless, he had a clammy face, the pallid look of a man who had just gotten over a shock. He peered into my face, then into that of the cowboy next to me, then into Lawson's, and, if ever in my life I beheld relief, I saw it then. That was all I needed to know, but I meant to find out more, if I could.

"Who're you?" I asked quietly.

He gazed rather arrogantly down at me. It always irritated me to be looked down at that way.

"Say, don't be smart with me, or you'll get it good," I yelled, prodding him in the side with the cocked gun. "Who are you? Quick!"

"Bo Snecker," he said.

"Any relation . . . what relation to Bill Snecker?"

"His son."

"What'd you hide here for?"

He appeared to grow sullen. "Reckoned I'd be as safe in Longstreth's as anywhere."

"Uh-huh. You're taking a long chance," I replied, and he never knew, or did any of the others, just how long a chance that was.

Sight of Steele's bloody breast remained with me, and I had something sinister to combat. This was no time for me to reveal myself or to show unusual feeling or interest for Steele. Since Steele had abandoned his search, I had nothing to do now but let the others decide what disposition was to be made of Snecker.

"Lawson, what'll you do with him?" I queried, as if uncertain now that the capture was made. I let Snecker go and sheathed my weapon.

That seemed a signal for Lawson to come to life. I guessed he had not much fancied the wide and somewhat variable sweep of the cocked gun.

"I'll see to that," replied Lawson gruffly, and he pushed Snecker in front of him into the hall. I followed them out into the court. This was at the back of the house.

As I had very little further curiosity, I did not wait to see where they went, but hurried back to relieve Miss Longstreth and Ruth. I found them as I had left them — Ruth quiet and pale, Miss Longstreth nervous and distressed. I soon calmed their fears of any further trouble or possible disturbance. Miss Longstreth then became curious and wanted to know who the rustler was.

"How strange he should come here," she said several times.

"Probably he'd run this way or thought he had a better chance where there was dancing and confusion," I replied, lying glibly.

I wondered how much longer I would find myself keen to shunt her mind from any channel leading to suspicion.

"Would Papa have arrested him?" she asked.

"Colonel Longstreth might have made it hot for him," I replied frankly, feeling that, if what I said had a double meaning, it still was no lie.

"Oh, I forgot . . . the ranger!" she exclaimed suddenly.

"That awful sight . . . the whole front of him bloody . . . wet. Russ, how could he stand up under such a wound? Do you think it'll . . . kill him?"

"That's hard to say. A man like Steele can stand a lot."

"Russ, please go find him. See . . . how it is with him," she said, almost pleadingly.

I started, glad of the chance, and hurried toward the town.

There was a light in the little adobe house where he lived and, proceeding cautiously so as to be sure no one saw me, I went close and whistled low in a way he would recognize. Then he opened the door, and I went in.

"Hello, old son," he said. "You needn't look worried. Sling a blanket over that window so no one can see in."

He had his shirt off and had been in the act of bandaging a wound that the bullet had cut in the tip of his shoulder.

"Let me tie that up," I said, taking the strip of linen. "Uh-huh, shot you from behind, didn't he?"

"How else, you locoed lady charmer? It's a wonder I didn't have to tell you that."

"Tell me about it, anyway."

Steele related a circumstance, differing but little from other attempts at his life, and concluded by saying that Snecker was a good runner, if he was not a good shot. I finished the bandaging and stood off, admiring Steele's magnificent shoulders. I noted, too, on the fine white skin more than one scar made by bullets. I got an impression that his strength and vitality were like his spirit — unconquerable.

"So you knew it was Bill Snecker's son?" I asked when I had told him about finding the rustler.

"Sure. Laramie pointed him out to me yesterday. Both the Sneckers are in town. From now on we're going to be busy, Russ."

"It can't come too soon for me," I replied. "Shall I chuck my job? Come out from behind these cowboy togs?"

"Not yet. We need proof, Russ. We've got to be able to prove things. Hang on at the ranch yet a while."

"This Bo Snecker was scared stiff till he recognized Lawson. Isn't that proof?"

"No, that's nothing. We've got to catch Longstreth and Lawson redhanded."

"I don't like the idea of you trailing along alone," I protested. "Remember what MacNeal told me. I'm to kick. It's time for me to hang 'round with a couple of guns. You'll never use one."

"The hell I won't!" he retorted with a dark glance of passion. I was surprised that my remark had angered him. "You fellows are all wrong. I know *when* to throw a gun. You ought to remember that rangers have a bad name for wanting to shoot. And I'm afraid it's deserved."

"Did you shoot at Snecker?" I queried.

"I could have got him in the back. But that wouldn't do. I shot three times at his legs . . . tried to let him down. I'd have made him tell everything he knew. Say, but he ran. He was too fast for me."

"Shooting at his legs! No wonder he ran. He savvied your game, all right. It's funny, Vaughn, how these rustlers and gunmen don't mind being killed. But to cripple them . . . rope them . . . jail them . . . that is hell to them. Well, I'm to go on, up at the ranch . . . falling further in love with that sweet kid . . . instead of coming out straight to face things with you?"

Steele had to laugh, yet he was more thoughtful at my insistence. "Russ, you think you have patience, but you don't know what patience is. I won't be hurried on this job. But I'll tell you what . . . I'll hang under cover most of the time when you're not close to me. See? That can be managed. I'll watch for you when you come in town. We'll go in the same places. And in case I get busy, you can stand by and trail along after me. That satisfy you?"

"Fine," I said, both delighted and relieved. "Well, I'll have to rustle back now to tell Miss Longstreth you're all right."

Steele had about finished pulling on a clean shirt, exercising care not to disarrange the bandages, when he stopped short to turn squarely and look at me with hungry eyes.

"Russ, did she . . . show sympathy?"

"She was all broken up about it. Thought you were going to die."

"Did she send you?"

"Sure. And she said hurry," I replied.

I was not a little gleeful over the apparent possibility of Steele being in the same boat with me.

"Do you think she would have cared if . . . if I had been shot up badly?"

The great giant of a ranger asked this like a boy, hesitatingly, with color in his face.

"Care! Vaughn, you're as thick-headed as you say I'm locoed. Ray Longstreth has fallen in love with you. That's all. Love at first sight. She doesn't realize it. But I know."

There he stood, as if another bullet had struck him, this time straight through the heart. Perhaps one had — and I repented a little of my over-confident declaration. Still, I would not go back on it. I believed it.

"Russ! For God's sake! What a terrible thing to say," he ejaculated hoarsely.

"No. It's not terrible to say it . . . only the fact is terrible," I went on. "I may be wrong. But I swear I'm right. When you opened your coat . . . showed that bloody breast . . . well, I'll never forget her eyes. She had been furious. She showed passion . . . hate. Then, all in a second, something wonderful, beautiful broke through. Pity . . . fear . . . agonized thought of your death. If that's not love . . . if . . . if she did not betray love, then I never saw it. She thinks she hates you. But she loves you."

"Get out of here," he ordered thickly.

I went, not forgetting to peep out at the door and to listen a moment, then I hurried into the open, toward the ranch. The stars were very big and bright, so calm, so cold, that it somehow hurt me to look at them. Not like men's lives surely.

What had fate done to Vaughn Steele and to me? I had a moment of bitterness — an emotion rare with me. Most rangers put love behind them when they entered the service and seldom found it after that. But love had certainly met me on the way, and I now had confirmation of my fear that Vaughn was hard hit.

Then the wildness, the adventurer in me stirred to the wonder of it all. It was in me to exult even in the face of fate. Steele and I, while balancing our lives on the hair-trigger of a gun, had certainly fallen into a tangled web of circumstances not calculated in the role of rangers.

I went back to the ranch with regret, remorse, sorrow knocking at my heart but, notwithstanding, that tingling alive to the devilish excitement of the game.

I knew not what it was that prompted me to sow the same seed in Ray Longstreth's breast that I had sown in Steele's. Probably it was just a propensity for sheer mischief — and just as probably a certainty of the truth, a strange foreshadowing of a coming event.

If Ray Longstreth did love him, perhaps through her this event might be made to seem less tragic. Somehow love might save us all. That was the shadowy portent, flitting in the dark maze of my mind.

At the ranch dancing had been resumed. There might never have been any interruption of the gaiety. I found Miss Longstreth on the look-out for me, and she searched my face with eyes that silenced my one last qualm of conscience.

"Let's go out in the patio," I suggested. "I don't want anyone to hear what I say."

Outside in the starlight she looked white and very beautiful. I felt her tremble. Perhaps my gravity presaged the worst. It did presage one thing — about Vaughn.

"I went down to Steele's 'dobe, the little place where he lives," I began, weighing my words. "He let me in . . . was surprised. He had been shot high in the shoulder, not a dangerous wound. I bandaged it for him. He was grateful . . . said he had no friends."

"Poor fellow. Oh, I'm glad it isn't bad," said Miss Longstreth. Something glistened in her eyes.

"He looked strange . . . sort of forlorn. I think your words . . . what you said . . . hurt him more than the bullet. I'm sure of that, Miss Longstreth."

"Oh, I saw that myself. I was furious. But I . . . I meant what I said."

"You wronged Steele. I happen to know. I know his record along the Rio Grande. It's scarcely my place, Miss Longstreth, to tell you what you'll find out for yourself, sooner or later."

"What shall I find out?" she demanded.

"I've said enough."

"No. You mean my father and Cousin Floyd are misinformed or wrong about Steele? I've feared it this last hour. It was his look. That pierced me. Oh, I'd hate to be unjust. *You* say I wronged him, Russ? Then you take sides with him against my father?"

"Yes," I replied in a very low tone.

She was keenly hurt and seemed defiant, despite an effort to shrink from me.

"It's only natural you should fight for your father," I went on. "Perhaps you don't understand. He has ruled here for so long. He's been . . . well, let's say, easy with evil-doers. But times are changing. He opposes the ranger idea, which is also natural, I suppose. Still, he's wrong about Steele . . . terribly wrong, and it means trouble."

"Oh, I don't know what to believe!"

"It might be well for you to *think* things out for yourself."

"Russ, I feel as if I couldn't. I can't make head or tail of life out here. My father seems so strange . . . though, of course, I've only seen him twice a year since I was a little girl. He has two sides to him. When I come upon that strange side . . . the one I never saw . . . he's like a man I never knew. I want to be a good and loving daughter. I want to help him fight his battles. But he doesn't . . . he doesn't satisfy me. He grows impatient and wants me to go back to Louisiana. That gives me a feeling of mystery. Oh, it's all a mystery!"

"True, you're right," I replied, my heart aching for her. "It's all a mystery . . . and trouble, too, for you. Perhaps you'll do well to go home."

"Russ, you suggest I leave here . . . leave my father?" she asked.

"I advise it. You've struck a . . . a rather troublesome time. Later, you might return, if . . ."

"Never. I came to stay, and I'll stay," she declared, and there her temper spoke.

"Miss Longstreth," I began again, after taking a long, deep breath, "I ought to tell you one thing once more about Steele."

"Well, go on."

"Doesn't he strike you now as being the farthest removed from a ranting, brutal ranger?"

"I confess he was at least a gentleman."

"Rangers don't allow anything to interfere with the discharge of their duty. He was courteous after you defamed him. He respected your wish. He did not break up the dance. This may not strike you particularly. But let me explain that Steele was chasing an outlaw who had shot him. Under ordinary circumstances he would have searched your house. He would have been like a lion. He would have torn the place down around our ears to get that rustler. But his action was so different from what I had expected, it amazed me. Just now, when I was with him, I learned . . . I guessed . . . what stayed his hand. I believe you ought to know."

"Know what?" she asked. How starry and magnetic her eyes! A woman's divining intuition made them wonderful with swift-varying emotion.

They drew me on to the fatal plunge. What was I doing to her — to Vaughn?

Something bound my throat, making speech difficult.

"He's fallen in love with you," I hurried on in a husky whisper. "Love at first sight! Terrible! Hopeless! I saw it . . . felt it. I can't explain how I know, but I do know. That's what stayed his hand here. And that's why I'm on his side. He's alone. He has a terrible task here without any handicaps. Every man is against him. If he fails . . . you might be the force that weakened him. So you ought to be kinder in your thoughts of him. Wait before you judge him further. If he isn't killed, time will prove him noble instead of vile. If he is killed, which is more than likely, you'll feel the happier for a generous doubt in favor of the man who loved you."

Like one stricken blind, she stood an instant, then, with her hands at her breast, she walked straight across the patio into the dark, open door of her room.

CHAPTER NINE

Cleaning Out Fairdale

Not much sleep visited me that night. In the morning — the young ladies not stirring and no prospects of duty — I rode to town.

Sight of the wide street, lined by its hitching-posts and saddled horses, the square buildings with their ugly signs, the something unfinished yet old, the lounging, dust-gray men at every corner — these awoke in me a significance that had gone into oblivion overnight.

That last talk with Miss Longstreth had unnerved and wrought strangely upon me. Afterward, waking and dozing, I had dreamed, lived in a warm, golden place where there were music and flowers and Ruth's sprite-like form leading me on after two tall, beautiful lovers, Ray and Vaughn, walking hand in hand. Fine employment of mind for a ranger whose single glance down a quiet street pictured it with dark-garbed men in grim action, guns spouting red, horses plunging.

In front of Laramie's restaurant I dismounted and threw my bridle. Jim was unmistakably glad to see me.

"Where've you been? Morton was in an' powerful set on seein' you. I steered him from goin' up to Longstreth's. What kind of a game was you givin' Frank?"

"Jim, I just wanted to see if he was a safe rancher to make a stock deal for me."

"He says you told him he didn't have no yellow streak an' that he was a rustler. Frank can't git over them two hunches. When he sees you, he's goin' to swear he's no rustler, but he *has* got a yellow streak, unless ... "

This little, broken-down Texan had eyes like flint striking fire.

"Unless?" I queried sharply.

Jim breathed a deep breath and looked around the room before his gaze fixed again on mine. "Wal," he replied, speaking low, "me an' Frank allows you've picked the right men. It was me that sent them letters to the ranger captain at Austin. Now who in hell are you?"

It was my turn to draw a deep breath. I had taken six weeks to strike fire

544

from a Texan whom I instinctively felt had been a prey to the power that shadowed Fairdale. There was no one in the room except us, no one passing or near. Reaching into the inside pocket of my buckskin vest, I turned the lining out. A star-shaped, bright, silver object flashed as I shoved it, pocket and all, under Jim's hard eyes. He could not help but read: United States Deputy Marshal.

"Son of a bitch," he whispered, cracking the table with his fist. "Russ, you sure run true to me. But never as a cowboy."

"Jim, the woods is full of us."

Heavy footsteps sounded on the walk. Presently Steele's bulk darkened the door.

"Hello," I greeted. "Steele, shake hands with Jim Laramie."

"Hello," replied Steele slowly. "Say, I reckon I know Laramie."

"Nit. Not this one. He's the old Laramie. He used to own the Hope So saloon. It was on the square when he ran it. Maybe he'll get it back . . . pretty soon. Hope so."

I laughed at my execrable pun. Steele leaned against the counter, his gray glance studying the man I had so oddly introduced. Laramie in one flash associated the ranger with me — a relation he had not dreamed of. Then, whether from shock or hope or fear I know not, he appeared about to faint.

"Laramie, do you know who's boss of this secret gang of rustlers hereabouts?" asked Steele bluntly.

It was characteristic of him to come sharp to the point. His voice — something deep, easy, cool about him — seemed to steady Laramie.

"No," replied Laramie.

"Does anybody know?" went on Steele.

"Wal, I reckon there's not one honest native of Pecos who *knows*."

"But you have your suspicions?"

"We have."

"You can keep your suspicions to yourself. But you can give me your idea about this crowd that hangs round the saloons . . . the regulars."

"Jest a bad lot," replied Laramie with the quick assurance of knowledge. "Most of them have been here years. Others have drifted in. Some of them work odd times. They rustle a few steers . . . steal . . . rob . . . anythin' for a little money to drink an' gamble. Jest a bad lot. But the strangers as are always comin' an' goin' . . . strangers thet never git acquainted . . . some of them are likely to be *the* rustlers. Bill an' Bo Snecker are in town now. Bill's a known cattle thief. Bo's no good, the makin' of a gunfighter. He heads thet way. They might be rustlers. But the boy, he's hardly careful enough for this gang. Then there's Jack Blome. He comes to town often. He lives up in the hills. He always has three or four strangers with him. Blome's the fancy gunfighter. He shot a gambler here last fall. Then he was in a fight in Sanderson lately. Got two cowboys then. Blome's killed a dozen Pecos men. He's a rustler, too, but I reckon he's not the brains of thet secret outfit, if he's in it at all."

Steele appeared pleased with Laramie's idea. Probably it coincided with the one he had arrived at himself.

"Now, I'm puzzled over this," said Steele. "Why do men . . . apparently honest men . . . seem to be so close-mouthed here? Is that a fact or only my impression?"

"It's a sure fact," replied Laramie darkly. "Men have lost cattle an' property in Fairdale . . . lost them honestly or otherwise, as hasn't been proved. An' in some cases when they talked . . . hinted a little . . . they was found dead. Apparently held up an' robbed. But dead. Dead men don't talk! Thet's why we're close-mouthed."

Steele's face wore a dark, somber sternness. Rustling cattle was not intolerable. Western Texas had gone on prospering, growing in spite of the horde of rustlers ranging its vast stretches, but this cold, secret, murderous hold on a little struggling community was something too strange, too terrible for them to stand long. It had waited for a leader like Steele, and now it could not last. Laramie's revivified spirit showed that.

The ranger was about to speak again when the clatter of hoofs interrupted him. Horses halted out in front.

A motion of Steele's hand caused me to dive through a curtained door back of Laramie's counter. I turned to peep out and was in time to see Floyd Lawson enter with the red-headed cowboy called Brick. This was the first time I had ever seen Lawson come into Laramie's. He called for tobacco.

If his visit surprised Jim, he did not show any evidence of it. But Lawson did show astonishment as he saw the ranger, and then a dark glint flitted from eyes that shifted from Steele to Laramie and back again.

Steele leaned easily against the counter, and he said good morning pleasantly. Lawson deigned him no reply, although he bent a curious and hard scrutiny upon Steele. In fact, Lawson evinced nothing that would lead one to think he had any respect for Steele as a man or as a ranger.

"Steele, that was the second break of yours last night," he said finally. "If you come fooling 'round the ranch again, there'll be hell."

It seemed strange that a man who had lived west of the Pecos for ten years could not see in Steele something which forbade that kind of talk. It certainly was not nerve Lawson showed. Men of courage are seldom intolerant, and with the matchless nerve that characterized Steele or the great gunmen of the day there went a cool unobtrusive manner, a speech brief, almost gentle, certainly courteous. Lawson was a hot-head Louisianian of French extraction, a man evidently who had never been crossed in anything, and who was strong, brutal, passionate, qualities that in the face of a situation like this made him simply a fool.

The way Steele looked at Lawson was a joy to me. I hated this smooth, dark-skinned Southerner. But, of course, an ordinary affront like Lawson's only earned silence from Steele.

"I'm thinking you used your ranger bluff just to get near Ray Longstreth," Lawson sneered. "Mind you, if you come up there again, there'll be hell!"

"You're damned right, there'll be hell!" retorted Steele, a kind of high ring in his voice. I saw thick, dark red creep into his face.

Had Lawson's incomprehensible mention of Ray Longstreth been an instinct of love — of jealousy? Verily, it had pierced the depths of the ranger, probably as no other threat could have.

"Ray Longstreth wouldn't stoop to know a dirty blood-tracker like you," continued Lawson hotly. His was not a deliberate intention to rouse Steele. The man was simply being rancorous. "I'll call you right . . . you cheap bluffer! You four-flush! You damned interfering, conceited ranger!"

Long before Lawson ended his tirade, Steele's face had lost the tinge of color, so foreign to it in moments like this, and the cool shade, the steady eyes like ice on fire, the ruthless lips had warned me, if they had not Lawson.

"Lawson, I'll not take offense, because you seem to be championing your beautiful cousin," replied Steele in slow, biting speech. "But let me return your compliment. You're a fine Southerner! Why, you're only a cheap four-flush . . . damned . . . bull-headed . . . *rustler!*"

Steele hissed the last word. Then for him — for me — for Laramie — there was the truth in Lawson's working, passion-blackened face. Lawson jerked, moved, meant to draw. But how slow! Steele lunged forward. His long arm swept up. Lawson staggered backward, knocking a table and chairs, to fall hard in a half-sitting position against the wall.

"Don't draw," warned Steele.

"Lawson, git away from your gun!" yelled the cowboy, Brick.

But Lawson was crazed by fury. He tugged at his hip, his face corded with

RANGERS OF THE LONE STAR

purple welts, malignant, murderous, while he got to his feet. I was about to leap through the door when Steele shot. Lawson's gun went ringing to the floor. Like a beast in pain Lawson screamed. Frantically he waved a limp arm, flinging blood over the white tablecloths. Steele had crippled him.

"Here, you cowboy," ordered Steele, "take him out. Quick!"

Brick saw the need of expediency, if Lawson did not realize it, and he pulled the raving man out of the place. He hurried Lawson down the street, leaving the horses behind.

Steele calmly sheathed his gun. "Well, I guess that opens the ball," he said as I came out.

Laramie seemed fascinated by the spots of blood on the tablecloths. It was horrible to see him rubbing his hands there like a ghoul.

"I tell you what, fellows," said Steele, "we've just had a few pleasant moments with the man who has made it healthy to keep close-mouthed in Fairdale."

Laramie lifted his shaking hands. "What'd you wing him for?" he wailed. "He was drawin' on you. Shootin' arms off men like him won't do out here."

I was inclined to agree with Laramie.

"That bull-headed fool will roar and butt himself with all his gang right into our hands," Steele rejoined. "He's just the man I've needed to meet. Besides, shooting him would have been murder for me."

"Murder!" exclaimed Laramie.

"He was a fool, and slow at that. Under such circumstances could *I* kill him . . . when I didn't have to?"

"Sure, it'd been the trick," declared Jim positively. "I'm not allowin' for whether he's really a rustler or not. It just won't do, because these fellers out here ain't goin' to be afraid of you."

"See here, Laramie. If a man's going to be afraid of me at all, that trick will make him more afraid of me. I know it. It works out. When Lawson cools down, he'll remember, he'll begin to think, he'll realize that I could snap a shot at more than his arm. I'll bet you he goes pale to the gills next time he even sees me."

"That may be true, Steele. But, if Lawson's the man you think he is, he'll begin that secret underground bizness. It's been tolerable healthy these last six months. You can gamble on this. If thet secret work does commence, you'll have more reason to suspect Lawson. I won't feel very safe from now on. I heard you call him a rustler. He knows thet. Why, Lawson won't sleep o' nights now. He an' Longstreth have always been after me."

"Laramie, what are your eyes for?" demanded Steele. "Watch out. And now here, see your friend, Morton. Tell him this game grows hot. Together you approach four or five men you know well and can absolutely trust. Say, there's somebody coming. You meet Russ and me tonight out in the open, a quarter of a mile straight from the end of this street. You'll find a pile of stones. Meet us there tonight at ten o'clock."

The next few days, for the several hours each day that I was in town, I had Steele in sight all the time or knew that he was safe. Nothing happened. His presence in the saloons or any place where men congregated was marked by a certain uneasy watchfulness on the part of almost everybody, and some amusement on the part of a few.

It was natural to suppose that the lawless element would rise up in a mass and slay Steele on sight. But this sort of thing never happened. It was not so much that these enemies of the law awaited his next move, but just a slowness peculiar to the frontier. The ranger was in their midst. He was interesting, if formidable. He would have been welcomed at card tables, at the bars, to play and drink with the men who knew they were under suspicion. There was a rude kind of good humor even in their open hostility. Besides, one ranger or a company of rangers could not have held the undivided attention of these men from their games and drinks and quarrels, except by some decided move. Excitement, greed, appetite were rife in them.

I marked, however, a striking exception to the usual run of strangers I had been in the habit of seeing. The Sneckers had gone or were undercover. Again I caught a vague rumor of the coming of Jack Blome, yet he never seemed to arrive. Moreover, the goings-on among the habitués of the resorts and the cowboys who came in to drink and gamble were unusually mild in comparison with former conduct. This lull, however, did not deceive Steele and me. It could not last. The wonder was that it had lasted so long.

There was, of course, no post office in Fairdale. A stage arrived twice a week from Sanderson, if it did not get held up on the way, and the driver usually had letters, which he turned over to the keeper of a little store. This man's name was Jones, and everybody liked him. On the evenings the stage arrived, there was always a crowd at his store, which fact was a source of no little revenue to him.

One night, so we ascertained, after the crowd had dispersed, two thugs entered his store, beat the old man, and robbed him. He made no complaint. However, when Steele called upon him, he rather reluctantly gave not only descriptions of his assailants, but their names. Steele straightway went in search of the men and came across them in Lerett's place. I was around when it happened. Steele strode up to a table which was surrounded by seven or eight men, and he tapped Sim Bass on the shoulder.

"Get up. I want you," he said.

Bass looked up lazily to see who had accosted him.

"The hell you say!" he replied impudently.

Steele's big hand shifted to the fellow's collar. One jerk, seemingly no effort at all, sent Bass sliding, chair and all, to crash into the bar and fall in a heap. He lay there, wondering what had struck him.

"Miller, I want you. Get up," said Steele.

Miller complied with alacrity. A sharp kick put more life and understanding into Bass.

Then Steele searched these men right before the eyes of their comrades, took what money and weapons they had, and marched them out, followed by a crowd that gathered more and more to it as they went down the street. Steele took his prisoners into Jones's store, had them identified, returned the money they had stolen, and then, pushing the two through the gaping crowd, he marched them down to his stone jail and locked them up.

Obviously the serious side of this incident was entirely lost upon the highly entertained audience. Many and loud were the coarse jokes cracked at the expense of Bass and Miller and, after the rude door had closed upon them, similar remarks were addressed to Steele's jailer and guard who, in truth, were just as disreputable-looking as their prisoners. Then the jocose crowd returned to their pastimes, leaving their erstwhile comrades to taste the sweetness of prison life.

When I got a chance, I asked Steele if he could rely on his hired help, and, with a twinkle in his eye that surprised me as much as his reply, he said Miller and Bass would have flown the coop before morning.

He was right. When I reached the lower end of town next morning, the same old crowd, enlarged by other curious men and youths, had come down to pay their respects to the new institution. Jailer and guard were on hand, loud in their proclamations and explanations. Naturally they had fallen asleep, as all other hard-working citizens had, and, while they slept, the prisoners made a hole somewhere and escaped.

Steele examined the hole, and then engaged a stripling of a youth to see if he could crawl through. The youngster essayed the job, stuck in the middle, and was with difficulty extricated. Whereupon the crowd evinced its delight. Steele, without

CLEANING OUT FAIRDALE

more ado, shoved his jailer and guard inside the jail, deliberately closed, barred, and chained the iron-bolted door, and put the key in his pocket. Then he remained there all day without giving heed to his prisoners' derision and threats. Toward evening, having gone without drink infinitely longer than was customary, they made appeals to which Steele was deaf.

He left the jail, however, just before dark. When we met, he told me to be on hand to help him watch that night. We went around the outskirts of town, carrying two heavy double-barreled shotguns Steele had gotten somewhere. Taking up a position behind bushes in the lot adjoining the jail, we awaited developments. Steele was not above paying back these fellows in their own coin.

All the early part of the evening gangs of half a dozen men or more came down the street and had their last treat at the expense of the jailed guard and jailer. These worthies yelled for drink — not water — but drink, and the more they yelled, the more merriment was loosened upon the night air.

About ten o'clock the last gang left to the despair of the hungry and thirsty prisoners. Steele and I had hugely enjoyed the fun and thought the best part of the joke for us was yet to come. The moon had arisen and, though somewhat hazed by clouds, had lightened the night. We were hidden about sixty paces from the jail, a little above it, and we had a fine command of the door.

About eleven o'clock, when all was still, we heard soft steps back of the jail and soon two dark forms stole around in front. They laid down something that gave forth a metallic clink — likely a crowbar. We heard whisperings and then low, coarse laughs. Then the two rescuers, who undoubtedly were Miller and Bass, set to work to open the door. Softly they worked at first, but, as that door had been put there to stay, and they were not fond of hard work, they began to swear and make noises.

Steele whispered to me to wait until the door had been opened and then, when all four presented a good target, to fire both barrels. We could easily have slipped down and captured the rescuers, but that was not Steele's game. A trick met by trick, cunning matching craft, would be surest of all ways to command respect.

Four times the workers had to rest, and once they were so enraged at the insistence of the prisoners, who wanted to delay proceedings to send one of them after a bottle, that they swore they would go away and quit the job altogether. But they were prevailed upon to stay and attack the stout door once more. Finally it yielded, with enough noise to have awakened sleepers a block distant, and, forth into the moonlight, came rescuers and rescued with low, satisfied grunts of laughter.

Just then Steele and I each discharged both barrels, and the reports blended as one in a tremendous boom. That little compact bunch disintegrated like quicksilver. Two tumbled over. The others leaped out, and all yelled in pain and terror. Then the fallen ones scrambled up and began to hobble and limp and jerk along after their comrades.

Before the four of them got out of sight they had ceased their yells but were moving slowly, hanging on to one another in a way that satisfied us they would be lame for many a day.

The next morning at breakfast Dick regaled me with an elaborate story about how the ranger had turned the tables on the jokers. Evidently in a night the whole town knew it. Probably a desperate stand of Steele's, even to the extreme of killing men, could not have educated these crude natives so quickly into the realization that the ranger was not to be fooled with.

That morning I went for a ride with the girls, and both had heard something and wanted to know everything. I had become a news carrier, and Miss Longstreth never thought of questioning me in regard to my fund of information. She showed more than curiosity. The account I gave of the jail affair amused her and made Ruth laugh heartily.

Ray questioned me also about a rumor that had come to her, concerning Floyd Lawson. He had wounded himself with a gun, it seemed, and though not seriously injured was not able to go about. He had not been up to the ranch for days.

"I asked Papa about him," said Ray, "and Papa laughed like . . . well, like a regular hyena. I was dumbfounded. Papa's so queer. He looked thunderclouds at me. When I insisted, for I wanted to know, he ripped out . . . 'Yes, the damn' fool got himself shot, and I'm sorry it's not worse.' Now, Russ, what do you make of my dad? Cheerful and kind, isn't he?"

I laughed with Ruth, but I disclaimed any knowledge of Floyd's accident. I hated the thought of Lawson, let alone anything concerning the fatal certainty that sooner or later these cousins of his were to suffer through him.

Ruth did not make these rides easy for me, for she was sweeter than anything that has a name. Since the evening of the dance I had tried to avoid her. Either she was sincerely sorry for her tantrum or she was bent upon utterly destroying my peace. I took good care we were never alone, for in that case, if she ever got into my arms again, I would find the ground slipping from under me. Despite, however, the wear and constant strain of resisting Ruth, I enjoyed the ride. There was a charm about being with these girls.

Then perhaps Miss Longstreth's growing curiosity in regard to Steele was no little satisfaction to me. I pretended a reluctance to speak of the ranger, but, when I did, it was to drop a subtle word or briefly tell of an action that suggested much. I never again hinted the thing that had been such a shock to her. What was in her mind, I could not guess. Nevertheless, I divined that some of her curiosity, perhaps the greater part, was due to a generous nature not entirely satisfied with itself. She probably had not abandoned her father's estimate of the ranger, but absolute assurance that this was truly just did not abide with her. For the rest she was like any other girl, a worshiper of the lion in a man, a weaver of romance, ignorant of her own heart.

Not the least talked about and speculated upon of all the details of the jail incident was the part played by the store-keeper, Jones, who had informed upon his assailants. Steele and I both awaited results of this significant fact. When would the town wake up — not only to a little nerve, but to the usefulness of a ranger?

Three days afterward Steele told me a woman accosted him in the street. She seemed a poor, hard-working person, plain-spoken and honest. Her husband did not drink enough to complain of, but he liked to gamble, and he had been fleeced by a crooked game in Jack Martin's saloon. Other wives could make the same complaints. It was a God's blessing for such women that Ranger Steele had come to Fairdale. Of course, he could not get back the lost money, but would it be possible to close Martin's place, or at least break up the crooked game?

Steele had asked this woman, whose name was Price, how much her husband had lost, and, being told, he assured her that, if he found evidence of cheating, not only would he get back the money, but also he would shut up Martin's place. Steele instructed me to go that night to the saloon in question and get in the game. I complied, and, in order not to be too carefully sized up by the dealer, I pretended to be well under the influence of liquor. By nine o'clock, when Steele strolled in, I had the game well studied, and a more flagrantly crooked one I had never sat in. It was barefaced robbery.

Steele and I had agreed upon a sign from me, because he was not so adept in the intricacies of gambling as I was. I was not in a hurry, however, for there was a little freckle-faced cattleman in the game, and he had been losing, too. He had sold a bunch of stock that day and had considerable money, which evidently he was to be deprived of before he got started for Del Rio. Steele stood at our backs, and I could feel his presence. He thrilled me. He had some kind of effect on the others, especially the dealer, who was honest enough while the stranger looked on.

When, however, Steele shifted his attention to other tables and players, our

RANGERS OF THE LONE STAR

dealer reverted to his crooked work. I was about to make a disturbance, when the little cattleman, leaning over, fire in his eye and gun in hand, made it for me. Evidently he was a keener and nervier gambler than he had been taken for. There might have been gun play right then if Steele had not interfered.

"Hold on!" he yelled, leaping for our table. "Put up your gun!"

"Who're you?" demanded the cattleman, never moving. "Better keep out of this."

"I'm Steele. Put up your gun."

"You're thet ranger, hey?" replied the other. "All right! But just a minute. I want this dealer to sit quiet. I've been robbed. And I want my money back."

Certainly the dealer and everyone else around the table sat quietly while the cattleman coolly held his gun leveled.

"Crooked game?" asked Steele, bending over the table. "Show me."

It did not take the aggrieved gambler more than a moment to prove his assertion. Steele, however, desired corroboration from others beside the cattleman, and one by one he questioned them. To my surprise, one of the players admitted his conviction that the game was not straight.

"What do you say?" demanded Steele of me.

"Worse'n a hold-up, Mister Ranger," I burst out. "Let me show you."

Deftly I made the dealer's guilt plain to all, and then I seconded the cattleman's angry claim for lost money. The players from other tables gathered around, curious, muttering. And just then Martin strolled in. His appearance was not prepossessing.

"What's this holler?" he asked, and halted as he saw the cattleman's gun still in line with the dealer.

"Martin, you know what it's for," replied Steele. "Take your dealer and dig . . . unless you want to see me clean out your place."

Sullen and fierce, Martin stood, looking from Steele to the cattleman and then the dealer. Some men in the crowd muttered, and that was a signal for Steele to shove the circle apart and get out, back to the wall.

The cattleman rose slowly in the center, pulling another gun, and he certainly looked all business to me.

"Wal, ranger, I reckon I'll hang 'round an' see you ain't bothered none," he said. "Friend," he went on, indicating me with a slight wave of one extended gun, "jest rustle the money in sight. We'll square up . . . after the show."

I reached out and swept the considerable sum toward me, and, pocketing it, I, too, rose, ready for what might come.

554

"You-all give me elbow room!" yelled Steele at Martin and his cowed contingent.

Steele looked around, evidently for some kind of implement, and, espying a heavy axe in a corner, he grasped it, and, sweeping it to and fro as if it had been a buggy whip, he advanced on the faro layout. The crowd fell back, edging toward the door. One crashing blow wrecked the dealer's box and table, sending them splintering among the tumbled chairs. Then the giant ranger began to spread further ruin about him.

Martin's place was rough and bare, of the most primitive order, and, like a thousand other dens of its kind, consisted of a large room with adobe walls, a rude bar of boards, piles of kegs in a corner, a stove, and a few tables with chairs. Steele required only one blow for each article he struck, and he demolished it. He stove in the head of each keg. When the dark liquor gurgled out, Martin cursed, and the crowd followed suit. That was a loss!

The little cattleman, holding the men covered, backed them out of the room, Martin needing a plain, stern word to put him out entirely. I went out, too, for I did not want to miss any moves on the part of that gang. Close behind me came the cattleman — the kind of cool, nervy Texan I liked. He had Martin well judged, too, for there was no evidence of any bold resistance. But there were shouts and loud acclamation, and these, with the crushing blows of Steele's axe, brought a curious and growing addition to the crowd.

Soon sodden thuds from inside the saloon and red dust pouring out the door told that Steele was attacking the walls of Martin's place. These adobe bricks, old and crumbly, were easily demolished. Steele made short work of the back wall, and then he smashed out half the front of the building. That seemed to satisfy him.

When he stepped out of the dust, he was wet with sweat, dirty, and disheveled, hot with his exertion — a man whose great stature and muscular development expressed a wonderful physical strength and energy. And his somber face, with the big gray eyes like open furnaces, expressed a passion equal to his strength.

Perhaps only then did wild and lawless Fairdale grasp the real significance of this ranger. Steele threw the axe at Martin's feet.

"Martin, don't re-open here," he said curtly. "Don't start another place in Fairdale. If you do . . . jail at Austin for you."

Martin, livid and scowling, yet seemingly dazed with what had occurred, slunk away, accompanied by his cronies. Steele took the money I had appropriated, returned to me what I had lost, did likewise with the cattleman, and then, taking out the sum named by Mrs. Price, he divided the balance with the other players who had been in the game. Then he stalked off through the crowd, as if he knew that men who slunk from facing him would not have nerve enough to attack him even from behind.

"Wal, damn me!" ejaculated the little cattleman in mingled admiration and satisfaction. "So thet's Lone Star Steele, hey? Never seen him before. All Texas, thet ranger!"

I lingered downtown as much to enjoy the sensation as to gain the different points of view. No doubt about the sensation. In one hour every male resident of Fairdale and almost every female had viewed the wreck of Martin's place. A fire could not have created half the excitement. And in that excitement both men and women gave vent to speech they might not have voiced at a calmer moment. The women, at least, were not afraid to talk, and I made mental note of the things they said.

"Did he do it all alone?"

"Thank God a man's come to Fairdale."

It almost seemed that all the women were glad, and this was in itself a vindication of the ranger's idea of law. The men, however — Blandy, proprietor of the Hope So, and others of his ilk, together with the whole brood of idle gaming loungers, and in fact even storekeepers, ranchers, cowboys — all shook their heads sullenly or doubtfully. Striking, indeed, was the absence of any joking. Steele had showed his hand, and as one gambler said: "It's a hard hand to call."

The truth was this ranger service was hateful to the free and easy Texan who lived by anything except hard and honest work, and it was damnably hateful to the lawless class. Steele's authority, now obvious to all, was unlimited. It could go as far as he had power to carry it.

From present indications that power might be considerable. The work of native sheriffs and constables in western Texas had been an honest farce, an utter failure. If an honest native of a community undertook to be a sheriff, he became immediately a target for the rowdy cowboys and other vicious element. Many a town south and west of San Antonio owed its peace and prosperity to rangers, and only to them. They had killed or driven out the criminals. They interpreted the law for themselves, and it was only such an attitude toward law — the stern, uncompromising, implacable extermination of the lawless — that was going to do for all Texas what it had done for part.

Steele was the driving wedge that had begun to split Fairdale — split the honest from dominance by the dishonest. To be sure, Steele might be killed at any moment, and that contingency was voiced in the growl of one sullen man who said: "Wot the hell are we up against? Ain't somebody goin' to plug this ranger?"

It was then that the thing for which Steele stood — the ranger service, to help, to save, to defend, to punish with such somber menace of death as seemed embodied in his cold attitude toward resistance — took hold of Fairdale and sank deeply into both black and honest hearts. It was what was behind Steele that seemed to make him more than an officer — a man.

I could feel how he began to loom up, the embodiment of a powerful force — the ranger service — the fame of which, long known to this lawless Pecos gang, but scouted as a vague and distant thing, now became invested in a clearer light, that of a ranger in the flesh whose surprising attributes included both the law and the enforcement of it.

When I reached the ranch, the excitement had preceded me. Miss Longstreth and Ruth, both talking at once, acquainted me with the fact that they had been in a store on the main street a block or more from Martin's place. They had seen the crowd, heard the uproar, and, as they had been hurriedly started home by the attendant Dick, they had encountered Steele, stalking past.

"He looked grand!" exclaimed Ruth.

Then I told the girls the whole story in detail.

"Russ, is it true just as you tell it?" inquired Ray earnestly.

"Absolutely. I know Missus Price went to Steele with her trouble. I was in Martin's place when he entered. Also I was playing in the crooked game. And I saw him wreck Martin's place. Also, I heard him forbid Martin to start another place in Fairdale."

"Then he does do splendid things," she said softly, as if affirming it to herself.

I walked on, having gotten a glimpse of Colonel Longstreth in the background. Before I reached the corrals, Ruth came running after me, quite flushed and excited.

"Russ, Uncle wants to see you," she said. "He's in a bad temper. Don't . . . don't lose yours, please."

She actually shook my hand. What a child she was — in all ways except that fatal propensity to flirt. Her statement startled me out of any further thought of her. Why did Longstreth want to see me? He never noticed me. I dreaded facing him — not from fear, but because I must see more and more the signs of the guilt of Ray Longstreth's father.

He awaited me on the porch. As usual, he wore riding garb, but evidently he had not been out so far this day. He looked worn. There was a hinted, furtive shadow in his eyes. The haughty, imperious temper, despite Ruth's conviction, seemed to be in abeyance.

"Russ, what's this I hear about Martin's saloon being cleaned out?" he asked. "Dick can't give particulars."

Briefly and concisely I told the colonel exactly what had happened. He chewed his cigar, then spat it out with an unintelligible exclamation.

"Martin's no worse than the others," he said. "Blandy leans to crooked faro. I can't stop it. I've tried to stop that, anyway. If Steele can ... more power to him!"

Longstreth turned on his heel then and left me with a queer feeling of surprise and pity. He had surprised me before, but he had never roused the least sympathy. How probable was it that Longstreth was, indeed, powerless, no matter what his position? I had known men before then who had become involved in crime, yet were too manly to sanction a crookedness they could not help.

Miss Longstreth had been standing in the door. I could tell that she had heard. She looked agitated. I knew she had been talking to her father.

"Russ, he hates the ranger," she said. "That's what I fear. It'll bring trouble on us. Besides, like everybody here, he's biased. He can't see anything good in Steele. Yet he says ... 'More power to him!' I'm mystified, and, oh, I'm between two fires."

Steele's next noteworthy achievement was as new to me as it was strange to Fairdale. I heard a good deal about it from my acquaintances, some little from Steele, and the concluding incident I saw and heard myself. Andy McVey was a broken-down rustler whose activity had ceased and who spent his time hanging on at the places frequented by younger and better men of his kind. As he was a parasite, he was often thrown out of the dens. Moreover, it was an open secret that he had been a rustler, and the men with whom he associated had not yet, to most of Fairdale, become known as such.

One night McVey had been badly beaten in some back room of a saloon and carried out into a vacant lot and left there. He lay there all that night and all the next day. Probably he would have died there had not Steele happened along.

The ranger gathered up the crippled rustler, took him home, attended to his wounds, nursed him, and in fact spent days in the little adobe house with him. During this time I saw Steele twice at night, out at our rendezvous. He had little to communicate but was eager to hear when I had seen Laramie, Morton, Lawson, Longstreth, and all I could tell him about them, and the significance of things in town.

Andy McVey recovered, and it was my good fortune to be in the Hope So when he came in and addressed a crowd of gamesters there.

"Fellers," he said, "I'm biddin' good bye to them as was once my friends. I'm leavin' Fairdale. An' I'm askin' some of you to take thet good bye an' a partin' word to them as did me dirt.

"I ain't a-goin' to say if I'd crossed the trail of this ranger years ago thet I'd turned 'round an' gone straight. But mebbe I would . . . mebbe. There's a hell of a lot a man doesn't know till too late. I'm old now, ready fer the bone pile, an' it doesn't matter. But I've got a head on me yet, an' I want to give a hunch to thet gang who done me. An' that hunch wants to go around an' up to the big guns of Pecos.

"This Lone Star ranger was the feller who took me in. I'd died like a poisoned coyote but fer him. An' he talked to me. He gave me money to git out of Pecos. Mebbe everybody'll think he helped me because he wanted me to squeal. To squeal who's who 'round these rustler diggin's! Wal, he *never* asked me. Mebbe he seen I wasn't a squealer. But I'm thinkin' he wouldn't ask a feller thet, nohow.

"An' here's my hunch. Steele has spotted the outfit. Thet ain't so much, mebbe. But I've been with him, an' I'm old, figgerin' men. Jest as sure as God made little apples, he's a-goin' to stop thet outfit . . . or he's a-goin' to kill 'em."

CHAPTER TEN

Enter Jack Blome

STRANGE that the narrating of this incident made Ray Longstreth unhappy. When I told her, she exhibited one flash of gladness, such as any woman might have shown for a noble deed, and then she became thoughtful, almost gloomy, sad. I could not understand her complex emotions. Perhaps she contrasted Steele with her father; perhaps she wanted to believe in Steele and dared not; perhaps she had, all at once, seen the ranger in his true light and to her undoing. She bade me take Ruth for a ride and sought her room. I had my misgivings when I saw Ruth come out in that trim cowgirl suit and look at me as if to say, this day would be my Waterloo.

She rode hard and long ahead of me before she put any machinations into effect. The first one found me with a respectful demeanor but an internal conflict.

"Russ, tighten my cinch," she said when I caught up with her.

Dismounting, I drew the cinch up another hole and fastened it.

"My boot's unlaced, too," she added, slipping a shapely foot out of the stirrup.

To be sure, it was very much unlaced. I had to take off my gloves to lace it up, and I did it heroically, with bent head and outward calm, when all the time I was mad to snatch the girl out of the saddle and hold her tight or run off with her or do some like fool thing.

"Russ, I believe Ray's in love with Steele," she said soberly, with the sweet confidence she sometimes manifested in me.

"Small wonder! It's in the air," I replied.

She regarded me doubtfully. "It *was*," she retorted demurely.

"The fickleness of women is no new thing to me. I didn't expect Waters to last long."

"Certainly not when there are nicer fellows around. *One,* anyway, when he cares." A little brown hand slid out of its glove and dropped to my shoulder. "Make up. You've been hateful to me lately. Make up with me."

It was not so much what she said as the sweet tone of her voice and the

560

nearness of her that made a tumult within me. I felt the blood tingle to my face.

"Why should I make up with you?" I queried in self-defense. "You're only flirting. You won't . . . you can't ever be anything to me . . . really."

Ruth bent over me, and I had not the nerve to look up.

"Never mind things . . . really," she replied. "The future's far off. Let it alone. We're together. I . . . I like you, Russ. And I've got to be . . . to be loved. There! I never confessed that to any other man. You've been hateful when we might have had such fun. The rides in the sun . . . in the open with the wind in our faces. The walks at night in the moonlight. Russ, haven't you missed something?"

The sweetness and seductiveness of her, the little luring devil of her, were no more irresistible than were her naturalness, the truth of her. I trembled even before I looked up into her flushed face and arch eyes. After that I knew, if I could not frighten her out of this daring mood, I would have to yield despite my conviction that she only trifled. As my manhood, as well as duty to Steele, forced me to be unyielding, all that was left to me seemed to be to frighten her.

The instant this was decided, a wave of emotion — love, regret, bitterness, anger — surged over me, making me shake. I felt the skin on my face tighten and chill. I grasped her with strength that might have been needed to hold a plunging, unruly horse. I hurt her. I held her as in a vise. The action, the feel of her, her suddenly uttered cry wrought against all pretense, hurt me as my brutality hurt her, and then I spoke what was hard, passionate truth.

"Girl, you're playing with fire!" I cried out hoarsely. "I love you . . . love you as I'd want my sister loved. I asked you to marry me. That was proof, if it was foolish. Even if you were on the square, which you're not, we couldn't ever be anything to each other. Understand. There's a reason, besides your being above me. Now listen. Stop playing with me. I can't stand it. If you don't, I'll . . . I'll . . . "

Whatever I meant to say was not spoken, for Ruth turned deathly white, probably from my grasp and my looks as well as my threat. I let go of her and, stepping back to my horse, choked down my emotion.

"Russ!" she faltered, and there was womanliness and regret trembling with the fear in her voice. "I . . . I am on the square."

That had touched the real heart of the girl.

"If you are, then play the game square," I replied darkly.

"I will, Russ . . . I promise. I'll never tease or coax you again. If I do, then I'll deserve what you . . . what I get. But, Russ, don't think me a . . . a four-flush."

All the long ride home we did not exchange another word. The traveling gait of Ruth's horse was a lope, that of mine a trot, and, therefore, to my relief she was always out in front.

As we neared the ranch, however, Ruth slowed down until I caught up with her. Side by side we rode the remainder of the way. At the corrals, while I unsaddled, she lingered.

"Russ, you didn't tell me if you agreed with me about Ray," she said finally.

"Maybe you're right. I hope she's fallen in love with Steele. Lord knows, I hope so," I blurted out.

"Why?" she asked curiously.

I bit my tongue. There was no use in my trying to be as shrewd with women as I was with men. I made no reply.

"Misery loves company. Maybe that's why," she added. "You told me Steele lost his head over Ray at first sight. Well, we . . . all have company. Good night, Russ."

That night I told Steele about the singular effect the story of his treatment of McVey had had upon Miss Longstreth. He could not conceal his feelings. I read him like an open book. If she was unhappy because he did something really good, then she was unhappy because she was realizing she had wronged him. Steele never asked questions, but the hungry look in his big eyes was enough to make even a truthful fellow exaggerate things.

I told him how Ray was dressed, how her face had changed with each emotion, how her eyes had burned and softened and shadowed, how her voice had been deep and full when she admitted her father hated him, how much she must have meant when she said she was between two fires. I divined how he felt, and I tried to satisfy in some little measure his craving for news of her. When I had exhausted my fund and stretched my imagination, I was rewarded by being told that I was a regular old woman for gossip.

Much taken back by this remarkable statement, I could but gape at my comrade. Irritation had followed shortly upon his curiosity and pleasure, and then the old sane mind reasserted itself, the old stern look, a little sad now, replaced the glow, the strange eagerness of youth on his face.

"Son, I beg your pardon," he said, with his hand on my shoulder. "We're rangers, but we can't help being human. To speak right out, it seems two sweet and lovable girls have come, unfortunately for us all, across the dark trail we're on. Let us find what solace we can in the hope that somehow . . . God only knows how . . . in doing our duty as rangers we may yet be doing right by these two innocent girls. I ask you, as my friend, please do not speak again to me of . . . of Miss Longstreth."

I left him and went up the quiet trail with the thick shadows all around me and the cold stars overhead. I was sober in thought, sick at heart for him as much as for myself, and I tortured my mind in fruitless conjecture as to what the end of this strange and fateful adventure would be. I discovered that less and less the old wild spirit abided with me, and I became conscious of a dull, deep-seated ache in my breast, a pang in the bone.

From that day there was a change in Ray Longstreth. She became feverishly active. She wanted to ride, to see for herself what was going on in Fairdale, to learn of that wild Pecos country life at first hand. She made such demands on my time now that I scarcely ever found an hour to be with or near Steele until after dark. However, as he was playing a waiting game with the rustlers, keeping out of the resorts for the present, I had no great cause to worry. Laramie was slowly gathering together a band of trustworthy men, and, until this organization was complete and ready, Steele thought it better to go slow.

It was of little use for me to remonstrate with Miss Longstreth when she refused to obey a distracted and angry father. I began to feel sorry for the colonel. He was an unscrupulous man, but he loved this daughter who belonged to another and better past side of his life. I heard him appeal to her to go back to Louisiana, to let him take her home, giving as urgent reason the probability of trouble for him. She could not help, would only handicap him. She agreed to go, provided he sold his property, took the best of his horses, and went with her back to the old home to live there the rest of their lives. He replied with considerable feeling that he wished he could go, but it was impossible. Then that settled the matter for her, she averred.

Failing to persuade her to leave Fairdale, he told her to keep to the ranch. Naturally, in spite of his anger, Miss Longstreth refused to obey. She frankly told him that it was the free, unfettered life of the country, the riding here and there, that appealed so much to her.

Longstreth came to me a little later, and his worn face showed traces of internal storm. "Russ, for a while there I wanted to get rid of you," he said. "I've changed. Ray always was a spoiled kid. Now she's a woman. Something's fired her blood. Maybe it's this damned wild country. Anyway, she's got the bit between her teeth. She'll run till she's run herself out.

"Now, it seems the safety of Ray, and Ruth, too, has fallen into your hands. The girls won't have one of my cowboys near them. Lately they've gotten shy of Floyd, too. Between you and me I want to tell you that conditions here in Pecos are worse than they've seemed since you-all reached the ranch. And bad work will break out again . . . it's coming soon. I can't stop it. The town will be full of the hardest gang in western Texas. My daughter and Ruth would not be safe if left alone to go anywhere. With you, perhaps, they'll be safe. Can I rely on you?"

"Yes, Colonel Longstreth, you sure can," I replied. "I'm on pretty good terms with 'most everybody in town. I think I can say none of the tough set who hang out down there would ever make any move while I'm with the girls. But I'll be pretty careful to avoid that bunch and particularly strange fellows who may come riding in. And if any of them do meet us and get gay, I'm going for my gun, that's all. There won't be any talk."

"Good! I'll back you," Longstreth replied. "Understand, Russ, I didn't want you here, but I always had you sized up as a pretty hard nut . . . a man not to be trifled with. You've got a bad name. Ray insists the name's not deserved. She'd trust you with herself under any circumstances. And the kid, Ruth, she'd be fond of you if it wasn't for the drink. Have you been drunk a good deal? Straight, now, between you and me."

"Not once," I replied.

"Floyd's a liar then. He's had it in for you since that day at Sanderson. Look out you two don't clash. He's got a temper, and, when he's drinking, he's a devil. Keep out of his way."

"I've stood a great deal from Lawson, and guess I can stand more."

"All right, Russ," he continued, as if relieved. "Chuck the drink and cards for a while and keep an eye on these girls. When my affairs straighten out, maybe I'll make you a proposition."

Longstreth left me material for thought. It must have been more than the presence of a ranger in town that gave him concern, or the willfulness of his daughter. There must be internal strife in the rustler gang with which we had associated him. Perhaps a menace of publicity, rather than risk, was the cause of the wearing strain on him. I began to get a closer insight into Longstreth, and in the absence of any conclusive evidence of his personal baseness I felt pity for him.

In the beginning he had opposed me just because I did not happen to be a cowboy he had selected. This latest interview with me, amounting in some instances to confidence, proved absolutely that he had not the slightest suspicion that I was otherwise than the cowboy I pretended to be. Another interesting deduction was that he appeared to be out of patience with Lawson. In fact, I imagined I sensed something of fear and distrust in this spoken attitude toward his relative. Not improbably here was the internal strife — between Longstreth and Lawson — and there flashed into my mind, absolutely with good reason, the idea that the clash was over Ray Longstreth.

I scouted this intuitive idea as absurd, but, just the same, it refused to be dismissed. As I turned my back on the coarse and exciting life in the saloons and gambling hells, and spent all my time, except when sleeping, out in the windy open, under blue sky and starry heaven, my spirit had an uplift. I was glad to be free of that job. It was bad enough to have to go into those dens to arrest men, let alone living with them, almost being one.

Ray Longstreth noted a change in me, attributed it to the absence of the influence of drink, and was glad. Ruth made no attempt to conceal her happiness, and, to my dismay, she utterly failed to keep her promise not to tease or tempt me further. She was adorable, distracting. We rode every day and almost all day. We took our dinner and went clear to the foothills, to return as the sun set. We visited outlying ranches, water holes, old adobe houses famous in one way or another as scenes of past fights between rustlers and ranchers.

We rode to the little village, Longstreth, and half way to Sanderson, and all over the country. There was no satisfying Miss Longstreth with rides, new places, new faces, new adventures. And every time we rode out, she insisted on first riding through Fairdale. And every time we rode home, she insisted on going back that way. We visited all the stores, the blacksmith, the wagon shop, the feed and grain houses — everywhere that she could find excuse for visiting. I had to point out to her all the infamous dens in town and all the lawless and lounging men we met.

She insisted upon being shown the inside of the Hope So, to the extreme confusion of that bewildered resort. I pretended to be blind to this restless curiosity. Ruth understood the cause, too, and it divided her between a sweet gravity and a naughty humor. The last, however, she never evinced in sight or hearing of Ray.

It seemed that we were indeed fated to cross the path of Vaughn Steele. We saw him, working around his adobe house. Then we saw him on horseback. Once we met him face to face in a store. He gazed steadily into Ray Longstreth's eyes and went his way without any sign of recognition. There was red in her face when he passed and white when he had gone. That day she rode as I had never seen her, risking her life, unmindful of her horse. Another day we met Steele down in the valley, where, inquiry discovered to us, he had gone to the home of an old cattleman who lived alone and was ill. Last, and perhaps most significant of all these meetings, was the one when we were walking tired horses home through the main street of Fairdale, and we came upon Steele just in time to see him in action.

It happened at a corner where the usual slouchy, shirt-sleeved loungers were congregated. They were in high glee over the predicament of one ruffian who had purchased or been given a poor, emaciated little burro that was on his last legs. The burro evidently did not want to go with its new owner who pulled on a halter and then viciously swung the end of the rope to make welts on the worn and scarred back. If there was one thing that Ray Longstreth could not bear, it was to see an animal in pain. She passionately loved horses and hated the sight of a spur or whip.

When we saw the man beating the little burro, she cried out to me: "Make the brute stop!"

I might have made a move had I not on the instant seen Steele heaving into sight around the corner. Just then the fellow, whom I now recognized to be a despicable character named Andrews, began to bestow heavy and brutal kicks upon the body of the little burro. These kicks sounded deep, hollow, almost like the boom of a drum. The burro uttered the strangest sound I ever heard issue from any beast, and it dropped in its tracks with jerking legs that told any horseman what had happened.

Steele saw the last swings of Andrews's heavy foot. He yelled. It was a sharp yell that would have made anyone start. But it came too late, for the burro had dropped.

Steele knocked over several of the jeering men to get to Andrews. He kicked the fellow's feet from under him, sending him hard to the ground. Then Steele picked up the end of the halter and began to swing it powerfully. Resounding smacks mingled with hoarse bellows of fury and pain. Andrews flopped here and there, trying to rise, but every time the heavy knotted halter beat him down.

Presently Steele stopped. Andrews rose right in front of the ranger, and there, like the madman he was, he went for his gun. But it scarcely leaped from its holster when Steele's swift hand intercepted it. Steele clutched Andrews's arm. Then came a wrench, a cracking of bones, of scream of agony. The gun dropped into the dust, and in a moment of wrestling fury Andrews, broken, beaten down, just able to moan, lay beside it. Steele — so cool and dark for a man who had acted with such passionate swiftness — faced the others as if to dare them to move. They neither moved nor spoke, and then he strode away.

Miss Longstreth did not speak a word while we were riding the rest of the way home, but she was strangely white of face and dark of eye. Ruth could not speak fast enough to say all she felt. I, of course, had my measure of feelings. One of them was that, as sure as the sun rose and set, it was written that Ray Longstreth was to love Vaughn Steele.

I could not read her mind, but I had a mind of my own. How could any woman, seeing this maligned and menaced ranger, whose life was in danger every moment he spent on the streets, in the light of his action on behalf of a poor little beast help but wonder and brood over the magnificent height he might reach if he had love — passion — a woman for his inspiration?

It was the day after this incident that, as Ray, Ruth, and I were riding homeward on the road from Longstreth, I caught sight of a group of dark horses and riders swiftly catching up with us. We were on the main road in plain sight of town and passing by ranches. Nevertheless, I did not like the looks of the horsemen and grew uneasy. Still, I scarcely thought it needful to race our horses just to reach town a little ahead of these strangers. Accordingly, they soon caught up with us.

They were five in number, all dark-faced except one, dark-clad, and superbly mounted on dark bays and blacks. They had no pack animals, and, for that matter, carried no packs at all. Four of them at a swinging canter passed us, and the fifth pulled his horse to suit our pace and fell in behind Ruth and me.

"Good day," he said pleasantly to me. "Don't mind my ridin' in with you-all, I hope?"

Considering his pleasant approach, I could not but be civil. He was a singularly handsome fellow, at a quick glance under forty years, with curly, blond hair, almost gold, a skin very fair for that country, and the keenest, clearest, boldest blue eyes I had ever seen in a man.

"You're Russ, I reckon," he said. "Some of my men have seen you ridin' 'round with Longstreth's girls. I'm Jack Blome."

He did not speak that name with any flaunt or flourish. He merely stated it. Blome, the rustler! I grew tight all over.

Still, manifestly there was nothing for me to do but return his pleasantry. I really felt less uneasiness after he had made himself known to me. And without any awkwardness I introduced him to the girls. He took off his sombrero and made gallant bows to both.

Miss Longstreth had heard of him and his record, and she could not help a paleness, a shrinking, which, however, he did not appear to notice. Ruth had been dying to meet a real rustler, and here he was, a very prince of rascals. But I gathered that she would require a little time before she could be natural. Blome seemed to have more of an eye for Ruth than for Ray.

"Do you like Pecos?" he asked Ruth.

"Out here? Oh, yes, indeed!" she replied.

"Like ridin'?"

"I love horses."

Like almost every man who made Ruth's acquaintance, he hit upon the subject best calculated to make her interesting to free-riding, outdoor Western men. That he loved a Thoroughbred horse himself was plain. He spoke naturally to Ruth with interest, just as I had upon first meeting her, and he might not have been Jack Blome for all the indication he gave of the fact in his talk. But the look of the man was different. He was a desperado — one of the dashing, reckless kind — more famous along the Pecos and Rio Grande than really more desperate men. His attire proclaimed a vanity seldom seen in any Westerner except of that unusual brand, yet it was neither gaudy or showy.

One had to be close to Blome to see the silk, the velvet, the gold, the fine leather. When I envied a man's spurs, then they were indeed worth coveting. Blome had a short rifle and a gun in saddle sheaths. My sharp eye, running over him, caught a row of notches on the bone handle of the big Colt he packed. It was then that the marshal, the ranger in me, went hot under the collar. The custom that desperadoes and gun-fighters had of cutting a notch on their guns for every man killed was one of which the mere mention made my gorge rise.

At the edge of town Blome doffed his sombrero again, said "Adios," and rode on ahead of us. It was then I was hard put to keep tracks of the queries, exclamations, and other wild talk of two very much excited young ladies. I wanted to think. I needed to think.

"Wasn't he lovely? Oh, I could adore him!" rapturously uttered Miss Ruth Herbert several times, to my ultimate disgust.

Also, after Blome had ridden out of sight, Miss Longstreth lost the evident effect of his sinister presence, and she joined Miss Herbert in paying the rustler compliments, too. Perhaps my irritation was an indication of the quick and subtle shifting of my mind to harsher thoughts.

"Jack Blome!" I broke in upon their adulations. "Rustler and gunman. Did you see the notches on his gun? Every notch for a man he killed! For weeks reports have come to Fairdale that soon as he could get around to it he'd ride down and rid the community of that bothersome fellow . . . that Lone Star ranger. He's come to kill Vaughn Steele."

CHAPTER ELEVEN

Ray and Vaughn

THEN, as gloom descended on me with my uttered thought, my heart smote me at Ruth's broken: "Oh, Russ. No. No!"

Ray Longstreth bent dark, shocked eyes upon the hill and ranch in front of her, but they were sightless. They looked into space and eternity, and in them I read a truth suddenly and cruelly revealed to her — she loved Steele.

I found it impossible to leave Miss Longstreth with the impression I had given. My own mood fitted a kind of ruthless pleasure in seeing her suffer through love as I had intimation I was to suffer. But now, when my strange desire that she should love Steele had its fulfillment, and my fiendish subtleties to that end had been crowned with success, I was confounded in pity and the enormity of my crime. For it had been a crime to make, or help to make, this noble and beautiful woman love a ranger, the enemy of her father, and surely the author of her coming misery. I felt shocked at my work. I tried to hang excuse on my old motive that through her love we might all be saved. When it was too late, however, I found that this motive was wrong and perhaps without warrant.

We rode home in silence. Miss Longstreth, contrary to her usual custom of riding to the corrals or the porch, dismounted at a path leading in among the trees and flowers.

"I want to rest . . . to think before I go in," she said.

Ruth accompanied me to the corrals. As our horses stopped at the gate, I turned to find confirmation of my fears in Ruth's wet eyes.

"Archie," she said — I had told her my middle name which she had since abbreviated to her taste and now tended to use it all the time — "it's worse than we thought."

"Worse? I should say so," I replied.

"It'll about kill her. She never cared that way for any man. When the Longstreth women love, they love."

"Well, you're lucky to be a Herbert," I retorted bitterly.

"I'm Longstreth enough to be unhappy," she flashed back at me, "and I'm

Herbert enough to have some sense. You haven't any sense or kindness, either. Why'd you want to blurt out that Jack Blome was here to kill Steele?"

"I'm ashamed, Ruth," I returned with hanging head. "I've been a brute. I've wanted her to love Steele. I thought I had a reason, but now it seems silly. Just now I wanted to see how much she did care. Ruth, the other day you said misery loved company. That's my trouble. I'm sore . . . bitter. I'm like a sick coyote that snaps at everything. I've wanted you to go into the very depths of despair. But I couldn't send *you*. So I took out my spite on poor Miss Longstreth. It was a damn' unmanly thing for me to have done."

"Oh, it's not so bad as all that. But you might have been less abrupt. Archie, you seem to take an . . . an awful tragic view of your . . . your own case."

"Tragic? Hah!" I cried like the villain in a play. "What other way could I look at it? I tell you I love you so I can't sleep . . . or do anything."

"*That's* not tragic. When you've no chance . . . then . . . that's tragic."

Ruth, as swiftly as she had blushed, could change into that deadly sweet mood. She did both now. She seemed warm, softened, agitated. How could this be anything but sincere? I felt myself slipping, so I laughed harshly.

"Chance! I've no chance on earth."

"Try!" she whispered.

But I caught myself in time. Then the shock of bitter renunciation made it easy for me to simulate anger.

"You promised not to . . . not to . . . ," I choked. My voice was hoarse, and it broke — a state surely far removed from pretense.

I had seen Ruth Herbert in varying degrees of emotion, but never as she appeared now. She was pale, and she trembled a little. If it was not fright, then I could not tell what it was. But there were contrition and earnestness about her, too.

"Archie, I know. I promised not to . . . to tease . . . to tempt you any more," she faltered. "I've broken it. I'm ashamed. I haven't played the game squarely. But I couldn't . . . I can't help myself . . . I've got sense enough not to engage myself to you, but I can't keep from loving you. I can't let you alone. There . . . if you want it on the square! What's more, I'll go on . . . as I have done . . . unless you keep away from me. I don't care what I deserve . . . what you do . . . I will . . . I *will!*"

She had begun falteringly, and she ended passionately. Somehow I kept my head, even though my heart pounded like a hammer, and the blood drummed in my ears. It was the thought of Steele that saved me. But I felt cold at the narrow margin. I had reached a point, I feared, where a kiss, one touch from this bewildering creature of fire and change and sweetness would make me put her before Steele and my duty.

"Ruth, if you dare break your promise again, you'll wish you never had been born," I said with all the fierceness at my command.

"I wish that now. And you can't bluff *me*, Mister Gambler. I may have no hand to play, but you can't make me lay it down," she replied.

Something told me Ruth Herbert was finding herself, that presently I could not frighten her, and then . . . then I would be doomed. "Why, if I got drunk, I might do anything," I said, cool and hard now. "Cut off your beautiful chestnut hair for bracelets for my arms."

Ruth laughed, but she was still white. She was indeed finding herself. "If you ever get drunk again, you can't kiss me any more. And if you don't . . . you *can*."

I felt myself shake. With all of the iron will I could assert, I hid from her the sweetness of this thing that was my weakness and her strength. "I might lasso you from my horse, drag you through the cactus," I added with the implacability of an Apache.

"Archie!" she cried. Something in that last ridiculous threat had found a vital mark. "After all, maybe those awful stories Joel Harkness told about you were true."

"They sure were," I declared with great relief. "And now to forget ourselves . . . I'm more than sorry I distressed Miss Longstreth, more than sorry because what I said wasn't on the square. Blome, no doubt, has come to Fairdale after Steele. His intention is to kill him. I said that . . . let Miss Longstreth think it all meant fatality to the ranger. But, Ruth, I don't believe that Blome can kill Steele any more than . . . than *you* can."

"Why?" she asked, and she seemed eager, glad.

"Because he's not man enough. That's all, without details. You need not worry, and I wish you'd go tell Miss Longstreth . . . "

"Go yourself," interrupted Ruth. "I think she's afraid of my eyes. But she won't fear you've guessed her secret. Go to her, Archie. Find some excuse to tell her. Say you thought it over . . . believed she'd be distressed about what might never happen. Go . . . and afterward pray for your sins, you strange, good-natured, love-meddling cowboy devil, you!"

For once I had no retort ready for Ruth. I hurried off as quickly as I could walk in chaps and spurs. I found Miss Longstreth sitting on a bench in the shade of a tree. Her pallor and quiet composure told of the conquering and passing of the storm. Always she had a smile for me, and now it smote me, for I, in a sense, had betrayed her.

"Miss Longstreth," I began awkwardly yet swiftly, "I . . . I got to thinking it over, and the idea struck me . . . maybe you felt bad about this gunfighter, Blome, coming down here to kill Steele. At first I imagined you felt sick just because there might be blood spilled. Then I thought you've showed interest in Steele . . . naturally *his* kind of ranger work is bound to appeal to women . . . you might be sorry it couldn't go on . . . you might care."

"Russ, don't beat about the bush," she said, interrupting my foundering. "You know I care."

How wonderful her eyes were then — great, dark, sad gulfs with the soul of a woman at the bottom. Almost I loved her myself — I did love her truth, the woman of her that scorned any subterfuge. Instantly she inspired me to take command over myself.

"Listen," I said, "Jack Blome has come here to meet Steele. There will be a fight. But Blome *can't* kill Steele."

"How is that? Why can't he? You said this Blome was a killer of men. You spoke of notches on his gun. I've heard my father and my cousin, too, speak of Blome's record. He must be a terrible ruffian. If his intent is evil, *why* will he fail in it?"

"Because, Miss Longstreth, when it comes to the last word, Steele will be on the look-out, and Blome won't be quick enough on the draw to kill him. That's all."

"Quick enough on the draw? I understand, but I want to know more."

"I doubt if there's a man on the frontier today quick enough to kill Steele in an even break. That means a fair fight. This Blome is conceited. He'll make the meeting fair enough. It'll come off about like this, Miss Longstreth. Blome will send out his bluff . . . he'll begin to blow . . . to look for Steele. But Steele will avoid him as long as possible, perhaps altogether, though that's improbable. If they do meet, then Blome must force the issue. It's interesting to figure on that.

"Steele affects men strangely. It's all very well for this Blome to rant about himself and to hunt Steele up. But the test'll come when he faces the ranger. He never saw Steele. He doesn't know what he's up against. He knows Steele's reputation, but I don't mean that. I mean Steele in the flesh, his nerve, the something that's in his eyes. Now, when it comes to handling a gun, the man doesn't breathe who has anything on Steele. There was an outlaw . . . Duane . . . who might have killed Steele, had they ever met. I'll tell you Buck Duane's story some day. A girl saved him, made a ranger of him, then got him to go far away from Texas."

"That was wise. Indeed, I'd like to hear the story," she replied. "Then, after all, Russ, in this dreadful part of Texas life, when man faces man, it's all in the quickness of hand?"

"Absolutely. It's the draw. And Steele's a wonder. See here. Look at this."

I stepped back and drew my gun.

"I didn't see how you did that," she said curiously. "Try it again."

I complied, and still she was not quick enough of eye to see my draw. Then I did it slowly, explaining to her the action of hand and then of finger. She seemed fascinated, as a woman might have been by the striking power of a rattlesnake.

"So men's lives depend on that! How horrible for me to be interested . . . to ask about it . . . to watch you. But I'm out here on the frontier now, caught somehow in its wildness, and I feel a relief, a gladness to know Vaughn Steele has the skill you claim. Thank you, Russ."

She seemed about to dismiss me then, for she rose and half turned away. Then she hesitated. She had one hand at her breast, the other on the bench.

"Have you been with him . . . talked to him lately?" she asked, and a faint rose tint came into her cheeks. But her eyes were steady, dark, and deep, and peered through and far beyond me.

"Yes, I've met him a few times . . . around places."

"Did he ever speak of . . . of me?"

"Once or twice, and then as if he couldn't help it."

"What did he say?"

"Well, the last time he seemed hungry to hear something about you. He didn't exactly ask, but, all the same, he was begging. So I told him."

"What?"

"Oh, how you were dressed, how you looked, what you said, what you did . . . all about you. Don't be offended with me, Miss Longstreth. It was real charity. I talk too much. It's my weakness. Please don't be offended."

She never heard my apology or my entreaty. There was a kind of glory in her eyes. Looking at her, I found a dimness hazing my sight, and, when I rubbed it away, it came back.

"Then . . . what did he say?" This was whispered, almost shyly, and I could scarcely believe the proud Miss Longstreth stood before me.

"Why, he flew into a fury, called me an . . . " Hastily I caught myself. "Well, he said if I wanted to talk to him any more not to speak of you. Sure he was unreasonable."

"Russ . . . you think . . . you told me once . . . he . . . you think he still . . . ?"

She was not facing me at all now. She had her head bent. Both hands were at her breast, and I saw it heave. Her cheek was white as a flower — her neck darkly, richly red with mounting blood.

I understood. And I pitied her, hated myself, and marveled at this thing, love. It made another woman out of Ray Longstreth. I could scarcely comprehend that she was asking me, almost beseechingly, for further assurance of Steele's love. I knew nothing of women, but this seemed strange. Then a thought sent the blood, chilling, back to my heart. Had Ray Longstreth guessed the guilt of her father? Was it more for his sake than for her own that she hoped — for surely she hoped — that Steele loved her?

Here was more mystery, more food for reflection. Only a powerful motive or a self-leveling love could have made a woman of Ray Longstreth's pride ask such a question. Whatever her reason, I determined to assure her, once and forever, what I knew to be true. Accordingly I told her in unforgettable words, with my own regard for her and love for Ruth filling my voice with emotion, how I could see that Steele loved her, how madly he was destined to love her, how terribly hard that was going to make his work in Fairdale.

There was a stillness about her then, a light on her face which brought to my mind thought of Ruth when I had asked her to marry me. "Russ, I beg you . . . bring us together," said Miss Longstreth, "bring about a meeting. You are my friend."

Then she went swiftly away through the flowers, leaving me there, thrilled to my soul at her betrayal of herself, ready to die in her service, yet cursing the fatal day Vaughn Steele had chosen me for his comrade in this tragic game.

That evening in the girls' sitting room, where they invited me, I was led into a discourse upon the gunfighters, outlaws, desperadoes, and badmen of the frontier. Miss Longstreth and Ruth had been, before their arrival in Texas, as ignorant of such characters as any girls in the North or East. They were now peculiarly interested, fascinated, and at the same time repelled. Miss Longstreth must have placed the rangers in one of those classes, somewhat as Governor Stone had and her father, too. Ruth thought she was in love with a cowboy whom she had been led to believe had as bad a record as any. They were certainly a most persuasive and appreciative audience.

So, as it was in regard to horses, if I knew any subject well, it was this one of dangerous and bad men. Texas, and the whole developing Southwest, was full of such characters. It was a very difficult thing to distinguish between fighters who were badmen and fighters who were good men. However, it was no difficult thing for one of my calling to tell the difference between a real badman and the imitation four-flush. I told the girls the story of Buck Duane, the famous outlaw and ranger. And I narrated the histories of Murrell, most terrible of blood-spillers ever known to Texas; of Hardin, whose long career of crime ended in the main street in Huntsville when he faced Buck Duane; of Sandobal, the Mexican terror; of Cheseldine, Bland, Alloway, and other outlaws of the Rio Grande; of King Fisher and Thompson and Sterrett, all still living and still busy, adding notches to their guns.

I ended my little talk by telling the story of Amos Clark, a criminal of a higher type than most badmen, yet infinitely more dangerous because of that. He was a Southerner of good family. After the war he went to Dimmick County and there developed and prospered with the country. He became the most influential citizen of his town and the richest in that section. He held offices. He was energetic in his opposition to rustlers and outlaws. He was held in high esteem by his countrymen. But this Amos Clark was the leader of a band of rustlers, highwaymen, and murderers. Captain MacNeal and some of his rangers ferreted out Clark's relation to this lawless gang and in the end caught him red-handed. He was arrested and eventually hanged. His case was unusual, and it furnished an example of what was possible in this wild country. Clark had a son who was honest and a wife whom he dearly loved, both of whom had been utterly ignorant of the other and wicked side of his life.

I told this last story deliberately, yet with some misgivings. I wanted to see — I convinced myself it was needful for me to see — if Miss Longstreth had any suspicion of her father. To look into her face then was no easy task. But, when I did, I experienced a shock, though not exactly the kind I had prepared myself for. She knew something. Maybe she knew actually more than Steele or I. Still, if it were crime, she had a marvelous control over her true feelings.

Jack Blome and his men had been in Fairdale for several days. Old Snecker and his son, Bo, had reappeared, and other hard-looking customers, new to me if not to Fairdale — these helped to create a charged and waiting atmosphere. The saloons did unusual business and were never closed. Respectable citizens of the town were awakened in the early dawn by rowdies, carousing in the streets.

Steele kept pretty closely undercover. He did not entertain the opinion, nor did I, that the first time he walked down street he would be a target for Blome and his gang. Things seldom happened that way, and, when they did happen so, it was more accident than design. Blome was setting the stage for his little drama.

Meanwhile Steele was not idle. He told me he had met Laramie, Morton, Zimmer, and that these men had approached others of like character. A secret club had been formed, and all the members were ready for action.

Steele also told me that he had spent hours at night, watching the house where Floyd Lawson stayed when he was not up at Longstreth's. Lawson had almost recovered from the injury to his arm, but he still remained for the most of the time indoors. At night he was visited, or at least the house was, by strange men who were swift, stealthy, mysterious — all that merely kindly disposed friends or neighbors would not have been. Steele had not been able to recognize any of these night visitors, and he did not think the time was ripe for a bold holding up of one of them. Nevertheless, he was sure such an event would discover Lawson, or someone in that house, to be in touch with crooked men.

Laramie had forcibly declared and repeated that some deviltry was afoot — something vastly different from Jack Blome's open intention of meeting the ranger. Laramie was right. Not twenty-four hours after his last talk with Steele, in which he advised quick action, he was found behind the little bar of his restaurant with a bullet hole in his breast, dead. No one could be found who had heard a shot.

It had been deliberate murder, for upon the bar had been left a piece of paper rudely scrawled with a pencil:

ALL FRIENDS OF RANGER STEELE LOOK FOR THE SAME.

Later that day I met Steele at Laramie's and was with him when he looked at the body and the written message which spoke so tersely of the deadly enmity toward him. We left there together, and I hoped Steele would let me stay with him from that moment.

"Russ, it's all in the dark," he said, "but I feel Lawson's hand in this."

"I thought of him first," I replied.

"Why?"

"Hard to say. Because I remember his face at Laramie's that day you winged him. Because Jim swore you were wrong not to kill instead of cripple him. You *were* wrong."

"No, Russ, I never let feeling run away with my head. We can't prove anything on Lawson."

"Come on, let's hunt him up. I'll bet you I can accuse him and make him show his hand. Come on."

That Steele found me hard to resist was all the satisfaction I got for the anger and desire to avenge Laramie that consumed me.

"Old son, you'll have your belly full of trouble soon enough," replied Steele. "Hold yourself in. Wait. Try to keep your eye on Longstreth at night. See if anyone visits him. Spy on him. I'll watch Lawson."

"Don't you think you'd do well to keep out of town, especially when you sleep?"

"Sure. I've got blankets out in the brush, and I go there every night late and leave before daylight. But I keep a light burning in the 'dobe house and make it look as if I were there."

"Good. That worried me. Now, what's this murder of Laramie going to do to Morton, Zimmer, and their crowd?"

"Russ, they've all got blood in their eyes. This'll make them see red. I've only to say the word, and we'll have all the backing we need."

"Have you run into Blome?"

"Once. I was across the street. He came out of the Hope So with some of his gang. They lined up and watched me. But I went right on."

"He's looking for trouble, Steele."

"Yes, and he'd have found it before this, if I just knew his relation to Longstreth and Lawson."

"Do you think Blome a dangerous man to meet?"

"Hardly. He's a genuine badman, but for all that he's not much to be feared. If he were quietly keeping away from trouble, then that'd be different. Blome will probably die in his boots, thinking he's the worst man and the quicker one on the draw in the West."

That was conclusive enough for me. The little shadow of worry that had haunted me in spite of my confidence vanished entirely.

"Russ, for the present, help me do something for Laramie's family," Steele went on. "His wife's in bad shape. She's not a strong woman. There are a lot of kids, and you know Laramie was poor. She told me her neighbors would keep shy of her now. They'd be afraid. Oh, it's tough! But we can put Jim away decently and help his family."

Several hours after this talk with Steele I took Miss Longstreth and Ruth out to see Laramie's wife and children. I knew Steele would be there that afternoon, but I did not mention this fact to Miss Longstreth.

We rode down to the little adobe house, which belonged to Mrs. Laramie's people and where Steele and I had moved her and the children after Laramie's funeral. The house was small, but comfortable, and the yard green and shady. If this poor wife and mother had not been utterly forsaken by neighbors and friends, it certainly appeared so, for to my knowledge no one besides Steele and me visited her.

Miss Longstreth had packed a big basket full of good things to eat, and I carried this in front of me on the pommel as we rode. We hitched our horses to the fence and went around to the back of the house. There was a little porch with a stone flooring, and here several children were playing.

The door stood open. At my knock Mrs. Laramie bade me come in. Evidently Steele was not there. So I went in with the girls.

"Missus Laramie, I've brought Miss Longstreth and her cousin to see you," I said cheerfully.

The little room was not very light, there being only one window and the door, but Mrs. Laramie could be seen plainly enough as she lay, hollow-cheeked and haggard, on a bed. Once she had evidently been a woman of some comeliness. The ravages of trouble and grief were there to read in her worn face. She had not, however, any of the hard and bitter lines that had characterized her husband. I wondered, considering that Longstreth had ruined Laramie, how Mrs. Laramie was going to regard the daughter of an enemy.

"So you're Granger Longstreth's girl?" queried the woman, with her bright black eyes fixed on her visitor.

"Yes," replied Miss Longstreth simply. "This is my cousin, Ruth Herbert. We've come to nurse you, take care of the children, help you in any way you'll let us."

There was a long silence.

"Well, you look a little like Longstreth," said Mrs. Laramie finally, "but you're not *at all* like him. You must take after your mother. . . . Miss Longstreth, I don't know if I can . . . if I ought to accept anything from you. Your father ruined my husband."

"Yes, I know," replied the girl sadly. "That's all the more reason you should let me help you. Pray don't refuse. It will . . . mean so much to me."

If this poor, stricken woman had any resentment, it speedily melted in the warmth and sweetness of Miss Longstreth's manner. My idea was that the impression of Ray Longstreth's beauty was always swiftly succeeded by that of her generosity and nobility.

At any rate, she had started well with Mrs. Laramie, and, no sooner had she begun to talk to the children, than both they and the mother were won. The opening of that big basket was an event. Poor, starved little beggars. I went out on the porch to get away from them. My feelings seemed too easily aroused.

Hard, indeed, would it have gone with Jim Laramie's slayer, if I could have laid my eyes on him then. However, Miss Longstreth and Ruth, after the nature of tender and practical girls, did not appear to take the sad situation to heart. The havoc was wrought in that household. The needs now were cheerfulness, kindness, help, action — and these the girls furnished with a spirit that did me good.

"Missus Laramie, who dressed this baby?" Miss Longstreth asked presently.

I peeped in to see a dilapidated youngster on her knees. That sight, if any other was needed, completed my full and splendid estimate of Ray Longstreth.

"Mister Steele," replied Mrs. Laramie.

"Mister Steele!" exclaimed Miss Longstreth.

"Yes, he's taken care of us all since . . . since . . . " Mrs. Laramie choked.

"Oh, so you've had no help but his," replied Miss Longstreth hastily. "No women? Too bad. I'll send someone, Missus Laramie, and I'll come myself."

"It'll be good of you," went on the older woman. "You see, Jim had few friends . . . that is, right in town. And they've been afraid to help us . . . afraid they'd get what poor Jim . . . "

"That's awful!" burst out Miss Longstreth passionately. "A brave lot of friends! Missus Laramie, don't you worry any more. We'll take care of you. Here, Ruth, help me. Whatever is the matter with baby's dress?"

Manifestly Miss Longstreth had some difficulty in subduing her emotion.

"Why, it's on hind side before," declared Ruth. "I guess Mister Steele hasn't dressed many babies."

"He did the best he could," said Mrs. Laramie. "Lord only knows what would have become of us. He brought your cowboy, Russ, who's been very good, too."

"Mister Steele, then, is . . . is something more than a ranger?" queried Miss Longstreth with a little break in her voice.

"He's more than I can tell," replied Mrs. Laramie. "He buried Jim. He paid our debts. He fetched us here. He bought food for us. He cooked for us and fed us. He washed and dressed the baby. He sat with me the first two nights after Jim's death, when I thought I'd die myself. He's so kind, so gentle, so patient. He has kept me up just by being near. Sometimes I'd wake from a doze an', seeing him there, I'd know how false were all these tales Jim heard about him and believed at first. Why, he plays with the children just . . . just like any good man might. When he has the baby up, I just can't believe he's a bloody gunman, as they say.

"He's good, but he isn't happy. He has such sad eyes. He looks far off sometimes when the children climb 'round him. They love him. I think he must have loved some woman. His life is sad. Nobody need tell me . . . he sees the good in things. Once he said somebody had to be a ranger. Well, I say, thank God for a ranger like him!"

After that, there was a long silence in the little room, broken only by the cooing of the baby. I did not dare to peep in at Miss Longstreth then.

Somehow I expected Steele to arrive at that moment, and his step did not surprise me. He came around the corner as he always turned any corner, quick, alert, with his hand down. If I had been an enemy, waiting there with a gun, I would have needed to hurry. Steele was instinctively and habitually on the defense.

"Hello, old son! How are Missus Laramie and the youngsters today?" he asked.

"Hello yourself! Why, they're doing fine!" I stepped into the room after him. "I brought the girls down . . . "

Then in the semi-shadow of the room, across Mrs. Laramie's bed, Ray Longstreth and Steele faced each other. That was a moment! Having seen her face then I would not have missed sight of it for anything I could name. Never so long as memory remained with me would I forget. She did not speak.

Ruth, however, bowed and spoke to the ranger. Steele, after the first start, showed no unusual feeling. He greeted both girls pleasantly.

"Russ, that was thoughtful of you," he said. "It was womankind needed here. I could do so little . . . Missus Laramie, you look better today. I'm glad. . . . And here's baby, all clean and white. Baby, what a time I had trying to puzzle out the way your clothes went on! Well, Missus Laramie, didn't I tell you . . . friends would come? So will the brighter side."

"Yes, I've more faith than I had," replied Mrs. Laramie. "Granger Longstreth's daughter has come to me. There for a while after Jim's death I thought I'd sink. We have nothing. How could I ever take care of my little ones? But I'm gaining courage to . . . "

"Missus Laramie, do not distress yourself any more," said Miss Longstreth.

"I shall see . . . you are well cared for. I promise you."

"Miss Longstreth, that's fine!" exclaimed Steele with a ring in his voice. "It's what I'd have hoped . . . expected of you."

It must have been sweet praise to her, for the whiteness of her face burned out in a beautiful blush.

"And it's good of you, too, Miss Herbert, to come," added Steele. "Let me thank you both. I'm glad to have you girls as allies in part of my lonely task here. More than glad for the sake of this good woman and the little ones. But both of you be careful. Don't stir without Russ. There's risk. And now I'll be going. Good bye. Missus Laramie, I'll drop in again tonight. Good bye."

Steele backed to the door, and I slipped out beside him.

"Mister Steele . . . wait!" called Miss Longstreth as he stepped out.

He uttered a little sound like a hiss, or a gasp, or an intake of breath, I did not know what, and then the incomprehensible fellow bestowed a kick upon me that I thought about broke my leg. But I understood and gamely endured the pain.

Then we were looking at Ray Longstreth. She was white and wonderful. She stepped out of the door, close to Steele. She did not see me. She cared nothing for my presence. All the world would not have mattered to her then.

"I have wronged you," she said impulsively.

Looking on, I seemed to see or feel some slow, mighty force gathering in Steele to meet this ordeal. Then he appeared to me as always — yet, to me, how different!

"Miss Longstreth, how can you say that?" he returned.

"I believed what my father and Floyd Lawson said about you . . . that bloody, despicable record! Now I do not believe. I see . . . I wronged you."

"You make me very glad when you tell me. It was hard to have you think so ill of me. But, Miss Longstreth, please don't speak of wronging me. I *am* a ranger . . . and much said of me is true. My duty is hard on others . . . sometimes on those who are innocent, alas. But God knows that duty is hard, too, on me."

"I *did* wrong you. In thought . . . in word. I ordered you from my home as if you were, indeed, what they called you. But I was deceived. I see my error. If you entered my home again, I would think it an honor. I . . . "

"Please . . . please don't, Miss Longstreth," interrupted poor Steele. I could see that gray beneath his bronze and something that was like gold deep in his eyes.

"But, sir, my conscience flays me," she went on.

There was no other sound like her voice. If I was all distraught with emotion, what must Steele have been?

"I make amends. Will you take my hand? Will you forgive me?"

She gave it royally, while the other was there pressing at her breast.

Steele took the proffered hand and held it, and did not release it. What else could he have done? But he could not speak.

Then it seemed to dawn upon Steele that there was more behind this white, sweet, noble intensity of her than just the making amends for a fancied or real wrong. For myself, I thought the man did not live on earth who could have resisted her then. And there was resistance. I felt it. She must have felt it. It was poor Steele's hard fate, to fight the charm and eloquence and sweetness of this woman when, for some reason unknown to him, and only guessed at by me, she was burning with all the fire and passion of her soul.

"Mister Steele, I honor you for your goodness to this unfortunate woman," she said, and now her speech came swiftly. "When she was all alone and helpless, you were her friend. It was the deed of a man. But Missus Laramie isn't the only unfortunate woman in the world. I, too, am unfortunate. Ah, how *I* may soon need a friend!

"Vaughn Steele, the man whom I need most to be my friend . . . *want* most to lean upon . . . he is the one whose duty is to stab me to the heart, to ruin me. *You!* Will *you* be my friend? If you knew Ray Longstreth, you would know she would never ask you to be false to your duty. Be true to us both! I'm so alone . . . no one but Ruth loves me. I'll need a friend soon . . . soon.

"Oh, I know . . . I know what you'll find out sooner or later. I know *now!* I want to help you. Let us save life, if not honor. Must I stand alone . . . all alone? Will you . . . will you be . . . ?"

Her voice failed. She was swaying toward Steele. I expected to see his arms spread wide and enfold her in their embrace.

"Ray Longstreth, I love you!" whispered Steele hoarsely, white now to his lips. "I must be true to my duty. But if I can't be true to you . . . then, by God, I want no more of life!"

He kissed her hand and rushed away.

She stood a moment, as if blindly watching the place where he had vanished, and then, as a sister might have turned to a brother, she reached for me.

CHAPTER TWELVE

The Eavesdropper

WE silently rode home in the gathering dusk. Miss Longstreth dismounted at the porch, but Ruth went on with me to the corrals. I felt heavy and somber, as if a catastrophe was near at hand.

"Help me down," said Ruth. Her voice was low and tremulous.

"Ruth, did you hear what Miss Longstreth said to Steele?" I asked.

"A little . . . here and there. I heard Steele tell her he loved her. Isn't this a terrible mess?"

"It sure is. Did you hear . . . do you understand why she appealed to Steele, asked him to be her friend?"

"Did she? No, I didn't hear that. I heard her say she had wronged him. Then I tried not to hear any more. Tell me."

"No, Ruth. It's not my secret. I wish I could do something . . . help them somehow. Yes, it's sure a terrible mix. I don't care so much about myself."

"Nor me," Ruth retorted.

"You. Oh, you're only a shallow, spoiled child! You'd cease to love anything the moment you won it. And I . . . well, I'm no good, you say. But their love. My God, what a tragedy. You've no idea, Ruth. They've hardly spoken to each other, yet are ready to be overwhelmed."

Ruth sat so still and silent that I thought I had angered or offended her. But I did not care much, one way or another. Her coquettish fancy for me and my own trouble had sunk into insignificance.

I did not look up at her, though she was so close I could feel her little restless foot touching me. The horses in the corrals were trooping up to the bars. Dusk had about given place to night, although in the west a broad flare of golden sky showed bright behind dark mountains.

"So *I* say you're no good?" asked Ruth after a long silence.

Then her voice and the way her hand stole to my shoulder should have been warning for me. But it was not, and I did not care.

"Yes, you said that, didn't you?" I replied absently.

"I can change my mind, can't I? Maybe you're only wild and reckless when you drink. Missus Laramie said such nice things about you. They made me feel so good."

I had no reply for that and still did not look up at her. I heard her swing herself in the saddle.

"Lift me down," she said.

Perhaps at any other time I would have remarked that this request was rather unusual, considering the fact that she was very light and sure of action, extremely proud of it, and likely to be insulted by an offer of assistance. But my spirit was dead. I reached for her hands, but they eluded mine, slipped up my arms as she came sliding out of the saddle — and then her face was very close to mine.

"Archie," she whispered.

It was torment, wistfulness, uncertainty, and yet tenderness all in one little whisper. It caught me off my guard or indifferent to consequences. So I kissed her, without passion, with all regret and sadness. She uttered a little cry that might have been mingled exultation and remorse for her victory and her broken faith. Certainly the instant I kissed her she remembered the latter.

She trembled against me, and, leaving unsaid something she had meant to say, she slipped out of my arms and ran. She assuredly was frightened, and I thought it just as well that she was.

Presently she disappeared in the darkness, and then the swift little clink of her spurs ceased. I laughed somewhat ruefully and hoped she would not be satisfied. Then I put away the horses and went in for my supper.

After supper, I noisily bustled around my room and soon stole out for my usual evening's spying. The night was dark, without starlight, and a stiff wind rustled the leaves and tore through the vines on the old house. The fact that I had seen and heard so little during my constant vigilance did not make me careless or the task monotonous. I had so much to think about that sometimes I sat in one place for hours and never knew where the time went.

This night, the very first thing, I heard Lawson's well-known footsteps, and I saw Longstreth's door open, flashing a broad bar of light into the darkness. Lawson crossed the threshold, the door closed, and all was dark again outside. Not a ray of light escaped from the window.

This was the first visit from Lawson for a considerable stretch of time. Little doubt there was that his talk with Longstreth would be interesting to me. I tiptoed to the door and listened, but I could hear only a murmur of voices. Besides, that position was too risky. I went around the corner of the house.

Some time before I had made a discovery that I imagined would be valuable to me. This side of the big adobe house was of much older construction than the back and larger part. There was a narrow passage about a foot wide between the old and new walls, and this ran from the outside through to the patio. I had discovered the entrance by accident, as it was concealed by vines and shrubbery. I crawled in there, upon an opportune occasion, with the intention of boring a small hole through the adobe bricks. But it was not necessary to do that, for the wall was cracked, and in one place I could see into Longstreth's room.

This passage now afforded me my opportunity, and I decided to avail myself of it in spite of the very great danger. Crawling on my hands and knees very stealthily, I got under the shrubbery to the entrance of the passage. In the blackness a faint streak of light showed the location of the crack in the wall. I had to slip in sidewise. It was a tight squeeze, but I entered without the slightest noise. If my position were to be betrayed, it would not be from noise.

As I progressed, the passage grew a very little wider in that direction, and this fact gave rise to the thought that in case of a necessary and hurried exit I would do my best by working toward the patio. It seemed a good deal of time was consumed in reaching my vantage point. When I did get there, the crack was a foot over my head. If I had only been tall like Steele. There was nothing to do but find toe-holes in the crumbling walls and, by bracing knees on one side, back against the other, hold myself up to the crack.

Once with my eye there I did not care what risk I ran. Longstreth appeared disturbed. He sat, stroking his mustache. His brow was clouded. Lawson's face seemed darker, more sullen, yet lighted by some indomitable resolve.

"We'll settle both deals tonight," Lawson was saying. "That's what I came for. That's why I've asked Snecker and Blome to be here."

"But suppose I don't choose to talk here?" protested Longstreth impatiently. "I never before made my house a place to . . . "

"We've waited long enough. This place's as good as any. You've lost your nerve since that ranger hit the town. First, now, will you give Ray to me?"

"Floyd, you talk like a spoiled boy. Give Ray to you! Why, she's a woman, and I'm finding out that she's got a mind of her own. I told you I was willing for her to marry you. I tried to persuade her. But Ray hasn't any use for you now. She liked you at first, but now she doesn't. So what can I do?"

"You can make her marry me," replied Lawson.

"Make that girl do what she doesn't want to? It couldn't be done, even if I tried. I haven't the highest opinion of you as a prospective son-in-law, Floyd. But, if Ray loved you, I would consent. We'd all go away together before this damned miserable business is out. Then she'd never know. And maybe you might be more like you used to be before the West ruined you. But, as matters stand, you fight your own game with her, and I'll tell you now, you'll lose."

"What'd you want to let her come out here for?" demanded Lawson hotly. "It was a dead mistake. I've lost my head over her. I'll have her or die. Don't you think, if she was my wife, I'd soon pull myself together? Since she came, we've none of us been right. And the gang has put up a holler. No, Longstreth, we've got to settle things tonight."

"Well, we can settle what Ray's concerned in right now," replied Longstreth, rising. "Come on. We'll go ask her. See where you stand."

They went out, leaving the door open. I dropped down to rest myself and to wait. I would have liked to hear Miss Longstreth's answer to him. But I could guess what it would be.

Lawson appeared to be all I had thought him, and I believed I was going to find out presently that he was worse. Just then I wanted Steele as never before. Still, he was too big to worm his way into this place.

The men seemed to be absent a good while, though that feeling might have been occasioned by my thrilling interest and anxiety. Finally I heard heavy steps. Lawson came in alone. He was leaden-faced, humiliated. Then something abject in him gave place to rage. He strode the room. He cursed.

When Longstreth returned, he was now appreciably calmer. I could not but decide that he felt relief at the evident rejection of Lawson's proposal.

"Don't fume about it, Floyd," he said. "You see I can't help it. We're pretty wild out here, but I can't rope my daughter and give her to you as I would an unruly steer."

"Longstreth, I can *make* her marry me," declared Lawson thickly.

"How?"

"You know the hold I got on you . . . the deal that made you boss of this rustler gang?"

"It isn't likely I'd forget," replied Longstreth grimly.

"I can go to Ray . . . tell her that . . . make her believe I'd tell it broadcast . . . tell this Ranger Steele, unless she'd marry me."

Lawson spoke breathlessly, with haggard face and shadowed eyes. He had no shame. He was simply in the grip of passion. Longstreth gazed with dark, uncontrolled fury at his relative. In that look I saw a strong, unscrupulous man fallen into evil ways, but still a man. It betrayed Lawson to be a wild and passionate weakling.

I seemed to see also how, during all the years of association, this strong man had upheld the weak one. But that time had gone forever, both in intent on Longstreth's part and in possibility. Lawson, like the great majority of evil and unrestrained men on the border, had reached a point where influence was futile. Reason had degenerated. He saw only himself.

"But, Floyd, Ray's the one person on earth who must never know I'm a rustler, a thief, a red-handed ruler of the worst gang on the border," replied Longstreth impressively.

Floyd bowed his head at that, as if the significance had just occurred to him. But he was not long at a loss.

"She's going to find it out sooner or later. I tell you, she knows now there's something wrong out here. She's got eyes. And that meddling cowboy of hers is smarter than you give him credit for. They're always together. You'll regret the day Russ ever straddled a horse on this ranch. Mark what I say."

"Ray's changed, I know, but she hasn't any idea yet that her daddy's a boss rustler. Ray's concerned about what she calls my duty as mayor. Also I think she's not satisfied with my explanations in regard to certain property."

Lawson halted in his restless walk and leaned against the stone mantelpiece. He squared himself as if this was his last stand. He looked desperate, but at the moment showed an absence of his usual nervous excitement.

"Longstreth, that may well be true," he said. "No doubt all you say is true. But it doesn't help me. I want the girl. If I don't get her, I reckon we'll all go to hell."

He might have meant anything, probably meant the worst. He certainly had something more in mind. Longstreth gave a slight start, barely perceptible, like the switch of an awakening tiger. He sat there, head down, stroking his mustache.

I almost saw his thought. I had long experience in reading men under stress of such emotion. I had no means to vindicate my judgment, but my conviction was that Longstreth right then and there decided that the thing to do was to kill Lawson. For my part, I wondered that he'd not come to such a conclusion before. Not improbably the advent of his daughter had put Longstreth in conflict with himself.

Suddenly he threw off a somber cast of countenance, and he began to talk. He talked swiftly, persuasively, yet I imagined he was talking to smooth Lawson's passion for the moment. Lawson no more caught the fateful significance of a line crossed, a limit reached, a decree decided, than if he had not been present. He was obsessed with himself. How, I wondered, had a man of his mind ever lived so long and gone so far among the exacting conditions of Pecos County? The answer was, perhaps, that Longstreth had guided him, upheld him, protected him. The coming of Ray Longstreth had been the entering wedge of dissension.

"You're too impatient," concluded Longstreth. "You'll ruin any chance of happiness if you rush Ray. She might be won. If you told her who I am, she'd hate you forever. She might marry you to save me, but she'd hate you. That isn't the way. Wait. Play for time. Be different with her. Cut out your drinking. She despises that. Let's plan to sell out here, stock, ranch, property, and leave the country. Then you'd have a show with her."

"I told you we've got to stick," growled Lawson. "The gang won't stand for our going. It can't be done unless you want to sacrifice everything."

"You mean double-cross the men? Go without their knowing? Leave them here to face whatever comes?"

"I mean just that."

"I'm bad enough, but not that bad," returned Longstreth. "If I can't get the gang to let me off, I'll stay and face the music. All the same, Lawson, did it ever strike you that most of the deals the last few years have been *yours?*"

"Yes. If I hadn't rung them in, there wouldn't have been any. You've had cold feet, Owens says, especially since this Ranger Steele, has been here."

"Well, call it cold feet if you like. But I call it sense. We reached our limit long ago. We began by rustling a few cattle at a time . . . when rustling was laughed at. But as our greed grew, so did our boldness. Then came the gang, the regular trips, the one thing and another till, before we knew it . . . before *I* knew it, we had shady deals, hold-ups, and *murders* on our record. Then we *had* to go on. Too late to turn back."

"I reckon we've all said that. None of the gang wants to quit. They all think, and I think, we can't be touched. We may be blamed, but nothing can be proved. We're too strong."

"There's where you're dead wrong," rejoined Longstreth emphatically. "I imagined once, not long ago . . . I was bullheaded . . . who would ever connect Granger Longstreth with a rustler gang? I've changed my mind. I've begun to think. I've reasoned out things. We're crooked, and we can't last. It's the nature of life, even in wild Pecos, for conditions to grow better. The wise deal for us would be to divide equally and leave the country, all of us."

"But you and I have all the stock . . . all the gain," protested Lawson.

"I'll split mine."

"I won't . . . that settles that," added Lawson instantly.

Longstreth spread wide his hands, as if it was useless to try to convince this man. Talking had not increased his calmness, and he now showed more than impatience. A dull glint gleamed deep in his eyes.

"Your stock and property will last a long time . . . do you lots of good when Steele . . . "

"Bah!" croaked Lawson hoarsely. The ranger's name was a match applied to powder. "Haven't I told you he'd be dead soon . . . any time . . . same as Laramie is?"

"Yes, you mentioned the . . . the supposition," replied Longstreth sarcastically. "I inquired, too, just how that very desired event was to be brought about."

"Blome's here to kill Steele."

"Bah!" retorted Longstreth in turn. "Blome can't kill this ranger. He can't face him with a ghost of a show . . . he'll never get a chance at Steele's back. The man don't live on this border who's quick and smart enough to kill Steele."

"I'd like to know why?" demanded Lawson sullenly.

"You ought to know. You've seen the ranger pull a gun."

"Who told you?" queried Lawson, his face working.

"Oh, I guessed it, if that'll do you."

"If Jack doesn't kill this damned ranger, I will," replied Lawson, pounding the table.

Longstreth laughed contemptuously. "Floyd, don't make so much noise. And don't be a fool. You've been on the border for ten years. You've packed a gun and you've used it. You've been with Blome and Snecker when they killed their men. You've been present at many fights. But you never saw a man like Steele. You haven't got sense enough to see him right if you had a chance. Neither has Blome. The only way to get rid of Steele is for the gang to draw on him, all at once. Then he's going to drop some of them."

"Longstreth, you say that like a man who wouldn't care much if Steele did drop some of them," declared Lawson, and now he was sarcastic.

"To tell you the truth, I wouldn't," returned the other bluntly. "I'm pretty sick of this mess."

Lawson cursed in amaze. His emotions were all out of proportion to his intelligence. He was not at all quick-witted. I had never seen a vainer or more arrogant man.

"Longstreth, I don't like your talk," he said.

"If you don't like the way I talk, you know what you can do," replied Longstreth quickly.

He stood up then, cool and quiet, with flash of eyes and set of lips that told me he was dangerous.

"Well, after all, that's neither here nor there," went on Lawson, unconsciously cowed by the other. "The thing is, do I get the girl?"

"Not by any means . . . *except* her consent."

"You'll not make her marry me?"

"No. *No*," replied Longstreth, his voice still cold, low-pitched.

"All right. Then *I'll* make her."

Evidently Longstreth understood the man before him so well that he wasted no more words. I knew what Lawson never dreamed of, and that was that Longstreth had a gun somewhere within reach and meant to use it.

Then heavy footsteps sounded outside, tramping upon the porch. I might have been mistaken, but I believed those footsteps saved Lawson's life.

"There they are," said Lawson, and he opened the door.

Five masked men entered. About two of them I could not recognize anything familiar. I thought one had old Snecker's burly shoulders and another Bo Snecker's stripling shape. I did recognize Blome in spite of his mask, because his fair skin and hair, his garb and air of distinction made plain his identity. They all wore coats, hiding any weapons. The big man with the burly shoulders shook hands with Longstreth, and the others stood back.

The atmosphere of the room had changed. Lawson might have been a nonentity for all he counted. Longstreth was another man — a stranger to me. If he had entertained a hope of freeing himself from this band, of getting away to a safer country, he abandoned it at the very sight of these men. There was power here, and he was bound.

The big man spoke in low, hoarse whispers, and, at this, all the others gathered around him, close to the table. There were evidently some signs of membership not plain to me.

Then all the heads were bent over the table. Low voices spoke, queried, answered, argued. By straining my ears, I caught a word here and there. They were planning. I did not attempt to get at the meaning of the few words and phrases I distinguished, but held them in mind so to piece all together afterward. Before the plotters finished conferring, I had an involuntary flashed knowledge of much, and my whirling, excited mind made reception difficult. When these rustlers finished whispering, I was in a cold sweat.

Steele was to be killed as soon as possible by Blome, or by the gang going to Steele's house at night. Morton had been with the ranger. He was to meet the same fate as Laramie, dealt by Bo Snecker, who evidently worked in the dark like a ferret. Any other person known to be communing with Steele, or interested in him, or suspect of either, was to be silenced. Then the town was to suffer a short deadly spell of violence, directed anywhere, for the purpose of intimidating those people who had begun to be restless under the influence of the ranger. After that, the big herds of stock were to be rustled off the ranches to the north and driven to El Paso.

The big man, who evidently was the leader of the present convention, got up to depart. He went as swiftly as he had come and was followed by the slender fellow. As far as it was possible for me to be sure, I identified these two as Snecker and son. The others, however, remained.

Blome removed his mask, which action was duplicated by the two rustlers who had stayed with him. They were both young, bronzed, hard of countenance, not unlike cowboys. Evidently this was now a social call on Longstreth. He set out cigars and liquors for his guests, and a general conversation ensued, differing little from what might have been indulged in by neighborly ranchers. There was not a word spoken that would have caused suspicion.

Blome was genial, gay, and he talked the most. Lawson alone seemed uncommunicative and unsociable. He smoked fiercely and drank continually. All at once he straightened up as if listening.

"What's that?" he called suddenly.

The talking and laugher ceased. My own strained ears were pervaded by a slight rustling sound.

"Must be a rat," replied Longstreth in relief.

Strange how any sudden or unknown thing weighed upon him. The rustling became a rattle.

"Sounds like a rattlesnake to me," said Blome.

Longstreth got up from the table and peered round the room. Just at that instant I felt an almost inappreciable movement of the adobe wall which supported me. I could scarcely credit my senses. But the rattle inside Longstreth's room was mingling with little dull thuds of falling dirt. The adobe wall, merely dried mud, was crumbling. I distinctly felt a tremor pass through it. Then the blood gushed with sickening coldness back to my heart and seemingly clogged it.

"What in the hell!" exclaimed Longstreth.

"I smell dust," said Blome sharply.

That was the signal for me to drop down from my perch, yet despite my care I made a noise.

"Did you hear a step?" queried Longstreth.

No one answered. But a heavy piece of adobe wall fell with a thud.

"There's somebody between the walls!" thundered Longstreth.

Then a section of the wall fell inward with a crash. I began to squeeze my body through the narrow passage toward the patio.

"Hear him!" yelled Lawson. "This side!"

"No, he's going that way," yelled someone else.

The tramp of heavy boots lent me the strength and speed of desperation. I was not shirking a fight, but to be cornered like a trapped coyote was another matter. I almost tore my clothes off in that passage. The dust nearly stifled me.

When I burst into the patio, it was not one single instant too soon. But one deep gasp of breath revived me, and I was up, gun in hand, running for the outlet into the court. Thumping footsteps turned me back. While there was a chance to get away, I did not want to meet odds in a fight. I thought I heard someone running into the patio from the other end.

I stole along, and, coming to a door without any idea of where it might lead, I softly pushed it open a little way and slipped in.

CHAPTER THIRTEEN

In Flagrante Delicto

A LOW cry greeted me. The room was light. I saw Ruth Herbert, sitting on her bed in her dressing gown. Shaking my gun at her with a fierce, warning gesture to be silent, I turned to close the door. It was a heavy door, without bolt or bar, and, when I had shut it, I felt safe only for the moment.

I gazed around the room. There was one window with blind closely drawn. I listened and seemed to hear footsteps retreating, dying away. Then I turned to Ruth. She had slipped off the bed to her knees and was holding out trembling hands, as if both to supplicate mercy and to ward me off. She was as white as the pillow on her bed and terribly frightened.

Again with a warning hand commanding silence, I stepped softly forward, meaning to reassure her.

"Archie. Archie," she whispered wildly.

I thought she was going to faint. When I got close and looked into her eyes, I understood the strange dark expression in them. She was terrified because she believed I meant to kill her, or do worse — probably worse. She had believed many a hard story about me and had cared for me in spite of them.

I remembered, then, that she had broken her promise, she had tempted me, led me to kiss her, made a fool out of me. I remembered, also, how I had threatened her. This intrusion of mine was the wild cowboy's vengeance. I verily believed she thought I was drunk. I must have looked pretty hard and fierce, bursting into her room with that big gun in hand. My first action then was to lay the gun down on her bureau.

"You poor kid!" I whispered, taking her hands and trying to raise her.

But she stayed on her knees and clung to me. "Archie! It was vile of me," she whispered. "I know it. I deserve anything . . . anything! But I am only a kid. Archie, I didn't . . . break my word . . . I didn't make you kiss me just for vanity's sake. I swear I didn't. I wanted you to. For I care . . . Archie . . . I can't help it. Please, forgive me. Please let me off this time. Don't . . . don't . . . "

"Will you shut up!" I interrupted, half beside myself. And I used force in

593

another way than speech. I shook her and sat her on the bed. "You little fool, I didn't come in here to kill you or do some other awful thing, as you think. For God's sake, Ruth, what do you take me for?"

"Archie, you swore . . . you'd do something terrible if I . . . tempted you . . . any more," she faltered.

The way she searched my face with doubtful, fearful eyes hurt me.

"Listen," and with the word I seemed to be pervaded by peace. "I didn't know this was your room. I came in here to get away . . . to save my life. I was pursued. I was spying on Longstreth and his men. They heard me, but did not see me. They don't know who was listening. They're after me now. I'm Special United States Deputy Marshal Sittell . . . Russell Archibald Sittell. I'm a ranger. I'm here as secret aid to Steele."

Ruth's eyes changed from blank gulfs to dilating, shadowing, quickening windows of thought. "Russ-ell Archi-bald Sittell," she echoed. "Ranger. Secret aid to Steele."

"Yes."

"Then you're no cowboy?"

"No."

"Only a make-believe one?"

"Yes."

"And the drinking, the gambling, the association with those low men . . . that was all put on?"

"Part of the game, Ruth. I'm not a drinking man. And I sure hate those places I had to go in, and all that pertains to them."

"Oh, so that's it. I knew there was something. How glad . . . how glad I am. Archie. Archie."

Then Ruth threw her arms around my neck, and without reserve or restraint began to kiss me. It must have been a moment of sheer gladness to feel that I was not disreputable — a moment when something deep and womanly in her was vindicated. Assuredly she was entirely different from what she had ever been before.

There was a little space of time — a sweet confusion of senses — when I could but meet her half way in tenderness. Quite as suddenly, then, she began to cry. I whispered in her ear, cautioning her to be careful, that my life was at stake. After that she cried silently, with one of her arms around my neck, her head on my breast, and her hand clasping mine.

So I held her for what seemed a long time. Indistinct voices came to me and

594

footsteps seemingly a long way off. I heard the wind in the rosebush outside. Someone walked down the stony court.

Then a shrill neigh of a horse pierced the silence. A rider was mounting out there for some reason. With my life at stake I grasped all the sweetness of that situation. Ruth stirred in my arms, raised a red, tear-stained yet happy face, and tried to smile.

"It isn't any time to cry," she whispered. "But I had to. You can't understand what it made me feel to learn you're no drunkard, no desperado, but a man . . . a man like that ranger."

Very sweetly and seriously she kissed me again.

"Archie, if I didn't honestly and truly love you before, I do now." She stood up and faced me with the fire and intelligence of a woman in her eyes. "Tell me. You were spying on my uncle?"

Briefly I told her what had happened before I entered her room, not omitting a terse word as to the character of the men I had watched.

"My God! So it's Uncle Granger! I knew something was very wrong here . . . with him . . . with the place . . . the people. And right off I hated Floyd Lawson. Archie, does Ray know?"

"She knows something. I haven't any idea how much."

"This explains her appeal to Steele. Oh, it'll kill her. You don't know how proud . . . how good Ray is. Oh, it'll kill her."

"Ruth, she's no baby. She's got sand, that girl . . . "

The sound of soft steps somewhere near distracted my attention, reminded me of my peril and now, what counted more with me, made clear the probability of being discovered in Ruth's room.

"I'll have to get out of here," I whispered.

"Wait," she replied, detaining me. "Didn't you say they were hunting for you?"

"They sure are," I returned grimly.

"Oh, then you mustn't go. They might shoot you before you got away. Stay. If we hear them, you can hide under my bed. I'll turn out the light. I'll meet them at the door. You can trust me. Stay, Archie. Wait till all quiets down, if we have to wait till morning. Then you can slip out."

"Ruth, I oughtn't to stay. I don't want to . . . I won't," I replied, perplexed and stubborn.

"But you must. It's the only safe way. They won't come here."

"Suppose they should? It's an even chance Longstreth'll search every room and corner in this old house. If they found me here, I couldn't start a fight. You might be hurt. Then . . . the fact of my being here . . . " I did not finish what I meant, but instead made a step toward the door.

Ruth was on me like a little whirlwind, white of face and dark of eye, with a resoluteness I could have not have deemed her capable of. She was as strong and supple as a panther, too. But she need not have been either resolute or strong, for the clasp of her arms, the feel of her warm breast as she pressed me back — these were enough to make me weak as water.

My knees buckled as I touched the chair, and I was glad to sit down. My face was wet with perspiration and a kind of cold ripple shot over me. I imagined I was losing my nerve then. Proof beyond doubt that Ruth loved me was so sweet, so overwhelming a thing, that I could not resist, even to save her disgrace.

"Archie, the fact of your being here is the very thing to save you . . . if they come," Ruth whispered softly. "What do I care what they think?"

She put her arms around my neck. I gave up then and held her as if she indeed were my only hope. A noise, a stealthy sound, a step froze that embrace into stone.

"Up yet, Ruth?" came Longstreth's clear voice, too strained, too eager to be natural.

"No, I'm in bed, reading. Good night, Uncle," replied Ruth instantly, so calmly and naturally that I marveled at the difference between man and woman. Perhaps that was the difference between love and hate.

"Are you alone?" went on Longstreth's penetrating voice, colder now.

"Yes," replied Ruth.

The door swung inward with a swift scrape and jar. Longstreth half entered, haggard, flaming-eyed. His leveled gun did not have to move an inch to cover me. Behind him I saw Lawson and, indistinctly, another man.

"Well, I'll be damned!" cursed Longstreth. He showed amaze. "Hands up, Russ."

I put up my hands quickly, but all the time I was calculating what chance I had to leap for my gun or dash out the light. Risk was too great for Ruth.

I was trapped. And fury, like the hot teeth of a wolf, bit into me. That leveled gun — the menace in Longstreth's puzzled eyes — Lawson's dark and hateful face — these loosened the spirit of fight in me. If Ruth had not been there, I would have made some desperate move.

Longstreth barred Lawson from entering, which action showed control as well as distrust. "You lied!" he said to Ruth. He was hard as flint, yet doubtful and curious, too.

"Certainly I lied," snapped Ruth in reply.

She was cool, almost flippant. I awakened to the knowledge that she was to be reckoned with in this situation. Suddenly she stepped squarely between Longstreth and me.

"Move aside," ordered Longstreth sternly.

"I won't! What do I care for your old gun? You sha'n't shoot Russ or do anything else to him. It's my fault he's here in my room. I coaxed him to come."

"You little hussy!" exclaimed Longstreth, and he lowered the gun.

If I ever before had occasion to glory in Ruth, I had it then. She betrayed not the slightest fear. She looked as if she could fight like a little tigress. She was white, composed, defiant.

"How long has Russ been in here?" demanded Longstreth.

"All evening. I left Ray at eight o'clock. Russ came right after that."

"But you're undressed for bed!" ejaculated the angry and perplexed uncle.

"Yes." That simple answer was so non-committal, so above subterfuge, so innocent, and yet so confounding in its provocation of thought that Longstreth just stared his astonishment.

I started as if I had been struck. "See here, Longstreth . . . ," I began passionately.

Like a flash Ruth whirled into my arms, and one hand crossed my lips.

"It's my fault. I *will* take the blame!" she cried, and now the agony of fear in her voice quieted me. I realized I would be wise to be silent. "Uncle," began Ruth, turning her head, yet still clinging to me, "I've tormented Russ into loving me. I've flirted with him . . . teased him . . . tempted him. We love each other now. We're engaged. Please . . . please don't . . . "

She began to falter, and I felt her weight sag a little against me.

"Well, let go of him," said Longstreth. "I won't hurt him. Ruth, how long has this affair been going on?"

"For weeks . . . I don't know . . . how long."

"Does Ray know?"

"She knows we love each other, but not that we met . . . did this . . . "

"I should hope not. I . . . "

Light, swift steps — the rustle of silk — interrupted Longstreth and made my heart sink like lead.

"Is that you, Floyd?" came Miss Longstreth's deep voice, nervous, hurried. "What's all this commotion I hear . . . ?"

"Ray, go on back," ordered Longstreth.

Just then Miss Longstreth's beautiful agitated face appeared beside Lawson. He failed to prevent her from seeing all of us.

"Papa! Ruth!" she exclaimed in consternation. Then she swept into the room. "What has happened?"

Longstreth, like the devil he was, laughed when it was too late. He had good impulses, but they never interfered with his sardonic humor. He paced the little room, shrugging his shoulders, offering no explanation. Ruth appeared about ready to collapse, and I could not have told Ruth's lie to Miss Longstreth to save my life.

"Ray, your father and I broke in on a little Romeo and Juliet scene," said Floyd Lawson with a leer.

Then Miss Longstreth's dark gaze swept from Floyd to her father, then to Ruth's attire and her shamed face, and finally to me. What effect the magnificent wrath and outraged trust in her eyes had upon me.

"Russ, do they dare insinuate you came to Ruth's room?"

For myself I could keep silent, but for Ruth I began to feel a hot clamoring outburst swelling my throat.

"Ruth confessed it, Ray," replied Lawson.

"*Ruth!*" A shrinking, shuddering disbelief filled Miss Longstreth's voice.

"Ray . . . I told you . . . I loved him . . . didn't I?" replied Ruth.

She managed to hold up her head with a ghost of her former defiant spirit.

"Miss Longstreth, it's a . . . ," I burst out.

Then Ruth fainted. It was I who caught her. Miss Longstreth hurried to her side with a little cry of distress.

"Russ, your hand's called," said Longstreth. "Of course, you'll swear the moon's green cheese. And I like you the better for it. But we know now, and you can save your breath. If Ruth hadn't stuck up so gamely for you, I'd have shot you. But . . . at that I wasn't looking for you. Now clear out of here."

I picked up my gun from the bureau and dropped it in its sheath. For the life of me I could not leave without another look at Miss Longstreth. The scorn in her eyes did not wholly hide the sadness. She who needed friends was experiencing the bitterness of misplaced trust. That came out in the scorn, but the sadness — I knew what hurt her most was her sorrow. I dropped my head and stalked out.

CHAPTER FOURTEEN

A Slap in the Face

WHEN I got out into the dark, where my hot face cooled in the wind, my relief equaled my other feelings. Longstreth had told me to clear out, and, although I did not take that as a dismissal, I considered I would be wise to leave the ranch at once. Daylight might disclose my footprints between the walls, but, even if it did not, my work there was finished. So I went to my room and packed my few belongings.

The night was dark, windy, stormy, yet there was no rain. I hoped as soon as I got clear of the ranch to lose something of the pain I felt. But long after I had tramped out into the open, there was a lump in my throat and an ache in my breast. And all my thoughts centered round Ruth. What a game and loyal little girl she had turned out to be. I was absolutely at a loss concerning what the future held in store for us. I had a vague, but clinging, hope that after the trouble was over, there might be — there *must* be — something between us.

Steele was not at our rendezvous among the rocks. The hour was late. Among the few dim lights flickering on the outskirts of town I picked out the one of his little adobe house, but I knew almost to a certainty that he was not there. So I turned my way into the darkness, not with any great hope of finding Steele out there, but with the intention of seeking a covert for myself until morning.

There was no trail, and the night was so black that I could see only the lighter sandy patches of ground. I stumbled over the little clumps of brush, fell into washes, and pricked myself on cactus. By and by mesquite and rocks began to make progress still harder for me. I wandered around, at last getting on higher ground, and here in spite of the darkness felt some sense of familiarity with things. I was probably near Steele's hiding place.

I went on till rocks and brush barred further progress, and then I ventured to whistle. But no answer came. Whereupon I spread my blanket in as sheltered a place as I could find and lay down. The coyotes were on noisy duty; the wind moaned and rushed through the mesquite. But, despite these sounds and worry about Steele and the never-absent haunting thought of Ruth, I went to sleep.

A little rain fell during the night, as I discovered upon waking, but it had not been enough to cause me any discomfort. The morning was bright and beautiful, yet somehow I hated it. I had work to do that did not go well with that golden wave of grass and brush on the windy open. I climbed to the highest rock of that ridge and looked about. It was a wild spot, some three miles from town.

Presently I recognized landmarks given to me by Steele, and I knew I was near his place. I whistled, then hallooed, but got no reply. Then, by working back and forth across the ridge, I found what appeared to be a faint trail. This I followed, lost, and found again, and eventually still higher up on another ridge, with a commanding outlook, I found Steele's hiding place. He had not been there for perhaps forty-eight hours. I wondered where he had slept.

Under a shelving rock I found a pack of food, carefully protected by a heavy slab. There was also a canteen full of water. I lost no time getting myself some breakfast, and then, hiding my own pack, I set off at a rapid pace, heading for town. I had scarcely gone a quarter of a mile, had, in fact, just reached a level, when sight of two horsemen halted me and made me take to cover. They appeared to be cowboys, hunting for a horse or a steer. Under the circumstances, however, I was suspicious, and I watched them closely and followed them a mile or so around the base of the ridges, until I had thoroughly satisfied myself they were not tracking Steele. They were a long time working out of sight, which further retarded my venturing forth into the open.

Finally I did get started. Then, about half way to town, more horsemen in the flat caused me to lie low for a while and make a wide detour to avoid being seen. Somewhat to my consternation it was afternoon before I arrived in town. For my life I could not have told why I knew something had happened since my last visit, but I certainly felt it and was proportionately curious and anxious.

The first person I saw whom I recognized was Dick, and he handed me a note from Ruth. She seemed to take it for granted that I had been wise to leave the ranch. Miss Longstreth had softened somewhat when she learned Ruth and I were engaged, and she had forgiven my deceit. Ruth asked me to come that night after eight, down among the trees and shrubbery, to a secluded spot we knew. It was a brief note and all to the point. But there was something in it that affected me strangely.

I had imagined the engagement an invention for the moment. But after danger to me was past Ruth would not have carried on a pretense, not even to win back Miss Longstreth's respect. The fact was, Ruth meant that engagement. If I did the right thing now, I would not lose her. But what was the right thing?

I was sorely perplexed and deeply touched. Never had I a harder task than that of the hour — to put her out of my mind. I went boldly to Steele's house. He was not there. There was nothing by which I could tell when he had been there. The lamp might have been turned out or might have burned out. The oil was low. I saw a good many tracks around in the sandy walks. I did not recognize Steele's. As I hurried away, I detected more than one of Steele's nearest neighbors peering at me from windows and doors.

I went to Mrs. Laramie's. She was up and about and cheerful. The children were playing, manifestly well cared for and content. Mrs. Laramie had not seen Steele since I had. Miss Longstreth had sent her servant. There was a very decided change in the atmosphere of Mrs. Laramie's home, and I saw that for her the worst was past, and she was bravely, hopefully facing the future.

From there I hurried to the main street of Fairdale and to that section where violence brooded, ready at any chance moment to lift its hydra head. For that time of day the street seemed unusually quiet. Few pedestrians were abroad and few loungers. There was a row of saddled horses on each side of the street, the full extent of the block. I went into the big barroom of the Hope So.

I had never seen the place so full, nor had it ever seemed so quiet. The whole long bar was lined by shirt-sleeved men, with hats slouched back and vests flapping wide. Those who were not drinking were talking low. Half a dozen tables held as many groups of dusty, motley men, some silent, others speaking and gesticulating, all earnest. At first glance I did not see anyone in whom I had especial interest. The principal actors of my drama did not appear to be present. However, there were rough characters more in evidence than at any other time I had visited the saloon.

Voices were too low for me to catch, but I followed the direction of some of the significant gestures. Then I saw that these half dozen tables were rather closely grouped and drawn back from the center of the big room. Next my quick sight took in a smashed table and chairs, some broken bottles on the floor, and then a dark sinister splotch of blood. I had not time to make inquiries, for my roving eye caught Frank Morton in the doorway, and evidently he wanted to attract my attention.

He turned away, and I followed. When I got outside, he was leaning against the hitching rail. One look at this rancher was enough for me to see that he had been told my part in Steele's game and that he himself had roused to the Texas fighting temper. He had a clouded brow and looked somber and thick. He also seemed slow, heavy, guarded.

"Howdy, Russ," he said. "We've been wantin' you. There's ten of us in town, all scattered 'round, ready. It's goin' to start today."

"Where's Steele?' was my first query.

"Saw him less'n an hour ago. He's somewhere's close. He may show up any time."

"Is he all right?"

"Wal, he was pretty fit a little while back," replied Morton significantly.

"What's come off? Tell me all."

"Wal, the ball opened last night, I reckon. Jack Blome came swaggerin' in here, askin' for Steele. We all knew what he was in town for. But last night he came out with it. Every man in the saloons, every man on the streets heard Blome's loud an' longin' call for the ranger. Blome's pals took it up, an' they all enjoyed themselves some."

"Drinking hard?"

"Nope . . . they didn't hit it up very hard. But they laid foundations. Of course, Steele was not to be seen last night. This mornin' Blome an' his gang were out pretty early. But they traveled alone. Blome just strolled up an' down by himself. I watched him walk up this street on one side an' then down the other just a matter of thirty-one times. I counted 'em. For all I could see, maybe Blome didn't take a drink. But his gang, especially Bo Snecker, sure looked on the red liquor.

"By eleven o'clock everybody in town knew what was comin' off. There was no work or business, 'cept in the saloons. Zimmer an' I were together, an' the rest of our crowd in pairs at different places. I reckon it was about noon when Blome got tired, paradin' up an' down. He went in the Hope So, an' the crowd followed. Zimmer stayed outside so to give Steele a hunch in case he came along. I went in to see the show.

"Wal, it was some curious to me. I've lived all my life in Texas, but I never before saw a gunman on the job, so to say. Blome's a handsome fellow, an' he seemed different from what I expected. Sure, I thought he'd yell an' prance 'round like a drunken fool. But he was cool an' quiet enough. The blowin' and drinkin' was done by his pals. After a while it got to me that Blome gloried in this situation. I've seen a man dead set to kill another all dark, sullen, restless, but Blome wasn't that way. He wasn't thinkin' about Steele. He didn't seem at all like a bloody devil. He was vain, cock-sure. He was revelin' in the effect he made. I had him figured all right.

"Blome sat on the edge of a table, an' he faced the door. Of course, there was a pard outside, ready to pop in an' tell him if Steele was comin'. But Steele didn't come in that way. He wasn't on the street just before that time, because Zimmer told me afterward. Steele must have been in the Hope So somewhere. Anyway, just like he dropped from the clouds, he came through the door near the bar. Blome didn't see him come. But most of the gang did, an' I want to tell you that big room went pretty quiet.

"'Hello, Blome, I hear you're lookin' for me,' called out Steele.

"I don't know if he spoke ordinary or not, but his voice drew me up same as it did the rest, an' . . . damn me! . . . Blome seemed to turn to stone. He didn't start or jump. He turned gray. An' I could see that he was tryin' to think in a moment when thinkin' was hard. Then he turned his head. Sure Blome expected to look into a six-shooter. But Steele was standin' back there in his shirt sleeves, his hands on his hips, an' he looked more man than anyone I ever saw. It's easy to remember the look of him, but how he made me feel, that isn't easy.

"Blome was at a disadvantage. He was half sittin' on a table, an' Steele was behind an' to the left of him. For Blome to make a move then would have been a fool play. He saw that. So did everybody. The crowd slid back without noise, but Bo Snecker an' a rustler named March stuck near Blome. I figured this Bo Snecker as dangerous as Blome, an' results proved I was right. Steele didn't choose to keep his advantage, so far as position in regard to Blome went. He just walked 'round in front of the rustler. But this put all the crowd in front of Steele, an' perhaps he had an eye for that.

"'I hear you've been looking for me,' repeated the ranger.

"Blome never moved a muscle, but he seemed to come to life. It struck me that Steele's presence had made an impression on Blome which was new to the rustler.

"'Yes, I have,' replied Blome.

"'Well, here I am. What do you want?'

"When everybody knew what Blome wanted and had intended, this question of Steele's seemed strange, on one hand. An' yet, on the other, now that the ranger stood there, it struck me as natural enough.

"'If you heard I was lookin' for you . . . you sure heard what for,' replied Blome.

"'Blome, my experience with such men as you is that you'll brag one thing behind my back an' you mean different when I show up. I've called you now. What do *you* mean?'

"'I reckon you know what Jack Blome means.'

"'Jack Blome! That name means nothin' to me. Blome, you've been braggin' around that you'd meet me . . . kill me! You thought you meant it, didn't you?'

"'Yes . . . I did mean it.'

"'All right. Go ahead!'

"The barroom became perfectly still, except for the slow breaths I heard. There wasn't any movement anywhere. That queer gray came to Blome's face again. He might again have been stone, I thought, an' I'll gamble everyone else watchin' thought Blome would draw an' get killed in the act. But he never moved. Steele had cowed him. If Blome had been heated by drink or mad or anythin' but what he was just then, maybe he might have throwed a gun. But he didn't. I've heard of really brave men gettin' panic like that, an', after seein' Steele, I didn't wonder at Blome.

"'You see, Blome, you don't want to meet me, for all your talk,' went on the ranger. 'You thought you did, but that was before you faced the man you intended to kill. Blome, you're one of these dandy, cock-of-the-walk four-flushers. I'll tell you how I know. Because I've met *real* gunfighters, an' there never was one of them yet who bragged or talked. Now don't you go 'round blowin' any more.'

"Then Steele deliberately stepped forward an' slapped Blome on one side of his face an' again on the other.

"'Keep out of my way after this, or I'm liable to spoil some of your dandy looks.'

"Blome got up an' walked straight out of the place. I had my eyes on him, which kept me from seein' Steele. But on hearin' somethin', I don't know what, I turned back an' there Steele had got a long arm on Bo Snecker, who was tryin' to throw a gun. But he wasn't quick enough. The gun banged in the air, an' then it went spinnin' away, while Snecker dropped in a heap on the floor. The table was overturned, an' March, the other rustler, who was on that side, got up, pullin' his gun.

"But somebody in the crowd killed him before he could get goin'. I didn't see who fired that shot, an' neither did anybody else. But the crowd broke an' run. Steele dragged Bo Snecker down to jail an' locked him up."

Morton, having concluded his narrative, was evidently somewhat dry of tongue, since he produced knife and tobacco and cut himself a huge quid.

"That's all so far today, Russ, but I reckon you'll agree with me on the main issue . . . Steele's game's opened."

I had felt the rush of excitement, the old exultation at the prospect of danger, but this time there was something lacking in them. The wildness of the boy that had persisted in me was gone now.

"Yes, Steele has opened it, and I'm ready to boost the game along. Wait till I see him! But, Morton, you say someone you don't know played a hand in here and killed March."

"I sure do. It wasn't any of our men. Zimmer was outside. The others were at different places."

"The fact is, then, Steele has more friends than we know, perhaps more than he knew himself."

"Right. An' it's got the gang in the air. There'll be hell tonight."

"Steele hardly expects to keep Snecker in jail, does he?"

"I can't say. Probably not. I wish Steele had put both Blome and Snecker out of the way. We'd have less to fight."

"Maybe. I'm for the elimination method myself. But Steele doesn't follow out the gun method. He will use one only when he's driven. It's hard to make him draw. You know these desperate men aren't afraid of guns or fights, yet they're afraid of Steele. Perhaps it's his nerve, the way he faces them, the things he says, the fact that he has mysterious allies."

"Russ, we're all with him, an' I'll gamble that the honest citizens of Fairdale will flock to him in another day. I can see signs of that. There were twenty or more men on Laramie's list, but Steele didn't want so many."

"We don't need any more. Morton, can you give me any idea where Steele is?"

"Not the slightest."

"All right. I'll hunt for him. If you see him, tell him to hole up, and then you come after me. Tell him I've got our men spotted."

"Russ, if you ranger fellows ain't wonders!" exclaimed Morton, with shining eyes.

Steele did not show himself in town again that day. Here his cunning was manifest. By four o'clock that afternoon Blome was drunk, and he and his rustlers went roaring up and down the street. There was some shooting, but I did not see or hear that anyone was hurt. The lawless element, both native to Fairdale and those visiting, followed in Blome's tracks from saloon to saloon. How often had I seen this sort of procession, though not on so large a scale, in many towns of wild Texas. The two great and dangerous things in Fairdale at the hour were whiskey and guns. Under such conditions the rustlers were capable of any mad act or folly.

Morton and his men sent word flying around town that a fight was imminent and all citizens should be prepared to defend their homes against possible violence. But despite his warning I saw many respectable citizens abroad whose quiet, unobtrusive manner and watchful eyes and hard faces told me that, when trouble began, they wanted to be there. Verily Ranger Steele had built his house of service upon a rock. It did not seem too much to say that the next few days, perhaps hours, would see a great change in the character and a proportionate decrease in number of the inhabitants of this corner of Pecos County.

Morton and I were in the crowd that watched Blome, Snecker, and a dozen other rustlers march down to Steele's jail. They had crowbars, and they had cans of giant powder which they had appropriated from a hardware store. If Steele had a jailer, he was not in evidence.

The door was wrenched off, and Bo Snecker, evidently not wholly recovered, was brought forth to his cheering comrades. Then some of the rustlers began to urge back the pressing circle, and the word given out acted as a spur to haste. The jail was to be blown up. The crowd split, and some men ran one way, some another. Morton and I were among those who hurried over the vacant ground to a little ridge that marked the edge of the open country. From this vantage point we heard several rustlers yell in warning, then they fled for their lives.

It developed that they might have spared themselves such headlong flight. The explosion appeared to be long in coming. At length we saw the lifting of the roof in a cloud of red dust, and then heard an exceedingly heavy but low detonation. When the pall of dust drifted away, all that was left of Steele's jail was a part of the stone walls. The building that stood nearest, being constructed of adobe, had been badly damaged.

However, this wreck of the jail did not seem to satisfy Blome and his followers, for amid wild yells and huzzahs they set to work with crowbars and soon laid low every stone. Then with young Snecker in the fore they set off uptown. If this was not a gang in fit mood for any evil or any ridiculous celebration, I greatly missed my guess. It was a remarkable fact, however, and one that convinced me of deviltry afoot, that the crowd broke up, dispersed, and actually disappeared off the streets of Fairdale.

The impression given was that they were satisfied. But this impression did not remain with me. Morton was scarcely deceived, either. I told him that I would almost certainly see Steele early in the evening and that we would be out of harm's way. He told me that we could trust him and his men to keep sharp watch on the night's doings of Blome's gang. Then we parted.

It was almost dark. By the time I had gotten something to eat and drink at the Hope So, the hour for my meeting with Ruth was about due. On the way out I did not pass a lighted house until I got to the end of the street and then, strange to say, that one was Steele's. I walked down past the place, and, though I was positive he would not be there, I whistled low.

I halted and waited. He had two lights lit, one in the kitchen and one in the big room. The blinds were drawn. They were light-colored blinds and transparent. I saw a long dark shadow cross one window and then, a little later, cross the other. This would have deceived me had I not remembered Steele's device for casting the shadow. He had expected to have his house attacked at night, presumably while he was at home, but he had felt that it was not necessary for him to stay there to make sure. Lawless men of this class were sometimes exceedingly simple and gullible.

I bent my steps across the open, avoiding road and path, to the foot of the hill upon which Longstreth's house stood. It was dark enough under the trees. I could hardly find my way to the secluded nook and bench where I had been directed to come. I wondered if Ruth would be able to find it. Trust that girl! She might have a few qualms and come shaking a little, but she would be there on the minute.

I had hardly seated myself to wait when my keen ears detected something, then slight rustlings, then soft steps, and a dark form emerged from the blackness into the little starlit glade. Ruth came swiftly toward me and right into my arms.

That was sure a sweet moment. Through the excitement and dark boding thoughts of the day, I had forgotten that she would do just this thing. And now I anticipated tears, clingings, fears. But I was agreeably surprised.

"Archie, are you all right?" she whispered.

"Just at this moment I am," I replied.

Ruth gave me another little hug, and then, disengaging herself from my arms, she sat down beside me. "I can only stay a minute. Oh, it's safe enough. But I told Ray I was to meet you, and she's waiting to hear if Steele is . . . is . . . "

"Steele's safe so far," I interrupted.

"There were men coming and going all day. Uncle Granger never appeared at meals. He didn't eat, Ray said. Floyd tramped up and down, smoking, biting his nails, listening for these messengers. When they'd leave, he'd go in for another drink. We heard him roar someone had been shot, and we feared it might be Steele."

"No," I replied steadily.

"Did Steele shoot anybody?"

"No. A rustler named March tried to draw on Steele, and someone in the crowd killed March."

"Someone? Archie, was it you?"

"It sure wasn't. I didn't happen to be there."

"Ah! Then Steele has other men like you around him. I might have guessed that."

"Ruth, Steele makes men his friends. It's because he's on the side of justice."

"Ray will be glad to hear that. Archie, she doesn't think only of Steele's life. I believe she has a secret pride in his work. And I've an idea what she fears most is some kind of a clash between Steele and her father."

"I shouldn't wonder. Ruth, what does Ray know about her father?"

"Oh, she's in the dark. She got hold of papers that made her ask him questions. And his answers made her suspicious. She realizes he's not what he pretended to be all these years. But she never dreams her father is a rustler chief. When she finds that out . . . "

Ruth broke off, and I finished the sentence in thought. "Listen, Ruth," I said then, "I've an idea that Steele's house will be attacked by the gang tonight, and destroyed same as the jail was this afternoon. These rustlers are crazy. They'll expect to kill him while he's there. But he won't be there. If you and Ray hear shooting and yelling tonight, don't be frightened. Steele and I will be safe."

"Oh, I hope so. Archie, I must hurry back. But, first, can't you arrange a meeting between Ray and Steele? It's her wish. She begged me to. She must see him."

"I'll try," I promised, knowing that promise would be hard to keep.

"We could ride out from the ranch somewhere. You remember we used to rest on the high ridge where there was a shady place . . . such a beautiful outlook? It was there I . . . I . . . "

"My dear, you needn't bring up painful memories. I remember where."

Ruth laughed softly. She could laugh in the face of the gloomiest prospects.

"Well, tomorrow morning, or the next, or any morning soon, you tie your red scarf on the dead branch of that high mesquite. I'll look every morning with the glass. If I see the scarf, Ray and I will ride out."

"That's fine. Ruth, you have ideas in your pretty little head. And once I thought it held nothing but . . . "

She put a hand on my mouth. "I must go now," she said, and rose. She stood close to me and put her arms around my neck. "One thing more, Archie. It . . . it was dif . . . ferent telling Ray we . . . we were engaged. I lied to Uncle. But *what else* could I have told Ray? I . . . I . . . Oh . . . was it . . . ?" She faltered.

"Ruth, you lied to Longstreth to save me. But you must have accepted me before you could have told Ray the *truth*."

"Oh, Archie, I had . . . in my heart! But it has been a long time since you asked me . . . and . . . "

"You imagined my offer might have been withdrawn. Well, it stands."

She slipped closer to me then, with that soft sinuousness of a woman, and I believed she might have kissed me had I not held back, toying with my happiness.

"Ruth, do you love me?"

"Ever so much. Since the very first."

"I'm a marshal, a ranger like Steele, a hunter of criminals. It's a hard life. There's spilling of blood. And any time I . . . I might . . . All the same, Ruth . . . will you be my wife?"

"Oh, Archie! Yes. But let me tell you, when your duty's done here, that *I* will have a word to say about your future. Archie, it'll be news to you to learn I'm an orphan. And I'm not a poor one. I own a plantation in Louisiana. I'll make a planter out of you. There!"

"Ruth! You're rich?" I exclaimed.

"I'm afraid I am. But nobody can ever say *you* married me for my money."

"Well, no, not if you tell of my abject courtship when I thought you a poor relation on a visit. My God, Ruth, if I *only* could see this ranger job through safely and to success."

"You will," she said softly.

Then I took a ring from my little finger and slipped it on hers.

"That was my sister's. She's dead now. No other girl ever wore it. Let it be your engagement ring. Ruth, I pray I may somehow get through this awful ranger deal to make you happy . . . to become worthy of you."

"Archie, I fear only one thing," she whispered.

"And what's that?"

"There will be fighting. And you . . . Oh, I saw into your eyes the other night when you stood with your hands up. You would kill anybody, Archie. It's awful. But don't think me a baby. I can conceive what your work is . . . what a man you must be. I can love you and stick to you, too. But, if you killed a blood relative of mine, I would have to give you up . . . I'm a Southerner, Archie, and blood is thick. I scorn my uncle, and I hate my cousin. And I love you. But don't you kill one of my family. I . . . Oh, I beg of you, go as far as you dare to avoid that."

I could find no voice to answer her, and for a long moment we were locked in an embrace, breast to breast and lips to lips — an embrace of sweet pain. Then she broke away, called a low, hurried good bye, and stole like a shadow into the darkness.

An hour later I lay in the open starlight among the stones and brush, out where Steele and I always met. He lay there with me, but, while I looked up at the stars, he had his face covered with his hands. For I had given him my proofs of the guilt of Ray Longstreth's father.

Steele had made one comment: "I wish to God I'd sent for some fool who'd have bungled the job!"

This was a compliment to me, but it showed what a sad pass Steele had come to. My regret was that I had no sympathy to offer him. I failed him there. I had trouble of my own. The feel of Ruth's clinging arms around my neck, the warm, sweet touch of her lips remained on mine. What Steele was enduring I did not know, but I felt that it was agony.

Meanwhile time passed. The blue, velvety sky darkened as the stars grew brighter. The wind grew stronger and colder. I heard sand blowing against the stones like the rustle of silk. Otherwise it was a singularly quiet night.

I wondered where the coyotes were and longed for their chorus. By and by a prairie wolf sent up his lonely lament from the distant ridges. That mourn was worse than the silence. It made the cold shudders creep up and down my back. It was just the cry that seemed to be the one to express my own trouble. No one hearing that long-drawn, quivering wail could ever dissociate it from tragedy. Finally it ceased, and then I wished it would come again.

Steele lay like the stone beside him. Was he ever going to speak? Among the vagaries of my mood was a petulant desire to have him sympathize with me. I had just looked at my watch, making out in the starlight that the hour was eleven, when the report of a gun broke the silence. I jumped up to peer over the stones. Steele lumbered up beside me, and I heard him draw his breath hard.

CHAPTER FIFTEEN

The Fight in the Hope So

I COULD plainly see the lights of his adobe house, but, of course, nothing else was visible. There were no other lighted houses nearby. Several flashes gleamed, faded swiftly, to be followed by reports, and then the unmistakable jingle of glass.

"I guess the fools have opened up, Steele," I said.

His response was an angry grunt.

It was just as well, I concluded, that things had begun to stir. Steele needed to be roused. Suddenly a single sharp yell pealed out. Following it, came a huge flare of light, a sheet of flame in which a great cloud of smoke or dust shot up — then, with accompanying darkness, burst a low, deep, thunderous boom. The lights of the house went out — then came a crash.

Points of light flashed in a half-circle, and the reports of guns blended with the yells of furious men, and all these were swallowed up in the roar of a mob. Another and a heavier explosion momentarily lightened the darkness and then rent the air. It was succeeded by a continuous volley and a steady sound that, though composed of yells, screams, cheers, was not anything but a hideous roar of hate. It kept up long after there could have been any possibility of life under the ruins of that house. It was more than hate of Steele. All that was wild and lawless and violent hurled this deed at the ranger service.

Such events had happened before in Texas and other states, but, strangely, they never happened more than once in one locality. They were expressions, perhaps, that could never come but once. I watched Steele through all that hideous din, that manifestation of insane rage at his life and joy at his death, and, when silence once more reigned, and he turned his white face to mine, I had a sensation of dread. And dread was something particularly foreign to my nature.

"So Blome and the Sneckers think they've done for me," he muttered.

"Pleasant surprise for them tomorrow, eh, old man?" I queried.

"Tomorrow? Look, Russ, what's left of my old 'dobe house is on fire. The ruins can't be searched soon. And I was particular to fix things so it'd look like

I was home. I just wanted to give them a chance. It's incomprehensible how easy men like them can be duped. Whiskey-soaked. Yes, they'll be surprised."

He lingered a while, watching the smoldering fire and the dim columns of smoke curling up against the dark blue.

"Russ, do you suppose they hear up at the ranch and think I'm . . . ?"

"They heard, of course," I replied. "But the girls know you're safe with me."

"Safe? I almost wish to God I was there under that heap of ruins, where the rustlers think they've left me."

"Well, Steele, old fellow, *almost* is not quite. Come on. We need some sleep."

Then, with Steele in the lead, we stalked away into the open.

Two days later, about the middle of the forenoon, I sat upon a great flat rock in the shade of a bushy mesquite, and, besides enjoying the vast clear sweep of gold and gray plain below, I was otherwise pleasantly engaged. Ruth sat as close to me as she could get, holding to my arm as if she never intended to let go. On the other side Miss Longstreth leaned against me, and she was white and breathless, partly from the quick ride out from the ranch, partly from agitation. She had grown thinner, and there were dark shadows under her eyes, yet she seemed only more beautiful.

The red scarf with which I had signaled the girls waved from a branch of the mesquite. At the foot of the ridge their horses were halted in a shady spot.

"Take off your sombrero," I said to Ruth. "You look hot. Besides, you're prettier with your hair flying."

As she made no move, I took it off for her. Then I made bold to perform the same office for Miss Longstreth. She faintly smiled her thanks. Assuredly she had forgotten all her resentment. There were little beads of perspiration upon her white brow. What a beautiful mass of black-brown hair, with strands of red or gold. Pretty soon she would be bending that exquisite head and face over poor Steele, and I, who had schemed this meeting, did not care what he might do to me. Pretty soon, also, there was likely to be an interview that would shake us all to our depths, and, naturally, I was somber at heart. But, though my outward mood of good humor may have been pretense, it certainly was a pleasure to be with the girls again way out in the open.

Both girls were quiet, and this made my task harder, and perhaps in my anxiety to ward off questions and appear happy for their own sakes I made an ass of myself with my silly talk and familiarity. Had ever a ranger such a job as mine?

"Ray, did Ruth show you her engagement ring?" I went on, bound to talk.

Miss Longstreth either did not notice my use of her first name, or she did not object. She seemed so friendly, so helplessly wistful.

"Yes. It's very pretty. An antique. I've seen a few of them," she replied.

"I hope you'll let Ruth marry me soon."

"Let her? Ruth Herbert! You haven't become acquainted with your fiancée. When . . . ?"

"Oh, next week, just as soon . . . "

"*Archie!*" cried Ruth, blushing furiously.

"What's the matter?" I queried innocently.

"You're a little previous."

"Well, Ruth, I don't presume to split hairs over dates. But, you see . . . you've become extremely more desirable . . . in the light of certain revelations. Ray, wasn't Ruth the deceitful thing? An heiress all the time. And I'm to be a planter and smoke fine cigars and drink mint juleps. No, there won't be any juleps."

"Archie, you're talking nonsense," reproved Ruth. "Surely it's no time to be funny."

"All right," I replied with resignation.

It was no task to discard that hollow mask of humor. A silence ensued, and I waited for it to be broken.

"Is Steele badly hurt?" asked Miss Longstreth presently.

"No. Not what he or I'd call hurt at all. He's got a scalp wound, where a bullet bounced off his skull. It's only a scratch. Then he's got another in the shoulder, but it's not bad, either."

"Where is he now?"

"Look across on the other ridge. See the big white stone? There, down under the trees, is our camp. He's there."

"When may . . . I see him?" There was a catch in her low voice.

"He's asleep now. After what happened yesterday, he was exhausted, and the pain in his head kept him awake till late. Let him sleep a while yet. Then you can see him."

"Did he know we were coming?"

"He hadn't the slightest idea. He'll be overjoyed to see you. He can't help *that*. But he'll about fall upon me with harmful intent."

"Why?"

"Well, I know he's afraid to see you."

"Why?"

"Because it only makes his duty harder."

"Ah," she breathed.

It seemed to me that my intelligence confirmed a hope of hers and gave her relief. I felt something terrible in the balance for Steele. And I was glad to be able to throw them together. The catastrophe must fall, and now the sooner it fell, the better. But I experienced a tightening of my lips and a tugging at my heartstrings.

"Ruth, what do you and Ray know about the goings-on in town yesterday?" I asked.

"Not much. Floyd was like an insane man. I was afraid to go near him. Uncle wore a sardonic smile. I heard him curse Floyd . . . oh, terribly! I believe he hates Floyd. Same as day before yesterday, there were men riding in and out. But Ray and I heard very little and conflicting statements at that. We knew there was fighting. Dick and the servants, the cowboys, all brought rumors. Steele was killed at least ten times and came to life just as many. I can't recall . . . don't want to recall . . . all we heard. But this morning, when I saw the red scarf flying in the wind . . . well, Archie, I was so glad I could not see through the glass any more. We knew then Steele was all right, or you wouldn't have put up the signal."

"Reckon few people in Fairdale realize just what *did* come off," I replied with a grim chuckle.

"Russ, I want you to tell me," said Miss Longstreth earnestly.

"What?" I queried sharply.

"About yesterday . . . what Steele did . . . what happened."

"Miss Longstreth, I could tell you in a few short statements of fact . . . or I could take two hours in the telling. Which do you prefer?"

"I prefer the long telling. I want to know all . . . all about him."

"But why, Miss Longstreth? Consider. This is hardly a story for a sensitive woman's ears."

"I am no coward," she replied, turning eyes to me that flashed like dark fire.

"But why?" I persisted.

I wanted a good reason for calling up all the details of the most strenuous and terrible day in my border experience. She was silent a moment. I saw her gaze turn to the spot where Steele lay asleep, and it was a pity he could not see her eyes then.

"Frankly, I don't want to tell you," I added, and I surely would have been glad to get out of the job.

"I want to hear . . . because I glory in his work," she replied deliberately.

I gathered as much from the expression on her face as from the deep ring of her voice, the clear content of her statement. She loved the ranger, but that was not all of her reason.

"His work?" I echoed. "Do you want him to succeed in it?"

"With all my heart," she said with a white glow on her face.

"My God!" I ejaculated.

I just could not help it. I felt Ruth's small fingers clutching my arm like sharp pincers. I bit my lips to keep them shut. What if Steele had heard her say that? Poor, noble, justice-loving, blind girl! She knew even less than I hoped.

I forced my thought on the question immediately at hand. She gloried in the ranger's work. She wanted with all her heart to see him succeed at it. She had a woman's pride in his manliness. Perhaps, with a woman's complex, incomprehensible motive, she wanted Steele to be shown to her in all the power that made him hated and feared by lawless men. She had finally accepted the wild life of this border as something terrible and inevitable, but passing. Steele was one of the strange and great and misunderstood men who were making that wild life pass.

For the first time I realized that Miss Longstreth, through sharpened eyes of love, saw Steele as he really was — a wonderful and necessary violence. Her intelligence and sympathy had enabled her to see through defamation and the false records following a ranger. She had had no choice but to love him; and then a woman's glory in work that freed men, saved women, and made children happy effaced forever the horror of a few dark deeds of blood.

"Miss Longstreth, I must tell you first that" — I began, and hesitated — "that I'm not a cowboy. My wild stunts, my drinking and gaming . . . these were all pretence."

"Indeed! I am very glad to hear it. And was Ruth in your confidence?"

"Only lately. I am a United States deputy marshal in the service of Steele."

She gave a slight start but did not raise her head.

"I have deceived you. But all the same, I've been your friend. I ask you to respect my secret a little while. I'm telling you because otherwise my relation to Steele yesterday would not be plain. Now, if you and Ruth will use this blanket, make yourselves more comfortable seats, I'll begin my story."

Miss Longstreth allowed me to arrange a place for her where she could rest at ease, but Ruth returned to my side and stayed there. She was an enigma today

— pale, brooding, silent — and she never looked at me, except when my face was half averted.

"Well," I began, "night before last Steele and I lay hidden among the rocks near the edge of town, and we listened to and watched the destruction of Steele's house. It had served his purpose to leave lights burning, to have shadows blow across the window blinds, and to have a dummy in his bed. Also, he arranged guns to go off inside the house at the least jar. Steele wanted evidence against his enemies.

"It was not the pleasantest kind of thing to wait there, listening to that drunken mob. There must have been a hundred men. The disturbance and the intent worked strangely upon Steele. It made him different. In the dark I couldn't tell how he looked, but I felt a mood coming in him that fairly made me dread the next day.

"About midnight we started for our camp here. Steele got in some sleep, but I couldn't. I was cold and hot by turns, eager and backward, furious and thoughtful. You see, the deal was such a complicated one, and tomorrow certainly was nearing the climax. By morning I was sick, distraught, gloomy, and uncertain.

"I had breakfast ready when Steele awoke. I hated to look at him, but, when I did, it was like being revived.

"He said, 'Russ, you'll trail alongside me today and through the rest of this mess.'

"That gave me another shock. I want to explain to you girls that this was the first time in my life I was backward at the prospect of a fight. The shock was the jump of my pulse. My nerve came back. To line up with Steele against Blome and his gang . . . that would be great!

"'All right, old man,' I replied. 'We're going after them, then?'

"He only nodded.

"After breakfast I watched him clean, oil, and reload his guns. I didn't need to ask him if he expected to use them. I didn't need to urge upon him Captain MacNeal's command.

"'Russ,' said Steele, 'we'll go in together. But, before we get to town, I'll leave you, circle, and come in at the back of the Hope So. You hurry on ahead, post Morton and his men, get the lay of the gang, if possible, and then be at the Hope So when I come in.'

"I didn't ask him if I had a free hand with my gun. I intended to have that. We left camp together and hurried toward town. It was near noon when we separated.

"I came down the road, apparently from Longstreth's ranch. There was a crowd around the ruins of Steele's house. It was one heap of crumbled 'dobe bricks and burned logs. It was still hot and smoking. No attempt had been made to dig into the ruins. The curious crowd was certain that Steele lay buried under all that stuff. I walked around with a busy tongue.

"One feature of that night assault made me ponder. Day-light discovered the bodies of three dead men, rustlers, who had been killed, the report went out, by random shots. Other participants in that affair had been wounded. I believed Morton and his men, under cover of the darkness and in the melee had sent in some shots not calculated upon in the program.

"From there I hurried to town. Just as I had expected, Morton and Zimmer were lounging in front of the Hope So. They had company, disreputable and otherwise. As yet Morton's crowd had not come under suspicion. He was wild for news of Steele, and, when I gave it and outlined the plan, he became as cool and dark and grim as any man of my kind could have wished.

"He sent Zimmer to get the others of their clique. Then he acquainted me with a few facts, although he was non-committal in regard to my suspicion as to the strange killing of the three rustlers. Blome, Bo Snecker, Hilliard, and Pickens, the ringleaders, had painted the town in celebration of Steele's death.

They all got gloriously drunk except old man Snecker. He had cold feet, they said. They were too happy to do any more shooting or mind what the old rustler cautioned. It was two o'clock before they went to bed.

"This morning, after eleven, one by one they appeared with their followers. The excitement had died down. Ranger Steele was out of the way, and Fairdale was once more wide open, free and easy. Blome alone seemed sullen and spiritless, unresponsive to his comrades and their admirers. And now, at the time of my arrival, the whole gang, with the exception of old Snecker, were assembled in the Hope So.

" 'Zimmer will be smart enough to drift his outfit along one or two at a time?' I asked Morton, and he reassured me. Then we went into the saloon.

"There were perhaps sixty or seventy men in the place, more than half of whom were in open accord with Blome's gang. Of the rest, there were many of doubtful repute, and a few that might have been apparently neutral yet all the time were secretly burning to help any cause against these rustlers. At all events, I gathered that impression from the shadowed faces, the tense bodies, the too-evident indication of anything but careless presence there.

"The windows were open. The light was clear. Few men smoked, but all had a drink before them. There was the ordinary subdued hum of conversation. I surveyed the scene, picked out my position so as to be close to Steele, when he entered, and sauntered around to it. Morton aimlessly leaned against a post. Presently Zimmer came in with a man, and they advanced to the bar. Other men entered as others went out.

"Blome, Bo Snecker, Hilliard, and Pickens had a table full in the light of the open windows. I recognized the faces of the two last-named, but I had not, until Morton informed me, known who they were. Pickens was little, scrubby, dusty, sandy, mottled, and he resembled a rattlesnake. Hilliard was big, gaunt, bronzed, with a huge mustache and hollow, fierce eyes. I never have seen a grave-robber, but I imagine one would look like Hilliard. Bo Snecker was a sleek, slim, slender, hard-looking boy, marked dangerous, because he was too young and too wild to have caution or fear.

"Blome, the last of the bunch, showed the effects of a bad night. You girls remember how handsome he was, but he didn't look it now. His face was swollen, dark red, and, as it had been bright, now it was dark. Indeed, he looked sullen, shamed, sore. He was sober now. Thought written on his clouded brow. He was awakening now to the truth that the day before had branded him a coward and that had sent him out to bolster up his courage with drink. His vanity had begun to bleed. He knew, if his faithful comrades had not awakened to it yet, that his prestige had been ruined. For a gunman, he had suffered the last degradation. He had been bidden to draw, and he had failed of nerve. He breathed heavily. His eyes were not clear. His hands were shaky. I almost pitied this rustler who very soon must face an incredibly swift and mercilessly fatal ranger . . . face him, too, suddenly, as if the grave had opened to give up its dead.

"Friends and comrades of this center group passed to and fro, and there was much lazy, merry, talk, though not very loud. The whole crowd was still half asleep. It certainly was an auspicious hour for Steele to confront them. No man knew the stunning, paralyzing effect of surprise better than Steele. I, of course, must take my cue from him or from the sudden development of events. But Jack Blome did not enter into my calculations. I gave him, at most, about a minute to live after Steele entered the place.

"I meant to keep sharp eyes all around. I knew, once with a gun out, Steele could kill Blome's comrades at the table as quick as lightning, if he chose. I rather thought my game was to watch his outside partners. This was right and, as it turned out, enabled me to save Steele's life.

"Moments passed, and still the ranger did not come. I began to get nervous.

Had he been stopped? I scouted the idea. Who could have stopped him, then? Probably the time seemed longer than it really was. Morton showed the strain, also. Other men looked drawn, haggard, waiting, as if expecting a thunderbolt. Once in my roving gaze I caught Blandy's glinty eye on me. I didn't like the gleam. I said to myself I'd watch him, if I had to do it out of the back of my head. Blandy, by the way, is . . . *was* I should say . . . the Hope So bartender."

I stopped to clear my throat and got my breath.

"*Was,*" whispered Ruth. She quivered with excitement.

Miss Longstreth bent eyes upon me that would have stirred a stone man.

"Yes, he was once," I replied ambiguously, but mayhap my grimness betrayed the truth. "Don't hurry me, Ruth. I guarantee you'll be sick enough presently.

"Well, I kept my eyes shifty. And I reckon I'll never forget that room. Likely I saw what wasn't really there. In the excitement, the suspense, I must have made shadows into real substance. Anyway, there was the half-circle of bearded, swarthy men around Blome's table. There were the four rustlers . . . Blome, brooding, perhaps vaguely, spiritually, listening to a knock . . . there was Bo Snecker, reckless youth, fondling a flower he had, putting the stem in his glass, then to his lips, and lastly into the buttonhole of Blome's vest . . . there was Hilliard, big, gloomy, maybe with his cavernous eyes seeing the hell where I expected he'd soon be . . . and last, the little dusty, scaly Pickens, who looked about to leap and sting some one.

"In a lull of the general conversation, I heard Pickens say, 'Jack, drink up an' come out of it. Every man has an off day. You've gambled long enough to know every feller gits called. An', as Steele has cashed, what the hell do you care?'

"Hilliard nodded his ghoul's head and blinked his dead eyes. Bo Snecker laughed. It wasn't a different laugh from any other boy's. I remembered then that he killed Laramie. I began to sweat fire. Would Steele ever come?

"'Jim, the ole man hed cold feet, an' he's give 'em to Jack,' said Bo. 'It ain't nothin' to lose your nerve once. Didn't I run like a scared jackrabbit from Steele? Watch me, if he comes to life, as the old man hinted.'

"'Mebbe Steele wasn't in the 'dobe at all. Aw, thet's a joke! I seen him in bed. I seen his shoulder. I heard his shots comin' from the room. Jack, you seen an' heerd same as me.'

"'Sure. I *know* the ranger's cashed,' replied Blome. 'It's not that. I'm sore, boys.'

"'Deader'n a doornail in hell,' replied Pickens, louder, as he lifted his glass. 'Here's to Lone Star Steele's ghost! An', if I seen it this minnit, I'd ask it to waltz with me.'

"The back door swung violently, and Steele, huge as a giant, plunged through and leaped square in front of that table. Someone among them let out a strange, harsh cry. It wasn't Blome or Snecker ... probably Pickens. He dropped the glass he had lifted. The cry had stilled the room, so the breaking of the glass was plainly heard.

"For a space that must have been short, yet seemed long, everybody stood tight. Steele, with both hands out and down, leaned a little, in a way I had never seen him do. It was the position of a greyhound, but that was merely the body of him. Steele's nerve, his spirit, his meaning was there, like lightning about to strike. Blome maintained a ghastly, stricken silence. Then the instant was plain when he realized this was no ghost of Steele, but the ranger in the flesh. Blome's whole frame rippled as thought jerked him out of his trance. His comrades sat stone-still. Then Hilliard and Pickens dived without rising from the table. Their haste broke the spell.

"I wish I could tell it as quick as it happened. But Bo Snecker, turning white as a sheet, stuck to Blome. And the others failed him, as he had guessed they would fail. Low curses and exclamations were uttered by men, sliding and pressing back, but the principals were mute. I was thinking hard, yet I had no time to get to Steele's side. I, like the rest, was held fast. But I kept my eyes sweeping around, then back again to that center pair.

"Blome slowly rose. I think he did it instinctively because, if he had expected his first movement to start the action, he never would have moved. Snecker sat partly on the rail of his chair, with both feet square on the floor, and he never twitched a muscle. There was a striking difference in the looks of these two rustlers ... Snecker had burning holes for eyes in his white face. At the last he was stanch, defiant, game to the core. He didn't think. But Blome faced death and knew it. It was infinitely more than the facing of foes, the taking of stock, preliminary to the even break. Blome's attitude was that of a trapped wolf about to start into savage action ... nevertheless, it was also the pitifully weak stand of a ruffian against ruthless and powerful law.

"The border of Pecos County could have had no greater lesson than this ... Blome face-to-face with the ranger. That part of the border present saw its most noted exponent of lawlessness a coward, almost powerless to go for his gun, fatally sure of his own doom. But that moment ... seeming so long, and really so short ... had to end. Blome made a spasmodic upheaval of shoulder and arm. Snecker a second later flashed into movement.

"Steele blurred in my sight. His action couldn't be followed. But I saw his gun, waving up, flame red, once . . . twice . . . and the reports almost boomed together.

"Blome bent forward, arm down, doubled up, and fell over the table and slid to the floor. But Snecker's gun cracked with Steele's last shot. I heard the bullet strike Steele. It made me sick as if it had hit me. Steele never budged. Snecker leaped up, screaming. His gun went clattering to the floor. His left hand swept to his right arm, which had been shattered by Steele's bullet. Blood streamed everywhere. His screams were curses, and then ended, choking him in rage hardly human. Leaping, he went down on his knees after the gun.

" 'Don't pick it up!' called Steele, and his command would have checked anyone save an insanely maddened youth. For an instant it even held Snecker. On his knees, right arm hanging limp, left extended, and face ghastly with agony and fiendish fury, he certainly was an appalling sight.

" 'Bo, you're courtin' death!' called a hard voice from the crowd.

" 'Snecker, wait! Don't make me kill you!' cried Steele swiftly. 'You're only a boy. Surrender! You'll outlive your sentence many years. I promise clemency. Hold, you fool . . . !'

"But Snecker was not to be denied his last game move. He scrabbled for his gun. Just then something, a breath perhaps, or intuition . . . I'll never know what . . . made me turn my head. I saw Blandy, the bartender, deliberately aiming a huge gun at Steele. If he had not been so slow, so sure, I would have been too late. I whirled and shot. Talk about nick of time! Blandy pulled trigger just as my bullet smashed into his head. He dropped dead behind the bar, and his gun dropped in front. But he had hit Steele.

"The ranger staggered, almost fell. I thought he was done, and, yelling, I leaped to him. But he righted himself. Then, as I wheeled again, someone in the crowd killed Bo Snecker as he wobbled up with his gun. That was the signal for a wild break for outdoors, for cover. I heard the crack of guns and whistle of lead. I shoved Steele back of the bar, falling over Blandy as I did so.

"When I got up, Steele was leaning over the bar with a gun in each hand. There was a hot fight, then, for a minute or so, but I didn't fire a shot. Morton and his crowd were busy.

"Men ran everywhere, shooting, ducking, cursing. The room got blue with smoke till you couldn't see, and then the fight changed to the street. Steele and I ran out. There was shooting everywhere. Morton's crowd appeared to be in pursuit of rustlers in all directions. I ran with Steele and did not observe his condition until suddenly he fell down in the street. He looked so white and so bloody I thought he'd stopped another bullet and . . . "

Here Miss Longstreth's agitation made it necessary for me to halt my story, and I hoped she had heard enough. But she was not sick, as Ruth appeared to be. She simply had been overcome by emotion. And presently, with a blaze in her eyes that showed how her soul was aflame with righteous wrath at these rustlers and ruffians, and how, whether she knew it or not, the woman in her loved a fight, she bade me go on.

So I persevered, and, with poor little Ruth sagging against me, I went on with the details of that fight. I told how Steele rebounded from his weakness and could no more have been stopped than an avalanche. For all I saw, he did not use his guns again.

Here, there, everywhere, as Morton and his squad cornered a rustler, Steele would go in, ordering surrender, promising protection. He seemed to have no thought of bullets. I could not hold him back, and it was hard to keep pace with him. How many times he was shot at, I had no idea, but it was many. He dragged forth this and that rustler and turned them all over to Morton to be guarded. More than once he protected a craven rustler from the summary dealing Morton wanted.

I told Miss Longstreth particularly how Steele appeared to me, what his effect was on these men, how toward the end of the fight rustlers were appealing to him to save them from these new-born vigilantes. I believe I drew a picture of the ranger that would live forever in her heart of hearts. If she were a hero-worshiper, she would have her fill.

One thing that was strange to me — leaving fight, action, blood, peril out of the story — was the singular exultation, for want of some better term, that I experienced in recalling Steele's look, his wonderful, cold, resistless, inexplicable presence, his unquenchable spirit that was at once deadly and merciful. Other men would have killed where he saved. I recalled this magnificent spiritual something about him, remembered it strongest in the ring of his voice as he appealed to Bo Snecker not to force him to kill.

Then I told how we left a dozen prisoners under guard and went back to the Hope So to find Blome where he had fallen. Steele's bullet had cut one of the petals of the rose Snecker had playfully put in the rustler's buttonhole. Bright and fatal target for an eye like Steele's.

Bo Snecker lay clutching his gun, his face set rigidly in that last fierce expression of his savage nature. There were five other dead men on the floor, and, significant of the work of Steele's unknown allies, Hilliard and Pickens were among them.

"Steele and I made for camp then," I concluded. "We didn't speak a word on the way out. When we reached camp, all Steele said was for me to go off and leave him alone. He looked sick.

"I went off, only not very far. I knew what was wrong with him, and it wasn't bullet wounds. I was near when he had his spell and fought it out. Strange how spilling blood effects some men. It never bothered me much. I hope I'm human, too. I certainly felt like a . . . an awful joy when I sent that bullet into Blandy's bloated head in time. And I'll always feel that way about it. But Steele's different."

CHAPTER SIXTEEN

Torn Two Ways

STEELE lay in a shady little glade, partly walled by masses of uprearing rocks that we used as a look-out point. He was asleep, yet far from comfortable. The bandage I had put around his head had been made from strips of soiled towel, and, having collected sundry bloody spots, it was an unsightly affair. There was a blotch of dried blood down one side of Steele's face. His shirt bore more dark stains and in one place was pasted fast to his shoulder where a bandage marked the location of his other wound.

A number of green flies were crawling over him and buzzing around his head. He looked helpless, despite his giant size, and certainly a great deal worse off than I had intimated and, in fact, than he really was. Miss Longstreth gasped when she saw him, and both her hands flew to her breast.

"Girls, don't make any noise," I whispered. "I'd rather he didn't wake suddenly to find you here. Go 'round behind the rocks there. I'll wake him and call you presently."

They complied with my wish, and I stepped down to Steele and gave him a little shake. He awoke instantly.

"Howdy, old son. Want a drink?"

"Water or champagne?" he inquired.

I stared at him. "I've some champagne behind the rocks."

"Water, you locoed son of a gun!"

He looked about as thirsty as a desert coyote; he also looked flighty. I was reaching for the canteen when I happened to think what a pleasure it would be to Miss Longstreth to minister to him, and I drew back.

"Wait a little." Then with an effort I plunged. "Vaughn, listen. Miss Longstreth and Ruth are here."

I thought he was going to jump up he started so violently. I pressed him back.

"*She* . . . ? Why, has she been here all the time? Russ, you haven't double-crossed me?"

"Steele!" I exclaimed. He was certainly out of his head. "Pure accident, old man."

He appeared to be half stunned, yet an eager, strange, haunting look shone in his eyes.

"Fool!" he exclaimed.

"Can't you make the ordeal easier for her?" I asked. "This'll be hard on Ray. She's got to be told things."

"Ah," breathed Steele, sinking back. "Make it easier for her . . . Russ, you're a damned schemer. You *have* given me the double-cross. You have, and she's going to."

"We're in bad, both of us," I replied thickly. "I've ideas, crazy enough maybe. I'm between the devil and the deep sea, I tell you. I'm about ready to show yellow. . . . All the same, I say, see Miss Longstreth and talk to her, even if you can't talk straight."

"All right, Russ," he replied hurriedly. "But God, man, don't I look a sight . . . ? All this dirt and blood!"

"Well, old man, if she takes that bungled mug of yours in her lap, you can be sure you're loved. You needn't jump out of your boots. Brace up, now, for I'm going to bring the girls."

As I got up to go, I heard him groan. I went around behind the stones and found them.

"Come on," I said. "He's awake now, but a little queer. Feverish. He gets that way sometimes. It won't last long."

I led Miss Longstreth and Ruth back into the shade of our little camp glade. Steele had gotten worse all in a moment. Also the fool had pulled the bandage off his head. His wound had begun to bleed anew, and the flies were paying no attention to his weak efforts to brush them away. His head rolled as we reached his side, and his eyes were certainly wild and wonderful and devouring enough.

"Who's that?" he demanded.

"Easy there, old man," I replied. "I've brought the girls."

Miss Longstreth shook like a leaf in the wind.

"So you've come to see me die?" asked Steele in a deep and hollow voice.

Miss Longstreth gave me a lightning glance of terror.

"He's only off his head," I said. "Soon as we wash and bathe his head . . . cool his temperature, he'll be all right."

Miss Longstreth dropped to her knees, flinging her gloves aside. She lifted Steele's head into her lap. When I saw her tears falling upon his face, I felt worse than a villain. She bent over him for a moment, and one of the tender hands at his cheeks met the flow of fresh blood and did not shrink. "Ruth," she said, "bring the scarf out of my coat. There's a veil, too. Bring that. Russ, you get me some water . . . pour some in the pan there."

"Water," whispered Steele.

She gave him a drink.

Ruth came with the scarf and veil, and then she backed away to a large stone and sat there. The sight of blood had made her a little pale and weak. Miss Longstreth's hands trembled, and her tears still fell, but neither interfered with her tender and skillful dressing of that bullet wound. Steele certainly said a lot of crazy things.

"But why'd you come . . . why're you so good . . . when you don't love me?"

"Oh, but . . . I do . . . love you," whispered Miss Longstreth brokenly.

"How do I know?"

"I'm here. I tell you."

There was a silence, during which she kept on bathing his head, and he kept on watching her. "Ray!" he broke out suddenly.

"Yes . . . yes."

"That won't stop the pain in my head."

"Oh, I hope so."

"Kiss me . . . that will," he whispered.

She obeyed, as a child might have, and kissed his damp forehead close to the red furrow where the bullet had cut.

"Not there," Steele whispered.

Then blindly, as if drawn by a magnet, she bent to his lips. I could not turn away my head, though my instincts were delicate enough. I believe that kiss was the first kiss of love for both Ray Longstreth and Vaughn Steele. It was so strange, so long, and somehow beautiful.

Steele looked rapt. I could only see the side of her face and that was white, like snow. After she raised her head, she seemed unable, for a moment, to take up her task where it had been broken off, and Steele lay as if he really were dead. Here I got up, and, seating myself beside Ruth, I put an arm around her.

"Dear Ruth, there are others," I said.

"Oh . . . Archie . . . what's to come of it all?" she faltered, and then she broke down and began to cry softly.

I would have been only too glad to tell her what hung in the balance, one way or another, had I known — but, surely, catastrophe. Then I heard Steele's voice again, and its huskiness, its different tone, made me fearful, made me strain my ears when I tried, or thought I tried, not to listen.

"Ray, you know how hard my duty is, don't you?"

"Yes . . . I know . . . I *think* I know."

"You've guessed . . . about your father?"

"I've seen all along you must clash. But it needn't be . . . so bad. If I can only bring you two together . . . ? Ah, please don't speak any more. You're excited now, not just yourself."

"No, listen. We *must* clash, your father and I. Ray, he's not . . . "

"Not what he seems! Oh, I know, to my sorrow."

"*What* do you know?"

She seemed drawn by a will stronger than her own. "To my shame I know. He has been greedy, crafty, unscrupulous . . . dishonest."

"Ray, if he were only that. That wouldn't make my duty torture. That wouldn't ruin your life . . . . Dear, sweet girl . . . forgive me . . . your father's . . . "

"Hush, Vaughn. You're growing excited. It will not do Please . . . please . . . !"

"Ray, your father's . . . chief of this . . . gang that I came to break up."

"My God, hear him . . . ! How dare you . . . ? Oh, Vaughn, poor, poor boy, you're out of your mind. Ruth, Russ, what shall we do? He's worse. He's saying the most dreadful things. I . . . I can't bear to hear him."

Steele heaved a sigh and closed his eyes. I walked away with Ruth, led her to and fro in a shady aisle beyond the rocks, and tried to comfort her as best I could. After a while, when we returned to the glade, Miss Longstreth had considerable color in her cheeks, and Steele was leaning against the rock, grave and sad. I saw that he had recovered, and he had reached the critical point.

"Hello, Russ," he said. "Sprung a little surprise on me, didn't you? Miss Longstreth says I've been a little flighty while she bandaged me up. I hope I wasn't bad. I certainly feel better now. I seemed to . . . to have dreamed."

Miss Longstreth flushed at his concluding words. Then silence ensued. I could not think of anything to say, and Ruth was silent.

"You all seem very strange," said Miss Longstreth.

When Steele's face turned gray to his lips, I knew the moment had come.

"No doubt. We all feel so deeply for you," he said.

"Me? Why?"

"Because the truth must no longer be concealed."

It was her turn to blanch, and her eyes, strained, dark as night, flashed from one of us to the other.

"The truth. Tell it, then." She had more courage than any of us.

"Miss Longstreth, your father is the leader of this gang of rustlers I have been tracing. Your cousin, Floyd Lawson, is his right-hand man."

Miss Longstreth heard, but she did not believe.

"Tell her, Russ," Steele added huskily, turning away.

Wildly she turned to me. I would have given anything to have been able to lie to her. As it was, I could not speak. But she read the truth in my face. And she collapsed as if she had been shot.

I caught her and laid her on the grass. Ruth, murmuring and crying, worked over her. I helped. But Steele stood aloof, dark and silent, as if he hoped she would never return to consciousness. When she did come to and began to cry, to moan, to talk frantically, Steele swaggered away, while Ruth and I made futile efforts to calm her. All we could do was to prevent her doing herself violence.

Presently, when her fury of emotion subsided, and she began to show a hopeless, stricken shame, I left Ruth with her and went off a little way myself. How long I remained absent, I had no idea, but it was no inconsiderable length of time.

Upon my return, to my surprise and relief, Miss Longstreth had recovered her composure or, at least, self-control. She stood, leaning against the rock where Steele had been, and at this moment, beyond any doubt, she was supremely more beautiful than I had ever seen her. She was white, tragic, wonderful.

"Where is Mister Steele?" she asked.

Her tone and her look did not seem at all suggestive of the mood I expected to find her in — one of beseeching agony — of passionate appeal to Steele not to ruin her father.

"I'll find him," I replied, turning away.

Steele was readily found and came back with me. He was as unlike himself as she was strange. But, when they again faced each other, then they were indeed new to me.

"I want to know . . . what you must do," she said.

Steele told her briefly, and his voice was stern.

"Those . . . those criminals outside of my own family don't concern me now," she said then. "But can my father and cousin be taken without bloodshed? I want to know the absolute truth."

Steele knew that they could not be, but he could not tell her so. Again she appealed to me. Thus my part in the situation grew harder. It hurt me so that it made me angry, and my anger made me cruelly frank.

"No. It can't be done. Longstreth and Lawson will be desperately hard to approach, which'll make the chances even. So, if you must know the truth, it'll be your father and cousin who'll go under . . . or it'll be Steele or me . . . or any combination, as luck would have it . . . perhaps all of us."

Her self-control seemed to fly to the four winds. Swift as light she flung herself down before Steele, against his knees, clasping her arms around him.

"Good God! Ray, you mustn't do that," implored Steele. He tried to break her hold with shaking hands, but he could not.

"Listen! Listen!" she cried, and her voice made Steele, and Ruth and me also, still as the rocks behind us. "Hear me! Do you think I beg you to let my father go, for his sake? No! No! I have glorified in your ranger duty. I have loved you because of it. But some awful tragedy threatens here. Listen, Vaughn Steele. Do not you deny me, as I kneel here. I love you. I never loved any other man. But not for my love do I beseech you. There is no help here unless you forswear your duty. Forswear it! Do not kill my father . . . the father of the woman who loves you. Worse and more horrible it would be to let my father kill you! It's I who make this situation unnatural, impossible. You must forswear your duty. I can live . . . no longer if you don't. I pray you . . . ."

Her voice had sunk to a whisper, and now it failed. Then she seemed to get into his arms, to wind herself around him, her hair loosened, her face upturned white and spent, her arms blindly circling his neck. She was all love, all surrender, all supreme appeal, and these alone, without her beauty, would have made her wonderful. But her beauty! Would not Steele have been less than a man, or more than a man, had he been impervious to it? She was like some snow-white exquisite flower, broken, and suddenly blighted. She was a woman then in all that made a woman helpless — in all that made her mysterious, sacred, absolutely and unutterably more than any other thing in life.

All this time my gaze had been riveted on her only. But, when she lifted her white face, tried to lift it, rather, and he drew her up — and then, when both white faces met and seemed to blend in something rapt, awesome, tragic as life — then I saw Steele. I saw a god, a man as beautiful as she was. They might have stood — indeed, they did stand — alone in the heart of a desert — alone in the world — alone with their love and their agony.

It was a solemn and profound moment for me. I faintly realized how great it must have been for them, yet all the while there hammered at my mind the vital thing at stake. Had they forgotten, while I remembered?

It might have been only a moment that he held her. It might have been my own agitation that conjured up such swift and whirling thoughts. But, if my mind sometimes played me false, my eyes never had. I thought I saw Ray Longstreth die in Steele's arms. I could have sworn his heart was breaking, and mine was on the point of breaking, too.

How beautiful they were together. How strong, how mercifully strong, yet shaken he seemed. How tenderly, hopelessly, fatally appealing she was in that hour of her broken life. If I had been Steele, I would have forsworn my duty, honor, name, service for her sake. Did I even have mind enough to divine his torture, his temptation, his narrow escape? I seemed to feel them, at any rate, and, while I saw him with a beautiful light on his face, I saw him also ghastly, ashen, with hands that shook as they groped around her, loosing her only to draw her convulsively back again.

It was the saddest sight I had ever seen. Death was nothing to it. Here was the death of happiness. He must wreck the life of the woman who loved him and whom he loved.

I was becoming half frantic, almost ready to cry out at the uselessness of this scene, almost on the point of pulling them apart, when Ruth dragged me away. Her clinging hold then made me feel perhaps a little of what Miss Longstreth's must have been to Steele. Yet, how different the feeling when it was mine! I could have thrust them apart, after all my schemes and tricks to throw them together, in vague, undefined fear of their embrace. Still, when love beat at my own pulses, when Ruth's soft hand held me tight, and she leaned to me — that was different. I was glad to be led away — glad to have a chance to pull myself together.

But was I to have that chance? Ruth, who in the strife of emotion had been forgotten, might have to be reckoned with. Deep within me some motive, some purpose, was being born in travail. I did not know what, but instinctively I feared Ruth. I feared her because I loved her.

My wits came back to combat my passion. This hazel-eyed girl, soft, fragile creature, might be harder to move than the ranger. But could she divine a motive scarcely yet formed in my brain? Suddenly I became cool, with craft to conceal.

"Oh, Archie! What's the matter with you?" she queried quickly. "Can't Ray and Steele, you and I ride away from this bloody, bad country? Our own lives, our happiness, come first, don't they?"

"They ought to, I suppose," I muttered, fighting against the insidious sweetness of her. I knew then I must keep my lips shut or betray myself.

"You look so strange. Archie, I wouldn't want you to kiss me with that mouth. Thin, shut lips . . . smile! Soften and kiss me. Oh, you're so cold, strange. You chill me."

"Dear child, I'm badly shaken," I said. "Don't expect me to be natural yet. There are things you can't guess. So much depended upon . . . Oh, never mind! I'll go now. I want to be alone . . . to think things out. Let me go, Ruth."

She held me only the tighter — tried to pull my face around. How intuitively keen women are. She felt my distress and that growing, stern, and powerful thing I scarcely dared acknowledge to myself.

Strangely, then, I relaxed and faced her. There was no use trying to fool these feminine creatures. Every second I seemed to grow farther from her. The swiftness of this mood of mine was my only hope. I realized I had to get away quickly and make up my mind after that what I intended to do.

It was an earnest, soulful, and loving pair of eyes that I met. What did she read in mine? Her hands left mine to slide to my shoulders, to slip behind my neck, to lock there like steel bands. Here was my ordeal. Was it to be as terrible as Steele's had been?

I thought it would be, and I swore by all that was rising grim and cold in me that I would be strong. Ruth gave a little cry that cut like a blade in my heart, and then she was pressed close against me, her quivering breast beating against mine, her eyes, dark as night now, searching my soul.

She saw more than I knew and with her convulsive clasp of me confirmed my half-formed fears. Then she kissed me — kisses that had no more of girlhood or coquetry or joy or anything but woman's passion to blind and hold and tame. By their very intensity I sensed the tiger in me. And it was the tiger that made her new and alluring sweetness fail of its intent. I did not return one of her kisses. Just one kiss given back — and I would be lost.

"Oh, Archie, I'm your promised wife," she whispered at my lips. "Soon, you said. I want it to be . . . soon. *Tomorrow!*"

All the subtlety, the intelligence, the cunning, the charm, the love that made up the whole of woman's power breathed in her pleading. What speech known to the tongue could have given me more torture? She chose the strongest weapon nature afforded her. And had the calamity to consider been mine alone, I would have laughed at it and taken Ruth at her word.

Then I told her in short, husky sentences what had depended on Steele — that I loved the ranger service, but loved him more; that his character, his life, embodied this service I loved; that I had ruined him; and now I would forestall him, do his work, force the issue myself or die in the attempt.

"Dearest, it's great of you," she cried. "But the cost. If you kill one of my kin, I'll ... I'll shrink from you! If you're killed ...? Oh, the thought is dreadful. You've done your share. Let Steele ... or some other ranger ... finish it. I swear I don't plead for my uncle or my cousin, for their sakes. If they are vile, let them suffer. Archie, it's *you* I think of. Oh, my pitiful little dreams. I wanted so to surprise you with my beautiful home ... the oranges, the mossy trees, the mockingbirds. Now you'll never ... never come."

"But Ruth, there's a chance ... a mere chance I can do the job without ... "

Then she let go of me. She had given up. I thought she was going to drop and drew her toward the stone. I cursed the day I ever saw MacNeal and the service.

Where, now, was the arch prettiness, the gay, sweet charm of Ruth Herbert? She looked as if she were suffering from a desperate physical injury. And her final breakdown showed how, one way or another, I was lost to her. As she sank on the stone, I had my supreme wrench, and it left me numb, hard, in a cold sweat.

"Don't betray me. I'll forestall him. He's planned nothing for today," I whispered hoarsely. "Ruth ... you dearest, gamest little girl in the world. Remember, I loved you ... even if I couldn't prove it ... your way. It's for his sake. I'm to blame for their love. Some day my act will look different to you. Good-bye."

CHAPTER SEVENTEEN

Russ Sittell in Action

I RAN like one possessed of devils down that rough slope, hurdling the stones and crashing through the brush, with a sound in my ears that was not all the rush of the wind. When I reached a level, I kept running, but something dragged at me.

I slowed down to a walk. Never in my life had I been victim of such sensations. I must flee from something that was drawing me back. Apparently one side of my mind was unalterably fixed, while the other was a hurrying conglomeration of flashes of thought, receiving of sensations. I could not get calmness.

By and by, almost involuntarily, with a fleeting look backward as if in expectation of pursuit, I hurried on faster. Action seemed to make my state less oppressive. It eased the weight upon me. But the farther I went on, the harder it was to continue. I was turning my back upon love, happiness, success in life, perhaps on life itself. I was doing that, but my decision had not been absolute.

There seemed no use to go on farther until I was absolutely sure of myself. I received a clear warning thought that such work as seemed haunting and driving me could never be carried out in the mood under which I labored. I clung onto that thought. Several times I slowed up, then stopped, only to tramp on again.

At length, as I mounted a low ridge, Fairdale lay bright and green before me, not far away, and the sight was a conclusive check. There were mesquites on the ridge, and I sought the shade beneath them. It was the noon hour, with hot, glaring sunlight, and no wind. Here I had to fight it out.

If ever in my varied life of exciting adventure I strove to think, to understand myself, to see through difficulties, I assuredly strove then. I was utterly unlike myself. I could not bring the old self back. I was not the same man I once had been. But I could understand why. It was because of Ruth Herbert — the gay and roguish girl who had bewitched me — the girl whom love had made a woman — the kind of woman meant to make life beautiful for me.

I saw her changing through all these weeks, holding many of the old traits and graces, acquiring new character of mind and body, to become what I had just fled from — a woman sweet, fair, loyal, loving, passionate. Temptation assailed me. To have her tomorrow — my wife! She had said it. Just one little twenty-four hours, and she would be mine — the only woman I ever really coveted — the only one who had ever found the good in me. The thought was alluring.

I followed it out — a long, happy stage ride back to Austin, and then by train to her home where, as she had said, the oranges grew, and the trees waved with streamers of gray moss, and the mockingbirds made melody. I pictured that home. I wondered that long before I had not associated wealth and luxury with her family. Always I had owned a weakness for plantations, for the agricultural life with its open air and freedom from towns. I saw myself, riding through the cotton and rice and cane, at home in a stately old mansion, where longeared hounds bayed me welcome, and a woman looked for me and met me with happy and beautiful smiles.

There might — there would be children. And something new, strange, confounding with its emotion came to life deep in my heart. There would be children! Ruth, their mother, I, their father. The kind of life a lonely ranger always yearned for and never had. I saw it all, felt it keenly, lived its sweetness in an hour of temptation that made me weak physically and my spirit faint and low.

For what had I turned my back on this beautiful, all-satisfying prospect? Was it to arrest and jail a few rustlers? Was it to meet that mocking Longstreth face to face and show him my shield and reach for my gun? Was it to kill that hated Lawson? Was it to save the people of Fairdale from further greed, raid, murder? Was it to please and aid my old captain, MacNeal of the Texas Rangers? Was it to save the service to the state? No — a thousand times no. It was for the sake of Steele. Because he was a wonderful man. Because I had been his undoing. Because I had thrown Ray Longstreth into his arms.

That had been my great error. This ranger had always been the wonder and despair of his fellow officers — so magnificent a machine — so sober, temperate, chaste — so unremittingly loyal to the service — so strangely stern and faithful to his conception of law — so perfect in his fidelity to duty. He was the model, the inspiration which fighting Texas had developed to oppose wildness and disorder and crime. He would carry through this Fairdale case, but even so, if he were not killed, his life would be ruined. He might save the service, yet at the cost of his happiness. He was not a machine. He was a man. He might be a perfect ranger, still he was a human being.

The loveliness, the passion, the tragedy of a woman, great as they were, had not power to shake him from his duty. Futile, hopeless, vain her love had been

to influence him. But there had flashed over me with subtle, overwhelming suggestion that not futile, not vain was my love to save him. Therefore, beyond and
above all other claims, and by reason of my wrong to him, his claim came
first.

It was then there was something cold and death-like in my soul. It was then
I bade farewell to Ruth Herbert. For I knew, whatever happened, that of one
thing I was sure — I would have to kill either Longstreth or Lawson. Snecker
could be managed. Longstreth might be trapped into arrest, but Lawson had no
sense, no control, no fear. He would snarl like a panther and go for his gun, and
he would have to be killed. This, of all consummations, was the one to be calculated upon.

And, of course, by Ruth's own words, that contingency would put me forever
outside the pale for her. I did not deceive myself. I did not accept the slightest
intimation of hope. I gave her up. And then for a time regret, remorse, pain,
darkness worked their will with me.

I came out of it all bitter and callous and sore — in the most fitting of moods
to undertake a difficult and deadly enterprise. Miss Longstreth completely slipped
my mind. Ruth became a wraith as of someone dead. Steele began to fade. In
their places came the bushy-bearded Snecker, the olive-skinned Longstreth with
his sharp eyes, and the dark, evil-faced Lawson. Their possibilities began to loom
up, and with my speculation returned tenfold more thrilling and sinister the old
strange zest of the manhunt.

It was about one o'clock when I strode into Fairdale. The streets for the most
part were deserted. I went directly to the hall where Morton and Zimmer, with
their men, had been left by Steele to guard the prisoners. I found them camping
out in the place, restless, somber, anxious. The fact that only about half the
original number of prisoners were left struck me as further indication of Morton's
summary dealings. But, when I questioned him as to the decrease in number, he
said bluntly that they had escaped.

I did not know whether or not to believe him. But that didn't matter. I tried
to get in some more questions, only I found that Morton and Zimmer meant to
be heard first.

"Where's Steele?" they demanded.

"He's out of town, in a safe place," I replied. "Too badly hurt for action. I'm
to rush through with the rest of the deal."

"That's good," Morton said. "We've waited long enough. This gang has been
split, and, if we hurry, they'll never get together again. Old man Snecker showed

up today. He's drawin' the outfit in ag'in. Reckon he's waitin' for orders. Sure he's ragin' since Bo was killed. The old fox will be dangerous if he gets goin'."

"Where is he now?" I queried.

"Over at the Hope So. Must be a dozen of the gang there. But he's the only leader left we know of. If we get him, the rustler gang will be broke for good. He's sent word down here for me to let our prisoners go or there'll be a damn' bloody fight. We haven't sent our answer yet. Was hoping Steele would show up. An' now we're sure glad you're back."

"Morton, I'll take the answer," I replied quickly. "Now there're two things. Do you know if Longstreth and Lawson are at the ranch?"

"They were an hour ago. We have word. Zimmer saw Dick."

"All right. Have you any horses handy?"

"Sure. Those hitched outside belong to us."

"I want you to take a man with you, in a few moments, and ride 'round the back roads and up to Longstreth's house. Get off and wait under the trees till you hear me shoot or yell, then come fast."

Morton's breast heaved. He whistled as he breathed. His neck churned. "God Almighty! So there the scent leads. We always wondered . . . half believed. But no one spoke . . . no one had any nerve." Morton moistened his lips. His face was livid; his big hands shook. "Russ, you can gamble on me."

"Good. Well, that's all. Come out and get me a horse."

When I had mounted and was half way to the Hope So, my plan as far as Snecker was concerned had been formed. It was to go boldly into the saloon, ask for the rustler, first pretend I had a reply from Morton, and then, when I had Snecker's ear, whisper a message supposedly from Longstreth. If Snecker was too keen to be decoyed, I could at least surprise him, then run for my horse.

The plan seemed clever to me. I had only one thing to fear, and that was a possibility of the rustlers having seen my part in Steele's defense the other day. That had to be risked. There were always some kind of risks to be faced.

It was scarcely a block and a half to the Hope So. Before I arrived, I knew I had been observed. When I dismounted before the door, I felt cold, yet there was an exhilaration in the moment. I never stepped more naturally and carelessly into the saloon.

It was full of men. There were men behind the bar, helping themselves. Evidently Blandy's job had not been filled. Every face near the door was turned toward me, dark, intent, scowling, malignant they were, and made me stiffen my resolve.

"Say, boys, I've a word for Snecker," I called, quite loudly. Nobody stirred. I swept my glance over the crowd but did not see Snecker. "I'm in some hurry," I added.

"Bill ain't here," said a man at the table nearest me. "Air you comin' from Morton?"

"Nit. But I'm not yellin' this message."

The rustler rose and in a few long strides confronted me.

"Word from Longstreth," I whispered, and the rustler stared. "I'm in his confidence. He's got to see Bill at once. Longstreth sends word he's quit . . . he's done . . . he's through. The jig is up, and he means to hit the road out of Fairdale."

"Bill'll kill him, surer'n hell," muttered the rustler. "But we all said it'd come to thet. An' what'd Lawson say?"

"Lawson? Why, he's cashed in. Didn't you'all hear? Reckon Longstreth shot him."

The rustler cursed his amaze and swung his right arm with fist clenched tight. "When did Lawson git it?"

"A little while ago. I don't know how long. Anyway, I saw him lyin' dead on the porch. An' say, pard, I've got to rustle. Send Bill up quick as he comes. Tell him Longstreth wants to turn over all his stock an' then light out."

I backed to the door, and the last I saw of the rustler he was standing there in a scowling amaze. I had fooled him all right. If only I had the luck to have Snecker come along soon. . . . Mounting, I trotted the horse leisurely up the street.

Business and everything else was at a standstill in Fairdale these days. The doors of the stores were barricaded. Down side streets, however, I saw a few people, a buckboard, and stray cattle. When I reached the edge of town, I turned aside a little and took a look at the ruins of Steele's adobe house. The walls and debris had all been flattened, scattered about, and, if anything of value had escaped destruction, it had disappeared. Steele, however, had left very little that would have been of further use to him.

Turning again, I continued on my way to the ranch. It seemed that, though I was eager rather than backward, my mind seized avidly upon suggestion or attraction, as if to escape the burden of grim pondering. When about half way across the flat, and perhaps just out of gunshot sound of Longstreth's house, I heard a rapid clatter of hoofs on the hard road. I wheeled, expecting to see Morton and his man, and was ready to be chagrined at their coming openly instead of by the back way. But this was only one man, and it was not Morton.

He seemed of big build, and he bestrode a fine bay horse. There evidently was reason for hurry, too. At about one hundred yards, when I recognized Snecker, complete astonishment possessed me.

Well, as it was, I had ample time to get on my guard. In wheeling my horse I booted him so hard that he reared. As I had been warm, I had my sombrero over the pommel of the saddle. And, when the head of my horse blocked any possible sight of movement of my hand, I pulled my gun and held it concealed under my sombrero.

This rustler had bothered me in my calculations. And here he came galloping alone. Exultation would have been involuntary then but for the sudden shock, and then the cold settling of temper, the breathless suspense. Snecker pulled his huge bay and pounded to halt abreast of me. Luck favored me. Had I ever had anything but luck in these dangerous deals?

Snecker seemed to fume. Internally there was a volcano. His wide sombrero and bushy beard hid all of his face except his eyes, which were deep-set furnaces. He, too, like his lieutenant, had been carried completely off his balance by the strange message, apparently from Longstreth. "Hey! You're the feller who jest left word fer someone at the Hope So?" he asked.

"Yes," I replied, while with my left hand I patted the neck of my horse, holding him still.

"Longstreth wants me bad, eh?"

"Reckon there's only one man who wants you more."

Steadily, I met his piercing gaze. This was a rustler not to be long victim to any ruse. I waited in cold surety.

"You thet cowboy, Russ?" he asked.

"I was . . . and I'm not!" I replied significantly.

The violent start of this violent outlaw was a rippling jerk of passion. "What'n hell!" he ejaculated.

"Bill, you're easy."

"Who're you?" he uttered hoarsely.

I watched Snecker with hawk-like keenness. "United States deputy marshal . . . Bill, you're under arrest."

He roared a mad curse as his hand clapped down to his gun. Then I fired through my sombrero. Snecker's big horse plunged. The rustler fell back, and one of his legs pitched high as he slid off the lunging steed. His other foot caught in the stirrup. This fact terribly frightened the horse. He bolted, dragging the rustler for a dozen jumps. Then Snecker's foot slipped loose. He lay limp and still and shapeless in the road. I did not need to go back to look him over. But to make assurance doubly sure, I dismounted and went back to where he lay. My bullet had gone where it had been aimed.

As I rode up into Longstreth's courtyard and turned in to the porch, I heard loud and angry voices. Longstreth and Lawson were quarreling again. How my lucky star guided me! I had no plan of action, but my brain was equal to a hundred lightning-swift evolutions. The voices ceased. The men had heard the horse. Both of them came out on the porch.

In an instant I was again the lolling, impudent cowboy, half under the influence of liquor.

"It's only Russ, and he's drunk," said Floyd Lawson contemptuously.

"I heard horses trotting off there," replied Longstreth. "Maybe the girls are coming. I bet I teach them not to run off again. . . . Hello, Russ."

He looked haggard, thin, but seemed amiable enough. He was in his shirt-sleeves, and he had come out with a gun in his hand. This he laid on a table near the wall. He wore no belt.

I rode right up to the porch and, greeting them laconically, made a show of a somewhat tangle-footed cowboy dismounting. The moment I got off and straightened up, I asked no more. The game was mine. It was the great hour of my life, and I met it as I had never met another.

I looked and acted what I pretended to be, though a deep and intense passion, an almost ungovernable suspense, an icy sickening nausea abided within me. All I needed, all I wanted was to get Longstreth and Lawson together or, failing that, to maneuver into such a position that I had any kind of chance. Longstreth's gun on the table made three distinct objects for me to watch and two of them could change position.

"What do you want here?" demanded Lawson.

He was red, bloated, thick-lipped, all fiery and sweaty from drink, though sober at the moment, and he had the expression of a desperate man in his last stand. It *was* his last stand, though he was ignorant of that.

"Me . . . ? Say, Lawson, I ain't fired yet," I replied in slow-rising resentment.

"Well, you're fired now," he replied insolently.

"Who fires me, I'd like to know?"

I walked up to the porch, and I had a cigarette in one hand, a match in the other. I struck the match.

"I do," said Lawson.

I studied him with apparent amusement. It had taken only one glance around for me to divine that Longstreth would enjoy any kind of a clash between Lawson and me.

"Huh! You fired me once before, an' it didn't go. Lawson, I reckon you don't stack up here as strong as you think."

He was facing the porch, moody, preoccupied, somber, all at the same time. Only a little of his mind was concerned with me. Manifestly there were strong forces at work. Both men were strained to the last degree, and Lawson could be made to break at almost a word. Longstreth laughed mockingly at this sally of mine, and that stung Lawson. He stopped his pacing and turned his handsome, fiery eyes on me.

"Longstreth, I won't stand this man's impudence."

"Aw, Lawson, cut that talk. I'm not impudent. Longstreth knows I'm a good fellow, on the square, and I have you sized up about OK."

"All the same, Russ, you'd better dig out," said Longstreth. "Don't kick up any fuss. We're busy with deals today. And I expect visitors."

"Sure. I won't stay around where I ain't wanted," I replied.

Then I lit my cigarette and did not move an inch out of my tracks. Longstreth sat in a chair near the door. The table upon which lay his gun stood between him and Lawson. This position did not invite me to start anything. But the tension had begun to be felt. Longstreth had his sharp gaze on me.

"What'd you come for, anyway?' he asked suddenly.

"Well, I had some news I was asked to fetch in."

"Get it out of you, then."

"See here now, Mister Longstreth, the fact is I'm a tenderhearted fellow. I hate to hurt people's feelin's. And, if I was to spring this news in Mister Lawson's hearin', why, such a sensitive, high-tempered gentleman as he would go plumb off his nut."

Unconcealed sarcasm was the dominant note in that speech. Lawson flared up, yet he was eagerly curious. Longstreth probably thought I was only a little worse for drink, and, but for the way I rubbed Lawson, he would not have tolerated me at all.

"What's this news? You needn't be afraid of my feelings," said Lawson.

"Ain't so sure of that," I drawled. "It concerns the lady you're sweet on . . . an' the ranger . . . you ain't sweet on."

Longstreth jumped up. "Russ, has Ray gone out to meet Steele?" he asked angrily.

"Sure she has," I replied.

I thought Lawson would choke. He was thick-headed anyway, and the rush of blood made him tear at the soft collar of his shirt. Both men were excited now, moving about, beginning to rouse. I waited my chance, patient, cold, all my feelings shut in the vise of my will.

"How do you know she met Steele?" demanded Longstreth.

"I was there. I met Ruth at the same time."

"But *why* should my daughter meet this ranger?"

"She's in love with him, and he's in love with her."

The simple statement might have had the force of a juggernaut. I reveled in Lawson's state, but I felt sorry for Longstreth. He had not outlived his pride. Then I saw the leaping thought — would this daughter side against him? He seemed to shrivel up, to grow old while I watched him. Lawson, finding his voice, cursed Ray, cursed the ranger, then Longstreth, then me.

"You damned, selfish fool!" cried Longstreth in deep, bitter scorn. "All you think of is yourself. Your loss of the girl. Think once of me . . . my home . . . my life."

Then the connection subtly put out by Longstreth apparently dawned upon the other. Somehow, through this girl, her father and cousin were to be betrayed. I got that impression, though I could not tell how true it was. Certainly Lawson's jealousy was his paramount emotion.

Longstreth thrust me sidewise off the porch. "Go away," he ordered. He did not look around to see if I came back.

Quickly I leaped to my former position. He confronted Lawson. He was beyond the table where the gun lay. They were close together. My moment had come — the game was mine — and a ball of fire burst in my brain to race all over me.

"To hell with you!" burst out Lawson incoherently. He was frenzied. "I'll have her or nobody else will!"

"You never will," returned Longstreth stridently. "So help me God. I'd rather see her Ranger Steele's wife than yours."

Absorbing that shock, Lawson leaned toward him, all hate and menace in his mien. They had forgotten the half-drunken cowboy.

"Lawson, you made me what I am," continued Longstreth. "I backed you . . . protected you, finally went in with you. Now it's ended. I quit you. I'm done."

Their gray, passion-corded faces were still as stones.

"Gentlemen," I called in clear, high, far-reaching voice with the intonation of authority, "you're both done!"

They wheeled to confront me, to see my leveled gun.

"Don't move! Not a muscle! Not a finger!" I warned.

Longstreth read what Lawson had not the mind to read. His face turned paler gray, to ashen.

"What d'ye mean?" yelled Lawson fiercely, shrilly.

It was not in him to obey my command, to see impending death. All quivering and strung, yet with perfect control, I raised my left hand to turn back a lapel of my open vest. The silver shield flashed brightly.

"United States deputy marshal in service of Ranger Steele."

Lawson howled like a dog. With barbarous and instant fury, with sheer, impotent folly, he swept a clawing hand for his gun. My shot broke his action as it cut short his life.

Before Lawson even tottered, before he loosed the gun, Longstreth leaped behind him, clasped him with left arm, quick as lightning jerked the gun from both clutching fingers and sheath. I shot at Longstreth — then again — then a third time.

All my bullets sped into the upheld, nodding Lawson. Longstreth had protected himself with the body of the dead man. I had seen red flashes, puffs of smoke, had heard quick reports. Something stung my left arm. Then a blow like wind, light of sound yet shocking in impact, struck me, knocked me flat. The hot rend of lead followed the blow. My heart seemed to explode, yet my mind kept extraordinarily clear and rapid.

I raised myself, felt a post at my shoulder, leaned on it. I heard Longstreth work the action of Lawson's gun. I heard the hammer click, fall upon empty shells. He had used up all the loads in Lawson's gun. I heard him curse as a man curses at defeat.

I waited, cool and sure now for him to show his head or other vital part from behind his bolster. He tried to lift the dead man, to edge him closer toward the table where his gun lay. But, considering the peril of exposing himself, he found that task beyond him. He bent, peering at me under Lawson's arm.

Longstreth's eyes were the eyes of a man who meant to kill me. There was never any mistaking the strange and terrible light of eyes like those. More than once I had a chance to aim at them, at the tip of Longstreth's head, at a strip of his side. I wanted to make sure. Suddenly I remembered Morton and his men. Then I pealed out a cry — hoarse, strange, yet far-reaching.

It was answered by a shout.

Longstreth heard it. It called forth all that was in the man. He flung Lawson's body off. But, even as it dropped, before Longstreth could recover to leap as he surely intended for the gun, I covered him, called piercingly to him. I could kill him there or as he moved. But one chance I gave him.

"Don't jump for the gun! Don't! I'll kill you! I've got two shells left! Sure as God, I'll kill you!"

He stood perhaps ten feet from the table where his gun lay. I saw him calculating his chances. He was game. He had courage that forced me to respect him. I saw him measure the distance to that gun. He was magnificent. He meant to do it. I would have to kill him.

"Longstreth, listen!" I cried, very swiftly. "The game's up. You're done. But think of your daughter. I'll spare your life . . . I'll give you freedom on one condition. For her sake. I've got you nailed . . . all the proofs. It was I behind the wall the other night. Blome, Hilliard, Pickens, Bo Snecker are dead. I killed Bill Snecker on the way up here. There lies Lawson. You're alone. And here come Morton and another to my aid. Give up! Surrender! Consent to demands, and I'll spare you. You can go free back to your old country. It's for Ray's sake. Her life, perhaps her happiness, can be saved. Hurry, man. Your answer."

"Suppose I refuse?" he queried with a dark and terrible earnestness.

"Then I'll kill you in your tracks. You can't move a hand. Your word or death. Hurry, Longstreth. I can't last much longer. But I can kill you before I drop. Be a man. For her sake. Quick. Another second now. . . . By God, I'll kill you."

"All right, Russ. I give my word," he said, and deliberately walked to the chair and fell into it, just as Morton came running up with his man.

"Put away your guns," I ordered them. "The game's up. Snecker and Lawson are dead. Longstreth is my prisoner. He has my word he'll be protected. It's for you to draw up the papers with him. He'll divide all his property, every last acre, every herd of stock as you and Zimmer dictate. He gives up all. Then he's free to leave the country, and he's never to return."

CHAPTER EIGHTEEN

Through the Valley

LONGSTRETH looked strangely at the great bloody blot on my breast, and his look made me conscious of a dark hurrying of my mind. Morton came stamping up the steps with blunt queries, with anxious mien. When he saw the front of me, he halted, threw wide his arms.

"There come the girls!" suddenly exclaimed Longstreth. "Morton, help me drag Lawson inside. They mustn't see him."

I was facing down the porch toward the court and corrals. Miss Longstreth and Ruth had come in sight, were swiftly approaching, evidently alarmed. Steele, no doubt, had remained out at the camp. I was watching them, wondering what they would do and say presently, and then Longstreth and Morton came to carry me indoors. They laid me on the couch in the parlor where the girls used to be so often.

"Russ, you're pretty hard hit," said Longstreth, bending over me with his hands at my breast.

The room was bright with sunshine, yet the light seemed to be fading.

"Reckon I am," I replied.

"I'm sorry. If only you could have told me sooner. Lawson, damn him! Always I've split over him."

"But the last time, Longstreth."

"Yes, and I came near driving you to kill me, too. Russ, you talked me out of it. For Ray's sake! She'll be here in a minute. This'll be harder than facing a gun."

"Hard now. But it'll . . . turn out OK."

"Russ, will you do me a favor?" he asked, and he seemed shamefaced.

"Sure."

"Let Ray and Ruth think Lawson shot you. He's dead. It can't matter. And you're hard hit. The girls are fond of you. If . . . if you go under . . . Russ, the old side of my life is coming back. It's been coming. It'll be here just about when she enters this room. And by God, I'd change places with you if I could."

"Glad you . . . said that, Longstreth," I replied. "And sure . . . Lawson plugged me. It's our secret. I've reason, too, not . . . that . . . it . . . matters . . . much . . . now."

The light was failing. I could not talk very well. I felt dumb, strange, locked in ice, with dull little prickings of my flesh, with dim rushing sounds in my ears. But my mind was clear. Evidently there was little to be done.

Morton came in, looked at me, and went out. I heard the quick, light steps of the girls on the porch and murmuring voices.

"Where'm I hit?" I whispered.

"Three places," Longstreth said. "Arm, shoulder, and a bad one in the breast. It got your lung, I'm afraid. But if you don't go quick, you've got a chance."

"Sure I've a chance."

"Russ, I'll tell the girls, do what I can for you, settle with Morton, and clear out."

Just then Ray and Ruth entered the room. I heard two low cries, so different in tone, and I saw two dim white faces. Ruth flew to my side and dropped to her knees. Both hands went to my face, then to my breast. She lifted them, shaking. They were red. White and mute she gazed from them to me. But some woman's intuition kept her from fainting.

"Papa!" cried Ray, wringing her hands.

"Don't give way," he replied. "Both you girls will need your nerve. Russ is badly hurt. There's little hope for him."

Ruth moaned and dropped her face against me, clasping me convulsively. I tried to reach a hand out to touch her, but I could not move. I felt her hair against my face. Ray uttered a low, heart-rending cry, which both Longstreth and I understood.

"Listen, let me tell it quick," he said huskily. "There's been a fight. Russ killed Snecker and Lawson. They resisted arrest. It . . . it was Lawson . . . it was Lawson's gun that put Russ down. Russ let me off. In fact, Ray, he saved me. I'm to divide my property . . . return so far as possible what I've stolen . . . leave Texas at once and forever. You'll find me back in old Louisiana . . . if . . . if you ever want to come home."

As she stood there, realizing her deliverance, with the dark and tragic glory of her eyes passing from her father to me, my own sight shadowed, and I thought, *if I were dying, then it was not in vain.*

"Send . . . for . . . Steele," I whispered.

Silently, swiftly, breathlessly, they worked over me. I was exquisitely sensitive to touch, to sound, but I could not see anything. By and by all was quiet, and I slipped into a black void.

Familiar heavy, swift footsteps, the thump of heels of a powerful and striding man, jarred into the blackness that held me, seemed to split it to let me out. I opened my eyes in a sunlit room to see Ruth's face all lined and haggard, to see Miss Longstreth fly to the door, and the stalwart ranger bow his lofty head to enter.

However far life had ebbed from me, then it came rushing back, keen-sighted, memorable, with agonizing pain in every nerve. I saw him start. I heard him cry, but I could not speak.

He bent over me, and I tried to smile. He stood silent, his hand on me, while Ray Longstreth told swiftly, brokenly what had happened. How she told it! I tried to whisper a protest. To anyone on earth, except Steele, I might have wished to appear a hero. Still, at that moment I had more dread of him than any other feeling. She finished the story with her head on his shoulder, with tears that certainly were in part for me.

Once in my life, then, I saw him stunned. But, when he recovered, it was not Ray that he thought of first, nor of the end of Longstreth's power. He turned to me.

"Little hope?" he cried out with the deep ring in his voice. "No! There's every hope. No bullet hole like that could ever kill this ranger. Russ!"

I could not answer him. But this time I did achieve a smile.

There was no shadow, no pain in his face such as had haunted me in Ruth's and Ray's. He could fight death the same as he could fight evil. He vitalized the girls. Ray began to hope. Ruth lost her woe. He changed the atmosphere of that room. Something filled it — something like himself, big, virile, strong. The very look of him made me suddenly want to live; and all at once it seemed I felt alive. And that was like taking the deadened ends of nerves, to cut them raw, and quicken them with fiery current. From stupor I had leaped to pain, and that tossed me into fever.

There were spaces, darkened mercifully, shutting me in. There were others of light, where I burned and burned in my heated blood. Ruth, like the wraith she had become in my mind, passed in and out. Ray watched and helped in those hours when sight was clear. The fever passed, and with the first nourishing drink given me I seemed to find my tongue, to gain something.

"Hello, old man," I whispered to Steele.

"Oh, Lord, Russ, to think you would double-cross me the way you did."

That was his first speech to me after I had appeared to face around from the grave. His good-humored reproach told me more than any other thing how far from his mind was the thought of my death. Then he talked a little to me, cheerfully, with that directness and force characteristic of him always, showing me that the danger was past, and that I would now be rapidly on the mend. I discovered that I cared little whether I was on the mend or not.

When I had passed the state of somber unrealities, then the hours of pain, and then that first inspiring flush of renewed desire to live, an entirely different mood came over me. But I kept it to myself. I never even asked, for three days, why Ruth never entered the room where I lay. I associated this fact, however, with what I had imagined, her shrinking from me, her intent and pale face, her singular manner when occasion made it necessary or unavoidable for her to be near me. No difficulty was there in associating my change of mood with her absence. I brooded. Steele's keen insight betrayed me to him, but all his power and his spirit availed nothing to cheer me.

I pretended to be cheerful. I drank and ate anything given me. I was patient and quiet. But I ceased to mend. Then, one day, she came back, and Steele, who was watching me as she entered, quietly got up and without a word took Ray out of the room and left me alone with Ruth.

"Archie, I've been sick myself . . . in bed for three days," she said. "I'm better now. I hope you are. You look so pale. . . . Do you still think . . . brood about that fight?"

"Yes, I can't forget. I'm afraid it cost me more than life."

Ruth was somber, gloomy, thoughtful. "You weren't driven to kill Floyd?" she asked.

"How do you mean?"

"By that awful instinct, that hankering to kill, you once told me gunmen have."

"No. I can swear it wasn't that. I didn't want to kill him. But he forced me. As I had to go after these two men, it was a foregone conclusion about Lawson. It was premeditated. I have no excuse."

"Hush. Tell me, if you confronted them, drew on them, then you had a chance to kill my uncle?"

"Yes. I could have done it easily."

"*Why*, then, didn't you?"

"It was for Ray's sake. I'm afraid I didn't think of you. I had put you out of my mind."

"Well, if a man can be noble at the same time he's terrible, you've been. . . . Archie . . . I don't know how I feel. I'm sick, and I can't think. I see, though, that you saved Ray and Steele. Why, she's touching happiness again, fearfully yet really. Think of that. God only knows what you did for Steele. If I judged it by his suffering, as you lay there about to die, it would be beyond words to tell. But, Archie, you're pale and shaky now. Hush! No more talk!"

With all my eyes and mind and heart and soul I watched to see if she shrank from me. She was passive, yet tender, as she smoothed my pillow and moved my head. A dark abstraction hung over her, and it was so strange, so foreign to her nature. No sensitiveness on earth could have equaled mine at that moment. And I saw and felt and knew that she did not shrink from me.

Thought and feeling escaped me for a while. I dozed. The old shadows floated to and fro. When I awoke, Steele and Ray had just come in. As he bent over me, I looked up into his keen gray eyes, and there was no mask over mine when I looked up at him.

"Son, the thing that was needed was a change of nurses," he said gently. "I intend to make up some sleep now and leave you in better care."

From that hour I improved. I slept. I lay quietly awake. I partook of nourishing food. I listened and watched, and all the time I gained. But I spoke very little, and, though I tried to brighten when Steele was in the room, I made only indifferent success of it.

Days passed. Ruth was almost always with me, yet seldom alone. She was grave where once she had been gay. How I watched her face, praying for that shade to lift. How I listened for a note of the old music in her voice.

Ruth Herbert had sustained a shock to her soul almost as dangerous as had been the blow at my life. Still I hoped. I had seen other women's deadened and darkened spirits rebound and glow once more. It began to dawn upon me, however, that more than time was imperative if she were ever to become her old self again.

Studying her closer, with less thought of myself and her reaction to my presence, I discovered that she trembled at shadows, seemed like a frightened deer with a step always on its trail, was afraid of the dark. Then I wondered why I had not long before divined one cause of her strangeness. The house where I had killed one of her kin would ever be haunted for her. She had said she was a Southerner and that blood was thick.

When I had thought out the matter a little further, I deliberately sat up in bed, scaring the wits out of all my kind nurses. "Steele, I'll never get well in this house. I want to go home. When can you take me?"

They remonstrated with me, and pleaded, and scolded, all to little avail. Then they were persuaded to take me seriously, to plan, providing I improved, to start in a few days. We were to ride out of Pecos County together, back along the stage trail to civilization.

The look in Ruth's eyes decided my measure of improvement. I could have started that very day and have borne up under any pain or distress. Strange to see, too, how Steele and Ray responded to the stimulus of my idea, to the promise of what lay beyond the wild and barren hills.

Steele told me that day about the headlong flight of every lawless character out of Fairdale, the very hour that Snecker and Lawson and Longstreth were known to have fallen. He expressed deep feeling, almost mortification, that the credit of that final coup had gone to him, instead of to me. His denial and explanation had been only a few soundless words in the face of a grateful and clamorous populace that tried to reward him, to make him mayor of Fairdale.

Longstreth had made restitution in every case where he had personally gained at the loss of farmer or rancher, and the accumulation of years went far toward returning to Fairdale what it had lost in a material way. He had been a poor man when he boarded the stage for Sanderson, on his way out of Texas forever.

Not long afterward I heard Steele talking to Miss Longstreth in a deep and agitated voice. "You must rise above this. When I come upon you alone, I see the shadow, the pain in your face. How wonderfully this thing has turned out when it might have ruined you. I expected it to ruin you. Who but that wild boy in there could ever have saved us all?

"Ray, you have had cause for sorrow. But your father is alive and will live it down. Perhaps, back there in Louisiana, the dishonor will never be known. Pecos County is far from your old home. And even in San Antonio and Austin a man's evil repute means little. . . . Then the line between a rustler and a rancher is hard to draw in these wild border days. Rustling is stealing cattle, and I once heard a well-known rancher say that all rich cattlemen had done a little stealing. Your father drifted out here, and like a good many others he succeeded. It's perhaps just as well not to split hairs, to judge him by the law and morality of a civilized country. Some way or other he drifted in with badmen. Maybe a deal that was honest somehow tied his hands and started him in wrong.

"This matter of land, water, a few stray head of stock had to be decided out of court. I'm sure in his case he never realized where he was drifting. Then one thing led to another, until he was face to face with dealings that took on crooked form. To protect himself he bound men to him. And so the gang developed. Many powerful gangs have developed that way out here. He could not control them. He became involved with them, and eventually their dealings became deliberately and boldly dishonest. That meant the inevitable spilling of blood sooner or later, and so he grew into the leader because he was the strongest. Whatever he is to be judged for, I think he could have been infinitely worse."

When he ceased speaking, I had the same impulse that must have concerned Steele — somehow to show Longstreth not so black as he was painted, to give him the benefit of a doubt, to arraign him justly in the eyes of rangers who knew what wild border life was.

"Steele, bring Ray in," I called. "I've something to tell her."

They came quickly, concerned probably at my tone.

"I've been hoping for a chance to tell you something, Miss Longstreth. That day I came here, your father was quarreling with Lawson. I had heard them do that before. He hated Lawson. The reason came out just before we had the fight. It was my plan to surprise them. I did. I told them you went out to meet Steele . . . that you two were in love with each other. Lawson grew wild. He swore no one would ever have you. Then Longstreth said he'd rather have you Steele's wife than Lawson's. I'll not forget that scene. There was a great deal back of it, long before you ever came out to Fairdale. Your father said that he had backed Lawson . . . that the deal had ruined him . . . made him a rustler. He said he quit. He was done.

"Now, this is all clear to me, and I want to explain, Miss Longstreth. It was Lawson who ruined your father. It was Lawson who was the rustler. It was Lawson who made the gang necessary. But Lawson had not the brains or the power to lead men. Because blood is thick, your father became the leader of that gang. At heart he was never a criminal. The reason I respected him was because he showed himself a man at the last. He faced me to be shot, and I couldn't do it.

"As Steele said, you've reason for sorrow. But you must get over it. You mustn't brood. I do not see that you'll be disgraced or dishonored. Of course, that's not the point. The vital thing is whether or not a woman of your high-mindedness had real and lasting cause for shame. Steele says no. I say no."

Then, as Miss Longstreth dropped down beside me, her eyes shining and wet, Ruth entered the room in time to see her cousin bend to kiss me gratefully with sisterly fervor. Yet it was a woman's kiss, given for its own sake.

Ruth could not comprehend. It was too sudden, too unheard of, that Ray Longstreth should kiss me, a man she did not love. Ruth's white, sad face changed, and in the flaming wave of scarlet that dyed neck and cheek and brow I read with mighty pound of heart that, despite the dark stain between us, she loved me still.

CHAPTER NINETEEN

Convalescence

FOUR mornings later we were aboard the stage, riding down the main street, on the way out of Fairdale. The whole town turned out to bid us farewell. The cheering, the clamor, the almost passionate fervor of the populace irritated me, and I could not see the incident from their point of view. Never in my life had I been so eager to get out of a place. But, then, I was morbid, and the whole world hinged on one thing.

Morton insisted on giving us an escort as far as Del Rio. It consisted of six cowboys, mounted, with light packs, and they rode ahead of the stage. We had the huge vehicle to ourselves. A comfortable bed had been rigged up for me by placing boards across from seat to seat and furnishing it with blankets and pillows. By some squeezing there was still room enough inside for my three companions, but Steele expressed an intention of riding mostly outside, and Miss Longstreth's expression betrayed her. I was to be alone with Ruth. The prospect thrilled while it saddened me. How different this ride from that first one, with all its promise of adventure and charm.

"It's over," said Steele thickly. "It's done. I'm glad, for their sakes . . . glad for ours. We're out of town."

I had been quick to miss the shouts and cheers. And I had been just as quick to see, or to imagine, a subtle change in Ruth Herbert's face. We had not traveled a mile before the tension relaxed about her lips, the downcast eyes lifted, and I saw beyond any peradventure of doubt a lighter spirit. Then I relaxed myself, for I had keyed up every nerve to make myself strong for this undertaking. I lay back with closed eyes, weary, aching, in more pain than I wanted them to discover.

I thought and thought. Miss Longstreth had said to me: "Russ, it'll all come right. I can tell you now what you never guessed. For years Ruth had been fond of our cousin, Floyd Lawson. She hadn't seen him since she was a child. But she remembered. She had an only brother who was the image of Floyd.

"Ruth obviously loved Arthur. He was killed in the Rebellion. She never got over it. That left her without any family. Floyd and I were her nearest kin. How

652

she looked forward to meeting Floyd out here! But he disappointed her right at the start. She hates a drinking man. I think she came to hate Floyd, too. But he always reminded her of Arthur, and she could never get over that. So, naturally, when you killed Floyd, she was terribly shocked. There were nights when she was haunted, when I had to stay with her.

"Vaughn and I have studied her, talked about her, and we think she's gradually recovering. She loved you, too, and Ruth doesn't change. Once, with her, is for always. So let me say to you what you said to me . . . do not brood. All will yet be well, thank God!"

Those had been words to remember, to make me patient, to lessen my insistent fear. Yet, what did I know of women? Had not Ray Longstreth and Ruth Herbert amazed and nonplused me many a time, at the very moment when I had calculated to a nicety my conviction of their action, their feeling? It was possible that I had killed Ruth's love for me, though I could not believe so — and it was very possible that, still loving me, she might never break down the barrier between us.

The beginning of that journey distressed me physically; yet, gradually, as I grew accustomed to the roll of the stage and to the occasional jars, I found myself easier in body. Fortunately there had been rain, that had settled the dust, and a favorable breeze made riding pleasant, where ordinarily it would have been hot and disagreeable.

We tarried long enough in the little hamlet of Longstreth for Steele to get letters from reliable ranchers. He wanted a number of references to verify the ranger report he had to turn in to Captain MacNeal. This precaution he took so as to place in MacNeal's hands all the evidence needed to convince Governor Stone. And now, as Steele returned to us and entered the stage, he spoke of this report.

"It's the longest and the best I ever turned in," he said with a gray flame in his eyes. "I sha'n't let Russ read it. He's peevish because I want his part put on record. And listen, Ray. There's to be a blank line in this report. Your father's name will never be recorded. Neither the governor, nor the adjutant general, nor Captain MacNeal, not anyone back Austin way will ever know who this mysterious leader of the Pecos gang might have been.

"Even out here very few know. Many supposed, but few knew. I've shut the mouths of those few. That blank line in the report is for a supposed and mysterious leader who vanished. Jack Blome, the reputed leader, and all his lawless associates are dead. Fairdale is free and safe now, its future in the hands of roused, determined, and capable men."

We were all silent after Steele ceased talking. I do not believe Ray could have spoken just then. If sorrow and joy could be perfectly blended in one beautiful expression, they were in her face.

By and by I dared to say: "And Vaughn Steele, Lone Star ranger, has seen his last service?"

"Yes," he replied with emotion.

Ruth stirred and turned a strange look upon us all. "In that case, then, if I am not mistaken, there were two Lone Star rangers . . . and both have seen their last service!"

Ruth's lips were trembling, the way they trembled when it was impossible to tell whether she was about to laugh or cry. The first hint of her old combative spirit or her old archness. A wave of feeling rushed over me, too much for me in my weakened condition. Dizzy, racked with sudden shooting pains, I closed my eyes, and the happiness I embraced was all that sweeter for the suffering it entailed.

Something beat into my ears, into my brain, with the regularity and rapid beat of pulsing blood — not too late! Not too late! Not too late!

From that moment the ride grew different, even as I improved with leaps and bounds. Sanderson was behind us — the long, gray, barren between Sanderson and the Rio Grande beyond it — Del Rio for two days, where I was able to sit up — all behind us — and before us the eastward trail to Uvalde. We were the only passengers on the stage from Del Rio to Uvalde. Perhaps Steele had so managed the journey. Assuredly he had become an individual with whom traveling under the curious gaze of strangers would have been embarrassing.

He was most desperately in love. And Ray, all in a few days, while riding these long, tedious miles, ordinarily so fatiguing, had renewed her bloom, had gained what she had lost. She, too, was desperately in love, though she remembered her identity occasionally, and that she was in the company of a badly shot-up young man and a broken-hearted cousin.

Most of the time Ray and Steele rode on top of the stage. When they did ride inside, their conduct was not unbecoming. Indeed, it was sweet to watch, yet it loosed the fires of jealous rage and longing in me, and certainly upon Ruth. Gradually she had been losing that strange and somber mood she had acquired, to brighten and change more and more. Perhaps she divined something about Ray and Steele that escaped me. Anyway, all of a sudden she was transformed.

"Look here, if you people want to spoon, please get out on top," she said.

If that was not the old Ruth Herbert, I did not know who it was. Miss Longstreth tried to appear offended, and Steele tried to look insulted, but they both failed. They could not have looked anything but happy. Youth and love were too strong for this couple, whom circumstances might well have made grave and thoughtful. They were magnet and steel, powder and spark. Any moment, right before my eyes, I expected them to rush right into each other's arms. When they refrained, merely substituting clasped hands for dearer embrace, I closed my eyes and remembered them, as they would live in my memory forever, standing crushed together on the ridge that day, white lips to white lips, embodying all that was beautiful, passionate, and tragic. And I, who had been their undoing, in the end was their salvation. How I hugged that truth to my heart.

It seemed, following Ruth's pert remark, that after an interval of decent dignity Ray and Steele did go out upon the top of the stage.

"Archie," whispered Ruth, "they're up to something. I heard a few words. I bet you they're going to get married in San Antonio."

"Well, it's about time," I replied.

"But oughtn't they take us into their confidence?"

"Ruth, they have forgotten we are upon the earth."

"Oh, I'm so glad they're happy!"

Then there was a long silence. It was better for me to ride lying down, in which position I was at this time. After a mile Ruth took my hand and held it without speaking.

My heart leaped, but I did not open my eyes or break that spell even with a whisper.

"Archie, I must say . . . tell you . . . " She faltered, and still I kept my eyes closed. I did not want to wake up from that dream. "Have I been very . . . very sad?" she went on.

"Sad and strange, Ruth. That was worse than my bullet holes."

She gripped my hand. I felt her hair on my brow, felt her breath on my cheek. "Archie, I swore . . . I'd hate you if you . . . if you . . . "

"I know. Don't speak of it," I interposed hurriedly.

"But I don't hate you. I . . . I love you. And I can't give you up!"

"Darling! But, Ruth, can you get over it . . . can you forget?"

"Yes. That horrid black spell has gone with the miles. Little by little, mile after mile, and now it's gone! But I had to come to the point. To go back on my word. To tell you, Archie, you never, never had any sense."

Then I opened my eyes and my arms, too, and we were reunited. It must have been a happy moment, so happy that it numbed me beyond appreciation.

"Yes, Ruth," I agreed, "but no man ever had such a wonderful girl."

"Archie, I never . . . took off your ring," she whispered.

"But you hid your hand from my sight," I replied quickly.

"Oh, dear Archie, we're crazy . . . as crazy as those lunatics outside. Let's think a little."

I was very content to have no thought at all — just to see and feel her close to me.

"Archie, will you give up the ranger service for me?" she asked.

"Indeed, I will."

"And leave this fighting Texas, never to return till the day of guns and rangers and badmen and even breaks is past?"

"Yes."

"Will you go with me to my old home? It was beautiful once, Archie, before it was let run to rack and ruin. A thousand acres. An old stone house. Great mossy oaks. A lake and river. There are bear, deer, panther, wild boars in the breaks. You can hunt. And ride! I've horses, Archie, such horses! They could run these scrubby broncos off their legs. Will you come?"

"Come? Ruth, I rather think I will. But, dearest, after I'm well again, I must work," I said earnestly. "I've got to have a job."

"You're indeed a poor cowboy out of a job. Remember your deceit. Oh, Archie! Well, you'll have work, never fear."

"Ruth, is this old home of yours near the one Ray speaks of so much?" I asked.

"Indeed, it is. But hers has been kept under cultivation and in repair, while mine has run down. That will be our work, to build it up. So it's settled, then?"

She looked inquiringly at me, with a soft blush.

"Well, if you are so dense, try to bring back that Ruth Herbert who used to torment me. How you broke your promises! How you leaned from your saddle! Kiss me, Ruth!"

Later, as we drew close to Uvalde, Ruth and I sat in one seat, after the manner of Ray and Vaughn, and we looked out over the west where the sun was setting behind dim and distant mountains. We were fast leaving the wild and barren border. Already it seemed beyond that broken rugged horizon with its dark line silhouetted against the rosy and golden sky. Already the spell of its wild life and the grim and haunting faces had begun to fade out of my memory.

Let newer rangers, with less to lose, and with the call in their hearts, go on with our work till soon that wild border would be safe. The great Lone Star state must work out its destiny. Some distant day, in the fullness of time, what place the rangers had in that destiny would be history.